PRAISE FOR THE SCIENCE FICTION OF L. E. MODESITT, JR.

"Modesitt provides the very best in science fiction—thrilling adventure viewed through the crucible of the human spirit."

—*Romantic Times*

GRAVITY DREAMS
A Barnes & Nob‌

"L. E. Modesitt, Jr., is a writer de͏‌‌‌‌‌‌‌‌‌‌‌‌‌‌‌‌‌‌‌‌ anity on the world. This concern shows͏‌‌‌‌‌‌‌‌‌‌‌‌‌‌‌‌‌‌‌‌ *War* and science fiction such as *The Eco͏‌‌‌‌‌‌‌‌‌‌‌‌‌‌‌‌‌‌* *Reve-lator*. It is thus no surprise to see i͏‌‌‌‌‌‌‌‌‌‌‌‌‌‌‌‌‌‌‌‌ *...vity Dreams*. . . . The space adventure side of the tale͏‌‌‌‌‌‌‌‌‌‌‌ that many readers want, and they will be thoroughly satisfied. Modesitt never fails on that level. But he is more than an adventure writer; he is also quite a thoughtful fellow, and I found his musings on the need for responsibility in a high-tech society the more fascinating aspect of this novel."

—*Analog*

"Modesitt does a fine job creating a believable world where citizens are exhorted to accept complete responsibility for their actions and genetically 'rehabilitated' if they do not. . . . The novel is loaded with enough hard science and space opera elements to please the author's large and avid body of fans."

—*Publishers Weekly*

ADIAMANTE

"Because he dares to be explicit about first principles, the narrative assumes the shape of an intellectual suspense story: How can the manifestly decent people of Old Earth defend themselves against aggression without violating their deeply held beliefs? The answer is both morally persuasive and emotionally wrenching."

—*The New York Times*

"The book has strong military action, slick social maneuvering, and a good deal of psychological tension."

—*San Diego Union-Tribune*

THE PARAFAITH WAR

"L. E. Modesitt, Jr., has a knack for getting to the heart of the matter. His world is complex and believable, and his characters crackle with life. *The Parafaith War* is a well-crafted study of society and personality."

—*Affaire de Coeur*

"With echoes of both Joe Haldeman's *The Forever War* and Robert A. Heinlein's *Starship Troopers*: dense, gritty, strong on technical detail."

—*Kirkus Reviews*

TIMEGODS' WORLD

TIMEDIVER'S DAWN
THE TIMEGOD

L. E. Modesitt, Jr.

TOR®

A TOM DOHERTY ASSOCIATES BOOK
NEW YORK

TIMEGODS' WORLD

This book comprises the novels
Timediver's Dawn, copyright © 1992 by L. E. Modesitt, Jr., and
The Timegod, copyright © 1993 by L. E. Modesitt, Jr.

This book is printed on acid-free paper.

Design by Jane Adele Regina

A Tor Book
Published by Tom Doherty Associates, LLC
175 Fifth Avenue
New York, NY 10010

www.tor.com

Tor® is a registered trademark of Tom Doherty Associates, LLC.

ISBN 0-312-87495-2

First Omnibus Edition: August 2000

Printed in the United States of America

0 9 8 7 6 5 4 3 2 1

CONTENTS

TIMEDIVER'S DAWN

For Wendy, Margot, and Mimi

Just because,
although each of you knows why.

■

THINK OF A world of witches, of high technology and space travel, of science and superstition. A world on the verge of changing inhabitable planets into green pastures and endless forests, a world so short of energy resources that all fuels are grown or captured from the sun.

You say there is no such world? Or that it is only our world, dressed up for a storyteller's pleasure?

Set aside your doubts . . . this world was as real as any you will know . . . and learn about the timedivers' dawn. Perhaps it began here:

"MERYN." THE SLIGHT, sandy-haired woman looked as though she carried perhaps a score of years, until she gazed upon one, and the darkness behind her eyes delivered the weight of centuries.

"Yes, Mother." The second woman, also slender and sandy-haired, could have been a twin to the first, except for the lesser depth of her eyes.

"It's time."

"I know."

"There can be no more witches in Eastron. Not now. Not with the empress of Westron's demands, and the weaknesses in the Duchy."

"But the Bardwalls still stand. . . ."

"And they will, and you may always return to look upon them. You must make a place among the people of Westron and learn their technologies. Our time has gone and will not come again for centuries. Not until they have stripped the last metals from the ground. Not until they have been hurled from the skies."

"Mother?"

"Yes."

"Do you really believe that?"

"Daughter, I know that Eastron is dying, and all the villagers and all the gentry will blame it on the witches. Because of the duke our faces are too well known. So I will face the empress with him, come what may, and you will survive."

"Mother!"

There is no answer, for the older witch has vanished.

The younger woman looked around the retreat, then continued placing her few things in the pack, which will be all that she can carry on her instant yet long journey.

IT SEEMS SO simple. It is not. It could have begun here as well:

"WITCH! WITCH!"

Thud! Crack!

One rock, then another, struck the whitewashed wall.

Their target, a stocky boy-child with strawberry blond hair, a dazed expression, and shoulders already overbroad, looked down from the low wall where he balanced. Looked down at the whitewashed surface where the rocks had struck near his feet, then back at the gathered handful of women, crippled veterans, and the priest.

". . . like his mother . . ."

". . . dead . . . thank Verlyt . . . !"

Crack! Whmmmpt!

"Suffer not a witch, nor a witch's child . . ."

The boy looked from one face to another, back and forth, as if seeking reassurance.

Crack!

One of the rocks struck his shoulder, hard enough to stagger him.

"Witch! Witch! Witch!" The chant began in earnest, echoing between the walls, drowning out the occasional low rumble of dry cloud thunder. Thunder that promised nothing but clouds that delivered no rain, no respite.

"Witch! Witch! Witch . . . !"

Crack!

Suddenly, the boy's dazed expression vanished and his face screwed up, as if he were about to cry. In a single motion, he tightened his lips and jumped down on the far side of the wall, away from the crowd, and began to run.

Pad, pad, pad, pad . . . ! The alleyway remained silent for an instant, the villagers momentarily silenced.

"Witch! Witch! Witch . . . !" The chant took on an even more frantic note.

Some of the veterans dragged themselves over the wall and hobbled or ran, knives in the hands of those who still had hands, after the fleeing child. Others turned back into the main street and dashed around toward the other end of the alley into which the child had fled.

"Witch! Witch! Witch . . . !"

Thud! Thud, thuuddd, thhuuddd . . . The heavy roll of the priests' drums supplemented the chant.

From huts and houses, from the vintners and the villas, the pursuers gathered, pounding down street and alley, tearing through house and hovel.

"There he is!"

"... witch-child ... !"

"SUFFER NOT A WITCH TO LIVE, NOR A WITCH'S CHILD!" boomed the amplified voice of the priest.

The boy, backed into a narrow niche between two walls behind the produce market, held a rock in each hand, waiting.

Crack! The first rock from a villager slapped against the wall.

Crack! Thud! Crack! Thud! The past experience of the rock throwers showed as stone after stone bounced against and around the boy.

He threw one stone back. It missed. He threw the other.

"Devil! Witch-child!"

Overhead, the dry thunder rumbled, and the dry clouds churned.

A rivulet of blood dribbled down the boy's face, no longer expressionless, but filled with rage, even as the tears diluted his blood into pinkish streaks.

Crack! Thud! Thud!

"Gone!"

"... damned witches ... ! reclaimed their own ..."

The small niche in the walls was empty, vacant but for rocks and streaks of blood upon the walls.

"... YOU HAVE RECLAIMED YOUR BIRTHRIGHT FROM THE WITCHES THIS DAY ..." bellowed the amplifier.

A third of a world away, two soldiers paused by the roadside to investigate a heap of clothing.

"Kid ... been beaten ..."

"Forcer!"

"Frillen, now what? Another discarded sack that has to be an aggrebel?" The heavy-set and silver-haired forcer glared at the two as he spoke.

The trooper pointed. "Kid. Beaten. He's still breathing."

"He'll live. Put him in the rear freighter with Garchuk. He looks strong. The ConFed home will take him. Now, let's get moving."

The two troopers shrugged. One lifted the boy and marched toward the military freight steamer. The other followed the ConFed forcer.

■■

"... AND NOW, IN the presence of the unknowable and the almighty, we wish you the greatest success in your striving to bring us all another world for all people, in peace, for our successors and their successors ..."

The face of the gray-haired and young-faced Emperor of Westron faded from the solideo link, to be replaced by the coat of arms of the Hrtallen.

"Rather impressive," observed the stocky man, his red hair somehow bushy in spite of its close-cropped nature.

"Isn't that the nature of royalty? To be impressive, I mean?" Her voice held an edge.

"That doesn't make young Hrtallen any less impressive. Besides, getting his formal support for the Mithrada planetforming can't hurt once the initial enthusiasm dies down."

"Assuming he isn't the politician his mother was."

"Lorinda."

"I know. It had to be done. The Eastron anarchy was a danger to everyone, but did they have to be so damned thorough? All the time that white-haired and sweet-faced old harpy was displaying motherly concern, her peacemakers were rooting out anyone who could pronounce the word anarchy."

The Imperial coat of arms faded from the screen, to be replaced in turn by an official Imperial newscaster in the traditional blue and gold. "That was the sendoff speech of the emperor, dedicating the unified Queryan mission designed to turn Mithrada into the second habitable planet within our solar system."

The view switched to an ancient circular brownstone tower, flying two banners, one the Westron flag, and the second bearing a sheaf of grain crossed with a single red flower—a ryall.

"But there are those who doubt the practicality and wisdom of tampering with the Mithradan ecosphere, such as it is. One of the doubters, here at the University of Vrecallitt, is Academician Terril Josset . . ."

"Turn it off, Harlon," snapped Lorinda. "One thing worse than a sincere emperor is an insincere and misguided academic."

The screen returned to a view of the stars before the *Hope*, as it edged inward toward the orbit of the sun's second planet, toward its mission to reform and cool the blistering wastes of Mithrada. To strip the heavy atmosphere and rebuild the planet in the image desired by men and women. To mine the only concentrations of metals within even impractical possibility, now that the thin outer asteroid belts had been stripped of what could be found.

∎∎∎

I WAS BORN in Bremarlyn, which no longer exists, like most of the cities and towns of Westron, the great western continent. Then it stood about one hundred kays east of Inequital.

Bremarlyn had little to distinguish it except that it contained the regional revenue office of the Imperial Government. My father was a solicitor in the service of the Crown, and he served as the local tax prosecutor of a government and a world that has passed into history.

My thoughts, scattered as they are, will be included in the sealed section of the Archives, while I still retain the power to ensure both their inclusion and the sealing of the records. Some things are best lost, but vanity being what it is, I have settled for censorship over oblivion. Anyone who does unlock the seals will, I trust, also read the factual supplements and data before coming to a final judgment on my follies.

Consecrated to the Temple as Sammis Arloff Olon, I still go by Sammis, although some persist in trying to distinguish me by using my original surname. That too shall pass, at least in another dozen millennia. Time flows more slowly these days, now that Query has left the seasons of the single-night moth and entered the long afternoon of the Immortals.

Why did it happen? How?

No one can answer the first question. As for the second, for me, it began with a dream.

In the dream I stood above four roads. There were no vehicles, no power wagons, no silent steamers, no gliding electrovans, just four roads.

One was gold, cold as the dark between stars.

One was black, and the heat rose from it as from the Grand Highway in summer.

One was red and smelled like memories.

And the last was blue, bright blue like tomorrow's dawn.

Despite the dream of these roads, then I had no special love of travel, nor do I yet. Everything I needed was in Bremarlyn—from the creek where I built dams to see how high I could raise the water behind my assembly of stones and sand to the fields where we played centreslot. No, I cannot say I had close friends, but we all played together most of the time, and, when we did not play, we fought.

In my first dream of the crossroads, I merely stood there paralyzed and unable to set foot on any road. Fear did not prevent me from taking that step. I could not move. Nor could I speak nor sigh. So I watched the four roads, somehow suspended above them, as each disappeared into its colored distance.

The four were not a crossroads exactly, and in the distance that was not distance, each split and splintered into hundreds of different directions, until each created its own horizon—blue, red, black, and gold. Yet all directions were the same, and every road went in all directions.

Wherever I was, watching the roads, it was cold, bonechilling cold.

Then, abruptly, as I wished to return to my bed and its comfort, I was there, sprawled on cold quilts. Cold quilts, as if I had not been sleeping there during my dream.

Feeling exhausted, though I had done nothing in my dream but watch, I slept . . . deeply. And I did not dream. Not then.

While I seldom remembered most of my dreams, the four roads remained with me, with their promise of anticipation and memory, heat and chill, long after I had roused myself from my quilts, long after I pulled on my Academy uniform and trudged off to classes.

IV

"MALFUNCTION ON SENSOR, alpha three, quad four, red." The metallic tone of the speaker reverberated through the module.

The monitoring officer's fingers seemed to meld with the keyboard while she accessed the network controlling the defective sensor. Her eyes widened as the data scripted out on the bluish screen before her. The sensor showed a temperature of 3° absolute positive, barely above absolute zero. On Mithrada, less than 120 million kays from the sun, that was patently impossible, not on a planetary surface so hot that water had never occurred in liquid form.

Shaking her head as if to clear her thoughts, she keyed the reset function.

Bleep.

The remote readings from the sensor on the planet below remained the same, long after the fractional units it took for the reset command to travel to the remote command network on the high plateau of Mithrada's northern hemisphere.

She took one deep breath, then another, before glancing at the sealed portal that separated the monitoring module from the rest of the planetary reformation station.

"Malfunction on sensor, beta six, quad three, orange. . . .

"Malfunction on sensor, gamma three . . .

"Malfunction on sensor, omicron eight . . .

The console before her blazed with maroon malfunction lights, bright points of brilliance that seared at her senses.

"Malfunction on sensor, delta four . . ."

With a sigh, she returned her attention to the original malfunctioning sensor and keyed the reset function again. And waited, ignoring the rising maroon tide that turned the module twilight-colored. And waited.

Bleep.

The sensor now registered a reading of 60° AP with a trend rate indicating a return to normal, for Mithrada, of close to 800° AP within one standard unit.

"Malfunction on sensor . . ."

The number of maroon lights continued to increase, even as the temperature on the first sensor continued to rise.

The monitoring officer ignored the more recent failures, finally blanking the row of screens above her on which the lights had flared. Then she returned her attention to the first failure, shaking her head slowly.

"Lorinda? What in Hell is going on planetside?" The intercom speaker carried a male voice.

"Tell you in a demistan. It looks like an impossible planetary cold wave." Her voice was hard, clipped, her eyes still on the sensor data.

"A cold wave? Are you all right?"

"Stop patronizing me, Harlon. This many data points don't lie. We've lost all temperature-sensitive remotes in four dozen subsectors. They all showed near-instantaneous temperature drops of eight hundred degrees."

"That's impossible."

"Malfunction in sensor, epsilon five . . .

"Malfunction in sensor . . ."

Lorinda cut off the audio warning system.

"Did you hear those, Harlon? Tell me which is less impossible— identical malfunctions of nearly a hundred randomly located sensors on eight different remote nets . . . simultaneously? Or one hundred severe temperature anomalies?"

"The whole system must be shot to hell . . ." came his reply.

"That could be, but there's an easy enough way to check. Have meteorology check the changes in surface winds. If it's not the sensors, there will be severe local changes."

"You think so?"

"I know so . . . if it's climate-caused. Check it out."

She shifted her monitoring to another early malfunction, which showed the same pattern of abrupt heat loss, followed by a gradual return toward normal Mithradan levels.

Her fingers began a series of calculations, based on the proximity of the apparent temperature drops to each other. With each input, and the resultant analysis, the frown on her face became more severe.

She removed the damper from the bank of display screens, and the module turned twilight-purple again. The light was so depressing that she immediately reblanked the screens. Lorinda hesitated a moment when the last screen analysis scripted out in front of her. Then she touched the intercom.

"Control central, this is monitoring. Analysis of sensor malfunction patterns indicates event is planet-based and not created from system failure."

"How do you know, monitoring?"

"Analysis of temperature gradients between malfunctions. Something . . . somethings . . . are acting like an absolute heat sink."

"Infraheat scan supports that, control central. So does preliminary met data . . ."

"Great . . . so rather than an understandable catastrophic equipment malfunction, we now have an impossible natural occurrence."

Lorinda shook her head in the privacy of the monitoring module. Not impossible—it had happened. And certainly not natural. Of that, she was all too sure.

THE SCIENTIST IN the pale blue tunic ran her left hand through her short-cut sandy hair, then tapped the light stylus on the console.

Looking up for a moment around the small windowless room, she pursed her lips. The gesture gave her face an elfin cast, which vanished as she concentrated and touched the keyboard.

On the screen before her, a title appeared in the formal script of Westra: "Project Vanish—Case III."

Her fingers played the keyboard again, and the angled script disappeared, replaced by a full-length view of a tall woman standing on a raised platform, surrounded by monitoring equipment. The subject wore a wide belt clustered with sensors over a plain singlesuit.

Abruptly, the woman on the screen vanished, leaving the platform empty.

The sandy-haired woman viewing the screen froze the image and studied it. Then she backtracked the visual, instant by instant. In one scan, the subject was present. In the next she was not.

Finally, the scientist touched the keyboard to remove the visual and replace it with the data from the monitoring equipment. The data readouts showed the same pattern. The subject's disappearance was instantaneous. No faded signals, no attenuation, only an absolute cut-off simultaneous on all equipment through the entire monitoring range.

The woman in blue pursed her lips again, ignoring the notation at the bottom of the arrayed data.

"Subject A-102-Green failed to return. No body found. No explosions noted simultaneously with disappearance. No other coordinated energy phenomena. Chronological analysis inconclusive."

Her fingers touched the console, almost as if independently of her thoughts, and the index returned to the screen. For a time, she regarded the first page of the lengthy index.

Evidence—that there was plenty of—but verifiable, measurable results indicating success? None to date—except her own personal observations, and they would not be considered objective, not to mention the questions they would raise.

At last, she blanked the index and stood, a woman with an almost elfin face, wearing the pale blue of a scientist. The severity of her hair and clothing hinted at the age she might have been. The smoothness of her complexion and the pale fairness of her skin indicated an age far younger than the expression in her eyes or the position which she held in the scientific hierarchy.

She sighed so softly that the expression was nearly soundless as she pressed the stud which put the computer system on standby. Just as soundlessly, she rose and stood before the darkened console, her eyes sweeping over the equipment for a last time, as if such a search could uncover the key she continued to seek.

Her steps were light, but slow, as they whispered her departure from the small modest office on an afternoon when most others had celebrated the holiday proclaimed by the emperor.

VI

"ALL THE ANOMALIES center here." The technician pointed to a circled area on the screen. "The general direction of movement is toward the planetary southwest—right along that line."

The officer frowned and gestured toward a series of triangles farther along in the direction outlined by the technician. "I assume those represent our planetary stocks."

"Just what we have there, sir."

"How much metal and support gear there?"

"About six months' worth. That's an estimate."

"And if whatever these things are freeze that, we lose six months of production equipment?"

"More than that. Don't forget we had to soft-land all of that, and we lost two of the landers doing it."

"Verlyt!" For a time, the slender man studied the screen and the gradual motions, and the abrupt temperature drops. Then he pointed again. "What's here, if anything?"

"That's the break between the two networks."

"Could we direct the equatorial laser and the microwave collector to focus on that point when the sensors indicate that's where these . . . these . . ."

"Frost Giants is what the recon types call them."

". . . things . . . these things are centered?"

"You want to fry them when they hit that point?"

"That's the idea. We can get plenty of energy from the orbital stations. What we don't have is more equipment, and for some reason that's exactly what your Frost Giants are interested in freezing."

"Do we know what will happen, sir?"

"No. But it can't be much worse than losing the entire planet-forming project, can it?"

The technician frowned. "I guess not, sir. I guess not. But what if the Frost Giants object?"

"It's their planet. If they kick us off, they kick us off, but there can't be more than a few. We may have to rethink, and maybe we can't complete the project, but we need to keep them away from the soft-landed equipment.

"That's my first objective. Then we'll see what happens."

VII

FIRST, THERE WERE the rumors. The Academy was always a place for rumors.

"Sammis, did you hear about the problems on Mithrada? Parts of the planet are freezing . . ."

I didn't even bother to answer. Astronomy had taught me enough about Mithrada to show how ridiculous that was. Hot enough to boil water, not to mention the higher atmospheric pressure there.

". . . serious . . . they called my brother off leave . . ."

". . . they're lifting the banned weapons, the big nuclear ones . . ."

At that point, Old Windlass walked in. We didn't have to stand, but were supposed to become silent, immediately.

". . . rebels from Eastron . . . do you think?"

". . . none of them left . . ."

"Master Olon, our lesson is *Carnelia*. I would appreciate it if you would turn your attention to whether *Carnelia* is a tragedy in the true sense of the word. You, too, Master Kryrel." Old Windlass—that was what we all called him, although his real name was Dr. Wendengless—would have discussed literature if the world had been crumbling and the schedule said it was time for literature.

"Uhhh . . ."

"Come now. Is *Carnelia* a tragedy? Yes or no? Surely, you must have *some* opinion."

"No, sir. *Carnelia* is a comedy disguised as a tragedy." My idea was not setting well, and all my plans for stringing along with Windlass's fondness for classifying everything as a tragedy had vanished because I had been listening to Jeen Kryrel and thinking why the rumors about Mithrada couldn't be correct.

"A comedy? Pardon the pun, gentlemen, but surely you jest? A comedy?"

"Yes, sir. I mean no, sir. If you take away the trappings of a court, and all the formalities, the situation is really a farce. Just because she had a single romp with the wrong nobleman, she's threatening to commit suicide? By throwing herself into a lily pond? And she drowns in waist-deep water? How can you take that seriously?"

"Master Sammis!" There was a pause. "How do you know the water is waist-deep in the Major Royal?"

"I checked in the Archives when I was in Inequital last week with my mother. The original plans say the pond was built to a quarter rod depth. It was later bricked up to a handspan, but at the time of *Carnelia*, I assume that it was the deeper level." Actually, I really hadn't done all that much research. I'd been discussing it with my mother, and she had mentioned the depths. But she was always right, and Old Windlass wouldn't know the difference.

"And where in the Archives did you find this wonderful information?"

"In the background information on the history of the Palace Major."

Windlass really looked confused, then. Started mumbling to himself, something about the material not being in the public domain. Finally, he looked up. "All right, Master Sammis . . . even if the Major Royal were only a quarter rod deep, you are missing the point through a technicality—"

Jeen was trying to keep from laughing, and Trien was grinning, and if Windlass saw them I was going to be in big trouble.

"—that Carnelia, indeed all the early Western royalty, placed an inordinate emphasis on sexual purity, perhaps because of the lower-class stigma attached to sexually transmitted diseases before the availability of modern medical techniques, and partly because of the need to ensure a clear line of royal descent in order to avoid a repetition of the chaos created by the Fylarian Fragmentation . . ."

I had to hand it to Windlass. He could talk his way out of anything.

". . . so you are correct in saying that in the modern context Carnelia's actions seem farcical. But that is not the question, Master Sammis. Are her actions farcical for the time and the society in which she existed? Are they? Come now?"

"It still seems like she overreacted, but it's hard to say, sir." I could have argued it either way.

"Master Sammis, last week you were disciplined for your reaction to criticism by a comrade of your performance during the centreslot title game. In fact, upon one occasion you failed to place an inflated rubber bladder inside a loose section of netting in the middle of a grassy field. This failure did not affect your survival, your future, or your status. It should not have affected your self-esteem, given your overall athletic reputation, despite your size. Yet you were so threatened by a mere verbal criticism that you employed bodily violence.

"Carnelia's whole value system and life may be threatened by her thoughtless action. Yet you, who react violently to a meaningless criticism of a generally meaningless game, are going to tell me that context is not important?"

Jeen was still grinning, but now he was laughing *at* me.

"No, sir."

"So you might consider accepting that context is vital in evaluating value systems?"

"Yes, sir."

"Master Kryrel . . ."

For some reason, freezing on Mithrada didn't seem quite so impossible after Old Windlass finished with me.

VIII

Some dreams never quite go away. So it was with my dream of the crossroads with its blue and red and gold and black directions that were all the same and all different.

Some nights that dream would flash before me, and then I would dream no more. Other nights, I would find myself moved from the crossroads in one direction or another, buffeted on invisible currents that were no less strong for not being felt or seen, until I was carried almost through a black chill wall into some place or time. Almost, but not quite, carried through that barrier, as though I stood behind a curtain where I could see most of what went on.

One dream was especially vivid. Or perhaps I recalled it because it so closely paralleled what actually occurred.

I had been carried into those black chill curtains that looked into another world, or so it seemed, and stood within a tower that glittered, inside and out. The tower was suffused with an energy that made it a beacon of sorts on both sides of the black curtain. No matter how I tried to look at the walls, they refused to stay in focus, even less than the other objects and people I could see from my obscured perspective.

Yet one thing was clear. The tower did not exist. Yet it was concretely there in my night/dream vision. I could see people walking through that tower. Some few looked ordinary. Ordinary as they looked, they were suffused with the same sort of energy as the tower itself, on a lesser scale.

Far less frequently, I could see others, dressed in tight black uniforms, who radiated a far greater sense of energy. In the most vivid of these dreams, the one that stuck with me, I could see one of the men in black more clearly than the others. He was below average in height, and far smaller than the colorful and uniformed giant who stood beside him. Yet the power which suffused him left the taller figure a mere shadow beside him.

The smaller man seemed graceful, with a narrow face and sandy hair. The strange part was that he stopped talking to the giant and looked straight at me, though I was certain no one could see me, ghost shadow that I was behind the black curtains of time or space or whatever.

I could feel his green eyes burning as he fixed them on me. And then he nodded and made a sign in the air that seemed like a benediction. The giant swung his head toward the smaller man, who answered before turning away from me and leaving me in that no-time place where reality and dreams seemed to almost meet.

The man seemed familiar, too familiar. Why had I seen him? What did the energy levels mean?

Before I could ponder the question, I stumbled from the blackness.

And was in trouble—serious trouble.

I did not wake in merely cold covers, or standing by my bed, as had happened once or twice when I had dreamed about the crossroads. I found myself standing in a winter rain, still wearing but a long nightshirt, and barefoot, at the foot of the stone walkway leading to the front door.

Whhhsssssttt . . . click, click, click, . . .

The half-frozen rain pelted down in sheets, as it always did in the Ninis storms, each sheet sweeping across the road and down the valley, followed by a break in the wind, cold ice drizzle, and then another pounding sheet of ice droplets striking hard enough to raise tiny welts on unprotected skin.

Most of my skin was either barely protected or totally uncovered.

Part of my mind was protesting. It was too early in the year for such a violent and chill storm. The afternoon before I had been picking chysts from the trees along the stone fence that separated our grounds from the Davniadses', and I had taken my tunic off. That's how warm it had been.

The changed weather wasn't paying any attention to my mental protests, but continued to raise welts on my skin and drench my nightshirt.

So I hurried gingerly toward the overhang of the front doorway, each bare foot planted as carefully as possible on the slick stones.

Not carefully enough, I discovered, as my bare feet slipped from beneath me and my posterior and flailing hands slapped down on the cold stones.

Scrabbling and edging along across stones that were slick as glass and cold as deep winter, I finally managed to reach the overhang and dry stones underfoot. From there getting inside was easy. I opened the heavy door and took three steps until I stood on the polished slate of the entry hall in an instant pool of water, with a few icicles hanging from the edge of my nightshirt.

Only after I was inside the house did I begin to shiver, either from relief or the accumulated impact of cold.

In those days no one in Bremarlyn locked or bolted doors. Why would we? Westron was prosperous; what little crime there might be was punished severely; and few of the lower classes traveled.

The hall was chill, chill enough that normally I would have worn a robe, but that cold was like a warm hearth compared to what I had left outside. What chilled me most was my soaking nightshirt. I wasted little time in stripping it off and carrying it to the kitchen where I wrung it out. Still naked, I took some rags and went back into the entry hall and wiped up the puddle I had left.

According to the big clock at the foot of the formal stairs, dawn was still some time away.

During the whole episode, I heard nothing from the maid down below, or from my parents above, but that may have been because any slight noise I made had been drowned out by the wind and the sound of the ice rain on windows and walls.

Then I put the rags in the empty wash bucket, hoping that Shaera would either think she had overlooked them or not want to mention the problem when she discovered them on the morrow.

Taking my damp nightshirt with me, I tiptoed up the back stairs to my room. I opened the window briefly, got pelted by the rain again, and closed it. After laying the wet nightshirt on the stone sill, I rummaged through my closet and found my other nightshirt, which, as a proper scholar in training, I was not to wear for another day. I yanked it on and climbed under the cold quilts, and began to shiver in earnest.

How had I gotten outside? Had I been sleepwalking? Did the dream have anything to do with it? What?

Surely I would have fallen on the ice going down the walk, and I swore that the chill of the ice underfoot and the rain had been too sudden for an awakening from a nightmare. Had I been sleepwalking, wouldn't I have wakened as soon as the cold and rain struck me, not all the way down the walk?

The questions seemed endless, but, surprisingly, shivers or not, I fell asleep before I could figure out answers that made sense.

When I woke the next morning, it was to a blaze of light. My first thought was that I had been transported to the tower of my night dream vision.

I heard nothing for a moment, but I could smell the odor of burnt sausage, which meant that Shaera was attempting breakfast. While she kept the large house spotless, she attacked cooking as if, like cleaning, it were to receive the full force of her ability and vigor. Full vigor meant high heat and overcooked meats and scorched breads.

The blaze of light came not from some dream tower, but from the sun flaring through and reflecting off the ice that coated the trees, the ground, and even the stones of the roadway.

I struggled from under my quilts, seeing that my breath did not quite turn to steam in the air of my bedroom, and went to the window.

The nightshirt was semi-frozen, and I lifted my hands.

The hall light was on, and that told me that the solar power units on the roof had begun to operate. They had been expensive, my father said, but he had always worried about relying totally on the electric current delivered through the semi-ceramic cables from the Imperial power authority. The power authority, of course, received its electricity from the satellite links, which had been the primary reason for the Westron space effort.

By pressing my nose close against the glass, I could see most of the front walk from the window. I pressed and looked. The walk was coated in ice, although it was beginning to steam as the solar cells warmed the coils beneath. There were darker patches where the ice was thinner that could have been footprints. But there was really no way to tell.

I turned and leaned against the wall, wondering which uniform I should wear to school, and realized my posterior was sore, very sore. From what I could see, lifting the nightshirt and craning over my own shoulder at the reflection of my backside, I had the beginning of a nasty bruise.

So I had not been dreaming. Now I was going crazy. First, out-of-season freezing rain, and now dreams about strange towers that left me rods from where I went to sleep.

"Sammis!"

My father's call halted any further speculation, since I had only a few minutes before I would be expected at the table, and fewer minutes after that if I wanted a ride in the steamer that would halve the walk to the Academy. My father did not believe in making things easier, nor did he believe in making things artificially harder. If he were going my way on part of his drive to work at the Imperial offices in Bremarlyn, I could ride as far as our paths converged . . . if I were ready, and if he had no other plans.

I raced for the washroom, mine alone, and certainly one of the few advantages of being an only child.

As I completed washing my face, I looked into the mirror. The face of my dream, the face of the man who had looked at me through the curtains of blackness, had been my face—older, more experienced, and unlined, but my face.

That made the whole mystery less real. How could I ever see myself anywhere? It had to have been a dream.

Since the sun promised to warm the ice, I chose a midweight uniform, the same blue and silver tunic over dark blue trousers, with the black boots we all had to wear.

"Sammis!"

"Coming!" I grabbed my pack and cloak and tumbled down the front stairs, taking a quick look at the spot on the floor behind the front door. No sign of water or water damage.

Both of them were at the table. Mother was dressed to go to the city—Inequital, not Bremarlyn—with leather dress boots, wide trousers and matching jacket. Of course, she would be wearing the flynyx coat Father had given her for their anniversary and driving the gold steamer. An independent woman, my mother, despite my father's importance as the preeminent regional solicitor of taxes and commerce. That he could also claim to be a descendent of the old dukes of Ronwic did not disturb her either. Nor did it seem to impress her. Little of pomp seemed to faze her.

I could tell she had been up early and had completed her morning workout, although she had probably not taken a run, as she usually did. Once or twice I had tried to follow her regimen and decided against it. She was only a shade taller than I was; but underneath her careful tailoring were muscles it would take years before I could match. Yet she never made an issue about it. She just got up and did it, without fail, every morning.

She had taken a degree herself, in economic theory and practice, and had published one or two monographs, claiming that it had been "just to keep her hand in," whatever that meant. She also was far more physical than my father, both with her own exercise room in the cellars and her ongoing classes in Delkaiba—that was the old Westron martial art. All the same, I was never quite sure what she did while I was in school or on her infrequent but long and solitary "vacations." Neither she nor my father ever mentioned it. And, somehow, my innumerable questions never quite got answered.

"Have some sausage, Sammis. Need some protein, not just starch."

I reached for the least burned sausage on the platter.

"What do you think about this business on Mithrada?"

"What business?" I was looking for an unburned roll, preferably to avoid having to take another sausage.

"The strange reports about the project problems. You don't discuss it in school?"

My mouth was full. So I nodded. I hadn't paid that much attention. So the emperor wanted another planet. There was still plenty of room in Westron, and more than that in Eastron.

"Waste of money. Terrible waste of tax revenues . . ." mumbled my father.

My mother frowned, which was also strange. Usually she wore an exercise singlesuit to breakfast and never showed other than a pleasant disposition. Again, she changed the subject quickly. "Are you sure that uniform is warm enough?"

"Ice storm was a freak," I mouthed. "Melting off already."

"Don't talk with your mouth full." That was Father.

"All too many freak occurrences," murmured Mother, so softly that Father, with his bad ear that he refused to have examined, heard nothing.

I looked at her, and she shook her head minutely, as if to tell me not to ask. I didn't. Instead, I grabbed the last roll, taking bites first from an almost ripe chyst and then from the roll.

Father pursed his lips and took a last sip from his cup.

"Coming?"

I swallowed the last mouthful, wiped my face, and nodded.

"Meet you at the steamer."

IX

"WHAT HAPPENED . . . ?"

"Get the lights!" That was Jeen Kryrel. He'd been trapped in his uncle's silo as a youngster, still didn't like darkness, even dim corners.

The buzz of the overhead lamps had disappeared with the lights themselves.

"Silence!" Dr. Yellertond's voice cut right through the gloom of the laboratory.

Since I hadn't been looking forward to the lab anyway, the power loss was almost welcome. The heavy slatetopped tables and the aged wood cabinets reeked of sulfur and flame . . . and of age. My father had gone to the Academy, and his father.

"You may remain at your stations while I check with the magister. You may talk *quietly*. Anyone whose voice I can hear will draw holiday duties."

The groan at that was clear. Dr. Yellertond loved to assign holiday duties.

"First power failure I've been in . . ."

"Do you suppose it was the satellite relay?"

"Probably just an interrupter here."

I didn't say anything. There had already been too many coincidences, and the power loss had something to do with the Mithrada situation. For some reason, I thought about my mother. She had not been planning to go to Inequital the night before. Yet she had been up and dressed, and very preoccupied.

She had friends in the capital—that was why she spent so much time there, she said, but that would not have explained her worried expression. She never looked worried. And the ice storm—that was unusual.

"What do you think, Sammis?"

"Yes, what's the runt think?"

What I thought about was giving Reylin a broken leg. My mother had instructed me in Delkaiba, just enough to make me cautious about trying to use it. But Reylin was always asking for a lesson of sorts.

"I think that the lights are going to stay out—for a long time." The words popped out before I could draw them back.

"Now the runt's a prophet . . ."

Already the lab was getting chilly, or it seemed that way to me, and the sulfur smell was more pungent than usual. The bruise I had gotten in falling on the icy front walk in my nightmare, or whatever, hurt if I sat on the lab stool wrong.

"Silence!" Dr. Yellertond was standing in the laboratory doorway.

The murmurs and whispers vanished into the gloom of the big classroom.

"The power outage is not local, but stems from a failure in the satellite relay systems. You are all dismissed. Anyone who does not live within walking distance of the Academy may wait in the library or the main anteroom of the administration building."

The tall, thin professor watched as we gathered books and notes together, and as we trooped out into the corridor, boots scuffling on the polished stone floors.

Like everything else in Westron the Academy was constructed mostly of stone, with slate roofing on heavy timbers. Interior walls were either paneled or plastered and replastered.

That was because most of the petroleum and iron had been exhausted by the First Civilization, or so Dr. Editris had said. He claimed the failure of the few Eastron oil reserves had led to the fall of the Eastron Republic . . . but that was history. I wondered if my father would be home when I got there, or if I would have to avoid Shaera by myself. Certainly, if the power link had failed for the Academy, there would be no power for the small Imperial complex at Bremarlyn, or for the Revenue Court.

". . . could be serious . . ."

". . . first time we've been dismissed in mid-day . . ."

Dr. Yellertond kept swinging around to find someone to glare at, but every time he started to turn the whispers disappeared. Allyson once had told me that the whispers at the girls' academy—it was called Tyrnelle House—were far worse.

Were they sending the girls home from Tyrnelle? If so, I could go over to the Davniadses. That would be better than staying at home with Shaera, who, for all her well-intentioned energy, would try to find something for me to do that I was really supposed to do. Allyson was interesting to talk to, even if she did look down on me.

"Silence!" The word had always been Dr. Yellertond's favorite, and he was not opposed to overusing it.

By then, we had all straggled into the central robing hall, where our lockers lined the walls. More than half the upper classes were already there, and Dr. Yellertond winced as the whispers washed over and around him. The man should have been a mystic or a retreat academic, not a teacher of young adults.

Finally, he shrugged, as if to wash his hands of us, and made a vague gesture, muttering something I could not hear.

"Are we officially dismissed?" I asked Loiren, who was grabbing a heavy winter cloak from his locker, right next to mine.

"That's what the assistant magister announced, just before old quiet-ass brought you guys in."

I grabbed my own cloak. I'd tried to take the lightweight one that morning, but Shaera and my mother had forced the heavier one on me, and it was hard to argue against both of them successfully. Since I'd wanted to catch the steamer ride with Dad—it did save me nearly a kay in walking—I'd taken the heavy black one.

Once I had the cloak, I took the pack, but I left all the books.

"You aren't taking your studies?" asked Loiren in surprise as he closed his locker.

"Why bother? It should be a few days before we get power back, and they'll have to review anyway."

"It's your head, Sammis."

I ignored Loiren. He meant well, but there were too many coincidences, and I wanted to get to the Davniadses.

Outside, it was still cold and sunny, and the wind coming up the hill from the west chilled my ears immediately. A good forty others were already marching down toward the road where most, I suspected, would find steamers to take them home. The bells in the Academy's temple were ringing to announce dismissal.

From the east, I could hear the lighter tones from Tyrnelle House, occasionally disappearing in the whistle of the wind. Clutching my cloak around me tighter, I was glad that I had not been successful in arguing for the lighter-weight overwear. Trudging down the paving stones toward the highway, I hunched up inside the heavy wool.

Clouds were piling up on the horizon, and it looked like another storm was pelting Inequital. While the capital wasn't visible from the low hills of Bremarlyn, I'd been there enough to imagine what it must be like, with sheets of heavy rain pouring through kay after kay of three, four, and even five story buildings—and the Grand Tower. Some of the anarchists claimed that the emperor and, before her death, his mother the Grand Empress, had used their power to keep other towers from being built.

Hoping my mother had left before the storm had hit, I whistled one or two notes of the Marching Song, but the wind was too bitter to keep whistling. So I put my head down and lengthened my steps. Despite my size, I could walk, or run, faster than anyone at the Academy. Not that I was about to in the cold.

By the time I started along the walking trail by the highway, uphill most of the way, my nose was running from the cold. The clouds from the west had begun to shut off the sunlight, and the wind was building up into a gale, bringing with it an acrid odor.

Half a kay further, and I was looking for the occasional steamer that might be headed my way, but most people lived on the eastern side of Bremarlyn. We lived on the more isolated side, closer to Inequital and to the Revenue Court where my father practiced.

Another half a kay, and I had reached the side road that wound gently toward our land. My ears were numb, and my breath made me look like a malfunctioning steamer myself. The ground crackled underfoot, and whatever the storm brought it wouldn't be rain, but snow or ice. Overhead, the clouds were thickening into an ugly gray.

Wheeep! Wheeep!

Waving from the window of the Davniadses' slate gray steamer was Allyson. I stumbled over the half-frozen turf and into the rear seat. Allyson and her mother were in the front.

"You look frozen, Sammis. What on earth are you doing out in this?"

"Mother's in Inequital, and Father is at work. At least he was. It was sunny when I left the Academy."

"I do hope your mother is all right, Sammis. All the communications links with the capital are out, just like the power." Germania Davniads was a big woman with a tiny voice. Allyson had her father's booming voice and both parents' build, but she wasn't overweight like her mother. She had a nice figure and a nice smile. She was a good head taller than me, not to mention a year or so older.

As the steamer hummed up the road, I readjusted my cloak. There was no heat, though, and while I could feel the circulation returning to my fingers and toes, the absence of wind alone was not enough to immediately thaw me out.

"I do hope Jerz managed to leave Jillriko early. He took the runabout." Germania kept her eyes on the winding road as her small voice continued. "It's such a long trip back, especially if the rain gets heavy, and that can easily happen at this time of year . . ."

Allyson half-turned and ran her eyes over my cloak. "It's too cold to rain, Mother. Don't you think so, Sammis?"

"Ice or snow, I suppose."

"I do hope that it isn't ice. The runabout is so light, and the hill to our place is so steep . . . Sammis, would you like me to run you all the way up to your doorway?"

"What . . . ?"

"Mother wanted to know if you wanted to come over and have hot cider, or if you had to get home immediately," added Allyson quickly.

"Cider sounds good . . ."

"Then we'll just take you to our place. All right, Mother?"

"If you think that is all right, dear. But won't your father and mother worry? Especially in this weather . . . and if it gets icy . . ."

By then, the steamer was nearing the turnoff for our drive. I looked up. A pair of soldiers stood by the drive, each carrying some sort of weapon.

"Just keep going, Mother." Allyson's voice was commanding.

"If you say so . . . dear . . . but . . . what are those men doing there? Doesn't your father work for the government, Sammis? Is there something wrong?"

Germania kept driving toward the Davniadses', and the soldiers watched us go without even turning their heads.

I felt cold again—very cold. Why would soldiers be stationed at our house? Did it have something to do with all the coincidences, or with the power losses?

Allyson was looking at me. She raised her eyebrows.

I shrugged, and shook my head. "Don't know." My words were barely more than mouthed.

She nodded.

Although I continued to study the lower part of our grounds until we started up the wide drive to the Davniadses', nothing seemed changed—except for the soldiers.

"Here we are . . . I do believe that I will put the steamer in the locker. The weather will not do it any good, and we certainly don't plan to go anywhere . . ."

"Sammis?"

"No. When it's time to go home, I'll just take the back path. It's

sheltered most of the way, and it's quicker than driving." More important, I could take it and not be seen. Perhaps someone in a case my
father had been prosecuting had made a threat against him. That had
happened once several years ago, and we had soldiers guarding the area
for weeks. But nothing had ever happened.

The steamer hummed to a stop inside the locker building.

"Mother, if you would see to the cider, Sammis and I will drain the
tank and close up . . ."

"If you wouldn't mind . . ."

"It's certainly no problem," I volunteered.

"Would you like your cider straight . . . or with chyst?"

I opened the door and scrambled out, carefully checking the hinges
before closing it. "With chyst, please."

The drainage hose was in about the same place as in our locker, and
I unrolled it, attaching the funnel clip to the end. The gray steamer—
the name plate said Altera—had one of the new side pipe drains, which
made it easy.

Unless it was going to be cold enough to freeze, steamers didn't need
to have their water drained, but Mother—she was the mechanical one—
always insisted that both of ours be drained whenever they were not in
use. Allyson didn't object when I began to drain the water. It was almost
clear, the sign of a well-maintained vehicle.

Allyson was topping off the etheline, presumably so that she did not
have to do it in the morning. But etheline never froze, not in Bremarlyn,
anyway, although in places like Southpoint all the steamers had to have
heating systems built into the water and fuel bunkers and even into the
steamers themselves.

I finished draining off the water and closed the steamer's drain valve,
then began coiling the hose. My hands were getting numb again, from
the chill and the water I had spilled on them. Even inside the locker I
could see the steam from my breath.

"How are we going to have hot cider?" I asked. "There's no power
and no sunlight."

"There's a small etheline burner in the kitchen. Mother insisted on
it, and it does come in handy." Allyson was wiping her hands on the
towel by the pump handle.

Straight black hair, but twisted up at her neck, dark blue eyes, and
a warm smile—Allyson was nice-looking, and I enjoyed being around
her, but more as if she were an older sister. She was just so much taller,
and older, in so many ways, than I was.

"Do you really know what's going on at your house?"

"No. It could be like two years ago, when that oil merchant was caught cheating on his revenue payments and threatened to have us all boiled in flynyx oil. We had some soldiers then."

Allyson touched my shoulder. I jumped.

"Sorry. You looked upset."

"I am. My mother left for Inequital this morning, and she was worried. Very worried, and she's *never* worried."

"What does she do? Nobody knows, for all the years you Olons have lived here. That house was, what, your grandfather's?"

"Right. It was Grandfather's, but I never met him."

Allyson motioned toward the locker door. She was wearing some kind of scent, like flowers, and it smelled good on her. "The cider should be ready, and you could use some. What about your mother, though?"

That was another thing I liked about Allyson. She didn't play the verbal games so many girls did. Not with me, at least. She just said what she had in mind.

"I really don't know. She travels a lot, and she's published some monographs. She doesn't talk about it." Even in the courtyard between the locker and the main house it was cold. I stopped and let Allyson handle the door latch. It was her door, and she was wearing gloves. I'd left mine at home.

The courtyard was cold, but because the Davniadses had left more of the woods around their place, the wind was less. Except for the drive, you would scarcely have known a house was there.

"You don't know what your own mother does?"

"I've asked. She's never answered, and when she doesn't want to answer, she doesn't. Period. Besides, you know that."

Allyson shook her head, as she made sure the latch was secure. "I know, but I was hoping . . ."

We walked quickly up the dozen steps to the rear door that led to the kitchen. The warmth of the house felt good, but I wondered how long the stored energy would last. That was the problem with solar heat, especially when it was cloudy for days on end. Thank Verlyt that Bremarlyn had lots of sun.

"Allyson? Sammis? The cider is set up in the side room, and there's a fire in the grate. I'm resting up here, but I'll be down later."

So we hung up our cloaks in the back closet, and I followed Allyson up to the side room, where I found the explanation for at least some of the warmth. The Davniadses had a small wood-burning stove grate instead of a solar storage drum or a fireplace. A small table was set with two cups and two plates. In the center was a serving platter with cheeses, three or four crumb rolls, and several slices of chyst, in addition to the wedge set by one cup.

"Wood-burning?"

"Father insisted on some room that could be heated during storms if we lost the electric power link. There's one upstairs as well. Mother is probably having her cider there."

I took the chair by the chyst cider, and Allyson sat down across from me. For the first time in hours, my ears felt comfortable. I unbuttoned the collar of my tunic, sipping the warm cider slowly and realizing just how cold it had been outside.

"That's snow." Her voice was softer. Her hands cradled the cup as she looked out through the double glass of the two wide windows.

Outside, the snow drove by the window, almost like white rain, it was so heavy.

"Verlyt! I'd better get home. No one knows where I am!"

"Sammis. Wait a bit. You said yourself that no one's likely to be home. And a few minutes more won't make that much difference. You need to warm up and have something else to eat."

Still on the edge of my chair, I reached for one of the crumb rolls, forcing myself to eat it slowly, with an occasional sip of cider. Nothing seemed to make sense—not the snow, for we seldom had snow in Bremarlyn; nor the cold, which was more like Southpoint; nor the soldiers. Especially not the soldiers.

"The soldiers again?"

I nodded, since my mouth was full.

"It doesn't make much sense." Allyson paused. "Could your mother be one of the Hands?"

". . . ouughchchouupphh . . ." I had all I could do to keep from choking on the spot. My mother, my well-educated and scholarly mother, an Imperial Hand? One of the emperor's unknown but highly trusted agents?

"Well . . . it does make sense, Sammis. She travels, and no one, not even her family, knows where. She is brilliant and well-educated. She is in fantastic shape, and no one in Inequital or anywhere else would know anything about her."

All of what Allyson said was true, but the whole idea was ridiculous. My well-tailored and devoted mother? With her flynyx coat?

"No, that's ridiculous . . ."

"Then why the soldiers?"

"You might as well ask 'Why the snow?', Allyson." I shrugged. "It's got to be tied up with the Mithradan mess . . . but without power we can't even hear the news."

"You don't have batteries?"

"Do you?"

"No . . . Father says they're too expensive."

I grinned. "Sounds like mine." I knew I needed something to eat. The midday meal at the Academy had been yellow fish stew, which tasted worse than it sounded. But I wanted to gulp the rolls and cheese down and start home. My guts were tightening just thinking about Allyson's suggestion, which made far too much sense. And I was afraid that the soldiers around my home meant nothing good. Nothing at all good.

"Now I've got you worried, don't I?"

"Just a little . . ."

Her hand touched mine, covered it, and I sat there, enjoying her touch and still worrying.

"Let me come with you."

I shook my head. "No. If there's no problem, then there's no reason for you to freeze. If there is a problem, I wouldn't want you involved."

She nodded, understanding what I meant. The roundups after the Eastron cleanup had been thorough, very thorough.

I slowly chewed a second slice of cheese, not tasting it. I swallowed and felt it settle like ice in my stomach. Even a sip of cider didn't seem to warm the cold weight there. So I stood up.

Allyson did also. "Please be careful."

"I'll try." I tried to grin, but it was forced.

"Before you go . . . let me show you something."

Show me something? Allyson displayed concern, but not the almost romantic implications of her statement.

She blushed as I considered her words.

"That sounds . . . different . . . from what I meant . . . just follow me . . ." She went from the side room into the kitchen and then opened a narrow doorway leading downward into a lower level of the house, toward the old servant's quarters, not that very many of the gentry had servants any longer, as we had Shaera. But the stairway was clean, as was the hallway. At the end was a heavy door to the outside, which opened onto the rear hillside underneath the veranda.

I'd seen the door from the lawn before, and wondered where it went. Now I was seeing it from the inside. Although the lower level was not heated, it wasn't that cold, and I could feel the residual warmth from above and from the main solar tap.

Allyson stepped back from the outside doorway and eased open one of the hallway doors into a small room with a single bed—one covered mattress on a simple wooden frame—and a lamp. The room had no window, and the walls were a clean but old cream plaster.

"There are quilts on the foot of the bed . . . here . . . and I'll leave the door unbolted. There is still a lock, but the key will be under the rock on the right."

"Why?" I whispered, knowing I didn't have to, but figuring that this invitation did not exactly have familial approval.

"If no one knows you're here, then they can't say you are, and Mother always has to tell everything. This way, if there's something wrong, you can at least have a place where you won't freeze. I'll see if I can find some warmer clothes and some food."

We both knew what she was saying. If the soldiers were not a protective detail, then anyone who helped me was in danger of losing everything as well. Even in making shelter available in a hidden fashion Allyson was risking a lot.

It would be only a while before her father arrived home, and he certainly, knowing Jerz Davniads, would ask the soldiers what was happening.

"I should be going . . ."

"I know."

Neither one of us said anything as we climbed back up the old stairs to the kitchen. As I pulled on my cloak, Allyson handed me a pair of faded leather gloves.

"You'll need them. Bring them back when you can."

I nodded, still having to look up at her.

Creaakkkk . . . whssllllsss . . .

The wind nearly tore the kitchen door from my hands as I stepped out into the chill. The afternoon looked more like twilight. The tiny white flakes fell as thick as a summer thundershower.

Not looking back, I plunged into the storm and down the back lawn, where the snow was almost ankle deep, nearly falling several times before I reached the trees and the narrow path that wound along the hillsides toward our house.

Chhichiii . . .

A grossjay jabbered from the evergreen branches, his call the only sound above the hissing of the snow and the whining of the wind.

By the time I was five rods into the woods, I could not even tell, looking over my shoulder, that there was a house uphill from where I walked. The path seemed longer than usual; my ears were numb; and my toes tingled by the time I reached the gate in the old stone wall. The wooden gate itself had been removed when my father was a boy. Only a gap in the stonework remained. The wall marked the boundary between our lands and the Davniadses', and on the other side were the remnants of Grandfather's orchards, mostly chyst, but some pearapple.

A hint of an acrid odor in the air tugged at my nose, and I stopped short of the gate, knowing that to return through the wall led to more than I really wanted to handle. Edging up the gap, I studied the path, but there were no prints in the snow, no sign of anyone this far down in the orchards.

The house was still a good hundred rods or more uphill, and the straggling remnants of the old orchards ran to within twenty rods of the back terrace.

After I went through the wall, my steps were even more deliberate, and I left the path, walking instead from tree to tree, pausing and looking uphill. The acrid odor got stronger and stronger, but I could see nothing through the trees—not until I was almost to the top end of the orchard.

The light from the fire lit up the entire house, and the row of soldiers formed a cordon around it. None of them were looking out into the storm, but at the burning house. All of them had weapons leveled.

I scuttled up into the lower branches of a pearapple, trying to sort it out, trying to keep my guts from turning inside out.

Why were they burning the house? And who were they?

I watched for a time, conscious of the cold creeping through me, as the flames continued to leap into the storm. Despite the fire and the cold, none of the soldiers relaxed in their scrutiny of the house.

One figure, presumably an officer, walked the outer perimeter. The second time he passed within a few rods of the tree where I was huddled on the back side of the trunk, peering around at the destruction. That was when I saw the shoulder patch, saw and recognized the emblem of the ConFed Marines, the same marines who were the shock troops in the Eastron occupation. The same marines whose intelligence service had handled rounding up the Eastron sympathizers.

Why were they burning my house? Why did they keep studying it as if something were hidden inside?

CCCRRRUMMMPPPP!

I had to hang on to the tree as it shook with the force of the explosion.

All of the marines were flattened on the snow. Some moved, as the fire burned even higher, sending billows of black smoke up into evening. Others looked as though they would never move.

Although I did not know what had caused the explosion—certainly it had not been expected by the marines—none of those who survived were likely to be favorably inclined toward anyone or anything associated with the house. Slipping down from the tree, I managed to stagger on unsteady feet through the still-heavy snow toward the path to the Davniadses'.

By now, the powdery stuff reached well over my ankles and showed no signs of stopping. Between the oncoming night and the clouds, the darkness made each step uncertain.

I kept looking back, but by the time I reached the wall I could see only a dim glow through the branches and the snow. The wind had not died down, but increased and whipped the edges of my cloak.

When I finally reached the Davniadses' lawn, it was a sea of white, churned by the wind. Only a few lights were on, probably etheline lamps or candles. Although the wind might have covered my tracks, I circled the lawn and edged up partly from the side, staying far enough from the veranda wall so that the drifting snow would cover my steps, concealing any sign that would show I knew in advance where I was going.

Probably a vain precaution, one way or another, but that was what I did.

The key was where Allyson had said it would be, although it took me some time to find it in the dark, and even more time to brush snow back in place. Neither the door nor the lock creaked, for which I was thankful.

Closing the door and latching it was more difficult because it was hard to see in the near-total darkness, and I had neither flash nor glow rod. Then, because I wanted to make no noise at all, my progress to the servant's room was even slower. As I opened that door, I discovered I could see, barely. A dim glow rod lay on the single small waist-high wardrobe, next to a small package.

First, I shook out my cloak in the corner away from the door and wardrobe, and brushed the loose snow off my Academy uniform. Then I unlaced my boots and took them off. My toes began to sting as feeling returned. I spread out the cloak, hoping it would dry somewhat, and put the boots next to them.

There was no note by the rod or the package, which contained some dried meat and fruit, several slices of bread, and other wrapped items I could not determine, as well as a small tool kit.

My uniform was damp and clammy. Off it came, and I draped it over the wardrobe and began to shiver even more violently. The two quilts helped, and I curled into a ball on the old bed, trying to sort things out.

Nothing was very clear, nothing at all. The marines had orders to burn the house, and that was a punishment only sanctioned by the emperor for traitors and their families. I knew we weren't traitors.

How long I lay there, I don't know, but finally the shivers stopped and my eyes closed, and I could appreciate not being caught in the fire or the cold of the storm. I think I slept.

THE BLOND WOMAN appeared in a recess off the Fountain Court, shadowed in darkness. Her hair was bound tightly, and she wore a dark single-piece military coverall and formfitting dull black boots. Around her waist was a military-style equipment belt bearing a number of items, including a projectile pistol.

The Fountain Court was deserted, except for a single Imperial guard who stood at the closed bronze doors to the Inner Palace.

The woman slipped an insignia onto each collar and a glistening badge into the holder on her chest as she walked toward the guard. Her breathing was deep, but even, as if she were recovering from heavy exertion.

Making no attempt to conceal her steps, she marched toward the guard.

"Halt. Who goes there?"

"Major Erlynn."

"Advance and be recognized." The guard raised the wide-angle shredder and turned it toward the major.

The woman vanished. The guard squinted, leaning forward . . .

Crack! He slumped to the floor with a broken neck from the single blow delivered by the major who had appeared next to him.

The major surveyed the ConFed Marine uniform, and shook her head slowly.

Even through the heavy and ancient walls, she could hear the crowd noise rising as the mobs roared in their surge toward the palace. She had checked the main gate, but those guards had either left or been removed. The gate mechanism had been disabled as well. The broadsides scattered throughout Inequital were slickly printed, far too slickly for revolutionaries in a world that had neither seen nor tolerated revolt for decades.

Another military coup attempt, using the unrest created by the aliens on Mithrada?

A single guard. That was almost planned treason, and now nothing she could do would stop the fall of the emperor. All she could do to complete her duty was to ensure the usurpers would not profit either. She turned and vanished.

A flash of light blistered from down the court, momentarily illuminating the fallen figure.

"Damned witch."

"She won't save him this time."

Within moments, the mob had begun to pour through the Fountain Court toward the Imperial apartments.

A quarter of a continent away, a woman still wearing the insignia of a major appeared behind the operator of a lighted full-wall console.

Crack!

The operator slumped dead in the seat.

Without moving the body, the major leaned over and touched the control room locks before she began entering a new set of coordinates.

Brinnnggg!

Ignoring the alarm that she had known her actions would trigger, she entered the override codes she was not supposed to have. She touched the launch controls, one after the other, until the signals had been sent to the remaining orbital satellite, the one without personnel, the one untouched by the Enemy. As she waited for the return signal, the one which she must answer with a second confirmation, she could hear the cutting lasers being wheeled to the heavy doors.

Hssssstttttt . . .

The sound and smell of molten metal began to permeate the small room.

A single amber light flashed, then another, until five lights were lit. She entered a second set of codes, and triggered them.

Ssssssstttttt!

A narrow beam lanced through the hole in the doors, needling through the woman's body.

"Pray I did right . . ." She muttered the words, staggered, then vanished, leaving only several drops of a sticky black substance on the tiles.

Outside the doors, the lasers hissed a moment longer.

Across the solar system, five satellite launch doors opened, waiting for the return signal that would unleash sunfire on the Enemy.

XI

AGAIN, THERE WAS the dream of the crossroads, the red and the blue, the black and the gold, and they were even more real, as if I only had to wish to step through the black curtain and stand upon that uncertain intersection.

I held back, almost as if there were something to wait for.

Then—perhaps it was a door opening, a footstep on the staircase, but the faintest of sounds—and I was awake, heart beating quickly and staring at the closed door.

Although the room was dark, except for the dimness of the glow rod, it could have been morning for all I knew. I did not think so, not with the tiredness and the soreness I still felt. Finally warm, I was wrapped in the two old quilts that Allyson had laid out for me.

Another faint step, and I relaxed slightly. The tread was too light for Jerz Davniads—he shook the floors when he moved. Even the stone of the cellar hallway would have resounded. That meant either Allyson, her much older sister Isolde, or their mother.

Whssssppp . . .

A robed figure slipped inside the doorway, carrying a second glow rod.

"Sammis?"

I nodded, relieved that it was Allyson, then whispered as I realized she couldn't see me. "Here. On the bed."

By now I could see a rueful grin. "Where else would you be?"

"What time is it?"

We were still whispering.

"Close to midnight." She sat down on the very edge of the bed, her high-necked robe wrapped tightly around her. "Father stopped by your drive, not long after you left . . . Sammis, those were ConFed Marines, and they wouldn't talk to him. They wouldn't even let him go until they had checked his name and position and searched the runabout."

"I know. I know. They burned the house . . ." My voice caught. Despite myself, I had trouble talking. ". . . kept watching the house, with weapons, ready to shoot anyone who tried to get out . . ."

"Sammis . . . why? What were you doing?"

"Nothing . . . you know Dad . . . all the trouble he took for the court . . . all the years . . . and his father . . ." I shook my head. In the darkness it seemed only half real, yet I was hiding in the Davniadses' servant's quarters.

"Your mother?" She extended a hand, and I took it.

"I just don't know . . . never . . . never would have believed it . . ."

"We're leaving in the morning, Father says. That means midday."

"Leaving . . . ?"

"Sammis, things are much worse than we thought. Father says that the whole Mithradan expedition was wiped out, including the space stations there. The power link was destroyed. There were riots in Inequital, and the broadcast video channels are off the air. There are some audio channels broadcasting, but from the east. Nothing from the capital."

I was tired, and sore, and my back was still bruised from the dream fall I had taken—had it only been a day earlier? None of it made sense.

All I could do was shake my head. I couldn't even say anything. I think my cheeks were wet, because even with the glow rods I had trouble focusing.

"Are you all right? No, that's a stupid question . . ." Allyson put an arm around my shoulders, and until she steadied me, I hadn't realized that I was shaking all over. "You can hold on to me. Just hold on to me."

I did. As if she were the only thing solid in a dissolving world, as if she were the only warmth in winter.

One of her hands, cool and warm at the same time, brushed my hair out of my face, kneaded the back of my neck to ease some of the hurt, some of the stiffness.

"Move over a little," she suggested. "My feet are cold."

And I did that too, as she lay down next to me, holding me almost as tightly as I held her.

When I could see again, clearly, Allyson was staring at the ceiling, even though she still had one arm around me, and I had both of mine around her.

"Worried?" My voice was unsteady.

"Me?" She kept looking at the ceiling.

"You."

For a while, neither one of us said anything. I thought I could hear the whistle of the wind outside. Otherwise, the house was silent.

"Yes. Father says that we'll be safer at the summer place in Olviad. It was originally a family refuge from the Ronwic times. The gray steamer . . . is special . . . too. Father used to race, you know."

"Your father wants to wait out the storm?"

Allyson nodded. "He wasn't happy about that, but he said there wasn't any choice. The marines upset him. He didn't say much, but I could tell he was worried. Mother doesn't understand anything. And Isolde—she was in Inequital, but father says there's nothing to be done . . . nothing to be done . . ."

By then, Allyson was shaking. So I told her, "Hold me. Just hold me. I'm right here."

And she did, and I think we both shook, hanging on to each other, knowing that a familiar world was coming apart, and not knowing why.

Outside, the wind whistled softly, on and off, as if the storm might be dying down.

Inside, behind the timber and stone and plaster, Allyson and I held each other, trying to hold off the storm, or what it had so suddenly come to represent, our feelings jumbled together between us and the quilts.

"I need to get back upstairs . . ."

"I know . . ."

"Father will be checking here in the morning, and . . ."

"I know that, too." Jerz Davniads was a friendly man, but he would certainly not hesitate to turn me in to the marines if he thought it would improve the chances of his family's survival. He might not think so, and wouldn't turn me over unless it would help. But there was no sense in risking it.

"Sammis . . . ?" Allyson turned her face toward me, her long hair brushing my cheek.

"Ummm."

"I wish it had turned out differently."

"So do I."

She leaned toward me, letting her lips touch, then warm, mine.

I held Allyson more tightly, feeling for the first time, really, how soft she felt against me, and how sweet she smelled.

"I have to go . . ."

"I know . . ." I knew, but I didn't have to like it. If her father woke up and went searching for his daughter, or couldn't sleep and wanted to prepare for the trip, I didn't want him making his way to the cellar. Neither did I want to let go of Allyson.

"I don't want to go, Sammis."

"I know."

"But I have to." She kissed me again, and then pushed away from me and swung her feet to the floor, reclaiming her slippers. "I have to . . ."

"I know." I felt stupid and helpless repeating the same words time after time, and all I wanted then was to keep holding on to Allyson.

She took her glow rod and slipped to the door. "I've left everything I could get for you . . ." Her voice was a whisper.

"If you hadn't . . . I don't know what . . ."

Her shoulders trembled as she took the three or four steps from the sagging old bed to the door. She was gone before I could even finish my sentence, and I was staring at a softly closed door. A closed door on what might have been. A door closed on . . . but there was no point in dwelling on that.

Queryan memories are long, and the round-ups and the burnings of the Eastron sympathizers, and of the witch-wraiths before that, had been pounded into my head by my own father.

For a long time, I lay in the jumbled quilts as the room cooled, thinking about nothing, then trying to decide what I could do, or where I could go. For everyone in Bremarlyn would know me, and in this time of chaos, no one would stand up for me—no one but Allyson, and she had done what she could. That was more than enough to get her burned should anyone discover it.

I got up and smoothed out the bed, folding the quilts as I recalled they had been folded. I checked my own uniform, which remained slightly damp, and put it on. Strangely, my cloak was dry, and my boots had never been damp inside.

After dressing as quietly as possible, I looked through what Allyson had brought—and thanked her mentally again. Not only was there the food and the tool kit, but also a small hatchet and a folding knife with several blades, and a folded square of waterproof ground cloth. All the non-food items were dusty, which probably meant that they wouldn't be missed, but all looked serviceable.

I took my nearly empty pack and placed everything in it, except for the knife, which went into my pocket, and the gloves Allyson had given me earlier. Then I pulled on the cloak and the gloves and swung the pack into place.

The door from the room opened easily. I stopped to listen. Not a sound from upstairs—although I had not expected any, since it had to be well before dawn. Still, my steps were light, if not noiseless, as I slipped to the big latched door.

Hssst . . . click. Despite my best efforts, the latch rasped.

I held my breath and listened. No sounds, except for the moaning of the wind outside.

Holding the door against the wind so it would not swing inside and hit the wall, I stepped into the night—or the predawn darkness.

Overhead, I could see some stars between the swirls of fast-moving clouds. The wind was light and skitterish, with gusts of warm air, then cooler air. From what I could see in the dim light, most of my tracks had been covered by snow and wind.

Since there wasn't much I could do about hiding my tracks, I walked to the far end of the wall, where the double stone steps came down to the lawn. The higher ones were clear of snow. Glancing up at the windows and seeing no light, I walked up two steps in the snow, and then turned and retraced my path to the lower door. From there I walked backwards along the wall until I neared the point where the other set of steps went up toward the courtyard and the kitchen. They were clear in the center, and my prints did not show.

The courtyard was dusted with snow, but only in the west corner had it drifted more than a finger deep. By scuffing my boots side to side, I obscured my prints enough that they did not look recent, and with the hint of warmth in the wind, after sunrise they might not be visible at all.

Like our drive, the Davniadses' was raised a handspan or so above the lawn, and the center part had been windswept. I checked the house, but there were no lights. Going down the drive was a risk, but Jerz Davniads wasn't the sort to chase me without considering the consequences— assuming he saw me at all. And taking the drive left fewer tracks.

It might be days before snow left parts of the woods path. Besides, anyone could be coming or going down the drive. Only Sammis Olon would be using the woodlands path.

At the curve in the drive, just before it entered the woods on its slope down to the road, I looked back at the house. In a way, I had hoped to see a single candle, or something. But the windowpanes were dark, and the hot-cold wind whistled across my cloak. I watched for another moment, then waved to Allyson, or no one, and began the hike downhill.

XII

"THE WITCHES OF Eastron? What a strange conceit, coming as it did from the only non-monarchial culture in Queryan history. Yet the thread of the so-called 'witches' appears in folklore, literature, and even in diaries for a period of close to a millennium.

"The references span four phases of government, including the Fylarian Fragmentation, and demonstrate remarkable consistency . . .

". . . women (or men) who did not age, who were seen in places too far apart for them to have travelled the distance, who displayed remarkable skill and dexterity, who avoided war and violence, even for the best causes . . .

"None of the attributes of the so-called 'witches', except for the rapid travel, and that could have been mere coincidence, are that remarkable, especially given the extraordinary hatred that devolved, either in Eastron or Westron, upon those accused of being witches. Yet even into modern times, the witchcraft charge has been used . . .

"All in all, the remarkableness of the conceit has been its continuation, given the mildness of the evils attributed to such witches—they lived a long life, possibly an endless one, and they could travel far distances in the blink of an eye. Yet such charges destroyed whole families in the early days of Eastron and even into the founding of the Westron Chartered Monarchy . . ."

> Archival Text Fragment
> Temporal Guard Archives
> Quest, Query
> 1200 N.G.E

XIII

I KEPT TO the side of the Davniadses' drive, and to the edge of the road after that. There was nowhere else to go—not by the road.

Father said that there had been talk of extending the road until it reached the Wayland Highway on the other side of the hills, but the Engineers had never started the work. My choices were clear—blunder through the still snowy hills or risk the road in the darkness before dawn, accompanied by wind and chill, before the marines started their usual canvass of the area and all the residents.

Like the Davniadses' drive, the crown of the road was clear.

Click . . . click . . . crunch . . .

My steps sounded louder in my ears than they probably did in fact, but the sound spurred me to set my feet more carefully on the downgrade.

Once I reached the sweeping ninety-degree turn above our driveway, I stopped and listened. Silence, but that didn't mean anything. Not where the ConFed Marines were concerned. I edged off the road and into the snow-covered grassy depression that was almost a ditch—on the opposite side of the road. Stepping through the snow, I kept my head low. Before long, I reached the point across the road from the low stone pillars that marked our drive.

Whhhsttt . . . whssssss . . .

Only the whisper of the wind broke the stillness—that and the sound of my breath.

Was there still a guard by the pillars? A marine detachment watching the smoldering ruins of the house built by my great-great-grandfather?

I glanced toward the pillars, but could see nothing but two smudges of gray against the shadows of the evergreen hedge and the overhanging trees. As I strained to make out whether there was a guard posted, the dream impression of the red-blue, gold-black intersection returned, somehow right behind my eyes, even closer than in my dreams.

Crack.

The sound had come from behind me. I could feel eyes on my back, and I grasped in some way for the dark intersection, knowing that only that could save me, if anything could.

Without understanding how, I was on the other side of the black curtain, seeing through a veil the snow-drifted depression where the three marines looked down on a set of footprints that came from nowhere and went nowhere.

From that no-time place, I could hear nothing, but one of the ConFeds made the ward gesture from the Verlyt rites. Another had a shredder aimed at where I would have been, where I had been instants before.

Suspended there, I dared not move, not that I could. So I watched as the three marines stomped through and around where I had been. Finally, one followed my tracks backward until they reached the hard stones of the road and disappeared.

My unplanned disappearance in plain sight might lift suspicion from Allyson and her family, since I hoped that the marines would not walk hundreds of rods back uphill and through the Davniadses' courtyard to compare footsteps in the snow. At least, I hoped I had left no tracks in the snow between the two places.

As I hung out of time, waiting, a marine reappeared with an officer, a tall and burly man. The marine pointed to my footprints, gesturing, then shaking his head. The burly man seemed to be exasperated, doing some pointing himself, jabbing a finger toward the marine, who kept backing up.

Even though I could feel nothing where I was suspended, I could tell that I was getting tired. The veil, or curtain, seemed to flicker in front of my eyes. What could I do?

My thoughts jumped back to the ConFed Marines guarding the house, and as they did, the scene through the black curtain wavered, then refocused, and I was standing in the orchard, still behind the curtain of time or place. But this time I knew that as soon as I willed it, I could be in the orchard.

With the marine tents, and the row of coffins laid out, some drifted over with snow, I did not want to reappear there. Not at all.

The Academy? No . . .

Finally, I concentrated on a place where I used to hike with Mother—the Long Wall Trail above the town, on the far side of Bremarlyn. I knew I could not go very far, but I *had* to go somewhere.

I thought, hard, and tried to visualize the trail and the way station, especially the way station, the one-windowed old log cabin.

Crrshhh . . . thud . . .

Sprawled on the trail, perhaps fifty rods from the way station, I looked around quickly. By now, the dim light of predawn lent everything a ghostly aura.

Chiichiii . . . chchiichii . . . An enormous grossjay stared down from the overhead branch at the interloper stretched out on the trail.

On this side of Bremarlyn, the snow did not seem to have been quite so heavy, and the temperature was markedly warmer. Not enough that I could do without cloak and gloves, but enough that I was comfortable in what I wore.

Sitting up slowly, I continued to look around. I did not stand. My knees felt like water, and I had a splitting headache.

Even the idea of trying to call up that contradictory mental intersection made me wince. Right now, that was for emergency travel.

Chichiii . . . chchiiichi . . .

No other recent footprints marked the mix of loose dirt and drifted snow, and the grossjay's scolding seemed more of a greeting.

The Long Wall Trail was more of a summer path, anyway.

Finally, I gathered my feet under me and lurched upright in the dawn. And, after a time, I managed to stagger to the way station.

The latch was rusty, but functional. I scrambled until I found an old wooden bar and slid it into place. Then I looked around in the dimness.

Some little light filtered in from the cracks in the wooden shutters that covered the unglassed window. My feet left tracks in the thin layer of dust that blanketed everything.

Inside were two benches and a table, all of rough wood polished only by time and summer usage. But the bench was as welcome as any soft chair anywhere. Off came the pack, and out came the food. I was so

hungry I was drooling. A growl from my guts reminded me not to gulp
it down whole. Beginning with a dried chyst, I chewed each bit thoroughly.

With the first mouthful, my shakes began to abate. After I finished
the chyst and a chunk of tough but welcome jerky, interspersed with
several sips from the small water bottle Allyson had packed, the headache began to lift.

Clearly, my out-of-time or out-of-place travel took energy, lots of it,
and I had started out with an empty stomach.

Sitting there in the way station, I tried to call up the black curtain
and the contradictory intersection. While I could bring them into mental focus, the effort set off another headache. The warning was sufficient,
and I relaxed and started in on a dried pearapple.

After that, I studied the way station. Four log walls, one with a
shuttered window, and one with a heavy door. The roof was not raised,
but angled. The log wall which had the door was lower than the back
wall, and three timbers, each a handspan wide, ran from front to back.
The angle also provided the overhang for the unrailed front porch I had
ignored during my staggering entrance.

Just the summer before, Mother and I had sat there, watching the
rain come down.

"Not many people come here any more, Sammis," she had said.
"We're not the physical people I . . . we once were."

She had always looked younger than she was, just as I did. On the
way up the trail, someone had noted that it was nice to see a brother
and sister on such friendly terms. I was too embarrassed to make the
correction, and she had just smiled an amused smile.

Yet I knew she was older than my father. That's what the marriage
book had shown.

In the early winter dawn, I dropped back from that memory, cut as
if by a knife at the thought that I might never see either my mother or
father again.

I carefully rewrapped the food, leaving out one last piece of jerky,
and replaced the remainder in my pack. As I chewed, I tried to sort out
everything that had happened in the last few days.

First, someone or something had attacked the ConFederation forces
on Mithrada and apparently destroyed the planet-forming stations and
most of the spacecraft—if the rumors were correct. At least some of the
orbital power stations were damaged or destroyed. Nothing was being
broadcast from Inequital and from the west. A detachment of ConFed
Marines had burned my family's ancestral home. Strange storms and
weather had struck Bremarlyn and perhaps much of Westra. Yet there

were no strange aircraft, no battles nearby, and no other military forces.

Last of all, somehow, I was learning to travel, or slide out of places and into places, and that travel took as much effort as playing a whole centreslot game, maybe more.

What was I going to do? I had some theoretical knowledge, a little skill with woodworking tools. Small for my age, if stronger than many a head taller, and looking even younger than my size—I couldn't pass as a casual laborer. Not with my gentry talk and uncalloused hands. Or as an orphan of sorts. The gentry didn't abandon children—ever. There were too few.

I didn't have an answer, but I couldn't stay in the woods for too long. And I had no idea how I would be able to find my parents—or what had happened to them without having the same thing happen to me.

For the moment, the problems had to subside with the waves of exhaustion that swept over me. I staggered to my feet and pushed one of the two benches around the table and got both of them side by side. With the pack as a pillow and my cloak as a blanket, I went to sleep. Without a single dream, for the first time in days.

XIV

ON THE CONSOLE screen in the laboratory a map appeared, one illustrating the outline of a continent in relief. In addition to the greens and browns depicting different elevations were traceries of red dashed lines. All the dashed lines either began or terminated at the same point near the center of the continent.

The researcher in blue sitting before the screen tapped in a series of commands, and the map vanished, replaced by a chart resembling a star map. She touched the controls, and a three-dimensional version of the star chart appeared. In the center was a red dot, and a handful of red dashed lines curved outward from the red dot. Most ended with a circled black star.

With a frown, the researcher touched the keyboard again. The star map vanished, replaced in turn by a chart listing names, with four columns of entries after each name.

A black star preceded the majority of the names, and those the researcher ignored as she studied in turn the entries following each unstarred name.

Occasionally, she sighed, and the noise echoed in the dimness.

Once the console flickered, as did the power panel lights on the monitoring equipment arrayed around a bare raised platform to her right. The platform stood in roughly the middle of the laboratory, sur-rounded at equidistant points by four consoles with screens.

Only the console occupied by the lone researcher was functioning.

The researcher glanced at the screen before her, then at the series of inked designs she had added on one side of the hard copy of the report beside the keyboard.

Again, the lights flickered, then failed, plunging the room into dark-ness and wiping the screen blank.

Sighing once more, the researcher waited, as if to see whether the power would return.

Wheep.

With the return of the lights, the screen relit, but displayed only a featureless blue.

The woman touched several keys, and the screen went black. She took a deep breath, then lifted the thin report that lay on the flat space to the right of the screen and slid it into the drawer in the console under the screen, shaking her head as she did so. Her sandy blond hair flared slightly with the movement, then bounced as she rose fluidly from the chair, and walked toward the bare platform in the middle of the labo-ratory.

Click. Her fingers turned off the monitoring equipment on the right hand side of the platform.

When all the power light panels were dark, she stepped upon the platform and looked around, taking another deep breath, as if attempt-ing a plunge into icy cold water.

With a sad smile, she vanished.

The room remained unpowered, but waiting.

Outside, the emergency etheline generator coughed, and the single set of lights illuminating the console where she had been seated flick-ered.

The researcher reappeared on the platform, smiling but shaking her head.

Droplets of water cascaded from her onto the platform. Her blue tunic and trousers were soaked, and the thin fabric clung to her like a second skin, outlining a slightly curved and youthful figure.

The lights flickered one last time and went out, leaving the window-less laboratory in near-total darkness, as the emergency generator coughed on the last drops of etheline.

The researcher walked surefootedly toward the doorway, leaving be-hind a trail of damp footprints that had already begun to fade as she slipped from the laboratory.

XV

THE LONG WALL Trail ended nearly five kays from the outskirts of Herfidian, itself a good twenty kays east of Bremarlyn by the Eastern Highway. None of the way stations had offered anything but shelter.

While shelter was indeed welcome amid the continuing strange alternation of snow and ice rain and sunlight and crisp fall afternoons, food was my biggest problem. Water was available from the cascades and the brooks, for the temperature never dropped far enough to freeze more than skim ice over running water. The abrupt changes in temperature had spoiled most of the wild fruits and berries. I had found one blue chyst in a copse of trees near the second way station. The blues are terribly bitter, but nearly a dozen were clear and edible.

I ate one on the spot and put the others in my pack, hoping to save what dried food was left as long as possible.

Rabbits were plentiful, and curious. But I had no way to kill them at a distance, and didn't seem to be able to stalk them. More important, I still didn't like the thought of killing them. Even at home, I'd never been a big meat-eater. Neither had Mother, and my father had teased her about it, saying that it was the secret to her youthfulness.

From the ridge line part of the trail, I had noticed some other strange changes. In places, huge circles appeared to have been cut out of the forest, and nothing remained but a fine dust. Those places seemed to be near the Eastern Highway, some distance from the trail, and the only things that were left standing were natural hills or the heavy foundation stones of barns or buildings.

It looked like the work of an enemy, because the destruction appeared to be just in or around the inhabited places. But who was this unseen enemy?

While I wasn't about to find out in the hills, trudging along the Long Wall Trail toward the east, I also wasn't in a hurry to make myself visible. What I could have used was a bath or a shower. Despite the earlier snows and sleet, the air was still dusty, so much so that I often found myself sneezing as I made my way eastward.

When I finally stood by the stone marker—the one that said "Long Wall Trail, in memory of Kenth, last Duke of Ronwic"—that signified the end or the beginning of the trail, depending on which way you were going, I still had no real idea what I would do. I couldn't live in the woods, and I had no living relatives—except a second cousin of my father's that I had met exactly once who lived somewhere in Inequital.

The sky was overcast, and the strange dark cloud pillars continued to dominate the western sky, in the general area of Inequital, although the capital itself was farther than I could have seen. A light mist was falling. The air was mostly warm, although the occasional strange cold gusts still accompanied the warmer mist. The dirt of the trail below me was unmarked, sheltered by a double row of overhanging firs. Behind the firs were the usual mix of Westron trees, most of the leafy ones well toward losing their summer foliage and having but scraggly winter leaves.

The marker sat about a hundred rods above the Eastern Highway. Why the trail ended near no town was a mystery to me, but I had never asked. All I knew was that I had another five kays to walk, and that I was getting hungry, and that I wanted a bath.

The last seemed most unlikely. Food was probable, one way or another, and walking was certain for now. I didn't dare waste the energy on place-sliding, not unless I was faced with an emergency, or worse.

Before I headed toward the highway, I unstrapped my pack and set it on top of the flat stone marker, unfastened it, and removed the last blue chyst. After three days, even the blue ones didn't taste too bad. I needed some energy, and otherwise there were only a few sticks of jerky and two small chunks of cheese left. Those I wanted to save.

Allyson had done well, but like all good things her provisions were about to end. When I finished the chyst, nibbled all the way down to the hard seed, I tossed it into the deep brush to my right.

Swwiiissshh.

A grossjay swooped after it, almost catching the seed before it struck the ground. Times had apparently been hard for the birds as well. Grossjays were not known for their fondness for chyst seeds.

I pulled the pack back on, shrugging my shoulders to try to relieve the stiffness that seemed permanent. Then I started down the trail, staying on the short grass on the side, avoiding the slippery combination of dirt and mud in the middle.

The line of firs ended halfway to the highway, and I pulled up short, staying in their shade, as I could hear the rumble of a vehicle in the distance. Instead of walking along the road, stupid in any case, I kept under the overhang of the trees, where I stumbled every so often. While most of the trees were light-leaved for winter, between the mist and the evergreens, I wasn't as exposed as I would be closer to the road, and I could hide quickly. The idea of hiding and skulking around bothered me, but being picked up by the ConFeds would have bothered me a lot more—especially since I didn't know why they were after my family . . . and presumably me.

After about a kay, the rumbling increased in pitch, and I dropped behind a pine, waiting.

Over the hill from the west they came, clear even from a distance. First came a steamer, black, with a flag on the front bumper. The flag was the ConFed banner. Then there were two open steam freighters, carrying full loads covered with tarps. Last came an armored steamer, the kind with the composite ceramic plates and a turret gun. The armored steamer was wreathed in vapor as it rattled along.

In my whole life, I had never seen such a detachment on the Eastern Highway, not near Bremarlyn, so far from Eastron, even father from the Northern Isles—although that conflict had been over even before my father was born.

So I crouched in a hollow behind the pine and waited for them to pass out of sight. The wait wasn't all loss, though. In looking around, I saw what might have been a stunted pearapple, behind the firs to my left, toward Herfidian. As I waited, watching, I marked the pearapple location and studied the steamer as it hum-hissed past my pine tree, less than five rods away. Double-tiered and totally enclosed, that black steamer was easily twice the size of my father's official steamer. The black finish was wearing thin and beginning to show the reddish ceramic beneath, and the faded purple stripe along the side, across both doors, was also heavily scratched.

I could feel the ground vibrate as the rest of the road convoy neared. The dull gray freighters looked newer, but still battered. Unlike the steamer, their cabs were open, and one had the windscreen folded down. Both were heavy-laden, with what appeared to be machines under the tarps. An armed ConFed stood in the guard booth at each corner of the cargo bay of each freighter. Eight armed ConFeds—in the center of Westron, thousands of kays from the old borders. And they weren't looking bored. I shrank down further behind the pine as the freighters neared. The guards had weapons out and kept scanning the roadside.

How anyone would catch them I couldn't imagine. All four were travelling nearly as fast as a normal runabout.

But someone had, clearly, because one of the armored guard booths on the first freighter had projectile holes in it and a dull reddish smear on the shattered composite underneath.

I decided not to move as the freighters passed, waiting for the laboring armored steamer to come into my now-restricted view.

The gray double plates were scratched, some of the scratches almost bleeding with red as the ceramic composite beneath showed through.

The turret had a steel shield around the gun port. An armored steamer with some steel—that was something else. Steel wasn't that easy to come by any more.

The acrid odor of old steam, old oil, and hot rubber permeated the area as the armed steamer rumbled past. It was the three-axle type, with shields over the double tires, and the gun in the top turret kept swiveling from point to point, although thankfully not in my direction.

I stayed in the hollow behind the pine until the ConFed vehicles had disappeared over another low hill, and until the sound and vibration were gone as well. The bitter smell of abused machinery remained.

I recalled the pearapple. Before I checked out the possibility of fruit, I made my way deeper into the brush, and relieved myself. Seeing the ConFed convoy had created a sudden urge for such relief.

Then I pushed through the thickets of dead summer brush to the tree. Although the birds and weather had taken a toll, I found two partly good fruits. Using the old knife Allyson had left me, I cut away the rotten parts and ate the rest right there.

After wiping the knife clean on some dried grass, and then on the hem edge of my cloak, and doing the same with sticky fingers, I made my way back to the edge of the highway and resumed hiking toward Herfidian.

As I neared the top of a low hill, perhaps the third after the place where I had encountered the convoy, something seemed wrong. My steps slowed, ears alert, eyes looking for a wisp of steam in the air. Sniff . . . sniff—even trying to detect a hint of the scent of oil and steam.

Only the sound of a grossjay broke the stillness as I edged forward.

I shook my head as I saw the emptiness that began just below the crest of the hill. Nothing but a few huge boulders rose out of the circular expanse of dust. It was though a giant lumberman had taken an axe and swung it at ground level in a circle, and then burned everything to dust—except the dust was a fine brownish powder, not gray or black like ashes, and there was no smell of burning. I thought I remembered the place . . . before . . . a water station with the old inn maintained more out of sentiment than anything else. My father had claimed the inn still served one of the better evening meals in the Bremarlyn area.

Where the inn and its outbuildings had stood were only buried lumps, foundation stones covered with shifting dust. The old high firs were gone, as was the steep-pitched barn that dated back to the time of wagons and beasts.

". . . *cccah* . . . *cuhh* . . . *CHEW* . . ." Once the fine dust got into my nose, I couldn't stop sneezing until my eyes were thoroughly running and my shoulders hurt from the violence of the sneezes. Had anyone been around, I would have been helpless.

Finally, I gathered myself together, just short of the dusty wasteland that seemed to stretch nearly a kay before me. Only the tracks of ConFed convoy through the thinner cover over the road itself marred the dust, so light that it seemed to shift with even the slightest breath of air.

How the steamers had made it through I wasn't certain, but there was no way I was going to survive the sneezes and convulsions that each step would generate. Going around the edge would add another kay to the distance to Herfidian—assuming Herfidian was still there and not a dusty wasteland. Assuming I did not run into the ConFed Marines.

I sat down on a fallen log for a moment to think, to think and to recover from my sneezing attack.

Something had destroyed the inn, something that had left only dust, and that something seemed to strike populated areas. I had seen the circular spaces from the trail, though none were actually out in the woods. But the presence of the ConFeds meant that some outposts had survived.

Shrugging, I got up. There wasn't that much choice. So I began to struggle along the edge of the destruction. The trees and brush closest to the actual destruction looked more as if they had been winter-killed than burned, but would extreme cold have the same effect as fire and create an ash-like dust?

By the time I regained the road, or the sheltered edge under the firs that bordered the highway, indeed had bordered all the highways, the afternoon was nearly gone. And I had no handy way-stations in which to shelter myself. So I kept putting one foot in front of the other.

Twice more the rumble of freighters pushed me out of sight—once into the ditch and once behind a thicket. These freighters were also guarded by ConFed Marines bearing nasty looks and nastier weapons.

As the day waned into twilight, and as I neared the top of each hill, I edged over carefully, afraid of what I might find.

Herfidian was in more of a valley, cut by the Oligar River, as I recalled, and the trade section was the part closest to Bremarlyn.

Had been the closest to Bremarlyn. The same circle of destruction was evident on the western side of the river. The eastern side looked untouched by that destruction, but I could see the shanties and tents and smell the open fires from more than a kay away.

Some order prevailed. The road had been swept clear of dust, or used enough to keep it mostly clear. That, and there was some sort of gate guarding the old stone bridge that crossed the Oligar. In the early evening light, I could see someone lighting a set of torches there. A soldier of some sort, for the outline of the weapon on his back was clear.

Soldiers and more soldiers!

If I walked down the road, the soldiers would have me, and some might know who I was. But with the river to the south and the swamps to the north . . .

So I retreated into the bushes and relieved myself again. After that, I found a grassy spot behind a tree, out of sight of the road. Once my pack was off, out came the last chunk of cheese and several fractured pieces of jerky. I chewed them slowly, savoring the last taste of each.

I curled up, just to rest—and woke to another set of rumbling wheels. Not that it could have been long, but the lights of the steamers against the thicket and trunks made me squirm even flatter to the ground until all three were past and rumbling down to the guarded bridge.

I thought about the place-sliding. Could I use it to at least get past the bridge?

That wouldn't be a problem, but I'd have to be careful where I ended up. The old Herfidian had been a worn-out trade town, dying bit by bit, and the enemy's destruction of the western part had probably just hastened the inevitable. Off in the older eastern part had been the metalworks where the smiths had built the land steamers and freighters, using the river mills for power.

Supposedly, Jerz Davniads's grandfather had made his fortune by developing a strain of oilseed plants from which etheline was distilled. Idly, I first wondered what had happened to the great oilseed plantations of the north, then briefly wished I had an etheline heater. But wishing was not about to deliver me a heater, and the soldiers below would spot the light anyway.

I sighed and put on my pack. Then, sitting in the hollow behind a fir trunk, partly sheltered from the evening wind that still bore the bitter cold-burnt odor of enemy destruction, I tried to call up the red-blue-gold-black crossroads of my mind. This time, surprisingly, I could summon the image easily, and with almost no effort I dropped behind the black curtain of no-time.

East Herfidian was no longer just metalworking, but an armed camp. Combat-ready ConFeds patrolled the streets. The metalworkers were busy now, apparently repairing military equipment. Seeing from behind the curtain was a strain, and East Herfidian did not appeal to me.

What about further east, toward Jillriko, or Halfprince?

I let my mind carry my seemingly disembodied self farther east, farther from Bremarlyn, farther from Inequital. The Eastern Highway itself seemed more permanent, as if it stretched through time, than the trees or buildings.

Half of Jillriko was gone, and the town looked nearly deserted.

Halfprince also looked empty.

Beyond Halfprince were the marshes, the damps, where the Faiyren River emerged from several creeks and the marshes before twisting downward and back to Jillriko.

Hot springs intertwined with the creeks, and a mist often covered the small valleys, especially in winter.

My view from behind the black curtain began to flicker, and I could tell that I was running out of time. The damps looked more hospitable than two deserted towns and one ConFed camp. So I looked for a clearing . . . or something . . .

—and dropped heavily into mushy grass anchored in mud.

With the darkness spinning around me, I took a deep breath. My eyes cleared, although the bushes were dark shapes against the darker shadows of the trees. The mud and grass underfoot comprised a shadow carpet whose different elements could be felt, but not seen.

Chhhiccciiii.

The sound of the grossjay reassured me as I squished toward drier ground, just looking for a place to sit down.

The odors of mud, swamp, rotting wood and plants filled my head, almost with a jolt compared to the cold no-sense feeling that accompanied my undertime travel.

My boots were holding up well to the mud, tramping, and wet, but the clothing looked more like a shapeless working outfit than the sharp-creased dress uniform that I had worn to the Academy on a morning not that long ago.

As I eased my way from the muddy grass up onto a hillock, the stillness made me edgy. Silence meant people, and the kind of people that went to the damps were not the kind I wanted to meet in the dark. As if I had any choice about it.

My vision began to spin again, and I sat down on the ground, next to a spindly fir. My attempt to rest was too late, and I could feel the darkness sweep over me, even darker than the oncoming night.

XVI

"WHERE'D HE COME FROM?"

"Steps start in the middle of the grass . . ."

"Must be the Enemy."

At first I thought the voices were from a dream, but I could feel my back and shoulders aching, and I wanted to shiver in the cold. Besides, it was clearly light. Had I slept through the night?

Where was I? Then I remembered my attempt to avoid the ConFeds at Herfidian . . . the damps. I was lying somewhere in the damps, recovering from an excess of my mental sliding from place to place. My head was splitting. Even the faint light of dawn was hard on my closed eyes.

"Too young for them, and he's human. One of the spacers said They had four arms and were like giants. That's what Lyron said."

"Damned witch, then."

"Pretty young for that."

"Witches always look young."

"Ever seen a witch?"

Slitting my eyes, I tried to see who was discussing me so coldly, as if I were not even there.

"He's waking up!"

"Open your eyes, boy—slow-like, and keep your hands in the clear."

I did exactly as I was told.

Two bearded men and a woman stood there. They all had long hair. One of the men had crossbow aimed at my midsection. A crossbow— for Verlyt's sake.

"Looks old, but it works, faster than you could blink your eyes and disappear." That was the woman. Her hair was dirtier than the shapeless man's jumpsuit she wore, and it looked like it had been dragged through most of the mud of the damps.

The stench that came from the three made the odor of rotting vegetation smell clean.

"Why you here?" Neither man was more than a shade taller than I was, but the one with the dirty white beard had shoulders like an ancient smith's, and his voice rumbled.

"Trying to avoid the ConFeds."

"The ConFeds? Near here?" The two men exchanged glances.

"Not that near. They've taken over Herfidian, and they're sending armed steamers along all the roads."

"Why would they do that?" Her voice was sharp, almost shrill, and I could see that her teeth were rotten. That proved she was not just lower class, but maybe criminal as well.

I stretched, slowly, still watching the man with the crossbow, and eased into a more comfortable sitting position. My head throbbed with each movement, and my stomach heaved.

"You sick?" asked the woman.

"No. Hungry. Tired. Damned little sleep, and less food."

"Where's your family, boy? Those clothes cost some."

"Gone. Dead . . . I think . . . Enemy . . . while I was coming home from school . . ."

"No other kin?" This came from the younger man, the first time he had spoken.

"A cousin in Inequital."

"Why'd you leave home? What town?"

"The marines were burning and looting . . ."

Again, the three exchanged worried looks.

"What town?" snapped the woman.

"Bremarlyn . . ." I didn't know about the burning and looting, but they shouldn't have, either.

"Far way to come on foot . . ."

"He didn't come on foot! Damned witch." That was the older man, who kept the crossbow steady on me.

I just sat there, head throbbing, without enough energy to move, trying to keep from puking my empty guts out.

"He's no witch," concluded the woman, "or not much of one. Good witch could have disappeared twice by now."

"What?"

"How?"

"You took your eyes off him twice. That's all it takes, just an eyeblink." She stared at me. "So do you help us, or does Vran kill you, and we turn you into a couple of days' rations?"

I shrugged, knowing that the sweat was beading up on my forehead. "Rather help you, given the choice."

"For now, boy, you got the choice. Hold out on us, and you won't wake some fine morning. My name's Sylvie. That's Vran. And that's Weasel. It's not his name, but he hasn't told us his real name, and we don't ask."

"Sammis," I volunteered.

"Sam will do."

I hated Sam, but now wasn't the time to be choosy. "Fine. Can I stand up?"

"No. You stand up that green, and you'll rip your guts out." From beneath her shapeless garments, she pulled a brown shape and extended it. "It's tough, but your teeth are young."

Tough wasn't the word for the morsel of travel bread, and it had flecks of mold which I brushed away. But after the second bite, my headache lost its edge, and my stomach began to quiet.

"Slower . . ." commanded Sylvie. "You want to lose that, too?"

I obliged her, even though Vran had lowered the crossbow. The small piece of bread would make me feel better, but it wasn't about to provide enough energy for me to leave the company of the three, one way or another. Feeling the looseness of my trousers, I was beginning to realize that my unusual travel took energy, a lot of energy. And I didn't have any. So I chewed, very slowly and very carefully.

My headache subsided to a dull ache, and my guts postponed any further protests.

"Up," grunted Vran.

I eased myself to my feet, still feeling weak.

"What's in the pack?"

"Not much."

"Good to carry forage, boy," said Sylvie.

I didn't like the way she looked at me, or the way she said "boy," as if there were something more implied. I shrugged. "Where to?"

"That way." Vran gestured with the crossbow toward a gradual slope up from where we stood, not that anything in the damps was particularly far above the marshlands.

With one slow step after another, my guts and head still filled with a dull ache, my feet found their way up a narrow path that was all but invisible.

In time, I stood beside a lean-to sheltered by an ancient boulder and an interwoven black thorn thicket. The limbs composing the frame of the lean-to were a mixture of smoothed, dark and ancient wood, and greener partly leaved branches clearly added later to something that had been abandoned until recently.

"Not much, but hard to find. Out of the winds, even the big ones, boy. Not that I wouldn't mind a bit more warmth on a cold night."

I shivered.

"Sylvie . . . the kid's hungry and cold, and you're treating him like raw meat." The man called Weasel spoke for the first time, and his tone was more cultured than that of the other two. His voice was harder, though.

"Jealous now, Weasel?"

Weasel snorted.

"Then take him with you, and find us something to eat."

I sat down on a fallen and half-rotten log and waited to see what they would say. While the hunger pangs in my stomach had lessened, the light-headedness persisted.

"He's in no shape to go far . . ."

"You won't either," rumbled Vran through his tangled and dirty white beard. He lifted the crossbow, then let it drop.

The man called Weasel looked calmly at Vran. "You rely on weapons too much." Then, without waiting for a reaction, his eyes fixed on me. "And you, young man, have clearly never been exposed to real danger. Not until recently. Can you stand?"

"I think so."

"Then stand, and let us see what forage we can find."

I took a deep breath, letting it out slowly, and eased to my feet. The light-headedness was replaced with a subdued headache, and my stomach growled.

"Let's go."

I let my steps follow Weasel's. Before we had edged our way back along the narrow path and through the swamp firs, I could see the reason for his name. Athletic as I had been at school, I felt like an ox trundling after him. His footsteps were silent, while each step of mine sounded with hisses and crackles.

We wound down toward the marsh itself. There the swamp grasses surrounded an expanse of open water.

Weasel looked back, studied me, and motioned for us to stop. "Verlyt-damned idea for you to be on your feet."

I agreed, but saying so wasn't going to do me much good. So I didn't.

Weasel rummaged through his shapeless jacket. "Catch."

It was a battered but almost ripe and unspoiled chyst.

"Just eat it slowly. Little bites. Real little bites."

I nodded and took one bite. Weasel watched. Almost as soon as I had swallowed the first bite, I could feel the headache lifting. My stomach growled.

Weasel nodded. "Hypoglycemic."

"What?"

"Blood sugar. Too low, and you don't function. Probably runs in . . . your family." He grinned a nasty grin. "But that will be our little secret, won't it, young man?"

"If you say so. I don't think I have much choice at this point." So far as I could see, I had no skills, not like a tradesman or apprentice. I couldn't use my place-diving ability without regular meals, and I had no way to leave the damps without food.

"You don't. Vran would like to use that crossbow on you."

I couldn't help shivering.

"It's not that bad. Vran . . . he just wants to show who's boss."

I took another small bite of the chyst.

"You look like you could take another step or two. Watch how I put my feet down, and try to do the same. You're not as noisy as Vran, but anyone could still hear you coming, and you don't carry a crossbow like him. Try to keep your head down more."

Attempting to emulate his footsteps, I followed as we skirted the highest swamp grass in a round-about trip toward the northern end of the marsh. Every once in a while, I took another small bite of the chyst.

Weasel had to wait for me more than once, but he never said anything, just turned and went on once I caught up. Finally we came to a spot where the barely perceptible trail vanished. He nodded at me, then walked straight toward the marsh.

I shrugged and followed, trying to find the firm footing Weasel used. I was successful in gnawing the chyst right down to the seeds, but not in always finding firm footing.

Squuuushhh.

Weasel turned and glared.

I held up my hands apologetically.

He shook his head sadly and turned, brushing through the shoulder-high grass so quietly that he sounded like the faintest of breezes. I sounded like a winter storm.

He was easing a woven basketlike structure from the waters of an inlet off the main part of the small lake in the center of the marsh. Inside were several objects.

Up came a second basket box, also with several creatures inside.

Weasel pulled a worn sack from his belt and emptied each basket in turn.

Both baskets went back into the water.

"There's actually enough for all of us tonight."

"Enough what?" I kept my voice low.

"Crayfish."

"Crayfish?"

"Sort of like freshwater lobsters."

I knew about both lobsters and crayfish. I just wasn't certain how hungry I was. Then my stomach growled, and I remembered that I had eaten the chyst, bite by bite, down to the seeds.

"Still hungry, Sam?"

I nodded reluctantly.

Weasel looked around, then started back along a different route.

I couldn't see the new route either, and I was beginning to sweat under the heavy cloak as even the damps warmed up in the midday.

Abruptly, Weasel stopped. At first, nothing caught my eye, but in the midst of the swamp grass was a greenish cactuslike plant. I watched as he bared a bulbous greenish-brown root and sliced a chunk out of it, splitting the chunk in two. The inside was whitish.

"Here."

"What is it?" I took the slimy chunk of root.

"Kind of swamp lily, but the root's mostly starch. Tastes like sawdust, but it's good for you." He used his knife to cut a small chunk and put it in his mouth. Even his lips puckered a bit. "Didn't say it tasted good, Sam. I said it was good for you."

I used my knife to cut a small chunk of the waxy white root. I looked at it. My stomach growled. I looked at it again, and my stomach growled again. So I ate it.

The swamp lily tasted like waxy sawdust, except I would have preferred the sawdust. And each piece seemed to swell as I chewed it. I had to make a special effort to swallow each bit. But it all stayed down, and my stomach stopped growling.

"Enough. Let's get back before Vran gets upset and starts looking for a reason to use that crossbow."

I had almost—almost—forgotten the broad-shouldered old man with the ancient weapon.

We were nearly halfway back to the hidden campsite before I realized that my headache was gone and that my stomach had stopped growling, but I still wasn't about to recommend swamp lily root except in dire circumstances.

XVII

CHIRRRIIITT . . . CHIRRRIITTT!

I jumped, almost throwing my cloak aside. The tree toad had seemed to be calling from inside my ear. The sudden movement reminded me how stiff I was from sleeping on the ground. Not quite the ground itself—Weasel had shown me how to put fan leaves over fir branches to keep the worst of the dampness from me, but I still felt cold and wet as I slowly eased into a sitting position, pulling the cloak around me, trying to get ready for the morning routine.

Get up; follow Weasel, either through the swamp or along the ravines, and forage anything that was edible. Then bring it back, rest, and repeat the process in the afternoon. How long had it gone on? It seemed like forever, but probably the ordeal had lasted less than an eightday.

I glanced over at the lean-to. That was where Sylvie lay. She had caught the damp fever first. Huddled into a ball in a corner of the lean-to, her shakes rustled the branches.

Hsst . . . hsst, hsst, hsst . . . hsst . . . hsst, hsst, hsst . . .

The pattern was nearly regular, almost like rain, except that it rarely rained in the damps. Instead there was an almost continual ground fog and mist that kept everything damp, all the time. That's why every damper's hutch, lean-to, or cave, for the few who had staked out the bouldered area at the southern end of the marshes, had a fire pit—as much to ward off the damp as for cooking or heat itself. Not that there was a lot to cook over those fires, especially not with the heavy unseasonable rains and the cold winds that had rotted and stripped even the winter fruits and those that were usually edible for months after harvest, like the chysts.

Weasel was nowhere in sight, but had clearly been up earlier, since a wisp of smoke rose from the fire pit.

Whatever else the Enemy had done, they had ruined the weather and the crops, even the fruit trees.

As on so many days, the wind whistled through the swamp firs, and the mists and clouds were so heavy that not even the outline of the sun was visible. I shivered, either from the chill, although my cloak, bedraggled as it had become, was certainly warm enough, or from watching Sylvie suffer.

Thwapppp. The slap caught me unaware and dropped me into the muddy grass.

"Damned witch . . . you did it to her . . ."

Vran was waving his crossbow. Luckily for me, it was not cocked. But that wouldn't take him long, not with his muscles, especially fueled by anger.

Although I gathered my feet under me, I remained on the ground, wondering if I would have to dive away from him in plain sight and reveal that I was in fact one of those damned witches.

"More than likely, she got it from cleaning one of those swamp rats." Weasel's voice was matter-of-fact. The long knife he normally carried in his belt was out, and he was testing the edge with his thumb.

"Sticking up for the witch again?"

"Hardly. Witches don't ever get sick. So if she caught it from him, he's not a witch."

While I was seldom sick, I'd had my share of illnesses growing up. All I could figure was that since I had not been ill in the damps, where everyone seemed to suffer, that Weasel thought I never was sick.

"Hunnnh?" Vran missed Weasel's subtleties. "Swamp rats?"

"Never mind. We'll get some of that marsh rice. Boil it, and maybe Sylvie can eat that."

Vran looked at the huddled heap that was Sylvie.

The cold morning wind whistled again, and I stifled a shiver, looking from Vran to Weasel and back again.

Weasel turned without saying another word. Vran kept looking at Sylvie. I scrambled to my feet, grabbed my pack, and followed Weasel.

Once past the swamp firs shielding the camp, he did not head north for the marsh, but instead southward toward the main branch of the creek that eventually became the Faiyren River. Before long we were nearing the cut the river had worn through the low hills that bordered the swamps.

I could hear the low rushing roar of the river where it billowed from the damps into the small canyon that turned into Faiyren Gorge. We were nearing the pond above the rapids where, sometimes, Weasel had been able to catch migrating wetbill ducks with his snares.

He stopped and turned to face me. "What are you going to do, Sam?"

I knew what he meant. Sylvie was going to die. Vran would blame me, and nothing would stop him from using the crossbow. Nothing.

I shrugged, aware somehow in that post-dawn chill that another change was coming. "Have to leave, I guess. Unless you have some other ideas."

"If you really had to, you could have left days ago."

I didn't answer that question. I shrugged again. "Nowhere to go. Can't do much of anything, except read and write and do some math. That doesn't count for much right now."

For the first time, Weasel looked puzzled. "What do you mean? There are always jobs for clerks, or bookkeepers."

"Not now. Stores are all looted, those that are left. ConFed Marines control the roads. They've burned out most of the gentry, at least between Bremarlyn and here."

Weasel's mouth dropped open. "Why didn't you say anything about that?"

"I thought you knew."

"Sam, nobody in the damps knows *anything*. We knew there was an Enemy, and some damage to the capital, and a few soldiers on the road. Other than that . . ." He spat on the ground. "This is the place where you go when there's no place else to go, when even the back alleys of Horesard and West Inequital won't take you in."

"Between the Enemy and the looters, most of the towns are gone," I added. "Not much food, either."

Weasel wasn't looking at me at all. He just kept shaking his head. Finally, he grinned. "The main road is downhill and about two kays southwest. If you head east, you should reach Esterly in about a day. You'd better get moving."

I shook my head.

"Long story, Sam. Vran will be after both of us before too long. One way or another, there's a chance I'm clear. You say Bremarlyn's gone?"

I nodded.

"You know the prosecutor there?"

I did, but I wasn't about to admit that he was my father.

"No."

"You don't lie well, Sam. Is he still alive?"

I shrugged. "I don't think so, but I really don't know." That was the truth. I had no idea whether my father had died in the blaze. Somehow, I doubted that my mother had, but I felt I'd never know that for sure.

"That's good enough for me." He began to move, even more quickly, down the trail. Then he stopped, and turned, his voice low. "And you'd better keep moving or Vran will catch up to you."

Within moments, Weasel was out of sight.

I kept moving, until I was a good half kay downhill from the top of the rapids. The rumbling *swush* of the water at the top had subsided to a continuous rush. I slowed at the sight of a patch of wild onions and a flowering thorn. The thorn seed pods weren't bad, and the onions actually tasted pretty good. You couldn't eat too many at once, though.

I eased some onions out of the damp soil, wiped off one and ate it, forcing myself to chew it slowly and in small bites. I stashed a handful in my pack, and then began to pick some thorn seed pods. Maybe a half dozen were edible. They went into the pack. Nearby was a blue chyst tree, but it had been stripped clean, either by the squirrel rats or the weather or by some other damper.

Weasel, even in the days I had followed him, had shown me a few more things to put into my stomach, besides the obvious fruits. I'd even gained back some little bit of the weight I'd lost. My mother would have laughed, I knew, at my coming to eat whatever was generally edible. My father would have nodded sagely.

As I thought of them, I had trouble focusing on the tree or on narrow path, partly because I was shaking, and partly because the tears got in the way. But I couldn't stop any longer, not with Vran and his crossbow lurking behind me. So I straightened up and lurched down the path Weasel had started on—the one that led to Esterly.

Every once in a while I looked back over my shoulder, but I could see no one behind me.

"Freeze, damp rat!" The harsh voice had the ring of authority.

I froze, then slowly let my still-watering eyes turn toward the voice.

The Confed Marine uniform caught my eye first, then the shredder, which was aimed at my midsection.

From the noises on the other side of the trail, I could tell at least two others were in hiding. The grin on the marine's face dared me to run, as if he were just itching to turn the shredder on me.

Except for my eyes, I stayed frozen. If I had to, I could probably dive under the now and escape. But what good would that do—except deplete my fragile energy reserves?

"That's a very good swamp rat. Because you're so good at taking orders, we just might have a use for you, damper."

I didn't say a word.

"Don't you want to know, damper?" He paused, and his voice turned nastier. "Answer me!"

"Yes, sir."

"A polite damper. That I can hardly believe. Not too old, either. Might even be some hope for you, boy. Why are you here?"

"Looters . . . got my family, relatives . . . Enemy got the rest . . ."

"Well, you're in real luck today, boy." He stepped back, still keeping the shredder aimed at my midsection. "Just head straight down that trail to our camp. I'll be right behind you; so don't get any ideas."

I followed his instructions to the letter.

Another half kay further, at the base of the slope, were several tents and a portable stockade. Two ConFeds with shredders guarded the fence. Inside were three other men, two youngsters like me, and a bearded man who was about the same age as the forcer who had caught me.

"Just keep moving, swamp rat. Stop right by the gate there. And don't move."

A faint sickly odor drifted toward me, but it disappeared before I could place it. It was clear they wanted me alive, for whatever purpose, and that it would be easier to escape from the stockade later than attempt anything immediately.

"Got another one for you."

"Did you check him?"

"No. Thought you could do it."

One of the guards set his shredder aside, while the other two continued to keep theirs leveled at me.

"Let's see the pack."

I handed it over.

"Ugghhh . . ." He didn't even bother to empty out the onions and seed pods, or the partly moldy chyst in the bottom. Half of it was good. He dropped the pack by the gate. "We'll take the hatchet and the knife. Set them on the ground."

I did that as well, wondering why they bothered with the knife. A knife wasn't much against a shredder.

"You can keep the pack. Now get in there, and don't cause any trouble. Or you end up like that." He gestured toward what I thought was a stump, before I saw the flies and coagulated blood around the shredded flesh and bone.

". . . uuuggghh . . ." Somehow, I managed not to lose what little was in my stomach, but the remaining bitterness burned my throat.

"That's what happens if you don't follow orders, swamp rat."

Click.

He had opened the gate while I was trying not to retch my guts out. None of the other three men even looked toward the gate, although all three stared momentarily at me.

Three steps, and I was inside, clutching my tattered pack.

Clunk.

"No talking. Any of you."

I sat down and ate the good half of the chyst and another onion. After one look at what I was eating, the three others lost interest. Had I still been at the Academy, I probably would have lost interest too. If not all my appetite and then some. But I needed to keep up what strength I had left, and enough energy for one emergency escape.

After finishing off the onion, I stretched out and used the pack to cushion my head. Besides food, I needed sleep. My days in the damps had been short on both. The ConFeds weren't out catching people for an execution, which meant they had something in mind. At the worst it was probably slave labor—I hoped.

XVIII

"NONE OF YOU are good enough to be ConFed Marines! You're not even good enough to be second-rate Secos! You aren't even . . ."

Too tired to ignore the thin man with the hard eyes, I listened to him. Standing at attention with me were the others that the ConFeds had rounded up, perhaps a score in all. Hard bread and water—that was all we had been given, but with my onions, it hadn't been too bad. The hard-eyed man and the others had rousted us from the stockade at dawn and marched us into town. Esterly, I think, though I had never been that far east of Bremarlyn before.

". . . but you're all we've got left, and it's my job to turn you into an imitation of the real thing. If you live long enough, you just might make second-rate marines, and that's twice as good as anything else!"

Why we needed more military personnel after the unseen enemy had turned so much of Westron into dust was still unclear to me. The forcer in front of the ranks kept screaming about the need for discipline and the need for order, but most of the others would have scuttled back into the damps right then—except for the five ConFeds with their shredders and hard eyes ranging up and down our ranks.

So we listened and hoped for some bread, perhaps a ground apple.

"We can beat the Enemy—if we work at it! But looters, scroungers and drifters don't work. You aren't looters, scroungers, and drifters anymore. You're the property of the ConFeds Marines, and you're going back to work, and you're going to like it."

Somehow I still couldn't see how more ConFeds in uniform, toting shredders, taking food at weapon-point, and screaming at people, were going to defeat the Enemy. Hell, the Enemy thought we were ants—if the Enemy bothered to think about us at all.

"Any questions?"

I had plenty. All they'd get me was trouble. So my mouth stayed shut.

"No brains here? Any questions? Last chance for questions, you dullards."

"Why . . . why us?" stammered a thin youngster. "What good will more soldiers do?"

"Step forward, boy!" screamed the ConFed Forcer. His olive-colored singlesuit was dusty. So was his blotchy face, where it wasn't dirt-streaked with sweat.

The kid who asked the question didn't move.

"Bring him forward!"

One guard handed his shredder to another and walked up to the pale-faced youth. Yanked him right out of line and threw him into the mud in the middle of the road. The dust that seemed everywhere and the intermittent and unpredictable rains left mud puddles everywhere, even on the once-spotless Imperial highways.

The youngster, not even as old as I was, lay there for a second, then scrambled up and started to run.

Scrut . . . scrut . . . scrut . . . scrut . . .

The shredders were as terrible as they sounded. He didn't even look like chopped meat—more like blood pudding sprayed on the ground. If I'd had anything in my stomach, it couldn't have stayed there.

"That's the first rule, you worthless bodies. *No* questions. Not ever."

At least three of my companions were retching their guts out, but the forcer let them without even commenting. He just waited for them to finish. My stomach stayed knotted tight.

"Now line up. Double file. Double file, two abreast. Move it, and make an effort to keep in step. An effort, damn you! Move it! Move it!"

I held my guts together, somehow, and I marched westward, toward the ConFed complex at Herfidian, back toward Bremarlyn, toward Inequital.

We all marched, and kept marching. We marched past the way-station that had been Halfprince. We marched through the ford at Jillriko—the bridge and half the town, the western half, had been an enemy target—and through the empty eastern half of Jillriko, trying not to inhale too much of the ever-present dust, trying to breathe through cloth scarves that the ConFeds handed out.

The Faiyren River ran brown, like the creeks, and you could see an occasional trout floating belly up. The carp survived, I guess. They survived everything.

XIX

COMPARED TO THE days I had spent in the damps, the physical side of learning how to be a ConFed Marine wasn't bad.

A subforcer rousted us out before dawn, into the near-freezing cold, and put us through calisthenics. Then we went through hand-to-hand combat instruction and drills. After that came a field breakfast, generally hard bread, some sort of meat, dried fruit, and, if you were really hungry, grain porridge.

After breakfast, another group took us to a makeshift rifle range. Obviously, the rifle range part bothered the forcers. They had at least four subforcers behind us with shredders, and we were given single shot projectile rifles.

The bullets were little more than case-hardened clay, not real penetrating ceramic. But they made sure we expended all the ammunition on the range. Then we took the rifles back to some equally makeshift workshops, where we practiced cleaning the weapons. After we finished cleaning, we were led out on a five-to-ten kay quickstep march with full packs.

Halfway through the march came a quick midday ration, which we each had carried in our packs. The second half of the march always had some sort of obstacle—usually difficult, sometimes impossible. But we all tried. The forcers did nothing if you gave everything. One or two slackers didn't. We never saw them again.

After we returned to the camp—or temporary base, as it was called by the head marine, a burly man a good two heads taller than me who titled himself the Colonel-General Odin Thor—we listened to lectures. Some were on weapons. Some were on the situation in Westra, and how the marines were rebuilding the government structure after the wide-scale destruction by the Enemy.

Unlike many of the other unwilling recruits, I listened, trying to sort out fact and propaganda. You could even ask a question, provided the questions were factual and not questioning the ConFeds.

After the first few days, I could have left at any time, since I knew where the stores were kept and since I had regained the weight I had lost. But the same problem remained. Although some ConFeds had clearly fired my house, and probably killed my father, where would I go?

So I stayed, getting into better physical shape than I had even for athletics at the Academy, learning whatever I could, and keeping my mouth shut. I lost track of the days, blurring as they did into the onset of spring, but kept working, especially at the hand-to-hand. When I left the marines, I'd need it.

At night, sometimes when I wasn't totally exhausted, I practiced my sliding from place to place. No longer did the dives under the "now" leave me exhausted, but my appetite remained enormous.

"Never saw a small man pack away so much," observed Selioman. Probably in his late twenties, old style, he had been in the converted stables that served as barracks when we had arrived.

"I guess I'm just nervous."

"Nervous? Ha! You never get upset, Sammis. You look like you're waiting for something to happen."

I shrugged.

"Look. The forcers all see it. Don't you wonder why one is always watching you?"

"I hadn't thought about it."

"They have. If you weren't so young, Carlis would have made an example out of you early."

"Carlis?"

"The mean one, with the scar. He looks like he's ready to kill you when he sees you practicing out in the yard."

"Do you think I should give it up?" I had discovered that one of the younger subforcers, Henriod, had been a martial arts master, and I had asked him for some pointers in my limited free time. That had grown into a series of pre-dinner workouts. He could still best me, most times, but I was beginning to be able to use my undertime sight to anticipate most of his actions, and before long, I suspected, I would be able to beat him. Not that I could afford to let him, or Carlis, know that, especially if what Selioman had said was true.

"I wouldn't. Everyone, including the colonel-general, has heard how hard you work. Quitting would give Carlis an advantage and a way to say you were slacking off."

"Hmmmm."

But I thought about it, and took another tack, easing up on the martial arts and getting another subforcer named Weldin to instruct me on some of the marines' gear other than weapons. In practice, that meant the steamers and their accessory equipment. It also meant I spent most of my free time helping him and the maintenance crew clean the big beasts. Every few days, it seemed another one arrived from somewhere, often with a different paint scheme, sometimes even bearing the name of a hauling organization. Weldin and his crew, all men, cleaned them, repaired the ceramic and glass fiber panels where necessary, and re-painted each with the ConFed logo and colors. I generally got the grub-biest work available for the limited time I was free.

Still . . . what else was I going to do?

For one thing, I started eavesdropping, dropping out of sight for a few moments, from the few places where I wouldn't be bothered, like the outhouse the recruits had to use, to duck under the now and watch.

If I got the right angle, though I couldn't hear from the undertime, I could see, and I was beginning to read lips.

The most interesting place to watch was the room where the colonel-general had his maps of Westron. Often he and the experienced squads were gone for days at a time. The maps told some of the stories, because when he returned the one that showed the areas controlled by the ConFeds was usually changed, showing an ever-expanding wave of blue moving back toward Inequital.

About the time it was clear that winter would indeed end, they split us up and put us in with the regular squads—scouts, troopers, or maintenance. Because of my work with Weldin and the fact that I clearly had some mechanical ability, I was one of two who went to maintenance. Selioman was the other.

Henriod told me he was sorry I hadn't been selected for scouts, but both Carlis and Weldin had overruled him. I knew why.

Another batch of involuntary recruits arrived, and, then, Weldin called us together in the big barn that housed our dozen or so steamers.

"Now that we have recovered the capital area from the Enemy, the colonel-general and the scouts have retaken the ConFed base near Mount Persnol, the closest Imperial installation remaining to the capital." Weldin cleared his throat, then smiled. "We will begin transferring our operations there to reinforce a special project which offers us a chance to take the fight to the Enemy."

I kept my face blank. A special project to take the fight to the Enemy? An enemy that apparently could appear at will in much the same way as I could? The strategy maps and my limited undertime lip-reading had shown me nothing of that, but with a shade more free time in the evening, and the ability to walk the grounds behind the outlying wired fences, I had more opportunity to duck undertime. I resolved to use it as soon as possible.

XX

THE CONVOY—THREE freighters, the lead steamer, and the repaired armored steamer—waited, chuffing, on the stones of the Eastern Highway bridge at Herfidian, to head through the bridge gates toward the muddied and lifeless hillside. I was on the first freighter, lined up directly behind the lead steamer. Even in the winter-weight uniform, I wanted to shiver.

Watery gray light from a barely risen sun spilled through high and hazy clouds. In the chill morning air, both breath and the exhausts from the steamers cast thin white plumes from the bridge out across the marshes and the knee-deep water of the river.

In addition to the head gate guard, two squads of marines were turned out, weapons unlimbered, behind the stone ramps flanking the bridge gate—one squad on each side, both squads facing the muddy slope where the highway angled until it reached the brush and trees beyond the enemy's circle of destruction.

"Still clear, sir."

The subforcer received the report without a word and nodded to the gate guard, who in turn began cranking the heavy bridge gate open. That gate had been something else in the time before destruction. Once mother had driven me, in that superb golden steamer of hers, to Jillriko, and the Herfidian bridge had been without gates then. The part of Herfidian west of the river had also existed then. Now there were marines and gates, and only half of the central town remained.

As we lurched forward through the gate, with one hand I clung to the support rail. The other clutched the telescope that came with the lookout's perch where I teetered. My eyes strayed to the projectile rifle stowed in the holder next to me, ready for use. I hoped I wouldn't have to, but I recalled the holes and blood that had decorated the freighter I had seen from the roadside so many weeks before.

Whufff . . . chuff . . . whufff . . . With the slight coating of slippery mud dust on the highway stones, all the steamers began to strain once they reached the beginning of the incline.

Ccccrrrruuunnnch . . . Even with the freighter partway up the lower section of the hill, I could hear the sound of the bridge gate finally closing behind the armored steamer.

"Lookouts! Number one and four, rifles on standby. Two and three, cover the brush out there under the trees, out to the side."

Using my ability to slide out of the here and now to check the area from behind the non-time black curtain would have been safer scouting. It would also have revealed my secret and had me killed as one of the witches of Eastron. So I focused the scope out to my right, trying to see who or what might be hiding. One grossjay, patches of winter leaves on closed branches, and browned grasses flashed through the lens at me. We weren't supposed to use the scopes until *after* we spotted something. The restricted vision told me why.

Wuhhufff . . . chuff . . . skreee . . . The freighter lurched again as the driver overcorrected on one wheel.

Clunk! My head connected with the hard wooden railing of the sentry box.

"Verlyt!"

"Quiet!" snapped Carlis from beneath.

As I swallowed the blood from my just-bitten tongue, I steadied myself with my left hand and stowed the telescope.

Whuuuufff . . . chuuufff . . . whuff . . . In approaching the crest of the hill, the freighter lurched forward, ponderously, swaying side-to-side with each lurch. And with each lurch and each sway, my stomach lurched also.

Whhuuufff . . . skreee . . . whufff . . . chufff . . .

By now I could smell old oil and bitter steam. Had I eaten that morning, that food would already have found its way elsewhere.

"Don't eat if you've got freighter lookout," Selioman had told me. "If you puke on the freighter, Carliss'll make you clean all the puke out of the belts and gears—after you get there. It took Marin a week."

So I had stuffed some hard bread and an unripe but squishy pearapple into my pack for later. The cooks had just nodded.

Whhhuuufff . . . whufff . . . whuff. The lurching died down, and the engine sound steadied as we crested the hill and reached the flatter part of the road heading to and through Bremarlyn.

Swallowing hard, twice, I leaned out into the breeze, trying to take in some fresh air. What I inhaled had no oil scent, no steam, but the bitter odor of mold and dust, of death and destruction.

"Bandit at quarter one!"

I swiveled to the left to track Rarden's call, but the tarp-covered supplies blocked my view. Belatedly, I swung back to scan the quarter three area, trying to see if we were heading into an ambush.

Nothing moved except one gray bird on a a limb without even winter leaves and a dark ground dog hole.

"Fire at will!" shouted Carlis.

I unstrapped the rifle, lifted it into the swivel, and released the bolt lock.

Crump! Crump! Rarden let fire. One of the ceramic shells plowed up the ground not a dozen rods from the freighter.

"Hold your fire!" Carlis sounded disgusted. "Did you hit that ground dog, number one?"

"No, sir."

"Next time . . . never mind." Carlis waved the green flag from the cab to the freighters behind and to the bewildered lead steamer.

None of it made sense. Scattered bandits wouldn't attack an armed convoy with even one or two lookouts. And nothing, including spaceships and lasers, had been effective in stopping the enemy.

"Stow arms!"

After replacing the rifle, I studied trees, grass, holes in the ground, and occasional birds—usually grossjays.

By mid-morning, we were passing the site of the old inn, just flat mud and plastered dust, not quite covering the blackened and split foundation stones.

The one time I had eaten there on my birthday after leaving first childhood, Father had ordered me a blue chyst tart as a special treat. So splendid—I had looked at it and looked at it, not really wanting to eat it.

"Go ahead," he had said.

Mother had smiled her mysterious smile.

So I had eaten it bite by bite, forcing the last bites into an unwilling stomach. While the tart had been tasty, I still wished I hadn't eaten it, and mother knew that.

"Magnificent, isn't it?" Father had mumbled with his mouth full of his own tart.

I swallowed as the freighter continued its lurching past another memory and another place destroyed, past the two stones that were all that remained of the best meal in the region, and past the inn that led back toward Bremarlyn itself.

Two tumbled piles of black sand and stone sat on a bare hillside, bare except for rock and mud, so bare I did not recognize the East Hill entry to Bremarlyn at first. Then, it may have been the angle, since I had never looked down on the gates to Bremarlyn—or what remained of them.

While the steamers were not the quietest of machines, their hissings and chuffings were low enough and intermittent enough for me to hear the lack of other sounds. The smell of ash, not dust, clogged the air, and the clouds overhead seemed to thicken as the freighters whuffed up and past the ruined stonework.

Peering from the lookout, I strained to see what had befallen Bremarlyn. Blackened trunks and gray ashes dotted the west side of East Hill, little enough remaining of the town forest park.

The old Customs Port Building, dating from the early days of the Compact, which had served as the local library since the time of my great-grandfather, stood blackened, roofless, its windows glaring blindly into the gray-hazed noon. Of the two burned-out steamers in the side parking area, little remained except the shattered ceramic tubing trapped in charred and melted glass fiber panels.

Strangely, Bremarlyn had been spared total destruction by the enemy weapons. Instead, it appeared as though every dwelling had been torched . . . the more impressive the building, the greater the damage.

As the freighters hissed downhill, storing energy in their flywheels, my eyes searched for familiar places. Marshall Getana's villa—flattened as if by an explosion. Salmarn Hooste's estate—burned so thoroughly that the walls of the old stables had collapsed inward.

While few non-gentry had lived in Bremarlyn, even the more modest homes had not escaped the burnings. Havvy Sarston's home had been levelled—all four rooms. The same for Kryn Naerlta's cottage. And under the odor of fire and ashes was a sickly stench that reflected the rest of the corruption.

With a still-empty stomach, I managed to spit the bile welling into my mouth clear of the steamer, half-choking, half-retching the noth-ingness within.

Carlis ignored the lookouts, wearing as he did a strange half-smile I feared I understood. By the time he looked back up I had wrenched my guts back into semi-obedience and merely looked greenish.

At that moment, I wanted to choke him. I knew I could kill him at leisure—if I felt that way later. But I was sick, sick especially of pointless killing, and, scared as I was, sick of violence because of fear.

On the right as the convoy entered the central square was the meeting hall, now just four toppled walls and charred timbers. At least five steamers were buried under the rubble of the side wall, and the odds were that their owners were buried on the other side of the same wall.

So far as I could tell from my lookout's perch, swaying in the noon-time haze and chill, not a structure in Bremarlyn had been left intact. Every one had suffered either fire or explosive damage, or both. Not a single wall stood above shoulder height.

The two big community power receptors stood untouched. But the beamed power receptor grids had been removed. Removed, not de-stroyed. The antenna bases stood untouched, but the grids themselves had been unbolted. Why? It didn't seem to make much sense, because the power satellites themselves had not functioned since the day I had left the Academy.

In the windless depression beyond the square where the Eastern Highway turned to run arrow-straight toward Inequital, the sick stench of death even turned the ranker sitting by Carlis greenish. Carlis kept smiling. I kept trying to keep from gagging, if only to avoid cleaning the steamer.

After a time, when all the steam vehicles had chuffed through the ashes, and the smells, and the memories, the convoy reached cleaner air and the emptiness and open meadows of the Great Valley that separated Bremarlyn from the capital.

My guts stopped trying to turn inside out, and Carlis stopped smiling and started barking commands again.

XXI

WHUFF . . . CHUFF . . . WHUFFT, chuff, chuff . . .

I kept looking toward the west, trying to see when I might be able to pick out the famed towers of Inequital.

No steam freighter guaranteed a smooth ride. Each crack in the stone pavement, each joint, translated into a jolt high above the road.

The closer the convoy tracked the Eastern Highway toward Inequital, the more destruction and the less life there were. Bremarlyn had been bad enough, with the Academy a still-smoking ruin and the western half where Kryrel and Hargin and Solbar and so many classmates had lived yet another welter of arson and explosive devastation.

As the afternoon began to fade, the steamers reached two low stone gates, heavily weathered and each standing in a pile of sand. The wind picked up, whistling slightly and coming from the west. I nearly gagged again, cold as the air was across my face, from the odor of destruction and mold.

Belatedly, I recognized where we were as the highway widened. The gates marked the edge of the Imperial Preserve, but there were no trees, no bushes, no flowers. Even beyond them, where the towers should have stood, there was only dust and ash and destruction.

My stomach had taken too many shocks. This time, as the scale of the destruction hit me, it only turned over once or twice in protest. At the same time, the total absurdity of the colonel-general's plans seemed even more apparent. *We* were going to take the fight to an enemy that had leveled the largest city in our planet's history? An enemy that had done so without a casualty? An enemy we had no way of even finding?

"We'll be taking the road on the left at the crest of the next hill . . ." Carlis was telling the rating at the steamer's controls. ". . . leads toward Mount Persnol . . ."

I looked back toward the flattened low hills, still not believing that nothing remained of Inequital, nothing of the capital where my mother had disappeared.

The steamer lurched, jamming me into the side of the sentry box as it turned onto the narrower stone road that headed directly south toward the mountains. My mother had called them hills, comparing them most unfavorably to the Bardwalls of Eastron.

"The Bardwalls are mountains, Sammis," she had said. "Compared to them, most of the mountains of Westra are mere hills." Strangely, in retrospect, I had never asked how she knew. She knew so much, often revealed merely in passing, that it had never occurred to me to ask until I no longer could.

The wind began to pick up, colder than in the valley. By the time we reached the crest of the second hill, I had refastened all the clips on my parka, and there were traces of rime ice along the depressions beside the road.

The road, not quite wide enough for two big freighters to pass comfortably, looked older than the Eastern Highway, with actual ruts worn in the stone. How long that had taken I could not guess, but it meant that the road probably predated the Westron Monarchy and might have even been built when some Eastron Duke ruled the area.

Ahead, to the right, on my side, I could see a lump or pile of something near the crest of the third hill. Each hill was a little higher than the one before. The fences were still in good repair, untouched by the fires that had gutted the plantation houses and the freeholder's houses.

I focused the telescope on a lump off the shoulder of the road—a burned-out steamer, reduced to a heap of ceramic parts and tubing, and ashes from the now-burned frame. A non-military vehicle, without the metal framing of a ConFed or Security steamer.

When we were within a dozen rods, I saw the gaping holes in the tubing, holes that could only have come from military weapons. The rust was not as heavy as on the wrecks at Bremarlyn, and the ashes were still nearly black.

I glanced down at Carlis, who watched the way ahead as intently as the lookouts, and wondered if the steamer had been merely trying to escape the ConFeds. Since Carlis was not smiling, he hadn't had anything to do with it.

Not one of the ConFeds, including the other troopers, gave the wrecked steamer more than a passing glance. I saw a glint of metal, like a buckle or pin, in the ashes. Then we were past the wreck and heading downhill again.

The road was quiet, except for the sounds of the convoy. Not even a single grossjay appeared on the wooden fences or by the scattered evergreens. Nor did any ground squirrels poke their snouts from burrows. I didn't see any burrows, either.

With each hill came fewer fences, fields, and meadows—and more trees. Older and taller trees. With each hill, Carlis's lips clinched tighter. And the shadows got longer, and the wind colder.

And I got hungrier, my stomach tightening into a dull aching knot.

As the convoy neared the top of a particularly long hill, with the steamer protesting more than usual, I caught sight of some life. Short piles of logs were laid out in stacks beside the road. Tree stumps lined both sides of the old highway, as did piles of ashes, whipped by the gusty wind like snow, where the brush had been burned.

"Camp coming up!" Carlis half-bellowed.

I curled my feet in my boots, trying to keep them from getting too numb. With my luck, and because my guts had rebelled so much, I was facing an even longer wait, if Selioman had been correct. Even if I hadn't puked my guts all over the freighter, at least twice Carlis had seen me losing control.

That probably meant cleanup detail.

Twheet! Twheet, twheet, twheet! I jumped, banging my sore thigh against the sentry box from the piercing whistle.

"Slow down. Watch for the flag on the right. The entry road is narrow. Take it easy." Carlis was squinting into the twilight, leaning forward.

I saw the flag before he did. "Flag on the right, sir! About twenty rods up, sir!"

"Slow it down." Carlis ordered the rating.

The steamer slowed and lurched, and I banged up against the sentry box again.

The wind gusts had subsided to a steady moaning, and my breath was beginning to form frost clouds. Even with the extra space provided by the felling of the trees nearest the old highway, I felt hemmed in by the height of those remaining, many of which towered close to fifteen rods above the plateau. Most of the stumps were broader than I was tall.

Black oaks grow slowly. I remembered one which had stood in front of our house, less than two handspans thick. My father told me that he had planted it himself when he had been about my age.

After the turn the convoy was headed west again, along the narrower stones of the side road toward the almost totally faded orange glow of a sun that had set behind the mountain hills. Another kay before brought us to a stone wall. The stones were gray-black, and the old-fashioned parapets by the gate looked down on me a lot more than I looked down to the ground.

Just the area in front of the closed and timbered gate was illuminated by the yellow of the etheline lights. The guard stations and the walls were dark.

The freighter sounded its whistle again, and I jumped.

The big freighter lurched to a stop.

Outside the gate, a single sentry appeared. Several lights flashed along the parapets to indicate that there were more guards waiting. Still, I thought the whole exercise was stupid. A raiding party would try any place but the front gate.

The walls dated back before the Resurgence, probably to before the time of the Eastron occupation. I figured they were that old because of the thickness. While the secrets of powder and guncotton had survived the ups and downs of Queryan history, with each fall more metal had been lost, and the struggling Westron baronies could not afford to use iron or lead shells, not if they wanted other more pressing tools, like lathes and pumps and steam engines. Stone balls were fired from the few bombards that could be sledged from siege to siege. Thick walls tended to defeat the use of the bombards.

"Identify yourself!" demanded the guard wearing the purple uniform of a Security officer.

"ConFed detachment two, sent by Colonel-General Odin Thor. The password is 'Vanish.' " Carlis's voice was merely a half-bellow.

One of the lights on the wall played over Carlis and the rating at the freighter controls, then dropped down to illuminate the stone pavement leading to the gate.

Creakkkk . . . urrummmbbblle . . . The gate began to open. The seco vanished back into the wall.

"Follow the line of torches to the barracks," called another voice. "Someone will meet you there to guide you to the unloading docks and the maintenance facilities."

Carlis nodded and grunted. The rating began torquing up the engine pressure, and, by the time the gates were fully open, we were rolling toward the darkness on the other side.

Whatever the installation had been before, it was big. In the early evening darkness, I could not see where the walls ended, only that they continued north-south without reaching a corner or turning point within light or shadow distance.

"Keep it slow . . ." added Carlis.

The line of torches curved to the right. To the left ran another road or street. Both seemed to be lined with foundations of a series of buildings long since taken down. Buildings that had been substantial—if the stone foundations were any indication.

Once the freighter came to the bottom of the incline, the road and the line of torches ran straight to a long two-story stone building able to hold hundreds of troopers. A steamer runabout, with functioning headlamps, waited before the building.

"Welcome to the project." The voice came from the steamer, clear, penetrating, ironic, and distinctly feminine. A woman stood on the running board of the steamer next to the empty driver's seat.

Even in the dim light from the torches and the freighter controls I could see Carlis's surprise. The forcer said nothing.

"Follow me," added the woman, swinging into the steamer in a single fluid motion.

"Go ahead. Follow her," snapped Carlis.

The last glimpses of twilight had completely faded by the time we traversed another half kay of old stone roads and right angle turns.

The convoy finally chuffed to a halt behind another ancient stone structure.

"Download team!"

I winced, wondering if Carlis would add me to the unloading and cleanup party for my failures to keep my stomach totally in line, but he glanced at me, than glanced away. "Road sentries—dismissed! Report to Subforcer Henriod for quarters and grub assignments. Engineers! Report to Subforcer Weldin . . ."

Carlis's instructions went on and on, but I put the sentry box in order, shouldered the projectile gun and climbed down. My legs were shaky, and I was very careful with the handholds and footholds. By the time my feet touched the hard pavement stones, Carlis was barking more orders to move the freighters to the unloading docks.

I retrieved my pack from the locker under the sentry box. It felt like a load of stones.

"Road sentries. Answer up." Henriod's voice was loud, but tired. "Rarden?"

"Here, sir!"

"Eltar?"

"Here, sir!"

"Sammis?"

"Here, sir!"

Henriod ran through a dozen names, then stopped, and cleared his throat. "We have quarters in the barracks building. On the second floor. Take any bunk you want in the open area. The rooms with double or single bunks are for officers, forcers, or subforcers.

"You'll have to walk back there. Stay in groups of three, at least. Keep your weapons until Janth and I get there with the locks for the armory. Late mess after unloading." He looked over the sorry appearance we presented. "Dismissed."

Eltar, Farren, and I walked back together, following the line of torches. The torches were attached to wooden piles that had once held broadcast light bulbs. The bulbs and their metal holders had been removed. After less than twenty rods, my shoulders began to ache from the weight of the light pack.

"Sammis?"

"Unnh?"

"You came from Bremarlyn . . . ?"

I didn't want to answer that one, but not answering would have been worse. Just from Carlis's comments, I had picked up on how little the ConFeds cared for the gentry.

"Um-hummm," I answered.

"Funny, you don't act that way," mused Eltar.

I shrugged. What could I say, really?

"You really gentry, Sammis?" asked Farren. He had a nose that made night-eagles look snub-nosed.

"It depends on how you figure it. My father was. My mother wasn't. I hope I got her common sense along with his name."

That got a chuckle from Farren.

"What's it like, being gentry?" asked Eltar.

Terwittt, terwittt. Some night bird punctuated Eltar's question.

I stumbled on a rough paving stone, although, between torches and stars, there was certainly enough light for me.

"I never thought of it that way," I finally answered. "I knew we had more than other people, but at . . . school there were sons of farmers, tradesmen, and mechanics. We lived in a large house, but many were larger. My father was from a long line of gentry, but my mother wasn't. She used to say that she didn't even know her own grandparents. Until everything fell apart, I never gave it much thought . . ." I cleared my throat. That was difficult because it was dry. "Why?"

"Why what?"

"Why did you ask?"

Eltar shrugged. "Always wanted to know. Mother died. Dad ran the store, and he always bowed to the gentry, and they dressed better, but they didn't look any smarter, and they didn't act any smarter. We were poor, and they barely seemed to notice us, except when the taxes were due or when the highway levies were demanded . . ."

". . . and when some young gentry lad showed up in a flashy steamer and made off with the pretty girls and dumped them back pregnant," added Farren.

I was tired, and there wasn't much else I could say. They were talking about things I'd never done or seen.

But, from what I'd overheard, they were the sort of things that had happened. I hadn't been old enough for that, and, besides, neither of my parents would have approved.

"You ever have a steamer?" asked Farren.

"No. Nor a girl," I admitted ruefully.

They both laughed, and by then we were walking up the last few rods to the barracks. Even Eltar, with all his size, kept shrugging his shoulders to keep the weight of his pack from stiffening his muscles.

XXII

THE LOW-SLUNG STEAMER runabout was back by the main entrance to the barracks, with a Seco guarding the purple machine. He carried a weapon I'd never seen before, a short-barreled gun not long enough to be a true projectile rifle nor short enough to be a handgun.

"Riot gun," observed Eltar quietly.

I must have looked puzzled.

"That's what the Secos used on the crowds at Wavertown."

"Wavertown?"

The three of us had stopped on the far side of the half-circle stone drive as we surveyed the Seco and the runabout. The security officer turned toward us, casually letting the weapon move in our direction.

"You didn't learn about Wavertown in school?" Farren's voice rose.

"No. What was Wavertown?"

"Wavertown was where the Secos killed two hundred miners for re-fusing to work the deep seams."

"The deep seams?"

"You're hopeless, Sammis," sighed Farren. "Look. All the easy metal is gone. At Wavertown, there were deep seams of iron ore. You know, the stuff they make steel from? The seams were so deep that a lot of miners got sick from the heat and the fumes. Some of them died. The government said they died from drinking too much etheline. The Secos took over the mines. The miners refused to go back to the deep seams. The miners held a public meeting, and the Secos surrounded them and ordered them to the mines. The miners refused. The Secos shot them. Two hundred died, and close to a thousand were wounded."

I shook my head. The Eastron Sympathy Revolt had been nothing like that. The southern miners had refused to support the war effort against Eastron and had sabotaged the mines so badly that they were never reopened. When the Secos had tried to stop the sabotage, the miners rose and tried to keep the troops from the mines until the de-struction was complete.

"Look, Sammis. You're gentry. Or you were. Do you think your folks were going to tell you that they beat down freemen and miners? And what about Nepranza?"

"What about it?" I asked softly. I'd never heard about it. "That was a long time ago."

"Nepranza was three-four years ago. What world were you in? Just because some minor lord got uppity when a few youngsters got too friendly with his daughters, the Secos murdered a dozen. Then they did have riots. The lord's girls were fine, they said, but a lot of the town's daughters weren't. They were dead, or wished they were."

I just kept shaking my head. Did they think that the newspapers would have hushed up the kind of massacre that Farren said had taken place? Or the supposed events in Nepranza? My pack felt like it weighed as much as the steamer that waited by the barracks.

"Do you really believe that drek about natural choice of the gentry?" Farren's voice was almost a shout.

The Seco was sneering openly as Eltar grabbed Farren's arm.

"Chill it, Farren. Sammis doesn't honestly know. Can't you see that?"

I wanted to slug them both—Eltar for being so damned condescending, and Farren for believing that all gentry had forked tongues and fangs. I didn't do either. I just walked away from them.

"Still gentry at heart . . ."

". . . just chill it . . . lost both parents . . . made it through Con-Feds . . ."

Just as I drew up to the runabout, careful even in my rage to keep a good distance from the dark-haired Seco with the riot gun, he swung to back to face the barracks door, and stiffened.

"Valtar? Have any of the ConFeds arrived back here?" The woman who had greeted Carlis so efficiently stood full in the torch lights, glancing past the Seco toward Eltar and Farren, who were still mumbling· about me. "Are those the first?"

I tried to keep my mouth shut as I studied the woman. She had sandy-blond hair that glinted in the light, and a figure that might almost have seemed boyish, with broad shoulders and narrow hips, until I saw her even narrower waist. Despite shoulders nearly as broad as mine and short hair cut square across the back of her neck, she was clearly feminine. Her face was almost elfin, except for the set of her jaw. I liked what I saw of her figure.

She reminded me of someone, but I was in no shape to remember who.

"Trooper." The words were directed at me.

"Yes, Colonel." I had no idea what she might be, but she radiated authority.

At my response, she smiled, a professional smile. Even so, the smile softened her expression momentarily, made her look years younger, close to my own age, before she wiped it away. She was attractive in a familiar sort of way, but that could have been because it had been so long since I had been around any real women. "We're a military project, Trooper, but not military. I'm Dr. Relorn." She studied me again. "How long before the rest of the troops arrive here?"

Her scrutiny left me feeling uneasy, as if she saw right through me.

"The other road scouts, about twelve in all, are on the way back. The unloading crews will be a while yet."

"You are?" she asked, the smile clearly gone.

"Sammis, ConFed maintenance, Doctor."

She frowned, then let the expression drop. "The barracks are yours. There's no power right now, but we should be able, now that you have some mechanics here, to get the standby steam generators on line within a day or two."

I would have liked to talk more, but Farren and Eltar were sauntering up the drive, and the Seco was positively scowling. So I inclined my head. "Thank you, Doctor. We appreciate it."

She nodded in return. "Good night." Again, her eyes seemed to look right through me. She smiled briefly, and it seemed for a moment as she and I were alone in front of the ancient stone barracks.

Then the smile was gone, and a doctor who acted like a colonel stood there. Probably twice my age for all that she looked young when she smiled. She turned, and I shook my head.

"Did you see *that?*" Farren's voice grated on my nerves. "She talked to you?"

Eltar was shaking his head slowly, whether at me or Farren I couldn't tell.

"Just to say that the barracks were ours and that we'd have power once we could get the standby steam generators working."

"Must be an old Imperial staging base," mused Eltar.

"Not used for military, either," I added.

"Trying to change the subject, Sammis? Hunh?"

"From what?"

"That lady you were giving the eye."

I sighed. Farren was obnoxious. "She acted just like a ConFed colonel, except she has her professional smile down better. And she acts like this is her base, not ours."

"Probably was . . ."

At that point, I didn't really care. Looking at the colonel-doctor or whatever she was had been nice, but I didn't see much future in it.

Besides, I was tired. My stomach hurt, and my head was close to spinning away on its own. "Let's find some bunks and then look for the mess."

"Good idea."

The doctor had been right. The barracks were ours. Completely. There wasn't a soul in the building. So we took three of the better bunks, ones with lockers built in underneath them.

The cold water was cold, and the hot water was lukewarm, indicating that something worked. I used liberal amounts of both to remove as much road dust, grime, and soot as possible. Even good steamers emitted some soot, and the ones that we had been using were in less than perfect condition.

By the time we had washed up, the rest of the road scouts had found their way into the barracks, followed by Janth and his locks for the armory.

"Let's have those weapons, now . . ."

I was more than glad to get rid of the projectile rifle, just wishing that he would hurry up and finish so that we could get something to eat. I felt as white as the ancient canvas mattress cover on my bunk.

"Field mess is being set up in the dining hall below. That's the big empty room at the back . . ." Janth went on, but I tuned it out, just waiting until we were dismissed to go eat.

After all, lack of food had landed me in the ConFeds, so to speak, and the ConFed organization's single greatest benefit to me had been the halfway square meals that allowed me to rebuild and maintain my strength.

"Sammis . . . just waiting to eat. Again . . ."

I tried to keep from smiling at the comments about my appetite, but I probably looked wolflike thinking about food. That was the way I felt.

"Dismissed."

I was second in line heading down the wide stone stairs toward the dining hall. Eltar liked to eat as much as I did. He was first. That was fine with me. Being first called too much attention to you, just like being gentry, or being an officer. Or a witch.

"Line up on the right! On the right!" Carlis's voice was unmistakable.

There was only one place to line up—on the right. So we did, with Eltar leading us on.

"Lukewarm field slop . . ."

"Boiled rat guts . . ."

". . . tasty rodent brains . . ."

The cooks were used to the comments, and the one who glared at us looked no different than usual as our boots echoed on the stone flooring.

Four long dusty tables had been dragged away from a stack on one side of the hall that must have held two dozen of the massive wooden trestles. The rest loomed there in the shadows cast by the field torches used in place of broadcast power globes or hard-wired lights.

The flickering light made the old building seem ancient, but its age wasn't my predominant concern as I shovelled a double helping onto the field tray.

. . . *grrrrr* . . . Both the light-headedness and my stomach were letting me know of my low energy state.

"You can eat that?" Farren sounded amused.

"He's a damper, Farren."

". . . cannibal type, you know, swamp rat eating swamp rat . . ."

I ignored Rarden's low-voiced comments and took two more slices of hard bread and one of the shriveled chysts that Eltar had spurned. Food was food, and, besides, the stuff we were getting was quite edible, if not exactly a gourmet's delight. My father had been the gourmet, not me. My mother had regarded food only as a necessity, not an end in itself.

I took the tray and sat down on one of the long benches across from Eltar. My light-headedness began to disappear with the first bite, as did the tightness in my stomach, and I forced myself to eat slowly, methodically chewing each bite.

"That good, hunnnh?"

Again, I ignored Rarden.

"That good, swamp rat?"

"Rarden!" Even I looked up at Carlis's bellow. The subforcer was standing almost at the end of the trestle table.

Rarden blanched. "Yes, sir!"

"Show some brains. That swamp rat is twice as tough and four times as poisonous as you. He has a hide thicker than a rhinopod. But he isn't going to let you insult him forever, and there wouldn't be enough of you left to stuff into a mess kit. So do us both a favor and shut your trap."

Carlis's tone showed he didn't think much of either one of us—except as raw troop fodder. Still, it got Rarden off my back—temporarily.

I returned near-full attention to the field rations and broke the second slab of stale bread in two, taking one bite of the rehydrated and undefined meat and one bite of the heavy bread, one bite of the meat and one bite of the bread, alternating until I finished it all. I saved the chyst until last.

Everyone was gone—except Carlis—when I stood to take the field tray back.

"Swamp rat . . ."

"Yes, sir?"

"Still so very polite. Swamp rat . . . just stay polite and listen to orders, and everything will be just fine."

"Yes, sir."

"You're so polite, swamp rat. You never do anything wrong that you can help. Why don't I trust you?" Carlis was sitting by himself at the very end of the trestle.

"Sir?"

"I don't trust you, swamp rat. I never will. And don't forget it."

"I won't, sir."

"I know you won't, swamp rat." Carlis shook his head, and looked back at his own partly eaten rations. "I know you won't."

Since I appeared to be dismissed, I left to go back to the corner of the barracks I had staked out for some sleep. The next morning would be the typically early ConFed dawn.

XXIII

LIFE AT THE new base was an improvement over the temporary encampment at Herfidian, especially once Weldin had managed to get the steam generators going. He claimed that they hadn't really been used in over a century.

I pretty much kept my mouth shut and tried to learn all that I could. While I didn't know much about the systems, at least I could understand the manuals. By reading them and watching what was going on, I learned some practical engineering of sorts.

In walking around the old base—we were never told its name, and maybe that had been lost along with all the other destruction—I realized something else. Less than a handful of Secos had held the base against the riots and raids. Aside from the Secos there were the technicians and some scientists, and the most powerful, it seemed, was the woman who had greeted us—Dr. Relorn.

No one told me that, but it was clear enough. She had the only personal guard and steamer.

While I had my own ways of finding out what was going on, I didn't start sliding under the now and snooping until we'd been at the base for several days and I was both rested and well fed. By then a second group of ConFeds had arrived, and the cooks were actually preparing food a cut above field rations. Not much, since it was still another season

until the harvest, assuming enough farmers had planted for there to be
a harvest.

After dinner that night, I lingered and cadged thirds, watching Carlis
shake his head sadly, and ate everything methodically. Then I walked
back outside, heading away from the gate and along one of the old worn
stone roads lined with foundations.

By the time I was half a kay from the barracks, twilight was fading
into early evening. I knelt down by one of the stone steps leading upward
to nothing and slipped under the now, sliding toward the technicians'
buildings.

As I headed toward the "reserved" section of the base, a faint spray
of lines appeared before me. "Before" isn't the right word, since you
really see with your mind and not your eyes in the undertime, and the
lines were more like a faint series of afterimages. But all of them radiated
from a single point near the center of a large single-story building.

The timbered building was newer than the two stone structures that
flanked it. Age is easy enough to tell from the undertime. Older things
seem solid. Newly built structures lack depth, and living things waver—
just a bit for trees to quicksilver for birds and other fast-moving, fast-
living creatures.

Following the lines backward, I found myself hovering undertime
before a single operating console and an empty platform surrounded by
other inactive equipment. At the console sat the doctor.

For reasons I could not explain, I slipped from the undertime behind
her and watched, with her, silently, as the screen displayed its images.

A man wearing a bulky atmospheric or water diving suit clambered
onto the platform, closed the suit's faceplate and vanished. The screen
blanked, then displayed a woman, wearing a less extensive version of a
self-contained breathing system, who also vanished.

The console shed the only light in the shadowed laboratory, a room
the size of a small equipment bunker that smelled of ozone and electronics.

"So you were in charge of the project?" I asked into the stillness.

She turned slowly in the swivel chair, as if she had known all along
that I had been there. "So far as I know, I still am."

"You knew I was watching."

She nodded, but remained in the swivel, apparently relaxed, even
though a stranger had appeared from nowhere.

"You can dive yourself. Otherwise you would have been more surprised."

For a moment, neither one of us moved.

All the heavy equipment dated from before the time the monarchy had limited the use of metals to bare essentials. That it had not been removed indicated either how important the project had been, how well-connected the doctor had been—or both.

Dr. Relorn continued to look at me, evenly, as though she were cataloguing my every feature.

I looked back—seeing a slender, sandy-haired woman with a narrow, elfin face and eyes that penetrated even through the gloom of the room. Her physical condition had to be good, just from her posture and aura.

"So why aren't you on the screen tapes?"

"I don't dive."

The words were matter-of-fact, but I could hear an edge to her voice.

"Why not?" I was surprised that I had the nerve to ask her.

"Do you know what you are?" Her reply came back to me almost as I finished challenging her.

"Me? I'm just a ConFed trooper, trying to get by."

"That's just not true, and you know it. You're gentry, and an heir of Eastron, if not—"

"No!" The last thing I needed was some idiot doctor blabbing about witches of Eastron. "Look, Doctor. I don't know where you've spent the last year or so, but every freeman and woman in Westron would be just as happy to cut the throat of any stray gentry youth they happened to run across—assuming there are any left outside of your fortress retreat here."

She didn't look convinced, but the anger was gone as quickly as it had appeared, and she looked younger, more relaxed. That her hair was as light as mine, if not lighter, was clear even in the dim light around us.

A muted roll of evening thunder punctuated the momentary silence.

"Why do they call you the swamp rat?"

I wondered how she had discovered that, but she was changing the subject all too successfully. "You never answered my question. Why didn't you try diving under the now?"

"Diving under the now?" Her eyebrows furrowed for a moment.

I could smell my own sweat, that and the odor of metal and oil and machinery. I shrugged. "That's what I call it."

"Why are you with the ConFeds?"

"Don't you understand yet?" I forced myself to be calm. She could probably fry me if she chose. That or put me on the run again. I sighed.

She smiled, and I found myself smiling in return. Her warmth was contagious, and the smile was genuine. Don't ask me how I knew. I knew.

"Why don't you sit down and explain?"

Looking around, I didn't really see anywhere to sit.

"My quarters are down the hall. It's convenient." She gestured vaguely behind her and to my left. "Was convenient," she added absently.

"Might not be convenient to me. If I'm not back in the barracks by last call, it's going to be difficult to explain."

"That's a while, isn't it?" Her voice was businesslike, as the smile faded.

"Enough for a short explanation, I guess."

After touching the console and blanking the screen, she stood in the near darkness, turned, and walked toward the door. The doctor walked the distance without a light. So did I.

Click.

A single lamp lit a low table and not much else. It flickered briefly, the way all the electric appliances did every now and again, the result of the imperfect system cobbled together with the backup generators. On each side of the table was a comfortable armchair.

"Would you like something to drink?"

"Water, please."

"Just water?"

"Just water." I sat down in the left-hand chair and waited. I could smell the faintest of fragrances in the air, just the hint of trilia.

"Here you are."

I took the narrow crystal goblet from her. "No servants?"

"No servants."

"Now, Dr. Relorn, you owe me an answer, and I owe you an explanation." I took a sip from the goblet, an antique similar to my father's Dyleraan, that probably dated back to the establishment of Westron.

"An answer." She leaned forward on the edge of the chair, somehow perched there, yet relaxed. "The question was why I did not attempt to dive, as you put it, 'under the now,' when I am the one running the project." She sat back slightly, as if waiting even as she spoke. "The simple answer is that mental travel—"

"Call it diving," I interrupted. I took another sip of the cold spring water that tasted as fresh as the water I had once scooped from the streams along the Long Wall Trail.

"—mental travel, or diving, is blind. You don't know where you're going, and I never liked traveling blind."

"But it's not. Besides, anywhere on Query—"

"We weren't looking on Query—"

My mouth dropped open for two reasons. First, I realized that other witches or divers might not really be able to see their destination. And second, Dr. Relorn was telling me that I could have travelled to other planets.

"—and the diving ability can take you forward or backward in time, but not in our solar system."

"But didn't you know you could travel from point to point on Query?"

"What for? You know the strength of the witch legends. Besides, what's the point of getting hurt in travelling a few thousand rods? If there's danger, the reward ought to be worth something. That's why we worked on it as an alternative to mechanical means of stellar travel—"

"Stellar? To other stars?"

"What do you think I've been talking about, Trooper Sammis?"

I shook my head slowly. The stars? I'd never thought about the stars. How much energy would that take?

"But the physical energy?" I couldn't help asking.

She nodded. "That's another reason. Mental travel takes less energy away from Query and even less outside our solar system. It takes more energy to travel from Westron to Eastron than to travel back centuries in the Serianese systems—even wearing one of those pressure suits you saw."

"Pressure suit?" Everything she said raised more questions.

"Other planets don't necessarily have breathable atmospheres."

I knew that. I just hadn't put the pieces together. After sipping, or gulping, from the goblet, I remembered she still hadn't answered my original question.

"But why didn't you dive?"

"I tried several short . . . dives . . . but I . . ." She shook her head. "I told you. I don't like doing things blind."

I could sense the fear. Her fear, and I knew. So I stood up and grasped her hands, trying not to think too much myself. Her fingertips were warm and ice-cold at the same time. "Now. Just let your mind relax. We're going to . . . Bremarlyn." I tried not to think about how supple and warm her hands were in mine.

"Bremarlyn . . . ?"

"No questions."

Diving under the now with the doctor was hard, especially at first, like dragging an anvil with my fingertips, afraid that I would drop her any instant. Once under the now, her fear washed over me like a black tide, almost blinding me and blotting my directional senses.

Fear—that was her blinder. I tried to push a sense of reassurance at her, a feeling of warmth. Her fear receded from me, but I could still detect it cloaking her, blinding her to our position in the undertime.

For all that, she burned in the undertime, swirling with those sparks I had noted earlier.

Even in forcing myself to ignore both her blackness and her brightness, I carried us to Bremarlyn, to an orchard I had known well. From the undertime, the area where I wanted to emerge appeared empty. In the starlight, the blackened walls of the old house gaped. Around us, the chyst tree leaves whispered in the summer night's breeze.

"Look," I said softly, remembering that I held the doctor's hands, before releasing them abruptly. "You did it. You know I couldn't have carried you. *You* did it."

"Are you always this direct?" Her voice was husky, yet amused.

"No . . . I've never dared. But . . ." I shrugged. With the scent of suddenly ripening chyst around me, I didn't feel like explaining. The last time I had stood in the orchard had been to see the fires which had been the beginning of the end for the old way of life on Query.

The doctor didn't say anything as she studied the ruined home, the overgrown grounds, and the neglected orchard.

"You could see," I added to break the silence, "and you will see . . ."

"Was that you?"

I knew what she meant. "Yes. Your fear blocks your sight from the undertime. You were so afraid to begin with that I had trouble seeing."

"You can see out from the undertime?"

I nodded. "Most of the time. You should be able to."

"Was this your home?"

"My family's. My father's, really. The ConFeds fired it at the beginning of the looting and burnings. All of Bremarlyn looks like this—or worse."

The breeze ruffled my hair and brought the bitterish scent of unripe chyst to us.

"We need to get back." I still worried about Carlis and the ConFeds.

"You're worried about your superiors? When you could leave the ConFeds any time?" Her tone was puzzled.

"You still don't understand, do you? Diving takes energy, plenty of it. And rest. When can you get either, when every freeman, every ConFed, is chasing you?"

The doctor raised her eyebrows. Despite the dimness of the starlight, the gesture was clear.

"Look. The ConFeds fired my house, killed my father. Every gentry house from Inequital to beyond the damps has been destroyed, either by the Enemy or by the ConFeds or someone else. The Enemy and the looters destroyed most of the crops." I could tell she still didn't understand.

"What would you have done? A student, one set of clothes, no money, no valuables, no food, no friends . . . you know that a single word is enough to show you're gentry. No skills to speak of and no family."

"I needed someplace to learn, to be fed, and to stop running." I shook my head in exasperation. "Let's go . . ."

"Where?"

"Back to your quarters."

Chicchichhii . . .

I smiled at the grossjay, then grabbed her hands, and dived. Grossjays never called at night.

"The woman . . ."

For an instant I had all I could do to force us under the now, but then the doctor relaxed just enough. Shadows converged on where we had stood, but not quickly enough. The troopers, ConFeds not under Colonel-General Odin Thor's command, for I would have known their postings, were after either me or the doctor . . . the woman. But why?

With the blurriness of the view and my own lightheadedness, I had all I could do to concentrate on getting us back to the doctor's quarters at the base.

On breakout, I released her hands, sat down, and took a long gulp of water from the goblet I had set on the table just minutes before.

"You are rather amazing, Sammis."

I ignored the comment. I was still thinking about the strange ConFeds.

"Would you like something to eat, or do you have time?"

"Yes. There's still a little time before I should go."

As she turned, I studied her. Certainly her figure was youthful, far more youthful than her age—like my mother. Her face was unlined, also like my mother. Was that for whom the troops had been waiting? But why? Was she still alive, or did someone just think so?

I took the last mouthful of water from the heavy goblet, tilting it back to get the last drops. The incipient headache began to fade.

"Will these help?" She offered a tray of biscuits.

"Perfect." I ate two at a single bite while she refilled the goblet. Another gulp, and another pair of biscuits, and another slow mouthful of water, and I began to feel normal.

"You ought to practice diving," I told her.

She reseated herself on the edge of the other chair, after setting the tray on the front center of the table. "I still can't see."

"Can you tell red and blue, black and gold?"

"Yes, but nothing outside the undertime."

"I couldn't at first, either. It takes practice."

"Yes. Perhaps we'll have time to discuss that. Later."

Her voice bore a faint huskiness, a trace of an accent or strangeness that seemed to come and go.

I still didn't know what she had been doing—except that her project had something to do with using the diving ability to visit other planets—even planets in other stellar systems. Why was Odin Thor interested? And what were the other ConFeds doing?

"You've been hiding your ability." Her tone was back to businesslike.

"Wouldn't you?"

"Under the circumstances, it's understandable. But I may be able to help you."

"Oh?"

"What if I tested for the ability? The colonel-general wants to use mental travel to rebuild Westron."

"How?" To say I was skeptical would have been an understatement. "It's hard enough to carry yourself from point to point."

"He doesn't know, but he's the type to grab for a useful tool even when he doesn't know how it could be helpful."

"Would you test all the ConFeds?"

"Why not? It might help remove some of the stigma. And I might find a few others."

That was a thought worth pursuing . . . if diving could be sanctified by science . . .

"Oh . . . time for me to go."

"Good-bye." That was all she said, as if someone dropping by from nowhere and disappearing back into nowhere were the most commonplace of occurrences.

Good-bye. All my questions—almost all of them—remained unanswered.

XXIV

"SAMMIS?"

At the time, I was trying to persuade an antique lathe to shave the tiniest edge of metal from one side of an unused generator casing in order to use it as a replacement for the original, which had shattered because Rarden had knocked a sledge into it. Some of the old metal was so brittle that it took scarcely more than a sharp blow to fragment it.

So much of the equipment Weldin had retrieved from the sealed underground bunkers was in that state. Some of it had to have been pre-disaster—perhaps two millennia old.

"Sammis!"

"Just a moment." I finally got the guide set the way I wanted and edged the casing into place. For someone who knew how to handle machinery, the adjustments would have been simple. I didn't, and they weren't.

One more pass, and the casing would fit the larger rotor shaft with adequate clearance, probably more than adequate clearance.

Rrrrrrr. . . .

I cut the power to the lathe and turned. Weldin was standing there.

"Yes, sir."

"After you get that fitted, get washed up, put on a clean uniform, and report to Janth."

"Janth?" Nothing I did had anything to do with the assistant armorer.

"All of you rankers are being tested by that doctor who used to run the base. The colonel-general has ordered it."

"Yes, sir."

I must not have looked too happy.

Weldin added, "Don't worry. If the doctor selects you, it will prob-ably mean easier duty."

"Yes, sir."

"Just finish up, and do it, Sammis. Colonel-General's orders."

There I was, being rescued from the ConFeds, and acting as though I were being thrown to the Secos.

The modified generator casing fit, not that I had had any doubt. All that remained was for me to drill out another hole where it joined the base plate. Then I fastened the new casing over the rotors and windings and all the other parts I didn't understand and fastened it in place. That gave us a functioning partial backup generator for the existing backup unit.

Next, I told Selioman before I left, to let him start out the testing.

"Why?"

"To be tested by that doctor . . . for something . . ."

Selioman shook his head. "Good luck. Whatever that is. I couldn't tell what she was testing for."

I shrugged.

Janth was pacing by the time I got to the armory. With him were Eltar and two men I'd seen, but didn't know.

"Let's go." Janth didn't even look at me as he paced out and down the corridor.

"Why so late?" Eltar's voice was pleasant, not probing.

"Caught me in the middle of repairing a generator."

Eltar nodded. He knew I was one of the few younger ConFeds who had any understanding of things mechanical or technical in nature. I didn't, of course. I just understood plans and prints and could read manuals.

Outside the barracks waited an antique open-benched steamer. The driver was a junior Seco.

A breeze ruffled the tattered pennant on the front quarter panel, and a dull rumble of thunder echoed from the direction of Mount Persnol. The overhead clouds promised rain, but not for a while.

Janth sat beside the driver on the padded bench seat. He took off his beret after a gust of wind threatened to blow it off. Eltar and I took the third bench, the last one in the back, without any upholstery.

Wheeep . . . Thud!

The steamer lurched forward.

Eltar cracked his elbow on the sideboard. I merely put splinters into my palm by grabbing the top of the sideboard on my side.

"Damned Secos. . . ." muttered the man in front of me.

Eltar muttered something less polite . . . and less audible.

"Shut it down," grumbled Janth. "All of you."

The junior Seco's shoulders slumped momentarily, as with a sigh. No Seco could have possibly have wanted to be isolated with a group of ConFeds. Although, as I thought about it, I had not seen any Secos except those attached to Dr. Relorn since the Enemy attacks had destroyed Westron.

Had they all been in Inequital when the Enemy had flattened it?

Some of the hills to the south were lit by a patch of sunlight pouring through an opening in the mostly cloudy sky. That one open space almost glittered, bright bluegreen. The clouds around it seethed, white and fluffy at the top and dirty dark gray at the bottom. Even as I watched, the clouds closed in and the distant sunlight began to fade.

The steam-wagon lurched uphill toward the laboratory complex.

"What's this all about?"

"You'll find out soon enough," grumbled Janth.

The steamer continued to whistle and lurch its way up the gentle incline, scarcely any faster than we could have marched.

In front of the main entry, off another stone-paved and circular drive, waited a pair of Secos, each armed with a riot gun. They stepped back as we scrambled out, adjusting their grasp on their weapons.

"Line up." Janth's voice was calm.

Without another word, we marched in through the entry door, Janth leading the way. He'd obviously been through the drill.

We marched down the center corridor, all the way to the back of the laboratory, then turned left, along the corridor I had walked myself with the doctor, until we reached the laboratory.

There were no guards outside the open door, and Janth barely hesitated before leading us inside and toward the platform in the center of the room.

Directional lights suspended from the ceiling outlined the platform. Where we lined up waiting to go up the wooden steps to the platform was half-lit by the scattering of the platform lights.

Dr. Relorn, wearing some sort of golden-brown tunic, sat before that screen, her sandy hair glinting in the reflected light. From where I stood, she looked much younger than the subforcer behind her, and almost like a girl compared to the height of the burly head ConFed.

Colonel-General Odin Thor stood beside her with a bored look, his face mostly in shadows. I was standing behind Eltar, wondering how the doctor would use the array of equipment to determine who might be a timediver.

"Next."

Janth nodded to Eltar, who stepped up on the platform.

Hmmmmmmmm . . .

Bzzzzzzz . . .

More from force of habit than for any other reason, I glanced at Eltar, first with my eyes, then with my thoughts, the way I did to dive under the now. None of the energy that surrounded me, or even Dr. Relorn, swirled around Eltar. He was just a quiet goldish blob.

Then I looked at the doctor—and the light swirls of gold and black eddied around her.

Another set of currents tugged at my mind, and I tried to scan the laboratory as well as I could without seeming too obvious.

Colonel-General Odin Thor! The head ConFed Marine himself was throwing off black and gold sparks in an undertime display that mirrored the doctor's.

I managed to catch my dropping jaw and turn the movement into a yawn.

Only the doctor saw it, and she frowned but briefly while ostensibly studying her instruments.

We had never talked about undertime sight, and I wondered if the doctor saw what I did, or whether I was some sort of freak in being able to see the time energies.

But I needed to tell her about the colonel-general—or was that how he had found her to begin with? What was their relationship? In our brief discussion, we hadn't talked about that either.

Right now, they were ignoring each other, but that didn't necessarily mean anything. Were they lovers? Or had the whole thing been coincidence?

Why did it matter? The doctor's private life was hers. So was the head ConFed's, and they both moved in orbits far above my present status.

"Next . . . next!"

"Sammis." Janth's bored voice turned exasperated. "Where's your mind, Trooper? Step up there."

Everyone in the laboratory turned to look at me.

"Sorry, sir." I stepped onto the platform.

Hmmmmmmmmmmmmm . . . cling, cling, cling!

Now, everyone was really looking at me. My nose itched, although the room couldn't possibly have been dusty.

"Some potential here, Colonel-General."

Odin Thor nodded calmly. "Doesn't surprise me. Always looked like witch-spawn. Do you want him?"

"We'll need some more tests . . ."

"He's yours, on loan, as long as you need him."

I tried to look puzzled, glancing from the colonel-general to Janth and back again. I opened my mouth, then closed it.

"Report to the doctor with your gear as soon as possible," Odin Thor ordered me, before turning to Janth. "Armorer, list him as support services to the Far Travel Lab."

"Off the platform, Trooper. Wait outside with the others who are done."

I shook my head slowly, as I took the three steps down to the stone floor of the laboratory. I wanted to tell Dr. Relorn about Odin Thor, if only to get her reaction. But I couldn't blurt out my discovery in front of everyone.

"Next . . ."

Outside, Eltar shook his head. "You going to be some sort of experimental type?"

"I don't know. Odin Thor looked happy enough to be rid of me. Rarden will certainly be pleased."

"What about you?"

"I don't know."

Janth came out of the laboratory.

"Sammis. Head back and clean out your gear. Be ready to go when the rest unload."

That was it. Period. I was detailed to the Far Travel Lab and Dr. Relorn.

XXV

WORKING FOR THE Far Travel Laboratory had some definite advantages—like a room of my own in the building next to the Lab. The immediate disadvantage? I had to go back to school . . . or learning.

I had not even put the kit bag that held all my worldly possessions on the graystone floor of the room before a thin and dark-haired man appeared.

"Sammis?"

"Yes?" I turned from the comfortable single bunk, complete with linens and a thick blanket.

"My name is Deric Ron Norften." He looked down on me, a good head taller even as he gave me a half bow of greetings.

"Sammis." I waited.

"Dr. Relorn asked me to look in on you, and to bring you these." He extended several thick bound notebooks, along with what appeared to be a stack of datacubes. "Do you know how to operate a console?"

"I used to be able to handle an Omega Vee, but that was a while ago."

"Our Gammas are trickier, I fear, but not impossible. Do you know where the briefing rooms are?"

I shrugged. "No. I know where this room is, where Dr. Relorn's laboratory is, and that's about it."

His soft chuckle erased his formality. "She can ignore a few details."

I nodded, trying to inventory the rest of the room as I did, taking in the two wooden armchairs, the narrow closet, the desk built into the wall, and the single window. A good three-quarters of a rod square, the room qualified as a ConFed officer's quarters. No wonder the colonel-general wanted to keep the technicians away from the troops.

"Do I get the tour?"

"Why don't you unpack? Then I'll be back, and you can see how we're laid out. After a quick tour, it will almost be time for dinner."

"And then?" I asked straight-faced.

"Why then . . . you get to work studying all this material."

"What's the point?"

"I thought . . ." He paused and his thin face screwed up slightly. ". . . at the proper time, Dr. Relorn will explain your assignment. I can say that you will need to know all this material before you can actually start your investigations." About three long steps, and Deric was depositing the notebooks on the otherwise bare desktop. He kept the data-cubes. "I'll be back shortly. Feel free to look around, but knock before you enter any of the rooms with closed doors. A number are occupied."

He half-bowed again and was gone.

Much classier than the colonel-general's minions, Deric was, but the bottom line was still the same. The good doctor wanted something from my scrawny carcass.

Unpacking into the closet and built-in drawers did not take long. Three sets of working uniforms and a single-dress uniform don't take up much space, even with underwear, belts, and a few toiletries. The biggest item was the foul-weather parka.

One thing I appreciated immediately. The room, the entire building, smelled clean. The sliding window had been left ajar, and a slight breeze brought the fresh smell of early summer inside. My nose itched slightly, probably from grass pollen, but I'd take pollen over filth any day.

The walls were plain goldenwood panels, with the faint cracks and scratches of age that matched the indentations in the graystone under-foot. The door itself was of the black oak that was tougher than iron-wood, but the latch was simple. The lock was a simple bolt.

Since I didn't feel like exploring at that moment, I folded the empty kit bag and put it on the top closet shelf. The notebooks beckoned, despite my lingering irritation with the doctor's cavalier assumption that I would automatically assume whatever duties she had in mind.

So I picked up the one on top. No title on the flexible cover. The page inside read, *Notes on Perceptual Thresholds in the Non-Time Interstice.*

Instead of standing around and waiting for Deric, I sat down in one of the wooden chairs and began to read . . . very slowly. Some phrases made sense and squared with what I had already experienced—

". . . travelling into the red represents apparent temporal re-gression . . . although whether such regression places the traveler into a backtime setting purely subjective in nature, a setting representing one of a series of alternative universes, or a flexible 'real' backtime position will require further observation . . .

". . . gold (cold) orientation is non-mass/non-energy oriented . . . black (hot) represents mass/energy concentrations . . . in a quasi-logarithmic representation . . .

". . . intensity of subjective color perception appears related to the apparent temporal velocity . . ."

—while others seemed so much gibberish . . .

". . . autonomous unwilled determinism . . . as a manifestation of free will . . .

". . . difficult if not impossible to ascertain the validity of the ancestral suicide theorem . . .

". . . mass-cubed energy progressions inapplicable . . . or apparently so . . ."

"Are you ready?" The thin-faced blond man was standing by the half-open door I'd never bothered to close. "The doctor would be impressed . . ."

"Nothing else to do, and I might as well learn what I'm supposed to learn. It might even come in useful."

He frowned, but I really didn't care. "This way, then." His voice wasn't quite as cheerful.

"Who lives here—on this level?"

"Several technicians and three travelers, at the moment, I believe, and you, of course."

I looked down the long straight corridor. On one side ran a line of windows, beginning at waist height and extending nearly to the inside roofline. On the other side were nearly a score of the heavy black oak doors.

Deric followed my eyes. "Only about half are occupied, now. A number of those associated with the project . . . left . . . with the disruptions."

I nodded, not wanting to say more.

"Doctor Relorn anticipates we will be adding several more from your contingent."

I shrugged. I didn't know all the ConFeds personally, especially some of the senior forcers or the newer recruits.

Deric wiped a stray wisp of his thin blond hair back off his high forehead and began to walk down the corridor in uneven long strides.

"The Security Forces are billeted on the level below, while the senior project members are either in the few quarters in the main laboratory or in the family quarters."

Deric only gestured at the first level corridor as we left the building. "Security quarters. On the first level on the other wing are the messing facilities."

"And the second level?"

"Empty quarters, for now."

His tone was so matter-of-fact that I didn't bother probing. I used my undertime sight to study Deric while we crossed the old stone-paved road to the main laboratory. Trying to walk and look undertime, I stumbled and almost crashed into the side of the graystone archway leading up the wide front steps of the laboratory.

Deric cast a few sparks into the undertime. Not many, but enough that he could probably travel short distances.

"Are you all right?"

I nodded. "Just looking and not watching where I was going."

"... *aaaccuuughhh* ..." My guide cleared his throat. "We'll take the right-hand corridor. The first few offices are for administration, although we have little of that now. Beyond the double doors is our mathematical section ..."

"Mathematical section?"

Deric raised his eyebrows again, this time further. "Someone has to calculate at least general directional vectors."

"Oh ..." I'd never needed vectors, but since I hadn't tried stellar travel, perhaps I just hadn't gone far enough to need them.

"Now that the main power net is gone, and we no longer have access to the mainframe at the university, we've had to simplify things somewhat."

I really didn't comprehend the complexity of the calculations he was describing. Still, I got the message. Mental travel or time-diving—whatever you called it—was a lot more complicated than I had realized. Either that, or I was more talented than the others. Or both.

We passed two open doors. The first held a young man sitting behind a desk, apparently waiting for something to happen or someone to enter. The second held an empty desk and chair, and several antique filing cabinets.

Next, we passed a closed door, with a wooden plate in the middle of the upper panel which proclaimed in gilded letters, "Mathematical Section."

Farther down the corridor, Deric opened an unmarked door and stepped inside. The room was larger than the plain black oak door would have indicated, long and narrow, with nearly a score of black and white consoles lined up against each wall. Several blocked doorways, and two lighter colored sections of wall paneling—each about a handspan wide—testified as to where interior walls had been removed.

Two men and three women were scattered along the rows, their backs to the aisle in the middle of the room. I wondered at the placement, since, for engineering hookup, it would have been easier to have placed the consoles back-to-back down the center. That arrangement would have allowed more privacy as well.

"Your console is number fourteen, over there."

I followed his gesture and walked as quietly as I could past a small dark-haired woman, who did not even glance up as I passed behind her.

Sure enough, on the console with the number fourteen was a brand-new nameplate—"Sammis."

A notebook, similar to the others I had already received, lay on the flat surface beside the screen, while several datacubes were racked next to the input slot.

I nodded. Dr. Relorn definitely did not waste time. I wondered how she would do in a showdown with the colonel-general.

"We'll come back later," Deric added, moving up beside me.

I sniffed back an itch in my nose, refraining from scratching it. The room smelled both of dust and of long use.

The tall, thin man shambled back out through the same doorway, then down past the two doorways blocked on the inside by consoles. He turned right down another corridor, which narrowed into a covered walkway leading to the west wing of the laboratory building.

"Here's the main travel laboratory."

As Deric opened the door, I recognized the big enclosed space again, and mentally located the doctor's quarters—down the corridor we had not taken.

"I've been here. That's where I was tested."

"Have you actually done any mental travel?" Deric's tone was bland.

"From what you indicate is possible, nothing at all."

"Well, learning it should be an interesting experience for you, then."

I stared around the empty laboratory from the half-open doorway, wondering where the good doctor was. "You don't operate this late?"

"We're working back up to a full schedule, but our operations were curtailed by the lack of power."

"I'm not sure I understand." How did the lack of electrical power have anything to do with time-diving?

"Without power, we couldn't run the gammas, or the necessary time-vectors for the travelers . . ."

It sounded like all their divers were as blind as the good doctor. That or they couldn't recognize what they saw. Trying to use charts in the undertime sounded difficult. Or were they trying to memorize them before diving? I shivered at the thought of all that memorization.

"What next?"

"Down below are the electronics shop and the equipment rooms . . ."

"Good. I'd like to see them." I said that because Deric clearly didn't want to show them to me.

With a shrug, he turned and waited for me to back away from the door before closing it.

As I looked down the hallway, I could see that the late afternoon shadows were fading under the clouds that gathered from the north.

"This way." Deric turned to head back the way we had come.

"What's down that way?" I pointed to the direction we had not gone.

"Just some guest quarters for visiting dignitaries." His steps were hurried as he led me through another hallway door into a staircase leading down. At the bottom, a second doorway opened onto a hall identical to the one above, except that it had no windows, not surprisingly, since it had to be below ground level.

We walked silently to the left, away from the side of the building holding the "visiting dignitaries' " quarters. After another ten steps or so, Deric halted. On the door of the equipment room was a square metal panel with numbered buttons. Deric punched several in quick succession.

Looking through the undertime, I caught the numbers—six, thirteen, twenty-seven—noted the pattern, and then nearly laughed. So long as the room was big enough to stand in, I could enter it whether it happened to be locked or not.

The doorway's modest size gave no clue to the size of the space— which sloped downward and into dim shadows beyond the range of an unaided eye. The doorway was nothing more than an interior building entrance to an equipment bunker that probably included the space under the parklike square across the stone-paved street from the laboratory.

I caught a glimpse of the pressure suits, interspersed with racks and racks of equipment I failed to recognize. In the gloom beyond the equipment racks, one object's general shape caught my attention, as much for its massiveness as for its purpose. A laser-cannon, or as near to it as possible. Supposedly, only a handful had ever been built because of the immense power demands. Now, it had to be useless without the broadcast power satellites.

Deric just stood there, not exactly barring my entry, but clearly indicating that I was not going to be allowed to wander through the entire equipment bunker.

So I just gazed around, and nodded. "Very impressive. Very impressive." Then I stepped back. "Anything else down here I should know about?"

"No. Not really. Down the other corridor are the disciplinary cells that were used before the Westron Monarchy. They were never removed when the structure was converted."

"Back for dinner, then?"

"I'll show you the dining area on the way back to your quarters. You'll have a little time to wash up. Evening meal is around 1800 for us."

"Fine." The ConFeds ate earlier, and my stomach was growling already.

The way back to my quarters was almost the same as the way we had come.

"You can take the walkway across, and those stairs . . ."

"If I take them now, and cross there . . . that will lead back to my room?"

"Exactly."

"And the facilities—showers?"

"Oh . . . I forgot. Just at the end of the hallway from your room."

"Do I just walk into dinner?"

"Yes. I'm afraid we don't have much ceremony. Your name has been posted, and the cook will expect you." Deric straightened, cleared his throat. "I do have one or two things to do . . ."

"I understand, and I can find my way back without any problem. Thank you very much."

"It was my pleasure."

He didn't sound convinced, and I'd just have to find out why.

XXVI

THE DINING SECTION of the quarters building appeared more like a restaurant than a military establishment—light wooden shutters on the inside of the windows and cloths on the dozen or so tables.

When I stepped through the double doors, I could see only five people—Deric and four others, three women and one man—all standing by a circular table.

"Sammis." Deric called.

"Deric." Nodding my head, I stepped toward the five. Except for Deric, I had met none of them. As I crossed the ten steps that separated us, the aroma of peffin filled my nostrils.

"Sammis, I'd like you to meet several of your fellow-travelers." Deric nodded toward a muscular red-headed woman. "This is Mellorie."

Mellorie's smile was instantaneous, and genuine, especially compared to Deric's. "It's nice to meet you, Sammis."

"It's nice to be here."

"This is Arlean, who runs the math and information section . . . and Gerloc, who found Sertis . . . and Amenda, who was our last brand-new traveler until the doctor found you."

Arlean looked like a librarian, with a narrow face and sharp eyes that missed nothing. Her smile was pleasant and showed even white teeth.

"Pleased . . ." Gerloc was about the same height as me, but rail thin, almost frail. His voice was deep, and contrasted with his sparse and wispy blond hair.

Amenda, slender and dark-haired, and half a head taller than me, nodded politely, but said nothing.

"The uniform . . . ?" asked Arlean, the mathematical librarian.

"Recruited straight from the ConFeds, Lady, with nothing to my name but uniforms."

"Looks like he's in shape, Arlean." Gerloc's tone was not quite mocking. "Arlean's always complaining that none of the male divers have enough muscle to carry all the monitoring equipment necessary."

I tried not to frown.

"Arlean is the one who coordinates the out-system data. Her library science background comes in handy," explained Deric.

Again, I had trouble understanding the continued obsession with data. Some of it made sense—like a general catalogue of the habitable or visitable plants and whether the air was breathable and the level of gravity. But collecting mountains of data when our entire civilization was falling in shards around us . . . ? When an unseen Enemy had leveled most of the cities? When every freeman's hand was set against education and knowledge and the gentry whom they held responsible for the disaster?

"You look rather doubtful . . . is it . . . Sammis?" Mellorie's voice was low, husky, and warm, far more sultry in a friendly way than I would have expected.

"I suspect I am."

"You're no farm boy ConFed, either."

"Mellorie, please introduce yourself to Sammis slowly," Deric suggested, with an edge to his tone. The edge bordered on a whine.

"I'm sorry, Deric." She curtsied to him and returned her glance to me. "Would you care to join us—Gerloc and Amenda and me—for dinner tonight?"

"I'd be honored."

"Enjoy your dinner, Sammis," added Deric. "I trust you will not mind if I occasionally introduce you to someone else."

"Not at all, Deric. Thank you again for the tour."

"Tour? Deric actually took the time to show you around?" Amenda's voice was low, though not as husky or low as Mellorie's.

"It was brief," I explained. "Just these two buildings, really."

"Still . . . ?"

"We should pick a table and sit down, even if we are to be saddled with peffin after all." Gerloc's tone was resigned.

Peffin stew or casserole sounded wonderful after ConFed slop. "Is it that bad?"

"No," answered Mellorie with a low laugh. "But Greffin serves it so often. But we've been eating it once every five days for more than a year."

That was a bit frequent for something as spicy as peffin stew. On the other hand, it was my first meal prepared with any care in nearly a year—or more.

Amenda pulled out one of the chairs at a circular table set for four.

I offered the chair across from her to Mellorie.

"Like I said, no ConFed farm boy."

I ignored the implication and sat on her left, facing the main doors, with Amenda on my left.

Gerloc took the last chair and sat, brushing his wispy blond hair off his high forehead after he edged his chair into place. "You're not obligated to tell us anything, Sammis, but we are curious . . ."

I took a sip of the water in the glass before me. "There's really not much to say. Born and raised in Bremarlyn, went to the Academy, escaped from the ConFeds who fired my family's house, escaped from the looters, and ended up being impressed by another group of ConFeds. When Dr. Relorn decided to test for . . . mental travel talent . . . I showed up as having it."

Mellorie nodded. "I thought so."

"Thought what, Mellorie?" asked Amenda.

"What I thought . . . that Sammis came from a good family and a solid background. Besides, he looks like a traveler."

"Old-style . . ." added Gerloc in a softer voice.

"I have been called witch-spawn, or worse." I had the feeling Mellorie had more to say, but had held her tongue.

Amenda shivered, as if the term were all too familiar.

Mellorie nodded.

Over her shoulder, I saw another threesome enter the dining area, none of whom I recognized, since neither of the two women happened to be Dr. Relorn.

"How would I put this . . . ?" Gerloc's voice was softer, pitched not to carry beyond the table. "Your . . . shall we say . . . experience level . . . ?"

"I don't know. No basis for comparison." Gerloc might be friendly, but I was reluctant to blurt out anything. "I can travel from point to point on Query. Too much travel burns a lot of energy, though."

Gerloc opened his mouth.

"I certainly have no experience in travelling to the stars or other planets. You discovered someplace called Sertis? Could you tell me about it?"

Gerloc closed his mouth, then took a sip of water.

Mellorie chuckled. "Guess what, Gerloc? He listens."

With a sheepish grin, Gerloc looked at Mellorie, then back at me. "I gather I don't have much choice."

"You're right. You don't," said Amenda pleasantly.

"I'll skip the details of how I stumbled onto Sertis, because they're in the notebooks you'll be reading. I'm pretty limited in terms of how far back or forward I can travel—seems to be in the neighborhood of fifteen hundred to two thousand years back and about half that forward. The forward side is always shady. That's because of the uncertainty factors, I gather . . ."

"You might try getting to the point . . ." Mellorie's voice was friendly.

"I will. I am simply not as direct as you are, Mellorie." Gerloc took another swallow and cleared his throat. "The point to which dear Mellorie refers is that Sertis doesn't change. The buildings are occasionally modified, but the population and technology are always the same, at least as far as any of us have been able to tell."

I frowned. "Does that mean we're different? Or they are?"

"They are." That was Mellorie. "We've found half a dozen other cultures out there, and they change. Dramatically, sometimes within local decades."

I was still frowning. So what difference did it make whether one culture on another planet in another solar system was stable?

"You look even more displeased, Sammis." Amenda's voice was softer, less persistent than Mellorie, yet removed.

"I'm new here." I swallowed, then spit out what I shouldn't have said. "Everything I hear still sounds like a research project. All very interesting, but so what? We've been destroyed by an unseen enemy, and our entire civilization is crashing around us, and we're gathering data?"

Now Amenda and Gerloc were the ones frowning.

I found myself wiping my forehead with the cloth napkin, a true social blunder, but sweat was oozing from my forehead, despite the room's coolness.

"Salads here." With that a waitress set a bowl before each of us.

"Thank you." My response was automatic.

The silence around the table lengthened as the waitress departed with a nod to me. No one else said anything. So I took a bite of the salad. Even with bitter reddish leaves interspersed with some mushrooms and wild onions, it was refreshing.

"What would you do, then?" Mellorie asked.

"I'm scarcely in charge," I mumbled with a mouth half-full of leaves and crunchy mushrooms that tasted of nut-bark.

"That's begging the question. You raised it."

Gerloc and Amenda looked from Mellorie to me, and back, as if they were watching a contest.

"Something useful."

Mellorie looked ready to snap back, when she smiled over my shoulder.

"May I interrupt?" Deric's question was only half-whine.

"Of course," Mellorie's voice dripped syrup.

I turned, caught a glimpse of a woman and found myself standing and bowing. The old traditions don't die.

"Sammis, I believe you know Dr. Relorn. I just wanted to reassure her that you had in fact arrived and were enjoying our hospitality."

"Everyone has been most hospitable, Deric. Most hospitable." I inclined my head toward my tablemates.

The doctor nodded politely under the makeup designed to make her look like an older woman trying to look young. "I'm glad to see you have been so well received, Sammis. Although I have interrupted an animated conversation, I do not intend to take much of your time."

"It's good to see you, Doctor, outside the testing laboratory, and I appreciate your efforts. Very much." I bowed slightly, again.

"He's quite the gentry, Doctor, isn't he?" observed Deric.

"I believe he is, Deric. But he also survived the ConFeds." She turned back to face me. "I hope you will enjoy working with us."

"I'm certain I will, Doctor, especially under your direction." I could have bitten my tongue for the last, particularly with Mellorie hanging on every word, but old habits die hard.

"Enjoy your dinner." With that, she and Deric turned and headed toward a table set for two.

I sat down.

"Can you doubt he's gentry born after that?" Amenda said to Gerloc.

"It was quite a performance, Sammis." The corners of Mellorie's mouth were twisted in a wry gesture.

I took the last mouthful of salad.

"Do you wish to honor us with your suggestions for what the laboratory should do amidst our crumbling culture?"

I set down my glass. "Pure knowledge isn't much help when you're facing someone armed with a riot gun or a crossbow. Within seasons, unless things change, we'll be out of both ammunition, arms, and food, with no way to resupply ourselves."

"So what do you want us to do?"

"I've been here one day, and I'm supposed to supply an answer?"

"That's good enough for now, I think." Mellorie's voice had turned much softer. "You're right. We see it too, but we don't have an answer either."

Amenda was suddenly looking at her nearly untouched salad.

Gerloc shrugged.

"You see, Sammis," continued Mellorie, "we don't have many action-oriented travelers left. Most of them left when the riots started."

I understood. All too well. Those who had remained were the cautious ones, the scared ones, or those with no place to go. I understood all right. I was just like them. "I understand."

"As a ConFed?" Amenda's tone was gentle.

"There are ConFeds, and there are ConFeds," noted Mellorie in a voice so low as to be little more than a whisper.

I ignored her observation. I didn't want to distinguish between Odin Thor's ConFeds and the ones that fired my home. "I understand—even as a ConFed. I didn't have much choice, you know. No family, no friends, and every time I opened my mouth I was tagged as gentry."

"You survived, though. That means you're not exactly as helpless—"

"Here is the famous peffin casserole," announced the waitress.

I still couldn't believe that the Far Travel Laboratory had cooks and serving personnel. The waitress wasn't young, probably in her early fifth decade, but she carried the casserole dish with authority and placed it in the center of the table, laying two serving utensils beside it.

"I'll serve," announced Amenda. "Sammis?"

I handed over my platter, glad to have escaped, even momentarily, the questions that Mellorie kept throwing at me.

"Gerloc?"

Thuddd . . .

"LAZY BOORNIKS. MISERABLE GENLOVERS! MOTHER-SWILLS!"

The shouts would have roused the damps, let alone the modest dining area. I found myself turning and on my feet, recognizing the voice.

Rarden was standing alone inside the doors bellowing. Looking through the undertime, I could see two other figures outside, but not who they were.

Because everyone seemed in shock, I was there even before the Seco who shadowed the doctor.

"Oh, it's the brave little swamp rat, is it? Ready to defend the gen-lovers . . . but you're one, too, aren't you?"

I just looked up at him.

"So now they've bought themselves a real ConFed . . . cause the Secos aren't enough."

I ignored the Seco coming up behind me and took another step toward Rarden, stopping just short of easy reach.

"Rarden. Get the hell away from here." I didn't even raise my voice.

"Threaten me, swamp rat . . . go ahead, threaten me."

"I don't make threats."

For some reason, he turned pale.

"You . . . always you . . ." He stumbled backwards and out the door.

I waited until he staggered back, and Selioman steered him down the corridor toward the outside entrance. Then I closed both double doors.

The Seco stood there holding the useless riot gun.

"Put that away. It won't scare any of the ConFeds, just make them kill you quicker." I walked around him.

Both Deric and the doctor were looking in my direction. I ignored them.

"No, he's not exactly helpless," muttered Mellorie. She flushed as she realized I had heard her comment to Gerloc and Amenda.

"I never said I was. I said I understood." I was tired of trying to justify anything. So I didn't. I just enjoyed the peffin casserole.

Neither of the other three said anything, either to each other, or to me, until the ubiquitous waitress collected the serving dish and our platters.

"Greffin is good with desserts," volunteered Amenda.

Since I hadn't had a dessert since before I had left the Academy, the idea sounded intriguing. "Such as?"

"Tonight is berrycream tort."

I hadn't cared much for desserts even when they had been available, and two bites were enough. I finished the tort on general principles. Desserts did contain an ample supply of calories.

Except for Mellorie's comment, everyone ignored my actions in running Rarden off, as if they were in bad taste. Yet Rarden would have destroyed the entire dining room to get attention. In terms of my father's background, though, my actions probably were in bad taste. My mother might have approved.

After dessert, Gerloc and Amenda rose together.

"Good night, Sammis, Mellorie."

I half rose. "Good night."

Mellorie nodded.

I reseated myself.

"You made quite an impression, Sammis."

"An unfortunate impression."

"You're a rare one," she mused, almost as if I were not there. "Your understanding is greater than your knowledge. You're not afraid to act."

"That's not quite true, Mellorie."

She just smiled.

She wasn't listening, exactly, and I was tired of explaining.

"Would you care to walk me back to my quarters?" She extended her hand as she rose from the straight-backed dining chair.

"I'd be honored, dear lady."

So I walked her to her doorway, which was less than half a corridor from mine. That was all I did.

XXVII

AFTER PULLING OFF my boots, I stretched out on the bed, leaving the window open and listening to the breeze. I intended to enjoy the rustle of black oak leaves and the touch of crispness to the evening that would disappear over the days ahead.

The mattress was firm, but not rock-hard like a ConFed pallet. The pillows emphasized the non-military nature of the Far Travel Lab.

For all the apparent friendliness of the dinner, and for all of the interest of Mellorie, including her almost-invitation into her quarters, things were just not what they seemed. None of them, except perhaps the doctor, appeared to understand that we had been attacked by an enemy we couldn't even find, and that Query was collapsing around them. They just seemed to be going through the motions.

Mellorie seemed to be the only one actually thinking, and I wondered how much that was from contrariness. Her on and off invitations left me confused.

Then there was the doctor, clearly made up to be as old as she claimed, rather than as old as she looked. I knew how old she could be, but I didn't believe it. The woman had to be decades older than me, for all that she looked like a young woman, for all that she wore severe and dowdy clothes to project an image older than she was. The silver streaks in her hair were probably dyed, since they didn't go all the way to the roots.

Outside, the twilight slowly faded into gloom, leaving my room, with its single wide window, even darker.

Chhhiritt, chhirritt . . . The sound of some night bird drifted through the open window.

Why had Dr. Wryan Relorn even listened to me on that night I had invaded her laboratory, let alone gone out of her way to have me transferred out of the ConFeds? If Deric were any example, her own senior staffers weren't exactly thrilled about my presence.

Nothing quite added up. The laboratory had been and still was gathering essentially useless data while it could have been performing a function vital to the Westron Monarchy. Except there wasn't a monarchy. There wasn't even a capital city. The nominal second-in-command verged on incompetent. Unless the doctor were keeping it to herself, no one had thought about redirecting the role of the divers to fit the current situation.

I shook my head, then stared into the darkness. Not that darkness was a barrier to someone who could look through the undertime. That raised another question—why couldn't the other divers see? Even Dr. Relorn seemed only to be able to see *from* the undertime, not through it.

Shrugging again, I sat up on the edge of the bed and pulled my boots back on. Waiting wouldn't provide me with any more answers.

As I slipped under the now for the short dive across to the other building, I wondered if anyone could track me in the same way I had found the doctor.

She was alone, sitting in one of the comfortable armchairs, leafing through a thick notebook.

"Greetings."

"Greeting, Sammis."

"You were expecting me."

"I thought you might show up . . . although I wasn't certain exactly when." She had removed the heavy makeup and looked years, if not decades younger. "You have some questions? Good. So do I."

I took the other chair without waiting for it to be offered. "Why don't your travelers do anything?"

She smiled faintly. "What would you have them do?"

"Everything is crumbling around us . . . couldn't they bring back some technology . . . something . . . ?"

"Such as?"

I felt like I were back in school. "What have I missed?"

She grinned. "Very bright . . ." After shifting her weight and crossing one trousered leg over another, she added, "You know none of my travelers can carry very much. That means we can't bring back metals—which we need—not in any meaningful quantity. We can't bring back equipment that we cannot understand, or that requires different power inputs. When you think about it, that doesn't leave much."

"What about knowledge?"

"How can you translate it into usable equipment?"

This time the silence stretched out as I thought and she silently waited. "I'm not educated, Doctor . . ."

"Just call me Wryan. You're far more educated than most people left around here, including the ones with degrees and honors."

Both her comments left me open-mouthed, at least momentarily. "I have to disagree, Doc—"

"Wryan." Her tone was no-nonsense.

"Are you called Wryan by the other divers?"

"No."

I shook my head, knowing from her tone that she wasn't about to explain. As she set down the notebook and leaned forward to place it on the low table, I watched, somehow taking in the grace of her movements.

Finally, I spoke again. "It still seems to me that we could benefit from what other cultures have to offer."

"We could—if we could find it, understand it, and copy it."

"Finding it . . ." I shut my mouth. What an idiot I had been! No wonder they had problems. None of them had learned how to see into real time from the undertime, and searching a culture by having to break out every time you went someplace would prove too exhausting for much productive effort. "I see . . ." But there was one item . . . and I saw that, too. "Weapons . . . is that why the colonel-general . . . ?

She nodded.

I realized there was something else I had not told her. "He's also a diver."

"The colonel-general? How do you know?"

I took a deep breath, wondering whether I could trust this doctor I scarcely knew, deciding I could, and thinking I was a fool for it. "The energies play around him the way they do around all the divers."

"In the undertime?"

"Yes."

"That was how you found me?"

It was my turn to nod.

"Who else knows?"

"About the colonel-general? No one I know of. I'm not sure he knows."

"That would make sense." She frowned, and I could see the darkness behind her eyes that was the only indication of her age. Otherwise, seated less than two paces from me, she could have been nearly a contemporary. "Does anyone else know how you found out."

"No. Probably shouldn't have told you . . ."

She smiled, and I couldn't help but feel better. The smile wasn't the professional one she had presented at dinner, but more impish . . . more personal.

I found myself smiling back.

"Would you like some cider? Hot?"

Hot cider? That last one who had offered me hot cider had been Allyson . . . had it been years ago?

"Are you all right?"

Her concern just made it worse, and at first I could barely keep from shaking. Then I couldn't, and I couldn't see, either. I could feel her hands on my shoulders, but she didn't say anything, and neither did I.

After a while, she handed me a small soft towel, and I wiped my face.

"I'm sorry . . ." She was kneeling next to my chair with one hand covering mine.

I just shook my head again, not really wanting to speak.

How long she stayed by me I didn't know, but when I looked at the small antique clock on the wall, the hands registered past midnight.

"Sorry . . ."

"Don't be . . . I'm glad I was here."

I just nodded.

"I meant it, Sammis."

"Talk to me . . . about you . . ."

"All right . . ." She shifted her position on the floor, and I let go of her hand. "Do you mind if I move? I think my legs are mostly asleep . . ."

"Oh . . . I didn't—"

"Don't worry about it." She reseated herself in the other chair and rubbed her calves with one hand. "There's not that much to say . . ."

But she did talk, about growing up as an orphan in the cold of Southpoint, having to sneak off when she realized she was not changing in looks, except to look more and more like her mother, the lady lost at sea and termed the "witch-captain." In posing as a wanton gentry daughter, she managed to accrue a degree or two from some of the lesser southern Westron universities, which she had used to get into the civil science bureaucracy . . .

". . . but it's getting late, and you're exhausted . . ."

I jerked upright, realizing I had not heard what she had been saying. "Not that tired . . ."

"You snored through my last three sentences." Her tone was gentle.

"You could be a princess, Lady."

"Wryan," she corrected.

"You could be a princess, Wryan. Even when you chastise, you make people feel good."

"A princess? All little girls want to be princesses." She paused. "Some of them get to be. Some decide it isn't worth the bother, but most of them never give up. There just aren't enough princes, and most of them are bastards."

That didn't make any sense at all. Finally, I asked, "What . . . I mean . . . princes?"

"You're tired, and we'll talk about it later. Was she nice?" Wryan stood up.

"Nice?" I had to think.

"The girl you remembered when I asked about the hot cider."

"Oh . . . it wasn't like that. She was very nice, and I never saw her again. I don't think she and her parents made it. No one else from Bremarlyn did, so far as I know."

She was next to me, and the faintest hint of trilia touched me. "Good night, Sammis."

"Good night." I still couldn't call her Wryan. "Good night."

Somehow, I made it under the now and back to my room. I got my boots off, but that was all, before collapsing onto the bed.

XXVIII

A WISP OF condensing water vapor floated from the steamer like a momentary banner in the cool of the early morning. The subforcer seated next to the technician at the controls checked the map, noting the steamer's position. While the topography and the road remained, most of the towns were no longer even recognizable.

"Should make Bremarlyn before long." observed the officer.

"Yes, sir. Nice day."

"Really wish we could get power at Herfidian, the way they do at the base camp on the plateau . . ."

The driver ignored the officer's comments and concentrated on the controls to guide the top-heavy steamer along the old stone-paved highway where it curved through a low point between two hillocks.

Crump!
"Verlyt!"
Crump!
"Power. Full power to the drive wheels! Down below—skirmish squad out! Skirmish squad out!"
"Sir? They're firing from in front of us!"
"Full power!"
Clang!
"Skirmish squad is clear, sir."
"Hunt down those bastards, Froman!"
"Yes, sir. Good luck."
Crump! Thud!
The steamer lurched.
"Full power!"
Crump!Crump!

XXIX

". . . IN THEORY, INTENSE gravitational relativistic pressures exerted by collapsed stellar masses should narrow the perception of 'black' pathways . . ."

I yawned. Just as I thought I might read three straight paragraphs of interest, the material lapsed into speculations. I had enough personal speculations not to have to worry about theoretical abstractions on the reconciliation of space-time theory with time-diving observations. And the personal speculations kept nagging at me, unlike the dry words on the screen.

Why did the doctor want me to call her Wryan? Why had a few kind words, well meant, dissolved me? Why did she seem to trust me? Or why, for Verlyt's sake, was I trusting her?

Without answers, I stifled another yawn and pushed onward through the theoretical material on time-diving, trying to ignore the questions at the back of my mind.

". . . even in the absence of empirical or validated experimental data, several facts are clear. . . ."

Clear as swamp water, I reflected, stretching and taking a quick look around the console room. Only Amenda and two other women I had not met were in the long room. None of them glanced up from their consoles.

My nose twitched from the faint odor of ozone. I rubbed it and shrugged my shoulders to release the tightness. Then I looked back at the screen.

". . . that the so-called time-paths are tied to the intensity of gravitational forces, or more precisely, to the proximity and concentration of mass and energy . . ."

I took a deep breath and forced myself to keep going through the text.

"Sammis?"

I looked up to see a tall figure standing just inside the doorway. Since Deric had caught me studying the material on my console, boring stuff if ever there was, I was more receptive to the interruption than I might have been. I waited. I didn't bother standing.

He ambled over. "Dr. Relorn would appreciate it if you would meet her in the main travel laboratory."

"Just a moment." I flipped to the front of the notebook to find the log-off code and used it. "Is that the big laboratory around the corner and across . . . ?"

"Right . . . but I'll go with you to make sure."

I didn't shrug, but felt like it. "All right." After stacking the notebooks on the shelf, I stood up. "Lead on."

Deric said nothing until we were in the corridor, where he took a half dozen steps, then stopped. "You were rather . . . effective . . . the other night at dinner . . . With your size . . . I mean . . . one wouldn't normally assume . . ."

"Rarden's always been after me. I felt it was my problem to solve."

"Do the others . . . ConFeds . . . feel the same way about you?"

"Deric, I wouldn't have the faintest idea. No one bothers me."

"Oh."

"How do your Secos feel? Like the one who reacted too late?"

"Karsnish?" Deric looked at the floor, then toward the end of the corridor.

I waited.

"Karsnish . . . understands why we need the ConFeds on our side . . . now . . ."

With a shake of my head, I turned and started toward the laboratory. Deric caught up quickly, but only to match steps with me.

He stopped outside the doorway. "Your colonel-general is there also."

The colonel-general? Why? Another setup? Had my trust in Dr. Wryan Relorn been misplaced after all?

I stepped inside, leaving Deric, who showed no intention of following me, outside.

She was standing by the same master console where I had first found her. She wore pale ice-green trousers and a matching short-sleeved tunic. Her eyes seemed to sparkle, though her mouth was stern, and she still wore the old lady makeup.

The head ConFed wore his usual off-purple fatigues, sharply creased, and his eyes followed me all the way from the doorway.

"The colonel-general has a request, Sammis." Her voice was neutral. I bowed slightly to them both, denying Odin-Thor the salute he would have liked.

"Trooper Sammis . . . you're still a trooper . . . on detail."

"Yes, Colonel-General . . . you wanted something . . ."

Odin-Thor cleared his throat, and his eyes centered on me.

I met his glare.

He cleared his throat again. Then, he blinked. His jaw tightened, and he pursed his lips. "Yes. You were from Bremarlyn. We have lost two supply steamers in the area. Both without any trace. I was hoping that someone from the Travel Laboratory would be able to find some sign of what happened."

He nodded at the doctor. "Dr. Relorn has informed me that none of her other travelers has the capability of . . . travelling . . . here on Query. With your background and training, I was hoping that you might be able to find out what happened."

I didn't like it at all. I glanced from the colonel-general to the doctor. Not only was she wearing the heavy makeup again, but there were dark circles under her eyes, almost too dark to be real. Her lips stayed tight after her statement.

"That might not be as simple as it sounds, Colonel-General. It takes a great deal of energy to use mental travel here on Query. I *might* be able to find out something if I knew what I was looking for and where it was supposed to be. There's no way that I can search the entire Bremarlyn area. I can get to specific points instantly, but it takes as much energy as though I'd spent half a day on a steamer getting there."

The ConFed leader nodded. "So you could check several points quickly, but not sweep an area?"

"I can sometimes tell if there's anyone nearby, but not always."

"Here's what happened. A regular convoy steamer from Herfidian to here disappeared. We sent a light armed steamer with a skirmish squad. It vanished as well. They both went by the highway—the Eastern Highway from Inequital toward Herfidian." The colonel-general glanced at Dr. Relorn, then back to me. "If you could even discover what happened—a wreck or attack, or if there's a large group of bandits . . . that would be most helpful."

"I'll do what I can, assuming that meets with your approval and the doctor's approval."

His frown was momentary as he turned toward her. "If you could—"

"If Sammis can help you, it would benefit all of us." The clarity and professionalism with which she spoke reminded me again that, despite her youthful looks under the makeup, Dr. Relorn probably had more experience than the colonel-general might ever have.

"Thank you, Doctor." He bowed.

"Not at all. You and your men have already done so much. We would only be repaying a portion of that debt." Her tone remained matter-of-fact.

He nodded again, and I tried to keep from shaking my head.

"Here is the general area where we think both groups disappeared." He extended a map, basically a reproduction of an Imperial road map, and pointed to an area highlighted in yellow, slightly east of Bremarlyn.

After studying the general topography, I straightened. "May I keep this for a while, sir?"

"Of course . . . ah . . . how long . . . ?"

"I'll try now. Trying isn't the problem, you understand. I just can't make many trips."

"Oh . . . I see . . ."

He didn't, and I looked at Dr. Relorn. "While I'm searching, Doctor, perhaps you could explain the energy deficits associated with diving. And . . ."

"I'll have something waiting for you, Sammis."

I thought I heard a trace more than professionalism there, but I wasn't sure.

XXX

SO I HAD lied to the great colonel-general? Was that so great a moral fault?

Dropping under the now, sliding away toward Bremarlyn and the apparently missing ConFeds, I still worried whether Odin Thor would find out about my ability to look at events from the undertime, whether Dr. Wryan Relorn would tell him what she knew, and how long it would take for Odin Thor to find out that I could do more than I said I could. Or would he find out at all?

I pushed the doubts and questions away, focusing instead on the hazy black path that carried me closer to Bremarlyn. Although I tried to follow the road, it didn't really work that way. What sliding under the now or diving through time really follows is the patterns of mass and energy concentrations, and you skip from concentration to concentration—in a way. It was hard to parallel a real road from the undertime, and after a few attempts I didn't even try.

Then I tried to locate a steamer backtiming. Backtime was what the red direction represented. But a steamer doesn't have that much energy, and I tried to latch onto the point source that I thought was a laser rifle.

Except that it disappeared. But energy just doesn't disappear. It dissipates when the rifle is fired. That was how I located one attack where I could see ConFeds firing shells from a short-tubed cannon that lofted shells over a hill and down around the steamer. Finally a shell blew the boilers and steam-cooked the subforcer and the driver.

Then the strange ConFeds just waited for the steam to clear, picked off the handful of survivors with projectile rifles, and appeared with a tug to cart off the wrecked steamer. All very dispassionately.

I could follow them, but nothing more. That squared with what I had read in the notebooks and with my own past experience. On Query, you can only enter and leave the undertime in your own subjective present. Period. No exceptions. Because the ambush took place in my past, I could only watch. And I could tell from my growing lightheadedness that the watching alone took some effort.

Before I was totally exhausted, I tracked the strange ConFeds back to a concealed tunnel less than five kays from the ruins of a house I knew well. While I was too exhausted to follow further, what I could see showed an elaborate underground installation, and an old one at that, with lots of metal and energy concentrations.

By then, black spots were interspersed with the light-headedness.

Still, breaking out in the laboratory was not particularly difficult. Standing up after I did was a real problem.

"Sammis . . . are you all right?" Dr. Relorn reached out to steady me.

With no strength and no ability to maintain my balance, I practically collapsed on her.

Her strength was far greater than I would have expected, and she eased me into one of the padded armchairs. The faint scent of trilia surrounded her, like a mist from my past.

While the colonel-general looked as though I had crawled from the sewer, his sour expression didn't stop his questions. "Did you find anything? What happened? Who did it?"

My head was pounding, and each question sounded like a thunderbolt.

"Just wait a moment, Colonel, and let him take a sip of this."

What she shoved under my nose was pungent, though not unpleasant. After just a sip or two, the headache began to subside.

"The whole steamer crew was ambushed . . . by a group of ConFeds . . . same kind of uniforms . . . tracked them to a hidden underground base near Bremarlyn . . ." Talking was a slight effort. So I stopped and took a full gulp from the narrow beaker that the doctor had handed me.

She was staring intently at me, but I couldn't understand the expression.

"So . . . they found it . . ." The colonel-general pulled at his chin. Then he looked at me. "Could you locate it on a map?"

"Why bother? I'll take you there . . . once I recover . . . in a day or so . . ."

If looks could have buried people, the doctor would have had me at the bottom of an ancient graveyard. But she said nothing.

I ignored her. Odin Thor, colonel-general or not, had to understand what he was playing with.

"What do you mean?"

"You're a latent diver, Colonel-General. So I'll take you there through the undertime, and you can mount your own assault from inside, if you want, while your troops hit the outside." I finished the beaker. "Do you have a map?"

He thrust it at me.

I ignored it, too. Instead, I closed my eyes and rested, almost in a trance.

"Trooper . . ."

"Colonel . . . don't push him—"

Even in my dazed state, I could recognize the steel in the doctor's words.

"—he did what you asked. You'll have answers as soon as he's able to give them. Mental travel is extremely fatiguing."

I was feeling better, but decided to keep my eyes closed.

"But he was only gone a few instants . . ."

"Wasn't Sammis one of your better trainees? Physically?"

"That's what they told me."

"That should tell you something about the physical effort required." I could hear the doctor's soft steps moving away.

"He only went a handful of kays. You say that you have mapped the stars." The colonel-general's voice was more like a rumble.

"If you will recall your earlier briefings, Colonel Odin Thor, it takes more energy to cross a room here on Query than to reach the nearest star."

"Then what good are your travelers?"

I wanted to open my eyes and enter the discussion, but even more to hear what the doctor might say. So I kept them closed a while longer and listened, listened to the soft footsteps and a gentle strong woman's voice.

"Could any dozen of your scouts found out what Sammis just did? Those are some of the immediate benefits. Over the longer term, once we find other civilizations, we should provide knowledge, better ways to generate or use energy—the possibilities are considerable."

"But for now, Doctor, I have to defend this base with rather limited resources. Not only against bandits, but against a renegade group of ConFeds."

"Odin Thor." Her voice was cold, and I almost sat up right then. "We know who the renegades are."

"Survival is a matter of strength, madam."

"We add to your strength."

"Just see that you do."

I yawned, groaned, and tried to imitate coming awake. It wasn't entirely an act.

Odin Thor still stood there like a tree that had scarcely moved, while the doctor was on the other side of the console. She began to rummage through a small locker and stacked something on a tray.

"Try these. They might help."

I rubbed the back of my neck where it ached, and the self-massage helped ease some of the remaining headache. Several bites of the crackers that tasted like the pungent liquid helped.

Odin had the map ready, waiting for the moment when I stopped stuffing my face, tapping his booted feet on the cracked insulating tiles of the laboratory floor. The fingers of his free left hand clenched and unclenched, clenched and unclenched, almost in rhythm to my chewing.

After a large pile of crackers, I began to feel better. "Could I see that map, Colonel-General?"

He glared. I stayed seated, since standing wouldn't have done me any good.

"Here."

"Here's a stylus, Sammis . . ."

The map had enough landmarks for me to be able to locate the stronghold of the real ConFeds. The fact that they were the real ones made it easier for me. A great deal easier.

"Be difficult to get them out . . ."

I shook my head. "Very easy. Very easy."

"I know the kind of installation they're in. Couldn't burn your way through with a battle laser . . ."

"They still have to breathe . . ."

The doctor turned whitish-green as she understood what I had in mind.

Odin Thor looked puzzled.

"Gas. Any kind of gas. Like the monarchy used on the Eastron installations that refused to surrender."

"But how . . . ?"

"Leave that to me, Colonel-General. My pleasure . . ."

XXXI

FROM SOMEWHERE IN the equipment bunkers, Janth came up with a case of gas grenades. I stared at the black mushroom-shapes. Each had a brilliant yellow danger warning, a set of crossed bones, painted on the top. The stemlike part was a handle.

"Ugly beasts, aren't they?" Janth frowned at the four on the armorer's table. On the floor remained a case. Two other grenades lay in the top layer of padding. "Should be another eighteen or so left there."

"They just left this lying in the old armory?"

"Verlyt, no. All the chemical stuff was in the sealed vault in the back. This was just the outer case. They had another airtight seal around this."

I leaned over to look at one of the black objects. A heavy metal ring protruded from one side of the mushroom's "cap." "What's this?" I pointed.

"Don't touch it. That's the arming ring. Once you pull that, the valve between the two gas fractions opens, and they combine."

"It just seeps out?"

"Not exactly, Trooper. Not exactly." Janth pursed his lips. "Been a long time . . . but . . . There's a lot of heat, which builds up as they combine. Eventually, you get an explosion. Combines the best of a frag grenade with the long-term kill power of the nerve gas."

"Eventually?" I managed to repress a shudder. "Nerve gas?"

"Paralyzes the nerves . . . you know, stops your brain. Stops your heartbeat. There's no cure."

"They used this . . . ?"

"Not since the Eastron revolt."

Since Eastron had been independent, as my mother had pointed out so often, the term "revolt" was inaccurate. "Can I pick one up? I need to know how heavy they are."

"Be careful, Trooper. That plastic should last forever, but that's got to be nearly a century old, and I really don't want it going off."

Neither did I. The grenade was heavier than the killer mushroom it resembled. Carrying more than three or four would be a problem. I put down the grenade and shook my head.

The slick paper of the instruction sheet was yellowed, and fine cracks ran from the central fold. The print of the instructions was crisp and black. So was the information. The Mark Delta contained enough nerve toxin to cover an area of fifty square rods in a no-wind condition. The toxin worked through contact, surface or inhalation, and one microjot (whatever that was) was sufficient to ensure lethality in ninety percent of the exposures.

There was also a bold-print warning.

DO NOT USE IN UNFAVORABLE WIND CONDITIONS!

The preferred method of delivery for the Mark Delta was with the projectile rifle modified launcher.

"Projectile rifle modified launcher?"

"None in the inventory. There haven't been for years."

I shrugged. The new preferred delivery method was the Sammis Mark One diver. "I'll be back when the time comes, Janth."

"That's what the colonel-general said, Trooper. Can't say I envy you."

Neither could I.

After walking around the corner, I slipped undertime and back to my room to think about the options again. I was glancing outside at the clouds over the southern peaks, having second thoughts about delivering death.

Tap, tap. Tap, tap.

"Yes?"

"Sammis?" The husky feminine voice was familiar.

"Come on in, Mellorie."

Wearing a clinging aqua coverall of some sort of soft material that indicated that she was very feminine, Mellorie eased open the unlatched door and stepped inside. She stopped. "When did you get back?"

"Just now."

"I didn't hear you in the corridor . . ." Her eyebrows were raised, and the corners of her eyes crinkled.

I tried not to grin. "I didn't come in that way."

"Oh . . ."

"I was down in the armory, getting a briefing on some antique weapons." I coughed to clear my throat.

Mellorie slipped into one of the chairs without waiting for the invitation I was reluctant to issue.

I sat on the foot of the bunk, not quite facing her. The wooden armchairs got uncomfortable after a while.

She crossed her ankles and sat up a little straighter. She pursed her lips before leaning forward.

As she did, I realized how deep the cut of her coveralls was, how much narrower her waist was than I had realized, and how shapely her breasts were.

I must have stared where I shouldn't have, because I could see her flush, the color rising from her neck into her lightly freckled and tanned face.

"Sorry . . ." I apologized.

"You are . . . rather direct . . ." Her voice was still throaty.

I looked away, shrugging. "Sorry. Dealing with women was a part of my education that I never reached." Outside the clouds had spread to cover the sun, and a breeze from the half-open sliding window ruffled my hair.

"You didn't have any sisters?"

"No sister. No brother." I continued to watch the clouds pile up over the mountains.

"What about your mother?"

"We didn't get around to talking much about women. I wasn't too interested . . . before the . . . disaster . . ."

"You liked your mother."

"Yes. I respected her, too." I still didn't want to think about her for too long.

"Any women friends?"

"In the ConFeds?"

"I meant before . . . and could you look this way? Please."

I shifted my weight and turned. Mellorie was sitting back a bit in the chair. The coverall still revealed too much for me to take easily.

"Thank you. I like looking at your face better." She crossed one leg over the other and twisted in the chair.

"They are uncomfortable."

She lifted her eyebrows.

"The chairs, I meant."

"Do you mind if I move?"

"Of course not. I said they were uncomfortable."

She uncrossed her legs and slipped to her feet, then sat down on the bed next to me. She brought with her the sweetness of ryall.

"Sammis . . . ?"

"Yes."

"If you wanted something, and you could have it now, but knew you couldn't keep it, would you take it now? Even if losing it would hurt?"

Mellorie's voice was low, and she wasn't looking at me.

I didn't look at her either, but I could feel myself stiffening, excited, and yet afraid I knew exactly what she meant.

"I suppose I would, if it were offered. I'm not up to just taking."

"I know. I could tell, but are you offering?"

"I . . . hadn't thought about it."

"Look at me . . ."

I did. Her brown eyes were clear, direct, her lips slightly parted.

Her hand touched mine, covered it, and tightened gently. The soft warmth of her touch sent a jolt up my arm.

I turned my hand in hers, returning the pressure.

"I'll take that for an offering."

I scarcely moved as her fingers touched my face, gently suggesting I turn toward her. I did, and found warm and soft lips on mine.

My hands were on her back and shoulders, and I realized she wore nothing under the clinging coverall.

"Gently . . . kiss me again."

Somehow . . . we ended up lying next to each other on the bed. The kisses lasted so long I was short of breath, and what breath I had was filled with the scent of ryall, and Mellorie.

Her hands slipped under my tunic, guiding it off me, and in time, I discovered that she had indeed been wearing nothing under the coverall.

I had been wearing plenty, but her hands were deft, and her warmth more than enough to balance the breeze from the afternoon thunderstorm that played over us.

Too soon was my release, and I felt cheated somehow.

"Just relax."

I couldn't. So I let my hands stroke her smooth skin, her soft hair, exploring the curves and lines I had always imagined, but never before felt.

She shivered. "I'm cold." She had some goose bumps on her back.

The blanket was soft enough, and warm enough, especially as close as we were. I began to kiss her neck, but I kept touching her skin.

The warmth began to return to her skin.

"Roll over," she directed.

So I did, and Mellorie began to massage my back, starting at the base of my neck and working down. She took a long time, and by the time she had reached more sensitive areas, neither one of us was interested in just touching.

The second time took longer, and I didn't feel cheated . . . at all.

I must have fallen asleep, because it was much later when the sound
of the thunder and the pelting rain woke me.

Mellorie was still curled next to me, but her eyes were open. One
hand rested on my shoulder.

"Did you sleep?" I asked.

"A little."

Crrasssh . . .

"Sammis . . ."

"Don't say anything," I told her. "Don't say anything."

In the craziness outside, in the storm, and inside, in me, there wasn't
any room for saying the obvious. Tomorrow was a long way off, and
while I hadn't known enough to love Allyson when we should have,
Mellorie had given me something I didn't want to lose before I had
to.

So I put my arms around her and held her while the thunder played
outside, and I think I cried, but neither of us said anything.

XXXII

ODIN THOR GLARED at the hand-drawn map on the plotting table, then
at me. His glance softened slightly, when he turned and looked at
Wryan—Dr. Relorn. The three of us stood each on a different side of
the table.

"You can't mean that," he repeated.

I sighed. "I do. The tunneled spaces are about ten rods wide and a
rod high, and there's about four hundred rods of tunnels all told. That's
a lot of cubic rods. To get total coverage of the tunnels would take
almost a gross of the gas grenades—without accounting for all the problems caused by walls and ventilation."

I could see Wryan rolling her eyes. "At the *outside*, I can make four
or five dives before I can't carry any more. That's if no one gives the
alarm. I can carry four or five of those monsters each time. That just
isn't enough for a brute force approach.

"What we've suggested will allow you to capture the remainder with
minimal casualties for our troops." I couldn't really call Odin Thor's
force the ConFeds. What Wryan had suggested was simplicity itself.
Don't try to cover the whole redoubt, but plant the grenades in the
ventilation systems and in the exit corridors.

"But we'll have to stand off so far that some of them will escape."

"Not many," I asserted.

Wryan shook her head sadly. "There will be a few left to murder."

Odin Thor looked away from her quickly, as though she were a rock snake.

I glared at him.

"And you, Trooper. I could have you shot tomorrow."

"Not if you want this mission carried out."

"True!" He laughed again, as if I had forgotten something important. "We'll see." Then he shook his head, as if our disagreement were of only passing interest. "How about the day after tomorrow?"

"Fine," I answered, just wanting to get the meeting over. "I'll start the drops just before first light."

Odin Thor glanced around the old laboratory, his eyes passing over the instrumented diving stage and taking in the shut-down consoles. "That should do it for now."

I nodded.

"Good day, Doctor. Good day, Trooper." His feet shook the floor as he left.

Click.

As the laboratory door shut behind him, we exchanged glances.

"He knows something we don't," I said.

"I'm sure he does, but we know something he doesn't."

Frowning, I looked at the dusty tiles before glancing back at Wryan. She wore a baggy blackish-green tunic over straight-cut gray-blue trousers—an ideal combination to make her cosmetics look garish and her face pale.

"We do? You, maybe. Not me."

"You know it, too, Sammis. You may not wish to recognize it."

A shivery feeling quivered down my back at the matter-of-fact tone.

"Do you want me to spell it out?"

Finally, I nodded.

"What's to keep you from applying a gas grenade to him in his sleep? Or anything else lethal? No guard or wall could stop you. Or me, assuming you teach me what you say you can." Her voice was flat.

I hadn't wanted to face that truth. Now Wryan was deliberately recalling it. Bad enough to think about killing faceless enemies who had tried to kill me and my family, but I owed Odin Thor *something*.

"Are you still willing to murder the ConFeds in their fortress?"

"They murdered my father and a lot of other innocents. They tried to kill me. And you, that one night."

She smiled gently, with a twist to her lips. "Don't make me a part of your decision, Sammis. If you do this, the blood will be on your hands."

"You don't have any on yours, Doctor?"

"It's Wryan, not doctor," she corrected me. "I have my share, more than my share. What you do remains for life, and that may be a *very* long time."

Again, she was acting as though I would be around forever. Even the witches all died. It just took longer; that was all.

"You're acting as if you don't want me to do this. You tell me that the blood will be on my hands, and that I can certainly stop Odin Thor."

She shrugged, and her gesture was like looking in a mirror. "This is your decision, and not anyone else's. You have to live with it—one way or the other."

"Wonderful. If I don't do something, we'll have a war between two groups of ConFeds who will destroy everything that's left. The other side might even win, and they want to kill me, and probably you. That leaves me a choice?"

She sighed. "It does. Don't you think the old witches of Eastron could have killed more than a few of their persecutors?"

"I thought they had."

"Some did; some didn't. Some left Eastron, took other names, had children, and avoided their heritage." She was looking intently at me.

"So . . . avoiding the problem is only a short-term solution. But the longer-term solutions have higher prices. Is that what you're telling me?"

"I'm just pointing out the alternatives."

"Why don't you decide?"

"Because." Again, there was that ghost of a smile, as she stepped away from the plotting table and the hand-drawn map. "Because it's your choice."

"Why, why, why do you insist on making it all my choice?" I was almost screaming.

"Because that is the way *you* will see it when you are older."

As her eyes caught mine, I could see a deep blackness behind the light piercing green, a glimpse of a darkness deeper than the undertime. I shivered where I stood, at having seen just that sliver of hell.

XXXIII

I LINED UP the grenades on the armorer's workbench in five groups of four.

"*Oooaaaah . . .*" yawned Janth, before covering his mouth.

I couldn't say I blamed him. Getting up well before first light is not conducive to alertness.

Even as he yawned, the assistant armorer's eyes never left the grenades, and his hand remained on the holstered butt of the projectile pistol. "How long before you make your first . . . trip . . . ?"

Concentrating on adjusting the equipment belt, I did not answer immediately. A quick release snap kept snagging. Finally, I got it unjammed. "Not very long. . . ."

"And how long between?" He was serious.

"No one briefed you?"

"Just that you'd be done before first muster. The colonel-general told me not to tell anyone."

I sighed. Secrecy about the mission was fine, but keeping the fundamentals of time-diving secret was just plain stupid. "I don't have time to tell you everything, but the duration between trips will be exactly the amount of time it takes me to place these," and I held up one of the black killer mushroom grenades, "at the other end. Actually diving undertime doesn't take any time at all. So . . . if I don't show up back here pretty quickly, you had better tell the colonel-general that there's trouble."

"How quickly?"

I had to shrug. "Can't tell you that because I don't know how long it will take to place them. Not very long, because I'll be back for the others."

I slipped four of the grenades into the release clips on my equipment belt. "Looks like it's time, Janth. Wish me luck."

"Luck, Trooper." He even smiled.

The first dive entry was smooth, splitting the now like a needle through a morning-still pond. The exit was almost as slick as I broke out in the middle of one of the four main ventilation ducts heading from the air-recirculating plant. The duct was carved from the rock and was wider than my armspan, though not much higher than the top of my head.

In quick motions that I had practiced with dummies Janth and I had put together, I released the four grenades from the equipment belt and spaced them equidistantly from the walls and each other. Then I pulled the arming pin of the first, then the second, the third, and the last. As I placed and armed the grenades, the forced air smelling of oil and metal whipped through my hair and past the squat and deadly black mushrooms. So heavy were the grenades that the wind that tore at me did not even rock them.

After dropping under the now as quickly as possible, I slid across the undertime from the hills of Bremarlyn back to Mount Persnol where the assistant armorer waited.

My second exit was still smooth.

"Quick there, Trooper."

"Hope we can keep it that way," I reached for the next of the black mushrooms. Janth clipped two of the second batch of grenades to my belt as I did two.

"Good—"

His sendoff was cut short as I dropped under the now, threading my way back along the silvery/gray/black undertime line I had travelled just moments before.

From what I could sense from the undertime, nothing in the underground ConFed base had changed between my departure and return.

Again, breakout was uneventful, and, in the second major ventilation duct, once more fighting the wind and odor of metal and oil, I placed and armed the grenades. This time my nose itched, almost enough to cause me to sneeze before I dropped undertime.

The trip back to Base was unpleasant—annoying, if you will. Imagine being suspended with the terrible itchy feeling and anticipation that comes just before a sneeze.

Kkkkatchhewww!!!

I felt like I had bruised every bone in my body, but I wiped my suddenly running nose on my sleeve and grabbed for another grenade.

"Cold there?" asked the assistant armorer as he clipped a second grenade to my equipment belt.

"No. Damned allergy . . . dust . . . oil . . ."

With that, I was gone again, back along the same track toward the real ConFed base to plant four more grenades in the third tunnel.

Again, there were no signs that my entries had been detected, or that the first two sets of grenades had exploded.

This time, fighting the wind and arming the grenades seemed harder. My nose itched and ran from the dusty metallic wind that swirled around me, but I still managed to get back undertime on schedule.

Breakout in the armory was a little rough. I came out above the floor level and staggered.

"Easy, Trooper." Janth steadied me.

I wiped my streaming nose on my sleeve again and grabbed for the next grenade.

"You all right?"

"So far. So far."

The fourth breakout in the ventilation system was even rougher.

Again, I was high, and dropped. It sounded to me like an explosion.

Clank.

I knocked over the last grenade as I tried to arm it.

CRRRUMMPPP!

The sound of the first grenade going off in the other duct sent me undertime, with the fourth grenade rolling free and unarmed. But there was no way I was staying.

The return was the worst yet. My head was beginning to ache. I wanted to tear my nose off because it itched so badly. While I didn't break out high, I did lurch out of the undertime off-balance, almost knocking Janth over.

KKKAATTCCHEWW!!!

"You all right?"

"No, but it's all shot if I don't make the last one."

I could tell the fifth dive would be my last for awhile. I could only fasten one grenade in the time Janth did three. But I staggered back undertime and let my mind carry me back to the ConFed Base.

I could still sense no action, but I wasn't looking for action, only for the two main exit locks.

No careful placement of grenades this time. I broke out in the empty center lock, and yanked the grenades off my belt, one after the other, arming them and dropping them on the floor.

The second lock was worse. I fell, bashed my elbow, and rolled over, yanking the first grenade clear.

BRINNNNGGGG!!!

Even I could tell that was an alarm.

I sort of flung the second grenade behind me as I dropped under the now.

Brattttttt. . . .

Whether the flechettes missed or I had ducked undertime before they reached me, I didn't know, and didn't care. White spots flickered in front of me and my head felt like it would explode.

Literally sliding out of the undertime, I ended up in a heap under

the edge of the armorer's work bench, sneezing with the little energy I
had left.

"Verlyt! You look like hell, Trooper."

"Thanks," I mumbled, still pretty much in a heap.

Click.

I could see a pair of trousered legs on the other side of the work
bench, trousers and booted feet.

"Who are you?" demanded Janth, reaching for the projectile pistol.

"It's all right," I rasped, trying to sit up.

"Dr. Relorn," snapped Wryan, "and if you want Sammis to recover,
you'd better let me give this to him."

Janth stood back, hand still on the gun, as Wryan put a beaker of
the bitter-tasting stuff she had poured down me once before under my
nose. I didn't wait this time. If I did, I wouldn't be in any shape to
drink it.

"You push yourself too hard," she said quietly.

"Not much choice," I said, between small sips.

"There's always a choice."

I didn't want to talk about it. "Janth?"

"Yes, Trooper?"

"Might as well stow the rest of the stuff back in the vault for now.
It either worked or it didn't."

"How soon will we know?"

"As soon as Odin Thor lets us know, or as soon as I recover enough
to check on it. But that won't be for awhile." I managed to struggle
into a half-sitting position.

Janth peered down at me. "I can see that."

"Take some more of this," ordered Wryan.

Janth took another look at me before beginning to replace the seals
on the grenade storage cases.

Thump. Creak. . . .

As the armorer worked, I took a mouthful. The liquid wasn't as bad
as swamp water in the damps, but the taste had little to recommend it.
The results were better than the taste. The flickering lights before my
eyes had disappeared.

"Can you get up?" Wryan asked.

"I'll be fine."

"Not for awhile, you won't," she corrected.

She was right. It took her hand, surprisingly strong for all its softness,
to help me to my feet.

"How did you know?" That question had escaped me while I was
trying to pull myself together.

"I just did." She shrugged. Her tone and gesture told me that she wasn't about to say more.

I looked over at Janth. "If the colonel-general is interested, I'll be recovering."

"I think you could use it, Trooper." He shook his head. "There's a lot more to that mental travel business than meets the eye, that's for sure."

Nodding at that, I took a first step toward the doorway. "Janth? The seals?"

For a moment, the assistant armorer looked blank. "But she got in."

"Sorry," I apologized. "I thought you knew. This is Dr. Relorn. She's the head of the entire travel lab."

The armorer inclined his head. "I'm sorry I didn't recognize you, but I hadn't expected you . . ."

"That's all right. I'm not at my best this early in the day."

But she was at her best. Without the makeup, she looked scarcely older than either Mellorie or Amenda. I'd thought she would look years younger without it, but this was the first time I'd seen her naturally in full light.

Her hair was mussed as well, and her tunic and trousers slightly creased, not quite up to the immaculate impression she usually projected.

Janth was still shaking his head as he undid the seals.

From the armory up through the tunnels to the first floor of the barracks had never seemed such a long walk. Outside, however, waited the steamer, the one I had first seen on a cool evening.

Wryan had said nothing since we had left the armory. Nor had I.

"How do you feel?" she asked once I was seated next to her.

"Better. Still shaky."

"I'll have some high-energy food sent to your room. You'll need that, and some sleep. By yourself," she added.

"Do you know everything?"

"No. But I've waited a long time, and seen a great deal. It's not surprising, and it's necessary. Whether I like it or not." While her tone was matter-of-fact, her voice did not ring quite true.

"Necessary? Whether you like what?"

She ignored my question. "You need to recover. I'm sure Odin Thor will want a report on the situation inside the ConFed redoubt, although he knows what it is. And you need to see for yourself. From the undertime."

The steamer was moving faster than I had expected, and Wryan took some of the corners nearly on two wheels.

"You never answered my question. What's necessary?"

"Mellorie, of course."

I decided not to ask any more questions of that nature, knowing I might not like the answers. Before I could have formulated any, the steamer screeched to a halt before the travel lab quarters.

"Are you all right to get up the stairs?"

"I'm fine. Just fine."

"Good. When you scout out the fortress, let me know what you find."

"I will. I certainly will."

"That would be helpful. Now, get some rest." She gave me a fleeting smile before speeding away in the steamer.

She was definitely not happy about my relationship with Mellorie, and didn't care if I knew it. Yet she had been there when I collapsed.

My steps up the stairs were slow. Very slow. I didn't see Mellorie. A tray of steaming food, including hot chyst cider, was waiting on my desk.

I pulled up one of the wooden armchairs and began to eat. Slowly. Although the amount of food seemed excessive, I plowed through it all. But I barely managed to get out of the uniform before sinking into the bed.

XXXIV

I SLEPT FOR most of the day, because it was late afternoon when I finally woke out of some nightmare I could not remember.

"You're finally awake." Mellorie's voice was a welcome relief. "You must have had some strange dreams."

"How long have you been here? Did I say anything?"

"Not long," she laughed softly. "You are suspicious." She paused, then uncrossed her legs, and moved from the chair to the bed next to me, running her fingers over my bare shoulders. "You were groaning, and I was about to wake you."

She wasn't saying something, but her fingers felt good kneading out the stiffness. So I waited.

Mellorie's hands stopped, and she put her arm around me and squeezed before letting go. "Your mind is somewhere else."

I nodded, stifling a yawn. "On food . . ."

"And?"

"I still have to find out how effective . . . my efforts . . . were . . ."

Mellorie stood up, not exactly looking at me or out the window, or anywhere. "Just what were you doing this morning, Sammis?"

"Killing people."

"Be serious."

"I am being serious. I killed some of the people who were killing our troops. I just don't know how many."

"The other ConFeds?" She was wearing a dark blue tunic and trousers, with matching, if scuffed, blue boots.

"You've heard about them?"

"They're the real ConFeds, aren't they?"

"Both groups are real. The others were in Eastron and did all the dirty work, though. At least from what I can tell."

"I hope you killed them all." Her voice wasn't husky. It was hard. "I hope you killed every single one of them."

The coldness of her words gave me a shiver, even as she turned to look directly out the window.

"Do you want to talk about it?" I asked.

"No."

"Are you certain?"

"I'm *very* certain, Sammis. Don't ever ask me again. Not if you care one bit for me." She still kept her face from me.

"That was why I asked . . ."

"I understand. But . . . just don't ask."

"All right. I won't." I slowly swung my feet onto the floor.

"If you don't mind . . . I don't feel well . . ." Her voice was brittle as well as hard. "I'll see you later." She walked to the door and let herself out without looking back.

Whatever had happened to her at the hands of the ConFeds was internal, or long ago, because there weren't any scars on her body. Scars on her soul—that was something else.

The light outside was dimming as another late afternoon storm built up.

The door Mellorie had left ajar blew shut with a gust that also brought the odor of rain into my room.

I was hungry, again. So I looked around. While I had been sleeping, someone had removed the tray and its dishes and replaced it with some fruits—chyst and pear-apple—and cheese, flanked by a small pile of biscuits. I sat down at the desk, uncomfortable chair and all, and ate every last bit, alternating the biscuits and cheese with the fruit.

A hot shower in the antique tiled stall remedied some of the lingering stiffness. After toweling myself dry, I pulled on another undress uniform.

Despite my growing dislike of the uniforms, I had nothing else to wear.

The roll of thunder outside indicated the oncoming storm might drop some needed rain.

I found myself licking my lips, staring at nothing. Should I report to Wryan? Odin Thor? Finally, I slipped under the now and out toward the hills of Bremarlyn. A ghost of a grayish thread was all that marked my morning route, probably invisible in the undertime to any diver who was not looking for it. Not that I was looking, suspended in the motionless chill of that place between worlds, between time, but the more I dived, the more I saw with my mind, rather than my eyes.

As I reached the underground redoubt, the silence struck me—the absolute lack of energy, almost that same lack of energy that had marked those places the enemy had obliterated. Here, near Bremarlyn, the grass waved in the breeze, and the trees gathered the sunlight, and Odin Thor's armored steamers and their crews lounged in the last warmth before twilight.

And beneath?

Nothing. Nothing but chill, silence, and darkness.

I reached out without breaking from under the now, trying to capture a mental image of the underground retreat of the real ConFeds, attempting to find those who had survived.

Nothing. Nothing but motionless machinery, and scattered lumps of flesh that had been men. Even in the sensationless undertime, the odor of death clogged my nostrils.

Knowing my time was limited, my strength not restored, and also aware that I needed to know what had happened, I eased myself backtime, red direction, careful that I should not overlap with my previous visit, even though you cannot contact yourself in the undertime . . . or in the now.

AAAAAAeeeeeeeeeeeeeeeeeeeeeeeeeeeeeeeeeeeeeeeeeeeeeeeeeee. . . . . . .

Nooooooooooooooooooo!!!!!!!!!!!!!!!!!!!!!!

. . . . .Verlytttt!!!. . . .

. . . dying . . . dying . . . dying . . .

Red lenses slashed across my eyes. Needles lanced my lips, and acid etched my throat. Breathing fire, I tried to rip my guts out, spew my innards across the cold of undertime . . . trying to escape the pyramiding agony . . .

Flares flashed across my visions . . .

. . . a thin man slashing his own throat . . .

. . . a woman grabbing a brain-spattered projectile gun from a dead ConFed's hand, to turn it against her own skull . . .

. . . a man with shaking hands injecting himself, biting his lips raw and trying to keep from screaming . . .

. . . a young soldier, crawling, scrabbling, leaving a pink frothed trail on the stone behind him . . .

. . . a captain, standing in the doorway of an underground barracks, propped against the casement, bringing up the heavy riot gun while trying to keep from shaking, trying to bring the gun to bear on the men writhing on the floor . . .

AAEEEIIIIIIIIIII/IIIIIIIII/IIIIIIIiiiiiiiiiiiiiiiiiiiiiiiii . . . The silent screams from the undertime chased me all the way back to the camp.

Uuuuuthuuuuupppppp . . . uuuutthhhuuuuppppp . . . uuupppthuuuupppp . . .

Despite the violence of the contractions and eruptions within me, it took a long time to empty my guts, and even longer for the dry retching to subside.

Longer still was it before I could stand and peel off my dishonored and soaked uniform and wad it up and stuff it into the empty rubbish bucket. I had to lean on the tile wall to be able to lather and wash myself clean. Hot as the water was, I shivered, and my teeth chattered. My knees threatened to buckle with each shiver, and each breath felt like it rasped my throat raw.

Would I ever feel clean inside again? I wondered, but not for long, because I needed every jot of strength I had to wend my way stark naked down the hallway to my room.

I did not make it under the quilt. Lifting even the coverlet was beyond me.

When I woke, I was in a strange room. Hanging tubes connected to needles seemed to run ice into my veins.

A cold sweat beaded on my forehead as I shivered under the weight of blankets that did not keep me warm.

I opened one eye.

A woman saw the gesture and scuttled from the light-walled area.

I licked my too-dry lips, swallowed, and waited for the room to stop circling around me.

While waiting, I fell asleep again.

The next time, I drifted into consciousness, feeling a hand that was simultaneously warm and cold upon my forehead.

"Sammis?"

"Ummmmm . . ." I meant to say "yes," but my tongue didn't fully cooperate.

"Just rest. You'll be just fine."

". . . uuuhhmmmm . . ." My mouth was swollen, and my tongue still refused to cooperate.

Why wouldn't I be fine? I'd just overextended myself by a factor of ten or so, but rest and intravenous replenishment should help.

At some point, I actually woke up clearheaded, and I was hungry— until I thought about food. I decided not to think about food and looked around.

Through the half-shuttered window blinds I could tell it was night. Clearly, more had affected me than simple exhaustion. Because I had not breached the undertime barrier, I could not have been poisoned by the gas grenades. The food left for me?

"Well, our sleeping prince has finally awakened . . ."

The heartiness of the doctor's voice instantly annoyed me. "How long have I been sick?"

"Feisty, he is, too. And that is a good sign . . ."

"How long?" I snapped.

"Let's see . . . about ten days . . ."

"TEN DAYS?" That was impossible.

"You're lucky to be alive, young man. Surviving nerve poison isn't exactly commonplace." She studied my eyes, and flashed a small light around.

"Nerve poison?"

"We don't know how you managed to get a small enough exposure to survive, but once you made it past the first few hours, it was just a matter of treating the symptoms. You're just lucky that your lady friend found you before it was too late." She was taking my pulse or listening to my heart.

"Lady friend?"

"But your signs are good, and I think we can get rid of this last tube and let you have clear liquids. The sooner, the better. You're too thin. All you travelers have too high a metabolic rate."

I wanted to say something.

"Not that any of you will ever get fat, but you'll starve on a diet that would feed a healthy farmer." She prodded my too-tight shoulder muscles. "Well, let's get started."

"Started?"

"Some high-protein, high-energy, clear liquids before you turn into a true shadow of your former self. Don't you feel light-headed when you work too hard for too long?"

I had to nod, feeling wrung out as well as light-headed.

"Tendency to chronically low blood sugars. Runs in the breed, I suspect. Now, let's get you something to drink."

"Water would be fine."

"Not enough. You want to end up with more tubes in you?"

"No."

"Didn't think so. I'll be right back. Or Nerlis will."

Nerlis?

As she swept out and opened the door, my view of the room improved with the increased light from the corridor outside. There wasn't much to see, just the bed, a plastic chair, a hospital-type table, and several thin structures on wheels draped with tubing. And one bouquet of sun daisies, framed by greens, with a card beside it, sitting on the window sill.

The flowers drooped, as if they had been there for some time.

Click, click, click.

Then the single overhead light flashed on, and my eyes watered.

"Let's get that out of you. I'm Nerlis, Trooper, and I'm glad to see you awake." She had short silvered hair, wrinkles, and a genuine smile.

"So am I. So am I." I coughed to clear my throat. "Where am I?"

"You wouldn't know; would you?" She laughed, a soft hoarse sound. "You're in the base infirmary. That's why you're still alive."

"But . . ."

"Everyone knew you had to go back. But it wasn't your fault. The armorer committed suicide, you know, after giving you the wrong weapons."

"Janth . . ."

"His family was killed in the looting after the enemy attacks. They say he's never been quite the same since. The colonel-general had worried about that, but there never were enough trained armorers." She busied herself with the needle attached to the tubing. "Look somewhere else, and relax."

"Somewhere else . . . ? All right."

"Aaaah . . . bring your arm up. That's it." She maneuvered a dressing into place where the needle had come out. "Now just hold your arm like that for a few minutes while I get the Sustain."

"Sustain?" I hated asking stupid questions.

"High-energy clear liquid," said Nerlis as she marched out of the room, her boot heels clicking on the tiles.

I licked my lips and tried to swallow. Tried, because my throat was so dry. Outside, the darkness was beginning to lighten, and I could see blurred clouds.

". . . in a little while . . ."

Nerlis's voice echoed down the corridor. She was talking to someone else. Their words were muffled. So I tried to shift my weight one-armed, leaving the dressing in place. How long before I could straighten my arm?

Click, click, click . . .

"Here we go." She was carrying a beaker of an off-purplish liquid and a cup, both of which she placed on the bedside table. After pouring a small amount into the cup, she held it up. "Take a sip. A *small* sip . . . and you can relax your arm. Any bleeding should have stopped by now."

My hands shook as I lifted the cup, easing a few drops into a mouth so dry that none even seemed to reach my throat. The second sip lubricated my throat, and a third may have reached my stomach.

"Wait a moment."

I put down the cup, marveling at how much effort three small sips took.

"Shouldn't be too long before some of the light-headedness starts to pass. Might be a minor stomach cramp or two."

"Uh . . ." Minor stomach cramp? I could barely keep from doubling over, and my forehead burst out in another cold sweat.

"Try to relax." Nerlis wiped off my forehead with a dry cloth, before folding it neatly and putting it on the bed-table next to the cup. "The reaction should pass quickly."

She was right about that, too.

"Another sip," she commanded.

I just looked at her.

She looked back at me.

I picked up the cup and took another series of small sips. My hands didn't shake the second time.

"The second set of cramps should be less violent."

They were. Instead of wanting to double up and die, I only felt like the three ConFeds had charged into my guts. I fumbled for the cloth and managed to wipe off my own forehead.

"Another sip?" I asked after the sweat and cramps passed.

"One more. Then wait for a while. You should start to feel better. You need to finish the entire beaker by midmorning." She started to leave, then turned back. "And no matter how good you think you feel, don't try to get out of that bed or sit up with your legs over the side."

"But . . ."

"You're dehydrated enough you don't need to use the facilities immediately, and we don't need you plastered face down on the stone."

"Yes, Nerlis."

"Thank you, Trooper." She left shaking her head.

I waited, then took another series of sips from the cup, and suffered through the entire process of cramps and cold sweats again. By the time

I had recovered from the third round of Sustain, I could see a gray, gray morning.

Wryan stood at the foot of the bed—from nowhere.

I gaped. It was one thing to surprise others, another to be surprised.

"Are you feeling better?"

"I thought you didn't dive?"

"I didn't." She smiled wryly. "But someone told me it was possible, and then left me hanging, and I worked on it."

"What really happened to me?" I found myself lowering my voice.

"Did you actually enter the ConFed fort?" The doctor was frowning, but she didn't look as formidable as before.

"No. Stayed strictly under the now. I'm not that stupid . . . but . . ." I shook my head. "Didn't seem to make that much difference . . ."

"It did. You'd be dead otherwise. Your reaction was from the mental feedback, I think, trying to convince your body to replicate the symptoms."

"Replicate?" I shivered. "Do you know . . . really know?"

Wryan just kept watching me, meeting my eyes.

". . . never . . . never . . . again . . ."

"Killing people, you mean?"

"Not that. Torturing them. Do you have any idea . . . ?" I was not just shivering, but shaking all over as the images pounded back at me.

"Try not to remember. Not just yet." Wryan's hands covered mine.

"Try not to remember? How . . . ?" That woman putting a gun to her head . . . or the man slashing his own throat . . . or the whole screaming, pounding pulsation of pain that had buried me . . . how could I not remember?

I could feel her hands tremble. "You felt it, too? You looked?"

"Not so closely as you did." Her face had paled momentarily.

"What happened?" As I freed one hand and used the cloth to wipe my forehead again, I was beginning to get an idea of what had occurred.

"They think you picked up traces of the nerve poison. You showed all the symptoms. The doctors claimed Odin Thor could be tried for murder. The nerve gas was banned throughout Query generations ago."

"Ahhhhh . . . and then the colonel-general claimed he thought it was only nausea gas to flush them out?"

"Exactly."

"Poor Janth."

"The armorer?"

I nodded.

"He really did suicide, Sammis. Not that I blame him."

"I don't either."

Slowly, as I stopped shaking, she removed her hands from mine and stepped back. I realized she had stopped wearing the makeup to make her look older.

I laughed harshly. "All that equipment's lost, at least for a season."

"Not nearly that long, unfortunately. The nerve gas will decompose within days." Wryan looked around. "You're not supposed to have visitors yet."

After the stimulation of seeing Wryan, and the reaction to those too-vivid memories, I felt drained again. So I reached for the Sustain. This time, the reaction was but a slight jolt and a damp forehead.

"Don't they understand? How horribly they all died? The background sheets said it was quick, not that it was like an eternal agony compressed into a thousand breaths. Even after. . . . even after . . . my father . . . no one . . . nobody . . . should die like that . . ."

"No . . . but you didn't know."

"Does that excuse it, Doctor?"

"No." Wryan looked straight back at me, her eyes clear. I respected her for that lack of evasion. "But it means you understand."

I had to lean back on the pillows, Sustain or no Sustain.

"You will have to kill again, Sammis. You know that. Chaos leads to violence, and some violence can only be halted by removing the causes."

Unfortunately, I knew what she meant. "Not now."

"No." She shook her head. "Not now." Looking around, she smiled faintly. "Good-bye."

She was gone, just like I had left her on those nights I had appeared in her quarters.

Click, click, click . . .

"Trooper? Who were you talking to?"

"Me?" I forced a grin. "Guess I was talking to myself."

Nerlis didn't believe me, but she just looked around, shook her head, and pointed to the cup. "Keep drinking."

"Yes, nurse." I reached for the cup again. It was going to be a long morning, a very long morning.

XXXV

ONCE I HAD struggled through the entire beaker of the Sustain, my recovery was a matter of time, and enough calories. I was ready to leave. Neither Nerlis nor Dr. Dyrell would agree.

"You have no bodily reserves, Trooper. None at all. Your immune system is depressed . . ." Dr. Dyrell, although hearty in tone, was less flexible than Odin Thor. ". . . and you probably never ate enough."

"I can't eat any more."

Dr. Dyrell just shook her round face at me. Her dark hair, peppered with gray, was so short and curly that it didn't even move. "You can't take in enough calories with three standard meals. You need a minimum of five full meals. Three or four and an equal number of heavy snacks will do the same thing." She glared at me. "Until you get some weight on that scrawny frame, you can't leave. Trying to do it overnight puts too much strain on your heart. We'll measure it out until we get you up where you belong.

"In the meantime, if you leave here using those mental travel tricks, it's your health. Maybe your death."

She wasn't joking. I had to go for the meals plus snacks routine. Five full meals I just couldn't take. Even after a day or two, I could tell the difference. Not that I looked much different, but I could use my undertime sight—and it was sharper—without feeling an instantaneous physical drain. Hard to believe that I had been operating on the edge of starvation, or that eating the diet of a healthy farmer had been insufficient.

Deric arrived with a stack of notebooks and the suggestion that I could spent my recuperation learning what every good diver should know. Most of the time, studying beat staring out the window, and gave me a welcome break.

Two days later, plowing through some overripe fruit and stale cheese and leafing through the third notebook, I heard footsteps.

"Sammis?"

"Mmmmpphhh . . ." With my mouth full, I just mumbled at Mellorie.

"Is that all you have to say?" She grinned momentarily. In her dark blue tunic and white trousers, she looked professional.

I shrugged, swallowing quickly. "Medical opinion was that I was near starvation. They won't let me out—officially—until I remedy that."

"Poor Sammis . . . you look a sight better than when they carted you out of your room. I'm sorry I didn't come earlier, but . . ." She looked down, then out the window, where high white clouds darkened into afternoon thunderstorms.

Something—more than just something—was bothering Mellorie.

"Do you want to talk about it?"

"No . . . but I should." She kept her back to me, with her hands clasped. "You . . . you thought . . . but I didn't. I couldn't. Not after Nepranza . . ." If she hadn't found me, who had? The doctor had said "woman friend."

"Nepranza?" I temporized. "That bad . . . ?" I didn't know what she was talking about.

"They said it wasn't that bad." Her voice was flat. "They say I must have been imagining things. They say that no one would have touched a child. Not the daughter of a lord. That's what they say. . . ."

Nepranza! The name connected. Farren had mentioned the place— molesting a lord's daughter . . . as if the only bad thing had been the killings of nearly innocent young men.

"They never talked to you?"

"My father wouldn't let them—before. He died in the riots. The ConFeds made sure of that. They made sure of a few other things."

"I see . . ." Not that I did. "Is that why you were attracted to me?"

Mellorie shrugged, still looking out the half-open window.

A roll of distant thunder punctuated her gesture.

"Yes."

I could barely hear her voice.

"Sammis . . ." She finally turned around, but she did not look at me. Her tunic was buttoned all the way to the neck. "Don't you understand? I was afraid. I knew you were sick, but I wouldn't go into your room. I wouldn't come see you until you were well." Mellorie finally looked up and into my eyes, almost glaring at me.

"Why don't you sit down?" I took a deep breath.

"You want me to stay? After I nearly killed you?"

"First," I sighed, "you didn't nearly kill me. I did. Second, there was nothing physically wrong with me. And third . . . we'll get to that. Now sit down. You owe me that."

She didn't owe me anything, but I wanted her to sit down.

"Do you know what happened?" I asked.

"They said you must have tried to check—"

"No. I'm smarter than that. I just wasn't prepared for the feedback. For all the deaths."

Mellorie's face went blank, as if a screen had covered it. "They deserved it. Every instant of it."

"Even the woman who took her lover's gun and blew out her own brains because the pain was so great? Or the boy who kept banging his head against the stone walls . . ."

"Don't talk to me about them . . . please . . . don't talk to me about them . . ."

"Mellorie . . . I damned near died because I picked up their deaths . . . my brain was trying to tell my body it was dying—five hundred times over. Do you know what it was like dying—"

"Stop it! Stop it, stop it, STOP IT!!!!" Mellorie lurched to her feet. She grabbed the railing at the bottom of the bed and shook it enough to make the heavy bed sway. "STOP IT!!!"

Click, click, click, click!

Nerlis stood in the doorway. I motioned her back, but she stayed there.

Mellorie didn't seem to notice. "All you can think about is their deaths! What about my sister? What about my father? What about me?"

"What about my father?" I asked quietly. "They burned him alive in his own house."

"Then how can you feel anything for them?" Her voice was lower.

"Because I felt every single one of them die. And nobody should have died like that."

"Would you do it again?"

"Would you do it?" I countered.

"In an instant. Would you?" A thin film of perspiration coated her forehead. "Would you do it again?"

"I don't know." I tried not to shake my head, but the images kept running through my thoughts—the woman grasping for the gun, the soldier with bloody fingers clawing his way along the floor . . .

"Goodbye, Sammis." She brushed the red hair back off her damp forehead with her right hand, as if nothing had happened. Her left still held the bed frame. "I hope you're back to normal before too long. Let's have dinner some time when you come back." Her face was almost expressionless. Then she grinned, and the falsity made her face look like a carnival mask. "Just mark it down as the hysteria of a pampered lady gentry. All right?"

Nerlis eased back into the corridor, although Mellorie had never even taken notice of her.

"Whatever you say, Mellorie. Whatever you say."

She let go of the bed frame. "I still like you, Sammis, but you don't understand. So let's just be friends. All right?"

I nodded slowly. "Friends."

"Friends." This time I got a faint smile, but a real one. For a long time, I looked blankly out the window, letting the breeze ruffle my hair, drawing in the air that bore the hint of the on-coming storm, and the ebbing scent of the one just departed.

"Are you all right, Trooper?"

"Call me Sammis, Nerlis."

A gust of wind tugged at my sheets, and Nerlis slid the window almost shut as the rain began to pelt against the pane. She went back into the corridor, presumably to check on other windows.

The rest of the cheese was still waiting, still stale. I could have eaten the chyst I had started, brown as it had become, if I'd been in the damps, but I picked up the pearapple instead and finished it in five bites. Then I took a deep swig of the Sustain, not because I liked the swill, but because I wanted out.

After that, I picked up the notebook, the one with the theories on the Laws of Time in it, and began to read again.

When the thunder and rain had died away, and the room was getting stuffy again, I tossed back the sheet and walked to the window, opening it wide. Then I went to the narrow wardrobe. Not a stitch of clothing.

I laughed. I hadn't been wearing anything when I had collapsed. I didn't get back into the bed, but wrapped the robe around me and sat in the chair.

Hatred. There was so much of it. Westron hated Eastron; the farmers and townies hated the gentry; the ConFeds hated the Secos; the gentry hated the Temple; and everyone hated the witches—and the Frost Giants. Mellorie was close to hating me because I refused to hate the people I had killed.

The room began to darken, both from the clouds and the twilight, but I wasn't cold. And I was tired of the bed, tired of lying around getting fattened up, tired of studying theories, no matter how valuable they might be.

"Your friend was a little upset." Nerlis carried a tray.

"Can I just eat it here?" I stood up, put the notebooks in a pile on the floor, and wheeled the bed table over.

Creeakkk.

"Turn it the other way." Nerlis set the wooden tray on the just-lowered table.

At its lowest setting, the table was higher than I would have preferred. What surprised me was that I was, if not hungry, certainly able to eat the food before me—slices of cold roast, jellied rice, sprouts, greens, and a pair of biscuits with some flambard preserves.

"Watching you eat just amazes me. You eat more than most guardsmen."

"It amazes me, too," I muttered between mouthfuls. I wanted out of the place, and, if it took eating everything in sight, so be it.

As I continued to munch, Nerlis left me with the diminishing pile of food and my thoughts.

The breeze had died as the air cooled, and outside the clouds were breaking up. In the west, the clouds glistened a greenish pink, underlit by the setting sun.

Terwhit . . . terwhit . . .

Whatever bird called, the sound was better than the harshness of the grossjays, those scavengers that had fed so well on the looting and burning following the Frost Giant attacks.

Terwhit . . . terwhit . . .

After pushing the table back from the straight-backed, two-armed wooden chair I stood and made my way to the window. Studying the dimming southern sky, and trying to pick out stars between the scattered clouds, I wondered if I could go undertime and follow a straight line to each.

The pinkness of the dying sunset faded into purple, then near-black.

One bright point of light emerged from behind a cloud. More properly, the fast-moving cloud left it unobscured in the evening, glittering and untwinkling above the dark and lightless building housing the Far Travel Lab.

Mithrada—the next planet inward from Query; host to the ill-fated planet-forming and metal-mining expedition that had brought on the Frost Giant attacks; evening or morning star to how many generations?

I tried to swallow the lump in my throat. When swallowing didn't help, I tried thinking. Except my thoughts skittered from crazy Mellorie to Allyson, and whether Mellorie could dive or not, I would have traded her for sweet, perceptive and intelligent Allyson without an instant's hesitation.

Those memories didn't help the lump in my throat, either, especially recalling lying in the darkness with Allyson, holding her and being held. In addition to a heavy throat, I was having trouble seeing, and my cheeks were wet. Above it all, Mithrada glittered, like a heartless diamond in the sky.

Terwhit . . . terwhit . . .

Hearing the unknown bird helped, and I hoped he or she would call

again, as I listened and the darkness deepened. In time, another cloud
obscured Mithrada, and I turned back to my bed.

"Oh . . ." I mumbled, barely keeping myself from jumping at the
sight of someone in the chair. I glanced through the undertime to avoid
the darkness.

The woman in the chair was Wryan, and there were deep circles under
her eyes. My food tray had been removed while I had thought and looked
and looked and thought. I hadn't even noticed.

"Troubles?" I asked. "I'm sorry. Have you been here long?"

"Not too long, and it was peaceful to sit here and watch you, and
listen to the wind." She paused. "There are always troubles, Sammis."
She took a breath that verged on a sigh before continuing. "I understand
that you had a few of your own this afternoon."

"Did Nerlis call you?" My tone was snappish.

"No. She told me when I came. It works better if I announce my
arrival officially." There was a trace of wryness in her tone.

I sat on the edge of the bed. My legs were a little stiff from standing
so long. Otherwise, I felt fine.

"Do you want to talk about it?"

I couldn't help grinning as she used the same words I had employed
earlier. "Yes . . . and no."

Wryan sat there waiting.

"Either Mellorie's not quite sane, or I'm not quite sane, or maybe
we're both crazy." I found that the table had been raised and moved
back to its place beside the bed. I took a gulp of Sustain before saying
another word. Verlyt, I wanted out.

Wryan sat there, leaning forward, her left arm propped on the chair,
her chin resting on her left hand, and her right arm loosely in her lap.

"She came to apologize about not being able to help me. She has
this . . . fear . . . about sickness. That didn't bother me—except that I
didn't realize I owe you—but when I tried to tell her what happened, she
didn't hear me."

Wryan watched, waiting for me to go on.

"It was easier for her to believe I was sick, and that she had let me
down, than it was for her to hear how horribly those ConFeds died. All
she said was that they deserved it. Every instant of agony. Because they
raped her—or worse." I shook my head. "I know she was hurt. I know
her father was killed at Nepranza. But she's alive. They're not. Some of
them were innocent.

"Like the woman who blew her brains out with her dead lover's gun.
She didn't rape Mellorie. Or the young soldier my age . . . or . . ." I slid

off the bed and walked back to the open window. For some reason, I didn't want to look at Wryan, perhaps because she was a woman.

"Some of them deserved the gas. But every one of them died. Odin Thor knew they would. I should have, but I was too busy proving that I could do it to think about what it meant. When they were all dying, it was a little too late."

"Would you bring them back?" Wryan's voice was soft.

The clouds had passed clear of Mithrada again, and the planet shone diamondlike just above the horizon.

"I said I didn't know."

"You know."

"You're right. I'd probably do it again, and I wouldn't bring them back. That makes me worse than Mellorie. Doesn't it?" I took my hands from the window frame and slowly turned to face Wryan. "Doesn't it?"

"Not necessarily. What would happen if you hadn't killed them? How many people would die? And who would they be?" She had leaned back in the chair.

"You're saying that it's all right to kill to stop more deaths? Hell! Why does there have to be so much hatred? So much killing?"

Wryan didn't have an answer. Neither did I.

Terwhit . . . terwhit . . .

I couldn't help but smile momentarily. The bird had a point. You sing when you can, not when someone wants you to. I glanced out the window, but, even looking into the undertime, couldn't locate the bird.

"Do you understand?" I asked Wryan.

"Understand what? That you killed real people? That some of them were innocent? That you hate yourself for doing it? Or that you know this is just the beginning?"

All of a sudden, with Wryan's last words, the room was cold, as cold as I had ever experienced, even in that dream ice-storm that had launched me into time-diving. "Just the beginning . . . ?"

I knew what she meant. The farmers weren't farming as much. The Frost Giants were out there somewhere. No one except Odin Thor's ConFeds had any way to hold things together. I stepped away from the breeze that ran through my robe and gave me a physical chill.

". . . just the beginning . . ." I sighed. "How bad is it?"

"Worse than that." She shook her head. "Odin Thor has his hands full with what amounts to two provinces of old Westron. Outside of that . . ." she shrugged. "Any place else, no one really farms . . . most of the crafters were killed with the gentry . . ."

The silence and the darkness stretched out between us.

Terwhit . . . terwhit . . . terwhit . . .

I smiled at the cheerfulness of the call. The bird was definitely right. "So we do what we can."

She was smiling also, though more faintly. "I suppose. What other choice is there?" Her quiet voice was firm.

The sound brought back another memory. "Thank you."

"You're welcome."

"How did you know?"

"I'm not sure. But I did."

Her tone told me not to pursue that question. I didn't. "You kept visiting me when I couldn't even think, when nobody thought I would live?"

"Yes."

"Why?"

"Because."

I grinned. "That's not good enough, Doctor."

"Because you gave me back part of myself."

That wasn't all, but it was enough. "You need some sleep." I took a step toward her, then stopped.

"I know."

"So . . . why don't you go get some? And have pleasant dreams?"

She stood up, looking ghostlike in the light-colored tunic and trousers. "I will."

"Thank you . . ." I wanted to say more, but couldn't say what . . . or why. Besides, she was probably a good century older than me. So I didn't.

"Good night, Sammis."

Click, click, click. . . . Her boots sounded lonely as she walked out, and I stood there for a long time. When I looked out the window, before climbing into the hospital bed, Mithrada had dropped below the horizon.

XXXVI

NERLIS AND DR. DYRELL officially discharged me two days after Mellorie and I "became friends." They also required all divers to come in for checkups every ten-day.

Gerloc, Amenda, and Arlean were all on the verge of starvation. So were several others I didn't know. One of the newest divers, a recruit ConFed named Jerlyk, was barely above the minimums. That led to a divers' nutrition chart, which ended up posted in the dining area.

In the meantime, between my efforts in the hospital and my efforts while on "light duty," I had finished all the background material on diving. At the end of the next ten-day, I was cleared to dive again.

"I have a loose end or two to follow," I told Wryan, after squeezing in to see her before Odin Thor arrived. He was already pacing down the hallway toward the main lab. "What I find out could be helpful."

"Such as?"

"Even though we can't break out on Query, except in real time, I could see backtime at least several days when I scouted the ConFed fort. I'd like to see what the limits are."

"Take it easy. We'll call it extended reconnaissance research for now." She smiled, almost sadly. "Good luck."

"Good luck to you. Odin Thor's almost here." I ducked out just as the colonel-general arrived. I avoided saluting him and was around the corner before he reacted.

"Trooper!"

I ignored the call, smiling, since I was out of sight. It was bad enough that circumstances required I do Odin Thor's dirty work without making him into a tin god. Besides, I had more important things to do.

After stopping by the snack table—another innovation of Wryan's—at the dining area and picking up cheese, hard biscuits, and fruit, I headed back to my room—by foot.

I had also gone back into conditioning, running and doing exercises. I didn't like them, but diving was clearly a strenuous business, and I was going to be in top condition. That was why Jerlyk and I met on the grassy square behind the quarters before every breakfast. After a few days, Gerloc and Amenda joined us, though neither could match us.

Grabbing some snack foods, I headed back to my room, which was fine with me. The next few subjective hours would be tough enough without any distractions.

Once inside, I eased the window wide open, trying to coax a breeze inside. For early fall, the weather was warm, almost hot. Entering the undertime too warm would make the entire dive uncomfortable.

After I opened the window and laid out my mid-morning snack, I sat before the desk and forced myself to eat all the elements of the semi-meal slowly, following it with a watered-down and tastier version of Sustain.

Then I stood up and walked around, trying to figure out what route I would take, but merely thinking about it didn't offer much insight.

Where and when I wanted to view was clear, although why was another question I didn't really want to address. Still . . . I had promised myself that I would try, and a promise was a promise, even to me.

After a last gulp of the Sustain, I stopped pacing and dropped through the now and into the undertime.

Not that I went all that far back, or even that far geographically— less than a year and less than two hundred kays—just back to Bremarlyn. Back to the evening of a freak snowstorm and the morning afterwards.

I could have tried to watch a scared youngster wearing a heavy uniform cloak slip down a snow-filled gully and disappear to avoid being shot. But I didn't.

Slipping further toward the dawn, I fought to see through the hazy barrier between the then and the undertime, as well as to see through the fat swirling flakes of the untimely snow.

As the indirect light of a dawn grayed by clouds waxed on that stately house I had not seen intact since then, I watched, trying to shift my view toward whatever had happened.

Did I really want to know?

I watched from outside the house. I could have drifted inside, looking at the Davniads, watching Allyson, but I would have felt somehow unclean, like a voyeur, or . . . a ConFed. So I watched from outside.

First, a puff of smoke fluffed from the chimney. I let myself drift further foretime, when the snowflakes had stopped and the light was brighter. Not yet mid-morning, but no longer early morning.

A figure—Jerz Davniads—opened the doors to the steamer locker. His breath trailed above him like a smoke plume.

Allyson appeared, moving quickly, with several bags, which she dropped by the steamer. Her father said something, but she did not even turn as she hurried back across the courtyard to the house to return with yet another pair of bags. Jerz waited until she had returned with the second set.

This time Allyson gestured at the bags and motioned toward the steamer. Jerz shook his head and walked back across the courtyard with her. They brought back four more bags, and Germania Davniads followed with two large baskets, which she put in the rear seat of the steamer. Allyson handed her father the bags as he placed five of them in the rear storage trunk.

As he lashed down the remaining bag on the storage rack, Germania slipped into the driver's seat and began the lightoff. Allyson stood by the locker door, but Jerz motioned her into the steamer. Then Allyson's mother backed the steamer out of the locker, set the brakes, and slid into the passenger seat. Jerz closed the locker before climbing stolidly into the driver's seat.

The steamer eased down the long drive, trailing a thin plume of white. At the road, the vehicle lurched slightly on some ice, but Jerz smoothly corrected and turned downhill toward the highway. He slowed as he approached the sweeping ninety degree turn above where our drive joined the road.

A single ConFed stood by the drive as the steamer slipped past. The marine turned and lifted his projectile gun.

Either Jerz Davniads did not see the weapon, or he ignored it, believing that no ConFed would turn a weapon upon a member of the gentry. The steamer continued on untouched, but the ConFed turned and sprinted up the drive.

I followed the steamer, now almost careening, as if the Davniadses had realized the danger.

Undertime, I could only watch, asking whether I wanted to know what had happened, hoping that they would, or had, escaped, and doubting as I watched.

Two military steamers waited at the spot where the road met the highway, and I could see another civilian steamer had been stopped. Some of the ConFeds were dragging one of the passengers out, a woman, and from the picture I got, I did not watch further, especially since there was nothing I could do.

I slipped time again, to the instant where the heavy Davniadses steamer plunged down the road. For an instant, the woman being assaulted by the ConFeds broke free, and tried to run toward the oncoming steamer. Her tunic had been mostly ripped away, and blood streaked across her uncovered shoulder and partly bared breast. Two ConFeds caught her and forced her down.

Jerz Davniads throttled up the steamer and aimed the heavy vehicle at the narrow shoulder of the road that offered the only chance of passage.

I refused to move closer in the undertime or to look at either Allyson or Germania, still hoping that the former steamer racer could bring them through.

The Davniadses' steamer edged the outside military vehicle and the bag lashed to the trunk ripped off. But the steamer was clear, skidding around the corner and onto the Eastern Highway, headed east, away from Inequital.

Then, I hoped—until a ConFed slammed a heavy black weapon onto a swivel and rammed it around, levelling it at the back of the steamer. *NOOOOOOOOO!!!!*

Laws or not, I slammed my mind against the barrier of the now. Once, twice, holding that scene suspended in stasis, trying, somehow, to stop what was going to happen.

. . . nooooo . . .

Try as I did, nothing happened. The ConFed stood there, ready to destroy Allyson and her family, and I could alter nothing. All I did was freeze myself in time to avoid seeing what would happen.

Another thrust at the undertime, and nothing changed, except I began to feel light-headed. Another jab, not nearly as forceful, and little flashing lights began to appear.

But the ConFed stood immobile with his shredder . . .

. . . and I finally watched . . .

I could almost feel the impact of the shredder on the steamer, and even through the undertime, the blast of flame from the ruptured cans of etheline was bright enough not to mistake.

Twisting forward in time, I skipped another blast of death and agony. Cowardly, but more death, more loss, I did not need. I had already lost Allyson twice. A third time, reliving the emotions of her death, I was not strong enough to undergo.

That was it. I watched just enough to see whether anyone else escaped. No one left the flaming mass that had been a heavy steamer.

Trying to swallow both a throat that felt swollen and tears that could not occur in the undertime, I moved forward to avoid watching more. That burned steamer I had seen before, on my trip to Mount Persnol, along with several others. I just hadn't recognized it or realized that had represented my last contact with Allyson. Not that it changed anything.

I had proved that, even if I couldn't emerge in the past, I could see some of it from the undertime. See more than I ever really wanted to see.

Releasing my hold on the undertime past, I let the time-paths carry me back to my room. Back to the sanitary facilities where I lost most of my mid-morning snack.

When the heaves stopped, I rinsed out my mouth with Sustain. The bitter taste served two purposes—restoring some minor measure of strength, and reminding me of—I didn't know what—but it was reminding me of something.

Then I slumped onto the bed. Outside, the breeze had stopped, and, inside, as I sat stewing, the sweat beaded up on my forehead.

My stomach had gotten too sensitive. What had happened to the youngster who had eaten swamp roots and held them down? Who had seen an innocent student shredded in front of him?

But I might have loved Allyson, given time, given a better world.

I wiped my forehead and took another sip of Sustain, from a new bottle.

Mellorie. She had lost her self-respect, and her family, and she hated the real ConFeds and wanted them all to die horribly. She couldn't accept anyone who didn't share that hatred.

And I didn't. The ConFeds I had murdered died in more agony than Allyson, than my father, or than Mellorie's family. Necessary as those ConFed deaths might have been, I did not have to share hatred. Responsibility . . . but not hatred.

I took another sip of warm Sustain. And another, wondering where the chain of hatred and death would end.

XXXVII

THE FIRST SIGN, which I overlooked because I was not that fond of sweets, came the night Greffin announced berrycream tarts would not be available.

"But . . . we've always had berrycreams . . ." protested Arlean.

"Since when? Since you became librarian when Orite left?" Gerloc's voice was calm, as if he were discussing the weather.

Arlean glared at the thin diver.

I went on eating the last of the buffalo stew. While buffalo was usually chewy, Greffin had clearly marinated it in something with the potency of acid, because it fell apart at the touch of a knife.

"Soon we'll be eating ConFed rations," sniffed Arlean.

"That's better than foraging in the damps." I kept my voice level.

"Too bad your taste didn't improve with the cuisine."

I tried not to wince at Mellorie's low-voiced comment.

Gerloc cleared his throat loudly. "We still have wheatcakes."

So I ate wheatcakes with sweet cream, noting loudly how much better they were than the delicacies of the damps, such as snake eyes and frond hearts.

The second sign came the first night Mellorie appeared on Jerlyk's arm, not long after the fall harvest.

Outside, the wind was whining, and, now that the crops couldn't use the moisture, a cold heavy rain beat against the old leaded glass panes.

Like me, Jerlyk had been a trooper with one of Odin Thor's units— the one operating well beyond Halfprince. Unlike me, he hadn't been cautious, and the armorer had reported his disappearance.

". . . and the colonel-general suggested I report here immediately," Jerlyk told me. "We lost two guards on the run before mine doing their collecting."

"Collecting? Collecting what?" I asked.

"Food supplies from the farming groups. That's what the outlying units do now—police against the hill bandits and protect the farmers and the towns against the looters. In return, they 'request' a share of the crops." Jerlyk was smallish, wiry, like me, but had jet black hair to go with the fair skin, and blue eyes that seemed to twinkle all the time.

"Is the looting that bad?" Mellorie leaned closer to him.

"It's gotten worse. The harvest wasn't that good . . ." Jerlyk's voice trailed off.

I understood. "The farmers need winter hold-out and seed for planting, and they resent a supply levy?"

"Right."

"But they wouldn't have even that without the ConFed patrols, would they?" asked Amenda.

"No," added Jerlyk between bites, "but they don't think that way."

They didn't, and Jerlyk and I had a chance to find out the details much sooner than I had anticipated.

Four days later, we were in the Far Travel Lab, in uniform, standing before the colonel-general and Wryan.

"Troopers, we have a problem. Some of the farmers are hoarding far more than they need." Odin Thor paused and cleared his throat.

I looked him straight in the eye. Jerlyk looked at the floor.

"We need the farmers to keep farming, but we need the surplus grain. That means we have to find out who's hoarding."

In no way did I want to dive and spy on the farmers, not so the ConFeds could destroy some poor farmer's harvest and home.

"This isn't the monarchy. We can't just take their food," continued Odin Thor. "If we do, they'll revolt and throw in with the bandits. If we don't let them know who's in charge, and distribute the surplus food, we won't have much of a society left by spring."

Wryan nodded before speaking. "What is your overall strategy? To use the divers to find out the hoarders, and then make them an offer they can't refuse?"

"Ahhhhhmmmmm," coughed the colonel-general. "What . . . well . . . that is the general idea . . ."

"What do we have to trade?" pursued Wryan. "Technical support, which they don't need . . . replacement parts, which have limited applicability."

"Etheline . . ." I suggested.

"Etheline?"

"The old ConFed fort has tanks and tanks of it," I noted. "And some of them aren't in the fort itself. It would take some cleaning up, but the farmers are going to need it for planting, even for heating this winter."

"You'd better get that trading program set up quickly," added Wryan.

Odin Thor looked puzzled, but said nothing.

"They could use old-fashioned stills to turn the grain we need to eat into alcohol, which would work almost as well as etheline." She added quietly, "Some people are already close to starvation. Some of those supplies will have to be reallocated if you want to keep local support."

The head ConFed nodded slowly as the implications sunk in. "Can you work with my staff to set up the details?"

"I would be happy to help there, Colonel. We need to announce that we will be helping the poorest and offering trades—"

"Above the supply levy," insisted the colonel-general.

I could see that, because all the farmers would claim poverty and lack of grain to hold out for the etheline.

"—before we start officially scouting around."

"I have to insist, Doctor, that at least my two troopers here start looking now. If we wait until the announcements are made to find out where the hidden stocks are, then we risk setting off looting between the farmers."

The colonel-general made sense. I didn't like it, but he made sense. Even Wryan bowed her head to his logic.

". . . and I would like you two to ride the next steamer out to Llordian. You are not to reveal you are divers."

I filled in the picture, not that I was particularly thrilled by the landscape. We were going to be tax-collectors. Tax-collectors have always had short life-expectancies in rural Westron.

"Colonel . . ." added Wryan.

"Yes, Doctor." Odin Thor was already glancing toward the door.

"My people will be able to post notices about food distributions for the needy at an instant's notice. I hope the redistribution effort will commence along with the collection and trading program." Wryan's voice was calm.

Odin Thor half-bowed. "I understand your concerns, Doctor. We wouldn't have it any other way."

"I do appreciate that, Colonel."

He started to leave, then twisted back. "The steamers leave tomorrow for Halfprince. The base there will run you out to Llordian."

"Yes, Colonel-General," answered Jerlyk.

I nodded.

Odin Thor fixed me with a stare, but said nothing.

"Good day, Doctor."

"Good day, Colonel."

After he had left, Wryan looked at us both. "Sammis, you need to stay."

Jerlyk glanced at me, then at the stern-faced doctor. "Then I will be leaving, Dr. Relorn."

She nodded curtly.

Jerlyk didn't quite double-time his way out.

I stood there, and she sat in her chair. Finally, she stood and walked toward one of the deserted consoles.

"You're playing with flame," I said.

"So are you. Why do you refuse to salute him? Or address him by title?"

"ME? Every time you call him colonel, he burns. His colonel-general rank is five grades above colonel."

Wryan smiled. "He was never confirmed in a rank above colonel."

"This business of posting notices . . . that was nearly a threat."

"No. It *was* a threat, and one we can carry out, if necessary. Without more popular support, we won't have anything. Odin Thor knows that."

I almost took a step toward her. Wryan wore the same off-tan tunic and trousers she seemed to wear every other day. The makeup was gone. I hadn't seen it in days. Now she wore her hair too short, but it didn't matter. She still looked not that much older than I did—at least to my unpracticed eye.

"Sammis?"

Her voice was so soft I almost didn't hear it.

"What?"

"Did you find what you were looking for?"

"No. She was dead. You knew that." My words dropped like stones. I hadn't told anyone. Who could I have told?

"Only because you already knew. You went back to confirm what your heart already had told you." Wryan's voice was gentle, almost as if she understood how watching Allyson die had hurt. I hadn't known it would hurt. How stupid can you be?

"I can definitely see some things on Query from the undertime— only for a few years either side of the now. That was enough."

"I can't. I've tried. I can do it on Sertis, but not here. I don't envy you that ability, not now." She pursed her lips, then walked back to the console, still lit. "Are you sure you're up to this spy mission?"

I shrugged. "It's better than the alternatives."

We both nodded simultaneously, and I wanted to laugh as we did so. I didn't, and neither did she, but there was a quirk to her mouth.

"You'd better go."

So I did, wondering why I enjoyed talking to a woman four times my age.

XXXVIII

FOUR CONFEDS STOOD in a rough square. Only one had a shredder. Two held handguns, and a fourth only a dress knife.

. Rough groupings of bearded men, women, and a few children encircled them. Gaunt face after gaunt face stared at the four, edging forward, backing them up to the statueless pedestal. Since the town was Llordian, the missing statue had probably been the old emperor.

"Killers . . ."

"Hogs! Oink! Oink! Oink!"

". . . genlovers!"

I frowned at the last epithet, but Jerlyk, standing beside me in the shadows, winced. So did the ConFed with the shredder.

The crowd, salted with a few crones and one white-bearded man with a single arm who stood a head taller than anyone else, reacted to the gesture.

"Genlovers! Genlovers! Genlovers . . . !"

Jerlyk whispered, "Means gentry-lover. Toady for the gentry."

"But why? Why the anger? We're the ones they should be angry at."

"Let's talk about it later, Sammis."

That made sense, because the tension in the town square was rising. If I appeared from nowhere and disarmed the ConFeds, then the crowd would kill them. I could still escape. The troopers couldn't.

The sun was strangely hot, like midsummer, and the warmth from the white walls of the trade quarter and from the pavement underfoot created heat shadows on the eastern walls of the square. The too-thin people in their drab and faded clothes, mostly unwashed, stood unmoved by the heat.

I wiped my forehead. After a ten-day plus of snooping around, I knew most of the townies were hungry. They had nothing to trade to the farmers. The ConFeds were protecting the farmers not just from the bandits, but from hungry townies.

Crack!

A single rock slammed into the pedestal behind the ConFeds. The lead trooper leveled the shredder.

"Go ahead! Throw another rock! Just give him the chance to use that shredder. He's a killer, and he'll kill all your children. So throw another rock!" The screaming voice cracked, but it was loud enough to break the heat-trance that had settled over the crowd.

Unfortunately, the voice was mine. The words were fine, but while I was wearing an unmarked tunic, it still looked too military. Or too gentrified.

"Genlover!" spat a boy who could not have been eight.

"The ConFed tax-collectors! It's them!"

"Bloodsuckers!"

Attention passed from the armed ConFeds in the square to the un-armed pair of ConFed tax-collectors in the alleyway adjoining the square.

"Now what?" hissed Jerlyk.

"I think we run."

So we did.

"Get them . . . bloodsuckers! Bloodsuckers! Genlovers! Genlovers!"

"Genlovers . . . genlovers . . . genlovers . . ." The words turned into a chant as the mob crowded into the alleyway.

We sprinted straight down the alley, then past the near-empty fruit stand and the orange-haired woman who stared as we pounded past.

". . . to the right . . ." I mumbled, trying to angle for the ConFed guard station by the western end of the town nearest the Eastern Highway.

"Look ahead . . ."

Jerlyk had a point. Some of the mob had left the square by the avenue and would reach the next corner before we would.

". . . then left . . ."

"That's a dead end . . ."

". . . climb . . ."

The low wall ahead, not even as high as my shoulder, would be easy enough to climb. Vaulting onto the flat section which turned out to be a covered storm drain, I glanced around. The other side was an empty yard, with empty racks that had once held lumber or timber—or something.

Some of the crowd headed around to cut us off.

"Down and out of sight, and dive. Out to the guard station."

I jumped down by the nearest lumber rack. No one could see us, and the windows in the back of the building were both shuttered and closed. We broke out of the undertime behind in the narrow space between the old town wall and the guard station. I stumbled and scraped an elbow on the wall.

"Verlyt!"

"So what did you scrape?" I asked, in between deep breaths, as I tried to catch my wind and simultaneously navigate my way toward the guard station.

"Forget it!" snapped Jerlyk.

We came around the corner just in time to meet the other four ConFeds racing in from the south end of the avenue.

The lead trooper, still carrying the shredder, opened his mouth, then shut it, then opened it again before stammering, "What . . . how . . ."

"Just a little misdirection. We almost didn't get clear."

The lead ConFed shut his mouth without saying a word.

The one behind him, a wiry man with copper hair, grinned. "We owe you, and I'm real glad to let you know that. I'm Nylen."

"Sammis."

"Jerlyk."

All the time we were talking, we were trotting toward the compound gate.

"Forcer! Forcer! Riot in the town!" yelled the man with the shredder.

Clang! Clang! Clang!

We were inside the compound, and the duty crew was already manning the guard towers and breaking out shredders and handguns. I found a projectile rifle thrust into my hands, and my way being directed toward a sandbagged position below the main guard tower.

To my left, the heavy wooden gate rolled shut. A pair of recruits began shoring it in place with the sandbags piled at each end. The post had been an old mail station, but somewhere along the line, someone had staked it out for military purposes, since it sat on the crest of a gentle hill at the western end of Llordian—the highest point amid the flat fields and sometime marsh grass.

I swallowed, listening to the shouting and muttering as the crowd flowed across the dusty parade ground toward the perimeter stockade. There didn't seem to be so many people once they were out in the open—scarcely a hundred or so, and mostly women and children, with a few disabled troublemakers like the tall one-armed man. Not even a challenge for the twenty or so armed troopers.

"There they are! Hiding behind their walls and guns!" The one-armed man's voice carried to the stockade.

One trooper lifted a projectile rifle. Before he could bring it to bear, a subforcer knocked it down and hissed something at the man.

"There they are! Protecting the rich hoarders and taking their cut while you go hungry! Look at them! They won't always have guns!"

The crowd milled around, listening to the high-pitched voice of the agitator.

The sweat rolled down my face, turning dust on my skin into mud.

Buzzzzz . . . buzzzzz . . . The black flies kept trying to land on my neck and bite, but I used a free hand to wave them away.

"See how they hide behind their guns! Do they look hungry? They aren't hungry. They don't have children who cry themselves to sleep."

"No, they don't have families any more. They already lost them!" That same stupid screaming voice again—mine. "At least you still have your children. At least we're trying to keep you from being killed in your sleep!"

"He's lying! Don't listen. He's lying!"

That was the wrong thing for the one-armed man to say. The crowd muttered, mumbled, and stopped.

"Why'd you say that?" demanded the subforcer who appeared at my elbow.

"Talk is cheaper than guns or bullets. And my family is dead." I turned to look at him.

"You . . ." he snorted. "I might have known."

At that moment, I nearly saw red. Bright red. But I just looked.

Finally, he looked to the side and walked away.

"Verlyt . . ." the oath was soft.

I glanced at the trooper beside me.

"Swashte will hate you for that."

"Probably." I didn't really care. Wryan had been absolutely right. Odin Thor would lose the entire province without a shot if he didn't get some food to those children. And soon.

As it became clear that the crowd had no intention of even halfheartedly storming the station, the senior forcer stood. "Stand down. First squad, hold the stockade. Purtell, deploy your men."

I ambled over to the station to turn in the projectile rifle.

Jerlyk grinned as he followed me. "Big mouth."

"Better than bullets," I repeated.

Swashte, the subforcer I had glared down, was talking to the senior forcer, Gleddell, and gesturing in my direction. Gleddell looked bored and shrugged. Swashte headed toward me.

"Trooper, I don't like your attitude. The senior forcer feels that you and I could use a little extra workout. Just to loosen up the muscles."

I shrugged. "If you think so."

"We could have a good match if you're not afraid of getting messed up."

"You sure that Gleddell doesn't want a disabled subforcer?"

"Verlyt, you really do have a mouth, Trooper. You really do."

I was tired of games. "What rules, Subforcer Swashte?"

"Just a friendly match, Trooper. Don't need rules for that, do we?"

"Not for a friendly match, I suppose. But if you should trip and break anything, I certainly wouldn't continue. What you do is up to you, of course." I stepped back and stripped off my tunic and equipment belt.

Swashte did the same and thrust his tunic and belt at a youngster right out of training.

"Ready, Trooper?"

I nodded, slipping into a balanced posture, half-looking into the undertime to anticipate his attack.

Quicker than he looked, Swashte feinted with a straightened left arm, then threw a half-kick at my back knee.

I could have played with him. Instead, I broke his planted leg and snapped his arm. Henriod had taught me well, and I cheated.

"Verlyt!"

"Did you see that?"

"Hell-fired killer . . ."

Gleddell had turned white, as he saw Swashte writhing on the ground.

I half-bowed to the grimacing subforcer. "I regret our friendly match was so short. Any time you want a rematch, I'd be pleased to oblige you."

Then I walked over to Gleddell. "I strongly suggest that Trooper Jerlyk's and my mission here is complete."

Gleddell shook his lank black hair off his forehead, ran his eyes over me as if he could not quite believe what he saw.

"Who are you?"

"Trooper Sammis, sir."

He glanced at my unmarked uniform, then at the ground. "Two nice bits of work today, Trooper, three if I understand what Nylen told me. I don't like any of them." He paused. "I hope I never see you again."

"Yes, sir."

"That's all."

I saluted him. It made him feel happier.

Everyone besides Jerlyk backed away as I walked back toward the barracks.

XXXIX

THE TRIP BACK from Llordian was long and boring. But the new diet must have helped. Neither one of us felt sick when we arrived back at base. Jerlyk hurried off, presumably to find Mellorie.

Somehow, despite that, I hoped Mellorie—or someone—would be waiting. No one was, and the room smelled musty. I opened the windows and let the wind in. The unseasonal warmth of Llordian was fading into normal early winter—wet, cold, and raw—still preferable to the mustiness.

Turning on the single lamp improved the gloomy late afternoon, and, after I had unpacked my few items, closing the window reduced the chill.

After taking care of my laundry, I braved the grimy shower and changed into a clean undress uniform, then headed for dinner—early.

Apparently, I wasn't the only one anxious for company. Gerloc was pacing, and Jerlyk had pulled out a chair from one of the unused tables.

Amenda walked in within minutes of me.

"Sammis, you're back." She was wearing a clean, if rumpled, blue tunic and trousers.

"So is Jerlyk. The ConFeds only like us in small doses. You're looking nice tonight."

She made a face. "How could you say that? The maids all left, and took all the small irons. I'm a rumpled mess."

"Advantage of ConFed uniforms, I guess. What else had been going on here?" I kept my tone light.

"Besides boring meals, a new diving schedule for everyone, and the disappearance of most of the support staff?"

"Greffin?" I hoped the chef at least would stay.

"He was still here at mid-day, but he was complaining to the doctor."

"Things are getting tough all over."

For some reason, Amenda nodded.

Then Mellorie walked in. Unlike Amenda or me, she had on another tailored coverall and a matching jacket which was definitely unrumpled. The scrape of Jerlyk's chair told me he had seen her as well. She looked past the rest of us and favored him with a smile that would have melted ice.

As I shook my head, Amenda cleared her throat. "What are you thinking?"

"Nothing . . . well . . . not nothing . . ."

"Are you jealous?" She seemed disinterested in the question, looking absently at Gerloc.

I had to laugh. "It was nice while it lasted."

"What did you mean about things being tough all over?" She acted as if her mind were in Eastron, or farther away.

Like me, I guess, making small talk. So I told her a bit about the problems at Llordian, just how the farmers didn't care if the townies starved, and how the ConFeds just wanted the supply levies.

"Sammis, don't you see?" Her eyes focused on me.

"See what? The farmers and the townies are going to be at each other's necks. Odin Thor doesn't have enough troops to police every area. Besides, if we take sides . . ."

Amenda nodded. "What will happen if we don't?"

I thought about that. "The townies will attack the farmers, and only the strong ones will survive."

"Will they?"

Amenda's question jolted me.

"Why wouldn't they?"

"The farmers are spread out. If they get together, that leaves their stores unprotected. Aren't there a lot more townspeople than farmers?"

Most of the successful farmers were the larger ones, who had their own equipment shops, even draft animals, and plenty of seed reserves. Some had enough hired hands to use as guards. Against petty bandits, at least. Their success against an enraged mob was another question.

"We're trading etheline for food, though."

"For how long, Sammis?"

I had to shrug. I didn't know.

"That brings up another question." Amenda pursed her lips, then tried to pat down her wrinkled tunic as Arlean walked through the doorway.

Arlean's tunic looked wrinkled, too, if not quite so rumpled as Amenda's.

"How long can the steamers run without parts?" pursued Amenda. "Even if the etheline-food trades and food taxes get us through this winter, what happens next year, or when we run out of etheline to trade?"

I didn't have a good answer, but I didn't have to come up with it right then.

XL

THE PORRIDGE WAS cold, and the brown bread was harder than ever. All the other divers had gone, late as I had staggered down.

I ladled the remaining congealed cereal into a large bowl and sprinkled it with a double handful of raisins, covering both raisins and porridge with molasses. A mess, but one with enough calories.

"Sammis?" I looked up from where I was shoveling the cereal in.

Deric's lips were tight, and he squinted, even though the morning skies were cloudy, and the lights in the dining area dim.

"Yes, Deric?" I mumbled. The heavy porridge tasted like glue, even with the handful of dried raisins I had poured over the glop. I missed the buns and the fresh fruit. Funny, how little you need luxuries when you're worrying about survival. Then, when you have them for a while, you miss them more than if you never had them.

"The colonel-general has requested your presence in his office."

"Does the doctor know?"

"She . . . asked me to convey the message."

I swallowed the last of the gray mess and followed it with a deep pull of water. "I'll head right there."

Deric turned and left without a word.

What did Odin Thor want?

Another ConFed I didn't know sat behind an empty desk outside the colonel-general's office.

"Sammis," I announced. "The colonel-general requested my presence."

"I'll tell him." The trooper, an arrogant-looking tough nearly as tall as Odin-Thor, remained seated.

Because I was me, I looked undertime to see what the esteemed colonel-general was doing. He was doing nothing at all, and doing it alone.

"The colonel-general is alone, and he's not engaged. So I suggest you tell him I'm here."

"I'll tell him when it's time."

I walked past him and toward the door.

His hand grabbed at my shoulder.

Thud.

The arrogant expression was replaced by a puzzled one as he looked up from the floor.

"Don't *ever* lay hands on me."

"The colonel-general . . ."

". . . will probably do absolutely nothing," added a new voice.

Henriod, the head of the scouts for Odin Thor, stood there. "It's good to see you again, Sammis. You've improved some more."

I shrugged. "I try. Jerlyk and I work out almost every day."

By now, the ConFed orderly had scrambled to his feet.

"Hasslek, this is former trooper Sammis." Henriod grinned. "Possibly the most dangerous man in either the travelers or the ConFeds." Then he looked at me. "Odin Thor was amused at what you did to Swashte. Told him that unless he got his act together, he'd set up a return match."

That didn't sound like Odin Thor at all. Not at all, not when he had been so adamant about not revealing that some ConFeds were divers.

Hasslek nodded and backed in through the door I had been about to open.

"If he's using me as a threat, things must really be getting tight."

Hasslek was standing in the door again, leaving it open. "The colonel-general will see you, gentlemen."

While I had been promoted a bit in Hasslek's regard, why Odin Thor wanted to see both Henriod and me was another question.

"Forcer Henriod, Trooper Sammis . . . if you would have a seat . . ." Odin Thor was all smiles.

I trusted him even less than before, but I sat down in the battered wooden chair next to the old and expansive red oak desk. Henriod sat in the chair next to me, leaving a vacant chair beside the closed outside window, which rattled in the morning wind.

"Sammis, how did you find Llordian?"

I shrugged. "Townies are close to starving, with no way to get food. Don't trust the farmers, but they trust us even less."

"Henriod, what is our current strength?"

"All bodies, sir?"

Odin Thor nodded.

"The main maintenance facility in Esterly still has about three hundred. Perhaps almost that many here. Another two hundred or so in places like Halfprince and Llordian. Add to that maybe . . . what? Fifty travelers . . . ? I'd say nine hundred, counting those I don't know."

"How many of the townspeople are able-bodied enough for even light ConFed duty?"

Henriod looked at me. I looked at Henriod. We both looked at Odin Thor.

"Not many," I volunteered. "Probably mostly women."

"The ConFeds don't take women," pointed out Henriod.

"Then you've got damned few . . ."

"So there are very few able-bodied townspeople left, but they threaten present food supplies and future crops. Is that a fair assessment?"

"Not totally, Colonel-General." Henriod had a thin sheen of perspiration on his forehead as he went on. "The townspeople are the only remnant of crafting skills left. Over time, their absence would be felt."

Their absence? What was Odin Thor proposing? Murder? Genocide?

"Anything else?"

"What about the next generation?" I asked.

Odin Thor almost smiled when he looked at me. "What about them, Sammis?"

"Without the townies, you won't have one," I blurted.

"There is that," admitted Odin Thor. "But, based on your observations and those of Forcer Henriod, I do not feel that the ConFeds—or your travelers . . . or timedivers, if you prefer—should continue to impose discipline where we are not wanted."

Odin Thor couldn't be serious.

"It's very simple, really," the Colonel-General continued. "We will remain only where we are wanted. Since Llordian seems to have mixed feelings about our presence and services, we will hold a totally free election. We'll even let them conduct it. If the townspeople and the farmers in the surrounding area want us to leave and vote for us to leave, we will."

"A truly honest election?" I asked.

"Why not? You indicated that it would be difficult to hold the place against a really determined mob without killing a large number of townspeople. We don't need to risk our limited manpower where we aren't wanted."

"But what about supplies?" asked Henriod.

"If we're careful, we have enough to last until early summer without any more levies, but I anticipate that some areas will request our presence."

"If the Llordians get to vote, won't you have to let others vote?" I asked.

"Absolutely. Because this is a first case, I would appreciate it if we make no announcements except in Llordian until after the election is completed." Odin Thor shook his head. "No. I'm not planning to use force if they vote us out. I expect the Llordians will. We can't stage elections all over the place at once. They will have to be phased so that we can pull out of areas that don't want us in an orderly fashion."

Henriod looked at me, and I looked at Henriod. Odin Thor was sincere in allowing the elections, but the whole thing still smelled.

"Why are we here?" Henriod's words reflected his puzzlement.

"You, Forcer Henriod, need to develop a withdrawal plan that will ensure we leave Llordian in a way that does not invite any attack or violence against us. That is very important. We must be perceived as impartial and not imposing our will by force in any way. That image could be endangered if any riots or outbreaks occur. That means the instant the vote is in, we must be on the way out, before it becomes known that we are leaving. Likewise, we cannot make advance preparations that can be seen or interpreted as evidence that we have decided to leave before the vote.

"Do you understand?"

Henriod nodded. I could understand why *I* would be concerned about such a withdrawal, but I couldn't see why Odin Thor would be.

"What about me?"

"Yes . . . Sammis. I have two reasons. First, you are in effect the ConFed's liaison with the travelers. Second, I would like you to use your diving ability to monitor and record the process at Llordian. We need to document on viewtape that we allowed full and free elections, that we left the area immediately, and any later follow-up. For rather obvious reasons and for this to be objective, we cannot have our observer visible after the elections."

I nodded. If any observer remained after the ConFeds left, he or she would certainly be a clear target. "Do we have any recording equipment left?"

Odin Thor smiled again. "We have some very good portable equipment which Eltar has restored. You can work with him, I trust."

Eltar? He still talked to me, unlike some of the others. "Yes, Colonel."

Odin Thor almost glared at me for using his real rank. "Will you make the arrangements for recording and let your fellow-travelers know that we will be holding free elections in Llordian, and, later, in other communities?"

I nodded. "Is there anything else?"

"For now that's all. When you're ready, get together with Eltar."

Odin Thor looked at Henriod. "Do you think you could have your plans ready by the day after tomorrow?"

"Shouldn't be a problem, sir."

"Good." Odin Thor stood. "Thank you both."

Since we were clearly dismissed, we left.

Outside in the chill under the gray clouds that promised freezing rain or worse, I stopped and looked at Henriod.

"Does this make sense?"

"In a way," answered the forcer. "We'd lose too many men if we had to put down wide-scale riots. If we didn't stop them, we'd lose any credibility."

"So you think Odin Thor is making a graceful withdrawal and using the free election bit to place the blame on the Llordians?"

Henriod shrugged. "That's the way it looks."

It did look that way, but I still kept remembering Odin Thor's smile.

My next stop was Dr. Relorn's office. She had some explaining to do, and she needed to know about Odin Thor's plans. I just dropped undertime and slid into the laboratory she used as an office.

She was alone, twiddling with one of the consoles.

"Greetings, Sammis." She turned in the swivel chair to face me. This time she had on a tan tunic and trousers. The cut was flattering, but not the color, which left her washed-out looking.

"You were expecting me."

"Who else would you tell about Odin Thor's latest scheme?"

She sounded so matter-of-fact that I felt like leaving. But no one else seemed to understand anything. So instead of leaving, I said nothing.

Neither did she.

I kept my mouth shut.

"Sammis . . . you can either accept the truth and keep growing up. Or you can pout, in which case I won't bother to spend time with you."

"Both you and Odin Thor are playing some type of game I still don't understand, and both of you are pushing me around."

Wryan looked at me, almost from head to toe. "Odin Thor is playing a game." She paused. "It could look like I am."

"Are you?"

"No. I try to tell you, but you don't want to hear it. And sometimes you don't hear what I say the way I meant."

If her words weren't an evasion, I hadn't ever heard one. "That's an evasion."

She grinned and looked like a youngster. "You're right."

I was getting tired of people deciding what was best for Sammis to know.

"I can only tell you that I have your best interests at heart." She smiled softly. "Mine, too, I hope."

Despite my anger, the softness and the near-wistful tone of her voice kept me from lashing out. Whatever she had in mind, it wasn't deadly or malicious, and that would have to do for the present. I shrugged.

"How about my quarters?" she asked. "It is warmer than here."

That was fine with me, and I followed her from the laboratory after she switched off the console and most of the lights. The laboratory seemed dark and ancient with the lights off, like a relic from the past.

Again, she flicked on the single lamp on the table, just like the first time I had visited her, and nodded toward a chair.

"Do you have anything . . . to eat?"

"You," she said, "are always hungry."

"Curse of the breed."

Wryan put out a plate with a chyst, a chunk of old yellow cheese, and a row of hard crackers. Before sitting down, she sliced several smaller pieces of cheese, taking one of the crackers and a slice for herself.

"Look who else is hungry," I had to mumble because my mouth was full.

She smiled, her mouth full as well.

"Odin Thor's going to offer open elections to the Llordians. Let them vote on whether the ConFeds stay or go. He thinks they'll vote us out. He wants me to play reporter and get the whole thing on viewtape."

Frowning, Wryan took another cracker and cut some more cheese. "After they vote no on the ConFeds, what does he plan?"

"He told Henriod to arrange for pullout, one that would get us out before anything happened. He wants me to tape the pullout and the aftermath."

Wryan finished chewing the cheese and hard cracker as she went for a pitcher of water and two tumblers—the heavy crystal ones that reminded me of my father's Dyleraan. She poured me a glassful, then one for herself. "You think he's telling the truth?"

"Yes. That's what bothers me."

"Did he say what he'll do in the other towns?"

"He said they could have elections, too, but they'd have to be phased. Why go to all that trouble? He didn't spend the last year building up all this power just to let it go."

"You're right. He didn't."

The chair was getting uncomfortable, and I shifted my weight. "So what is he doing? And what happened to his plan to attack the Frost Giants?"

"I don't know . . . for certain. But you had better make sure you do a good job recording what happens at Llordian."

Wryan had an idea of what the colonel-general was doing. She also wasn't telling.

"Why aren't you telling me?"

"I might be wrong. You need to figure out why people act the way they do without relying on me or on Odin Thor."

I swallowed hard on her words. Relying on her? Especially on Odin Thor? She wouldn't relent, and after I finished the cheese and the chyst, I left, diving back to my room before heading out to find Eltar.

XLI

CARRYING THE PORTABLE equipment that Eltar had put together wasn't all that difficult, and that alone showed me how much stronger I was getting. The equipment was easily twice the weight of the nerve gas grenades, and I had no trouble with it—provided I didn't try it when I was hungry.

"Sammis," protested Eltar the first time I popped back into the small corner of maintenance that Odin Thor had set aside for him, "I'll never get used to you appearing out of nowhere."

He did, though.

I started out by taking shots of Llordian proper—breaking out on the tops of buildings, odd corners, anywhere to provide an accurate picture. Getting the people was harder, and I finally ended up dressed like a ragged peddler. The pack contained all the gear except the hand-held recorder. Even that was difficult, since several times I had to sit for hours in dusty corners just to get a few minutes of tape when no one was looking. I tried to record from the undertime, but the equipment just didn't work there.

Getting shots of the posters announcing the referendum was easier. Since everyone crowded around each one posted, no one was watching a ragged peddler. Later, I went out at dawn and took some clear shots of the posters.

"You expect me to mix and splice and put together something that looks professional?" Eltar protested.

"No. Just something that looks honest and real."

"Honest and real—from you?" interrupted another voice—Rarden.

When I'd faced him down at the divers' mess, I thought I'd seen the last of the troublesome ConFed. "Yes, honest and real." I kept my voice cheerful.

Wearing a grease suit, he was carrying a toolbox for heavy maintenance work on the steamers. "This is *honest* work."

"Very honest work. Without the steamers, we'd be in big trouble."

"Not like your sneak thieving."

I shrugged.

"Not like sneak thieves," Rarden repeated.

"Rarden . . ." I answered slowly. "You don't like me, and I don't like you. If I wanted you dead, you would be, and no one could save your ass. So . . . why don't you think instead of opening your mouth without thinking?"

Both Rarden and Eltar turned pale.

When Rarden had carted his toolbox to the steamer at the far end of the bay, Eltar glanced at me, then at the floor. "Did you mean what you said?"

"What?" I replied absently, wondering why Rarden had hated me so much even before he had discovered I was a diver.

"That nothing could save him if you wanted him dead?"

At that point, I wished I hadn't said it. "Yes and no," I hedged. "Do you really want an answer?"

"I think I deserve one, Sammis." Eltar was still pale.

"You do." I sighed. "It's like this. What would happen if I appeared right behind Rarden with a projectile gun? Could he stop me?"

"Of course not."

"And who else could do that?"

"The other divers."

"But whom among them would want to?"

"Oh . . ."

"So . . . I could dispose of Rarden any time. But everyone would know it was me, and what would keep Carlis from keeping his own projectile rifle handy to pot me at a distance when I wasn't even aware of him?"

Eltar nodded slowly. "You need to eat and sleep just like everyone else. But . . ."

I knew where he was headed. "If . . . if I wanted to live like a total sneak thief and recluse the rest of my life, never trusting anyone, with every person's hand against me, like they were against the witches of Eastron, then I *might* be able to run around killing people. Except then, all the other divers would eliminate me as a danger. And they could."

The ConFed who might be my friend looked only slightly relieved.

I tried one more time. "Look, Eltar. I got caught by Odin Thor's men because there was no place else to go. Now it's going to get worse."

"What?"

"The farmers—those that are left—aren't farming enough to feed everyone. The townies are close to starvation, and everyone hates the ConFeds. There's enough food to go around now. What about next year?"

"Can't you, and the other divers . . ."

I sighed, loudly. "Eltar, this is about as much weight as I can carry, and I'm one of the stronger divers. Second, I'd have to find spare food to carry, and the situation here is the same all over Query."

"Oh . . ." Eltar looked pale again. I was doing great violence to his mental well-being.

I shrugged. "That's why I'm still supporting Odin Thor. He seems to be the only chance. Verlyt knows it's a slim one. And who knows if we'll ever get around to the Frost Giant problem?"

Nodding, Eltar turned to the workbench. "Let's see that last tape pack. Are you going out again soon?"

"Not until after noon meal." I handed over the tape pack I had extracted from the recorder.

"When are the elections?"

"Two days."

He laughed mirthlessly. "Then we'll see."

I nodded. We would indeed, but what we might see was another question.

XLII

ON THE DAY of the referendum in Llordian, the ragged and dirty peddler was back in harness, recording the happy Llordian townies as they cast their ballots.

My site was in the market, behind a pottery stand run by an old woman who never seemed to sell anything. I had set out various small carvings and trinkets in front of me, on the stone ledge next to the empty fountain—it had been empty the first time I saw Llordian and still was.

While I waited, I carved—mostly things like napkin rings and awkward grossjays. Terrible carvings, but sometimes people actually offered me something for them, usually a piece of fruit, a roll, or cast-off clothing. I took the food, but not the clothing.

I never spoke, just shook my head and pointed to my throat. By election day, the pottery woman just told people not to bother the mute peddler.

The townies all crowed as they stuffed paper ballot after paper ballot into the big boxes. A pair of armed ConFeds watched each box, but only to make sure no one walked off with it. They ignored the people stuffing in two or three ballots, all marked with big black crosses in the space indicating the ConFeds should leave.

"That one . . ." grunted a bearded man.

He pointed at a carved wooden ring, a crude copy of a silver napkin ring I had remembered from childhood.

I nodded as he held up a small copper—one of the few coins I had been offered. Then again, the napkin ring was one of my better efforts.

As he took the ring, the sound of a steamer hissing whispered into the square. Two large farmers, flanked with guards of their own, scanned the ballot box, but did not leave the steamer.

I risked getting caught and trained the recorder hidden in my pack at the disgusted look on the white-haired man's face. The younger farmer, as big as Odin Thor, but with skin like cream toffee, shook his head.

The steamer hissed again and picked up speed.

The bearded man, now walking from the dry fountain toward the steamer, spat on the stones in the direction of the farmers. An urchin—one who had tried to steal one of my wooden grossjays—made an obscene gesture. Two women hurried from the steamer's path, covering their faces with scarves. Another boy picked up a stone, only to have it knocked from his hand by his mother.

Not a single other farmer did I see, and, after I crept away in the late afternoon, I back-checked all of the other polling locations. No farmers to speak of.

Under the cover of darkness, Henriod implemented his pullout, and when the townies arrived the next morning brandishing the polling results, the old postal station that had been the ConFed fort was empty, the gate wide open.

I was hidden behind the low parapet on the roof, recording the faces, the dust, and the townies' indignation.

"Swine . . ."

". . . knew before we finished . . ."

". . . last of them . . ."

Crack . . . One desultory stone clacked against the open gate.

". . . anything left?"

A handful of older men, including the ubiquitous one-armed man, entered the main building, rummaged through every room. I could hear crashes and slams and other sounds.

In time, they left, empty-handed, grumbling, swearing, with the old postal station a shambles. So did I, bringing the footage back to Eltar.

Then I had noon meal, by myself, and took a nap.

Something was going to happen at Llordian later. When or what, I didn't know, but I could feel it. Because I couldn't explain it, I didn't even try and talk about it. Besides, Wryan seemed to be avoiding me, and no one else would understand.

So I slept, not well. First, my room was too cold. Then the sun came out and heated everything up, and I woke up sweating.

I wanted to dive out to Llordian and see what was happening, but figured that was unwise, at least on an empty stomach. That reasoning got me down to the snack table in the divers' mess, where I polished off two chysts, a large chunk of cheese and a handful of very hard crackers, all washed down with warm and almost sour citril.

Gerloc wandered in when I was finishing, nodded, picked up a chyst, and wandered out.

Was everybody avoiding me? Or was I giving off some sort of signal?

At the front door I looked south, up toward Mount Persnol, where the clouds were turning cherry pink in the late winter twilight, wondering what, if anything, might be happening in Llordian.

With a sigh, I walked back to my room and pulled on a black foul-weather sweater and the darkest trousers I owned, making a note that we really ought to develop a set of dark uniforms for time-diving. Then I added a dark jacket and gloves. If I were going to skulk around in the shadows, I might as well look like the shadows.

Recorder in hand, pack on back, I dropped under the now and slipped out to Llordian, breaking out on a little ledge on the top of the meeting house overlooking the square.

A heavy door shut somewhere.

". . . if you think . . .

". . . too young . . . at that price . . ."

Two figures whispered in the shadows nearly directly underneath my perch.

A bell rang softly in the distance.

Nothing was happening, and I was frowning. Then it struck me. Of course nothing was happening in Llordian.

My first breakout was on the roof of a long wooden porch on the front of a timber and stone farmhouse.

Scruff. I winced at the sound. The roof sloped, and I had skidded on the heavy tiles, trying to keep my balance.

"What's that? Scurrit? Scurrit!"

"There's nothing out there. Ferly would have hissed, or something."

"Keep your voices down," added another voice, hard and female.

I eased myself flat on the tiles, grateful their finish was rough enough to keep my place in spite of the gentle slope.

For a time, everything was silent, except for the whisper of the wind, which, light as it was, wasted no time in chilling me.

"Stop it," whispered the female voice.

"Annya, none of those townies will be around tonight. It'll take a couple of nights before they're convinced the ConFeds are gone."

"Maybe . . . but what did we hear? Ghosts?" The woman's voice was low.

"Could have been a branch scraping on the barn wall."

"Maybe. We'll wait a while. Then you watch until midnight . . ."

I didn't stay any longer.

After checking several other farms I had visited "officially" as a ConFed, I was convinced the farm woman was right. If the townies were going to attack any farms, it wouldn't be that night.

Which night? How long? I didn't know, and I wasn't about to tell Odin Thor. And Wryan wasn't about to do my thinking for me.

So, day by day, I kept checking and recording, watching as the townies whispered and the farmers worked towards spring, weapons always nearby.

XLIII

FIVE RAGGED FIGURES—three older men and two women—trudged up the hard dirt road, their feet barely raising the heavy dust under the bright late winter sun. The men wore blanket jackets with patches, the women old shawls, folded and refolded around them. All five had tattered trousers and shapeless shoes.

Two farmers armed with antique projectile rifles stood behind the wooden gate, their shoulders and heads outlined against the green-blue sky. Both wore heavy leather jackets—the kind that were quilted on the inside.

The five stopped a good rod from the gate. From the underbrush uphill, I caught both the townies and the farmers in the recorder.

"Peace," croaked the lead ancient.

"What do you want?" asked the heavier farmer, his brown hair shot with gray, as he leveled the weapon at the townspeople.

"Food . . . our children are hungry. Our gardens are bare, and the convoys have stopped coming."

"We need food . . ." protested a heavy-set woman.

"You don't look like it, woman."

"Our children need food." Her breath was a thin line of white smoke.

"We don't have any, not if we want to plant."

"You're hoarding it . . ." A thin woman at the back whined.

The farmer sighed. "You don't know . . . you know nothing . . ." His face was weathered and lined.

"You won't give us food?"

"There isn't any."

The younger farmer—not much older than I was—frowned.

"See . . . even *he* doesn't believe you." The white-haired whiner jabbed a finger.

"Just go on back to town." The older farmer gestured with the gun. The younger one leveled his own weapon.

"So we can watch our children starve while you hoard?"

"Woman, my seed grains wouldn't feed a handful of people, and then you'd have nothing next year."

"We won't last until next year."

The farmer gestured with the weapon again. "I can't help you."

"You won't . . ."

". . . Verlyt judge you, miserly . . ."

They turned back toward Llordian, their shoulders stooped and their feet scuffing. As the townspeople dwindled into stick figures straggling back along the road to Llordian, the younger farmer caught the older man's eyes.

"They'd just take everything because they're hungry now. If we gave them what we could afford, it wouldn't be enough. Then they'd be back demanding more. And more." The older farmer sighed.

"They will be anyway. At night."

The younger man looked down at the gate, then at the stone wall that ran gently uphill toward the thicket where I lay concealed. Finally, he looked back at the gate. "Think we should have asked those ConFeds for help?"

The older man shrugged. "Which thief do you ask into your home? Now, the ConFeds look better."

The younger man shrugged in turn and looked back up the road to the farmhouse. "Gero will be down in a while. Need to see about those etheline globes. You think tonight?"

The other shook his head. "Be a while yet."

XLIV

TORCHES. A LINE of the flickering lights showed the townies snaking through the darkness.

I didn't know how well the scene would record, but I did the best I could from an exposed hilltop overlooking the road. Then I dropped undertime.

Anger was a smoldering mist, compounded with fear, that shrouded the entire mob. It was a mob, carrying staffs, knives, a few dart rifles, and one or two projectile rifles—ConFed issue.

They didn't chant. They weren't marching, but there must have been more than a hundred of them walking up that dark and winter-dusty road.

At the head of the mob was a one-armed man. He gestured; he gesticulated; he exhorted.

They responded, flowing uphill toward the gate and a handful of farmers.

Since Odin Thor would most definitely want a record of the confrontation, I broke out near where I had recorded the first demands of the townies.

"Food . . . we want food . . . food . . . we want food . . ." The cracked voice of the one-armed man ran like an off-key note through the muttering chorus.

"Ready?" asked a voice from the darkness below me.

"Not yet. Wait until they get closer."

A spark flickered on the farm road, momentarily illuminating two men beside a wooden framework.

". . . food . . . we want food . . . food . . . we want food . . ."

The chorus swelled as the mob straggled toward the dark gate, oblivious to the farmers hidden there.

A blaze of yellow flame splashed across the clay of the road a few rods before the leading edge of the mob.

The chorus died into mutters—momentarily.

"Just go home, and no one will get hurt!" boomed a voice from the darkness behind and below me.

". . . food . . . we want food . . . food . . . we want food . . ." The one-armed man began the chant again, and the crowd picked up on his words.

This time the flame splattered nearly at the feet of the one-armed man.

"Just go home!"

". . . food . . . we want food . . . we want food . . ."

"AAEEEEEEeeeeee . . ." The blankets of a woman burst into flames.

"Killers! Killers! Get the killers!" screamed the one-armed man, as he grabbed a youth by the arm and pushed him toward the gate, running for an instant with him. Then he did the same with a young woman . . . and another man, older.

". . . food . . . we want food . . ."

Crack! One of the farmers' projectile rifles sounded, but I couldn't see anyone fall as the mob began to lurch toward the farmers.

The one-armed man kept alternating chants, either "get the killers" or "food . . . we want food" as the townies surged forward.

Crack! This time an older woman staggered.

By now, the smoldering oil and smoke gave a hellish atmosphere to the road. My own reaction was to slip under the now and take out the one-armed troublemaker, but I wasn't certain if that would make the situation better or worse. Then again, maybe I really didn't feel like either side deserved help.

Crack! Crack! Crack! This time the shots came from the mob.

"They got Gero!"

"We can do it!" screamed the one-armed man. "We want food . . . food . . . we want food . . ."

The mob surged toward the wooden gate, and the handful of farmers scrambled back up the road, leaving one lying face down by the wooden framework, and another trying to lift the wounded or dead man.

As he saw the mob pouring over and around the gate, the last farmer released the body, then bent down and lit the top globe on the pile of globes by the wooden framework. He sprinted uphill after the others.

The mob continued toward the down farmer.

WWWWHHHHHSSSSTTTTTTT!!!!! The entire pile of etheline missiles burst into flames, spewing fireballs in all directions and turning a good dozen townies into instant torches.

Using the light of the human bonfire, the farmers dropped three more townies. But the killings went almost unnoticed as the mob moved toward the farm buildings near the hill crest.

". . . food . . . we want . . . food . . ."

Somehow, the chant and the smell of burning flesh got to me, even if no one else paid attention. I retched.

"There's one on the hillside!"

I dropped undertime before both sides finished targeting the unmistakable sound of guts being turned inside out.

I could have carried off two or three people, but which ones, and where? And for what purpose? They would have hated me for not taking their part, or feared me for my ability, or both.

Instead, I staggered back to my not very clean quarters, washing off in the grimy facilities down the hall. Once again, no one noticed. Or if they did, they ignored me, smelling as I did of burning and death.

I don't think I slept, just lay there, thinking about bodies burning like torches, and that reminded me of Allyson.

At dawn, after a healthy helping of bland fare—porridge, cheese and hard crackers, I reshouldered my pack and started back to Llordian.

The morning light showed the trail of bodies up the road. I stopped counting after the first twenty. Besides the farmer shot in the first moments, I only found one other farmer's body.

Greasy black smoke wisps, interspersed with puffs of white smoke or steam, still smoldered from heaps along the road and from the blackened stone walls of the farmhouse, the silo, and the two barns. The tile roofs had collapsed into the buildings when the supporting beams had burned. A trail of corn betrayed someone's success at looting.

A few rods farther on a dark splotch stained the stone fence enclosing the small front yard of the farmhouse. Beside the stone walk, littered with small pieces of charred wood, lay a small hand-carved doll.

Overhead, the gray clouds emphasized the desolation. The wind kept the stench of burned grain and charred flesh from becoming overpowering, and I managed to hold back another round of retching as I recorded it all.

No livestock remained, but whether the farmers had recovered it or the townies had made off with it I couldn't tell. What I could tell was that the townies had destroyed far more than they obtained.

Chhichii . . . chichiii

Two grossjays perched in a bare-limbed tree.

Chhiichiii . . .

Another scavenger fluttered down out of sight on the road where most of the townies had died.

After another sweeping pan of the destruction, I dropped undertime, heading back toward Mount Persnol.

XLV

OVER THE NEXT ten-day, I recorded, after the fact, the results of another three attacks around Llordian. I refused to witness or record another attack in progress, since, short of killing off the townies wholesale, no reasonable solution was possible.

Wryan and I argued over it—one of the first real arguments we had.

"You don't think losing a leader will stop them?" I had asked late one night, since we still did not meet openly. She was sipping hot cider.

"No. It's a structural problem. Removing one person won't solve anything." Wryan set down her heavy mug.

"No one else can lead them so effectively."

"Sammis, that isn't the problem." She gave me an exasperated look, the kind that I hated, perhaps because my mother had done the same. So had Dr. Wendengless.

"They're starving."

Wryan shook her head. "They're hungry. They don't know what starving is. Not yet." The coolness in her voice chilled me.

"Then what is the problem?"

"You tell me."

"Why?"

"Because I can't afford to do your thinking for you."

Sounding like the difficult student I didn't really want to be, I asked again. "Why?"

"That's enough. Sometimes . . ." She gave me an exasperated sigh this time, not just a look.

"All right," I conceded. "They don't understand the entire concept of seed grain."

"They don't care, but that's not the real problem."

I almost sighed. "They hate the farmers, and they hate us."

Wryan shrugged, as if to ask what else was new.

"The farmers don't trust them."

"True."

"So . . . that's the problem."

"That is *a* problem, but it's not the critical one." She yawned. "Now, it's late, and you'll probably have to record more disasters for Odin Thor—"

"You agree with all this recording? With Odin Thor letting Llordian tear itself apart?"

"Yes. It's the only thing. It may not work."

I shook my head. Sometimes she was so warm, and others . . . well, then she was the cool and calculating Dr. Relorn.

I dropped back undertime to my single room and its stack of equipment and viewtapes to think over what she had said. I didn't get to sleep immediately, not with the old memories of smoke and a burned-out steamer and the newer recollections of greasy smoke, blackened empty walls, and the charred heaps that had been people.

Of the three attacks around Llordian, two had resulted in burnouts like the first one I had observed. In the third, the farmers had killed nearly fifty townies—mostly with the etheline firebombs—and someone had picked off the one-armed man.

The morning after our argument, I began another undertime sweep of the Llordian area—only to find another small and burned-out farm. Few if any of the farmers had gotten away.

Most of the grain had been carted off in the farm's own steam truck. I found it stored in an old house in Llordian, guarded by three townies armed with ConFed-issue projectile guns.

At least one slaughtered hog was being roasted in a pit contrived in the dry fountain in the town square.

More important, urchins acting as sentries had been posted on every road leading to Llordian. I dropped in out of nowhere and told Odin Thor.

"Getting organized, are they?" He just smiled. "Very interesting. Just keep a close watch, Sammis, if you would. Let me know what happens."

"Don't you think we should do something?"

"What?" asked the colonel-general, smiling his false smile. "They don't like us. They certainly don't want us around. You think I should risk our forces for people who would attack us?"

I shrugged. What he said was certainly true. Yet it rang false.

"Let me know as things develop," he repeated, looking at the door.

I got the hint. "I will." I dropped undertime.

As I wandered around my room, straightening it up for lack of anything better to do, and using the sinks in the facilities to wash uniforms, I wondered if I could look foretime, to get a hint of what might happen.

According to all the texts and materials Deric had forced on me, and whose "training" I was ignoring on the pretext of the Llordian assignment, other divers could break out in future times in other planetary systems.

So . . . after I hung up the uniforms and made a desultory effort at cleaning up the sanitary facilities somewhat, I went and stuffed my body. Then I reviewed the notebooks on future breakouts.

By mid-afternoon, I had pulled back on the heavy black sweater and dropped under the now, heading for Llordian. Hanging over the square, undertime, I edged myself toward the blue direction, gently pushing. That was the easy part. I didn't even feel light-headed.

Seeing what would happen in the future was another question.

At first, the outlines of the town flickered and fuzzed, much as they normally looked from the undertime, even in the "now." Then, further uptime the barrier to seeing Query became solid gray. That was what most divers normally saw. I pushed further into the blue, and the gray barrier dissolved into more of a grayish haze.

Through the haze, I could make out one thing clearly. Most of Llordian was gone in whatever future I was watching. I concentrated harder, not moving farther foretime, in trying to make out some hint of what might happen. The haze remained, but I could see two images superimposed on each other.

One view was of unkempt and grass-dotted dunes. The other was of a fountain, the same dry fountain from the Llordian central square, surrounded by a low wall. The hills beyond the wall were covered with grasses and scattered trees.

My head was aching, but the two images shifting back and forth were the best I could do before retreating back to my room. The room was empty and cold. Some days the power wasn't on in the afternoons. That was to provide enough for the maintenance facilities.

I kept the heavy sweater on and sat on the edge of the bed.

No matter what happened, Llordian was dead. In one case, it looked like a lot more than Llordian was dead, but drawing a conclusion from just one part of a continent could be dangerous.

If Llordian was dead for all practical purposes, why did Odin Thor and Wryan both think it was important? And why wouldn't either one tell me?

XLVI

MORE ATTACKS AND burnings in Llordian and occurred over the next ten-day.

Then the elders and farmers of another farming town, Felshtar, came to Odin Thor complaining about the ConFed levies. Odin Thor asked for an election. They voted—sixty percent for the ConFed departure— and Henriod pulled out the ConFed troops. Two days later, the Felshtar townies attacked a small farm. The farmers retaliated by burning an outlying house.

About the same time, the Llordian farmers mounted an attack on the once-empty Llordian houses where grains had been taken and stored.

I eased back into Llordian as the ragged peddler, trudging down the road from Halfprince. Even from the edge of town, the stench was nearly unbearable, in spite of the cold south wind. The old postal building had been pressed into service as lodgings, and two women, armed with ancient scatterguns, stood by the nearly closed gate.

The town's wall facings that had been white-washed and flecked with silver were scraped, scarred, and covered with dust and blackish grit. An odor of charred flesh and burned wood lingered in the air. Dark reddish blotches stained the curb stones.

In the square, the pottery lady's stand was a crushed pile of fabric and broken wood, interspersed with colored clay shards. By the still-dry fountain stood the empty spits where the stolen and slaughtered hogs had been roasted, with a heap of days-old bones kicked into a corner. A rat gnawed at one in the gray mid-morning light.

One whole row of dwellings on one side of the square had been fired, and the roofs had collapsed in on themselves. Two bent men glanced at me, then returned to scavenging items and carrying them to the small wagon.

"You!"

I turned slowly, letting the hidden recorder in my pack pan the destruction. A thin man, almost as tall as Odin Thor, silver hair streaked with soot or worse, wearing a farmer's jacket over a mechanic's grease suit, aimed a projectile gun at me. He wasn't a farmer, not with the projectile holes in the jacket, and the prison brand on his forehead.

"What you doing here?"

I looked around wide-eyed, reached slowly for one of the trinkets I had carved, ready to drop undertime instantly. He leveled the gun directly at me as I displayed a badly carved napkin ring.

"Oh, it's you. The mute boy." He shook his head. "Get out of here. No one has anything. The farmers will shoot you just like us, maybe faster."

I looked puzzled, pointed to the pottery stand.

"Merdith? They got her, too. She didn't want to lose her pots." He snorted. "Swine! Starve us . . . hoarders . . ." The man almost forgot me, then stopped and gestured with the gun back toward the Halfprince road. "Go on. Someone might shoot you because they don't know you. Go on!"

I nodded, let my shoulders sag, and plodded back the way I had come, toward the postal building—the ex-ConFed fort—that had become the latest housing in Llordian.

Something seared through my shoulder. I staggered undertime, holding to my concentration like a precious jewel until I fell on breakout right in front of Nerlis, the nurse in the infirmary.

"Sorry . . ." I think I said.

When I woke up again, I was lying on a flat table with Dr. Dyrell using a long instrument on my chest. The fire redoubled and dropped around me like a prickly red haze.

How long I drifted there, I don't know, except that I was in a room where people seemed to come and go, and look at me, and come and go. Wryan came at least once. So, I think, did Odin Thor. Even in my haze Wryan stood out like a silver star.

When I woke up for real, there were, again, all sorts of tubes attached to me, and a large flexible pad across my left shoulder and chest.

Nerlis arrived within instants.

"Well . . . are you really awake?"

I nodded.

She shook her head slowly, not quite fondly, but not totally disap-provingly. "You get into more trouble . . ."

I just looked at the mass of tubes connected to me.

She followed my eyes. "Those stay there until we're sure you're not starving again."

"When . . . can . . . I . . . eat?" My voice felt rusty, and my throat was dry.

She laughed. "That's a good sign. Let's try liquids, first. There's noth-ing wrong with your digestive system."

I glanced to the window as she checked me, before bustling out for the liquids she had promised. Outside were high soft white clouds and a bright green-blue sky, almost springlike.

Wryan arrived shortly, dropping from nowhere into the infirmary room. She glanced over the tubing. "I think I've seen you like this before."

"Doctor . . ." acknowledged Nerlis, returning with a beaker. She barely hesitated before bringing it up to my lips.

The first sip was hard, so dry were my lips and mouth. The second was easier. The third hit my stomach like a centreslot ball to the groin. I'd forgotten the impact of Sustain on an empty stomach, but my body brought back the recollection instantly.

Nerlis wiped the sweat off my forehead, then nodded. "He's all yours, Doctor Relorn. I'll be back in a while to disconnect the tubes."

Wryan pulled the chair closer to the bed. "Sammis . . . who told you that you were invulnerable?"

I didn't want to answer that one.

"Walking into Llordian . . ." she didn't finish her statement.

"All right . . . was stupid." I took another sip of Sustain with a shak-ing hand. "Should I have dived in and recorded and disappeared?"

"Why not?" Wryan's voice was calm.

"How about the witches of Eastron?"

"It's a different time and a different place." She looked at me criti-cally. "You should be dead, you know?"

I didn't ask why, not wanting to move much.

"Your wounds weren't survivable, according to Dr. Dyrell." She stood up and pointed a finger at me. "But you're still not invulnerable."

I yawned. All of a sudden, I felt tired.

"I'll talk to you later."

As I recovered over the next ten-day, I discovered that the remaining farmers had nearly leveled Llordian, but not before the last remnant of the townies had attacked and leveled a dozen more farms—empty because the farmers had retreated to one they had made into a stronghold.

The townies attacked, and three quarters of them were wiped out—as were nearly half the farmers and most of the stored crops and seed grain.

At Felshtar, nearly the same thing had happened, because the farmers, hearing what had happened at Llordian, waited until the next townie attack. Then they burned the entire town, while the townies were out burning every farmhouse they could reach.

Jerlyk made some tapes of the destruction.

Algern, another town near Esterly, complained about the ConFed levies. Odin Thor showed them the tapes, then sent a handful of townies and farmers by steamer to Llordian. They didn't even ask for an election. They did ask, after talking with Wryan, for a committee of townies and farmers, under ConFed supervision, to verify townie food needs and farmer supplies.

By the time I was well enough to leave the infirmary, I had figured out what had to be done, if we were to avoid self-destruction and get back on the road to dealing with the Frost Giants.

Wryan didn't encourage me or oppose me. What she said was, "If you think so, go ahead and persuade everyone."

I didn't have to persuade everyone, just Odin Thor.

XLVII

THE SUNSHINE THAT had promised an early spring vanished as we walked into the colonel-general's office. My shoulder still twinged when I stretched too far, but the redness of the scars had already begun to fade.

Odin Thor stood behind his desk and peered at me, and I still didn't know whether Wryan was really behind me or not. At least, she'd agreed to come.

"The divers can't stay here any longer."

"Why not, Trooper Sammis?"

"First, because it makes your troopers uneasy. Second, because they need to adjust to the real world. And third, because this base isn't suited to rebuilding the future." My voice almost squeaked, but I got it all out.

Wryan said nothing, just stood there with a faint smile on her face.

Odin Thor smiled even more broadly. "My troopers will do what I say."

"Not necessarily."

"Oh . . . ?"

"Not if I tell them your big secret—that you're a diver yourself."

For once, the colonel-general looked surprised. He opened his mouth, then shut it. Then he just sat there.

"You, madame." he finally said, "Do you believe such an absurdity?"

"Colonel," she said with a wry twist to her lips, "what I believe is not the issue. Is it?"

Odin Thor glanced toward the closed door, then looked at me. "What could you possibly gain by making such a statement?"

"Look," I said, hoping the words came out the way I had rehearsed them. "What happened at Llordian and Felshtar showed that right now people only respect force. They also try to destroy what they don't want to understand. I'm a diver. I'm not a trooper, and I never will be again."

Odin Thor's hairy eyebrows furrowed.

"Do you really think you could keep me from destroying most of your forces—if I had to?"

"You wouldn't."

"Not unless you forced him," added Wryan.

Odin Thor stepped back. "Let's start this over." He resumed the false jollity. "Why don't you just explain this whole wonderful scheme of yours?"

"It's not wonderful. It's designed for survival." I cleared my throat. "It's simple when you think about it. From the divers' viewpoint, they have to sleep, and get rest. If the ConFeds are three buildings away, some of the divers are always vulnerable. Plus, several of them have had rather unpleasant prior experiences with ConFeds.

"Second, the divers are still living in the past. They still look at what they're doing as a research project. They need to become more self-reliant, and building their own camp will require that. In addition, the ConFeds are already beginning to resent having to support the divers. If the divers support themselves, then they're not a drain on the ConFeds. And the ConFeds are going to need every man possible to maintain some sort of order in the next year or so." I rubbed my shoulder, recalling Llordian.

"Now . . . you asked about you. If you are known to be a diver, and divers can neutralize people at will, no one is likely to challenge you. But . . . you can't make that known until the divers, who, presumably, would be viewed as your power base, are out of easy physical reach of the ConFeds."

Odin Thor paced back toward me. A good two heads taller than me, he radiated physical power. "Why couldn't I just remove you?"

"Because you can't survive over the long term without divers," interjected Wryan.

"I beg your pardon?" Odin Thor's politeness was strained.

"Look," I almost shouted. "Your damned steamers are your lifelines. They're more than half ceramic, and there's not a ceramics facility left on the planet. Where are the etheline refineries? The Enemy—the Frost Giants—whatever they are, leveled all the factories and took out the solar satellite links. We can reach them. You can't. *Maybe* in time we could repair them. You can't. How long will those standby generators last?"

Odin Thor wasn't stupid. "All of that may be true, but what good are your divers? There's not an engineer among them, you two excepted."

I swallowed. "We can bring small things back from other planetary systems. Weapons, certainly tools, some limited metals. Perhaps technology."

Odin Thor raised his eyebrows.

"We've already proved to be able to provide instant communications."

He looked out the window. "You're telling me I have no choice."

"Not exactly," added Wryan. "Sammis is telling you that over the long term you have no choice."

"Madame, I am not that short-sighted. I have no choice. Will you keep your bargain?"

"We have to," I added. "For the same reason. We have to be viewed as helpful. Otherwise, any time a diver appears, we'll be back in the old witches of Eastron days, having to hide and run."

"I'm not sure I believe that."

"If I bring Weldin copper wire, iron plates or scavenge materials from ruins in Eastron, he can rebuild a generator for power generation. I can't build one."

Odin Thor said nothing, looked out at the clouds.

Wryan nodded faintly.

"All right. What comes first?"

I'd thought about that. First, the divers brought raw materials and goodies for the ConFeds. Then, they decided they wanted their own village, not an armed camp, with some strong hints from Odin Thor that he really couldn't guarantee day-in, day-out security unless the divers were in a less accessible location.

Odin Thor would let his men—gradually—bring in women. Only

willing ones, and the divers could police that. With the women would come children. That would take care of some resentment against there being female divers and no female ConFeds.

"Sit down, why don't you?" I suggested.

Wryan smiled faintly from behind Odin Thor as she pulled up a chair. Odin Thor turned and retreated behind his desk.

I sat in the chair right before him. It would be a long morning.

XLVIII

NONE OF THE divers really liked the whole plan. Mellorie liked getting away from the ConFeds, but protested the idea that *she* would have to help build the new divers' village, with her own hands yet. Arlean liked leaving the ConFeds and the walls, but disliked the isolated location on the other side of Mount Persnol, and hated the idea of leaving the library where it was. But she didn't want to hand-carry it, along with all the equipment, to the village.

Gerloc protested having to be a porter, perhaps because he didn't want to admit he was relatively fragile as a diver. Jerlyk didn't like having to set up defenses for the new village—minor as they were— when the apparent protection of old Camp Persnol had been so great. Amenda said nothing, but looked relieved and sad simultaneously.

Deric protested the loudest.

". . . most absurd . . . idiotic idea . . . throwing away a generation of research . . . going back to nature . . . mind over matter doesn't work without technology . . ."

By the time he had repeated himself three times, even Gerloc and Arlean were looking away.

Then there was me. I protested, too, about the self-centeredness of everyone else, one afternoon as we stood in the far hills comparing on-site progress with the plans Deric had reluctantly developed. "Why do we have to drag everything out of everyone? Why can't they just understand? They're all hanging onto a time that's dead."

"Are you sure you don't see this new community as an easy way to bury the past and avoid facing unpleasant memories?" asked Wryan, turning toward me so that she didn't squint into the setting sun. Though it was late in the afternoon and the sun was about to drop behind Mount Persnol, the spring air was still warm.

"Of course not."

Wryan looked at me.

I shrugged. "A little, maybe."

"You realize we need more divers." Wryan continued as if she had not mentioned unpleasant memories.

"Why do we need more divers?" I kicked a small limb away from the stone foundation.

She gestured around the foundation stones, mortar troughs, and stacked beams that were eventually supposed to be a divers' cottage. A rutted muddy track in front of the foundations showed on the neatly drafted plans as a stone-paved roadway.

"Not enough people," I ventured.

"You just might show signs of brilliance, Sammis."

From her tone, I gathered I had missed more than I had grasped. So I tried again. "If Odin Thor is going to succeed, he needs more than we can get . . ."

That wasn't it. Wryan just kept looking from the plans and to the foundations.

"If Odin Thor doesn't succeed . . ." That wasn't it either. Finally, I rubbed my shoulder—still aching at the end of long days—and thought. "Oh . . . if he *does* succeed . . ."

Wryan nodded. "Correct. Can you take some time tomorrow morning to get this back on track?" She pointed to the plans. "Then you can start searching in the afternoon. Work with the crews in the morning, and search in the afternoon. We can't exactly forget that the Frost Giants are still out there, and we don't have enough divers if they return."

"Damned recipe for exhaustion . . ."

"You're brilliantly correct about that as well." She rolled up the plans. "These aren't getting built the way they should. I'll follow up on your searches in the morning, and work with the crews in the afternoon."

That was what happened. The building part was the easiest, actually less energy-consuming than diving, and gave me a few new muscles, lots of aches and blisters, and more than a few headaches.

"Why do we have to use so much stone . . . ?"

". . . not enough power tools. . . ."

". . . who made you Verlyt . . ."

". . . liked the old quarters better . . ."

Searching for new divers was almost a relief after those mornings. I didn't have to actually make the contacts—Wryan and Amenda handled that. In practice, it turned out to be simple . . . and time-consuming.

I could see the time energy controls through the undertime. That was the easy part. After that, I had to find out exactly who possessed the talent, which wasn't exactly easy when most of them didn't know they had it, didn't want to know, or tried to suppress it.

Then Wryan and Amenda had to decide how to approach the diver, or his or her parents or both.

"Let the parents come here, if they want." That had been Jerlyk's solution.

Not a bad idea, but—like so many good ideas—a little hard to sell. As a compromise, we ended up building two villages, separated by a fairly imposing ridge, and connected by a single narrow road. Originally, one location had been an Imperial forest research station and the other a Seco recreation center. Both were in poor shape.

One village, initially the Seco recreation center and somewhat larger, was for non-divers who wanted to stay with us, for young divers and their families, and for any relations of divers. The other was for divers alone. I hoped the distinctions would blur over time.

Needless to say, the mixed diver/non-diver village got underway much more quickly, once we actually transported the non-divers on site. It was nearly a day from the old camp by steamer, up through so many switchbacks on a narrow road that arrival anywhere would have been a relief.

One way or another, we struggled through the spring and early summer, finally finishing three good-sized cottages in the divers' village, with several others nearing completion. A small water-driven generator supplied some power, intermittently, although Wryan insisted on complete wiring.

The garden idea went better than the cottages, probably because by the end of spring, everyone was sick of flourcakes, dried chysts, and all the staples. Amenda spent almost every free instant in the sunlight, seemingly happy for the first time since I had arrived.

Once the first cottages were completed, most of us moved, except for Deric, who, surprisingly, had taken charge of quietly teaching Odin Thor how to be a diver.

By midsummer, we had located an additional two dozen divers, mostly with families. All but a handful lived in the mixed village.

Also by midsummer, Odin Thor was demanding the metals, goods, weapons, and technology I had promised.

XLIX

ONE THING LEADS to another, and pretty soon everything gets complicated. After the complications arrive, then anyone can screw it up. The idea I had proposed to Odin Thor had seemed simple—use time-diving to skim the surplus off other high-tech cultures in order to help rebuild

Query and to figure out how to deal with the Frost Giants.

Explaining doesn't explain anything.

The day after I could no longer ignore Odin Thor's demands, I fitted myself out with what I considered a diving uniform—tight-fitting black exercise trousers and tunic, with a light pair of black hiking boots, and an old thermal windbreaker from the bunkers under the old fort. I wore an equipment belt, the kind with concealed pouches and pockets, as well as the obvious gear, such as a small-caliber pistol, a knife, and some rope. The windbreaker was also black and long enough to cover the belt, knife, pistol and all. On top of it all I carried a small backpack, empty except for several days' dried foods, mostly fruits with some jerky.

Then there was the thin notebook, based on all the notes from Wryan and the other timedivers, which laid out a sort of map of the nearer stellar systems. My idea was simple enough, just to skim through the backtime to see if any cultures had developed ideas or items we could use—and carry. That was the big problem. Unless a timediver could lift an item, he or she couldn't bring it back. Some divers were barely strong enough to carry themselves, let alone additional loads.

The kitchen was empty when I sat down for a bite of breakfast— cheese and bread, washed down with some citril. Outside the flat and mismatched panes, the purple of early dawn faded toward gray as the sun neared the underside of the horizon. No one else was awake. Wryan would probably be the next one up, but I intended to be gone before she rose.

Saying good-bye to her was getting too hard, and there would be all too many good-byes over the days and seasons ahead.

I sliced off another hunk of cheese, sealed the wedge, and put it back in the cooler. The battery charge was running low, but there wasn't time to fix that right then. We missed the luxury of the broadcast power that had been one of the first casualties of the Frost Giant attack.

Paring the cheese into smaller slices, I put them on the second slice of rough grain bread and began to eat, finally washing the remnants down with the last of the citril in my mug.

The gray dawn became a grayer morning as I stood, seeing that there would be no sunrise, not with the heavy clouds overhead and the promise of more rain. After I rinsed out the mug and stacked it in the rack, I swung up my backpack.

"Ready to go, I see." Wryan stood by the open archway that led to the room the three women shared. Her sandy hair was tousled, and her small feet were bare, as if she had pulled on the sweater and trousers on the run.

"No sense in wasting time." I looked at her, nearly my size, almost eye to eye, and set the pack on the chair.

She smiled sadly.

I smiled back.

She grinned.

I grinned. "Not much good at good-bye."

"Neither am I."

Somehow, this time I knew what to do. I reached for her and pulled her close. In the end, she was holding me as tightly as I held her. She was shaking, as if she were crying.

I wanted to say something, but couldn't. So I kissed her forehead, and brushed away some tears.

Funny, it took me until then to realize I was shaking too, but Wryan touched my cheek and leaned back to look at me. I kissed her, but, again, she kissed me even as my lips reached for hers.

That was the first time we had held each other, or kissed.

For a long time after that lasting kiss, neither one of us could do anything but hold the other.

"You deserve better . . ." I had to say it. What was I but an under-educated and spoiled gentry brat who could time-dive and survive trouble? ". . . and I'm too young, too shallow for you . . ."

"Let me worry about that, Sammis. The age doesn't matter, not at all, not the way things are looking . . ."

"True . . ." I had to grin ruefully, but lost it when I felt she meant something else. "What do you mean?"

"That's my secret until you come back . . ."

"Working on my curiosity, then, Lady?"

Her arms were tighter around me, and I gave in, letting my lips find hers.

How much time passed, I did not know, but it was definitely later when we let go, except for two hands tightly intertwined.

"When you come back, we'll talk about it."

"About it?"

"My secret, as you call it. It's already becoming obvious, but . . ."

I nodded. Whatever she had discovered was not something that should get to Odin Thor, at least not until we had worked out how to handle it. That was becoming more and more our operating style.

She disengaged her hand from mine and straightened her sweater. "Now get out of here while we're still relatively intact."

I knew exactly what she meant. So I leaned toward her and brushed her lips, then leaned back and grabbed my pack. And I was undertime, knowing she was crying again and that I wasn't in much better shape.

That's why the first dive wasn't much of a dive, just enough to get me into the abandoned polar space station. I'd checked earlier, and it still had an atmosphere.

Staggering out of the undertime, I was ready to bolt if the air had disappeared or turned foul, but neither had happened. So there I was, hovering in the old operations center, swaying from side to side, ready to fall, except for the fact that I was weightless.

From the station's size and equipment, it had to have been the base from which the ill-fated Mithradan planet-forming had been launched and supported. While I could have floated as easily as finding a place to light, I felt better with the illusion of sitting and strapped myself into one of the operations' center chairs, in front of a dull black screen.

My hands were still shaking, and that had never happened before. Then again, something like Wryan had never happened before. If I didn't know better, I would have said that, tousled as she had been that morning, she looked more like my age than hers. Yet she had to be more like four times my age—at least.

But then, no one believed I was my own age either. People still thought of me as a school-age brat when they first saw me.

My thoughts were wandering because I did not want to deal with my entanglement with Wryan. So I pulled out the thin notebook and began to study the stellar/time maps I had so carefully tried to integrate.

Too many of the systems were blanks, meaning that they were either uninhabited or we had no information.

We couldn't risk losing any divers, and that was a circular problem too. A good diver could skip undertime without getting frozen stiff or suffocated, but the good divers were those who could transport what we needed.

At that point, I groaned. Once again, I had missed the obvious. Sitting in an orbital space station filled with space suits designed for at least some hostile environments, I had a solution.

I dropped undertime and popped back into the kitchen where Wryan was staring out the window over a cup of something.

"Don't move. I shouldn't be back, but here's an idea for the information we need—"

She looked at me, and from even across the room I could see her eyes were bloodshot.

"—on other systems." I had to plunge on or I'd stop, and then I'd never leave. "You know the big orbital station? The one involved in the Mithrada fiasco? It's got a bunch of space suits in it—not just one or

two like you had in the lab. Put the marginal divers in suits and get
them to scout systems. Just present time. If they find traces of civilizations or cultures, then someone else can follow up."

"Like you?"

"Or you," I added.

"Next time, we go together, Sammis Arloff Olon. Or you don't go."
I thought about that. "Let me think that over."

"Please do, and I'll put together a plan for your mapping idea while
you follow the leads you have. Now kindly get on your way . . . and be
careful."

I nodded and ducked undertime, swallowing as I did. I couldn't finish
the swallow until I popped back out in the space station. Then I began
looking at the maps.

Sertis was first on the list, a mere two stellar systems away.

L

SERTIS—WHAT SHOULD I say about the place?

Crowded, at least in the cities. I picked the largest one, at the inter-
section of a large river and a wide bay filled with a range of vessels.
Some were powered with energy flows I could sense from the undertime.
Others were clearly sailing ships.

With each dive I had become more and more sensitive to the flows
of energy from the now, perceived from the undertime. None of the
other timedivers could sense them, but I suspected some would develop
the ability with more experience. That made homing in on large energy
concentrations easy; cities particularly.

That was about the only easy part.

First, I'm not a linguist. The gabble of voices was just that—verbal
confusion. Second, the signs and written languages were even worse.
Third, what I was wearing was clearly enough to attract unwanted attention. The Sertians apparently were strong on flowing robes and hoods.
The men were mostly bearded, and the women wore colorful scarves.

The clothing was the easiest to remedy. Slipping under the now, I
located and liberated an appropriately-sized cloak, along with an exterior
belt and purse. After the Llordian mess, I was more than a little appre-
hensive about walking alone in places where my disposal would be easy
from a distance. So I stayed with the crowds near what seemed to be an
open market. The air was like an oven. Only the lack of humidity made

either the temperature or the odor bearable. And I had thought the damps were rank!

"Hslop?" A ragged child grinned at me. His face was almost squarish, and his hair was black and tight-curled around an olive face.

Since I didn't know what the urchin meant, I scowled.

"Hslop? Hslop?"

I just turned away, ducking between two substantial matrons, and moving toward a line of stands, each draped in purple.

Despite my hopes, I was still staggered. The first stand had a wide range of steel knives, real steel, laid out. I nodded and passed by.

"Hssilinglop?" asked the woman tending the stand.

I ignored her, wishing I could understand the language.

The second stand was more interesting, with an assortment of hand tools. I watched as the owner and a thin young man bargained over a hatchet. Finally, I drifted on, noting that the urchins still trailed me, at a distance.

A quarter of the way around the market, past the food stands and the fabrics, I found the power tools. Some of them looked like they ran on etheline, or some liquid hydrocarbon. One or two were battery-powered, but they were covered with a film of dust. Several were not familiar, but one looked like a tree saw. I could make out another saw with an assortment of circular blades that looked as though it would cut finished timbers and boards, and a power drill.

"Hssilinglop?" asked the stall tender.

I pointed to the circular saw, thinking that we could try it out. If it worked, someone like Gerloc could get some more.

"Res thorp."

Not knowing what "res thorp" meant, I pawed around in the purse that I had liberated, and offered a small silver coin—far less than an earlier customer had paid for the tree saw.

He held up four fingers, pointing to the silver coin. I didn't have four of them, but I did have a gold piece of some sort. So I held up two fingers. He gave me a sad face. I shrugged.

Finally, he held up three.

I winced, thinking about having to show the gold piece.

He shrugged and gave me two and a crooked finger. I guessed that was a half.

I scrabbled through the purse and came up with two silvers, and a quarter of a silver, it looked like, plus some smaller and lighter coins. I put them all on the wooden counter.

He shrugged, trying not to smile too much, and took them. I think the smaller coins added up to more than half a silver because he dragged out a carrying case and threw in all the blades, plus a wrench and a small can of lubricant.

I walked to the nearest alley and disappeared undertime. Someone else could certainly handle Sertis, even if I had to write a manual. That would provide goodies for both the divers and Odin Thor.

LI

COLLECTING WEAPONS IS hard work for a timediver. A knife I could carry, but it would be useless against a Frost Giant. A projectile rifle presented the same problem.

Nuclear weapons worked effectively on the Frost Giants. But nukes also destroyed large chunks of real estate and possessed too much mass for a timediver to carry. From what Wryan had determined, particle beams also would work, but not lasers. The difference was academic, since any particle beam ever built by Westron with enough force to fragment a Frost Giant wouldn't fit on a steamer, much less on a timediver's back.

Only high-tech worlds can build small and destructive weapons, and high-technology cultures tend to be shortlived because they are complex and require a continuing high level of education. There are always exceptions, but the exceptions presented another problem.

Not that either kind of high-tech system was hard for me to find because their energy use beat through the undertime like a flare.

High-tech meant unstable and short-lived or stable and lasting. The first of the longline high-tech cultures I found was Muria. That's what I called it, but who knows what they called themselves?

Tall and slender people, bipedal, with brains and eyes in their heads, finely scaled green skin and white silk hair. Scales and hair don't go together? On Muria they did.

Three sexes, or maybe four, and they all looked alike. The Murians had created a paradise. Golden-fronded trees lined paths that were permanent, yet cushioned every footstep and wound between close-linked clusters of hive houses. Each hive house group was separated from other groups by a varying mixture of orchards, forests, and low-effort cultivated fields. All their nourishment seemed to come from vegetation, but some of the fruits or vegetables looked more like meat.

It rained on Muria just enough, and the cloud patterns kept a favorable range of temperature and breezes. Just enough Murians were born, so that while the settlements changed, the total number of them stayed about the same. Murian medicine, or genetics, or culture, provided long lives, and Murian science had reduced power generation to small fusion generators. Too big to carry, but small enough to fit into a large closet. They were fusion powered, that I could tell from the energy flows.

I couldn't believe the planet. So I went backtime for two or three centuries. I couldn't see any differences. Then I went foretime, and there wasn't much change there, except that the locations of some towns changed.

After that, I started looking for weapons, and I couldn't find any. I could dive into hidden places, but those were very few. I could seize any document or text, but I couldn't read them. I could disassemble any machine, but those I understood I didn't need, and those I didn't understand I couldn't figure out.

Understand, these Murian people were intelligent—and nonviolent. Short of creating a one-person crime wave, there didn't seem to be any way I could persuade them to employ force. Violence was becoming a last resort for me, not that I hadn't employed it effectively.

The Murians had an interstellar drive, and a few explorers who used it. That was where I focused my efforts and where I came up with the duplicator, an accident if ever there was one, since I was looking for weapons.

Their interstellar ships were small, too small to handle distances without supplies and more spare parts and equipment. But they did well, quite well. So I continued to watch from the undertime until I discovered the strange gadget in the ship that duplicated everything from food to tools, with apparently no input except electrical power.

Then the real work began. I tracked a new ship backtime to its construction until I could watch a team of Murians install the duplicator. That night it was my turn.

The shell of the ship was quiet as I broke out of the undertime. No alarms, no bells, not even any energy flows. With my recently acquired Murian tools, I studied the duplicator up close—an elongated octagonal donut that fit on a cabinet about half the size of the kitchen table in our cottage. The central "hole" was where they put items to be duplicated and at first glance seemed limited to items about two handspans square. Because the Murians built most equipment in modular form, the size limit probably didn't cause that many problems. In any case, it was better than anything we had, because we had nothing to speak of, and less on the way.

The duplicator was in a separate compartment next to what I figured were the fusion generators. A glistening blue wire ran from the octagonal machine into a square junction box. In a few moments I had removed the cover of the junction box and set it out of the way on the green-gray deck.

The Murians liked their planet humid, and inside the ship was no exception. I stopped and wiped the sweat off my forehead and out of my eyes. A deep breath followed, and I ignored the musky smell that was part me, part leftover Murians.

Inside the junction box the glistening blue wire split into three smaller insulated filaments. The uncovered end of each filament was purplish. Each was wound around a metal plug the size of my thumb. With some effort, I carefully unhooked the insulated filament wires from the three plugs and withdrew the wire through the side opening in the junction box.

Now the duplicator was free of the power system, and all I had to do was release it from its mountings. That meant standing nearly on my head to release the bolts anchoring the machine to the built-in counter. There were eight bolts, and I had to rest after twisting each one free. Rested and wiped my forehead and tried to get the sweaty salt out of my eyes.

My tunic was dripping, and the ship definitely smelled like sweating human being by the time I twisted the last bolt free and laid it on the floor next to the seven others.

After wiping my forehead again, I tried to lift the duplicator. I could not break it free of the counter, although it seemed to wobble sideways. I let go and sat on the deck to catch my breath and to think.

One Murian had carried the device, and they weren't that much bigger than I was.

I took a swig from my small water bottle. Not that I really needed it in most circumstances, but it did make me feel more comfortable.

Next I checked under the counter, looking for another bolt or fastening. There weren't any. Then I studied the eight-sided machine itself, to see if there were brackets holding it on the sides. Nothing.

I pulled on it. Again, no result. I pushed it toward the bulkhead, losing my balance because it slid so quickly, then stopped cold just before hitting the bulkhead, apparently locked in place.

After some more experimentation, I discovered that it had been threaded through a series of "lock" positions on the metallic plastic bench top. Once I finally maneuvered it free, still having to stop to wipe the sweat off my forehead, I set it on the deck.

I rested, wondering if it would take this long for everything I attempted to make off with. Standing up, I checked the counter surface on which the duplicator had rested, running my fingers over the flat metallic plastic or plastic metal. The surface was absolutely smooth to my touch—absolutely.

I ran the Murian screwdriver, which had a triangular blade, over the surface. Again, nothing. Then I had another thought and pulled my own knife from my belt and drew it over the surface. It ran into a faint, barely detectable tackiness.

I frowned. The Murians had forged what amounted to a lock. More important, they had established some sort of directional bonds that weren't magnetic and which only operated in certain positions in certain directions. The duplicator could not have been lifted off that counter without destroying both duplicator and counter. The bolts had been there just to keep it from sliding around accidentally.

Looking down at the eight-sided machine with its short glistening blue wire, I had the feeling my troubles were only beginning. After repacking the Murian tools into my belt pouch, I picked up the duplicator and staggered undertime.

While it had taken me one straight dive to Muria from the Queryan orbital station, it took three subjective days and twenty rest breaks to get back to camp, breaking out in the small work room Wryan shared with me. I carefully eased the duplicator onto a solid bench and turned around to see Wryan coming through the doorway.

"You look like hell," she observed.

"Hell probably feels better."

"What did you bring back?"

"A duplicator. If we can get it to work."

"Duplicator?"

"It copies anything you put in the middle there—fish, fowl, or electronic components."

"How?"

I shrugged. "Don't know. But the only input is ship power."

"How much power? What kind? Alternating, direct, burst?"

I shrugged again. "How would I know? I never even finished the Academy. It does take a lot of power. A whole lot. I could feel that when the Murians used it."

"Murians?"

"Intelligent amphibian descended. Very cultured. *Very* advanced."

Wryan fingered the blue wiring. "Getting it to work could be a real problem. If this is the only power input, and it takes as much power as you say, we could be in trouble. And we'll probably need two anyway."

"Took me everything I had to get *one* of them back here."

"Even if it is a duplicator, how can we duplicate it? We'll need more than one."

My shoulders sagged. I hadn't thought about that, but she was right.

"Don't worry about it now. I'm going to have to study this first, and I'll probably need you to study one in operation to make sure we set this up right."

Since I didn't exactly feel like dragging another one of the duplicators across the galaxy any time soon, and since I would have gone to hell for Wryan, I just nodded. "In a day or so."

She looked at me. "In a week or so. Maybe longer. You need something to eat, and then some rest." Her eyes radiated concern, and, tired as I was, I only wished that they had radiated more than just that.

A thought struck me belatedly. "How did you know I was back?"

"I just knew."

I wanted to pursue that but couldn't figure out how, and besides, the room seemed shaky. I sat down on the bench.

"Are you all right?"

"I'll be fine."

She had an arm around me, helping me up. "You need something to eat. No blood sugar and no rest. Just lean on me."

So I did. Concern was better than nothing, if less than what I really wanted. We made it to the kitchen, and I slumped into a chair.

"What about the duplicator?"

"It can wait," answered Wryan as she began pulling items from the cooler. "It can wait."

LII

FINDING THE DAMNED duplicator was just the beginning of my problems.

"Sammis, this wire is superconductive."

I nodded as I munched through a half wedge of cheese. I never seemed to eat enough to keep me from running through my personal energy reserves.

"At room temperature." Wryan sipped something from a mug.

"I'm not sure I understand." As I looked up, I could see one of the new divers, Kerina, peer into the kitchen and withdraw. I could have checked by looking undertime, but didn't bother.

Wryan frowned. "Think about it. The duplicator takes enormous power. It all goes through this wire. That means that the wire and the insulation are both incredibly advanced. It also means that the duplicator is useless unless we can hook it to a power plant."

"We have several . . ."

"Not designed for this. Do the Murians?"

I nodded again, thinking about the ship generators. This time I was working on a chyst.

"Do they come in parts? This duplicator is modular." Wryan stood up and walked to the sink, where she rinsed out her mug and set it on the rack.

After a mouthful of chyst, I answered. "I don't know."

"We still may have some physicists left, Sammis. In a generation we won't, even with . . ."

"Translated loosely, if I don't come up with a miniature fusion plant that we can build, or duplicate, we're pretty much through."

Wryan smiled that sad smile. "That's one way of putting it."

"We do have an operating power plant."

"Yes. I'm not certain it will produce electrical power at the right frequencies for the duplicator. I don't know if we could produce the proper transformers, rectifiers, whatever it might take to convert it."

I sighed and looked at the kitchen floor. Before long I could see myself having to lift most of the Murians' technology, piece by piece, just because nothing matched and we no longer had the scientific expertise to make it match.

"Fine. I'll bring you back a fusion power plant. Except for the fuel. I'm not about to try that."

"My guess is that they use water."

"Water? Plain water?"

"That won't be the problem, Sammis."

"What will be?"

"Getting the power to create the first fields."

At that point, I gave up trying to understand, at least for the moment, and decided to concentrate on the problem at hand.

"Before I kill myself doing all this, Dr. Relorn, I want to strike a deal."

"Deal?" Wryan was clearly puzzled. "A deal?"

"I don't trust our dear colonel-general. Neither do you. So I want us to put together our first duplicator and fusion power plant complex someplace unknown to and unfindable by the good colonel-general. If it works, we'll supply both to the timedivers, without revealing our hidden facility, and we'll set up the second facility as if it were the first."

Wryan started grinning.

"Why are you grinning like an idiot?"

"You wouldn't believe me if I told you."

"Try me."

"Your deal was my next idea. I can even tell you what kind of location we need."

Wryan's idea was simple. We would find a high mountain location, preferably on the Bardwalls of Eastron, where no one went even before the annexation, near a stream with enough force to power a small hydro turbine. Wryan was confident she could re-engineer, one way or another, the output to generate the mag bottle for a fusion system.

"Only the mag bottle, you understand."

Sounded great.

Reality, as usual, intruded.

Right after we got the duplicator out of sight, I started hunting for a location. It only took us an afternoon to find the right place on the Bardwalls, a sheltered valley inaccessible except by a diver, with a southern exposure and even a set of caves we could, with only a little work, seal off for storage.

I began scavenging doors and frames from the wreckage of Bremarlyn for the largest cave and cobbled together enough to keep any possible animal intruders away.

Wryan began locating the equipment she needed, with what time she could spare from her work in administering, salvaging, and troubleshooting for the timedivers' villages.

Within days, Odin Thor showed up at our official workroom in the divers' village. He and his aide, a ninny called Verlin, who was nothing more than a directional guide for the good colonel-general, caught me actually working on planning out a phase of Odin Thor's weapons' scouting project, rather than ours. Once Deric had taught Odin Thor how to dive, within ten-days he had been replaced by Verlin.

I was sitting at the cottage table trying to figure out my next series of time sweeps for mid and high-tech cultures along a spiral arm of the galaxy. Wryan had theorized that the high percentage of what she called second-generation stars argued for a greater probability of inhabited systems. What second-generation stars had to do with anything was beyond me, but if Wryan said so there was a good chance it was so.

"Sammis! You promised us better weapons. Where are they?"

I hadn't really even had a chance to stand, not that I wanted to for Odin Thor, but, giving him the benefit of the doubt, I pushed my chair and waited for him to finish glaring. I was still holding the small ceramic tile I had been fingering as I had pondered where to begin the timediving sweeps.

"Colonel-General, I have already supplied tools. Gerloc and some of the other divers are providing new equipment. But there are only so many of us. I was to have three timedivers to help map the possible technical systems. All I have is Derika, because you said the equipment was more important."

Odin Thor opened his mouth.

I held up my hand. "Let me explain. A star system lasts for millions of years. Not all systems have habitable planets. Those that are habitable are used for only a fraction of their physical lifespan. An even smaller number of those have high-technology civilizations, and those civilizations do not last long."

"But you can time-dive!"

"Diving takes a fraction of an instant. That's true. But," I lied, "you know you cannot see real time from the undertime, and that means spending real time investigating each possibility. With just two time-divers, you cannot expect great progress in a mere few ten-days."

"You argue too much, Sammis. Former Trooper Sammis."

"Yes, Colonel-General. It is one of my faults, but I also do my best to produce. So let me."

Odin Thor knew that. So he glowered at me again and stomped out of the cottage kitchen. Verlin had not said a word, and he followed Odin Thor. The two of them stood by the vegetable garden that Tyra had planted and continued to cultivate. As they whispered to each other, it looked like a conspiracy, but it was only a discussion of where Odin Thor wanted to go next. He put his hand on Verlin's shoulder, as if congratulating the fellow, and they disappeared into the undertime.

I could sense the vortex. Odin Thor spent energy like water. That might be because he never felt what he was doing.

I decided to see if I could catch Wryan before Odin Thor did. My first thought was our hidden operational center in the Eastron mountains. I was so upset that I dropped undertime still holding on to the small ceramic tile I had been fingering.

When I emerged near the waterfall on the Bardwalls, the tile was flashing with flecks of timelight or energy or something. I set it on the ground and stared at it. A thought at the back of my mind tickled at me, some memory of something, but I could not exactly recall what. I picked the tile back up and studied it. The energy flows were looped into the undertime somehow, and my fingers had a tendency to skitter off the surface.

The tile was linked undertime, not totally either in or out of the now. Why hadn't anything like that happened before? To me or to anyone else?

Crack!

The noise was an impact on the boulder. The tile was unscathed, but there was a dent in the granite.

Plain old fired clay, wrapped into the undertime some way, was tougher than solid granite. If you could do that with stone or metal, what a building material you'd have. I could see it wouldn't work for weapons, even knives, because the time flows had made the tile hard to hold.

"Oh . . ." Then I remembered a long ago dream about a tower built with glittering stone. A real dive made half-asleep?

I picked up a chunk of stone the size of my fist and dropped undertime, then popped back out. There was no change in the stone that I could see or sense.

I sat down on the boulder to think.

Was it the clay? I picked up the tile and went undertime, and popped back out. The glitter was gone, and I could tell the tile was a plain and ordinary tile again.

I thought some more.

"Sammis? What are you doing?" Wryan was standing almost at my shoulder. Like me, she was almost undetectable when she went undertime or emerged. Strange how we seemed able to find each other.

"Thinking."

"Thinking? About Odin Thor?"

"I was. Came here looking for you. Try to tell you about his latest complaint—but I got sidetracked."

"He caught me with Jerlyk, trying to develop a full-time hydro generator for the diver's camp, enough to handle what we had in mind. If we were successful, we could always borrow it . . ."

"We need two . . . just like the duplicators."

"Damn." She shook her head. "You're right."

"What did the great colonel-general say?"

"We weren't keeping up with the needs of the marines and the Guard, and you were becoming impossible."

I grinned for a moment. "I'm glad he thinks so highly of me."

"You are impossible." She gave me a smile. "What sidetracked you?"

I told her about the tile and showed her the gouge on the boulder.

"Did you know you had the tile in your hand?"

"Not the first time."

"What about the second?"

As I saw where she was headed, I nodded. "But that won't work. You're implying that this time-protection only works if you aren't conscious of it."

"Time-diving is mind over matter, Sammis. What you can carry with you is a function of your strength of will."

"So you think that if I dive and concentrate on *not* carrying something, I can duplicate the effect?"

This time she was the one who shrugged.

I tried it—and was too successful. The tile fell out of thin air onto a rock outcropping and shattered.

Wryan tried it with one of the fragments and had similar results.

Then I recalled the looping fields around the tile and picked up a fist-sized rock and tried to slide undertime and replicate the fields. Wryan was watching when I dropped back into the now.

"It glitters a bit."

The once-dull stone shimmered, but the looping wasn't strong enough and seemed to unravel as we watched. That effort was a start, another skill to practice, along with everything else we had to do. As for erecting a tower or a building . . . I was not sure how I was going to link two stones together at all, but I knew it could be done, and that I would do it.

In the meantime, I still had to find a fusion power plant and another duplicator—and some weapons for Odin Thor before he got totally out of hand.

"Sammis . . . now what?"

I could feel myself grinning for no good reason at all. "We learn how to build buildings that are indestructible, duplicate the unduplicatable, steal the unstealable, and in general lay the foundation to become the gods of this corner of the galaxy."

Wryan gave me another one of those sad smiles. "Is that where we are headed?"

I stopped grinning. "Is there any choice?"

Neither one of us had much to say about that. So I left the rock fragment glittering on the ground, shot through with looped time energies, and slid undertime back to the cottage workroom, while Wryan went her way.

LIII

As USUAL, I ended up spending time on the wrong things. Instead of immediately looking for a way to get the Murian fusion plant or to find Odin Thor some weapons, I began wondering about time looping of materials.

One of my goals was personal. If Wryan and I could build a retreat that was time-warp protected and could be entered only by diving, not even Odin Thor would have much success getting at us.

So I spent most of the afternoon mentally playing with fields, trying to loop them around objects. One thing became clear. The composition of an object had less to do with the ease of time-warping than its mass. With one exception—nothing which contained electrical energy would stay warped out of time.

I carried a small battery under the now, just next to the cottage workbench, and looping the fields went fine. When I dropped back into the now, the strands of time-loop sprayed away from the ceramic case like water off a hot skillet. Once in the now, they just wouldn't stay looped.

The other thing that became clear was that the fields reinforced each other. I put two time-warped rocks next to each other, and the fields I had created intertwined.

Then I tried it by the brook with some mud. Mud? I didn't have mortar to play with, and I wanted to see whether you could mortar together two time-linked objects.

Yes . . . and no. I could attach the mud to the rock and loop it, or I could loop a bunch of mud and apply it. But I couldn't use unlooped mud between two time-warped objects.

My mud-slinging completed, I washed my hands in the brook and decided that, after I got something to eat, I would have to trudge back to Muria, or someplace, to find Odin Thor something vaguely resembling a destructive toy.

What troubled me was not that I wouldn't find it, but that I probably would. If it weren't for the vague and uneasy understanding that the Frost Giants were still lurking somewhere in the undertime, I would have told Odin Thor where to put his weapons.

The more we got into time-diving, the more likely they would be back, and we still didn't have the faintest idea of how to stop them.

So I dropped undertime for the cottage and some more to eat before heading back to Muria—or whenever.

LIV

THE PROBLEM WITH the energy pistol wasn't what it did. It drilled large holes in solid rock, metal and sundry other substances. It also weighed half a stone. Amenda couldn't even point it.

Wryan suggested I look for something lighter. I did. There wasn't.

So . . . what else could I do?

I pulled on my blacks one cloudy fall morning, smiled brightly, and announced I was off to find a lightweight energy weapon.

"Find one?" asked Wryan with a critical look. Even when she was critical and tousled, I wanted to hold her. And a bit more.

Instead I just nodded. "A few angles left to explore."

"Be *very* careful, Sammis." She looked dubious.

If she'd had any idea exactly what I was going to try, she would have been even more dubious. Then again, maybe she knew.

I dropped back to Ydris with the ease of routine. Finding the place had been an accident. Then, again, my whole life resembled an accident.

On one of my too frequent theft-trips to Muria, I noticed another one of those thin energy lines, one that wavered and blasted and screamed for all of its tenuousness. Being inherently curious, I came back. It was clearly a track made by a timediver, yet it was opaque to me. So I followed it—all the way back to Ydris. Back a good long ways, probably halfway to the end of my backtime range.

Ydris—home of rod-tall amphibians with dexterous claws and enormous brains. Ydris, where both brains and claws were employed in supporting a duel-based culture.

Lace towers rose from artificial lakes and held the sunrise, speared the sun, and held its light well into the night. Light and energy—the Ydrisians squandered them like water.

I took a score of dives to scout out Ydris, from the empty and arid poles where ice winds whistled across sea ice sculpted into knife-shaped dunes to the tropical jungles where each instant held battles between beasts so savage that even the Ydrisians avoided their own equator—except for the outcasts.

The cities, built of pale jade nearly as hard as time-warped granite, circled and twisted along narrow peninsulas too regular to be natural. And in those cities, well, Thor would have drooled.

Just in passing, I had liberated the heavy energy pistol for Odin Thor. That stopped his complaints about the wisdom of time-diving. Initially. Before the problems.

Problems? One of the ConFeds, Beran, put the whole pistol in a duplicator. Fuel cell/power source/battery and all. After the blast and flash that momentarily blinded a score of ConFeds drilling nearby, turned Beran into molecules too fine to discover, and sent three others to the infirmary, we discovered, at the cost of one duplicator, that attempting to duplicate stored power produced rather messy results.

Cleaning up required building another duplicator from scratch, steal-

ing another heavy energy pistol, and conducting a few educational lectures for dumb ConFeds.

Everything had more problems and angles than I ever anticipated.

So . . . I was diving back to Ydris, red-flashing into the past, knowing
what I had in mind, but not exactly how to do it.

First, I tracked back to where I had found the first energy pistol. Easy
enough. Then I traced that back to where it was manufactured—a small
black stone building on the end of a peninsula. No real help from that—
just a group of machines, each one stamping or forming or drawing
little parts that were assembled by another machine. It would have been
a good place from which to lift more pistols, but that wasn't the idea.

I lifted one pistol, barely emerging from the undertime, then dropped
further backtime, to the point where the factory was being built. In
time, I zeroed in on a single Ydrisian who was assembling a much larger
version of an energy weapon.

When he, it, she left the room, I deposited the smaller version.

That didn't work. The technician, researcher, whatever, nodded,
squawked, and made a few changes. I could scarcely feel a chill in the
time currents. So I reclaimed the weapon and looked at geography.

A cooler continent in the southern hemisphere was also a technical
center. I never did figure out the local politics or what passed for them,
but even from the outside and undertime, it was clear that the southern
continent and the northern continent did not exactly get along.

So I went back foretime and retrieved some more energy guns, as
well as a few other technical devices, and deposited them in various
locales on the southern continent, hoping. . . .

The jolt to the undertime was like a cold wind, shivering the timepaths around Ydris like leaves in a storm, and confirming that I'd done
something.

I had, all right.

When I returned to the time when I had picked up the pistol, all I
could see from the undertime was a shimmering flow of energy and a
sea of hot glass fused into strange shapes and emitting a hellish glare
quite discernible from the undertime.

That was the bad news. The good news was that a few hundred local
years earlier, the "new" Ydrisians had developed some much smaller and
more highly directed energy weapons, one of which was worn on the
foreleg, or whatever they used for manipulation.

It took awhile, but this time, I tracked down all the components,
including the miniature power cells just before they were energized.
And I brought them back.

Wryan was waiting.

"What did you . . ." she shook her head. "I felt it from here."

"Don't ask," I mumbled. I laid out the band on the work bench. "This should be able to be made into a wrist band, a gauntlet. Fires directed energy beams. Here's an uncharged power source. It holds about the equivalent of one of our fusion plant's energy for—I don't know exactly . . . and here's the key to the charger. I can get the rest later."

I slumped against the bench, feeling the blood drain from my face. "Sammis . . ."

Wryan's voice was coming from a distance, but I managed to sip from whatever she held in front of me. Then I could stand up—except my legs started to shake.

That wasn't physical.

I had only wanted to spur the Ydrisians into building smaller weapons—not into destroying themselves. They weren't admirable, and they fought all the time, but so did we.

I wondered if the Frost Giants looked at us that way.

"Sammis . . . ?"

Wryan's arm was around me. Her warmth and strength helped, but I wondered, absently, if my eyes were beginning to show the almost hidden blackness I sometimes glimpsed in hers.

LV

EVERYTHING APPEARED TO be improving. Between Gerloc and Amenda and the new divers like Kerina and Hadron and the use of the duplicators, we had gathered enough originals from Sertis and were producing enough tools and food to stop the levy on the farmers and to supply them with a few goods.

Wryan even worked out a continuous duplication stream for etheline.

The big hang-up was getting new fusion generators on line, but we had four of them operating officially. That didn't count Wryan's and my private one up in the Bardwalls.

With the batteries from Ydris, we even dispensed with the water turbines for the start-up fields.

Then, on the hills that had been Inequital, Odin Thor turned a work crew loose and leveled an area for a headquarters complex. Wryan and I—mostly me—prevailed upon him to let the divers build a tower/ monument in the center, one built with time-warped stone that would stand forever. I badgered Deric to design something that looked like my dream, and then took over as project manager, when I wasn't scouting or doing miscellaneous-type engineering.

It sounds easy, but it wasn't. I started to cart building stones from Bremarlyn and glowstones from Muria before it dawned on me after about two trips—we only needed one perfect stone of each type, plus a duplicator. Of course, it took time to assemble another fusion plant and duplicator, but Odin Thor lent me some discipline cases, not that they remained that way.

And, yes, the gauntlets. Wryan and I made several modifications to them, one of which involved time-warping. Unless a diver could warp time around the gauntlets after donning them, they didn't work. The field didn't have to last, but its creation was the first step in arming them. I insisted on the idea, and Wryan, swearing quietly under her breath, figured out how to do it. One circuit was all we needed, of course, since we could duplicate the rest. Strictly an arming circuit, but that particular feature ensured that they couldn't be removed from a diver and used by anyone else. That also meant some of the divers couldn't use them, but both Wryan and I were adamant about that safeguard.

There's nothing like nearing success in survival to ensure something goes wrong.

"Sammis . . ."

I was studying a cooler from Sertis, trying to discover how we could incorporate something to attach to the cooler to convert the cycle frequency from our handy dandy Murian fusion system into the Sertian equivalent. Then we could just duplicate the coolers and hook them up directly to the community power system. Yes, we had coolers, but they were big, cumbersome and didn't work all that well. They were murder to duplicate because it had to be done piece by piece, and replacing parts entailed standing on your head, sweating profusely, and swearing liberally—when you weren't muttering under your breath.

Along the way, I was trying, and often losing, in my efforts to ensure our tools, equipment, and appliances were roughly compatible and interchangeable. Aside from me and Wryan, who was too busy to do much about it, no one else cared. Why I did, I wasn't certain, but I seemed to get stuck caring about the details no one else bothered with, that and Odin Thor's interminable quest for weapons.

"Sammis . . ." Wryan's voice was cool.

I looked up.

"The Frost Giants are back."

I sat up so suddenly my head crashed into the work bench. "Uuufff . . ." I shook my head. "How do you know?"

"They froze two cottages in the other village."

"The other village? Why there?"

"Targeted the fusion plant, I think. They are energy seekers, as you may recall."

I scrambled to my feet. "Have you alerted any of the others?"

"Most everyone."

"Now what?"

"I was hoping you'd have an idea."

The problem was that I didn't. Except one that I didn't like.

"You're not going . . . ?" asked Wryan with a look at my face.

"Anyone else better suited?"

We both knew the answer to that one.

So I went and pulled on full gauntlets, diving suit, and went hunting for Frost Giants.

Finding the track from the village wasn't hard; it was almost bluish and jagged in the undertime. Nor was dropping backtime to see what had happened earlier in the day difficult, not that I could break out, but I could watch a hazy view.

Even from undertime, I shivered as the blocky figure sucked heat and energy from the fusion plant and the surrounding cottages. Frost Giant—a misnomer in some ways. The figure I saw was oblong, with two legs, and what appeared to be four wide and stubby arms. It wore no apparent clothing, except a bluish energy shimmer, and while it had a "head" of sorts, that was more a protrusion than a head resting upon a neck. It was cold, so cold that I felt it was sucking energy from the undertime as well.

Then it was gone, leaving a bright blue and jagged time-trail that seemed both sideways and backtime simultaneously.

I followed, although the effort was like ricocheting through a rock canyon on a high-speed steamer that bounced off every wall. Each "bounce" gave me a headache.

When the bouncing stopped, I was still undertime in the Queryan solar system. That was easy to figure because I couldn't break out from the undertime. The planet was Thoses, the one out beyond Query. Rumor had it that the First Empire had put a base there.

Someone had. Once. But the Frost Giants had frozen it solid, too.

From the undertime, all I could see was the energy drain and the collapse of empty domes and plastics into dust. Sure, it had happened a millennia or more before I was born, but watching it happen and being unable to do anything about it was unnerving.

As I shivered in the undertime, I worried. I worried a lot. The Frost Giants didn't seem all that bright, but more like some sort of cosmic energy grazer. And the trail from Query to Thoses had been without stops, as if they passed from solar system to solar system and grazed on all the artificial and natural heat and energy they could reach within their time range.

Another bright blue jagged trail, this one foretime, toward Mithrada. I dropped away and headed back to the divers' village.

The problem was simple, and nearly impossible. Unless we could either find a Frost Giant in real time, or in another time outside the Queryan system, we couldn't even try to attack it. I needed to talk to Wryan, to design some sort of tracking plan or strategy.

Execution I could handle, but not long-range planning. Not well.

LVI

"OUT OF MY WAY, Sammis." Even when he was trying to keep it down, Odin Thor's voice boomed. He twisted the bosses on the gauntlets to activate the microcircuitry.

When I looked at Odin Thor, I wished I'd never found Ydris. The gauntlets were too powerful for his ego. Bad enough for me, and I'd survived his damned ConFed Marines with no illusions of justice.

"They won't work very well in here, Odin Thor." I used both his last names to irritate him. Dangerous, but he lost most rudiments of logic when he was angry. "Or too accurately."

"Don't you ever say anything straight out, runt?" All of Colonel-General Augurt Odin Thor looked ready to assault me. Which would have been fine, except that was the moment Wryan walked into the travel hall, or what there was of it we had built.

"Dr. Relorn . . ." Odin Thor was all charm again, bowing low, almost from the waist. "I was about to depart to see if I could localize the latest manifestations of the Frost Giants. The ones that young Sammis here tracked across the cluster."

"You are so determined, Colonel. Do you think that it is necessary? Especially when we have no effective way of neutralizing individual Giants?"

"Madam, we know who the enemy is. That enemy has just destroyed another timediver's innocent family."

"What will you do once you find all the Frost Giants, Odin Thor?" I interjected.

"Keep track of them until we can destroy them. They'll be a threat until we do."

I wanted to know how Odin Thor could keep track of anything when he couldn't find his way across a room under the now. Instead, I asked, "Do you remember what happened the last time?"

Wryan shook her head, but I ignored her. This one wasn't going by logic.

"That was years ago!" snapped Odin Thor.

"Not to the Frost Giants. Barely an instant for them."

Wryan looked even more distressed, and I knew why.

"So we're going to cower in our half-built city and our half-built tower and hope they leave us alone? Hope they don't freeze another poor family with their curiosity? Can I tell my people that the great Doctor Relorn and her intrepid scout, who can avoid the Giants, wish to run and hide and leave them to face the terrible freezings? That you two have no wish even to track the Giants to warn them?"

"What are you going to do, great Odin Thor? Track them all over the galaxy until they get tired and turn on us again?"

Wryan was making motions behind Odin Thor's back for me to shut up, but it wouldn't make much difference. He was going to do what he was going to do, and we'd end up picking up the pieces again.

"Don't you understand?" By now he was bellowing.

Deric had dashed in from supervising the time-warping of the wall stones in the adjoining hall. Another young-looking diver who carried a youngster in a sack upon her back stood frowning in the archway.

"Understand what?" asked Wryan calmly.

"That the Giants are our enemy. That they will threaten us as long as they roam free through the galaxy."

By now, half a dozen divers had popped in, and, unfortunately, out. Word would be through the community within the afternoon, if not within instants.

I could see the handwriting on the wall, and it was written in blood. Mine and Wryan's especially.

Sighing loudly, I got their attention. Once again, it was my mess, a mess that I should have seen coming sooner.

The travel hall was silent, too silent.

"Why don't we discuss it at a full meeting of all the timedivers tonight? It affects everyone, and everyone should have a say in it."

"Great idea, Sammis!" boomed Odin Thor. His voice was not quite mocking. "What time?"

"After dinner . . . whenever you want . . ."

"I'll let you know." And the colonel-general was off, on foot. He couldn't afford the embarrassment of planet-sliding, since he still had little enough directional sense. He was smiling every step of the way.

Wryan looked over at me sadly. "You know what will happen."

"Got any better ideas, Doctor?"

"Do you?"

"Just one."

She did not ask, but continued to look at me sadly.

"Finding something that destroys Frost Giants before they destroy us."

"Ignorance rules again."

"Always has. Probably always will."

"How long will it take you to find something?" Wryan seldom wasted time on formalities or useless commentary.

"That's simple enough. Until I do or until there's nothing left unfrozen on Query."

"And now?"

I took her hand and held it, cool as it was. "You and I go over the possibilities." I leered a little bit.

That got a faint smile. "Not those possibilities . . ." She took her hand back.

"If you say so, but we really need a good physicist to talk with, assuming there's one alive somewhere. Who would know?"

"Jerlyk or Mellorie—they were with the university."

We touched hands and slid undertime, under the clinging black surface of the now, slipping sideways and out toward the half-built settlement on the hilltop below Mount Persnol. Thor was probably trying to calculate the directionality of his planet slide. Sooner or later, he'd come booming in with an energy swathe half a world wide. Not that more than a handful of our timedivers could sense the energy flows. But his dives, like him, were so violent that I winced whenever he broke out near me.

While I could detect Wryan in the undertime, as usual, there was no sense of feeling, no sense of movement, until we lanced back into the now, right in the middle of a cloudburst.

"Should have looked first," I sputtered.

Wryan let go of my hand and dashed through the muddy street and into a half-completed cottage. I followed, since the building did have a roof and the rain was pelting down in big, cold drops.

No one was working there, although several tools had been carefully laid out.

Wryan looked around, studying the footprints in the dust. "They were working earlier."

"Odin Thor?"

"Looks like it."

That was worse than I had thought, because he'd already organized at least some of the divers and was probably holding an informal meeting of his own right now. "Let's try to slide to Jerlyk's. Don't really want to wander through this rain."

Wryan took my hand this time, and we dipped under the now and finally emerged on Jerlyk's front stoop. I was shaking a bit. Even after all my practice, sometimes the little dives, where you're trying to hit a small point in the now, were still more tiring than the long ones in a different system. And, of course, no one had ever been able to backtime or foretime in our own system. That was one of the problems in dealing with the Frost Giants. They could and we couldn't. They had all time, and we had the now.

LVII

MY STOMACH JITTERED as I chewed through the marinated buffalo steak. Greffin was still a superb chef, not that we saw him much, but he only had to prepare one meal. The duplicator, and an idea of Mellorie's, made eating his creations possible at any time.

Mellorie—somehow, coming from her it made sense. She had simply asked whether the duplicator could only duplicate what was put in it, or if a duplicated pattern could be retrieved later.

I could have bashed my head on the wall. With that question, the reasons for the settings and the fact that some duplicators on Muria were linked to the lattice crystal memory banks made instant sense.

Jerlyk retrieved—stole, if you will—some blank crystals, and Wryan helped him and Mellorie in setting up a couple of master duplicators. We couldn't steal more than two initially, because of the effort required. While setting up a closet-sized fusion plant wasn't impossible, that was just the first step. You still had to do wiring and all the time-consuming details to put the infrastructure together.

But . . . if Wryan or I wanted to visit Mellorie's cottage, she and Jerlyk were happy to punch a button and provide us with one of Greffin's best meals, hot as the moment it was duplicated.

Wryan had done the honors just before we ate, insisting it was her turn.

So we sat there, at the cottage table, alone, since, with the construction of additional cottages, Kerina and Hadron had moved out and left the place to us. Derika had left even earlier.

"You're worried about the meeting tonight?" Wryan asked.

"Aren't you?"

"Of course. What are you going to say? It's your meeting."

That bothered me, too. I'd come up with the meeting because the divers and the ConFeds had to face reality together, but I had the feeling that Wryan and I were the only ones who cared about reality. So what could I say?

I took another sip of citril and another mouthful of the buffalo steak. Finally, I looked at the cabinets behind and above Wryan's shoulder. "I guess that I'll say what I said to Odin Thor."

"They won't like it." Her tone was not critical, just gentle, reminding me of the facts.

I knew they wouldn't like what I had to say. So we finished eating in silence.

Wryan and I arrived in the travel hall early, waiting to see who would appear. Gerloc and Amenda were already there, along with Mellorie and Jerlyk. In a corner, by himself, was Verlin. As soon as he saw me, Verlin popped out of sight.

"Off to tell everyone," I muttered under my breath.

Sure enough, within moments, divers and even a handful of ConFed forcers and subforcers—probably those living in the ConFed quarters near the half-built tower—arrived.

Then Odin Thor marched through the door and straight toward me.

"We're all here, Sammis. What do you plan to do about the Frost Giants?"

Everyone looked at me, and I wanted to dive right out from underneath their sight because almost every eye stared accusingly at me, as if I had created the problem. Then again, maybe that was just the way I felt.

Instead of speaking immediately, I took a long look around the room, trying not to swallow too hard as I did so.

"Well?" demanded the man who towered over me.

"I'll tell you what I'm going to do, Colonel Odin Thor. Then I'll tell you what I recommend we do. And then, all of you can do exactly what you please." You will anyway, I thought, without voicing it.

Odin Thor looked momentarily puzzled, but said nothing.

Nearly a hundred people clustered around Wryan and me in the big empty hall, and it was so silent you could hear every isolated cough, every foot scuffle.

"First," I said. "We have not developed or found a weapon which an individual diver can carry that will destroy a Frost Giant. I have found, as you all know, a number of weapons, and I am continuing to search for one which will do the job. In the meantime, I strongly suggest that we have a group of divers mount a general search of the more likely timepaths to provide a warning if another Giant or group of Giants appear to move our way.

"Right now, all we can do is avoid them. I will continue trying to find the necessary weapons—"

"Is that all?" asked Odin Thor, his voice barely below a bellow. "Is that all?"

I could sense the unrest rippling around the room. They were all looking for a miraculous solution from good young Sammis—the man who had brought them the duplicator, the gauntlets, and some idea of hope. And I didn't have an answer.

"Is that all?" repeated Odin Thor, his voice not quite mocking.

I looked at him, and my eyes were colder than a Frost Giant. "If you want to drag out the last one or two nuclear devices buried under Westron and invite every Frost Giant in the galaxy to come and attack, be my guest. But don't blame me."

There was actually a moment of silence, and I seized it. "I've told you what I can do, and what I will do. You have to decide what you want. You know where to find me."

And I left, diving undertime from where I stood, taking even Wryan by surprise. The damned idiots!

Wryan did not arrive until later.

"Proud of yourself?" she asked, her voice somewhere between dry and bitter.

"No. But we've given them damned-near everything, and we don't have a last miracle in hand. We don't have that many energy sources, and if we don't stir things up, we'll probably have enough time to find an answer. But Odin Thor doesn't want a good answer; he wants an answer now."

Wryan sighed, and her shoulders slumped for a moment. "Do you think your departure did any good?"

"I don't know. I do know that staying would have been worse, because I would have lost my temper."

Wryan looked at me. "That would have been worse, you think?"

"I don't think you can hold people's loyalty through force."

"You . . ." she stopped. "Well, it's done, and we'll have to see."

"What happened after I left?"

"Odin Thor delivered a long sermon on the need to bring the fight to the Frost Giants. He said that your first step was absolutely right, that we couldn't attack an enemy if we didn't know where they were. Then he went on to suggest that the ConFed techs would develop some 'traps' for any Frost Giant who attacked Query.

"Gerloc volunteered to put together the scouting patrols. And Odin Thor reminded everyone that you *might* just find an answer, but that the ConFeds would be ready whether or not you were successful or not." She smiled wryly. "All in all, he did a masterful job of taking control without directly slamming you, and—"

"In making me look like a spoiled brat," I finished.

"I didn't say that."

I sighed. "I have a lot to learn. But the whole thing just . . . I don't know . . . why do people put up with such falseness?"

"Because, unlike you, Sammis Arloff Olon, most people cannot live without certainty and hope, and Odin Thor is good at appealing to their needs."

She was right, and there wasn't much I could say. I just hoped I could find a weapon or a defense before Odin Thor found a nuclear device.

LVIII

FOR A WHILE, nothing happened. Gerloc's patrols found tracks and traces of one cluster of Giants, and the ConFeds continued to work on their trap. I was splitting my time trying to find weapons and trying to find a better way to track the Frost Giants.

If the Frost Giants descended upon Inequital from Mithrada, I could sense their undertime tracks, but actually breaking into those tracks or breaking out on Query would be blocked to me. Why?

Because, as Wryan explained it to me, according to the Laws of Time, foretiming and backtiming within your home system are not possible.

Had I, as a descendent of Query, been born on Sertis, would my home system have been Query or Sertis? Or would both be blocked to me? My gut reaction was that both systems would be blocked. Otherwise, a race with both interstellar colonies and time-diving abilities could screw up the entire universe. Then again, maybe I didn't like that idea because it was just the sort of thing that Odin Thor liked to get involved in.

Still, as I pulled on the insulated time-diving uniform—the material represented another theft from some out-system by Kerina—I knew I had to try the chance of backtracking the Frost Giants, if only to find out where they had come from before Odin Thor did. I knew from my earlier attempts that I could see some scenes, even if I could not act. Seeing and following those tracks might give me some hint of their origin.

Wryan had left early, presumably to talk to Odin Thor and try to keep him from mounting his nuclear attack on the isolated pocket of the Frost Giants that Gerloc had found in the globular cluster out beyond Sertis. I had no love of the Frost Giants or Odin Thor, but I had yet to see anything that a diver could carry that would destroy one of them. Even after my statement at the meeting, no one seemed to understand that. Or they didn't want to, as Wryan suggested.

After what the Frost Giants had done to Inequital, I wasn't interested in stirring them up without any way to neutralize them or destroy them.

If I could discover that the Frost Giants were spread across a good chunk of the galaxy, that *might* provide us some breathing room before Odin Thor started another witch-burning crusade, just like those of the Westron past.

So I pulled on the black uniform, the boots, and the equipment belt, including the heaviest gauntlets around, one of the few technological remnants of Ydris. With just one little push, I had shoved the Ydrisians from violence and fighting into such high-tech disaster that they had destroyed each other. While I might have wished otherwise, it had happened, and it would be difficult if not impossible for me to undo it. Besides, sadly, the divers needed the gauntlets for personal survival, and I wasn't about to go back to the witches of Eastron days, not after my own trials in the damps.

No one else was around in the cottage as I stuffed down a high-energy breakfast. I put some additional food in the thin backpack, mostly hard bread, cheeses and dried fruit and meat. After my first diving experiences, and after my stint in the hospital, I didn't feel comfortable without carrying some food. Then I sighed . . . and dived, letting my mind carry me sideways in time to the hilly plains that had been Inequital. While I could neither break out in the foretime or backtime on Query, nor see more than a few years past or future, there was nothing to prevent me from slipping backwards and watching for the tell-tale paths of the Frost Giants . . . or other timedivers.

As I suspected, near the present there were no traces or tracks, not the slightest "warping" of the time arrows that might indicate the passage of a traveler. Perhaps two or three years in the past the undertime twisted almost violently, so violently that I had to refocus my concentration to remain there. The clutter and distortion were so great, the blue twisting in upon the red and the black and gold interleaving with each other, that I forced myself farther into the red.

Farther backtime meant fewer trails and a chance to find a Frost Giant track discrete enough to trace back to another home planet or base.

That wasn't what I found.

Backtime of the Frost Giants, clear and thin as a razor, I found a time-line edged with crimson and vibrating with pain. Not that it was obvious, or that anyone else would have sensed the pain, because I've had Wryan ask about it. No one else can see more than a blur through the undertime, and no one else can sense strong emotions through the undertime. Wryan always thought it was funny that I have no empathy sense except through the time walls.

In this case, the pain was there. I almost missed it, and I had to have missed it before. But I was getting more sensitive with experience, and I was looking for that sort of thing. It wasn't really a backtime line, but a crosstime line, running from somewhere west of Inequital to Inequital itself, and then further to the east. Toward Esterly—or Bremarlyn. Maybe farther.

My blood was as cold as if a Frost Giant had appeared before me, and, even in the suspension of the undertime I felt like my heart was racing. Mentally, I took a deep breath. Mentally, because you have no physical abilities in the undertime. Everything is suspended—itches, elation, pain.

That was why my mind wanted to make my body shudder. If that trail represented what I feared . . .

Taking a mental hold of myself, I did my best to mark the timing and place of that crimson line. Then I dived back to the cottage.

No one was there.

I ate a chyst, and paced from the workroom to the kitchen area and back again. I went outside and looked around. The overcast looked like it was building to a storm that matched what was building inside me. I could almost see my breath steaming, and I shivered, but not from the cold.

Serla looked through the shutters from next door, but she must have seen my face, because she disappeared.

I walked back inside and cut some stale brown bread and two slices of yellow cheese. Tough chewing, but it gave me something to do.

Wishing Wryan were back, I paced back down to the workroom and looked at the new duplicator and the original of the Ydrisian handgun, the one that had led to my manipulations of Ydris, and set the change-winds howling down the corridors of time. Most of the butt and the area under the barrel were taken up by energy cells.

A thought occurred to me, and, while I waited, I jotted it down on the tablet by the bench.

"Time-diving energy flows. Diverted to energy cells for weapon power?"

After all, if the power inherent in time flows could be tapped for weapons, the whole problem of energy storage would be minimized.

Even if—I dropped the thought. Either it could be done or it couldn't.

I wished Wryan would appear, but I still didn't want to show my face down at the Marine camp. In Odin Thor's current mood, there was always the chance for some sort of "accident" to happen to me. He thought he still needed Wryan, but he had no use for me, now that he had the duplicator, the gauntlets, and the closet-sized fusion plant.

From the cluttered workroom I walked back to the kitchen and ate a pearapple. I looked out the window again. The thunderheads were building up to the south, and the sky was turning a purpled black.

A single jagged lightning bolt flared in the distance.

Tempted to eat something else, I deferred, mainly because my guts were feeling heavy. I still wanted to bite things, chew them. I kept pacing.

Heavy cold raindrops were striking the roof and the cottage walls and windows.

I could feel the undertime tension and turned to face the open space in the middle of the kitchen where Wryan would appear. She was wearing a black diving suit.

"I don't know which storm's worse—the one outside or the one inside," commented Wryan after taking a quick look at my face.

"Inside, this time. I need your opinion. Hold my hand and dive with me. Inequital, just before the Frost Giant attack."

"It wasn't exactly an attack, Sammis."

"This isn't about the attack . . ."

She looked at my face and asked, "Can I get something to eat? Will it wait that long?"

I didn't want to wait. I'd waited all morning, it seemed, but she looked pale, and, besides, who knew where the dive would lead? I nodded. "Anything special?"

"Just fix me some tea."

So I turned on the burner to heat the water, while she rummaged through the cooler. Then I nibbled another corner of the hard yellow cheese.

"What is it?"

I shook my head. "I'm not sure, but I have a feeling that it's not at all good."

"Is it the Frost Giants or Odin Thor?" She was fitting together a combination of sliced meats, greens, and cheese too thick to be properly called a sandwich.

"Something else. Very different."

"You are upset. Just let me finish. Sit down and stop pacing. I don't need indigestion, too."

Perching on the edge of the chair, I watched her. Even eating that monstrous sandwich, she looked graceful. When she picked up the heavy tea mug, she could have been handling the imperial china. Yet those slender hands were as strong as mine and a lot more skilled. She'd been a medical doctor before she'd gone into the time-diving research and probably had several careers before that, although I had never had the nerve to ask her about them. She made me feel so young, so hell-fired inexperienced, at times.

I reached for the cheese.

"Are you really that hungry?" Her eyes were smiling, but caring, too, at the same time.

"No. Nervous."

"I know. I'll be ready in a minute, but I haven't had anything to eat since dawn. Trying to explain Frost Giant migration patterns takes a lot of effort when Odin Thor doesn't really want to hear. But he finally got the point."

"Which was?"

"Migration patterns, by themselves, mean that there are probably many more Frost Giants lurking around and that it isn't wise to act until you know exactly how many. That's because they react to temporal and energy disruptions. Destroying Frost Giants will create both." She took a last bite of the sandwich, chewing it thoroughly, unlike me.

"How long will he wait?"

"Maybe ten days . . . unless we can find several other clusters of Giants."

"You know—"

"I know. You can't find weapons and track Frost Giants simultaneously. And you're the only one who can see clearly enough from the undertime."

"You can . . ."

"Not quite as well, and, besides, we agreed not to let him know that."

I shook my head. Concealing things from Odin Thor was always a two-edged sword.

"I'm about ready. Will I need anything special?"

"A medical kit . . . maybe . . . But I think it's too late . . . was too late a long time ago."

"Is this an off-system, back-time injury case?"

"I'm not sure."

"Just a moment." She left the kitchen.

I waited, but before I had a chance to grab another chunk of cheese she was back, strapping a small case to her equipment belt.

"And stay away from the cheese."

I shrugged, flushing slightly in spite of myself. "Then let's go." I extended my hand.

"Wait." Both her arms went around me, and she pulled us together, holding me tight, and somehow warming part of the chill inside me. "I know . . . I know . . ."

She knew me all right, too well, but she was also right, and I stood there and hung onto her, while her fingers crept up my back and kneaded away some of the tightness in my shoulders. After a time, she lifted her head from my shoulder and brushed my lips with hers. "All right?"

"Yes. Much better." I tried to smile, but took a deep breath instead.

Then we held hands and slipped undertime, crosstime toward Inequital. The thin crimson dive-line was still there, like a slash of blood at right angles to the Frost Giant tracks.

Perhaps Wryan tensed as I guided us along that line. I felt she did, but since our physical condition remained exactly the same as when we entered the undertime, any tension had to be strictly mental.

What I did not understand about the crosstime track was its intensity. All tracks faded over subjective time. At least all those I had run across did. Time-diving is a subjective mental feat. Only entry and breakout actually have an objective reality.

So why was this track so unfaded? I thought I knew, and I was scared.

All I could do was try to match our dive with that of the crimson track, trying to trace it to the end.

Reaching the end of the track was not that difficult, except that the diver had never broken out back into the now. The crosstime slide ran from somewhere west of Inequital through Bremarlyn and into Eastron . . . and stopped, as if the diver were suspended.

In peering into that backtime view of Query, I could only see a hazy view of the "then," a view of a cave of some sort, high in the Bardwalls, a cave filled with old-fashioned cabinetry and wardrobes and other objects I could not make out. Certainly, more than a cave.

Investigating the cave would not solve the problem of the suspended diver, and the screaming of the crosstime track that tore at both heart and soul.

With a mental shrug, I tried to look through the barrier that separated me from the endlessly fading energy that had to be another timediver. All I could gather was an endless scream, a mindless feeling of agony, that blotted out any sense of description.

I could sense the shakiness coming on for me, and, looking for a breakout point, chose the closest one—the current time position of the equipment cave.

Legs trembling, I glanced around the room, lit through a pair of diffused and hidden skylights, and took a deep breath. That was a mistake.

I knew . . . and my legs would not hold me, not while I shuddered and wept in the darkness. Not while Wryan held me and said nothing, though I could feel her tears mingle with mine.

Less than the thinnest of barriers separated us from that endlessly dying diver I knew too well, and that barrier might have been the length of eternity, for all that I could not cross it.

Nothing . . . nothing had I suffered, nor would I ever suffer, in comparison, even should I find some way to break that endless dive of agony.

In time—how long I did not know—I finally managed to gather myself together, shaking from more than one cause, and to sit up in the dim light. I could not look at anything too closely, especially not at the wardrobe with the one open door, as I grasped for my pack and a small chunk of hard bread. Offering Wryan a piece silently, I broke off a small chunk and chewed it slowly, thoroughly.

"How . . . terrible . . ."

I nodded. Banal as the word "terrible" was, what other word was there?

"To be trapped in an endless death . . . without the strength or consciousness to break out . . . even to die . . ."

". . . dying forever . . ."

"Sammis . . . I'm . . . sorry . . ." Her voice said more than the words. So did her hand as she squeezed mine. "You knew?"

"No . . . felt it . . . guessed it . . . I think . . ." I took another bite of the hard bread, trying to get enough energy back into my system to stop the shakes, to allow me to think.

One way or another, thought was all I had. Thought was all I had.

Wryan and I eventually chewed through the entire loaf, the cheese, the dried fruits and meats, although most of the bites were mine. By then the sun was dropping over the Bardwalls and the cave was lit only by some sort of emergency lamp that functioned still.

Wryan looked like hell, which was better than I felt.

"You knew your mother hadn't died in the fire, didn't you?"

"Yes. I couldn't explain why."

"You were close to her."

"Not exactly. We never spoke much. We just did things together. My father did all the talking."

"Could you tell when she was around? Could she tell when you were near?"

I had to think about that. In some ways, that had been another lifetime. "I think so."

She snorted. "You think so? How did you know she was here? And why did you insist I come, with a medical kit?"

Wryan definitely had me there.

"All right. I knew."

"That's important. There might be one way . . ."

"How? We can't touch her. We can't merge, and we're from two separate times."

"Whose mind controls the dive?"

"Hers . . ."

"So all you have to do is reach her thoughts . . . that's all."

"That's all? That sounds like reaching across eternity."

"Sammis."

I knew what she meant. I just wasn't sure about meshing with that agony again. Especially meshing and keeping my own sanity. The whole idea was insane. The thought of leaving anyone—let alone who that forever-dying diver was—in such endless agony was even worse.

"I'll be with you," Wryan added, taking my hand.

"Let's go." I closed my pack.

"What are you going to do . . . exactly?"

That was a good question, and one for which I had no ready answer. So I sat down on the floor. I didn't really want to touch anything. "I'm not sure. But I have to push as close as I can, try and force the barrier . . ."

". . . and . . . ?"

". . . don't know. Do I send reassurance? Or encouragement? Or strength?" I sighed. "Hell! I don't even know if this will work. How can I make her feel anything?"

"I don't know. It may not work."

"I know. But I have to try."

"*We* have to try."

I scrambled around in that dawn-lit retreat until I could hug her again. Then I pulled on my pack and checked my equipment.

"Ready?"

Wryan just nodded, and we took each other's hands, and eased under the now toward that endless scream.

The second time was worse.

In that undertime, drawn by the crimson line like an iron filing to a lodestone, the thin black curtain seemed to fade into dark translucence.

They say you can't smell in the undertime, but the odor of burning cloth and flesh seared my nose, throat, and lungs.

Somehow my thoughts reached for my mother, who had left to do her duty and never made it back, and—

. . . find the darkness . . . the shelter . . . no leads . . . must not . . . cannot . . . lead them back . . . not to Sammis . . . burns . . . Verlyt! Just hold on . . . just another instant . . .

Images flew at me and through me.

. . . Standing on the point of a narrow rock jutting out over a canyon, where a blue ribbon wound through dust-crimson rocks below, watching a night-eagle launch itself into the first flight of twilight, listening to another woman . . .

"You have a responsibility, Meryn. It will last longer than you can possibly conceive, past the fall of Eastron, perhaps beyond the fall of Westron. And should you let anyone know what you are, you will be called 'witch', and worse, and every man, every woman, and every child will rise against you. You will see most of your children die of old age . . ."

. . . Appearing from the shadows, slipping across the hard-packed dirt path to the stacked barrels and placing one flare, then another, then lighting them, both and dropping into the no-time place, feeling the explosions in the Westron camp from undertime, and knowing that the delays would be futile . . .

. . . Looking down at the inlaid casket of the duke, remembering the unlined face of years past, the blond hair before it silvered, the capable hands—before the onslaught of the ConFederation Marines of Westron, ignoring the whispers of the three women at the other side of the chapel . . . "How could she? After all the years, and looking like that. She has to be a witch . . . why he never remarried . . ."

. . . Running the wooded path, feet set quickly and silently in place, breathing easily and leaving the flat-footed soldiers of the empress gasping far behind, taking the trails where the steamers could not follow, enjoying the pure physical effort, the ability to leave the empress's best with their mouths gaping . . .

. . . Nodding at the round-faced solicitor, whose decency could not be disguised by his profession and position, wondering whether it would be a kindness or a mistake to accept his proposition, wondering if, this time, there would be a child, and hoping, again, that there would . . . "On my terms, Aldus? That is more than generous . . ."

. . . Looking down at the blond-haired boy infant, with the elfin face even so soon after birth, wanting to cry after so long, yet not daring to, and knowing that the long toll of years would be ending. ". . . forever may a she-witch live, until she is with child and mortal . . ."

. . . Seeing the fire, the flames, the shells from the ConFeds, and the crumpled body of a round-faced solicitor; knowing that Aldus wore the same puzzled expression in death that he had in life; seeing the houses of the Westron gentry fall, fired and shelled; seeing the empire crumple with each shell . . .

. . . Walking through the Fountain Court toward a single sentry; seeing the lone guard as a sacrifice against the mob howling toward the Palace walls; wondering what sacrifice would be called for; asking whether she could; knowing that her son would understand . . .

"No!" THOUGH I could not utter the word, I screamed it in that undertime prison, and the barriers between the three of us shivered—but did not shatter nor break.

. . . break out . . . now . . . somehow . . . Sammis . . .

One fragmentary thought—that was all—and the crimson thread I had held on to, locked my soul to, was gone, nothing more than a fast-fading memory.

You did it. That second thought was warmer, closer.

But . . . how . . . ?

I don't know. Isn't it better than diving in silence?

It was. Much better.

Shall we check the retreat?

No. *Leave her there. One death is enough.*

Wryan knew what I meant. There was no way to save her, and to find her dust and bones where they lay somehow was wrong. Wrong for me, anyway. I had my goodbye. Years late, but that's usually the way the ones that hurt come to you.

LIX

I WAS SHAKING again when I staggered into the kitchen of the cottage.

Wryan may have been, also, but I wasn't in the best of conditions to determine that as I slumped into one of the heavy wooden chairs.

Thump. Wryan hit the other chair harder than I had landed.

I put my head on the table, trying to sort it all out, from the memories of Eastron that were not mine to the views of me seen through my mother's eyes. I knew I had never been female, but I shivered at the memories of having been so, at the recollection of joy at my own birth, and the desperation . . .

"... Verlyt..." The exclamation stumbled from numb lips. Too much was happening—again—all too quickly. I lifted my head to look at Wryan.

Her face was pale. Mine probably was, too. Looking at her features was like looking at mine. Same elfin face. Same green eyes. Same not-quite-blond but sandy hair. Same wiry muscles.

"How long ... ?" I asked. My mouth was dry.

"How terrible ..."

I realized Wryan had not even heard my question, and I could see the darkness in her eyes. "The memories ... ?"

"Just through you ... mainly feelings, and that was more than enough."

It was hard just keeping my head up, splitting as it was with memories that were not mine, and yet that would always belong to me. I shivered again.

"How long?" I asked again, not wanting to deal with the memories or the still-raw remembrance of pain, and stench of burning flesh that clung to my nostrils.

"How long for what?"

"Look at me. What do you see?"

"I see you." Despite the pain in her voice, the wry warmth was still there.

"I look at you, and I see me. Just like my mother saw me."

"I know. I knew that from the day you arrived with Odin Thor. But you had to see for yourself. We're probably related, but how I couldn't tell you."

"How long?" I asked for the third time.

Wryan sighed. "Persistent, aren't you?"

"You're not?"

She shrugged, and it was eerie, seeing for the first time, really, myself shrug. "Not so long as your mother. About a century, give or take a year or two."

"So I'm in love with my mother's sister?"

"You never said you were in love."

"I am, and you know it, and I'm scared." I pushed back the chair and stood up, walking toward the window. The thin sunlight was dimming into dusk. Diving around the planet can play hell with your biological clocks. "I don't think you are. You've waited so long and hoped, and here I am."

"How do you know you're in love? And not looking for your mother?"

"Because I found her, and she's dead." Outside, a grossjay hopped along the raised brick curbing, looking for something to scavenge.

"I never knew your mother, Sammis."

"But the three of us all look alike. Too much alike for mere coincidence."

Wryan sighed. "All witches look alike."

"Then why don't all timedivers look alike?"

"Witches are timedivers, plus some different traits. Odin Thor is probably a stronger diver than either one of us, although he couldn't navigate his way from one side of the planet to the other without help." She stood up and went over to the cooler.

I followed her. Witches or timedivers or both, we were always hungry.

"Not much here."

"You didn't answer my questions."

Wryan took a bite from a pearapple and chewed it slowly. The color began to return to her face almost instantly. So I took out the last one and took a bite from it, hoping for some near-instantaneous rejuvenation myself.

"I can't. I grew up in the Southpoint orphan home. My mother was the captain of a Southpoint coaster, an independent woman who did as she pleased. But she died after I was born—or so the Ladies of Mercy told me. I asked about her when I was old enough to get away from the home's walls. Some of the oldsters remembered her—with a tinge of admiration and envy. But no one could or would say what happened to her, not to her daughter, or to any fifteen-year-old girl."

"How long ago was that?"

Wryan took several more bites from the pearapple before attempting to answer. "Long enough. I could be your grandmother in some ways, but it doesn't make any difference."

I had to shake my head. "Doesn't make any difference? Compared to you, what I know wouldn't fill a thimble, and you'll still be young centuries from now."

"So will you."

There was that. I chewed some more of the pearapple, trying to digest everything. My stomach was doing better than my mind.

"Sammis." Wryan's voice was soft.

I stopped and looked at her.

"What you are is more important than what you know. Especially now, because the whole world is changing."

I thought about that. The world was changing. More and more people with the time-diving ability. Even with fewer people after the onslaught of the Frost Giants, the infrastructure of Westron was tottering because of the continuing failure of fragile high technology. "Changing or collapsing?"

"That's up to us."

"And Odin Thor. He wants to build a military dictatorship."

She looked at me, and I looked at her, and I could see the darkness behind her eyes. What scared me then was the thought that she saw the same darkness behind mine.

One way or another, there would be no more war on Query. One way or another. Even if it took the witches of Eastron and their offspring and their talents.

LX

I WAS WRONG about the war, because I had forgotten about the Frost Giants. They hadn't forgotten about us, and Odin Thor hadn't forgotten about them.

EEEEEEEeeeeeeeeeeeeee . . .

The scream of the vest-pocket nuclear device vibrated even in the undertime, even from the geographic distance I had put between the trap and myself. The location was north of Inequital, almost a wasteland, that had yet to recover from the first Frost Giant attack. Then it had been industrial.

The trap? Simple enough. Odin Thor and Weldin had rigged a fusion power plant to run at full output and linked it to a modified arc furnace of some sort, figuring that the combination of heat and energy would be enough to tempt a Frost Giant into appearing. Then they rigged the nuclear device to a thermocouple trigger. The instant the temperature began to drop, the bomb blew.

Not terribly elegant, but effective.

. . . eeeeeeeeeeeeeeeeeeeee . . .

My head ached from the vibration and energy flashes that weren't supposed to have a physical impact in the undertime, and I was kays from the blast.

". . . noooooo . . ." The non-voice was mine, trying to close eyes that would not, could not, close in the undertime.

. . . blue flashes, like jagged edges of a mirror, cut through my head . . . an image of a small blue and blocky figure, four-armed, surrounded with warm blueness . . .

. . . a dull red plain . . . standing beside another blue-block figure
. . . reassuring heat . . . flashing back and forth . . .

. . . so much heat . . . pressure . . . like knives cutting from inside . . .

. . . and more blue shards knifing their way through my head, already
fading as they cut.

I time-staggered back to the divers' village, stumbling out of the
undertime and losing the contents of my guts right into the sink.

Cold water helped my appearance and that of the sink.

By the time Wryan appeared, I was back to normal, if pale.

"For someone who has created so much destruction, you certainly
have a nervous stomach," she observed, wrinkling her nose.

I went on cleaning up the mess, opening the window. The cold winter
air was preferable to the odor.

"Staying around to experience death close up doesn't do much for
me."

"I take it Odin Thor's trap was successful?"

"Too successful, I suspect." I dried my face, and folded the towel.
The wind almost lifted it off the rack. I slid the window half-closed and
took the chair across from Wryan. She was pale, though not as pale as
I was. "You? You felt it, too?"

"No." Her lips quirked. "You're not exactly good for my digestion.
I felt you feel that thing's death."

"Oh . . ."

I stood up, feeling the unease mount within me, the sense of an
avalanche overhanging. Opening the cupboard, I took out some hard
crackers, tossed one to Wryan, then caught the towel as a gust of wind
from the window blew it past me. After closing the window the rest of
the way, I began to chew on the cracker, slowly, until I was sure that
my stomach would take it.

The mental unease continued.

"All hell is breaking loose. Better warn all the divers. Shut down the
power plant—ours anyway."

Wryan looked blank. I just dropped undertime and sprinted for the
Bardwalls. I wanted something left to rebuild with, and the one power
plant, the duplicator and the parts we had stashed there would be
enough.

In the undertime, I could sense the distant rush of blue, but it wasn't
close . . . yet.

Wryan broke out as I was shutting down the system. The cold of the
location and the time-protected walls should have been enough to in-
sulate it from the Frost Giants. They couldn't easily get inside, nor pull

the energy through the walls, I didn't think, but there was no reason to provide that temptation.

"Do you think . . . ?"

"I know. Now let's tell whoever we can reach. I'll take Odin Thor."

Wryan's eyebrows raised a notch, even as she completed the shutdown I had started. Outside the double doors, the winter whistled, throwing more snow against the rocks below and building the drifts.

The retreat was mostly complete, with glowstones on the floor and some furniture, and the workroom we had moved from the cave. But we had not used it much, partly because of the time difference. Living a quarter of the way around the planet from where you spent most of your waking hours could be more than a little disruptive. Besides, who wanted to advertise it?

The cold—and the lack of energy—might protect us . . . that and the fact that the Frost Giants didn't seem to move much out of the now, except as a group or when pushed.

I could hope.

Wryan looked at me, although her face was dim in the low light from the storm outside, now that we had shut down the power.

We left, sliding across the now.

Odin Thor was sitting in his office, Weldin sitting across from him, and two other forcers, Carlis and someone I didn't know, in the other chairs. Each had a glass—old Imperial crystal recovered from who knew where—in his hand.

"What . . ." gaped Odin Thor, as I dropped into the space between the chairs.

"Sorry to disrupt your premature celebration, Colonel, but it appears as though you have made the Frost Giants really mad. A force of them is headed this way through the undertime, and I frankly have no idea how to stop them. You might think about dispersing your troops and personnel. That way, some of them *might* survive."

"It's your doing, witch," snapped Carlis.

I looked at the idiot. "I told him not to attack the Giants. And I told him then that we didn't have any way to stop them as a force. You all agreed to this idiocy over my strong objections. Now, you'll have to live with it."

I glanced undertime, feeling that the blue rush was nearer, but unable to judge how much nearer.

The unknown forcer, a heavyset and older man, nodded, then asked, "How long before these attacks start?"

"Assuming they stay close to the now—the present time reference—

I'd guess it might be a day, perhaps two, before the mass of Giants strikes Query."

"That soon?"

"I don't understand exactly how they travel the undertime, because it's hard to track unless you're right with them, but they move at an angle—that's the only way I can describe it . . ."

Odin Thor stood up, his face slightly flushed. "You have the—"

At that point, I lost it.

I slid under the now, inside his big arms, and cracked him on the jaw, then was back across the room before he could react.

"I could have killed you right there."

The room got very quiet, so quiet that the faint whine of the wind seemed like a shout.

Carlis looked at me with the look one gives a snake.

I almost smiled, but I was looking at Odin Thor. "You have blundered and blasted your way to power. And you almost saved Westron. But you couldn't wait. We gave you weapons and tools. We brought back the technology to make food. In time, we could have stopped the Giants. But you couldn't wait. I'll do my damnedest to find a way, but not because of you. And if you *ever* threaten the safety of the divers or the people again, you won't live long enough to realize what you did."

I looked at the others. "The only thing you can do is to scatter and stay away from power plants, hot areas, and large groups of people. I know it's winter, but this wasn't our idea. You can thank Odin Thor for it."

I dropped undertime and behind Odin Thor, touching the gauntlet bosses to deactivate his weapons, before moving aside and reappearing.

He glared as the gauntlets failed to trigger.

"You don't listen, do you?" I forced a smile. "Now, gentlemen, the choice is yours. Partly. The divers will tell all the women and children, and I think they'll choose survival. I hope I can find it in time."

I left, dropping back to the cottage to stoke up on food and equipment before beginning my solitary quest. Wryan was better at organizing people. I just hoped I would be as good at searching.

LXI

SOMETIMES THE ANSWERS are right in front of you, if you can only see what they mean. Or, perhaps it's more accurate to say that the pieces are all there, but it takes a new or different perspective to combine them to reach a solution.

Odin Thor had used one of the few remaining vest-pocket fusion devices to pot his Frost Giant. The Frost Giants, predictably, had retaliated, and what was left of Westron was generally uninhabited mountains, swamps, deserts, and whatever structures the divers had managed to warp undertime—like the unfinished tower.

Now the Giants were trying to track down individual divers, without too much success, because they were even noisier than Odin Thor in the undertime. Whether I liked it or not, we had to find something to stop them. And only massive jolts of energy, such as a fusion device or a massive particle beam, seemed to affect them.

The problem was simple enough.

We needed to destroy Frost Giants. Destroying Frost Giants took energy. The gauntlets worked fine, except they didn't handle the massive amounts of energy required. We could no longer produce those old-style energy-intensive weapons, and only a few of the fusion devices remained, far fewer than the total number of Frost Giants. Far fewer.

Not many high-tech races we could observe and steal from produced mass destruction energy weapons, or, for that matter, much in the way of any weapons at all. Those that did, like Ydris, produced weapons that were more like mobile forts.

The logic of what had to be done was simple enough. We needed to use *someone's* existing technology to apply enough energy selectively to individual Frost Giants. And whatever it was had to be light enough for a timediver to carry.

Simple and apparently impossible.

I went back to Muria. The gentle Murians weren't destructive, but they did have some interesting technology, and not all of it was obvious.

So I watched from the undertime, subjective day by subjective day, and scoured the planet from one island continent to another, from laboratories to the very small proto-factories they used. Each day, at first, I staggered back to Query, back to our retreat in the cliffs of the Bardwalls. At least there, I could look at the starkness of the cliffs and the play of the light in the canyon below. With the timewarped nature of the walls and the cold location, it apparently wasn't too attractive to the Frost Giants. Neither was the tower, still only half-completed, but who had time to build anymore?

Sometimes, Wryan wasn't there. Mostly she was, as if she knew when I would return.

"Any luck?"

"It's not a matter of luck, just perseverance," I mumbled through a full mouth.

"You've lost more weight." Her voice was gentle. "You can't keep this up for too much longer."

"Do I have a choice?" I swallowed some more of the underbaked bread, which had to have come from Sertis originally, via the duplicator. Without the duplicators, we already would have starved. All the fields were dust, along with the remaining Westron farmers.

Since Wryan didn't answer, I jammed some more bread and a hunk of unidentified cheese into my mouth and continued chewing. Then I swallowed some Quin. Drinking beer after diving can destroy your balance and then some, but I wasn't going anywhere for a while, and from Wryan's comments, I needed as many calories as my system could take, followed by as much sleep as I could get away with.

"How is it going?"

"You know. Otherwise, you wouldn't be out there day after day, killing yourself. You have to be careful. I don't want you ending up like—"

"I know." I cut off her words abruptly. Some comparisons, well meant as they may be, are too painful to hear. "What's the esteemed colonel doing?"

"He's located another vest-pocket device, and they're baiting another trap." Her thin face was as white as mine still felt.

The off-focus glimmer of the time-warped walls went even more off-focus as I swallowed, hard. Almost, almost, I felt as though I were falling through the armaglass into a two-kay-long drop to the Dyel below.

Wryan nodded, slowly. "Everyone is so bitter about the destruction that they can't wait."

Pushing aside the Quin, a bottle duplicated from the late Duke of Eastron's hidden private stock, I forced another mouthful of bread and cheese into my stomach. The room settled back into semi-solidity.

I joined Wryan in the headshaking, not having anything else to add.

My legs were rubbery when I tried to stand up, and the out-of-time glimmer of the retreat's walls flashed at me.

Wryan slipped under my arm and helped guide me into our bedroom, where I ended up sprawled face down on the old-fashioned bed. The last thing I remembered was her hands kneading the tightness out of my back.

When I woke, she was gone. But a faint spiciness remained around the pillow next to mine. The sun was well into the sky, almost straight over the canyon, lighting the tumbling waters of the Dyel so far below.

Rolling onto my back, still tangled in the quilt, I closed my eyes without drifting back to sleep.

Odin Thor . . . vest-pocket devices . . . Frost Giants . . . Wryan . . .

With a sigh, I struggled upright and swung my feet onto the glow-stones, another theft from the Murians, but one I was certain they would not have minded. The slight warmth in winter and slight chill in summer, and the everpresent luminescence made the retreat just a touch more special.

"Oooooo . . ." The exclamation was mine. Despite Wryan's ministrations of the night before, my shoulders still ached.

About then, the guilt hit. I'd been avoiding Odin Thor, while trying to track down a weapon, a way to drive off the Frost Giants. Wryan had to have been shielding me—again.

A hot shower helped, as did some more bread and cheese, along with a ripe chyst. Both guilt and aches subsided.

As I sat in the stool overlooking the canyon, the problem remained—how to concentrate enough energy in one spot when we couldn't even generate it. It was too bad we couldn't just toss them into a nearby sun—since there were plenty of those and they certainly had enough energy.

I ate a second chyst and then stood, heading for the sleeping room. There I began to dress, slowly.

Energy . . . Frost Giants . . . compactness . . . energy . . .

As the words drifted through my thoughts, I finished my pre-dive preparations.

This time. This time I was going to find what we needed.

LXII

EVEN FROM HER protected position, the woman shivered, though shivering was not physically possible, as if she could sense the absolute chill that lay only instants from her.

From where she viewed, through the dark lens of time, she could see both the flattening swirls of ambient energy flows being sucked into nothingness and less clearly, the new-formed snow cascading downward and the soft explosions of vegetation being frozen nearly instantaneously.

She concentrated and removed herself to another locale, only to find a circular gray-brown wasteland, covered with fog as the heat from the surrounding area poured back over the frozen surfaces. A wall of thunderclouds towered against the low mountains.

Again, she concentrated, this time on a plateau that had been tree-covered with a walled encampment centered upon it.

A series of pelting rains and gusty winds swept across another gray brown wasteland. In places, new gullies appeared in the waist-deep sludge of fragmented cellular matter that had been largely living days earlier, cut by the force of water and gravity. The stone walls stood stark where they had for centuries, now alone in rearing above the gentle undulations of the plateau surface. Stone and sludge. Just stone and sludge and rain.

Once more, the woman concentrated . . . and disappeared . . .

LXIII

NOW THAT I had steeled myself to develop whatever was necessary, I stayed on Muria, continuing to concentrate on discovering something that either concentrated energy, stored large amounts of energy, or transported that energy.

As far as I could discover, in sliding from undertime locale to undertime locale around the Murian systems, they had little need for storage of massive quantities of energy. Their closet-sized fusion generators and their light, thin, and all too durable superconducting cables took care of that aspect of energy.

In the end, the fact that I could sense energy flows from the undertime led me in the right direction—to a small series of structures located directly under the south magnetic pole of Muria. At the time, I didn't know it was the south magnetic pole, but Wryan later assured me that it had to be.

The complex seemed inactive, but the spray of energy ghosting around it in the undertime indicated that at infrequent intervals massive amounts of energy had been expended.

The initial observation was easy. The eight buildings, arranged as points of an octagon, were all closed and without inhabitants. So was the central eight-sided structure, which enclosed an eight-sided platform. In the center of the platform was a shimmering circular plate half a rod across and perhaps the thickness of my thumb. Connected to the plate were sixteen of the thin superconducting cables—apparently two from each outlying building.

A quick series of dives verified that each outlying building contained an inactive fusion power plant.

The ghostly energy lines looped around the plate, then, about a handspan above the metal, disappeared.

I dropped backtime, perhaps a local decade or so, before any activity appeared, and watched as three Murians employed what might have been a forklift to place a cube covered with the shimmering insulation used for their superconducting wires on the plate. A burst of energy from all fusion systems, and the box was gone.

That meant more backtiming, since there was no way to determine where the box had been destined. Instead I forced myself back to the construction of the facility, getting hell-fired close to my personal back-time limit, in order to follow the equipment back to its point of fabrication.

There were two plates. One went somewhere in an interstellar ship. The other went to the site where I had found it. That cinched it. The Murians had a matter transmitter. But they didn't use it often at all. And its use required the output of eight fusion generators at peak load.

Still . . . I wondered about the possibilities. So I went back a touch farther and liberated a set of the plates . . . and did a few experiments of my own. They worked. I didn't know much about physics, but when you can see the energy flows certain alternatives show a possibility. Like using the direct energy from a sun instead of one fusion generator—or eight generators.

It sounds easy. It wasn't, and it took subjective weeks before I was convinced that what I had in mind would work. That's the way it is with all brilliant discoveries. They become grunt efforts. Great ideas are easy. Getting them to work is the hard part.

After figuring out the pieces for my gadget, I had to get all the pieces home, all the time hoping that there was a home left for me to go back to. I suppose I could have checked in periodically with Wryan, but that would have taken twice as much subjective time as staying on Muria, and time was something we had little enough of in any case.

Carrying all of the equipment was a chore, requiring about three times the number of breaks and stops to get me back to our Bardwall retreat. At least the retreat, with its time-protected stone, would have survived the worst of any Frost Giant attacks.

Empty . . . and dusty—that was the way I found it. The single workroom off the minuscule kitchen showed no recent footprints.

"Wryan?" My voice echoed.

"Wryan?" Again, no answer.

"WRYAN!" *Wryan, Wryan, Wryan. . . .*

My stomach was so tight that I was shaking all over.

Had she run into the Frost Giants—or Odin Thor? Was I too late? Again?

As the questions swirled around in my head, I reached out and managed to steady myself on the long workbench. Another look through the archway told me that it was mid-morning in the Bardwalls, and there was no reason Wryan would be home in mid-morning. None at all.

That reasoning didn't calm either my guts or my shaking.

Wryan, dear, where are you?

"Sammis . . . are you all right?" She had apparently broken out in our sleeping room. Her light steps scuffed toward the kitchen.

"Where have you been?" The words came out before I had a chance to even think about them. Or glimpse her face.

She stopped silently in the archway, and I could see the exhaustion and the strain, the lines in her face, the blackness under her eyes, the sandy hair wisps framing the high cheekbones.

"Oh, Verlyt . . ." *Wryan . . . Wryan . . .*

"Wherever I was needed." Her voice was husky, in a way I had never heard, as if she had cried and cried. And then had to cry again.

There was so much to say, and no words for me to express those feelings.

Wryan took another step forward.

"I'm sorry . . ." It wasn't the right thing to say, but I said it anyway. "I'm sorry."

"The Woods are gone, and the Plain of Cannorra, and Camp Pers-nol . . ." She shook her head. "And, yes, one Frost Giant. One more Frost Giant. Two in all."

I let go of the bench to reach out to her, but the room began to spin. So I put my hand back down and concentrated on keeping my balance. Before saying anything more, I went to work unstrapping the equipment from the complex harness that wore me, rather than the other way around. I couldn't talk; so I might as well do something.

Clunkkkk.

Despite my best efforts, the main tube hit the work bench top harder than I had intended. That might have been because my hands were still shaking, and because the room kept trying to spin around me. The pair of plates in their insulation were all the rest that I could manage.

Clannkkk.

Rather than argue with my body, I sat down on the floor to finish disentangling myself from the rest of the components.

"Sammis!" Wryan didn't seem to mind the components, but her arms had trouble encircling both electronics and me, especially in the cramped space between the equipment bench and the timewarped stone wall.

"Sorry it took so long . . ."

"Some of us knew it would . . ."

Her arms stayed around me, and I could tell she was shaking, crying without tears, perhaps because she had no tears left to shed.

"I think I have what we need." What else could I say?

She held me, still without speaking, still shivering, although the workroom was warm enough for me to have begun to sweat. I scarcely smelled human, even to me, but Wryan didn't seem to mind.

"Let's get the rest of the equipment off you." Her arms squeezed me, then dropped away.

With her help, stacking the rest of what I had brought back took only a few moments longer, even if I kept having to take deep breaths and concentrate on keeping the universe steady.

"You need something to eat." Her voice was almost back to the no-nonsense tone of Dr. Wryan Relorn.

"Yes, Doctor."

"I'd hit you for that, but you'd fall over."

She was right, unfortunately, and I had to lean on her to get into the stool by the dusty counter. I just sat there while she tossed together something on a plate.

I ate it, more concerned with raising my blood sugar and with the exhaustion in Wryan's face than the details of what I was eating.

"You have something, too."

"Too tense to eat—"

"You've lost weight you can't afford—"

"You should talk, Sammis Arloff Olon . . ."

"Just humor your returning explorer and eat."

Finally, she sat down on the stool next to me. When she got around to it, she ate every bit as much as I did.

"So you couldn't eat?" I could feel the tiredness in every bone, and suddenly my bladder was demanding relief, but the room had lost its disconcerting tendency to whirl around my head. "Don't you feel better?"

"Yes." She tilted her head at me in that elfin way.

I waited.

"Outside of the divers, there are probably less than a million people left alive."

"In Westron?" That was hard to believe, even with the Frost Giants.

"Everywhere. There must be a thousand Giants. They've sucked the ambient energy out of everyplace where there might be people."

"Hell . . ."

"We can keep ahead of them, and we've saved some of the children, those of us who can carry them undertime. But they won't leave."

"Verlyt!"

She tilted her head again, wordlessly asking for my reason. I touched her shoulder, squeezed it gently, feeling both smooth black cloth and muscle before letting go. As close as Wryan was, I could smell the spiciness of her, that brought up thoughts of holding her, and more. But she was waiting for my explanation, and some hope of a solution. I just hoped I had it.

"Maybe later," she answered my unspoken question.

"Energy," I answered. "The plates tunnel matter or energy from point to point."

Her face screwed up.

"Drop one into a sun—timewarped—and the other near a Frost Giant. Should overload them. More energy than a particle beam or a small nuclear device."

She still looked puzzled. "Do you want a thousand gateways to the sun scattered all over Query?"

"Oh. . . ." I thought for a moment. "The timewarping will only last a short time once it starts passing energy."

"That's still a lot of energy." Wryan pursed her lips. "Why do you have to do it on Query?"

"That's where—oh . . ." As usual, I was still thinking in linear terms. There really was no reason why I couldn't backtime outsystem and plant the suntunnels. Given Wryan's Laws of Time, that wouldn't undo the deaths, although it might undo some of the environmental damage, but it wouldn't require baking the planet, except for the few Giants who decided not to leave and whom we couldn't track backtime.

"Are there any energy storage devices in that assortment you brought back?"

"No. Straight duplicating job, and the duplicates work."

"Then, after you take a short nap, after you take a shower, we need to start duplicating. And hunting."

So I took a shower, and a nap, and took care of a few other things, like hanging onto Wryan, who was hanging onto me, as if we had discovered each parting could be the last.

As I fell into the depths of sleep, I wondered how and why Wryan had arrived back so quickly at the retreat. But how seemed so much less important than the fact that she had.

LXIV

DUPLICATING THE SUNTUNNELS was the easy part, especially since Wryan and Jerlyk and a few of the other divers had, while I was hunting, moved one fusion plant and the duplicator into a small rebuilt and time-warped stone barn in the middle of Hardle, north Westron. The Frost Giants had ignored or avoided it.

Then I had to see if the theory actually worked in the real world. I decided that a few sunpoints in the colder areas of Query wouldn't hurt, not if they were areas already destroyed by the Giants.

Finding a Frost Giant would scarcely be difficult, not with close to a thousand of them grazing Query.

Wryan watched as I linked the two heavy discs to my equipment belt—one on each side. My breath was white steam in the cold of the barn.

Jerlyk looked at the glistening metal. "Are you sure this will work?"

"No. Do you have any better ideas?"

Jerlyk shook his head.

"Then I'd better see if it does. They can't destroy much more."

Wryan's lips brushed my cheek. "Try to take care."

I shrugged. Of course I would. Whether it would be enough was another question.

First, I dropped along the black arrow that led to the sun, forcing myself against the waves of time pressure that spewed from that nuclear depth. My experiments with time-warping made the drop-off of one disc possible. I just willed it out of the undertime. Clearly I couldn't have survived if I had tried to physically place it there. Solar surfaces and innards are not forgiving, even to timedivers.

Then, I just let the time pressure throw me back to Query, looking through the blue flashes from the Giants, seeking one that was isolated.

That didn't take long, either subjectively or objectively.

A strong and jagged blue trail led me to a plateau north of South-point.

Not being particularly heroic, nor caring to relive another being's death again, I didn't even break the surface of the now. Instead, I willed the disc out of the now and over the Giant—and mentally sprinted toward the retreat, dropping onto the glowstones.

. . . craccckkk . . .

Even though my break-out cut off the jagged blue flashes, I sat there shivering for several moments before looking for something to eat. I wasn't really hungry, but I wanted some time to pass before I re-entered the undertime.

I munched on more hard crackers and watched the wind whip snow from the Bardwall spires. After finishing two crackers, I dropped back under the now and headed back to Hardle.

My breath still came out white in the barn's air.

"Success?" asked Jerlyk.

"Probably. You go check." I wandered over to the wall map of Westron Wryan had taped to the stones. Duplicated, it had wrinkles and creases, even a red stain across the lower right corner. Red crosses surrounded with circles marked the destruction she had been able to verify. Where she had discovered the original map, who knew?

I pointed to the approximate location where I had dropped the suntunnel. "Should be right here."

Jerlyk looked from me to Wryan and back again. Wryan said nothing, just returned his glance.

"They can't touch you in the undertime. If you feel anything cold or blue, it didn't work." I added.

Jerlyk checked his gauntlets, straightened his belt and disappeared.

"The same problem?" asked Wryan. Her breath smoked in the cold, just like mine. She was wearing a heavy black fur-lined parka.

"Almost got clear this time. Went to the Bardwalls. Waited. Then I came here." I felt cold in the thin insulated jacket. So I put my hands up under the jacket, and walked toward the duplicator. "Take another set."

"You think it worked?"

"The only question is how long the links lasted. You calculated a maximum of—"

"That's enough to vitrify stone, Sammis."

"*If* your calculations were right, we ought to use them as much as possible on Query in deserted areas."

Wryan shrugged. "I suppose you're right."

"Two reasons."

"Two?"

I nodded. "First, who can track and attack the Giants? Me? You? Jerlyk? Maybe Mellorie. And Odin Thor and a guide."

"You forgot Kerina."

"Is she that strong?"

Wryan nodded.

"Anyway," I noted, "the second reason is a warning. We need to post the system, so to speak, to make sure that Frost Giants understand it's death to poach here."

"Are they intelligent enough—"

"I'd say so." Alien, but not without brains.

By now, I was wondering about Jerlyk. Of course, he dropped into sight as soon as I really began to worry.

He was bobbing his head enthusiastically. "It worked."

I didn't believe him so I followed up myself, probing backtime just enough to check. But he was right.

Wryan was also right. There was a section of ground a hundred rods across fused into solid rock glass.

So we went hunting, the three of us, without even telling Odin Thor.

By the end of the day, we had placed nearly a hundred suntunnels.

By the end of the ten-day, after notifying all the divers, we placed over a thousand.

We also lost four divers, including Arlean, who broke out and didn't make it back under the now before the tunnel triggered.

That left one problem—perhaps an even bigger one.

LXV

THE HALF-BUILT TOWER was untouched. So were the buildings around it, although they had been built by the ConFeds without time-warping the stones. They had used the duplicator, which Wryan and I had installed in the subbasement of the tower, for production of the building materials.

At the time, Odin Thor had complained about having to carry the stones and braces up the long ramp. The complaints about that hadn't resumed with the rebuilding.

A gaggle of summer lilies peered from the small flower bed planted by Jianne, one of the younger divers. Deric had insisted on flower beds around the tower. So we had flower beds. I stopped on the steps leading to the uncompleted south portal to look out at Mount Persnol, noting the too-frequent circular patches of brown on the lower slopes, wondering how many years before the vegetation erased the scars.

From the tower, I could not see where Camp Persnol had been, nor where the ill-fated non-divers' village had been. Both were gone, just a few stone walls rising from brown dust and rock.

"Sammis?" Amenda, fragile-looking in divers' blacks, appeared at the foot of the steps.

Two ConFeds, sweating in the sunlight as they toiled on the new ConFed administration building across the open space that was planned for a square by Deric, stopped and watched. One made an obscure sign, a ward against evil. The other laughed at him and said something, drawing an imaginary weapon, waving it in our direction. They both laughed.

"Yes." I waited for Amenda, although I was really waiting for Wryan. She looked overhead. "It's . . . impressive . . ."

I thought so, too. For all his finickiness, Deric understood something about architecture. Either that or he knew where to find good design. I didn't much care which as long as the results were good.

"The crystal lattices work . . ."

"Good." I nodded. She had taken over the library functions after Arlean had died. The lattices were a Ydrisian invention for storing information, practically indestructible and with unlimited capacity, it seemed. One lattice the size of my fist could hold all of the information that had been in the entire Far Travel Laboratory.

Unfortunately, Arlean's biggest problem was finding the knowledge to save. Most of the divers thought I was a little fanatical about my two projects—information storage and what I called the duplicator library— mint condition originals of any equipment we might need.

Already they saw the value of the second. So they just shook their heads about the first.

"What about the underground ConFed fort?"

Amenda shivered. "It takes a little getting used to, but I've located some engineering texts . . ."

"HUT . . . two, three, four. . . . HUT . . . two, three, four. . . ."

We both watched as a squad of ConFed recruits marched by the tower. They wheeled toward the ConFed building across the field that would one day be a square.

"HUT . . . two, three, four. . . ."

The forcer marching them wore a heavy Ydrisian energy pistol—a copy of the one I had originally brought back for Odin Thor, before I had been so successful in my time-meddling.

The sight of the energy weapon on the forcer's hip sent shivers down my spine. With a duplicator . . . every ConFed could have such a weapon . . . but it was too heavy for most people to use. Except for Odin Thor's troops. The gesture of the ConFed across the square took on more significance.

"Are you all right, Sammis?"

"Sorry, just thinking."

"About what?"

"I'd be interested in that as well," added another voice, one I knew well. Wryan appeared on the step next to me.

I squeezed her hand for an instant.

"Are you going to tell us?" asked Wryan.

I shrugged. "Just thinking. One of the reasons I was so effective as a diver was because of the physical conditioning I got from the ConFeds. One of the ongoing problems of too many divers has been lack of strength."

"You want to make the divers into ConFeds?" asked Amenda.

"No. Physical conditioning wouldn't hurt. Start with the younger ones . . ."

"Sounds like another one of your projects," added Wryan.

"I have to go . . ." pleaded Amenda.

"You don't . . ."

"Really . . ."

Wryan looked at me when Amenda had hastened toward her new crystal lattice library beneath the tower. "That wasn't all you were thinking."

"You don't miss much, my lady."

"Remember that. I am your lady." She smiled and waited.

"I wouldn't have it any other way."

Her smile faded.

I sighed, enjoying the breeze, but knowing she would wait longer than I could. The ConFeds halted by the uncompleted building and broke ranks. In instants, there were a score working there, instead of a handful.

"Odin Thor is good at discipline . . ."

"So are you," noted Wryan.

"I don't like it."

"What?"

I gestured toward the ConFeds. "They look like nothing's changed, ready to use what we've provided to take over the world."

"You could stop them." Wryan's voice was even.

"Why should I have to? It's better that it never gets started. I need to talk with Odin Thor."

Wryan frowned. "He doesn't listen very well. Still." Her face was troubled, yet faintly amused.

Across the field, the building rose, even as we talked.

I squeezed her hard, then let go. "No time like the present."

"What do you have in mind?"

"Call it a smaller force, a guard of some sort, half old ConFed, half new diver. Couldn't be any more ConFeds than divers."

Wryan pursed her lips. "He won't agree."

"I have to ask." First, I added.

"I'll come."

"No. If he doesn't see me as strong enough . . ."

She nodded, almost sadly. Then she squeezed my hand.

Walking through the uncompleted central hall toward the west wing, I could almost visualize what the tower would look like centuries into the future. And it would stand, more than centuries into the future. That I knew.

"Halt."

Outside Odin Thor's closed door—he had the only finished space in the tower, I suspected—stood a sentry. Hasslek. I remembered him.

"Hasslek, do I have to turn you into. . . ." I paused.

He had one of the energy guns pointed at me. He also had a nasty smile. I didn't like either.

Crack. Half-sliding under the now, I disarmed him with a chop to the wrist. Then I finished the job.

Thud. I let his unconscious body drop face-down on the glowstones, hoping he lost a few teeth in the process and gained a little more respect for his betters.

Opening the door without knocking, I stepped inside and closed the door behind me, not bothering with the useless lock.

Odin Thor pulled his polished black boots off the desk and stood up.

"Sammis, how good to see you." The stench of false jollity was almost nauseating. He must have seen something. He stopped. "Would you have a seat?"

I smiled as falsely as he had. "No. This won't take too long. Since when have you been issuing energy guns?"

Odin Thor looked at me, then walked toward the window. "Well, Sammis . . . it's like this . . ."

At that moment, I had the strangest feeling, as though Odin Thor and I were being watched from the undertime. I smiled, then gave the unseen figure I remembered the old Temple peace benediction.

Odin Thor, insensitive as he was, didn't even notice. He was watching the ConFed building crew. ". . . we really can't maintain the projectile weapons. And after we routed the Frost Giants, a lot of the men didn't feel really secure . . ."

I snorted. "We don't need a force like you're building."

"Oh, and how would you keep order? Or have you forgotten Llordian?" He turned from the window.

"No. That's why I want to propose something else."

He walked back to the big desk. I wondered where he had found it and how many men had worked to refinish it. "Such as?"

"How about a guard force composed half of divers and half of ConFeds? It ought to be called a guard, a civil or a temporal guard."

Odin Thor was shaking his head before I finished. "Won't work. You don't have enough divers." He smiled, again broadly and falsely. "But we could use a timedivers section in the ConFeds. You could head that up."

"I think you're missing my point. If we don't put the ConFeds and the divers together now, working side by side——"

"A lot of your divers are women . . ."

I'd thought of that. "I know. They're a great stabilizing influence, and they'll also reassure a lot of the remaining farmers and the few townies left." More important, in time, they'd change the whole character of the ConFeds.

"They aren't tough enough."

"Is Wryan tough enough?"

"Yes . . . but . . ."

"Fine. I'll guarantee the divers' physical conditioning."

Odin Thor was shaking his head violently. "It won't work. It won't."

I waited, knowing he'd find some way to reject my suggestion. Except it wasn't a suggestion.

"Sammis." He was back into false jollity again. "You've done wonders in finding tools, in getting weapons, and in helping destroy the Frost Giants. And in time, the whole planet will be properly grateful to you. Right now, though, they're scared of your timedivers. They need time to accept you. Setting up a divers section of the ConFeds would be a first step toward what you want."

It wouldn't, because Odin Thor would use us for all the dirty and hateful work, and then we'd be forever beholden to him for protection.

"I don't think so. We need a dual guard, and we need it now."

"Sammis, let's not be hasty. We have a planet to rebuild."

I took a deep breath, wondering how to set it up.

"Believe me, I have a lot more experience in this," he continued expansively.

"No." I smiled. "We'll do it my way. You, Wryan, and I will head up this guard."

"Sammis . . ." The phony heartiness disappeared, and his voice was heavy and rough. He also towered over me, even from a rod away.

Not that his size bothered me.

"There's no way I would ever agree to that. No way." His voice was honest and cold, and I liked that tone better than the phony jolliness.

I smiled. "But you will, Odin Thor. You will. Just think about it."

Then I dropped under the now, leaving him with a puzzled look on his face.

LXVI

ODIN THOR—WHY had I let the idiot who had created the mess get so far? That gesture of the ConFed had chilled me to the bone, bringing back all the old hate memories, the class distinctions . . .

But who was the idiot? Odin Thor or Sammis? I had known he would botch it up, but I had let him run the ConFeds. I had known killing the Frost Giants with nuclear weapons would fail, but I had let him use them.

Wryan, perched on a stool by the wide glass window, watched as I paced the glowstones. She sipped a beaker of citril.

"Still thinking about Odin Thor?" she asked.

I nodded.

"I let him get too far. Now . . ." I shrugged, stopping to watch the dark clouds form and reform over the needle peak of Frythia. In the twilight, they appeared even more threatening. As often as the clouds threatened the peak, assaulted it with thunder and infrequent lightning, it never changed. Neither would Odin Thor, not unless . . .

I walked to the bedroom, the glowstones warm under my bare feet, and began to pull on the blacks that had become my uniform, and by extension, I suppose, the uniform of the timedivers. Then came the black boots from Sertis, and the gauntlets, with the quick timeloop to arm them. Then a knife, a sharp one.

"Sammis? Are you sure?"

"Yes."

The tone of my voice must have indicated my intent and my resolve. Wryan shivered by the window, but her eyes remained strangely calm as she watched me complete my preparations.

I glanced again at the tip of Frythia, disappearing into the coming night, then took a deep breath and dropped under the now—

—and broke out in Odin Thor's new office, in the west wing of the tower, further around the globe that was Query, around to the site of lost Inequital, where the sun still shone.

"Sammis . . ." He was still in his fancy new ConFed uniform. He wore both the heavy energy pistol and gauntlets—a needless duplication.

But then, I had never seen him without them, not since I had given them to him.

"No. Call me Verlyt, or Hades, or fate, Odin Thor."

He wasn't slow, but I had seen his action coming and dropped sideways and undertime even before the energy sheeted off the time-protected stones behind where I had stood.

Crack! My stiffened hand slashed across his unprotected wrist.

"Fate, Odin Thor."

He tried to bring the gauntlets to bear again.

This time I dropped out of the undertime and slashed the other wrist. "Verlyt, Odin Thor . . ."

I slapped his cheek.

"Coward! Dancer!"

I answered his taunt with a well-placed kick that threw him onto the floor beside his enormous wooden desk.

"Why don't you just kill me?"

"Because," I answered from behind him, dropping undertime and reappearing again to finish the sentence, "you have to live to make amends."

"Coward! You can't kill me! You don't have enough nerve."

I slipped behind him, delivered another side kick hard enough to crack his ribs, and dropped away.

Another blow to the face, and I barely dropped undertime before his good arm clutched for me.

I watched for a moment from under the now, sliding with the real time as Odin Thor peered around the disordered office. One corner of his new desk smoldered where his gauntlets had burned it.

With help from my jab, he crashed into the chair, then teetered to the floor.

His own weight snapped the wrist.

". . . bastard . . ."

I watched in realtime from the corner behind him as he staggered upright, blood streaming down the back of his neck, one wrist off-angled.

"We're going to take—

"—a trip," I concluded from the opposite corner.

My knife nipped his right biceps, a little deeper than a surface cut. A cut across his thigh, and I was gone.

"... coward ... stand ... fight ... bastard ..."

"Fate, Odin Thor ..."

Another slice on the left biceps.

He stood there, panting, looking from one side of the room to the other, twirling to try to surprise me if I came up behind him. I let him twist and turn, twist and turn, just hanging in the undertime, waiting.

Another slash, this time across the back of his shoulder.

The room was smoky, laden with ozone, and reeking from Odin Thor's sweat and blood, the chairs strewn around. My own forehead was damp, my sleeves streaked with blood lost in the black fabric.

"... never take me ..."

I had to disagree. So I planted a fist in his gut, and an open-palmed slam on his chin.

Thud!

After hitting the stones, trying to cushion his fall with his good left hand, he turned, and I ducked undertime.

I was less delicate, with a kick to his jaw.

He was out, sprawled on the floor. His jaw was probably broken as well.

I took off his gauntlets, his knife, and the energy pistol, then bound his wrist up as well as possible. The jaw would need more professional help.

Sitting there, I sheathed my knife, after wiping it on his uniform, and waited until he began to wake up. Then I forced us both under the now.

... back toward Bremarlyn, toward a house being fired, and the agony of two people ...

... back toward a crossroads where an innocent girl was consumed in flames.

There I held Odin Thor, letting their agonies flow through me and into him.

... back to an underground camp where. ...

AAAAAAeeeeeeeeeeeeeeeeeeeeeeeeeeeeeeeeeeeeeeeeeeeeeeee ....

Nooooooooooooooooooooo!!!!!!!!!!!!!!!!!!!!!!!!

... *Verlytttt!!!* ...

... *dying ... dying ... dying* ...

Red lenses slashed across my eyes—again. Needles lanced my lips, and acid etched my throat. Breathing fire, I tried to rip my guts out, spew my innards across the cold of undertime ... trying to escape the pyramiding agony ...

Flares flashed across my visions . . . the visions I threw to Odin Thor—

. . . a thin man slashing his own throat . . .

. . . a woman grabbing a brain-spattered projectile gun from a dead ConFed's hand, to turn it against her own skull . . .

. . . a man with shaking hands injecting himself, biting his lips raw and trying to keep from screaming . . .

. . . a young soldier, crawling, scrabbling, leaving a pink-frothed trail on the stone behind him . . .

. . . a captain, standing in the doorway of an underground barracks, propped against the casement, slowly bringing up the heavy riot gun while trying to keep from shaking, trying to bring the gun to bear on the men writhing on the floor . . .

The second time, or was it the third—wasn't so bad, perhaps because I knew I wouldn't die, or perhaps because I threw all the agony at Odin Thor.

Then, before that muted pain could subside, for I knew the ConFed did not feel so sharply as I did, we dropped foretime to . . .

. . . Llordian, where on a black hillside lit by torches . . .

WWWWHHHHHSSSSTTTTTT!!!!! The entire pile of etheline missiles burst into flames, cremating a dozen townspeople as instant torches.

Using the light of the human bonfire, and shooting from the shadows uphill, the farmers dropped three more townies, as the mob began to trot toward the farm buildings revealed near the hill crest by the flames from the road.

". . . food . . . we want . . . food . . ."

Burning flesh, reeking, and the searing agony of death by fire, again charred my soul, and again, I poured it through the undertime link to Odin Thor.

Then, I staggered forward in the undertime, to . . .

EEEEEEEeeeeeeeeeeeee . . .

The scream of the vest-pocket nuclear device vibrated even in the undertime north of Inequital, from the wasteland that had yet to recover from the first Frost Giant attack.

. . . *eeeeeeeeeeeeeeeeeee* . . .

My head ached from the vibration and energy flashes that weren't supposed to have a physical impact in the undertime—and my soul wept from the old pain and from throwing it at Odin Thor . . .

". . . noooooo . . ." The non-voice was mine, trying to close eyes that would not, could not, close in the undertime.

. . . blue flashes, like jagged edges of a mirror, cut through my head.

. . . an image of a small blue and blocky figure, four-armed, surrounded with warm blueness. . . .

. . . a dull red plain . . . standing beside another blueblock figure . . . reassuring heat . . . flashing back and forth . . .

. . . so much heat . . . pressure . . . like knives cutting from inside. . . .

. . . and more blue shards knifing their way through my head, already fading as they cut.

I staggered back toward the now, wondering if I could take another jolt, knowing that Odin Thor needed one last agony. So we stopped and watched and found . . .

. . . a circular gray-brown wasteland, covered with fog as the heat from the surrounding area poured back over the frozen surfaces. A wall of thunderclouds towered against the low mountains.

. . . a plateau that had been tree-covered with a walled encampment centered upon it . . . covered with lifeless sludge, screaming with the death agonies of two hundred hapless souls . . .

. . . pelting rains and gusty winds sweeping across another gray-brown wasteland, where new gullies appeared in the waist-deep sludge of fragmented cellular matter that had been largely living days earlier, cut by the force of water and gravity. The stone walls stood stark where they had stood for centuries, now alone in rearing above the gentle undulations of the plateau surface. Stone and sludge. Just stone and sludge and rain beating down on the echo of another hundred deaths.

With a final push, I broke out within the west wing of the tower, almost losing my balance.

I dropped Odin Thor on the floor of his office, as gently as I could manage. His eyes were open, and he was breathing, although his fancy ConFed uniform was a mass of cuts and blood.

My guts were close to turning inside out, but I just stood there and watched until his self-awareness began to return, amazed that he was insensitive enough to recover at all. Asking myself if I should have exposed him to even more, although I wasn't certain I could have taken any more myself.

His eyes blinked, then came to rest on me.

"Fate . . . Odin Thor . . ."

". . . you . . . the damned deathgod . . ."

I shook my head. "That would have been easy. I want you to live with the feelings of all those deaths. If you ever put on that ConFed uniform again . . . if you ever think about forgetting . . . if you ever . . ."

Odin Thor shuddered and dropped his eyes from the blackness he saw in mine.

". . . and much as you hate me, we work together . . . because I'll always be here . . . always . . ."

I took a ragged breath, forcing back the still-felt screams of the dying, and the searing throbbing within my head. ". . . remember . . . death is easy . . . you ever *think* about playing emperor . . . I'll leave you dying . . . forever . . ."

He didn't look at me, but he didn't have to. He knew, and I knew.

Odin Thor would recover enough without me. He could get his own help. So I dropped back undertime and across continents to where I belonged.

Wryan was waiting, not that I expected otherwise, pacing before the black expanse of the window. She was looking toward Frythia, though the time difference between the retreat and the tower at Inequital ensured that mere eyesight saw nothing except the darkness.

That was all we often ever saw—the obvious light or dark.

Her eyes widened as she stepped toward me, then stopped.

Looking down, I could see why, with the blood splattered on the back of my hands, caked on my sleeves enough to be obvious despite the blackness of the fabric.

"You . . ." Her eyes were neither upset nor accusing, just asking.

"No . . . he is somewhat . . . scored. At least one broken wrist, some cracked ribs, and probably a broken jaw. That doesn't include the severely punctured ego."

My lady nodded slowly. "Now you know, and Odin Thor knows."

I shrugged. My shoulders ached, and my skull throbbed with the still-remembered agonies I had forced through myself to our would-have-been tyrant. "I suppose so. I suppose so."

It wasn't a question of supposing. Odin Thor knew. Knew that I had held him in the palm of my hand and judged him. Knew that I could visit death—or even worse—upon him. Knew that I understood death better than death itself, something that had taken me a long time to accept. But after feeling, individually, hundreds of deaths, I knew that death was not to be feared. Dying was another question, and I could leave Odin Thor dying endlessly.

I dropped the morbid thoughts and half-smiled at the sandy-haired woman who had trusted me more than I trusted myself.

Her hands took mine, those slender and strong fingers intertwining with mine, and I understood also why she had let the decision be mine.

"There's a lot to do . . ."

She shook her head. "Tomorrow will come. You've made sure of that—"

It was my turn to disagree. "*We* made sure of that."

"Then, hadn't we better make sure of us?" Her eyes sparkled like the sky over a rainbow, and her fingers tightened around mine.

She was right, of course.

THE TIMEGOD

To Christina,

for Elizabeth and Kristen

■

PICTURE A MAN, or, if you will, a woman, standing in an empty room, a plain hall lit by slow-glass panels and green glowstone floors.

The person standing there wears a black jumpsuit with a four-pointed star on the left collar and wide silvered wristbands. The bands contain microcircuitry.

Suddenly, the man, or, if you will, woman, is gone.

The slow-glass panels still light the hall.

Some time later—a few units, a few days, rarely longer—the traveler reappears in the same spot and walks out of the hall.

That is all there is to it, the base action of the Temporal Guard at Quest, the single city of the Immortals of Query, that hidden planet circling a very ordinary yellow sun in a very ordinary galaxy.

There's no such thing as a race of timedivers, you say, Immortals who ride the paths of time a million years or more, who manipulate cultures, lift and cast down civilizations in their corner of the galaxy?

Let us lay that question aside for a time.

■■

THE CHILD IN the cradle is male, crying, and has a smooth head covered with red fuzz. Still in his first seasons, his eyes glitter the green of witch fire.

He howls because his mother has dropped him back into his cradle. She cries because she dropped him. She ignores the pain of the faint burns on her hands and forearms.

The man, who has arrived in response to her crying, puts his arms around her as she sobs over the infant and asks, "He did what?"

Through her sobs, she answers. "Sleeping. Wet. Covers were soaked. Thought he would be happier dry. Picked him up, and he burned me. Burned me . . . me . . ."

She turns out of his arms and twists her forearms outward to show him the light red lines arrowing across her skin.

The man shivers within himself, but remains silent. He studies the picture of his own father on the wall above the cradle, looks back at the baby, and sets his jaw.

The woman follows his eyes and nods, but she says nothing either. This pain will pass.

CALL ME LOKI. It's as good a name as any, better than most, and besides, that's what my parents named me.

What better name for the grandson of Ragnorak, for the child of fallen heroes, fumbler in the complex intrigues of the Immortals, sometime god, timediver, and idiot-savant par excellence?

The dominoes of time have toppled, shoved into new patterns by the winds of change, those chill torrents that howl down the corridors of time, those black rays of timepath tossed carelessly out by each sun and vaulted and trod by the timedivers of Query in their ceaseless efforts to maintain their precarious position on the top of time's totem pole.

A too-florid description, perhaps, but accurate for all the verbosity.

I am serious. I have always been serious—too serious. Queryans are immortal, but nature balanced it nicely, since the genetic interlock required for fertilization, and the time-diving ability, kept births low—less than one per couple per millennium. And accidents do happen, time-diving ability or not.

Queryan timedivers ranged through time, and since time is space, so to speak, through space as well. As a precaution, all children were Locator-tagged at birth, although the talent didn't usually develop until later, nor fully until puberty.

Only a small percentage of us had innate navigational senses, and most Queryans never went far from Query. Backtiming or foretiming on Query itself is out. The Laws of Time are inflexible. If you dive at all on Query, you dive planet clear.

Still, all of this was far indeed from my mind on a spring day when I walked out of the house and across the ridge line toward the rocks where I so often played. How old was I? Old enough to speak, and not old enough to have received much schooling from either of my parents or from the tutors. Old enough to enjoy watching the birds soar over the valley below, and young enough that even small boulders were the ramparts of the old castles of Eastron—castles so ancient that they exist only in legend and in cryptic references in the Archives.

After the house was lost in the trees behind me, I stopped to watch a stone mouse nibble on a purple flower before I skipped a rock at him and watched him scamper between two boulders. The path I had worn along the ridge was clear enough to me, perhaps because there were so few paths, except close to our house, not that I saw many houses then.

My parents preferred to walk, in contrast to many on Query, at least in coming after me or summoning me for meals or my beginning studies.

That day, there were no studies, and when I reached the higher end of the ridge, I scrambled over the rocks and up into the stone jumble that was my castle.

First, I stood on the highest flat boulder, pretending I was the High Tribune in the Tower. Or maybe I was merely the emperor of ancient Westra. But the sun continued to beat down, and I decided to inspect the dungeons, a twisted cave almost directly beneath my high ramparts, but a cave that I could only reach by a shaded and narrow trail around the side of the rocky cliffside below the peak.

To think has always been to act, and I did, bouncing off the squared-off boulder and squirming through the narrow aperture created by an ancient fracture of another giant boulder and onto the trail. Holding onto various roots and branches, I scuttled along the trail until I could swing into the cool darkness of the cave—otherwise considered as the private dungeon of the duke of Eastron, or maybe of the king of the Perrsions vanquished by my grandfather so many years earlier.

RRrrrrrr . . . The low growl rumbled toward me, and I looked up and back into the cool darkness where two green-gold eyes set in golden-tan fur fixed on me. Time seemed to slow as I looked at the big cat, far bigger than I. Between his paws was a small animal—half-eaten—and blood smeared his jaws and yellow teeth.

I stepped backward, one step at a time, my eyes on the cat, for perhaps three steps, until the heel of my boot caught a rock and I flailed backward before landing hard on my backside.

RRRrrrrr . . . The cat decided on another meal—or a larger and more tasty one—and sprang.

I wanted to be somewhere else—anywhere. High and somewhere away from the cat . . . on top of the ridge. Why I didn't think of my house, I don't know, but I didn't.

There was a cold feeling, a sense of red and blue and gold and black, and I was teetering on top of my castle rampart, too close to the edge. I sat down. Then I shivered, and I could feel the tears rolling down my cheeks.

The faint puzzled growling from beneath convinced me that my sudden departure from the dungeon had been real enough. But what was I supposed to do next? Would the cat follow me?

"Very impressive, young fellow."

I sat up straight.

"Especially for a first time." She wore black, and she had a thin face, sort of like my mother's, but her hair was cut shorter, and it was sandy brown. Her eyes were a piercing green, almost as piercing as the cat's.

"I'm not a young fellow. I'm Loki."

"I know. That mountain cat is a very confused young hunter, and he might not attack you the next time, and you might be able to dive out of the way again. And you might not. But I would suggest that you leave the cave below alone."

"Why?"

"The cat is bigger than you are, Loki. He also has sharp teeth and claws." On her wrists were silver gauntlets that caught the sun as she turned and looked down on me. "It's time for you to head home."

For some reason, I obeyed her, looking back as I walked to the edge of the jumble and began to climb down. When I could see the top again, she was gone.

I burst through the door into the kitchen, where my mother was kneading bread dough. She even had an oven, not just a synthesizer. "You're back early."

"You'll never guess what I did. Never, never, never!"

"Then you'll have to tell me." She smiled. "Do you want some fruit? I have some pearapples here." She always pushed the fruit, and I always ate a piece or two.

I took the pearapple, but I didn't bite into it. "Don't you want to know?"

"Tell me, my hero." She kept kneading the dough.

"I ran into a mountain cat—a big one. He was in the dungeon . . . I mean the cave."

"How did you get away, or did you kill him with a sword?"

For some reason, I got angry then. "You don't believe me. It was a real cat, with green eyes, and it had a dead animal, and it jumped at me."

She stopped kneading the dough then and looked square in my eyes. "What happened then?"

I didn't really want to say, and I wished I'd kept the whole thing to myself. But I had so wanted to tell someone. "I wanted to get away, and I did. Somehow, I was on the top of the ridge again."

"What did it feel like?"

Again . . . I didn't want to say, but I did. "It was blue and red and gold and black and cold, and then I was there. And so was this woman. She had on a black jumpsuit, and she had big silver bracelets on her wrists."

My father walked into the kitchen from somewhere. "Where did you see this woman?"

"On the ridge, Dad. On top of the rocks. That was after I got away from the cat."

He looked at my mother.

"Loki was exploring the rocks again. Apparently, he surprised a mountain cat with its kill, and it attacked. He place-slid to the top of the ridge."

"Damned Locators." Then he looked at me. "Let's go sit down."

My mother just left the dough on the counter, and we all sat down in the comfortable chairs in front of the big window in the main room.

"Do you know what you did, Loki?" asked my father gently. "It's called diving, and almost everyone on Query can do it, but usually they're older than your handful of years before they learn how."

"You mean, I can do it again?"

He nodded. "But you have to be careful. You have to think about where you are going—very carefully. What would happen if you wanted to see the bottom of the ocean?"

"I'd see fishes."

"You'd also die, unless you could breathe water, and the water is so heavy it would squash you into a ball smaller than my little finger." He held up his hand and wiggled his finger.

That was my introduction to time-diving, or more precisely, place-sliding. Of course, the lecture didn't end there, but it got very repetitious, and my father insisted on making me slide around the house, right then and there.

After that we had dinner, and then, because it was later than usual with all the lecturing, it was bedtime. I thought I was tired until I lay down in my bed.

"When you dive places, just be careful, Loki." My mother squeezed me so tightly I squirmed. "Just be careful." Her cheeks were damp, and she was breathing quickly.

"I am careful. The big cat didn't get me, and no one else will either." All I wanted to do was practice sliding from place to place, but saying anything about it then didn't seem wise, even on a spring evening when I had passed some sort of test.

My mother finally let go of me and tiptoed out of my room, although I was fully awake, thinking about where I could go now that I did not have to get there just on foot.

"They're watching." I could hear my mother's voice.

"They want another hero for the Guard." My father's voice was cold. "Another would-be god."

"Not my Loki . . ."

But I wanted to be a hero, the one who vanquished the Perrsions, the one who foiled the enemies of Query, and I thought about everything I could do for a long time that spring night.

IV

MY TIME WITH the Guard—and everyone's—started with the Test.

In time, and in Time, there are turning points, pivots from which the change winds blow. The Test, that trial to determine whether a Queryan gets advanced training, membership in the Temporal Guard, or whether he or she stays a planet-slider for a long, long life—that was my first deliberate turning point . . .

On that morning that now may never have been, the sky of Query was green, with overtones of blue that made the hills circling the city of Quest and the peaks behind those hills stand out in even sharper relief than the clearest holo could project.

The morning was cloudless, as so many mornings in Quest are. I had place-slid to the park surrounding the Square, breaking out of the undertime with the thought-chill that always ends a planet-slide or a timedive.

The Tower of Immortals stands in the center of the Square, surrounded solely by grass and the low fireflowers that flicker scarlet under the golden-white sun. The fireflowers edge the glowstone walks leading to the Tower.

Although four portals open from the Tower, Queryans not belonging to the Temporal Guard enter only through the South Portal.

The Tower soars from its rectangular base into a dome which climbs to a spire. The Tower is out-of-time-phase, and the spire flares with the fires of a thousand suns captured in the timeless and untouchable depths of the faceted slow-glass facing. The oldest holos of the Tower from the Archives show no change, even though the mountains in the distance are a shade sharper and the nearer hills a trace harsher. While the city has altered in many particulars, the Tower of Immortals has not, except in name. Only a few records survive from the early days of the Guard, and they only mention the Tower.

As I stared at the Tower on that morning that may not have been, none of this crossed my mind. Too young to note the changes in the park or the buildings from century to century, and filled with the elation of becoming a Guard, I studied the Tower more as a present I was about to receive.

If you see a good holo of the Tower, you can see how the edges blur. That's because the walls of the Tower proper, except for the rectangular wings, are partly out-of-time-phase, which renders it effectively indestructible, as well as unchangeable. That's unless the Temporal Guard were to pull it down stone by stone. That's the way it was built, stone by stone, and, according to the stories, it took years, some say a century, but even then I found that hard to believe. Very little of the past is recorded, and not all of that is terribly precise or accurate.

I stood and stared, convincing myself that, red hair and all, I would be the first of my family in eons—that is, since my grandfather—to pass the Test and join the Temporal Guard. So few pass the Test who do not join the Guard that passing is regarded as tantamount to joining.

Wishing would not make it so, and, clutching my illusions, I began to walk up the glowstones to the South Portal. I could have slid right up to the entrance, but ceremony means much to all Queryans, particularly when a youngster elects to take the Test.

Readiness is a personal question, and no one, not my mother, nor my father, ever broached the question. Custom, I suppose.

The portals were dark, but the interior of the Tower was bright with slow-glass panels, glittering and lit with the light not only of golden suns but of red suns, blue suns, orange suns, and white suns. Yet for all the light, as I entered the Tower, I felt a sense of coolness, quiet, and peace.

Not that I hadn't been there before. With my parents, tutors, and friends, I had walked all the public corridors, the meeting halls, and the Hall of Justice.

Thinking about the Hall of Justice, I recalled the stories that Gerhalt had told about the trial of Orpheus, who used the Lyre of Heaven to bring down the Tribune Alcinor. Gerhalt told more stories than any of my tutors, and I suppose that they all had points. Anyway, the story was that Orpheus was sent to Hell and never arrived, but later I checked the Archives. The Archives were silent on that point. Mostly, the Archives contain scientific data, and records concerning other systems.

Before I realized it, I was at the archway to the Testing Hall in the West Wing of the Tower. It was called the Testing Hall by those not in the Guard, but the Travel Hall by Guards.

A tall woman, with white-blond hair and deep black eyes, waited.

I had heard that all the Guard participated in routine functions, and I concealed my surprise with a curt nod and a simple statement.

"Counselor Freyda."

Query had no distinction between civil and military, between compulsory and voluntary. The Tests determined who could join the Guard, and the Guard was the government. Ability determined position in the Guard, and the Counselors directed the Guards to implement the policies laid down by the Tribunes.

Nonetheless, I was surprised that Counselor Freyda, rumored to have been a close friend of my departed and possibly late grandfather, whom many had said I resembled, would be my examiner.

"Loki," she responded.

It was not a lack of warmth, I felt. Rather we are a laconic people, except perhaps for me. That's what comes from living until some accident in a planet-slide or a time fluke does you in. When you contact the same people over centuries, tight speech and good manners prevail, and the Counselor had always been impeccably correct.

"You need not take the Test." Her eyes smiled, knowing that I would.

The formal statement was necessary. Some Queryans never took the Test and used their talents only to travel around Query, even though it is actually easier to deep-time out-system, a fact never mentioned much by the Guard.

Counselor Freyda had always been an attractive woman, though in my youthful exuberance, I thought all Queryan women were attractive, beauty being a matter of degree. Even with formality, you get a different perspective when your life stretches before you to a possible infinity.

She rose from the simple straight-backed chair and led the way to the Travel Hall.

The Travel Hall is nothing more than a long, high, slow-glass-lit room at the end of the West Wing of the Tower. Some say it and the other parts of the Tower which are not out-of-time-phase, the two rectangular wings, were added later. Not much later, because no holos or old-fashioned pictures exist of the Tower without the two wings.

A series of small equipment rooms flanks the Travel Hall. The rooms open directly onto the Hall through small arches. The builders of the Tower liked arches.

In practical terms, the Travel Hall is actually outside the main time-protected walls of the Tower. So is the Infirmary. If you think about it, it makes sense.

Most Immortals can't planet-slide or time-jump from within the out-of-time-phase walls of the main Tower, and even those who can have a reduced range and more difficulty. That's why the Infirmary and Travel Hall are "outside." If you want a good dive or medical help in a hurry, most divers find it best to avoid the warping effect of the time-protected walls.

Freyda conducted me into one of the equipment rooms, the Counselors', where the slow-glass wall panels were flanked with heavy gold and black hangings. From the drawers of a carved chest, she took four wristbands, slipped one over each forearm, and handed the remaining pair to me.

I put them on, not having the faintest idea what they were for. She frowned, and her bands took on a luminous appearance. Mine remained dull silver.

"The first part of the Test is simple. Go undertime as far as you can, or until you feel me dragging at you. Then come back. If you have trouble, I'll bring you back. Do you understand?"

I was all too aware that we made a strange pair, with her height and black suit, so simple and stark next to my red. I had decided to wear red to the Test.

If I succeeded, I would wear black. No actual law, but those who serve or who have served in the Temporal Guard wear black. My father said it has been so since before his great-grandfather's time. Even then I wondered about the subtle impact of the unspoken, of those things which were just done.

Realizing that I had been daydreaming, I nodded abruptly.

Freyda nodded back and grasped my left wrist. Her fingers were firm and cool. I ducked undertime. Instead of latching onto the ground, I just concentrated on trying to force myself backtime, trying to turn the universe bright red like me. I could feel the redness flashing against the black of the timepaths.

Flashes of blue alternated with the sense of backtime red I was seeing, and I began to feel like I was dragging someone. Freyda was signaling. I went limp, blanked my mind, and let her carry us back to the Travel Hall.

"I doubt that we need other tests." Her voice was level, but with a trace of strain, it seemed to me.

Was there any question? I'd been confident of passing for as far back as I could remember. I'd been practicing fore- and backtiming on Query almost as long as I could read. Not that I could actually break out, given the Law of Non-Interference, but, oh, how I had practiced, enjoying the red and blue rushes back and forth in the undertime.

Freyda looked carefully away from me toward the far end of the Hall. "Custom, however, requires two other phases."

I tensed. What else was necessary?

"Next, slide off Query as you backtime."

"In any direction?"

"How do you determine direction, Loki?" The question was some-what pointed, perhaps because custom, again the unspoken, indicated that I should not have experimented with off-planet time-slides.

Embarrassed by my gaffe, I tried not to flush and stammered, "I'm not sure . . . there must be four. I mean, red and blue and gold and black, except that you could call gold and black, cold and hot. Somehow gold ought to be hot, but it's cold."

"So you've experimented on your own. I might have guessed. Have you followed a black line out-system and tried a breakout there?"

Was there a trace of a smile on her face?

"I've followed the lines a little way, but never tried a breakout."

That was certainly true. The Temporal Guard keeps its secrets. I wasn't about to break out somewhere or somewhen that wasn't favorable to my continued existence. I had followed the black timepaths both blue and red directions just up to breakout on a number of worlds, but I had no way of knowing whether they were cold asteroids, moons, or planets. I thought I knew, but when you're experimenting on the edge of the forbidden, you hold back. At least, I did then.

"All right. We can skip phase two. Follow any black line backtime, red direction, as far- or as near-time as you want. Pick a favorable break-out. If it's dangerous and you have trouble, I'll recover you."

I picked the strongest timepath until it branched, took what seemed a Queryan-sized trail to breakout.

Now, it's easy to say "followed" or "took," but unless you've been a timediver, the words don't mean much. You can move your body, but the work is all inside your head.

When I first started time-diving, I actually tried to walk through the undertime nothingness. That's a bad habit, like mouthing words when you read. Unless you break the habit, you'll never get any distance. You mentally "see" the paths and visualize the shade of red or blue. That's your acceleration back- or foretime. Most divers can't slide or dive off the planet's surface except along the black force lines, the arrows of the stars.

Some of the older races speculated that the suns throw time rays, as well as other energies. They do, and the black arrows, paths, call them what you will, are what we follow. You have to know when to get off. If you follow the strongest path to the end, you'd end up in the middle of some star. Not that you'd get that far. The distortion is so great even in the undertime that you'd have to force yourself beyond the mental abilities of all but the strongest Temporal Guards to approach close enough to injure yourself physically.

A knack, that's what it is.

A Guard can feel the "home" sense of the Tower of Immortals if he or she is near Query. Being both in and out of time, it acts like a beacon. Even if you lose your path you can home in on it.

During the Test, I was vaguely aware of all this, but hindsight makes for a better perspective . . . if you have the time.

With a quick shiver through the mind, and a brief session under the regenerator, I popped out onto my chosen destination, catching a glimpse of stars in a frozen sky, eyeballs bugging out. Gasping for breath, I ducked back undertime, my lungs feeling like they were ice-burned the whole subjective trip back, thinking through the pain what a dunce I'd been.

That's it. Pick an easy path; stick your nose out without even a question as to whether there's any air out there to breathe. I'd lost Freyda. Or she hadn't chosen to get frostbite of the lungs.

I fired myself back to Query and the Travel Hall, longing for warm fresh air the whole way. Freyda arrived a moment later.

"Like your grandfather. Rash. But stronger. With training, you'll do."

That was my Test.

Sounds simple . . . but either you can or you can't.

After passing my Test with Counselor Freyda, I slid home to wait the days or seasons before I was called for training, ready to bask in my parents' pride.

"I passed! I passed!" I shouted, plunging onto the porch where my parents were eating their midday meal.

"I didn't doubt you would for a moment," said my father, scarcely looking up from his fruit.

"I hope you'll be happy, dear," added my mother.

"But . . . I mean . . . not everyone . . ." I couldn't understand it. They were the ones who had told me all the legends of the Guard.

All of them, from the terrible losses of the Frost Giant Wars to the heroic deeds of Odin Thor, to the Triumvirate, even my grandfather Ragnorak . . . all the sacrifices made by the Guard to restore Query to the glory that had preceded the devastation of the Frost Giants.

I'd gone to sleep so many nights as a child looking at my father's shining gold hair, listening to him tell about the hardships that his father Ragnorak had endured on mission after mission for the Temporal Guard.

Now neither of them seemed overjoyed.

"You don't seem particularly pleased," I charged.

"If that's what you really want, dear," answered my mother, "we're both happy for you." She smiled so faintly it wasn't a smile, and turned back to her lunch, a wild salad she'd gathered from the woods behind the house.

Even my father didn't meet my eyes after the first few instants. He picked at his fruit silently.

I thought about sliding out into the mountains to be alone, but what difference did it make? I was apparently alone even at home.

My room was on the second level at the back, overlooking the small gorge at the other end of the ridge. The gorge separated the clearing where the house stood from the rest of the woods that sloped down over the lower hills. In the distance on a fair day, I could sometimes see the heights of the western Bardwalls over the evergreens.

I slumped into the hammock chair on the shady side of my small balcony and stared at the trees.

There was a tap at the door. Doors weren't really necessary, but were there as a matter of courtesy and custom. Also, short slides are more trouble than they're worth. Once when I was about ten, I guess, my door stayed locked for a full season. It didn't seem to matter. That was before I realized that my parents could slide around it if they had wanted to—they so seldom dived or slid that it never really occurred to me that they could. I don't think they ever did. The room got rather messy, but the question hadn't occurred to me.

"Come in," I called, knowing from the sharpness of the knock that it was Dad.

He opened the door quietly, came out, and sat in the highbacked stool closest to the hammock chair.

"You don't understand, Loki, and you're confused." He waved me to silence and went on. "How could your father, the son of the great Ragnorak, hero and Guard, be so casual about your decision to join the Guard? I can tell from your face. You're about to say that I couldn't make it, didn't pass my Test."

He smiled gently. "That's not quite true. I never even tried to take the Test. Nor did your mother. She's the great-granddaughter of Sammis Olon. I suspect, looking at you, we could have passed. That wasn't the question. My question was: What's the Guard for?"

What was Dad driving at? And why had he chickened out of taking his Test? Who was Sammis Olon?

"To protect us," I answered automatically.

"From what? Nobody's seen a Frost Giant in over a million years." His voice never lifted.

"That doesn't mean there aren't any. And what about the rest of the universe?" He just didn't seem to understand.

"What about it? There's no danger in it, particularly to you."

I couldn't understand him. "Then why did you tell me all those stories about the Guard? They were true, weren't they? *Weren't they?*"

"Yes, Loki, they were true. My father, your grandfather, destroyed promising civilizations, changed history on a dozen planets that were no real threat because of a million-year-old fear. When I told you those stories, I thought you would understand the Guard is a grubby and unnecessary business. Even the thunderbolts thrown by the Guards had a price. I tried to tell you that—how entire civilizations were changed so they would develop something, with no thought as to what those changes did. Ydris the mighty is no more—so we could have gauntlets that throw thunderbolts. I tried to portray the dangers, the horrors, and the arbitrary nature of meddling with Time and the lives of innocents."

"Innocents? What about the time the soldiers of the Anarchate blew off his wrist?" I remembered that one vividly. "Or the time he stopped the Perrsions from using a city-buster on Kaldir? Or—"

"Everything I told you was true," he interrupted, "or what my father told me. Lying wasn't one of his many vices."

"You were jealous of your own father! That's it!" I was seething.

He fixed me with a strange look in his eyes. "That's enough, Loki," he said calmly, almost gently. "I don't think we have that much more to talk about. Your mother wanted me to ask about your decision once more. Passing your Test doesn't mean you have to join the Guard, but I can see that your mind is made up. Arguing about the role of the Guard accomplishes very little."

He held up his hand to stop my objections and continued. "The entire nature of the Guard is subjective. It's a different world, a series of worlds. Your mother and I have tried to become as self-sufficient as possible here. We built the house with our own hands, harvest what we can from the lands and the woods. In the Guard, you will find machines to supply everything . . ."

He went on and on, telling me over and over, way after way, that the Guard was wrong in this, wrong in that. And he'd never been in the Guard. I wondered if he hated his father for being such a hero. Obviously, I wasn't going to have that problem.

I listened and didn't say a word until he finished.

"Thank you, Dad. Is there anything around here that needs to be done?"

He looked at me as if I'd climbed out from under a rock.

"You really don't understand, do you?" He flexed his forearms, ridged with the muscles developed from his years of manual self-sufficiency, and kept staring at me.

What was there to understand? For some strange reason, he was giving the Guard a trial and judging it guilty without any firsthand experience.

We sat there, maybe for twenty units, neither of us wanting to say anything. An odd picture—young man and a youth almost a man, yet one was father, one son. On Query you can't tell age by outward physical appearances.

Finally, Dad slipped off the stool, brushed his longish hair back off his forehead, and walked into the house. Before he left, he said, "You're welcome here as long as you want to stay, son." And damn it, he sounded like he meant it.

I kept watching the trees, as if I could see them grow or something. They didn't. The only thing that grew was their shadows.

The first few days of summer were like that. I couldn't take the sitting. I thought about Dad's comments on the Guard, the harsh conditions, the struggles, and I got scared. Just a little.

Why should I have been scared? I didn't know, but I started in with the ax and split a winter's worth of wood in a ten-day, and the hell with the blisters.

Next came the running. If the Guard wanted toughness, I intended to be ready. I've got heavy thighs and short legs. Do you know what running over sandy hills is like with small feet and short legs?

I tried to chase down flying gophers. Never caught one, but within ten-days I was getting pretty close before they disappeared into their sand holes.

At first, the temptation to cheat on the running, to slide a bit ahead undertime, was appealing, but I figured that wouldn't help my physical condition much. Besides, I could already slide from rock tip to rock tip without losing my balance.

Once when I was sprinting back across the clearing to the house, I caught a glimpse of Dad watching through the railings. I don't think he knew I saw him, and the expression on his face—pride mixed with something else, confusion, sadness—I didn't know.

Through all the quiet meals we shared those long ten-days, I knew they didn't understand, couldn't understand.

One morning a Guard trainee in black arrived with a formal invitation from the Tribunes for me to begin training.

Along with the invitation was a short list of what I was to bring, with the notation that nothing else was required.

That made packing pretty easy.

TEN OF US were ushered into a small Tower room with comfortable stools, a podium, and a wall screen.

Six young women, four young men—girls and boys really—we sat and waited. None of us knew each other, and with the reticence common to Query, no one said anything.

I couldn't stand it.

"I'm Loki." I glared at the tall girl. She had her black hair cut short, and, surprisingly, it suited her.

"Loragerd," she said gravely.

The other women were Halcyon, Aleryl, Shienl, Patrice, and Carrine. The men were Ferrin, Gill, Tyron. I thought women and men, but we were all at that age of being neither youth nor adult.

Like rocks on the beach, waiting, we sat.

Through the open archway marched a small man dressed in the black singlesuit of the Guard. On his left collar was a four-pointed silver star. His hair was so black it was blue, and his dark eyes glittered.

"Good morning, trainees. I'm Gilmesh, and this will be your indoctrination lecture." He settled himself behind the podium, studied each of us for a fraction of a unit, cleared his throat, and went on.

"First and foremost, the Guard relies on voluntary subjection to absolute discipline. By this I mean that you agree to live under the rules. The rules are few and absolute. We'll get to those shortly. But why do you think we have to do it this way?"

Dead silence. No one was about to volunteer anything, which was just as well because Gilmesh rushed on as if he hadn't expected an answer.

"The Guard is a small organization with a big job. We don't have the personnel to coddle discipline problems. Minor offenses merit special work assignments or dismissal. Major offenses normally result in a sentence to Hell and dismissal. High Crimes lead to a sentence on Hell and a chronolobotomy."

I understood everything but the last term. Most of us must have worn the same puzzled expression because he stopped and explained.

"Chronolobotomy . . . that's a condensation of a medical term I'm not certain I can remember, let alone pronounce. It means surgical removal of all time-diving abilities. Sometimes limited planet-sliding talent remains, but that depends on the individual."

At that point the room seemed a whole lot colder.

"Well . . . what does the Guard do?" asked Gilmesh, ignoring the chill he had created with his casual revelations. "The Guard is charged with the maintenance of civil order on Query, the elimination of possible threats to Query and other peace-loving races in our sector of the galaxy, and the encouragement of peace. That's it."

The four-pointed star emblem of the Temporal Guard flashed onto the wall screen. Seemed to me that the duties of the Guard gave it a lot of power. Of course, without the Guard, the Frost Giants had nearly wiped us out.

Gilmesh surveyed the ten of us.

"Any of you may drop out of the trainee program at any time in the next three years before we get to field training . . . and probably half of you will. If you decide to leave the Guard after that, you're responsible for two years of administrative duties or an equivalent sentence on Hell. Administrative duties are routine clerical or maintenance functions. In short, you'll be menials. In return, you'll receive restricted time-diving privileges to a number of systems. Is that clear?"

It was quite clear, even to a group of mixed-age youngsters. I was probably the youngest. We never did compare ages.

Gilmesh went on outlining more guidelines, rules, regulations, without arousing much interest until the end of his spiel.

"Academic training will take roughly four years, and diving training will start about two years from now. You will not—I repeat, *not*—attempt any time-diving on your own during this period until you are cleared by the Guard. Here's why."

The screen flashed on again, and the narrator began cataloguing the possible dangers of diving by untrained personnel. Impressive . . . airless planets, planets with poisonous atmospheres, predators, black holes, everything that could possibly go wrong.

It ended with a condensation of the Last Law. "No time manipulation by a member of a species can undo the death of any other species member from that same base system." Translated loosely, once a Queryan dies, no amount of time-fiddling by the Guard can undo that death. If you blow it and die, you stay dead. Dead is dead.

As I recalled from my tutors, the casualties among the earliest timedivers had been fantastic . . . well over eighty percent. I was begin-

ning to see why. You don't think about it as a child. You slide where
you want to on the planet, and even if you backtime or foretime on
Query itself, you can't break out. You feel safe.

Gilmesh ended the indoctrination lecture by giving us room assignments in the West Barracks. He dismissed us after telling us to locate
our rooms, drop off our gear, and report back in one hundred units.

We did and when we returned were directed to Special Stores for
uniform fittings. We each got four black singlesuits and a green four-
pointed star to go on the collar.

That was the beginning of the routine.

The classroom work didn't seem all that hard, not to me, but within
ten-days Shienl and Gill had left.

I enjoyed the mechanical theory class, taught by a blond giant of a
man named Baldur. Often he was units late or held us, and his explanations of the importance of mechanics in culture could be long-winded.

Baldur asked questions . . . lots of them . . . in a quiet light voice that
penetrated, made you listen.

"Tyron, I know you're not the most mechanically inclined trainee,
but you do have the capability to understand the basic outline of something as simple as a generator."

Tyron flushed and mumbled, "Is it that important?"

Baldur didn't raise his voice, didn't seem flustered, just asked another
question.

"Tyron, most cultures have a ruling class or elite or power structure.
That elite's position is normally based on its control of the available
technology, directly or indirectly, and its ability to direct the use of
resources. Control and direction are maximized when that elite understands the technology it directs. What happens when an elite loses its
collective ability to understand the basis of the technology it controls?"

"I don't understand. What does that have to do with generators?"

I didn't understand either, but both Loragerd and Halcyon nodded
as if they did, and Ferrin grinned.

"Loragerd?" Baldur asked.

"They begin to lose control. They aren't the elite any more."

"What about the Guard?" countered Ferrin.

I thought it was a dumb question.

"It's all dumb," protested Patrice. "Ruling classes don't just disappear. And the Guard's no elite."

Baldur never let it go with a simple resolution. "Is the Guard an
elite?"

Tyron suppressed a groan, I could tell, but I didn't see why. Sure,
the Guard was an elite. Pretty obvious.

"Yes," I burst out.

"Why don't you finish the logic for Tyron, then, Loki?"

What logic? I didn't have any, but I decided I'd better bumble through as well as I could.

"If the Guard is an elite," I started slowly, "then it must control some technology. If Guards don't understand technology, then the Guard will lose control." I paused before the immediate objection came to mind. "But the Guard has power because Guards can time-dive, and that's not based on technology."

"It's not?" responded Baldur. "How can you power stunners without generators? How can you stay warm and dry without heat or housing and not become a rootless society that shifts with the weather? I'll admit that the line is harder to draw for Query, but it's still valid."

He stopped, cleared his throat, and continued speaking. "That's something you all ought to think about. In the case of a mid-tech culture like Sertis, the example is clear . . ."

He launched into a description of how the local monarchs ruled through control of the water supplies—the water empire model, he called it.

We got back to generators before too long, and this time Tyron paid attention. Why the digression would have motivated him I didn't see. That was because I thought generators were more interesting than all that speculative stuff about elites and control—or Baldur's comments about excessive waste generation, but we found out about that firsthand later.

We had other courses, too, on the administrative law of the Guard, on meteorology, EQ biology, comparative weaponry . . . a whole mishmash.

The first year was sort of a crash backgrounder.

In the second year, along with more advanced mechanical and technical training, Baldur started us on simple equipment repairs in a side area of the Maintenance Hall.

Patrice protested.

"Why do we have to know how to put all this tangled junk back together? I'm not going to be a mechanic. I'm a diver."

Baldur just smiled. "Do you want an answer, or are you angry because it's difficult?"

Patrice glowered at him. "An answer."

"As a diver, you will be using this equipment, and you'll use it better if you understand it. Understanding only comes when you have a feel for it. Knowing how to repair it gives that feel. Besides, if we repair it, there's less waste, and that means less junk that trainees have to lug to Vulcan.

"Incidentally, Patrice," he finished with a milder tone, "no one in the Guard is *just* a timediver. We all have support jobs as well. If not in Maintenance, then in Linguistics, Medical, Assignments, Research, Archives, or what have you."

I remember Gilmesh mentioning that, but hearing it and starting in with oily metal and dented wrist gauntlets was something else.

Not that it was all work, by any means. Less than half our day was taken up with academic training those first two years.

Every so often I saw Counselor Freyda. She had me over to her quarters in Quest for dinner two, three times, told me about my grandfather. I guessed she followed my training because of old Ragnorak.

VI

IN THE THIRD year the pace stepped up. Not only was the academic load heavier, but we began full-scale physical training. Not just conditioning, but physical flexibility, hand-to-hand combat, weapons familiarization, even life-support equipment training—including deep-space gear.

Carrine resigned a ten-day into the third year, leaving seven of us.

One of the more interesting courses was taught by a Senior Guard called Sammis. "Attitude Adjustment" was the title. That didn't cover the half of it.

The day we started, Sammis lined us up on a field on the edge of Quest. Some of the training facilities were on the other side of Query, but from the field I could see the Tower over Sammis's shoulder.

We stood in the center of a series of posts of different heights. Each post had a tiny platform just big enough for both feet mounted on top.

Sammis waited in front of us until he had our attention.

"In this course you learn by doing. The first exercise is to slide from the top of one post to the top of the next. Like this."

He winked out and appeared on the platform top of the first post, disappeared and reappeared on the top of the second post. Like a jagged bolt of black lightning, he slid from post top to post top and reappeared back on the ground in front of us.

"Now you try it." He pointed at Ferrin. "You start."

Ferrin slid undertime to the first post, broke out with only one foot on the platform, lost his balance, tried to slide, started leaning before he could reorient, and fell to the grass. That first post wasn't much taller than knee-high. The injury was more to his pride than posterior.

Halcyon giggled. Sammis turned on her.

"Halcyon, you're next."

She made it to the third post before tumbling off.

Eventually, it was my turn. I took it carefully, and outside of wavering on the fourth or fifth post, made it through all fifteen platforms.

Sammis was frowning when I finished.

"Did I do something wrong?"

"No, no." He shook his head. "Just . . . nothing."

He left me standing there while he watched Loragerd fall off the platform of the second post.

No one else got past the fifth post that day. Didn't seem all that hard to me, but I'd been sliding from rock to rock in the hills behind the house ever since the day I met the mountain cat, and that was almost as far back as I could really remember.

Tyron called it a pointless exercise, but it wasn't. As Sammis explained after watching everyone (but me) fall off the tiny platforms, "This is to get you up to speed for real diving. In a lot of dives, where you end up could spell the difference between staying in one piece and becoming several. Some divers," and he seemed to have someone in mind, "are gifted enough to dive out of a waterfall while being thrown head over heels. Most of you will find you can't dive except from a relatively stable platform. If you land where you aren't supposed to, you won't be able to dive back."

Oh, it made sense, all right, and so did the "attitude adjustment" exercises that Sammis introduced in the ten-days that followed. Some of the trainees, like Loragerd and Ferrin, never could handle more than the simplest setups. Patrice got pretty fair at it.

We each had a different "final"—supposedly based on what Sammis thought we should be able to handle.

Sammis trotted, or slid, me out to a site on the western cliffs.

"Loki, this could be more than you can handle. I want to make it clear. This isn't a test for passing or failing. It was designed to demonstrate what you can and cannot handle. If you get into trouble, just slide clear. Do you understand?"

His face was kindly, almost worried. Most of the time he had an elvish cast to his features, hinting at mischief.

I nodded.

"The course is set up in increasing order of difficulty, but it's blind. You won't be able to see your next breakout stage until you reach the stage before. You are not to break out except next to the Locator flags.

At the last point, there is an envelope with your name on it. If you can, bring it back."

The whole setup got to me. At least before, I knew approximately where I was headed.

"You mean, somehow when I reach the first point, I'll see the second one."

"Tougher than that. At the first-stage flag is a vector direction arrow for the second stage. The same is true for the next, and so on. You may have only a moment to absorb that information before sliding. There are ten landing points. After the last, or when you stop, return here."

I wiped my forehead. The more I heard about this test, the less I liked it. Despite what Sammis said, I had the feeling there was more to it.

I stalled.

"You mean, I could be falling through midair trying to absorb more directions?"

He grinned. "Not quite that bad, but I wouldn't stay put very long."

"Where do I start?"

Sammis pointed to a flag fluttering below the top of a cliff overhanging the beach.

I nodded and slid, but I didn't break out immediately. Even though it's difficult, you can get some idea of what a landing point involves from the undertime, like looking up from beneath the water at twilight.

The ledge was narrow. Something white fluttered from the rock. I oriented myself undertime to break out facing the white object, presumably the flag and the directions to the next stage.

The ledge was even narrower than I had anticipated, and the wind gusted around me. The permaflex vector arrow attached to the flagstaff indicated a point on the rocks offshore. Even from the cliff tops I could see the surf crashing over them. In between the waves, I could see another banner. Belatedly recalling Sammis's injunction not to hang around, I slid again.

From the understream I watched the breakers and tried to locate the vector directions before I broke out on the rocks. I'd never tried really delaying a slide consciously before, but it seemed to work. The vector arrow was attached to the flagstaff.

I appeared on the wet and very slippery rocks, right after a substantial wave, hoping the area would be water-free for at least a unit or so, and concentrated on the vector. The arrow pointed back to the cliffs farther down the coast. The course pattern was apparently a zigzag along the coastline in order to prevent me from seeing more than one point ahead. I located the flag and slid undertime to avoid the breaker whose advance spray on my neck indicated it was about to crash over me.

From the undertime, point three was on a thin spike of rock jutting out from the cliffs. The spike wavered as the flag fluttered in the wind. Was the rock wavering, or was it my undertime perspective? I didn't like it at all. I decided to see if I could flash by it. You know, just take a quick peek and retreat undertime.

I'd never done a slide that way before, but I didn't like that flag placement.

I actually put a little weight on the stone for an instant and felt it give before I ducked back undertime. The vector arrow pointed to the base of the cliff below.

Sammis be damned. The course had been set up for keeps. But I was going to finish it and find out why.

Point four was established on a peninsula of fragmented rocks and jumbled stone. From the undertime I could see the white flag and the vague form of the vector arrow, but not much else. Each point was making me more wary of the whole exercise.

What was the latest catch?

Was there a tidal blowhole? A rocksucker flattened under the flag waiting for me to step down? Physical reactions are an illusion in the undertime, but I felt I shuddered as I hung there, thinking about the acid touch of a giant rocksucker snapping up around me.

How about coming out next to the rock at a slight angle in order not to be where the course designer planned for me to arrive? I was supposed to touch each point. How close?

Finally, and the non-time moments hung like icicles while I decided, I skipped through. My second guess had been correct. One of the largest rocksuckers I'd ever seen was draped flat over the rugged rocks, with a tentacle loosely encircling the white flagstaff.

I was back undertime virtually instantaneously, but even so, the rocksucker's sting-arms whipped through the space where I'd been fast enough for me to sense a sudden rush of air just before I slid undertime.

I missed the vector arrow in my haste to get clear.

Sliding back and positioning myself at a steeper angle to the flagstaff, I leaned in with another flash. The angle made it difficult, but after two more glimpses, I managed to determine the direction to point five.

The fifth flag was not at sea, nor high in the cliffs, but straight along the beach line to a level space on the sand.

I studied the flat circle around the flag from the undertime, but couldn't see anything out of order. I jumped onto the sand as close to the flagstaff as I could manage, focused on the vector arrow, and tried to locate point six.

I didn't get that far before I was tossed head over heels into the air by a blast of air that made a hurricane seem gentle. I felt strangely light.

I'd managed to memorize the directions, although I hadn't seen the flag for the next point. I slid undertime from my midair tumbling, mostly upright, and reoriented myself.

Given the nasty nature of the course, I somehow suspected the gadgetry involved with point six would have shortly reversed flow, and I would have found myself smashed into the hard sand. The farther along I got, the less happy I was getting about the test. The air-blast generator or whatever wasn't a test. There was no way for me to have known what was waiting and not much of a way to avoid it. The point had been deliberately designed to see if I could slide undertime after I'd been bushwhacked.

I put it behind me—for the moment—and slid in the direction the arrow had pointed. The slide seemed to take longer, but since it's all subjective in the undertime, the unseen examiners couldn't tell my fumbling so long as I located the seventh point.

The obstacle for point seven was clear. They, whoever "they" were, had lowered the flag from an overhanging cliff, letting it float in midair, a good fifty feet above a loose talus pile.

No way in the world I could obtain footing anywhere close to that flag, and even standing beneath it would have been dangerous.

I hovered there in the undertime, although that's not precisely how it works, trying to figure out how to get a look at the vector arrow. If necessary, I could flash through, fall, and dive out of the fall. The rocks below were just far enough and sharp enough that, if I goofed, I'd end up with more than a few broken bones.

I could give up, but somehow, someway, damned if the unknown "they" were going to get the best of me.

Well . . . if I could hang in midair in the undertime, why not in realtime? Not exactly the same, but it was worth a try. Maybe I could leave my heels in the undertime as sort of an anchor.

I tried it . . . and damned if it didn't work.

Offbalance and feeling like I was going to pitch forward, I was still hanging in midair in front of the damned flagstaff. I wasted no time and studied the locator diagram, glanced along the vector path, saw the glimmer of white, and jumped back undertime.

As I slid on a low angle back down to the surf line, I wondered what was next. So far I'd seen only single-item booby traps, but with three points left to go, I'd have been surprised if something weren't doubletrapped.

The white flag was there, all right, and I reached it before I thought

I would—again, a subjective reaction, but I hesitated before I broke out. From the undertime, I could dimly see the flag whipped by the spray and wind, located in the middle of more rocks in an overactive surf line. If I broke out there, I'd risk being pounded by the surf and tossed onto the rocky shore. But was that the clue?

I mentally pushed myself undertime close to the flag, searching for a clue. I wanted to kick myself when it penetrated. No small white rectangle where the vector arrow should have been. A phony point eight, short of where the real point eight was.

The actual point eight was in the middle of the long waves farther out, the tall flag anchored from beneath the water with no place to break out. I did the split-entry trick a second time, leaving my heels locked in the undertime, and as quickly as possible, studied the vector arrow pointing to the ninth flag.

It pointed up the coast and right into the middle of the lava cliffs. Right in the middle of the cliffs was an understatement.

The breakout point was a small cubical room hollowed from the solid rock without any windows or doors. I could tell as I circled the space in the undertime that it was surrounded with machinery of some sort.

Beginning to feel more than even abnormally nervous about the last stages of the damned test, my blood was both boiling and burning. The whole thing wasn't even close to an ordinary test.

From the undertime I could sense the power of the machines buried in the walls of the rock chamber. Even though I couldn't determine anything, I was betting they would be focused on me the minute I appeared.

Someone was more than bending the rules, and so would I. I slid back undertime to the beach below. I didn't exactly break out, not all the way, anyway, but I did manage to get a good chunk of rock, shuttled back undertime to point nine, and studied the chamber.

By wandering around the limp flag and straining to pierce the uncertainty that separates the "now" from the undertime, I could see a vector arrow sheet attached to the rock wall behind the staff.

Still skeptical, I mentally let go of the rock, and, since mind controls matter, it dropped into the chamber. For a long moment, nothing happened. Then a greenish light filled the other side of time, the "now," pervading the space in the rock.

Gas! If it were a test of capabilities, nothing fatal would be employed, only something painful or humiliating.

While the gas swirled around and clouded the chamber, I decided, foolishly, to flash-slide by the vector arrow and get a peek at the directions. I made one pass, far less than a unit in real-time, and managed to absorb the direction and approximate distance. The almost instantaneous slide still left my face stinging.

That's a disadvantage of time-diving. You're left suspended with whatever hurts until you break out. True of pleasure as well, which leads to some interesting permutations, I'd been told, but that was trainee gossip.

Point ten took a while to pin down—or up—subjectively, that is. The directions were confusing, but damned if I was going back for a second look and more gas burns.

That last point, once found, was simple enough. Locating it was what took the subjective time. The vector arrow had indicated an incredibly long, virtually vertical direction arrow. If the scale was correct, and I had no reason to disbelieve it, my last point had to be well above Query's surface.

Figuratively, I scratched my head over that conclusion, but decided to follow the vector arrow to the end.

In the dark above Query, I located an orbiting structure. Through the silver haze that divided the undertime from the objective "now," I could sense that the space station, if that was what it was, had been there for eons, if not longer. The outer spokes of the wheel were gouged and pitted, and one of the arms was holed through.

Guessing that a recovery point and the tenth flag would have to be in the hub, I wandered around in the undertime. The space chill seemed to seep into the undertime. Temperature changes weren't supposed to penetrate beneath the now, not according to what I'd gathered from my sneaky looks into the texts of the advanced time theory course. Our group wasn't scheduled for that until the final half-year.

Groping around half-blind in both the space darkness and the hazed undertime, the subjective time dragged out before I pinned down the elusive tenth flag in a small compartment with heavy metal doors at each end.

I hesitated. All I needed was a momentary appearance, and an envelope with my name on it. Yet every other spot had been trapped. By then, of course, the gas burns were getting to me. Subjective feelings, because the intensity was constant. I just wanted to get the test over with.

I knew whoever set the course was playing on my impatience, and I was tempted to sit up there in orbit for what seemed subjective hours until I figured out the latest catch.

Could it be the orbit itself? Was the chamber airless, and designed to catch me taking a deep breath of vacuum? Was some other equipment focused on the arrival point?

I snooped around as well as I could, discerned no equipment, could sense no energy concentration. Sometimes you can really feel them in the undertime because high energy does have the tendency to warp time itself.

Finally, I decided it had to be the location and the airlessness which were the tests. I made a flash-through appearance, just long enough to grab the envelope and to register if anyone had left any device to record my presence. The cold started to freeze my face, on top of the burning from the green gas, and I continued to seethe while I slid back down to the beach where it had all started. Breakout was welcome as the effects of gas and chill began to dissipate.

Sammis was waiting, sitting on the sand with his head in his hands and his knees drawn up, a morose look on his elvish face.

Some of my pent-up anger lessened on seeing him in that unguarded position, also strengthening my suspicion that he had not been the sole architect of the test course.

"Sammis," I said, my good resolves to keep my mouth shut evaporating rapidly, "here's your damned envelope." I practically threw it at him. He caught it automatically.

"Who the hell designed your little course?" I snapped.

He scrambled to his feet. I had the feeling I wasn't supposed to be back yet.

"Are you all right? How far . . ." He stopped and looked at the envelope. "You got through all ten?"

"I think so. At least if that airless hulk of a space station happened to be number ten, I got through all ten."

He made me recite all of them, and I did, rather impatiently. "Look," I said sharply as I finished responding to his grilling, "if I said I did all ten, I did all ten. I'm not about to lie to anyone about it. Damned if I'll lower myself by lying."

"What?" he asked. He paled slightly, I think.

Abruptly, I realized that I was still a trainee, and a fairly junior one at that. "I'm a little upset."

"I can understand that, Loki."

He still hadn't answered my question. I tried once more. "Sammis, who designed that course?"

"The final responsibility for evaluating the attitude adjustment skills of his trainees rests with the instructor."

That, or some variation, was all he said. I knew someone else was involved.

I just didn't know who.

VII

HE IS A cadet, wearing black. His instructor, in black as well, is a woman. The two of them walk into the empty hall.

"Now, Loki," she begins, "a long dive is no different from a planet-slide in theory, but it's even more important that you come to a full time-stop before you break out."

The cadet, a red-haired man shorter than his superior, nods.

At first glance, they would both appear perfect young adults, but a closer look at the woman's eyes would reveal a tightness and a bleached-out depth that shows even through the dark irises. She has seen more than the man, much more.

The corners of his mouth quirk upward for a moment, accentuating the oddness of his complexion. He is deeply tanned, but carries freckles and flaming-red hair, with green eyes that flash even as he stands motionless.

"Now," she commands.

VIII

THERE'S A HELL of a lot to Temporal Guard training. Advanced work is practically always conducted on a one-on-one basis. It has to be. Abilities vary so greatly from individual Guard to individual Guard that a standardized program would fail. Many of the older Guards themselves can only handle two-way dives to well-charted or nearby localities, such as Sertis. They couldn't have helped me much, although I suppose they were fine for someone like Ferrin.

Freyda was usually my field diving instructor. She wasn't as good as I was even then, but she was well acquainted with the impetuousness I displayed, and acted as a brake on my lack of caution. Freyda was nothing if not cautious.

She was so cautious that I was stunned to find out through casual gossip that she'd spent several years living with my grandfather Ragnorak before he had disappeared on a long-line, backtime dive.

Later, it made a bit more sense, when my own experience and the talk of others confirmed that the Counselor was cautious in every area but one. On Guard matters, however, she was all business and didn't hesitate in using whoever or whatever was best for the Guard.

"You're going to Sinopol with Baldur. That's for Procurement, and you'll need a complete cosmetic," Freyda announced one morning as I entered the training rooms.

"Sinopol?" I'd never heard of the place.

"Hunters of Faffnir, high-tech, about a million back. You need to get a briefing from Assignments and a full language implant. I mean *full,* with complete fluency. Then report to Cosmetics. You two leave tomorrow."

"Supplies?" I ventured.

"Power systems. Baldur will fill you in."

"No weapons from the Hunters of Faffnir?" I was pumping and decided they sounded like a war-oriented bunch.

"The culture's based on hand-powered weapons, personal combat—or massive destruction. There's not much in the way of economical weapons we don't already have. You're going as a bodyguard for Baldur and because he needs a high-powered diver to bring the generator back."

"We have generators," I ventured.

"This is better—much better, according to Baldur—and we're about to lose the opportunity to obtain it. Now . . . you need to get moving."

I got the picture. I was the porter for the heavy technological gadgets. Could be interesting even for a coolie. I buttoned my lip and marched over to Assignments, where Heimdall motioned me to an end console with a single abrupt gesture.

After I had the briefing tapes firmly in mind, Heimdall shoved me out the archway toward Linguistics. There I was laid out under the Gubserian language tank to absorb a complete dosage of Faffnirian.

The language tank is an experience in itself. When I tottered to my feet after an afternoon of high-speed implantation, I muttered my thanks in gibberish, gibberish to almost anyone in the Tower. It would have meant "Thank you . . . I think" to a Hunter of Faffnir.

Recalling the elaborate Code Duello of the Hunters, I belatedly realized that the doubt in my voice would have earned an immediate challenge from any full-fledged Hunter in Sinopol, but the young Guard tech, Ordonna, just smiled. She was used to the disorientation.

Although it was late by the time I reached Cosmetics, and I had hoped everyone had disappeared . . . no such luck. Two Guards were waiting. They slathered me with something over every pore of my body, popped me into a conditioner, pulled me out thirty units later, and shoved me in front of a mirror. I had dark brown skin. After covering my hair with another kind of gunk, they stuffed my head under some other electronic gadgetry. I came out with black hair so dark it had that incredible tinge of blue.

"You can either come back after you're done, and we'll reverse the changes, or wait. The bonding will break down in a couple of ten-days," the head cosmetician noted. "If you're on a long-term assignment, be back here for renewal in twelve days subjective. Good luck."

I trudged to the East Portal of the Tower and slid straight to my rooms in the West Barracks. I collapsed on my couch, barely remembering to set the wake-up for the next morning.

Baldur was waiting for me at the Travel Hall. "What did they tell you?"

"Standard briefing."

The big blond Guard—except now he was big and dark, like me—shook his head. "How's your hand-to-hand? Are you any good with a knife?"

"Nix on the knife. All right on the hand-to-hand." I was being modest. I was good on the hand-to-hand, partly because I cheat. I can't explain the mechanics, but I use my diving/sliding ability to speed up my reactions and motions. Never met another diver who could the way I can. Sammis could anticipate, and he was the best I knew.

"I hope you're better than that. The odds are a hundred percent that you'll have to fight at least once on this trip."

Such a comment seemed strange coming from Baldur, the gentle giant. He was really more of an engineer than a Guard.

"I'll do all right."

He pulled me over into a corner. "Loki, I've heard that you're the hottest Guard since Ragnorak or before. I've also heard that you forget to listen. Listen, please, and save both of us some trouble . . ."

He was off and running about the fantastic technology of the Hunters of Faffnir, their ultra-courteous social structure, and their nasty habit of challenging each other to fights on the slightest pretext. I tuned it out because I'd already gotten it from the briefing tapes.

Baldur meant well, but he went on and on.

Suddenly, he wasn't talking.

"Loki . . . I give up. You know it all. I hope you don't have to pay for it like Mimris did. Are you ready?"

"Sure." Who was Mimris? I wanted to know, but after that sermon I wasn't about to ask.

"We're sliding to the objective-now site of Sinopol before diving straight back. I'll need a breather in between. As it is, I can barely reach High Sinopol. That's one of the reasons for the trip and your presence." Baldur grimaced and brushed his long blue-black hair out of his eyes. Usually it was white-blond.

I knew I was diving along as a glorified porter, but why the rush?

After a million years, someone decided we needed a new type of generator? Heimdall and Freyda hadn't said a word, just pushed the buttons and sent me off. Baldur was bluntly admitting this dive was almost beyond him.

I looked at Baldur again, as if he were a different man.

"Beginning to wonder, aren't you?" He smiled wryly. "I should have started with our politics. Remember, we're a totally parasitic society. We're moving into a time-phase where the average diver can't reach many high-tech cultures. The Guard is reluctant to meddle and create artificially spurred high-tech systems. In the meantime, Terra and possibly Wieren may develop into high-tech cultures. Predicting is chancy, especially when our own lights could go out if we're wrong."

"What lights?" Baldur's words made sense, but not too much.

"Loki, can you build a generator, make a glowbulb, even forge a knife?"

"No. Can you?"

"As a matter of fact I can. But I spent four years on Sertis learning how to, and a couple more on Wieren. As far as I know, I'm the only one on Query who can build anything from scratch, or from raw metal. That's the point. We beg, borrow, and steal."

"We don't need to build that much. We have the duplicator."

"We stole that too, back at the very beginning." Baldur cut off the philosophy with a smile. "I'd rather not have to go to Sinopol. It's at the fringe of my ability. We need a certain compact generator, and you're about the only one who can lug that much metal a million years. So we're going. Please keep your lip sealed and act insignificant."

"But why do we need it?"

Baldur signed. "I just told you. We can't make technology. I can duplicate it and understand it, but not create it. It took me a long time to find this, but I can't lug it back myself."

I nodded. What else could I do? Baldur had spent a long time searching for this generator, and didn't want to lose it. Perhaps he was over-dramatizing, but who was I to dispute it? He'd convinced the Counselors and the Tribunes. Besides, I liked the thought of being indispensable.

"We'll break out in a small room I rented on a long contract. Then we'll round up enough of the local exchange to pay for the generator, pick it up, and return to the Travel Hall."

"Why do we even have to pay for it?"

"You'll see. Perhaps you could steal it. I can't." Baldur shook his head. "Hopefully, you'll return to regular training a little better equipped to understand than before."

I nodded politely again.

We walked over to the Travel Hall and suited up with outfits that
Baldur had obviously brought back on a previous dive.

I dressed. Someone had taken the time and care to tailor the gear for
me, and I wondered who. Then again, the way it stretched, it might
adjust to a wide range of body sizes. Basically, the Hunters wore black
bodymesh suits that covered everything but hands, feet, throat, and
head. The material was a flexible synthetic patterned in octagons. I tried
to nick the stuff with the razor knife that was part of the equipment
and couldn't even peel a sliver from it.

The mesh octagons were small and closely spaced over vital areas, but
there were some oddities. Like the right side of the chest was more
heavily armored than the left, and there was only the wide-spaced lighter
weave in the genital area. The mesh was more open on the arms and
legs, but the spinal column was heavily protected. A pair of shorts, a
sleeveless overtunic, a wide equipment belt, and boots completed the
uniform. Our wrist gauntlets were disguised as ceremonial bracelets.
Sounds unwieldy, but it was designed not to restrict movement at all.
The mesh actually stretched and contracted as necessary. Really an ingenious outfit.

"You look like you've worn that all your life," commented Baldur.

I couldn't say much to that, and didn't.

Baldur gestured, and we slid to Sinopol "now."

Sinopol of the present is nothing more than a handful of hovels
crouched around a shallow inlet of the Sea of Tarth, a pile of brown
heaps perched on a plateau above the choppy black waters of the dead
sea.

Looking at this scene of rustic poverty, listening to a boy whistle his
flock of ironhairs from sparse grazing into the rough stone-glass corral
for their evening slop, I found it hard to believe that an empire had
centered on the spot.

The Hunters of Faffnir had founded Sinopol a million and a half years
earlier. Then the high plateau was lower, the air sharper, and the water
dark green and filled with fish.

Sinopol the Fair lasted five thousand and one centuries. The city rose
for five thousand centuries and fell in less than a hundred years. For five
thousand centuries the Hunters hunted and conquered the systems of
the Anord Cluster. In the five thousandth century, the Hunters overran
the Technocracy of Llord, and there were no more conquests left in the
cluster. Anord Cluster is isolated by the Rift—impassable to large fleets.

Without conquest, the Hunters turned on themselves, first on the
fringes, then at the capital, and in the end the tallest towers of Sinopol
were fused flat into silicon block.

When the shepherds of Faffnir now dig their deep storm cellars—yes, the weather disturbances triggered by that mighty collapse have lasted a million years—they sometimes find a Bird of Pleasure sealed in the glass. Were they to dig deeper they would be astounded, but grubbing through ironglass with blunt spades is a tedious business. The poor shepherds dig only deep enough for survival from the devil storms that scour the top of that vast plateau that was once Sinopol.

Sinopol the Fair in the five thousandth century, the Great Millennium, was ringed with the eight glass blue towers of dawn guarding the corners of the city. The golden walls stretched the twenty kilos between each tower, double-walled, with each wall strong enough to stop a war cruiser at full acceleration. For all the brightness of the towers and the walls, for all the strength represented in the steelglass battlements, the city laughed, breathed with the merriment of a joyous people who sold the tools of war with a smile, their hair, that universal blue-black, cropped short, and their eyes flashing as they talked of the art of war, and sometimes, the war of arts.

For a Queryan Temporal Guard to stroll the streets of Sinopol required caution, Baldur had said, even after a body and hair coloration. The Hunters of Faffnir were hunters, even the city dwellers of Sinopol.

Strangers were prey. The slightest offense under the elaborate Code Duello led to a public challenge at any one of the many corner arenas, where smiling Hunters chose between the parties and laid bets on the outcome.

Since the high-tech era of Sinopol was a million years past, not many of the Guard had visited Sinopol or the Palace of Technology. Strictly speaking, the Palace wasn't a palace . . . rather a city within a city, surrounded with force screens shimmering green in the dusk and gold in the sunrise. Kilos of closed and cool arcades, scented year round with the smells of a summer evening, were lined with storefronts.

Did a Hunter want battle armor? The nearest information corner contained computerized directories of the enterprises located in the Palace. He could select from a variety: Armor Omnipotent, Body Block, the Body Guard, Corpus Electric.

After this buildup from the tapes and Baldur, arrival in Sinopol came as a shock. Baldur's rented room was a hole in the wall, a clean hole in the wall, but a hole in the wall, nonetheless.

Baldur wasn't in any shape to discuss the matter. While I could see that he wanted to get the whole thing over, under the body-dyeing job he was pale. I shoveled some rations in him, and then into me. Then I insisted he lie down on the single couch. He did and was out in less than a unit.

At first glance the room could have been anywhere on a dozen planets. Just a synthetic-veneered room with a couch, a table and two chairs for eating, an armchair, a corner full of cooking gear, and a separate room with funny-looking facilities for hygiene.

One window, and when I went to look out, trying to ignore Baldur's snores, another oddity struck me. Supposedly, this was a poor area, but the window was spotless. So were the others I could see. The air was clear. The orange sun made the whole city shimmer in the noon light.

I sat down in the big chair for a while, hoping Baldur would wake up, but he just kept snoring away. I tried to remember the briefing, running over one item at a time in my mind. Baldur kept sleeping.

I stood up. Somehow the chair didn't feel right. I studied it, but couldn't figure out why.

I walked back over to the window. Baldur snored and turned in his sleep. I checked the lock and bar on the doorway. I presumed it led to a hall. The security equipment was dusty. Baldur rolled back over, stopped snoring, and stayed asleep.

I'd had it. The mission's first step was to get a pile of stellars—the local currency—in order to buy the generator. Baldur had been more vague about the reasons, but he clearly believed that we couldn't or shouldn't steal the generator outright. I had to accept that. So I checked my outfit over once more, as carefully as I could.

Then I slipped undertime to take a look around Sinopol. I figured I could find my way back, but as a precaution I'd locked the location into my wristbands.

I made my first breakout into a quiet corner of the Palace of Technology and popped out when no one seemed to be looking. As I strolled through those endless halls, I put a few pieces together.

Item: Only the biggest and toughest-looking men walked alone.
Item: Women could and did walk unescorted.
Item: The smallest of the male Hunters were taller than I was. Most were at least Baldur's size.
Item: Stellars were carried in sealed belt pouches like mine, attached with the same synthetic as the bodymesh.

There wasn't much chance of liberating the coin of the realm through cutpursing.

A pair of young Hunters came out of a metal-mirrored emporium, their eyes swinging across the hall. The flowing script above the door they left proclaimed the store as "The Reflection of the Honorable Pursuit." A smoother translation would have been "War Reflects Honor."

The two Hunters didn't seem that much older than me. They walked quickly. I moved aside, recalling Baldur's recommendations to avoid trouble.

They moved in the same line.

I started to avoid them again, then saw the pattern. If I kept clear of them, I'd be called for cowardice or its socially acceptable equivalent. If I didn't, one or the other would brush me and claim that I had insulted his honor by not recognizing his passage.

The corridor was wide, well lighted, moderately traveled. The Faffnirians could smell a fight. People were already turning in anticipation before the two bullyboys started their final approach. Unless my neck was really at stake, sliding undertime with a crowd watching wasn't the best idea. All we needed was an entire high-tech culture looking for a stranger who disappeared in full public view. Baldur, not to mention Heimdall, would have my hide.

If I'd been Heimdall, or Freyda, even Baldur, I might have been able to plan a graceful way out. But I wasn't. I just kept marching straight ahead until the thinner one, and both were whipcord lean, like a Hunter of Faffnir sounded, brushed my shoulder.

"Honored young Hunter, I do believe you have conducted your passage with less than the requisite discretion," intoned the thin one. The elaborate phraseology underscored the deadliness of the game somehow.

"Honored old Hunter, I do believe you have contrived a lack of clearance in your own passage merely to reaffirm past glories," I responded. Better to be shot as an eagle than a dove.

His eyes widened slightly. His companion smirked, I thought.

"I regret," he retorted, "your passage from this veil will provide such an opportunity, for the Hunters need young hounds of spirit."

The "corner" arena was not far. Too close. After the first rush, I'd been tempted to disappear and try to reason with Baldur and company, but the thought of all the high-tech goodies of Sinopol being brought to bear on Baldur and me dissuaded me, as did the thought that Heimdall just might have recommended a tour on Hell for calling attention to the Guard.

No . . . better I fought out of it—if I could. I could always dive at the last minute before the lean Hunter tried to cut my throat—I hoped.

He folded his cloak and stepped over the circular edge of the "arena" etched on the faintly gritty stone glass pavement. All the pavements in the Palace of Technology pulsed with a faint light, but the "arenas" glowed reddish while the corridor floors glowed with a faint yellow.

I folded my own cloak, studying him as I did.

The knife would be more of a hindrance than a help. I decided I would throw it as soon as convenient.

"I favor the one with the spotted face."

I scanned the smooth brown faces around the circle before I understood the voice meant me. Damn! My freckles hadn't been covered totally by the cosmetic job, or the Hunters saw at slightly different frequencies. The two bullies had immediately gone for the difference, just like Baldur had said they would.

"He's smaller."

"But to reach his age with such blotches . . ."

"At three to two."

The companion Hunter stepped into the middle of the circle and began a spiel. "Is there no other way for the two honorable individuals to reconcile their difficulty?"

"I would accept only a profound apology and the necessary departure from the Hunters, and that with difficulty," replied the one I would have to kill or dive from. That was right. No honorable bloodletting, scratch-on-the-shoulder, old-chap stuff. One victor and one body would result.

"An apology will not suffice, not for one who provokes for mere vanity," I snapped, not thinking.

That didn't set well with the crowd. They lived for mere vanity. The mutter that went around the circle turned opinion against me. These people expected pointless duels.

"Arrogant young dog."

"Surprising what these young mongrels say."

There was more, little of it complimentary.

I was experiencing culture shock. I was not standing in a bloodstained arena, on sand baked by a sun burning overhead, with a bloodthirsty crowd jeering and cheering.

No . . . I was waiting in a wide, cool, and spacious corridor with the scent of trilia flowers, or something similar, wafting around me, with well-cloaked weapons shoppers stopping for a casual look, as if it were the most common sight in the world to see two young men getting ready to kill each other.

Maybe it was in High Sinopol in the Five Thousandth Century of Glory, but as a young, time-diving Temporal Guard from Query, I had more than a few reservations about the matter, including a real concern about my ability to get out of the mess anywhere near whole.

All too soon the formalities were over, and the Hunter was circling in on me. At first, I countercircled, trying to ignore the running comments from the bystanders. I felt slippery under the mesh armor.

"See . . . the mongrel backs off."

"Perhaps he is an imposter."

I couldn't help the slightest shudder at that. Imposters were dispatched beyond the veil on the spot—if discovered. Shuddering was a luxury, and almost my last one at that. Seeing the distraction, the Hunter came in quickly, light on his feet and perfectly balanced. His knife was like silver fire.

Somehow I avoided it and circled back, still holding onto my own knife.

"The young dog has speed. Most would have been gutted on the spot."

"If he is so quick, why does he let the other control the circle?"

Tactics were becoming clearer as we circled. Given the bodymesh armor, slashing was virtually useless. Any successful use of the knife would have to involve a clean and incapacitating thrust, or slashes across the head and neck. I owed my unscathed condition partly to that.

Now critical jeers came from the crowd, and not all were aimed at me.

"Can't you even finish a mongrel, proud Hunter?"

Sooner or later, he'd get careless with my lack of offense, I hoped.

Sooner it was. Perhaps enraged by the crowd, perhaps thinking me an imposter, he came in with his knife too wide. I threw my own blade at his neck, and half ducked, half slid, blurring almost into the undertime, right around his arm. I snapped his knife wrist with the moves Sammis had drilled into me so many times and virtually simultaneously crushed his throat with an elbow thrust.

For a moment, as he twitched before dying, I must have looked at the body stupidly.

"Have you ever seen a Hunter that fast?"

"So fast . . ."

"The knife was a decoy . . ."

The murmurs went around the circle. The bets were paid, and the bullyboy remaining, pale under his dark complexion, approached.

"Honored young Hunter, I apologize and regret any inconvenience that may have been caused."

I nodded curtly, choking down the nausea that kept climbing back up my throat.

Under the customs, I got the dead Hunter's weapons and his coin purse. The rest went to his clan or wife.

"I would be honored, Hunter of Honor," I managed, after receiving the dead man's knife, weapons belt, and purse, "if you would convey my understanding of the honor and bravery of such an esteemed Hunter to those who would be most concerned."

The ritual saved me. I wasn't sure I could have said anything original. After that, I had to reclaim my own knife. No one had even touched it. The sanitary-disposal vehicle rolled on soundless tires up to the body, lying alone in the arena, even before I had taken a dozen steps down the yellow corridor pavement.

A few older Hunters were standing at a distance, speculating among themselves. I walked toward the nearest narrow side corridor and, the instant I was alone, slid undertime and straight for Baldur's room.

I made it to the funny-looking hygiene facilities and thoroughly lost the contents of my stomach.

Two blows, delivered as taught, and a young man was dead on the glowing red stone glass. Everyone had smiled, especially the older merchant type who had bet on me. I recalled looking up from the crumpled body on the pavement to see him chuckling and collecting from a dour Hunter. Had that triggered the nausea?

Had it been the winning smile of the young lady after my glorious victory? Or the laughter? Or the realization that I had used techniques my opponent had no idea were possible? I'd cheated. Cheated him of his life, and no matter how I rationalized it, my own failure to avoid the confrontation played a big part in his death.

Baldur was standing at the door to the facilities as I washed up. I hadn't had time to close it. He understood, all right.

He nodded at the weapons belt and purse I'd dropped in the middle of the floor. "Just like you, Loki. You had to snoop around and get in over your head."

"How could they? How could I?" I hadn't had that much choice, but still . . . "I kept thinking that you or Heimdall could have avoided it. But, no, I had to get into a situation where either everyone in Sinopol would be looking for me or I had to kill somebody."

I sat down because I was shaking.

Baldur sat in one of the armless chairs and looked at me. "You know, Loki, you're probably one of the few Guards in centuries, besides Sammis, who's killed someone bare-handed. I assume you used hand-to-hand."

I mumbled an affirmative, and he went on.

"Most of the Hunters of Faffnir retire after a single tour or die in some sort of combat. Don't put too much guilt on yourself. But don't push it all away. It would be helpful if you retained some appreciation of life."

I was afraid Baldur might start preaching again. The feeling must have showed. He laughed.

"No, young killer, no sermons. One point. You killed one man, who possibly deserved it, and you feel the impact. Freyda, Eranas, Martel, and the others make decisions which kill, or leave unborn, millions. Odin Thor, for all his purported heroics, never killed anyone face-to-face with bare hands. He just sat back and roasted them. Think about it."

I didn't want to think about it. Instead I opened the purse.

Surprisingly, it was stuffed with stellar notes. Surprising, because I had not thought such a young Hunter would have carried so much. I handed them to Baldur.

"That's enough for us to go into phase two."

Phase two was gambling. Simple when I thought about it, and another reason why Baldur needed a good diver with him.

Casino-style parlors were scattered throughout Sinopol. We settled on one, Rafel's Bazaar of Chance, large enough so that substantial winnings were possible and not remarked overly, but plain and lower-class enough that minor breaches of etiquette would not result in duels.

My part started there. I jumped forward and recorded the payoff numbers and symbols on a chance gadget, logged them against the local objective time. Basically, the gadget was a gilded random-number generator, the kind that Baldur or I could have gimmicked. It was honest.

"Of course, it's honest," pointed out Baldur when I returned backtime with the information. "Under a duel-based society, how long would a crooked operator last . . . unless he was also the best fighter. Even then, someone would eventually kill him."

Baldur had a point.

Since I couldn't occupy the same space-time twice, after I'd given Baldur the information, I jumped ahead over my time in Rafel's and waited for Baldur on the corner outside. Because Sammis and Freyda were always insisting on it, I left myself wide unit margins—objective time—on both sides.

Since I didn't want to wait that long, I scanned the undertime future for Baldur's return before I broke out and dropped out in a deserted corner before walking back into plain sight. It still seemed like forever before Baldur lumbered out of the casino, blue-black hair over his forehead, but my enthusiasm for lone exploring had been damped. He didn't say anything, just pushed on. We took a moving slideway toward the Palace of Technology, drifting through the early evening like quiet ghosts among the laughing Faffnirians.

Two things struck me. Sinopol was clean. The term "immaculate" even could have been applied accurately. Second, each establishment seemed to be open around the clock. Each Faffnirian apparently adjusted his individual schedule to his liking or needs.

Like all Imperial cities, Sinopol reeked of money, reeked of power—from the fountains that bent light around falling water which twisted in midair, to the men and ladies of leisure who paraded the streets flanked with bodyguards who were dressed in matched golden mesh armor and little else, to the clean air scented with trilia flowers, all overlaid with the impression of absolute bodily cleanliness.

Baldur knew exactly where he was headed as we marched from slideway to slideway, liftshaft to liftshaft.

In a moment when no one was close, I asked, "How can a society with such person-to-person dueling run an empire than spans an entire cluster?"

"How would you keep a society lean and able to function over five thousand centuries?" he asked back.

High Sinopol contained more people than all of Query, and then some, and probably had a hundred times the creative spark. For all the wealth and technology applied to the streets and corridors of the city, for all the fantastic decorations, I saw nothing of the overelegant, nothing of the decadent, of the Sertian. Not exactly austere was Sinopol, but not overdecked either.

In the middle of a narrow corridor in the Palace of Technology, Baldur stopped abruptly. The script over the slit door stated, "The Power Place."

Baldur faced me.

"Remember, this is still Sinopol. Nothing is perfectly safe. Once I verify that the generator is complete, we're supposed to be able to wheel it out. But be ready to grab it and dive, if necessary. You worry about the generator, not about me."

He sounded so damned gloomy.

"You're what counts," I responded. "We can always get another generator."

"I don't think so. There's a funny twist in time around this generator, and they don't appear any later. Remember, Sinopol itself won't last much longer."

"Couldn't we go back earlier?"

"This is as far as I can go, and I'd rather not spend even more time educating you on what to look for and how to get it. Besides, you'd end up killing a bunch of Hunters, and then Heimdall would get into the mess." He took a deep breath.

"Let's get on with it."

He made it sound like a last chance. Just for one suitcase-sized fusion generator. I didn't see the big problem, but if he wanted to think that way, that was his prerogative.

The slit door to the generator shop remained sealed until Baldur placed a black disc in the slot. He shoved me inside before the knife edges of the portal snapped shut behind us.

We stood in a small room with a number of weapons nozzles pointed at us. The walls shimmered metallic blue, devoid of features beside the weaponry, some scanners, and five closed portals.

"Baldra, Hunter of the Outer Reaches, returns for what he has ordered, Honored Craftsman." Baldur practically groveled before the blank wall screen. I groveled too.

Energy fields crackled around the room, so much power concentrated that it probably bent the undertime. I could have made it out through the undertime before being fried . . . maybe . . . but there was no way Baldur could have.

The flow of energy waned, and another portal opened into a small showroom. Again, no one was present in the room, but a blocky object, about the size of a small trunk and covered with a shimmering black cloth, rested on a table. The table had legs wider than Baldur's, with heavy braces. Next to the table was an open case with an attached harness. There were small wheels at the bottom of the harness, presumably so that a combat trooper could either pack it or push it. I hoped I could push. The whole business looked heavy.

"You may enter, Baldra of the Outer Reaches . . . with your companion."

Baldur stepped forward. I kept a half-pace behind him. I began to see Baldur's problem. I could have lifted it clear, but I didn't have the faintest idea of what to look for. Baldur couldn't time-carry it, for all his superior physical strength.

What a tenuous web the power of the Guard rested on—a duplicator and generators stolen from Muria, information storage lattices from Ydris, food synthesizers stolen from who knew where . . . and the Guard always reaching, always searching out the gadgets necessary to keep Query functioning.

Baldur made a quizzical gesture as he lifted the cloth that glittered with a light of its own.

I caught a glimpse of what was under the black cloth. It wasn't any fusion generator. The unseen observer reacted, and the energy fields around us began to build. Maybe it was my imagination, but there was no room for error. I grabbed Baldur by the arm and slid undertime, diving forward. He didn't resist, and I brought us out into real-time near dawn in the rented room.

"That wasn't the generator, was it?"

"No. I don't understand what went wrong."

I did, or thought I did. Since it might have been my fault, I evaded the question. "Baldur," I began hesitantly, "I may be able to salvage this. I may not, but I have an idea. I'll be back in a few units."

I slid out undertime before he could protest.

If I was right, the actual generator had been on the table under the cloth until the time Baldur was gambling. My recovery was going to be tricky because I had a limited window. I was just lucky I'd been impatient and hadn't wanted to wait in objective time for Baldur. That meant I could use that time. Hopefully, the operator/craftsman at the Power Place had set up the real generator before we'd won the stake at Rafel's. If not, I'd have to try another approach.

I lucked out. From the undertime, I could tell that something had been set out. But I didn't break out—not at that subjective point.

I needed a replacement. Searching foretime a couple of days, I found a chunk of a grayish synthetic sculpture roughly the same size as the generator. It was piled in the back of what I judged to be a warehouse. No one was likely to miss it immediately.

Toting the synthetic contraption backtime to the Power Place, I located a nearby closet and stored the sculpture even farther backtime. Next I wandered around undertime until I located the command-and-control center of the Power Place. Back foretime I dived until the room was vacant, perhaps several days. When I broke out the whole place was a shambles. I fiddled around, my ears listening for someone, but no one ever came while I was there, until I found the main power control levers on a side panel.

With another dive back to the sculpture and to the first part of my window, I located the control room, and with a quick flash-through, cut the power to the entire Power Place.

I slid into the showroom where the generator—I hoped the real generator—was waiting and lifted the shiny black cloth. It looked real enough, although it was so dark I had to sort of look through the undertime. I made the switch and hoisted the real power equipment undertime.

The damned fusion generator may have been trunk-sized, but I could barely hang onto it with my arms and hands for the instants of subjective time it took me to struggle back to our rented room not long after dawn.

I was staggering as I broke out, but Baldur picked the generator out of my arms as if it were a toy.

I collapsed into the big chair. It even felt comfortable this time. "Is that it?"

I explained how I'd made the switch.

"You made the switch *before* we got to the Power Place, but in subjective terms it was later."

I nodded.

Baldur was no dummy. "That means that because you made the switch earlier in real-time, you had to rescue me, which meant that you had to make the switch."

I wanted to get away from the circular logic. Because I'd made the switch, I had to make the switch. Fine.

"Baldur, I've got to go back and grab that carrying case. I can't possibly hand-carry that generator back to Query without it."

"Hold it. You say the Power Place was a shambles after you went foretime?"

"Yes. Why?" What difference did it make?

"We'd better make sure that happens too." Baldur handed me a silver cube the size of my fist. "Energy reflector. Drop it as close to our back-time departure point as you can. It diverts energy back to the source. That's an oversimplification, but after it works you should be able to pick up the carrying case at your leisure."

I sighed, squared my shoulders, took a deep breath, and dived. I managed to get within a few units of the time we'd left the night before, made a flash-through breakout, and dumped the cube.

I waited for the energy flows to settle and broke out maybe thirty units before dawn. Baldur had underestimated the impact of his little cube—or the amount of energy focused on it. I doubted if a single circuit in the entire Power Place would work. Picking up the carrying case from the wreckage was a snap, and the scrapes and scars on it didn't bother me.

Back in the room, Baldur loaded me up with the damned generator.

"I'll see you later," he remarked as I dived.

For a moment, I wondered what he meant, but I recalled a bit of theory that Freyda had mentioned, and it made sense. Baldur had spent less objective time away from Query than I had. With all my doubling back and forth, I actually had been in the now longer than Baldur had, and that meant he would arrive back at the Travel Hall sooner than I would.

As I vaulted from timepath to timepath back toward Query, I

couldn't help wondering about the implications of the time-twists I'd created in Sinopol.

Baldur had been so relieved to get his new toy that he'd dismissed the paradoxes. Or maybe he was just more used to them, but I'd never snarled Time before.

There weren't any suitcase-sized generators later in Sinopol's timeline. Was that because we'd destroyed the one craftsman making them, or because no one else wanted anything that small?

I tried to figure out what came first. Had I caused the switch by imagining the energy buildup? Or had I reacted to actual buildup and a possible double-cross and thus set in motion the destruction of future generators?

Did that mean that we had to do what we did because we did what we did?

Then, too, there were no change winds, and that meant that we hadn't changed what was. Did that mean what we did had been fated all along?

I gave up on that one, but I still wondered why Baldur needed the small generator so badly, and why he couldn't just have described it and sent me after it. Or didn't they trust me to go off alone? Why couldn't they have waited until I knew more? Or was there something the generator was needed for now . . . *and* they didn't trust me?

I gave up trying to figure it out until I knew more. In practical terms, for the moment, it didn't matter.

By the time I broke out in the Travel Hall, Baldur had a small cart waiting for the generator. It went straight to Maintenance.

I went back to my rooms and to bed. I didn't even eat.

IX

IN A PARATIME *reality, a being stands in front of flames.*

Call the being an angel, for lack of a better term. His wings are silver and, folded behind him, dwarf his body. This angel is a student of the past, paradoxically, because he is not, yet is, and has no past. As he stands before the flames, he studies the wingless statue that is suspended in the midst of the fires.

The golden statue is of a god. Term him that, although his shape is mere humanoid, because as god he is casting a thunderbolt.

Set on the pedestal before the font is a tablet.

The angel-student-scholar turns his attention to the tablet, and his eyes widen as he recognizes the star chart.

A whisper of the change wind can be heard in the background, yet this is but a paratime reality, less than drifting smoke until the god acts.

Which god? That, too, waits for the change wind.

DEALING WITH TIME-DIVING season after season, and knowing you could be time-diving centuries later has a certain effect. It really doesn't take too long for Guards to set themselves apart, even as we guarded the people of Query.

Field training showed some of that separation quickly. As part of field training, we were rotated through the various functional duties of the Guard, such as Weather Observation, local Guard duplicator offices, and Domestic Affairs, with a longer stint in the Locator section. Locator was the people-tracing aspect of the Guard.

Locator and Domestic Affairs are the two Guard functions not located in the Tower, not even in the wings. The Tower is out-of-time-phase, and few Queryans can slide or dive into or out of the Tower.

If there is a serious problem—violence or a missing child—time is important. The out-of-Tower location of the domestic Affairs and Locator offices speeded up the process.

Basically, in Locator four or five Guards sit on stools behind plain black consoles around an open stage, waiting for upset Queryans to appear and pour out their Locator problems . . . usually a missing child, a childish prank, and occasionally a missing parent.

Two or three of the Guards who sit and wait were trainees. That was how I found myself staring at a blank Locator screen one afternoon.

What a comedown it was—to spend the morning in advanced field dive training, diving into a nowhere between stars and trying to orient yourself enough to dive back to Query without using the homing equipment and then to find yourself spending all afternoon—or worse, late at night or after midnight—propped in front of a blank console . . . waiting, sometimes for nothing.

Sometimes not. Sometimes a child disappeared.

"Guard Loki!" called the woman, breaking into my afternoon reveries. She knew my name because it was on the desk name plate. "My daughter's disappeared. I can't trace her anywhere."

"Her name?" I asked politely, because Gilmesh had pounded into my head that Guards, especially trainees, were always to be polite.

"Kyra Dierdre."

"Birth date?"

"Sixteen Jove 2,115,371."

I keyed it all into the console, added the MC—minor child—code because she was only eleven, and came up with the Locator tag number. Then I punched in the seeker controls.

"Undertime!" flashed the console in its flowing script. It doesn't really work that way, of course, because there's no objective duration to a dive, but the machines are designed to indicate simultaneous "bridges" between different objective locations as "undertime."

Even as I thought that, I tapped the studs and read the directions. Then I pressed the emergency buzzer so that Roggan, the duty supervisor, would know I was fast-tracking.

"One Red, South 34-337-45. EPB . . . Astarte."

I fed the coordinates into the microcircuits of my wrist gauntlets and timedived right from my stool. For an eleven-year-old to have gotten that far meant talent, and talent meant trouble, which was where she was headed.

The Guard tried not to lose many, but such accidents were still the leading cause of death among children. Young children's Locator tags were automatically monitored until they were ten for just that reason. Of course, Kyra had to be eleven, but that's just sometimes the way things are.

If Kyra broke out on an airless planet, I'd have to be there for the pickup within a unit or two to prevent physical damage. If I couldn't get to the breakout point in time, unless the child were unusually gifted, the results would be fatal.

I'd heard lots of talk about looping time to undo death, but you can't do it. Dead is dead. The metaphysics of it consumes hundreds of pages of theory, but dead is dead. That was the hard part about going after place-strayed children. Sometimes we got there too late.

Rescuing Kyra was standard. Under the Time Laws I couldn't make physical contact until after breakout, but I swept in behind her on a narrow time-branch that led to the airless moon called Astarte and followed her right to breakout. I came out right behind her, grabbed, and dived straight undertime. She barely had time for a gulp of vacuum or a chance to see the black ash and stars spilled across the sky like sugar.

Like an arrow I made for the Infirmary.

The medical technician looked up, almost bored, as we popped into view. His name was Hycretis.

"Vacuum burns, maybe," I said quickly.

The girl struggled, and I realized I was still holding her tightly. I let go, ready to grab her if she tried to move, ready to dive if she attempted it. But she did neither, just stood there once she stepped away from me.

Hycretis stepped forward. He did smile at her. "We need to make sure your face and eyes aren't hurt, and your lungs."

"I'm fine." Her voice teetered on the edge of tears.

"You probably are, but we'd like to check," Hycretis added. "What's your name?"

The blond-haired girl shook her head.

"Kyra," I added.

Kyra glared at me. I didn't know what to say. I'd just saved her from freezing solid, and she was glaring at me. So I stood there, waiting.

"Kyra," Hycretis said, very gently, "I'd really like to make sure you don't get sick."

"Why?"

"Sometimes, if you exhale where there's no air and it's cold, it blisters the inside of your lungs. We can fix that right now, and it won't take long, but if we wait, you'll be a very sick young lady."

"All right." She didn't look at me as she followed Hycretis.

I'd have to check back with him for the rest of the procedure after he finished, but, in the meantime, I couldn't do anything in the Infirmary. So I made for the Locator stage and my console.

Roggan was talking with the mother when I popped out. Both of them looked at me.

"She's all right. She broke out on Astarte—"

The mother paled.

"—but I got there in time. She's getting a checkup and probably a quick turn under the regenerator to make sure there's no lasting lung damage."

Roggan let out his breath.

"When can I get her?" The woman's voice was calm. Queryan stoicism—perhaps a touch of mist in her eyes, but no tears, no visible emotion.

"She'll have to be debriefed before she can go home," I said.

"What?"

"We don't want it to happen again. We might not be so lucky the next time. She's required to have additional cautionary instruction. Otherwise she might try a repeat." I shifted my weight, wondering why I was explaining and not Roggan.

"How long before I should come back?"

"About two hundred units," Roggan answered.

When the woman left, Roggan turned to me. "Why didn't you give more of a warning?"

"I didn't think I had much time. It was a long slide."

"You'll follow up with the cautionary procedures?"

I nodded.

"You're clear, and covered."

So I slid under the now and back to the Infirmary, where I walked in circles until Hycretis was done with Kyra.

Then I slid Kyra and myself to the training-center stage. We had to walk through the narrow stone archway. The training center wasn't in the Tower either, but across the main square of Quest from it. The room we entered was out-of-time-phase, and I didn't let go of Kyra's arm until we were inside.

She tried to slide. Strong kid. She faded slightly, but that was all she could manage. Better than a lot of the Guard could do, and she was only eleven, with a lot of development yet to come.

"All right, Kyra. Take it easy."

"Why?"

She had a good question, but at least I had the stock answer ready. "Because we don't want you killing yourself. Because we don't want you jumping to another airless moon . . . or worse."

She did shudder as she recalled Astarte.

"Sit down." I pointed to a comfortable stool facing the blank wall screen. She sat.

I punched the stud and triggered the series. Basically, it was similar to the briefing Gilmesh had given me the very first day of my own training, but worded more simply. Kyra had already received some of the material and would receive more under standard instruction within the next few years, whether or not she opted for the Test and the Guard. Most children don't show real time-movement abilities until close to puberty—and it's hard to get off Query without those abilities. They pick up planet-sliding by the time they can walk and talk coherently—sometimes earlier—which is why some Queryan homes with small children have inhibitors. An inhibitor field won't stop an adult or older child, but the static patterns are enough to stop smaller children . . . most of them.

Kyra was caught by the screen. No great surprise, since a hypnotic field was focused on her to intensify the material. Standard hazard list was the basis—the dangers of suns, airless planets, black holes, blizzards, radiation. The briefing also pointed out that she couldn't dive without concentration and discipline, so if she had gotten into a place where she was scared silly, she would have died because she couldn't dive.

Simplified, but the Guard's indoctrination series for wayward children laid it on thick—designed for the extraordinarily headstrong children whose will had outpaced the development of their rational facilities.

Some hundred fifty units later, I escorted Kyra back to Locator. She was a slim tall girl already, close to my shoulder in height, with piercing green eyes, a sharply pointed nose, and flowing blond hair. Before she turned to her mother, she fixed me with an absolutely black stare.

I stood there and took it, not really knowing what else to do. Finally, I smiled. She didn't.

Then the two of them disappeared, presumably for home. I sat back down on my stool in front of the console and keyed her name into the records as a likely prospect for the Guard. While she might not pan out, anyone that strong at eleven was likely to be one hell of a diver in another five or ten years.

Just for the hell of it, sitting there and fiddling with the console, I accessed my own Locator tag. The screen began flashing a series of directions and locations, ending up with my own position in Locator, all the locations in the appropriately condensed codes, of course.

I blanked the screen and scratched my head.

The console had given several dozen backtime locations for me. I'd been there, but I wasn't now. So how could the Guard locate a diver?

You couldn't, at least not easily, not unless you knew all the previous assignments. Then it clicked. That was why Heimdall and Assignments were so insistent that we recorded the times of all previous dives as soon as we got back to the Travel Hall. And that was also probably why the Guard tried to instill the habit of diving out of the Hall and returning there.

Presumably the Locator and Assignment records were available to other senior Guard officials. That meant a quick cross-check would eliminate past assignments and enable a disciplinary or rescue team to zero in on the latest "real" location.

They'd have to be careful, and then some. They couldn't pull a Guard out of a time-track he'd already established. It was funny in a way how the Guard could change a time-track not associated with Query, but could only reach a Queryan at the end of the time-trail—that is, the now.

That's because of the Laws of Time. They preclude most would-be paradoxes. Only the strongest divers can break out even close to an earlier objective backtime dive of another diver. Most can't.

I shook my head at the possible complexities of locating lost or strayed Guards and spent the rest of my duty tour waiting for another time- or place-lost child to track. It didn't happen that time.

But it happened often enough. Children will be children, especially young ones. Without the automatic analyzers and the inhibitors, there would be a lot more lost and hurt children on Query.

And children don't function on the same time frame as adults, not that it matters when Locator covers an entire planet. It's always breakfast for someone when you're ready for dinner, or the other way around.

That night I was tired, and I yawned. A senior Guard named Jaclynn was the supervisor, and she glared at me. It wasn't effective, because her eyes were muddy brown, and, frankly, I was too tired to really care. Sammis had showed up that morning with a refresher course on fitness. I think the idea was more to demonstrate that he could wear us all out.

So I yawned and looked at the console. It blinked red—bright red— and I stopped yawning and fed the home and destination coordinates into my gauntlets.

"I've got it!" I yelled, and dropped right into the undertime. That was before most of the others had even finished reading the warning, but I was always quicker than most—except maybe Sammis, and that could be why he bothered me so much.

There was a four-year-old on the loose in the Sand Hills of Eastron, or close enough. I hadn't learned the exact matches between the Locator coordinates and the geographical parallels, but I didn't need them— just to follow the line to the child.

Morning rises like thunder out of the Bardwalls and over that icy tower that is Seneschal and spills onto the Sand Hills. The River Scyllay winds through the hills, half sand and half twisted shapes of sandstone and black glass sculpted by the winds. The black glass dated to the Frost Giants, according to my father, but it can cut sharper than a laser, even while the most solid appearing bluffs and cliffs can collapse underfoot.

It took me three half-slides until I found the boy, building a pile of sand that must have been meant as a castle, sitting on a beach beside the now-placid River Scyllay. He couldn't have been more than three paces from the river.

I dropped out a hundred paces downriver and began to walk toward him, looking for trouble, like big sand snakes that could have swallowed the child whole—Ferrin said they were mutations from the Frost Giant times—or sand cats similar to the mountain cats. Personally, I worried about the snakes more, but as I walked, I didn't see any of the curved depressions they created, nor any holes in the undersides of the bluffs overlooking the river. There weren't any clouds over the Bardwalls, and that was a good sign that we wouldn't face a flash flood.

So I kept walking, ready to dive, as I neared the boy. He had silver-blond hair, even fairer than Baldur's, and he was piling sand around a

small black glass stone worn smooth by the river and the sand. He was
wearing blue night shorts that were wet on the cuffs and smeared with
damp sand.

"Hello," I said, squatting down, not too close, to view his work.

He looked up wide-eyed, shrinking back a little.

I smiled and waited.

He waited.

"I used to build castles."

He slowly lifted another handful of wet sand and plopped it on top
of his pile. "Mommy didn't want to come to the beach."

"I see."

"She said after breakfast."

I nodded. One of those morning children for whom breakfast time
was midmorning or midday.

"Are you almost finished?" I asked.

"No."

I could see his point. So I stood up and looked around, trying to
listen to see if anything else might be stirring, besides the red flies I
was brushing away.

The boy had several welts on his back already, but they didn't seem
to bother him.

"We need to go home," I suggested.

"Don't want to." He pushed another pile of sand onto the heap.

"Your mommy will be worried. She doesn't know where you went."

"I told her I was going to the beach."

"Did you tell her which beach?"

He smoothed the sand around the black stone. "No."

I checked the home coordinates on my gauntlets and reached for his
hand.

"Don't want to."

"I know." I waited some more. I kept looking for sand snakes and
cats. Maybe it was too early for them.

"All right. Hungry."

I think I was spoiling his fun by standing there, but I didn't argue,
just took his hand and followed the coordinates.

The house was in a village cluster in a valley not that far away. We
broke out right in front of the porch. It was quiet.

I tried not to sigh as we walked up the steps to the door. "Is this
your house?"

The boy nodded. I could see a set of elaborate wooden blocks at one
end of the porch. I hoped they were his.

I knocked on the door. Nothing. I knocked louder.

"Who the frig is it, Nerryn?"

"How would I know? It's not even past dawn."

That was an exaggeration. The sun had barely cleared the Bardwalls. I knocked again.

"Coming . . ."

The man's mouth dropped open when he saw the uniform. "Verlyt . . ." He shut his mouth as he saw the child. "Rykker . . . are you all right?"

"I went to the beach, Daddy."

The man looked at me.

"It happened to be a beach on the River Scyllay, right in the middle of the Sand Hills."

By now the mother was there, hugging the child and murmuring, "Are you all right, dear?"

"I'm hungry now."

I tried not to grin. "You might think about an inhibitor," I suggested. "At least for when you're asleep."

The two exchanged glances. "I thought you turned . . ."

"You didn't . . ."

I backed away silently, hoping they remembered to keep the inhibitor on while they were asleep. There really wasn't anything else I could do.

Rykker gave me a solemn wave, and I dropped back to Locator to enter another report. Then I went to my room in the West Barracks and collapsed.

Sometimes nothing happened, and sometimes . . .

One day, my watch tour was just about over—it was a morning tour—when Frey marched in and presented himself before my console. Frey was Freyda's son by her fourth or fifth contract.

He wasn't swinging the black light saber, and he was decked out in formal blacks, with his Senior Guard's four-pointed silver star positively glittering. My insignia was the gold and green of a senior trainee. At the end of the year, when we finished with Locator and Domestic Affairs probation, we'd all receive official full Guard status and could wear the solid-gold star.

The ranks were really quite few. After you became a Guard, years, centuries, could pass before the next promotion. The Senior Guards wore the four-pointed silver star. Counselors wore black stars edged with gold, and the three Tribunes had black stars edged with silver.

When I looked at the Guards I came in contact with, I wondered who was selected, by whom, and why. Freyda was a Counselor, and trying to be a Tribune when Martel stepped down, or so the gossip ran. Baldur was a Counselor, but Gilmesh, who had more service than either, and who was in charge of Personnel, was only a Senior Guard. So was Heimdall.

Frey had been promoted to Senior Guard a few years back and had been assigned to run Locator/Domestic Affairs when Wolflen had never come back from a scout run to Atlantea.

Frey was in a hurry.

"You're off at 1100?"

"Yes."

"Report to Domestic Affairs as soon as you're relieved. We need a second standby Guard with hand-to-hand skills."

He was gone. No explanation. No questions about my availability. Just report to Domestic Affairs.

I wondered if I were getting a reputation as a standby muscler as a result of Baldur's report on the Sinopol dive. I'd only had lectures on Domestic Affairs and wasn't scheduled to do my probationary work there until later in the year. For me, it was the last probation tour, but Ferrin had started there. Why had Frey ordered me as a backup Guard? For what?

By the time Ferrin had arrived to relieve me at 1050, I was itching to go.

"Know what's going on in Domestic Affairs?" I asked with a straight face.

Ferrin smiled, and his too-big teeth lighted his face like a glowbulb. He had picked it up. He catches everything. He might not have been much of a diver, but if anything were in the wind, his long thin nose and keen ears were the first to find out.

"Frey needs muscle, and he doesn't want to turn to Heimdall for it. You were selected, shining star."

I grinned back at him. Even though he was snoopy, and his lank black hair hanging over his forehead and his long nose gave him a vulture-like look, I had to like Ferrin. Always willing to help out, he did what he was supposed to do without griping and probably acquired more sheer knowledge from training than any two others put together.

"So why does Frey need me?" I had another question, stupid, but Ferrin could answer it, and I didn't need one of Gilmesh's sarcastic answers. "And why does he run both Locator and Domestic Affairs?"

"Do honey and soda bread go together?"

I thought for a moment, then shook my head.

Ferrin, ready to explain anything, plunged in. "Look, Loki, at what Locator does. Locator tracks people. Now, what does Domestic Affairs do? Handles the police functions. And how could it handle the police functions without being able to track people?"

It made sense. I hadn't had to track someone wanted by Domestic Affairs, but Loragerd had told me the story of her second watch at Locator, when the Guard's special Domestic Force had gone out with stunners after a man who had tried to storm Martel's house with an ax.

Using an ax against anyone or his home is bad enough, and it doesn't happen very often, but to lift an ax against the High Tribune . . . the wretch deserved a term in Hell for something like that.

The only problem was that he didn't get it.

The Domestic Force cornered him on a cliff edge under the Bardwalls, right below the Garthorn, but before they could stun him, he'd jumped off, and there was no way to match fall velocities, especially on Query. Besides, who'd want to take that kind of risk for a nut like that?

I'd asked Loragerd if she knew more about the incident, but she couldn't add much, only that the man had yelled something about the "tyranny of time" and screamed that he was tired of being a "poor, dumb sheep." His family claimed that the Guard had stunned him and just let him fall. But really, what difference did it make?

No trial. The matter was closed.

So why did Frey need me—a senior trainee? Ferrin still hadn't answered that question.

"What's so hot that Frey needs me?"

Ferrin stopped smiling. "I have not the glimmer of an idea, nor even the inkling of a conceptual hypothesis of a rational nature. Unfounded rumor would indicate that he requires someone with outstanding technical diving skills and of a physical nature, someone who is not beholden to Assignments."

Whenever Ferrin used the double-talk, he meant he couldn't verify what he said, that he was guessing. His guesses were better than most Guards' knowledge. His guess translated into Frey needing a junior goon who might be expendable, and he wanted to round up the goon without asking Heimdall's help.

I added my own guesses. Frey didn't need or didn't want a fully trained Guard, which I took to mean that the physical situation wasn't all that dangerous, but that there were some internal politics involved.

I nodded to Ferrin and signed over the console.

When I reported to Domestic Affairs at 1103, I was promptly greeted by Frey, Gilmesh, and a Guard I'd never met.

"Loki, this is Hightel." Frey made the introductions.

Hightel was stocky, broader than me, with rock-sandy hair and brown eyes, and seemed ready to burst out of his black jumpsuit. He smiled pleasantly. I decided he was the kind of Guard to be polite to.

"Greetings," I acknowledged, bowing slightly. I still couldn't resist pushing Frey a bit. "Could you please explain what I'm here for?"

"You didn't tell him?" asked Gilmesh.

"Press of time," admitted Frey.

Gilmesh's eyes flicked over Frey with a strange cast, I thought, but the look vanished in an instant. Hightel's face remained pleasantly impassive.

"It's fairly simple," began Gilmesh as Frey stood there without uttering a sound. "We have to move a miscreant from detention to the Hall for trial. Hightel would normally handle the situation, but there is a faint possibility that those sympathetic to the miscreant may attempt to interfere. You are present to ensure that no one interferes with Hightel."

At that, he handed me a stunner, deliberately setting it on full.

I didn't understand, but buttoned my lip. None of it made sense. If the miscreant were so dangerous, why drag a trainee, even a senior trainee, in as a second Guard? Frey was all too nervous, and Gilmesh too plausible. I still took the stunner.

"Miscreant" was the official term for those non-Guard Queryans who violated the Code. This particular miscreant must be something. I was interested to see what he or she looked like, to see why Frey and Gilmesh had pulled me in.

While some detention cells were in the Domestic Affairs building across the Square from the Tower, most cells were in the lower Tower levels. Made sense, because the construction of the Tower itself inhibited sliding and diving. Then the Guard added restrainer fields, a beefed-up version of the inhibitors used for children.

What the restrainers did was to scramble thought enough to prevent time-diving or sliding. Without something like that, it would have been impossible to confine most Queryans.

The four of us marched across the Square to the Tower, out of step, but who cared?

In the fall, and the seasons' temperatures vary only marginally in Quest except for midwinter when there is frost and an occasional snow, the fireflowers' scarlet was brighter, and they glowed into the twilight, often until midevening. They looked like they would pour perfume into the air, but they had no scent at all.

Hightel hadn't said a word. We marched down the ramps to the detention levels and still he said nothing. Frey pointed out the cell. Except for the restrainer fields, the thick walls, and the barred door, the windowless room might have passed for a comfortable, if austere, apartment.

"The executioners arrive, with a young one to be blooded as well. Lead on, servants of tyranny," declared the prisoner. Even without the flowery speech, he didn't look like a miscreant, but many people do not look like what they are.

Although we all had youthful builds and did not age physically, the man in the cell gave an impression of greater age—tiny lines in the corners of his eyes, a spade beard, faded green tunic and matching trousers, and handcrafted leather boots like my father made. He had light brown hair and a reddish beard, and his eyes sparkled as he spoke.

Neither Gilmesh nor Frey said a word. I did not either, trying not to frown at the mental static created by the fields—and the static I felt was outside the cell where the restrainer was focused.

Hightel was the one who spoke as he opened the door.

"Let's go."

He took the man by his arm. The prisoner couldn't slide or dive once he left the field area because he probably couldn't carry the bigger man with him. If he did, Hightel had the weapons and the training to subdue him after breakout, although my job would be to follow and assist him.

I noticed my palms were sweaty. I didn't know why, really. The trip had to be routine—just up the ramps and across the center of the Tower to the Hall of Justice. We didn't even go outside, and there were Guards everywhere we went.

I saw shadows around every corner, and no one said a word.

In the Hall of Justice, the Tribunes were waiting—all three of them—and that meant it had to be important. It only took one to decide most cases.

I breathed a sigh of relief when the prisoner was settled into the red "accused" box and the restrainer field was adjusted and trained on him. He didn't look dangerous, wasn't as big even as I was, but what do appearances indicate?

I eased myself into a corner of the section reserved for the Temporal Guard. Although no one had said anything, I assumed he'd require an escort back to the cell after the trial. Besides, I wanted to know why he was so dangerous.

The Hall of Justice is a magnificent place, lit with slow-glass panels brought from every type of colored sun in the galaxy, with seats enough for thousands, the whole Temporal Guard and more, and with the crystal dais for the Tribunes, the black podium for the Advocate of Justice, and the red stone box and podium for the accused. Every whisper from the front can be heard clearly to the last seat high in the soaring back of the Hall.

Martel was the High Tribune, flanked by Eranas and Kranos. They
sat quietly, waiting. The Advocate, silver mantle draped over her formal
black jumpsuit, stepped to her podium.

I drew in my breath as I recognized Freyda, the Counselor and my
advanced time-jump instructor.

"Honored Tribunes, honored Guards, honored citizens . . ." she began.

I looked around the Hall. A handful of Guards and a hundred or so
other spectators were scattered about, including a group of ten young
students and their instructor.

The name of the accused was Ayren, and he was charged with civil
disorder, theft, personal violence, and treason. To me, that seemed like
an odd combination.

Freyda offered the evidence—the testimony of a dozen witnesses, all
brief, what holo records there were—with a low-key approach. All of
the testimonies of the witnesses were taped, but they were on call should
the accused contest the factual content of the testimony.

Ayren chose not to challenge anything.

According to the evidence, the frail man in the red stone enclosure
had employed crude explosives to destroy the Domestic Affairs regional
office at Trifalls, used a stunner stolen from the wreckage of the office
to stun the first Guards who arrived to investigate, and had stood on
the ruins preaching the overthrow of the Temporal Guard and asking
every citizen to murder the next Guard he saw.

Fortunately, none of the few he had spoken to had taken his admo-
nition seriously.

Finally, Ayren tired of merely stunning Guards and, when the follow-
up Domestic Force arrived, attacked them with a crossbow stolen from
the Historical Museum.

Theft alone was almost an automatic sentence to Hell. Had to be.
Any Queryan could slide into anyplace big enough to hold him. A few
of the Guard could do better than that. So there was no real way to
safeguard any extensive set of personal belongings.

Our system had some compensating mechanisms—like the duplicator. Why steal common items when you could get your own from the
regional duplicating centers? Also, most Queryans had trouble carrying
large items. My diving equipment, for example, was stored in a chest
keyed only to my aura. The chest was locked, too heavy for most to
carry on a planet-slide, and too small to get inside.

And the Locator tags inserted at birth meant that you could never
escape the Guard, that miscreants could be tracked wherever and whenever they went.

All this didn't mean theft didn't exist, merely limited it because the stakes were low and the rewards few. Who wanted to be an Immortal and chained to a rock on Hell with eagles swooping and ripping at your guts, grounded by a temporal restraining field and fed by a bodily sustenance field that would not let you die?

Ayren hadn't got all that far with his stolen crossbow. One Guard—Dorik—had taken a bolt through the arm, probably through carelessness, but the other two Guards had stunned Ayren and carted him off to detention.

As the trial progressed, I got more and more confused. Ayren scarcely seemed crazy, but, with each damning charge, each report of assault or theft, each violent action, he either nodded in agreement or failed to contest the charge.

At the same time, Freyda imputed no motives, just cited each action, the corroborating evidence, and the applicable section of the Code. Her summary was brief and concluded with the blunt statement that "Ayren Bly, Green-30, did destroy the property of the people of Query, did willfully take goods belonging to others without intent to restore or replace, did attack with intent to murder, and did advocate the overthrow of the government by force. The evidence is clear and undisputed."

Not terribly eloquent, but sufficient, considering the wealth of evidence she had displayed on the screens.

Ayren declined to offer counter-evidence and rose to offer a closing statement, as was his right. By then, the students had left, and only a few spectators remained.

Ayren stood behind the podium. In the light from the slow-glass panels that illuminated the Hall, his eyes held the glitter of madness, and his voice was filled with the bitter fire of hate . . . or something more.

"Thank you, Advocate, Tribunes. My time here is worthless, a coin of gold buried in a charade of counterfeits . . .

"My speaking will not save me from Hell, nor will my words alter one iota the orbit of this doomed planet. But I must make the gesture, feeble as it might be, against the winds of time. For the winds of time do not die, but sleep, drowsing in the afternoon, waiting for the god of time to wake them and change the face of this hapless orb. There will be a god of time, and you will know him, though you know him not. And he will know you, and not all your power will stand against him in his anger. He will sweep away the mighty and the proud, and they will break into less than the dust of time . . .

"You have recorded the histories of dozens of races across the stars, but there are few records indeed of our history. One cannot learn from history when there is no history . . .

"I look around this Hall built by our predecessors. We rattle around in it like dried gourd seeds in a child's toy, playing out a charade of justice which is not justice. Nor is it law. Nor mercy. I do not expect these, nor should I, for I have agreed to let the charade continue until cometh the god of time . . .

"Do not condemn me to Hell because I violated the Code. Do not condemn me because I assaulted your agents of repression. If you must condemn me, condemn me for speaking the truth. Truth that you have yourselves condemned the people of a once-mighty planet to be your sheep, herded by a few blacksuits, beguiled by an easy life and meaningless toys, while you tear down the galaxy to protect your poor pastures and preserve your waning power. For your power surely wanes . . .

"Send me to Hell for trying to save the sheep from the shepherds who are no more than black wolves. Send me to Hell, if you must, but do not call it justice . . ."

There was more, but pretty much in the same vein—ranting and raving about the god of time who would put down the tyrannical Tribunes and the awful evil Guard. Poor bastard—didn't seem able to see the mountain for the boulders.

No one listened to him. Who would have, with his spouting such nonsense?

He wanted to tear down everything. Then what would happen? But he was too wrapped up in his madness to ask those questions, and he wouldn't have listened to the answers.

After Ayren finished, he bowed politely to Freyda, to the Tribunes, and sat down.

The fire had fled his eyes, and once more he was just a frail and tired man. For a single moment, I felt sorry for him.

The black curtain rose around the Tribunes from beneath the dias, but not for long. I didn't time it. When it dropped, everyone stood for the verdict. Fewer than twenty spectators remained.

The slow-glass panels were damped, except for those focused on the Tribunes. Martel picked up the black wand from the holder and pointed it at Ayren. "Ayren Bly, Green-30, the Tribunes and people of Query find you guilty as charged and sentence you to thirty years on Hell, and on your return to a full chronolobotomy, to enable you to serve Query as you are best able."

One of the spectators—a woman—maybe his daughter, contract-mate, or lover—collapsed. No one paid any attention to her as two

Guards I didn't know joined Hightel. Two grabbed Ayren and marched him out. The other one and Frey followed closely. They were taking him straight to Hell.

Still . . . no one noticed the fallen woman.

I walked over. She was clothed in a bright green jumpsuit which flattered her tan and golden hair. At that moment, she was crumpled in a heap against one of the benches.

I picked her up and laid her out straight on the bench, wondering if I should cart her over to the Infirmary. She was breathing normally, but was pale underneath the tan.

She recovered before I'd decided what to do, stared at me, and sat up, shaking slightly. Her eyes glanced around and then settled on me. "Are you going to send me to Hell too?"

"What on Query for?" I stammered.

"You're one of *them*. Isn't that what you do to everyone who doesn't agree with you?" She studied my trainee star, and an amused smile crossed her face.

"Only those who blow up buildings and try to kill innocent people."

"No Guard is truly innocent."

I was getting fed up with the conversation. I'd been worried about her, and she, whoever she was, was treating me like the criminal.

"So it's all right to blow up people you don't like if you can pin a label on them? That justifies it?" I demanded.

It didn't even register. She shook her head sadly, and asked, "Did you ever wonder what the past was really like? Did you ever ask yourself why we don't have heroes any more? Do you ever ask yourself why you do what you do? Not that I'd expect it of you. Or your type."

I mean, what could I have said? That I intended to be a hero? I didn't. So really, what was there I could have said?

She watched me for a moment. Then she turned and vanished.

Despite her words, I was impressed. Not many people can drop under the now inside the Tower. Not many at all.

Then I swallowed. Was she why Frey was worried? And who was she?

I didn't like going to find Frey. So I didn't. Instead, I tracked down Gilmesh in Personnel.

He looked up wearily from his stool and high desk when I came in, after proper announcement by a junior trainee I didn't know. "Yes, Loki?"

I told him about the woman, ending with my punch line: ". . . and she just dropped undertime right in the Hall of Justice."

Gilmesh looked at me. "And you think that's important?"

"Yes. Otherwise, you wouldn't have wanted an extra Guard. Were the Guards you usually use watching her?"

He actually grinned, but only for a moment. "You're not as dense as old Ragnorak, are you?"

I shrugged. "I wouldn't know."

He took a slow breath. "We don't know who she is."

I thought I understood. Locator tags don't work unless you know the tag number. You have to match the person and the name, and you can't sort the now by every Queryan—even with computers and data lattices.

"Should I have stopped her?"

Gilmesh shook his head. "Contrary to what that fool said, the Guard doesn't operate like that. We don't have any proof she's done anything." He sat up straighter. "So . . . go enjoy yourself, or whatever."

There wasn't much else I could do, except wonder, and that I could do on my own time. I wandered back to the West Barracks for something to eat.

XI

AFTER MY MYSTERIOUS assignment supporting Domestic Affairs, I thought my probationary work there would be interesting, certainly more interesting than tracking down strayed four-year-olds.

Things didn't turn out that way. My first assignment was inventorying, because I was a strong diver.

Marsten was a plain Guard, gold four-pointed star, who had completed the minimum fifteen-year term necessary for personal privileges. You could leave the Guard anytime after your service time exceeded your training time, but you didn't get privileges until after fifteen years. Anyway, Marsten was sticking around for a while, even though he didn't have to, maybe just until some more trainees graduated.

He plunked down a list on the table in front of me. "This is what each regional office is supposed to have in equipment. Your job is to make sure it's all there and operating. If it isn't, you come back to Stores or our main duplicator downstairs, and draw it or duplicate it, and charge it to that office on the main records, and then cart it out there."

He plunked down another list, a shorter one, but still several pages long. "Here are the regional offices. Just start at the beginning, and work your way through. You should average a couple of offices a day, maybe more when you get to the smaller ones."

I picked up the list of offices. There must have been close to a hundred. I hesitated, then asked, "Why do we have so many offices? Most people can get anywhere on Query."

Marsten just sighed.

I waited for an answer, and finally he did.

"Sure, hotshot, they can. Do you want two hundred or four hundred citizens milling around in one place all the time? Can't you see what a mess that would be?"

I felt stupid, but I just hadn't seen it. Just because you can do something doesn't mean it's a good idea.

"Sorry."

So I took the lists and studied them. The inventory lists separated items by big stuff and little stuff. The big stuff was obvious—things like fusion power system, small duplicator, data lattice system (fourteen lattices). Some of the small items were clear enough, things like stunners and batteries, but others seemed odd. Why would every Domestic Affairs office need twenty jugs of distilled water? Five would have been more than enough with a duplicator.

Then I picked the first office on the list, packed my inventory list into my jumpsuit, and slid out to Abiort, a two-room office halfway between Southpoint and the Callerin Peninsula. It was open only days, not nights, the way the seventy or so smaller offices were.

The duty Guard looked up, saw the green-edged star, and asked, "Inventory?"

I nodded, and she grinned. I wasn't sure I liked the grin, but I pulled out the list.

"Go to it," she said. "I can tell you that we're short of the mid-batteries and one stunner. Hystan dropped it into the river last ten-day."

I must have frowned.

"It happens. What's your name?"

"Loki."

"Look . . . we're a two-person office. If one of us takes off time to get supplies, that means we have to do all the inputting at headquarters, and that takes time, and then carry it back. What happens if there's a problem? The office isn't covered."

I looked toward the emergency stud on the front door.

"How do you think Frey would feel if the main office had to handle a local problem, or if the locals got the idea to bypass us?"

I got the idea. The whole inventory system was nothing more than the use of trainees to keep supplies updated, particularly in the smaller offices.

Abiort wasn't too bad. It took me a while, because I didn't know where things were, but, after going through it all, I added two jugs of water for the fusactor, the missing stunner with batteries. The big problem was carting in the sections for the battery recharging system and helping assemble that.

Part of the inventory system was also just make-work. With their duplicator, things like recording tapes for the holo cameras could be duplicated on the spot, but it seemed like the offices just let those slide until the trainees came along.

Then, after I checked off everything, I went back to Domestic Affairs in Quest and logged in the inventory approval and the replacement of the battery charging system. Batteries and power cells were always a real problem.

The duplicators have the nasty habit of exploding if you try to duplicate anything that stores energy. That means you can't duplicate most batteries, even uncharged, or equipment that has things like capacitors, without making a mess. Most Guard equipment doesn't have capacitors.

The Guard actually owns a battery factory on Sertis, and junior Guards get to ferry them back to Query, lots of them.

After the Abiort station came Addyma—halfway around the globe, about a thousand kilos north of the Sand Hills. Addyma was a larger regional office with perhaps five Guards permanently assigned and a round-the-day-and-night operation.

Addyma didn't need anything except a few large batteries, but the duty Guard—it was local midnight—wanted to talk.

"What was your last rotation?" she asked.

"Locator."

"That bothered me. I always wondered if I could find them fast enough, especially the children."

"Did you?" I asked that mostly out of courtesy, but partly out of curiosity.

She shrugged and looked out into the night, out beyond the glow lights that lit the path to the station. "I guess I was lucky. Some trainees weren't. Jystel—she came back to the Barracks so upset—some little boy wandered out of the house at night. His family had a place on the Faustools, you know the islands off of Point Hindrian?"

I nodded. I knew the Point, but not the islands. I hadn't studied every island on the planet. Who had?

"She didn't get there soon enough. He went over the cliff. She said the worst part was the father screaming at her like it was her fault that she didn't get to the boy fast enough. They didn't watch the child, and it's our fault."

"People expect a lot from the Guard."

"Too much, sometimes." She looked at me and the list. "You'd better get the batteries and get on with it. We're number two, and you've got another hundred and three to go."

"How do you know?"

"We all did inventory once." She grinned.

I went back and got the batteries, and she grinned again when I popped out with them. She had a nice smile, but I didn't ask her name, and I never saw her again.

I still had to go back and log in the batteries into the inventory before I took off for Aldfa—except it was another day station, and it was closed because it was halfway around the globe also. The same held true for Baisra. So much for doing things in order.

Basically, everything that happened while I was doing my probationary work in Domestic Affairs was like the inventory—dull and routine.

Even when somebody got called out of the regional offices, like Southpoint, in the middle of the night, all we did was wait at the regional duty desk and, if trouble showed, run to get a full Guard. I did some standby stints, but never even saw a citizen in trouble.

Then, the next day, I'd be back doing inventories or something equally stimulating or worse, like the trash detail.

Query's a clean planet. We like it that way, but we don't have any industry, even though we use a lot of equipment per person. So what happens to the old stuff? When you're young, it just disappears. Except it doesn't. Someone takes it somewhere.

The organic stuff goes down those little compact units in the sink which essentially use lasers to reduce it to its original, mostly harmless atoms. And because people put the wrong things down there, some get injured, and a lot of replacement units are drawn from the regional duplicator offices.

The busted units, along with everything from broken chairs to ripped linens, are supposed to be carried to the dumps on Vulcan. It's the nearest planet outside our system with no people and a breathable atmosphere. Probably two thirds of all Queryans can make the dive. That doesn't mean they all do. I've seen houses surrounded with piles of junk. Some people are slobs.

Other people can't carry stuff, especially heavy stuff, and they're supposed to put that in the bins outside the local Domestic Affairs offices. That makes the Guard, specifically the senior trainees like I was, the garbage disposers of last resort. Usually after you've done something stupid, like forgetting to carry supplies to someone, or oversleeping, you get outfitted with a nice heavy sack, a laser-cutter, and a list of Domestic Affairs stations.

So I'd slide out to Hyspol or Nurt or someplace I'd never heard of before I became a trainee for Domestic Affairs and land in front of a pile of junk, and slice and dice until I had a pile of smaller junk that fit in the sack. Then I'd slide out to Vulcan and dump it in this huge canyon, must have been a hundred kilos long. According to Baldur, the canyon's going to get filled with lava in another couple of million years anyway.

Then I'd go back and slice and dice, and cart another load. It really made you think about doing stupid things. Sometimes we got behind, and all the trainees and even some junior Guards got called in for a ten-day or so, and that's all we did. I hated it, but so did everyone else.

I mean, divers carting garbage around? That was the worst, but even that didn't last forever, and inventorying seemed a lot more desirable after the trash detail.

Then, one day, it was over—no more trash, no more inventory, no more probation. We weren't trainees.

Of course, for the actual induction into the Guard, there was a formal ceremony. Gilmesh, in his capacity as head of Personnel, made sure we showed up in formal blacks and marched the seven of us into the Hall of Justice and out before the Tribunes.

There actually were several hundred Guards in the Hall, the most I'd ever seen together at one time, and most of the Counselors. The Counselors all sat in the front row of the Guard section.

Gilmesh got up there before us and turned to the Tribunes. "I have the honor of presenting to the honored Tribunes and to the Temporal Guard assembled seven new Guards."

He read out our names and gave a brief statement about how we had completed all the requirements and were fully qualified to assume all duties of a Guard.

Then Martel addressed each of us one by one. The formula was exactly the same.

"Loki, do you understand the requirements of your duties, and that you voluntarily place yourself under the absolute strictures of your office and of the Guard for the duration of your service to Query?"

"I do." That was what we'd been told the proper response was.

After that Gilmesh pinned on—surprisingly awkwardly—the gold four-pointed star, and I stepped down, and Loragerd stepped up, and Martel went through the same formula with her.

After everyone got a star, Gilmesh stepped up again and made another short speech, a charge to us, really.

"You are now full members of the Temporal Guard, with all the privileges and responsibilities that accompany your position. Because responsibility can never be delegated, but only assumed, you and you alone are responsible for your actions. You have great powers, and equally great responsibilities, and you will be judged, not only by the Guard but by the Laws of Time, on the accomplishment of those responsibilities."

Then Martel made an even briefer statement.

"A single lapse in temporal responsibility almost allowed the Frost Giants to destroy Query. There are no responsibilities too small for your concern, nor none too great to be borne. Bear them both well."

Then we bowed to the Tribunes, turned and bowed to the Guard, and marched out.

That was it. I was a full Temporal Guard, and I really didn't feel that different.

XII

IN THE MIDDAY sun, a dwelling crouches in a overgrown meadow, its back to the trees. Beyond the meadow, a rocky ridge climbs toward a higher jumble of rock.

The intermittent splatters on the still-bright unfinished wood and the dusty permaglass testify that the dwelling is vacant. Tattered lynia flowers droop their violet fronds across the barely visible stones of the walk, those that the moss has not already crept over.

A breeze whispers its course across the open ground with the restrained promise that it will whistle when the clouds now hugging the horizon arrive later in the afternoon.

From thin air, a young man wearing a one-piece black jumpsuit appears in front of the structure.

He gawks at the building, at the dust-streaked panes, the overgrown stone walk that leads nowhere, as if he had not expected the desertion.

After a moment of hesitation, he walks briskly up the low steps to the porch and to the door.

"Greetings!" he bellows. A gust of wind heralding the clouds in the distance ruffles his bright red hair as he waits for a response.

The arched door opens at his touch.

He steps inside, and the hall echoes as his black boots strike the floor.

The house, for it could be termed that despite the years of desertion, is small, with hygiene facilities and a pair of bedrooms on the upper level and three rooms on the main level.

Dust blankets the simple furniture, the once-polished stone and wood floors that shine beneath the covering bestowed on them by time.

So well-built and preserved is the structure that the dust seems out of place.

The man in black, his face smooth and unlined enough to be considered that of a man scarcely more than a youth, tours the rooms in silence.

He returns to the dining area and looks at the polished table, which bears only a bronze bell. On the handle is a legend in a language he does not know.

After regarding the bell for a long time, a time long enough that the distant clouds are no longer so distant, he pockets the bell and returns to the front hall, face blank, shaking his head.

"Totally gone," he comments to no one, because there is no one to hear him. "Just vanished. Left everything . . . and didn't even tell me. Not even a note."

He frowns and takes out the bell. He replaces it in a pocket and shakes his head again. Then, after stepping onto the narrow stone front porch and carefully closing the heavy door behind him, he vanishes into thin air.

The clouds and rain have not arrived, but they will.

XIII

I WAS STILL stunned at the disappearance of my parents. Not that long after I became a full Guard—or when they knew I'd make it—they'd just vanished. What was the significance of the strange bronze bell on the table? Did it have any?

I'd worried about it, and finally I'd gone to Locator and asked if they could trace my parents. It took a while to dig up their codes, because I'd only known their names, but the Locator computers eventually did come up with full names and codes—and promptly informed me that my parents had ceased to exist a full season before.

They hadn't died—they just disappeared from the system.

But why? I just didn't understand. I'd talked to Ferrin, and he hadn't helped, and Loragerd had held me and talked, and that had helped, but I still didn't understand.

Then, on top of that, Gilmesh had summoned me into his office.

"You're going to spend a tour in the Domestic Affairs office in South-point," he informed me.

After diving across suns, and retrieving heavy metal generators from High Sinopol a million years past . . . I was going to local police duty? I couldn't believe it, and it must have showed.

"Everyone does Domestic Affairs at some time, sometimes before they get roving time-assignments," Gilmesh told me. "Even hotshot divers. Patrice is, just like you. You do well here, and then we'll see."

That just wasn't true, and we both knew it. Almost everyone else who had trained with me was in the junior Guard assignment pool—except for poor Patrice. Whenever some office needed something done or an extra body, they asked Gilmesh, and he assigned them. When they weren't diving, they did clerical and other routine chores—but they were in the Tower.

But we were lower than that, and I didn't know why.

"You're going to Southpoint. That's a major station."

That also meant more scutwork, I could tell. Major stations were open all the time, and I didn't have any doubts who would be handling the late shifts. At least, as a full Guard, I now had two rooms in the Citadel to go back to after duty.

Patrice went to another major station, except she was on the other big continent—Eastron—in a place called Ronwic.

The head Guard at Southpoint was Bossul. He'd just been made a Senior Guard after a good century of local patrol duty, and I doubted if he could have backtimed more than a few dozen centuries. He was dark, muscular, and he didn't like me. He didn't care that I knew it either.

"You're here for one reason, hotshot, and one reason only. You've got a reputation as a good diver and a mean bastard. We're going to use that for a while. Your job is real simple. You get to take care of the troublemakers and cart them off to detention."

I guess my parents had sheltered me. Troublemakers? The only troublemakers I'd ever run across were people like Ayren, or the woman in the green jumpsuit who didn't exist. And I wasn't even sure whether they were the best or worst in troublemakers.

"What kind of troublemakers?"

"All kinds." He had a nasty smile. "You'll find out."

And I did.

It couldn't have been much past sunset when a local citizen dropped out of nowhere and gaped at me. "Where's Bossul?"

"He's off duty, citizen. May I help you?"

He wasn't exactly convinced by my lack of age and mass, and the black uniform didn't seem to count for much, but he stammered out his problem. His name was Edwye, and he and his family lived on a lagoon north of Southpoint. Edwye and his contract-mate had a daughter.

From there even I could read the script, between the harried look on his face and his words. The daughter was attractive, or someone thought so, and vandalism and a nasty sort of Peeping Tomism were taking place. Someone had just left a nude picture of her, taken while she was bathing, with more than merely suggestive remarks, and promising to be there for a midnight rendezvous.

I didn't like it, but there wasn't much else to do but take a look. I flashed up to headquarters and asked for a standby. They sent a trainee down, and I followed Edwye out to the lagoon. The sands of the lagoon were silver in the starlight, and even the whitecaps on the ocean beyond glimmered in the early evening.

The house was long and narrow and old, but neat and clean—at least the main room where I met Mirte and Gyrlla was. The daughter was Mirte, and I could see the attraction. She was petite, with soft blue eyes, and honey skin, and white-blond hair, and a figure that had my heart racing. The picture the mother handed me didn't help. Mirte definitely had it all. But I swallowed and got on with it.

"When did this arrive?"

"Just a few units before I slid to get you."

I thought. There was a chance, just a chance, that an undertime trail might remain. The briefs said it was possible.

"I'll be back in an instant," I said, and dropped undertime, concentrating hard. The books were right. There was a trail . . . sort of . . . and it didn't go all that far—just over the hill and into a larger house on some sort of stilts that overlooked the river that wound into Southpoint.

I didn't break out, but looked into the now as well as I could. A bearded man was looking down at something that I was willing to bet was a duplicate of the picture dropped on poor Mirte. I checked the rest of the place from the undertime, but didn't see or feel anyone else around.

I slid back to Edwye's house. Everyone looked up.

"You weren't gone very long."

"I didn't need to be." I swallowed. Now what was I going to do? Did I wait? Or did I grab the guy? I decided to ask someone—that's an advantage of being able to dive. "I need to check out one more thing. It will take a couple of units. You should be all right."

They looked doubtful.

"Trust me," I said patiently, and I was gone.

Marsten's replacement was Zegl, an equally stolid woman, and she was the duty supervisor I dropped in on. She glared at me. "Now what?"

I explained in quick sentences and asked, "Do I grab him and his picture, or what?"

"Of course. We'll get the evidence after that. What if he dives out-system?"

I didn't mention that that wasn't a problem. I just thanked her and dropped out of the now next to the unnamed man who was still drooling over the picture of Mirte.

Drooling he might have been, but that didn't stop him from trying to stick me with a long thin knife. I used Sammis's training to break his wrist, stunned him with the standard-issue stunner, and checked the place again, this time in the now, but he still seemed to live alone. After that, I carted him off to detention in the Tower.

Zegl took charge of the miscreant there, and I gave the coordinates to the techs who would gather the evidence. One came with me to take holo statements from Edwye and his family. Zegl insisted that the holo tech for the family be a woman.

"It's all taken care of," I said. "This is Harleen. She'll need to take holo statements for the trial, and she'll take the picture for evidence."

"Who . . . what . . . who was it?" stammered Edwye.

"I don't know the fellow's name, but he has a beard and lives in a house on stilts on the other side of the hill toward the river. He also tried to put a rather long knife in me."

"But . . . how did you know?"

I shrugged. How could I explain, exactly? I temporized. "I found a duplicate of the picture . . . actually not a duplicate, but one like it."

"Smazal will kill us," mumbled the girl.

"I doubt that," I said. "He's in detention in the Tower with a broken wrist."

They looked blank.

Harleen looked at me. "You'd better get back to the office. After I'm done here, I'll stop there and get your statement."

So I slid back to the office and sent the trainee back to Quest. Nothing had happened while I was gone, and nothing happened the rest of my duty that night.

The next night, when I came on, Bossul was waiting.

"Pleased, hotshot?"

"About what?" I was confused.

"Every punkout in Southpoint is going to try something now, just to prove that they're better than Domestic Affairs."

"Why?"

"Because, hotshot, they hate the damned Guard, and don't you forget it."

"So what was I supposed to do?"

"Just what you did, but it's just the beginning. Good luck."

He still didn't like me, but he was right, and the warning helped. Nothing happened that night, but the next night, right after I sat down at the desk, I understood why there is a wall between the door and duty office.

Two sharp explosions occurred, and one of the front glow-bulbs shattered. Thanks to Bossul's warning, I went under the now and literally caught the perpetrator as he dropped into the now in his own basement, more like an arsenal.

He didn't even have a chance to look surprised when I stunned him.

Zegl actually looked pleased when she saw the arsenal. "Dumb luck and brute skill, but I like the results."

Frey, of course, never showed up or said a word, even if he were the head of Domestic Affairs. And I wasn't sure I liked the term "brute skill," but Bossul didn't bother me for a while.

The next time was worse. It was maybe a ten-day later. This time a man charged into the office with a Guard stunner—they were forbidden to civilians, even ex-Guards. I was so nervous that, when the door opened, I dropped under the now. So I wasn't there when the bolt went through where I should have been.

I got him from behind.

I also was beginning to get mad, but I couldn't figure out what to do. Did I have to keep being a sitting duck? So scared that I had to hide in the undertime in my own office?

I stayed scared, and I lost weight, and ate more, and worked out like hell with every exercise Sammis ever invented. And with each night and every sound, I ducked under the now.

In the end, I put twenty punkouts, as Bossul called them, into detention. They all got sentences to Hell and chronolobotomies. Southpoint got a lot more peaceful, but not even the rest of the Guards in the office talked to me much. But when they had an all-out trash cleanup, no one suggested I be assigned, even if I was junior.

I still had trouble figuring why the local toughs were so concerned about making a statement against Domestic Affairs. With duplicators, food synthesizers, and the like, no one had to go without or go hungry. So it wasn't as though they had a real reason for trying theft or vandalism or sexual assault. They were bound to lose, and they had to know it. Didn't they?

I never did answer that question, but finally, Frey sent a trainee for me. The head of Domestic Affairs was shaking his head when I came in.

"You sent for me?" I asked.

"You're coming back to the Tower. Pick up your gear from Southpoint and report to Gilmesh in the morning."

I couldn't figure that one, but I wasn't about to complain, not at all.

Bossul was waiting at Southpoint. I smiled politely at him, and I was nice. I just said, "I've learned a lot here, and I wish you well."

He responded in kind. "Good luck, hotshot. You'll need more than skill in the big-time 'now.'" He shook his head and walked back into his little office.

Tyrkas gave me a quick smile, the only one I ever got from her.

That was it. I slid under the now and back to Quest. After I had the first solid sleep in seasons, I freshened up in my room in the Citadel, pulled on a clean uniform, and walked back to Gilmesh's office.

He saw me for about twenty words' worth.

"Clean out the cabinets in the storage room. When you finish, tell Dorma and do whatever she wants until someone needs a diving errand."

That put me back in the real Guard, cleaning cabinets, fetching batteries from Sertis, and occasionally carrying recording equipment for some research operation. Those sounded wonderful, but they were dull, dull, dull, and tedious. All you did was lug holo equipment to some place and point, unpack it, let it record, pack it up, and bring it home. Usually, it was in deep space somewhere, which meant space armor, which was heavy and smelly. Then, after you brought the stuff back, someone analyzed it to make sure something wasn't going wrong somewhere in time or space.

But that was better than cleaning cabinets, detaining punkouts in Southpoint, or doing trash detail. I still remembered that with a shudder.

XIV

AFTER WHAT SEEMED years of running around fetching batteries and perfumes and exotic foods, I finally got an independent search mission— a special search of Heaven IV.

Although I was more than happy to do something more challenging, I wondered why, since I was still a very junior Guard, a fact that Gilmesh was always more than happy to reinforce. I thought Freyda might know and had gone to find her to see if she could answer the question. Sometimes she could help, and sometimes she couldn't. When I'd asked her about my parents' disappearance, she pointed out that it probably had to have been their choice. With Locator tags placed at birth or shortly thereafter in everyone's shoulder blades, and my parents' diving abilities, foul play, while it could not be ruled out, was unlikely. But she couldn't or wouldn't explain much further, except to say that sometimes people did wish to leave the protections of Query and managed to do so.

Still, she would talk to me, possibly more about a strange duty assignment than missing parents, but it had to be on duty hours because she made a policy, at least with me, of never talking about the Guard in a private setting.

She was outside of Personnel when I caught up with her.

"Why the Heaven IV search mission for me?"

"It's not for your charm, dear Loki. You're just about the only young Guard who can handle a split entry. It's a rare ability, as I keep telling you. You'll need it on Heaven IV. Anyway, it's a simple mission. Have fun."

She gave me a wry smile as she left me standing there. Freyda could always leave me speechless in those early years.

I headed for Assignments. The Assignments Hall is just inside the main part of the Tower, and the back side of the Hall follows the curve of the dome. Heimdall, the head of Assignments, had carefully placed his console in the middle of the curve on a low platform, with two lines of smaller consoles radiating out from his. Ostensibly, the arrangement allowed Guards consoles to study the briefing materials while being close enough to Heimdall to draw on his experience.

Interestingly enough, the access keys to the briefing files could only be actuated in the Assignments Hall, or by the private codes of the Counselors or the Tribunes.

Heimdall pointed at one of the consoles at the far end of the right row. "Heaven IV."

I pulled the stool up to the console screen and attempted to absorb the information on Heaven IV. The briefing was simple enough. A random holo surveillance of a "religious" meeting on Heaven IV had turned up what seemed to be mentions of miraculous appearances and disappearances from the skies.

To the suspicious Tribunes, any strange disappearance indicated the possibility of time-diving or planet-sliding—or other high technology—needing further investigation. Heaven IV was normally monitored by balloon-borne miniature holos, and the tapes weren't all that good. Because of the time lags in recovering the tapes and processing them, the reputed events had taken place some three hundred years earlier. My job was to confirm or deny the reports.

Heaven IV is at the edge of the area regularly monitored by the Guard, closer in to galactic center, and an odd planet to boot. The angels had a loosely held social structure, basically nontech, and for good reason, since they were peak dwellers and had limited access to the minerals of the planet.

They shared Heaven IV with the goblins, who were surface dwellers in the hot—and it was hot—lower levels. Heaven IV is a metal-poor, rugged planet with a thick graduated atmosphere.

The rest of the briefing was technical.

After struggling through it, I headed down to Special Stores, where the techs fitted me with a full-seal warm suit and supplied me with a miniature time discontinuity detector. Supposedly, the gismo was designed to point toward sudden changes in time fields, which would enable me to track down the case of the mysterious appearances and disappearances—if they even existed.

How did a population of less than ten million people support such high-tech gadgets? For the most part we didn't. We bought or took them, and sometimes improved on them, from various times and places.

Even stealing takes effort, information, and hard work. For example, scattered throughout the Guard were linguists who knew the major languages in use in each high-tech humanoid world in our sector.

Some of them lived there and learned the languages, but if the people were humanoid enough, we just kidnapped one and hooked him, her, or it into the input side of a language tank. That wasn't usually enough for the tank to give full fluency, and after that, one of the poor linguists ended up on a long-time assignment surviving and becoming fluent in the tongue.

The business of getting specific technology could be cutthroat at times, like when the Guard needed miniature weapons. The old Guard manipulated Ydris from mid-tech to high-tech with backtime tampering. Unfortunately, the higher technology also resulted in turning most of Ydris into fused glass.

Most people would rather forget that, and it was a long, long time ago.

Anyway, after I got all the gadgetry in hand, I pulled on the form-fitting warm suit, and took the rest of my standard diving equipment out of my storage chest with care. In the mid-afternoon, the equipment room we junior Guards shared was empty. So was the Travel Hall. I liked it that way.

The timedive back to the Heaven IV of three hundred years earlier was uneventful, smooth as silver, and breakout was on the dot. I expected that of myself, tried to avoid sloppiness. I always have.

The sky of Heaven is blue, bluer than the bluest sky of Terra, bluer than the bluest sea of Atlantea, and the pink clouds tower like foamed castles into the never-ending sky.

Angels on widespread wings soar from cloud to cloud, half resting on the semisolid cloud edges on their flights to and from the scattered mountain citadels that rear tall into the domain of the angels.

I looked down, and I could see a hell under the dark clouds below, the red shadows of the surface, and the squat black cities of the goblins.

I had the split-entry technique down pat, and I hung there with my toes tucked into the undertime, poised in midair.

After some units just soaking up the feel of the unlimited skies, I studied the time discontinuity detector dial which I was wearing above my wrist gauntlets. The needle was supposed to point to any discontinuity.

Every once in a while it would quiver, and I'd duck understream to narrow the distance. Whoever or whatever was causing the disturbances was doing it in short bursts, like a planet-slide, or quick in-and-outs. After having wasted more than a hundred units, I still hadn't succeeded in narrowing the area.

So I marked the real-time coordinates and set them into my gauntlets. Then I dived back foretime to Query.

The Travel Hall was deserted. I packed up my gear and started out of the Tower to get a hot meal and a good night's sleep. Hanging in chill midair, warm suit or not, was tiring, even for me.

Freyda intercepted me as I was heading for the West Portal. I answered the unasked question. "No. Took me all this time just to get within a revolution or two and half a planet. The detector's pretty rough."

"A few others have said that." She sounded relieved, maybe that I could get it to work at all. Then she inclined her head questioningly.

I knew what she meant. We walked out of the Tower of Immortals together, preserving the decorum of not sliding out of the Tower, and onto the west ramp that led through the fireflowers into the late twilight.

As we reached the edge of the glowing scarlet, Freyda stretched out her hand, and I took it, and we slid to her city quarters, high in the Citadel. She insisted on cooking, and for being a Counselor, Freyda is a good cook. She used simple food, simple recipes, the kind where skill is more important than the ingredients.

A contract wasn't in the offing, not between a very junior Guard and a Counselor. There wasn't just the age difference, but the status and experience differences.

Sometimes we talked together. Sometimes we slept together, but most times we went our own ways. We never talked about the Guard, and we never talked policy or politics, and it was probably a good thing for me we didn't.

For all her apparent gentleness off the job, Freyda believed with heart, soul, and body in the Tribunes and their powers, the Guard, and the system as it stood.

"Heaven IV?" she asked as we lay across from each other on the two low couches. The view of the Tower from her rooms in the Citadel was picture perfect. The spire of the Tower glittered like an arrow of light poised in front of the hills.

The Citadel was one of the few multiple dwellings in Quest and dated almost as far back as the Tower itself. Many Guards, like me, kept rooms there, and many, unlike me, had retreats elsewhere on Query. I had two rooms on a much lower level with almost no view, except of the side of the West Barracks. My rooms were too cramped for me, and I knew I'd eventually have to get a larger and more private place. But I had all the time in the world and was spending my free days exploring the tangles of time and the remote reaches of Query.

I spent a lot of time on mountaintops, in the quiet high forests under the Bardwalls. I've needed places alone as far back as I could remember, and before that. My mother told me I was sliding into strange corners around our isolated mountain home even before I could complete a full sentence.

I was also retrieved five times by the Locator section before I could talk, or so I was told. Some of that might have been parental exaggeration, but I doubt it. They didn't exaggerate much. Maybe I was a late talker.

"Loki?" Freyda asked. I realized I'd forgotten where I was, with my thoughts out on the empty needle peaks of Eastron.

I picked up a fistful of nuts before answering her question.

"Blue. Never seen such blue," I mumbled while chomping.

"I remember it," she said softly. "Years ago, Ragnorak took me. You're so like him, Loki. I couldn't hold a split jump, and he held me there in the air so I could see it—the cloud towers, the angels . . . If we were only angels, instead of temporal administrators of the galaxy."

"Just part of it," I reminded her. I already knew the galaxy was big.

She shook her head, and her eyes seemed less deep. "How do you like being a god, Loki?"

"No god, just a simple Guard."

She laughed, with overtones to her voice like a harsh silver bell and a sweet golden one at the same time. "No Guard, just a simple god, is more like you."

"Then you're a complicated goddess."

Times, she was all flame, like me, and times she was colder than the ice computer on Frost. Never knew which would come, fire or ice, but that night was fire, perhaps foreshadowing the future.

Freyda was gone when I woke the next morning, and that was strange
. . . for her to leave her rooms to me. On those few times I had stayed
the night, she'd at least wakened me before she left.

As I thought about it, I realized she'd never been to my quarters, nor
had I ever been to her retreat, not even when she'd had me for dinner
back when I had been in basic training. I knew she had a place in the
hills overlooking Quest. I'd heard Heimdall saying it had a fabulous
view, but I'd never been there at all.

You can know so little about your lovers, I guess, even your very
first.

I had to get back to the Travel Hall, back to Heaven IV, before
Heimdall rattled me for goofing off. After gulping down a few swigs of
firejuice, some cheese, and a piece of fruit, I cleaned up and pulled on a
new black jumpsuit Freyda had brought back from Textra for me. I
dropped the dirty one in my rooms and jumped as close to the Tower
as I dared.

Heimdall was checking the logs in the Travel Hall and smiled that
brilliant and meaningless grin of his when I walked in. "Back to Heaven,
or from it?"

I shrugged. We all had to put up with his crass mannerisms. He was
good at trend projections and organizing assignments. He was a lousy
diver. The older Guards called him "all-seeing," not quite mockingly.

I thought he talked too much and too sharply, but that could have
been because I disliked him.

"Heaven IV" was all I said.

He didn't respond, and I went into the equipment room and suited
up.

If anything, the blue sky was bluer, and the cloud towers pinker. All
in the mind, because I'd dived to a point not more than a few dozen
units after I'd left the day before.

I was in the right real-time. The needle on the detector kept jumping
and twitching.

After fifty units sliding around the blue skies, feeling colder and
colder, warm suit or not, watching angels soaring, occasionally fighting
with those black ice lances, ducking under the darker shadows of the
pink clouds, I decided I was making little or no progress.

I backtimed and broke out far enough earlier to see if I could discover
when the time discontinuities started. So wrapped up in my own
thoughts was I that I slipped out under a cloud shadow right next to a
pair of youngsters of opposite sexes, engaged as such youngsters are often
wont to be.

Not all humanoids are dual-sexed, but most are. It must go with hemispherical symmetry.

After the shock passed—me seeing them, and them seeing this wingless being looking much like them standing in midair—I shrugged it off and decided to confuse the issue. I threw a thunderbolt from my gauntlets at a passing birdlike creature. Perhaps it was the local equivalent of an eagle, but I vaporized it with one bolt.

Then I smiled at the pair and slid elsewhere—more carefully. Hopefully, no one would believe them if they talked. I knew the lingo, but they hadn't let out so much as a cheep.

The damned wrist time detector just wasn't accurate enough. If I couldn't find the perpetrator of the time discontinuities, I was positive no Guard could.

I dived back to Query and pooped out in the Travel Hall. After storing my gear, I located Heimdall. Not difficult, because he was reigning over the Assignments Hall from his central console.

I explained.

He called in Freyda, Frey, Gilmesh, and Kranos.

I explained again.

"Sterilize the whole atmosphere," recommended Heimdall.

Freyda frowned at that.

Frey, Freyda's son, was walking around the consoles twirling the light saber. He'd picked that up from some obscure group of galactic-wide do-gooders from near the end of his backtime limits. Watching his nervous gestures, I wondered who his father might have been. For that matter, I wondered how Freyda had entered five contracts. I couldn't imagine her in *one*.

Frey stopped pacing.

"What about a virus?" he asked.

"What?"

"Just find an angel and stun it. Take a tissue sample and bring it back. The gene laboratories on Weldin ought to be able to synthesize a virus that's fatal."

"Ingenious," muttered Heimdall. "Are you sure it won't be fatal to something else, like us?"

"If the biological engineers on Weldin can't do it right, no one can," Frey announced dogmatically.

I thought there were holes big enough in Frey's plan to march the whole Guard through, but no one was asking my opinion. I decided not to volunteer it.

"Why don't we just see what happens first?" asked Freyda. "Maybe it's just a fluke."

Kranos and Gilmesh nodded.

"See what you can find out, Loki."

I hadn't had much to eat before I'd left that morning; so before I headed back to Travel Hall, I slid out to Hera's Inn for a bite or three.

Ferrin was sitting at a table with Verdis, and they were so intent that neither looked up. A redhead a few years older than me, Verdis worked in Personnel when she wasn't diving.

Ferrin had been the first of our trainee class to get a real permanent assignment—Patrice's and my stints in Domestic Affairs local office didn't count. While I was playing local policeman in the depths of night in Southpoint or later running odd errands across Query and time for the Guard, and that meant Heimdall or Frey most of the time, Ferrin had been assigned to Locator. I hoped my turn would come before long—but not for something dull like Weather or Personnel.

As far as Ferrin and Verdis went, however, it wasn't romantic attachment that kept them from noticing me. Verdis was gesticulating, even pounded the table once. Ferrin wasn't grinning.

Since they obviously didn't want company, I picked out a scampig fillet from the synthesizer and wolfed it down with a beaker of firejuice. Both of them were as intent as ever when I left.

Patrice was the only one in the Guard equipment room when I got back to the Travel Hall. She was finishing her suit-up.

"Destination?" I asked casually.

"Sertis. Where else? Do they ever send junior Guards anywhere but to ferry batteries and delicacies?"

"Isn't it better than Ronwic?"

She shook her head. "There, I actually helped people who needed it and couldn't do it themselves."

"It'll get better," I said inanely.

"It better." She left without another word.

What she said about Ronwic nagged me. Why hadn't I felt that way? I'd just been a hired thug to put the local punkouts in line. I'd learned a bunch about tracing people through the undertime, but what was there to show for it? Twenty punkouts on Hell?

As I pulled on my warm suit and other gear, I wondered. Still, after less than two years in full Guard status, I was on independent search. Patrice was unhappy about being a porter, but I did that too, and I'd probably go back to it after Heaven IV.

No reason to be that bitter, I figured. We had time.

On Heaven IV, the sky was still blue, a thousand years foretime, the clouds pink, and the angels still flew.

Fewer angels than centuries before, it seemed, but plenty.

I checked the time discontinuity detector. Not once did it quiver. I quartered the planet, spent another fifty units, but didn't get one twitch on the detector.

I backtimed, splitting the difference. That brought me out about two hundred years foretime of real-time Query.

Same blue sky and pink clouds . . . fewer angels . . . no quivers on the detector. Quartered the planet again—but no time discontinuities registered on the detector. None.

There was a different feeling about this time, a feeling of aftermath, but I couldn't pin it down. Something had happened, I was convinced. I dived farther backtime, the realtime equivalent of Query "now."

On breakout, I found plenty of angels, plenty of pink clouds. Some of the pink cloud towers struck me as angular, regular, as if they'd been shaped.

I slid into one, found it hollow and filled with angels bearing pink ice lances. I dropped undertime before my presence registered, I thought.

I tried another survey of Heaven IV.

Something was brewing. The discontent, if I could call it that, permeated the endless skies.

Half the angels had the pink ice lances, and half were carrying black ones. The black lancers and the pink lancers avoided each other. But still nothing registered on the time detector.

I ducked undertime and emerged about a year later, more from curiosity than anything.

Everything was over but the moans. Damned few angels anywhere.

I backtimed about half a year and broke out in the middle of a pitched battle of the pink lances against the black lances.

I didn't believe it. All the information on Heaven IV stated that the angels were basic pacifists, and that only the goblins below had the warlike traits.

But believe or not, I was hanging in the middle of a war raging across the skies of Heaven.

I studied the time detector and found nothing.

I had a good idea I was never going to find anything, but I coppered my bets by trying a good double-dozen times/locales for spot checks. Nothing.

That's what I told Heimdall and Freyda.

"So now what should I do?" I asked.

"Drop it," ordered Heimdall.

"If it doesn't show up again," added Freyda, "there's no reason to worry. We'll just up the routine surveillance."

I had a funny feeling that the whole mess was self-fulfilling, but wasn't sure I could explain why. I didn't try either.

And part of the reason I didn't was that Freyda's voice seemed so distant. I could have been imagining it.

"Loki, report to Athene." Heimdall dismissed me.

As a very junior Guard, with no permanent assignment, I was shuffled from pillar to post. Sometimes it was Maintenance, sometimes Assignments, where Heimdall had me help prepare briefing tapes, but most often it was Special Stores.

Athene used a lot of the unassigned Guards. Special Stores was in charge of procurement, responsible for getting the items we couldn't make by sending Guards off to buy, beg, borrow, or steal what was necessary.

Not that it was a bad section to work for, although the planets and times we saw were all stable and settled, and the junior Guards like me all dealt in simple ferrying operations or cash transactions, but after a while I wondered if there couldn't have been a better way to do it.

The more senior Guards came up with the cash and did the "steal" operations. Most non-time-diving people store valuables in locked enclosures. It's very simple for a trained Guard to dive directly inside and remove a portion of what passes for currency.

Usually we don't take much. What with our simplified culture, low population, and the use of the duplicating technology, we don't need many items.

After my fifth or sixth trip to Sertis to buy power cells, however, I had some questions. Not about the power cells and batteries. Some items don't duplicate, like anything that stores energy. The Guard who tried to duplicate a power cell was likely to end up with a fried duplicator and some holes in him. Perfumes don't duplicate either, for some reason, and a few foods can't be synthesized, but normally we just do without those.

But the power cell and battery operation was such a charade. I mean, I'd put on one of those burnoose things they wear on Sertis, dive there to a factory the Guard owned, walk in and lay down the currency for what was on the order, and pick up the batteries. Then I'd walk out and far enough away to disappear.

Perhaps because it was so late in the afternoon, perhaps because I was still unhappy with the outcome of the Heaven IV mission, I wondered a bit too loudly for Counselor Athene.

Athene was a bit of a tradition. According to my father, she had been the Counselor and in charge of Special Stores back when his father had been a trainee.

"Can't we ever make anything? Why didn't we just build a factory on Query?" I'd asked Halcyon.

We'd just finished checking the posting sheets to discover we'd been assigned a whole lot of trips to Sertis for power cells.

"What do you mean?" asked Athene.

I must have jumped. I hadn't realized anyone else was around.

"Well . . . uh . . . seems like we have to gather a lot from everywhere, and that we make nothing . . ."

"There is that," Athene said.

Halcyon stepped back. The twinkle in her eye told me that I was on my own. Not nastily—Halcyon's not like that—but she had sort of a "now you've stepped into it" look with mischief in it. That was the only way I could describe it, and maybe it wasn't quite like that. I really didn't understand women. That was getting clear.

I should have followed Halcyon's example and kept my mouth shut, but it was too late.

"Who do you think ought to make all the materials we import, and how?" Athene asked in her gentle voice.

Athene was one of those deceptive-looking Guards. Taller than I was, slender as a willow, with softly curled hair like spun gold, a small nose, put together with a soft voice, a stubbornness harder than the Bardwalls' granite, and slate-gray eyes that could burn hotter than a nova—that was Athene. I didn't think she ever forgot.

I didn't have a ready answer. I just didn't like the charades involved in getting power cells. I mean, why steal money to pay for a product produced by your own factory? And I didn't know who ought to man- ufacture power cells, batteries, perfumes, and the other things I'd already had to ferry across time and space. I just thought there had to be a better way.

"Do you have any suggestions, Loki?"

"Maintenance . . ." I suggested lamely, forgetting my resolve to keep my mouth shut.

"Not a bad idea. I wonder what Baldur would think about it."

I didn't care for the tone of speculation in her voice, but this time I didn't say a word.

"After you make your pickup this afternoon, I'd like to talk to you again. And remember to drape the burnoose properly. Don't wear it like you threw a blanket over you."

"Yes, Counselor," I said politely. Then I noted the rest of the details from the posting sheet, signed for the Sertian currency, and trudged down the ramp to the Travel Hall.

From nowhere, Halcyon joined me. "You had to open your head, didn't you?"

"Wasn't too sharp," I admitted. "Wonder what she's got in store for me when I get back."

We didn't say much as we got ready to dive. What else was there to say?

Sertis is high mid-tech or low high-tech—at least it has been for most of its recent history, and we basically just slipped from the now on Query to the now on Sertis.

In training once, I asked why we made so many trips there, but Gilmesh answered my question with a question: How much can you carry on a dive or slide? And that's the problem. So far the Guard hadn't run across any mechanical time-diving equipment. Just people, and that meant that anything that got carried across time was carried by some poor Guard, usually some poor junior Guard or trainee.

Needless to say, that limitation had a profound influence on the culture I grew up in.

The dive was as uneventful as usual. Just boring, in fact.

Halcyon and I made the pickup, burnooses adjusted properly, and turned the two cases of power cells over to the Special Stores supply desk, where a Senior Guard named Quetzal logged them in and shooed us away.

Halcyon wanted dinner. I wanted to face the music with Athene before logging out with Personnel for the day. My stomach was knotted up. I didn't like upsetting the Counselors, but I didn't know why. And Athene was a Counselor, maybe the oldest.

I presented myself at the archway into her corner of the Special Stores Hall.

"Loki, our talk will have to wait. Martel has announced his decision to step down."

I didn't understand, and my face must have mirrored my lack of comprehension. I just wanted to get it over with.

Athene walked over, and with the high boots and formal Counselor's blacks, she looked down at me by half a head or more. She half lifted her hand . . . let it drop. I thought she was going to ruffle my hair, and almost as if I weren't even there, she shook her head. Then she straightened and explained.

"If Martel steps down, we need to select a new Tribune."

Everything clicked. The new Tribune had to be a Counselor. So the Senior Guards balloted for a Senior Guard to be a Counselor. Then the ten existing Counselors and the new one decided among themselves who would be the new Tribune, and that could be anyone except the newest

Counselor. Once the new Tribune was selected, the three Tribunes selected who would be High Tribune. There was always a new High Tribune when a Tribune stepped down.

That was an oversimplification, but a roughly accurate summary, without going into the various ballots or the single right of refusal by the two remaining Tribunes.

Athene was getting prepared for her part in the selection. So she didn't have the time to put a junior Guard through her logical wringer, for which I should have been grateful. I wasn't. I wanted to get it over with.

More to delay her than for any other reason, I asked, "Have the Senior Guards selected the new Counselor?"

"No. I suspect Heimdall will be the one they pick."

She didn't elaborate. I couldn't see Heimdall as a Counselor, but since I wasn't a Senior Guard, it wasn't any of my business.

The Counselor selection process was over in a couple of days. How could it not be? Out of the two hundred Senior Guards, all but a handful were on Query or could be reached quickly. The others were recalled if they could be, and with almost everyone able to meet in the Hall of Justice, they picked Heimdall, just as Athene had predicted, within a few hundred units.

In the meantime, the Guard functioned. While it didn't happen too often, picking a Tribune wasn't such a big deal to the average Guard. At least, it wasn't to me. The office, rather than the holder, generated the respect.

With all my rationalization, I wasn't particularly happy to see Heimdall picked as the new Counselor.

I did not know all of the Counselors, and some I'd met in the course of my duties, without knowing they were Counselors until later. I was familiar with Freyda, Athene, Baldur, who'd taught us Maintenance as trainees, and now, of course, Heimdall.

Baldur had never said a word to indicate his position, and I couldn't recall him wearing the gold-edged black star of a Counselor. Maybe I did, and I hadn't noticed it.

The second day of the selection, while eleven Counselors and the two Tribunes were holed up picking a successor to Martel, I had lunch with Loragerd at Hera's Inn. It's always been a favorite with the younger Guards.

"What do you hear about the selection? How do they narrow it down from the ten?"

"Loki, sometimes you're so naive." She smiled and reached across the table to ruffle my hair. I liked that when she did it.

"What do you mean?"

"The choice is never that open. They've already narrowed it to a couple. I'd say Baldur or Justina."

"Justina?" The name was familiar, but I couldn't place her.

"You know, the stern, let-us-do-what-is-right-for-the-people type who runs Weather? She gave us the indoctrination, but left all the training up to Pertwees."

I had a hazy mental picture of a dark-haired woman, still, cold, and full of herself, a female version of Heimdall, in a way.

"Didn't know she was a Counselor."

"Can you imagine any Guard running such a tedious operation without some reward?"

"Some of the satellites are pretty run-down," I mentioned, recalling the one Sammis had stuck into my attitude adjustment test. "Where did they ever get them anyway?"

"Sometimes I think you do your best to forget history, especially if it doesn't square with legend. The stations predate the Guard. Some say that they're all the same station, duplicated piece by piece by the early Guard."

"Now, that's a legend."

She shook her head. "Can you imagine us building one today?"

I thought about it. I couldn't. I was still interested in the selection; so I changed the subject back.

"Which one do you think they'll pick?"

Loragerd took a sip of the dark ale she liked so much before answering. She was still wearing her hair as short as the first day we met as new trainees. "Baldur. He's fair and doesn't pick fights. A lot of the Counselors owe Justina something, but just considering her will pay that debt. I don't think they'd really pick a justice-over-mercy type for Tribune."

The logic made sense to me.

We were both wrong. When we reported back to Assignments for another round of cleaning off consoles and racking old tapes, after lingering longer over lunch than we should have, Heimdall was back in his high stool on the platform, with his new gold-edged black star in place.

"Who?" we asked in unison.

"Freyda," he answered. He seemed pleased, but who wouldn't after having been elected Counselor?

Glammis was sitting next to him, smiling broadly. That was one of the few times I'd seen her smile, not that I ran across her very often. She was the assistant supervisor of Maintenance, usually quite reserved.

She and Heimdall spent a lot of time together, but Loragerd told me that they'd never been contract-mates or even shared quarters.

Heimdall was in a good mood. He beamed at Glammis, even smiled at us.

"Loragerd, you can take off the afternoon. Loki, as far as I'm concerned, you're free also—but I understand Athene wants a word with you first."

I didn't think the Senior Guards or Counselors ever forgot anything. I trudged down the ramp from Assignments to Special Stores.

Athene was expecting me, and she didn't waste any time. "Loki, I've been thinking. I've had a chance to talk it over with Heimdall and Gilmesh, and some of the other Counselors, and the Tribunes. We all agree you need a permanent assignment. Since this assignment was my idea, I thought I ought to be the one who told you."

My stomach rolled into a tight little knot. When the powers-that-were didn't want to convey the good news themselves, it wasn't good news.

"We've decided on your first permanent support assignment."

She was repeating herself. I waited for the other boot to fall. Except for Ferrin, no one out of my trainee class had been made permanent. Maybe it wouldn't be too bad. I felt I could take Assignments, Special Stores, even Weather, or Archives.

"Maintenance."

I must have cringed.

"It's not that bad. Baldur says you're one of the few newer Guards with any mechanical aptitude at all. Besides, Heimdall thinks it will keep you busy."

Why was Heimdall so interested in keeping me busy?

"When do I report?"

"I'd say today, but the afternoon's basically a holiday. Make it first thing tomorrow. I'll tell Baldur to expect you then. Gilmesh already knows."

I bowed and said thank you. I was a bit dazed. Like Patrice had said years ago, divers didn't work in Maintenance, especially not crackerjack divers. And I was becoming a damned good diver, if not one of the best. Everyone said so. So why had they all decided to stuff me away in Maintenance?

I ran down Loragerd at Hera's Inn and asked the same question. She wasn't terribly sympathetic, but that might have been because she and Halcyon had been comparing notes on something, and I'd burst in.

"You're favored with one of the first permanent Tower assignments, while Halcyon and I are still carting perfume and power cells around, and immediately you slide here to tell us what's wrong with it. What did you want? Special assistant to Freyda in view of your past services?"

Loragerd was high on the dark ale, I figured, but the crack hurt.

"That's not it at all."

"Not completely anyway," chipped in Halcyon.

Loragerd brushed Halcyon's comment away with a wave and turned full face to me. "Sometimes you're so dense. Don't you see? All support jobs are dull. Do you want to lug supplies across time and keep records for Athene? How about keeping reports on population shifts for Gilmesh in Personnel? Or would you rather listen to citizen complaints at Domestic Affairs? Didn't you already get enough of that? Or do you want to listen to Frey's boasts and worry about getting sliced with that saber when he's not watching where he twirls it?"

I had to chuckle at the last. Loragerd always makes so much sense. Why couldn't I see it that way?

She reached over and touched my arm briefly.

"Other things will change too, Loki. Remember that."

What did she mean?

Then Loragerd switched the conversation back to the selection process. I didn't have a chance to comment. Halcyon looked peeved for a moment, but relaxed as Tyron and Ferrin wandered over.

"You know," began Tyron, dumping gossip on the table like a chunk of rockwood, "there's a rumor that the first Counselor selected for Tribune refused the election . . ."

"Who was it?" I snapped.

"Was it Justina?" asked Loragerd.

"Corbell? Athene? Baldur?"

Tyron shrugged. "I don't know. No one's saying, but it's never happened before, not that anyone can remember or that the Archives mention."

"But that sort of thing wouldn't be in the Archives," protested Ferrin.

I sipped my firejuice and let them discuss it. Despite the furor over the rumor, I was thinking about reporting to Maintenance. No one really understood. What real diver wanted to stand ankle-deep in oil and grease?

I left early, while the others were still singing and talking.

First, I slid up to a little ledge under Seneschal, high in the Bardwalls, and stared at the silver rivers in the canyons below. That ledge was the sort of place where I intended to have my own private retreat some day, a place where the only sound was the occasional hiss and flap of a night eagle or the whistling of the wind.

In my thin jumpsuit, I soon grew cold and slid back to my own quarters in the Citadel.

After a solid night's sleep, I reported to Baldur the next morning with my heart in my hands, so to speak.

He didn't let me voice my misgivings, and, sitting back in his plain stool, he started right in.

"A lot of Guards have the feeling that Maintenance is grubby, that we work ankle-deep in grease, oil, and grit. Now, take a good look around . . ."

Baldur stood a good head and a half taller than me, and with his light blue eyes and silver-blond hair, looked like a gentle sort of giant. His voice was mid-toned, a light baritone that cut through noise and distractions without being raised and without annoying. Baldur was instantly likable, yet conveyed solidity. But somehow no description really did him justice.

That morning, as he outlined Maintenance, I wished they had selected him Tribune, forgetting that, if they had, he wouldn't have been running Maintenance.

"Do you see any oil and grease?" he asked.

I didn't. At first glance, the huge Maintenance Hall seemed as light and airy as any of the other major Halls.

Baldur led the way to a corner area, well lighted and with a clear worktable and a comfortably padded, high-backed stool.

"Here's your space. The work you'll start with is replacing or repairing microcircuitry in wrist gauntlets and stunners. They get banged up so often it's simpler for us to repair than replace. Within the year, you will be able to repair any of the circuitry you see here from scratch. Then we'll go into more elaborate work."

That sounded elaborate enough.

The technical side was straightforward enough. Baldur demonstrated the console reference guides for the information on gauntlets and stunners, the micro-magnifier and the step-down microcircuit waldoes, and pointed out the bin where what I had to handle would be placed.

Next came a guided and detailed tour of the Hall, and we ended up back in his spaces.

"Sit down." He pointed at a vacant stool. I sat.

"Why is an understanding of machinery and electronics important to a Guard?"

"Because a Guard can't use to its fullest capabilities equipment he doesn't understand." That's what he had told us in training.

Baldur laughed.

"Well . . . you do remember those lectures. That's not all. I may say some things which will surprise you or shock you, but try to keep them in context.

"First, the Guard is composed generally of a group of polite barbarians. Second, barbarians have a tendency to destroy what they don't understand. That includes history. Third, most past Tribunes have historically understood that, from Sammis Olon on. Fourth, most Guards don't. Now, do you know what I mean by a polite barbarian?"

I didn't have the faintest idea, but decided to guess. "Someone who is polite, but doesn't understand?"

"What's polite? Understand what?"

I shrugged.

"Look at it this way, Loki. Most Guards know that if you push the stud on a stunner and point it at someone, it knocks them out. Why?"

I shrugged again.

"Then how did someone somewhere discover how to build one—by trying every possible piece of electronic gadgetry in the universe?"

I must have looked as blank as I felt.

Baldur grinned. "Pardon me if I got on my podium, but I can get intense on this subject."

I nodded, wondering where he was headed.

"I'll cut it short for now. It takes an understanding of physiology and electronics to design a stunner. On Query we don't have that knowledge. We never did. Oh, I've picked up the technical skills, and, like an educated animal, I can build one pretty much from scratch, given time, but I don't know why it works. No one on Query does. How about a wrist thunderbolt?

"Do you understand the simple chemistry behind a projectile gun? A linguistics tank?"

I'd never thought about it. Probably a whole lot of Guards hadn't either.

"That's what I mean by barbarians. Every culture has its barbarians, but in the average culture when there get to be too many barbarians and too few individuals who understand the technology, the culture collapses to a level where more people understand the mechanics of everyday life.

"On Query, no one understands the mechanics of everyday life. Nor that the Guard structure is all that really holds our system together. In the Guard, basically three functions are critical—Maintenance, the data banks of the Archives, and Special Stores.

"Maintenance does more than maintain things; we also teach Guards the basics of technology. You know about Special Stores, and the Archives basically store data."

"I thought the Archives had records of our history."

Baldur laughed softly. "A little history goes a long ways. Besides, someone has to write it. No . . . the data banks mainly contain hard technical information—everything from dive records to background material on out-system cultures."

I pondered that while Baldur went on.

"One of the reasons I give trainee lectures is to emphasize the importance of understanding the technology we use, but it's gotten harder and harder to get across, even in my lifetime. A related problem is power. Stored power can't be run through a duplicator. So we continue to duplicate the old Murian fusactors and to import various kinds of generators—but there's still the Law of Diminishing Output."

He paused and looked at me.

I didn't shrug, but I didn't know where he was going.

"If I duplicate ethylene to run a portable generator, the total energy generated by that generator will be less than the energy required to duplicate the fuel. That's why we need fusion power. But we have to duplicate the Murian fusactors piece by piece, and they still have to be assembled and tested.

"And Maintenance has to repair or replace all that equipment."

Baldur paused, studied me, and sighed.

"I can see I've just about overloaded your rational facilities. We'll talk more later. In the meantime, start by studying the schematics on the gauntlets until you can visualize them in your sleep. Draw them on the drafting board. If you don't understand the reasons for the circuits, read this." He dropped a thin book on the table.

"If you still have trouble, come find me."

I nodded and picked up the book and walked back to my new permanent-support work area and studied schematics and began to cross-reference them to the manual. It was slow. I hadn't gotten through more than twenty pages by the end of the day when Baldur told me to close up.

It seemed to go on like that for ten-day after ten-day, but it probably wasn't that long before I actually began to make some repairs—and after that, the manual made more sense.

After the gauntlets, Baldur began to give me other things, like stunners and restrainer field generators. At first, learning each new system was almost as hard as the gauntlets, but I kept at it.

It was better than being in Domestic Affairs or lugging power cells—a lot better.

XV

SAMMIS CAUGHT ME on the way into Maintenance. For some reason, a lot of things had jumbled together in my mind, from my parents' being gone to the police duties in Southpoint to the damned portable generator from Sinopol—and the generator question, unlike the other two, I might be able to figure out. But I was still having trouble figuring out the need for such a portable generator. Sure, it was a lot smaller than the closet-sized generators that powered most Guard operations, but why did we really need it? The old regular fusion generators worked fine, and because they were bigger, they also produced more power. So even Baldur's sermons on waste and power didn't answer that question. We had the generators, plenty of them. That still bothered me, and I was still trying to figure out the practical implications when Sammis touched my shoulder—lightly.

"Loki, Freyda and I have an assignment for you."

After his attitude adjustment test, even though it had been seasons earlier, I was skeptical of Senior Guard Sammis and any assignment he had.

"Yes?" I kept walking toward the dining hall in the West Barracks. Not many divers ate there, mostly trainees, but it was convenient when I didn't feel like I wanted to be on display at one of the inns. Besides, where else would I have gone?

"It's just an observational job on . . . well, we really don't have a name for the place."

"Then why do you need me?"

"Loki, call it part of your training." Sammis grinned in a too-friendly fashion.

I surrendered to the inevitable. "Tell me about it."

"It's all on the briefing tapes in Assignments. But, in short terms, something unusual is happening in this system. Planets are being moved, but we don't see any ships. The heat of the sun is changing, but it's not following the stellar sequence. Locator is picking up a lot of temporal shifts that can't be traced to the Guard."

I waited.

"And the only sign of life is on a gas giant, pretty far out from the sun." Sammis paused.

"Why me?"

"Because you're young and expendable," Sammis wisecracked back.

That was clearly all I was going to get from Senior Guard Sammis. "What am I supposed to ask Heimdall for? 'That place Sammis mentioned'?"

"The file key is 'Anemone.' "

"I appreciate it, Sammis." I gave the older Guard a half-bow. "But I'll still have to tell Baldur."

He was gone, and I went in to tell Baldur. He nodded and told me that I could finish up with the gauntlet repairs on my bench when I got back. So I walked back up the ramps to Assignments and asked for the Anemone briefing.

Heimdall sent me off to the end console, and I began to study the package. There wasn't much to study. About halfway through, it dawned on me, and I should have figured it out earlier, why I was expendable. Anemone wasn't Querylike. Gas giants aren't.

The Guard doesn't operate off Query with any technology that can't be carried by a single diver. So . . . that meant the Guard's exploration vehicle had to be a diver who could carry a lot, including the equipment to keep him alive in the now, since it's hard to get a real idea of a technology or a culture from the undertime. I was the exploration vehicle.

"Cumbersome" wasn't the word for the equipment, and Baldur fussed over every bit of it.

"Remember to check the full-spectrum readouts first. Even you couldn't survive a thermonuclear blast."

"How would anyone know I was there?"

"If the Frost Giants had had much in the way of brains, they could have. Sometimes I wonder how we've been lucky so long . . ."

It wasn't luck, exactly, I figured, but didn't get a chance to say so.

Baldur kept talking. "It would be easier if we just had deep-space travel. We could drop a flitter—"

"Flitter?"

"Sorry—pressurized atmospheric travel vessel—we could drop one of those right into the atmosphere, takes holos from there."

"It wouldn't exactly be unobserved," I pointed out.

Baldur laughed. "I don't think you understand just how alien these people are."

"They aren't people, Sammis said."

"In my view, anything that thinks is a person."

I had to think about that. Didn't flying gophers think a little? Where did you draw the line?

Finally, everything was ready, and there wasn't that much point in waiting. I carted everything over to the Travel Hall and checked and double-checked the equipment. Baldur fussed some more. Sammis was nowhere to be seen.

After a wave, or as much of a wave as possible in a portable man-worn tank, I twisted the helmet into place, made sure the oxygen worked, and dropped under the now, deeplining down and out.

The first sign that something was wrong occurred even before I reached the planet—a wall of time winds that shook me and my suit until we rattled. Now, undertime is subjective, but I still say that even the equipment rattled.

The whole system was like that. Black time vortices that twisted and turned in on themselves. Gold pyramids hovering in the undertime. I thought I saw a gold and black spiral turning in the undertime. I did. I saw a whole ring of them orbiting Anemone in the undertime.

I ducked away from them and dropped toward the planet, but not all the way to the ground, or whatever passed for it. The deep-space pressure suit was limited to handling about twenty atmospheres, and that meant I couldn't break out on the planetary surface—or anyplace particularly close. About the lowest point would have been at the break-point between the troposphere and stratosphere. That would have been pushing it. So I hung a split entry high in the thin swirling clouds, feeling like I weighed about ten times normal, and turned on all the gadgets Baldur had hung on me.

All of them registered something—the entire electromagnetic spectrum was filled, and though I wasn't that much of a technician or engineer, all the indicators were that something was generating a whole lot of patterns of sorts. Dealing with time energies you get the feel for energy patterns. They were there.

I looked around with my eyes. That didn't help much, because it just looked as though I were hanging in a gray soup. After a moment, I remembered Baldur's instructions and turned on the temperature discriminations in the suit visor.

The whole view changed.

To my right was a towering wall of slowly shifting blocks, dark green in color. To my left was another wall, but of a lighter green. In the middle, opposite me, three bluish spirals winked into existence, just as if they had popped out of the undertime.

The slight shiver in the now confirmed that.

I swallowed, recalling those gold and black spirals in orbit. What were these creatures?

The blue spirals swept in and stopped in a semicircle around where I hung, my boots sort of resting, the part that wasn't locked undertime, on what you might call a grassy plain between the canyon walls. Except that all of this was just a bunch of clouds.

I flicked off the discriminators for an instant and was back in the gray soup. There were three patches of darker gray towering up. Since I preferred color, I flicked back on the discriminators.

Now what? It had only taken the locals instants to find me.

A sort of static crackled around me, or my thoughts, almost like the eddies from a restrainer field, except there were images instead of static.

. . . *{A towering green cloud with nothingness in the center}* . . .

. . . *{Three perfect spirals—half-black, half-gold—turn slowly around a miniature pulsing red cube a mere fraction of the size of the spirals}* . . .

. . . *{From sweep of stars, mottled green/yellow tracks appear one by one leading to the cube, which turns an even uglier shade of red}* . . .

. . . *{Sun-black flames lick at the cube, which melts into a blue vapor and vanishes}* . . .

. . . *{Gold winds blow around the red cube, which fades into white and then into gold. Then the gold cube splinters into shards. Faint gold mists rise from the shards as they shrink until neither shards nor mists remain}* . . .

. . . *{The three perfect spirals turn and turn until the red cube slowly manifests faces which are split triangularly between black and gold}* . . .

I could get the feel of the debate—should they burn me, freeze me, or hope I'd conduct a rational dialogue? The problem was that I could sense what they were "saying" but didn't have the faintest notion of how to communicate with them.

Still, I tried to think at them, pushing an image of me, superimposed on top of the red cube.

Nothing happened, except more images dropped into my mind.

. . . *{The three spirals are joined by a larger spiral, spinning more slowly}* . . .

. . . *{A web of lines, in spiraled grids, settles over the red cube, anchoring it between the cliffs}* . . .

As that last image washed over me, I shuddered because I could feel the black lines falling, and I tried to dive undertime, but nothing happened.

Outside, with the discriminators, I could see that a larger blue spiral had appeared, and all four were twirling in an apparent pattern around me and my frozen suit.

Was I frozen, or the suit? I concentrated, thinking about diving under the now without the suit, and I relaxed. Whatever they had used to freeze the suit in time was linked to the suit, not to me.

I swallowed again. They apparently controlled their system through some form of mental power. I couldn't tell for sure, but I got the impression, as the outsider overhearing their mental images, that machinery, at least as we knew it, wasn't exactly involved.

. . . *{A rolling horizontal spiral, mostly black, rolls toward and over the red cube. After it passes, the cube is gone, but red streaks run through the spiral}* . . .

The last image definitely gave me the idea of being dissected or digested for information.

I couldn't move the suit undertime, but that didn't mean I couldn't use the equipment. So I used one arm to dig out the portable cannon—a shell thrower of sorts—fastened to the suit's thigh.

The shell exploded nicely above the top of the largest blue spiral.

. . . *{Sun-black flames flash from all four spirals toward the small red cube}* . . .

That made me angry. What was I supposed to do? I could hear them, but they couldn't hear me. They tried to keep me from diving and discussed me like some bug caught in a trap.

When I began to sense the blackness of the undertime starting to vibrate, I decided that it was time to leave, even if it meant leaving suit, sensors, and information behind. So I dived right out of the suit and under the now, almost sprinting away from Anemone.

Figuratively speaking, I didn't even look back.

I went through the change-wind barrier like a needle through coarse-woven fabric. Then I stopped, hanging outside the time walls of the system, to see if anything followed.

Nothing.

I waited in the undertime to see if any of the spirals appeared, but none did.

Without the suit and its gadgets I wasn't equipped to break out, but I decided to go foretime and see what I could discover. Pushing toward the blue was harder than normal, but I went as far as I could before heading back in-system.

I didn't get there. The time-wind wall was there, except it was farther in-system, and this time it was so solid I just about bounced back to Query. Then I backtimed, and discovered that the wall retreated and solidified not much after my own initial undertime track appeared, and I could sense the faint wail of the change winds.

The change winds—how can something be subjectively perceived as a wind with no objective correlation, but be based upon a multiple chronological readjustment? I thought it was a lot of jargon when we studied it, and I still did even while they were moaning behind and around me.

I felt like frowning, but you can't frown in the undertime. At least we can't, although I felt that the spirals could.

When I broke out in the Travel Hall, I was stark naked, and I must have blushed. Only Hightel was there, stripping off a burnoose or something and putting it in his chest.

"What happened to you?"

"I lost my equipment," I mumbled.

"Who was she?" He grinned.

"A large blue spiral about a kay high with a desire to roll over me."

"You play in rough company." He shook his head.

"Not by choice." I ducked back under the now and went straight to my room in the West Barracks. After pulling on another uniform, I dropped back to the Travel Hall. Then I went to find Sammis and Baldur.

It took a while, but we finally sat at a table in the corner of Assignments. Heimdall and Wryan, who was Sammis' partner, also joined us, but they pulled their chairs back a little, as if to indicate they were just observers.

No one said that much until I got to the point where I mentioned the undertime view of the spirals.

"They actually moved in the undertime?" Sammis asked.

"That's the way I saw it. But it seemed like it only happened in high-grav undertime spots."

"Could happen," Wryan interjected. Heimdall looked at her and cleared his throat. She looked at him, and he closed his mouth.

The next real questions came when we got to the images.

"Why didn't you try to communicate with them?"

"I did. I thought at them, and they didn't hear. I waved my arms, and they didn't pay any attention. Then they froze me in the now and started to think about dissecting me. That's when I got out the cannon."

"You didn't fire at them?"

"Of course not. I fired over their heads—or tops, or whatever their high points are. But then they got upset, and I left."

"You left the equipment?" asked Heimdall.

"If I hadn't left the equipment, I wouldn't have left at all. The whole undertime was turning very hot and black."

"Why didn't they bind you as well as the suit?" asked Sammis.

"A blind spot, I think. They don't have any idea of the extensive use of materials."

Sammis looked at Baldur, who shrugged.

"Sammis is probably right. If you look at the temperatures, gravities, and pressures involved . . ."

Sammis looked confused.

"At the surface of Anemone, ice would be harder than steel, but what would happen if you built a spaceship out of it? Or even a pressure suit?"

"We'll have to stop them," Heimdall insisted.

"Why?" Wryan asked. Her voice was dry. "We can send someone out to check what Loki found out about the time wall, but it would seem that their instincts are to retreat. Besides, we really don't want to go around destroying whole systems again, do we?"

Sammis coughed loudly. Everyone looked at him. "We're missing one simple point. If Loki couldn't break through their time barrier, how would you propose we do anything—unless you want to backtime a lot, and how could you guarantee success? Do you really want a repeat—"

Wryan coughed loudly. Sammis blushed, and went on more softly, "For that matter, barriers like that tend to be two-way."

"Besides, how could they hurt us?" Baldur followed on. "If they tried to break out on Query, they'd die instantly. They aren't into materials technology, and from what Sammis has said, they can't or won't venture out beyond the outer limits of their own system. Our own observations showed that they were building a second gas-giant planet. You don't go to that kind of work if there are easier alternatives."

"A gas giant?" I blurted.

"What else could they do?" Baldur asked.

I didn't know. I do know that the spirals hadn't seemed particularly nasty. They had debated what to do with me, if the images I'd received were accurate, and they hadn't chased me. They seemed to be able to move physically in the undertime, unlike us, but was that only a function of the high-gravity fields? Supposedly, time fields are linked to gravity. If we could live under ten or twenty gees, could we also move in the undertime?

There wasn't much way to find out, not that I could see.

"We'll have to bring this up to the Tribunes," Heimdall insisted.

Wryan, Sammis, and Baldur looked at each other.

"Can I get back to work?" I asked. There wasn't much I could add.

Baldur and Sammis looked at each other. Sammis shook his head, then added, "You need to file a trip report here in Assignments. Add it to the Anemone file."

"Now?"

"In the next day or so."

"I'll do it now."

"Fine, Loki," Baldur said wearily.

So I stood up and found an empty console, and entered everything I could remember. When I was done, I looked around, but they'd all gone. So I went back to my workbench and the pile of broken gauntlets, mainly trainees', that had been waiting for me.

XVI

WRAPPED IN FURS and close against a young lady with smooth, cool skin, I was dreaming, flying lightnings across a twilight sky. Though Loragerd lay by me, she was not within the dream, as I strode across massive black mountains to pull down night.

Fires streamed from my fingers, and the stars paled to nothing against the light I wielded . . .

A faint hum came from the clothes strewn behind the couches, leading me from the dream. I wondered about it, but let myself slip back into the clutches of sleep, drawing Loragerd closer.

Her black, pixie-cut hair was fluffed slightly, and the warm fragrances of trilia and cinnamon drifted from her body and enfolded us in the early morning.

Suddenly, two Guards I didn't know were shaking me out of my sleep.

Instantly awake, I threw the smaller Guard off my shoulders and into the wall. I'd seen him before, a brown-haired ferret who usually sat at a corner console and followed Heimdall around the Tower.

The other Guard stood there and leered at Loragerd, who had drawn the covers around her, since neither of us was wearing anything.

The first Guard was staggering up out of the corner where I'd thrown him. The leering one saw me turning toward him and stammered, "Heimdall . . . needs you now . . . in Assignments . . . Urgent . . . he said . . ."

"So? Was this necessary?" I wanted to take both of them and drop the bastards over the Sequin Falls.

"Heimdall sent us," apologized ferret-face, as if that excused anything and everything.

"And how did he know where we were?" I asked without thinking.

Nobody answered me, and I realized what a stupid question it had been. Heimdall had just sent them to Locator to get the coordinates, and there they were.

Looking at the pair, I noticed they were both bigger than I was. Not so big as Baldur, but big enough. I didn't care.

"Scram!" I growled. "We'll get there when we're dressed, and that will be a lot sooner if you get out of here."

The two exchanged glances, looked back at me, and winked out as they slid, presumably back to Heimdall.

I put my arms around Loragerd, who was shaking. Though the room was warm, I could feel the shivers and goose bumps on her normally satin-smooth skin.

"Are you all right?" I asked.

She gave a little headshake, and I hugged her again. We didn't say anything else. What else was there to say? We'd overslept when we should have been on duty. Junior Guards don't have any rights. Voluntary subjection to discipline and all that.

I wasn't shaking, but I was angry, and there wasn't anything I could do about it. As we dressed, Loragerd looked at me, a strange sort of look, but I could have been imagining it.

We didn't even have anything to eat. She headed to Linguistics, which was her permanent assignment, and I made for Assignments.

When I got there, I could have cut the silence with a light saber, Frey's or anyone else's. Heimdall was slumped in his high stool, and the despair poured from him like a river.

As he caught sight of me, he straightened, opened his mouth as if to shout, then clamped it shut. He waited an instant, then began curtly, "Glammis was on Atlantea. Fifty centuries back. Locator tag wavered, just went blank."

That meant the Locator console was receiving a signal, but one not linked to Glammis' thought pattern, which meant she was dead, deep-stunned, or near death.

I stared at Heimdall. The whole morning made sense. If there'd been anyone Heimdall had been close to, it had to have been Glammis, the slight woman with the stern face and dark curly hair. Why had Glammis been on Atlantea? She usually presided over the trainees and the mech shop with an iron hand. Baldur supplied the philosophy, Glammis the work.

She seldom went into the field, but Baldur had once mentioned that she had been considered a crack diver, centuries ago.

Heimdall glared at me and cleared his throat. I was supposed to say something.

"You want me to find her and bring her back?"

He nodded. I understood. Heimdall wanted ability, not just any diver, and there were doubtless problems. Sammis and Wryan were backtime and out-line, and Gilmesh was involved in a foretime plot on Curatol. So Heimdall had sent his troopers after me.

"Information?" I asked. I had a couple of units, if that.

"End console."

If I hadn't known Heimdall better, I would have sworn the iron Guard's voice was ready to crack.

In a funny way, I had to admire him. Me . . . if that had happened to Loragerd, I'd have gone off half-cocked no matter what. Heimdall knew his limits, understood he couldn't rescue Glammis and had to stand by helplessly as he tried to round up help.

Glammis's mission had been simple, according to the console. The mid-island people of fifty centuries earlier had developed a broadcast power transmitter. The results were strange, to say the least, since the measured output was considerably larger than the input at times, and at times there was no output despite continued input. The project had failed, and the generator later exploded.

Glammis had been so intrigued with the possibilities, considering the ongoing power problems, that she had decided to make the dive herself. Wasn't too surprising, when I thought about it. Divers who understood mechanical theory or engineering were few and far between. Glammis had been surprised that I knew what she was talking about even when I first started working in Maintenance.

I got the directional output from the console and headed for the Travel Hall. No waiting for languages, cosmetics, or special equipment—I threw on an equipment belt, clipped on a stunner, slipped on the wristbands, and dived.

A fast recovery, if at all. I wasn't happy about it. Messengers who confirm bad news are likely to become the recipients of gratuitous violence.

Death on the time-lines is funny. You can loop time, change the whole pattern of another culture . . . but dead is dead. Our own pasts and futures could not be directly changed by our own actions backtime of the now.

Atlantea was a strange planet, although every planet has its peculiarities. Atlantea has shallow seas and metallic deposits, with no moons and no tidal forces to speak of. The combination's not supposed to occur, especially not with intelligent life, but that's the way it was.

And Glammis was down.

I red-flashed the back trip, skipping from timepath to timepath, homing in on Glammis' signal from her Locator tag and power packs.

Sometimes the line between death and unconsciousness is terribly fine. If Glammis died—brain-dead death, objective time—before I had dived clear of Quest, she was dead, but if there were any sparks, she had an outside chance.

I was aiming for a breakout point right at the instant her Locator signal had shifted from active to passive. Theoretically, I could not back-time past her "now," but I was hoping I could power my way in sooner without the innate resistance of her conscious mind.

It was worth a try.

Undertime doesn't really have a color, but it feels gray, and your vision is limited. You can see "outside," or I can, into real objective time, but it's muddled, like looking up from beneath the water, silvered over and wavering, with flashes of light darting across your field of vision like minnows. Some divers can't see that much, and some can't see at all.

Time tension, like water tension, exists at the moment of breakout when you are showered with a spray of moments that slide off you with the emotional shock of icy rain.

Except this time I was bounced back undertime as soon as I broke out, my head reeling with the impression of time mirrored in time. I slid sideways fractionally and came out in a corridor.

The stench was ozone. The building atmosphere spelled out "power plant."

The directionals on the wrist gauntlets pointed toward a door closed and barred. The bar had melted, in effect welding itself to the frame.

No one was around, and from the dim light filtering through the skylights above, I figured it was either very early in the day or very late.

The feeling of time being warped grew as I walked up to the door.

I grabbed the crossbar and dived. The bar came with me—the door frame didn't. That's how the Law of Discrete Particles works. If the bar had been the same material as the frame, nothing would have happened.

I still couldn't slide or dive into the room, for whatever reason. I broke out, dropped the bar, forced open the door—it was a sliding type that had a tendency to jam—and walked into the generator room. I didn't know if that's what it was, but that's what it felt like.

The place was a mess. Two control stations were a fused mass, and I didn't need more than a quick glance to see that both controllers were dead.

With the currents of time swirling around me, it took every bit of concentration to walk across the ceramic floor to the dark-haired woman sprawled on her back. She was alive and breathing. But her mouth hung open, and her wide green eyes were empty.

I picked her up, hoping she didn't have any physical injuries, and caught the time tide boiling out of the generating equipment to throw us undertime and foretime toward Quest.

From the total lack of resistance I had in carrying her, I suspected that Glammis had literally lost her mind, but I'd leave that determination to the medical techs.

To keep things quick and simple, I just broke out with Glammis right in the Infirmary, and I staggered into the critical-care section as Hycretis came running. He didn't ask any stupid questions, and I helped him ease her under the regenerator and the diagnostic scan unit.

Hycretis focused on Glammis as if I weren't even there.

I stood there for a long moment, wondering why the room was vibrating, before I understood my legs were shaking. Then I tottered toward the cabinet I knew held the Sustain and gulped down a cup. That helped, but my legs weren't much better. So I plopped down on the edge of a vacant bed at the end of the ward. Then I lay back and closed my eyes.

"Damn you, Loki! Damn you!"

I felt myself being shaken like a rag doll. Was it a nightmare? I tried to roll over, but the buffeting wouldn't go away.

"What did you do? Deprive me of my only joy, would-be god? Torment me with an empty shell?"

Like a slowing top, the universe began to settle, and I woke up fully to find Heimdall grabbing my harness, shaking me, and screaming, tears streaming from his eyes, and saliva drooling from the corners of his mouth.

"Answer me! Answer me, would-be god!"

Heimdall slapped my face, and it hurt.

He had me just by the harness. I slid behind him with a quick dive barely under the tension of the now. He was still holding an empty harness and staring at the vacant space where I had been when I cracked him a solid one from behind. He went down like a breaker, foaming at the mouth, but out. Out cold.

I looked down at the poor bastard. "Too much strain, I think."

Both Hycretis and the two troopers holding him appeared stunned, for some reason.

"Let him go." I gestured at the two Guards.

They released their hold on the medical tech, but he didn't say anything.

"Heimdall was just under too much stress," I announced. "He really needs some medical care and some rest." I turned to the two thugs. "You two watch Heimdall and make sure that he gets rest. Keep out anybody but Counselors and Tribunes." They would anyway, and hopefully that would keep them out of further mischief.

"Hycretis, you do whatever's necessary for Heimdall—muscle relaxants, sedatives, whatever you think is suitable."

This time my words registered, and he nodded.

I checked the objective time. Seemed like I'd been gone forever, but the wall clock said one hundred units had elapsed from the moment I'd left the Travel Hall headed to Atlantea. I'd have bet that ninety units had been my sleep and recovery time.

"Glammis?" I asked Hycretis as he rummaged opened a cabinet and ran his eyes down the drawers.

"Physically, she's fine. Her mind's wiped clean. How I don't know. She has the thought patterns of practically an unborn child."

The Glammis we knew was gone. Heimdall had been right.

"Did you tell Heimdall?"

"How could I not tell him?" He pulled out a spray injector of something.

I thought of the two thugs behind us. Right. How could he not?

Another question was why I hadn't noticed that Heimdall seemed to be building and using a private army. That could wait. First, I needed to talk to Baldur.

I knew the answer to the power puzzle Glammis had been investigating, I thought. Baldur would know if my surmises were correct. I went down the ramps to Maintenance not quite at a run.

Baldur glared at me as I stood respectfully outside his area, taking deep breaths and refusing to go away.

"All right." He touched a stud on his console. "What is it?"

I recounted my travels to Atlantea, from the funny generating room where I'd rescued Glammis to the time currents and my diving difficulties.

". . . and I don't have a hard fact to go on, but if I had to guess, I'd say that they're tapping the time tides somehow and wrenching time out of its flow."

When I began, Baldur had a half-bemused, let's-humor-Loki look on his face. By the time I finished, he was running his stubby fingers through his white-blond hair. He did that when he was excited. Freyda told me that, but this was the first time I'd seen it.

"Fascinating concept—fascinating but dangerous. Let me think about it, Loki. Let me think about it."

As far as he was concerned, I had ceased to exist. Baldur was back in his world of numbers and concepts.

While I was deciding what I ought to do, I walked back over to my own work space and began to finish cleaning and running maintenance checks on a faulty duplicator that Frey had sent down from the Domestic Affairs weapons storeroom.

The duplicator wasn't faulty. Frey or someone else was. Someone had tried to copy some sort of hand weapon with a power pack in place. Luckily, there had only been a residual charge in the weapon, or Hycretis would have been scraping Frey and his light saber off the nearest wall.

As it was, in its discharged state, the power cell had released enough energy to melt down the weapon, the holding chamber, and warp the adjacent modules.

Boring . . . that's what repairs like that were. In spite of the light pouring in from the long windows and the airiness provided by the high ceilings, milling and otherwise breaking apart the fused modules and replacing the sections one by one was a tedious task. Some were so hopeless that all I could do was black-box them.

While I worked on the duplicator, a handful of trainees delivered several other busted objects to the bin Baldur had set up when I came to Maintenance.

All in all, I enjoyed being able to fix things, see a pile of metal turned back into a functional machine. As Baldur had pointed out, repairs were usually more efficient than sending trainees and junior Guards all over time to pick up more and more hardware when so often the repairs were minor.

Besides, there was another problem with merely black-boxing it all. Trash, waste . . . I'd hated the waste detail as a trainee. If cleaning up after Frey was boring, it was nothing compared to lugging busted stuff off to the dump on Vulcan. But if somebody didn't, we would have been buried. Still, the waste pile there stretched for kilos down that empty canyon, and I wondered what someone might think if they ever found it—someone besides the Guard, that is!

But Baldur insisted that I help lug off anything that I couldn't fix. So there was a personal incentive not to create too much waste.

As I finished the duplicator and rolled it back to the front where Frey's flunkies would pick it up, I saw someone standing in the shadows.

Loragerd.

With all the rush, and especially after dealing with Heimdall, I'd lost track of her. I looked down at the glowstones, wondering what I could say. The morning had to have been hell on her. I stepped toward her.

"Are you all right?" she asked.

I could feel my throat tighten. Here she was, waiting for me, asking how I was. What could I say? I didn't say anything—just shook my head and held her tightly.

"Loki." She leaned back and wiped my cheeks. "I'm fine, just fine. Heimdall was after you, and worried about Glammis. You handled everything except you. Freyda told me to take off early and find you. I did."

I still couldn't say anything.

After my fling with Freyda, our relationship had cooled, but she still worried. Imagine, sending Loragerd to look after me.

Imagine, Loragerd caring how I was. Me?

Ridiculous—except there I stood in the afternoon shadows of the ancient and time-protected machines holding Loragerd and shaking.

I finally relaxed enough so that we could walk back into my spaces. I shut down the equipment, and we had a short dinner at Hera's before going back to my rooms.

All night long, I kept waking up, wondering if someone would appear out of nowhere and grab me. Loragerd slept better, I thought. At least, she didn't wake up in fits and starts like I did.

On that long night, with my arms around Loragerd, wondering about the chain of tomorrows that loomed ahead, I kept recalling the shock of the morning. Seemed a lot longer ago than the same day.

I was going to get a place, even if I had to build it stone by stone, where no one could slide into it. Heimdall could rot in Hell before dragging me out of sleep.

Thinking that, knowing it would be so, in the early morning silence, I drifted into an uninterrupted sleep and did not wake again until the wake-up chimed.

Loragerd and I ate some juice, some fruit, and dressed. She left for the Linguistics Center before I was quite together, but within units I was headed for Maintenance. I made the Tower in a quick slide and hustled down the ramps from the west portal to see what Baldur had come up with.

From the look of his area, he'd been there all night. The circles under his eyes were blacker than ever, but he gave me a smile. That was, after I'd waited ten units or so for him to come out of his thought-world.

"Most intriguing problem, most intriguing, Loki, but I suspect a self-resolving one."

"What do you mean?"

"I've checked the files. Glammis located this device fifty centuries back, and the records show the station was abandoned and destroyed. The Atlanteans succeeded in transferring some energy across time. I've postulated a theoretical basis for the mechanism. I did have a head start; it parallels some theories I've been developing."

"I'm lost," I admitted.

He beamed faintly because I'd asked a question. A lecture was coming.

"If your conjecture is correct, and I suspect it is, the total of mass and energy—energy really, since mass is a stabilized form of energy, and that's simplifying it grossly—does not need to be constant. The average energy level of a given locale over objective elapsed time must approach some constant. Because of the forces involved—call them resistance for lack of a more precise term—it takes more and more power input per unit of output as the duration of operation increases.

"The Atlantean power plant was diverting energy from the nearer time levels. That was why you couldn't dive into the area immediately around the generator." Baldur stopped and gestured an end to his response, lifting his bushy blond eyebrows as if the conclusion was evident.

I didn't feel like guessing. "And?"

"There is a definite limit to the energy easily available to the generator. Within a few years, seasons, perhaps days, the generator will stop delivering power. Five, ten years later, left to itself, it might function again for a period before stopping. The idea isn't too bad for an emergency power source. It's really an energy concentrator more than a generator."

"The damned thing will quit by itself?"

"I'd calculate so. And . . ." Baldur launched into a detailed explanation of how and why, which I listened to with my thoughts elsewhere. I'd have to go back and check the Atlantean generator over a period of years before making a final report.

I've always disliked loose ends.

After that, I was going to discover the location I'd visualized for my private retreat—where Heimdall and his thugs couldn't track me down.

Baldur wound up his technical dissertation.

"Then I'll dive back and check out your theory."

"You doubt everyone, don't you?"

I grinned. He'd caught me out. "Let's say I have extreme difficulty accepting what I can't understand without some proof."

Baldur dismissed me with a nod, and I marched back up to the ramps to the Travel Hall. I should have checked in with Assignments, but I could claim I was acting under Baldur's orders if anyone complained.

The backtime trace on the Atlantean generator was a snap. At least, finding it provided no problems.

Ten years foretime from my pickup of the disminded Glammis, I came across not a malfunctioning power plant, nor an empty structure, but a fused and leveled pile of rubble, glazed over as if by a tremendously hot energy source.

I tried to locate the exact point of destruction, but couldn't. In one instant, five years objectively after Glammis's near demise, the complex stood, with high fences around it, vacant and nonfunctional. In the next unit remained only the glazed pile of junk.

No matter how I concentrated in the undertime, I couldn't identify that fraction of a unit when the destruction occurred. Between the two instants of time, I could only sense a vortex, a whirlpool of time, an instantaneous unleashing of power striking between the threads of time, yet a power totally separated from the Time surrounding those instants.

I recorded the results on the portable holo unit I'd carted along for that purpose, including some scenes of the Atlanteans practically barricading the complex. What else could they do? Close to the generators, machinery didn't work right, and they clearly had some idea of what was going to happen. So they stayed away.

I packed up the unit and dived back to the Travel Hall.

A few trainees were popping in and out of the Hall, but there was no one around I had to account to. I still logged the dive, before I took the holo unit and went and cornered Baldur again, not that it was hard because he seldom left Maintenance during the day.

"Not surprised," he commented tersely, for once trying to get rid of me. He'd solved the problem. I was the doubter. "Time recoil, showing the limits to which energy can be transferred."

I wandered back to my own area, thinking it over. I didn't understand the why of it, but that's the way Time is. You can only bend it so far before it strikes back.

Ferret-face was waiting for me.

I glared at him, still angry for his entry, and for what they'd done to Loragerd. He cowered. Damned if I knew why. He was an experienced Temporal Guard with the power of Heimdall behind him, and I was a junior Guard with no one behind me.

"Heimdall would appreciate seeing you in the Assignments Hall."

I still wondered about ferret-face's politeness, but that's not the sort of question you can ask.

Heimdall was back behind his console, as if nothing at all had happened the day before. His eyes were a bit bloodshot. That was all. His shoulder-length black hair was as smooth and stiff as ever, and the coldness he carried with him filled the Hall.

He got away with the longer hair because he wasn't an active diver, and now that he was a Counselor who would question it?

Intent as I was on Heimdall, I missed seeing Freyda at first. She was standing a few steps to the left of Heimdall.

"Honored Tribune, Counselor." I gave them both a half-bow.

Heimdall pointed to the chair on the platform next to his console. I plunked myself into it. Freyda seated herself next to Heimdall, and both of them looked at me from their higher stools.

Heimdall nodded at Freyda. She accepted whatever invitation it was and began. "You're to be commended for your recovery of Glammis. While she will need a total reeducation, there was no lasting physical or genetic damage. She may retain some residual memories and traits. That remains to be seen.

"Second, the Counselors have recommended that you be assigned to take over as assistant supervisor of Maintenance. Glammis will not be able to resume her duties for some time."

Was that an understatement. Glammis would take years to recover her skills, and there was no guarantee that the stimuli of her second childhood would lead her down the same mech-oriented path as her first had.

The promotion wasn't that much, if you thought about it. Maintenance had basically been the three of us, and off-and-on trainees. While Baldur would continue, obviously, as the supervisor of Maintenance, I'd have wide latitude . . . and more to do. I think Baldur just talked them into it to keep me from bothering him. But I could see the need to drag in some trainees as soon as I could, and I could also see the thinness of the pool of Guards with mechanical talents. That's what happens when you rely on duplicators.

I nodded again, and thanked Heimdall and Freyda for their confidence, vowed to follow the high standards of tradition, bowed once more, and was dismissed.

Back down the ramps to Maintenance I ambled, musing over the latest turn of events. The first thing to do was to move into Glammis's old spaces. She'd had better equipment and full access to the data banks for equipment.

Several days passed before I was satisfied with the results, and I'd rearranged the area three or four times before I got the layout I liked. By that time the repairs had piled up, and that meant I was working late for a good ten-day stretch catching up, because I was handling both what had gone to Glammis and what I'd handled.

I didn't feel that should be a permanent state of affairs.

Baldur agreed. "What do you suggest?"

"That you request the trainee with the best mechanical aptitude from the current third-year class for a hundred units a day."

"Fifty," replied Baldur.

I'd recommended one hundred units to get fifty, but I wasn't through. "I'd also suggest more routine maintenance help from the second-year trainees, like you used to require."

"If you want to run the operation, that's fine."

Surprisingly, Heimdall agreed. Maybe he thought it would keep me busy, or more involved with the Guard.

Narcissus was the third-year trainee, and I ended up giving him the same spiel Baldur had fed me—except I wasn't quite so successful.

"You seem awfully sure, Loki. I guess I believe you." That was his reaction.

I must have had some additional reaction to his doubts.

"I believe you," he stammered quickly. "I believe you."

I had wanted to tweak him with a thunderbolt to get my point across, but I hadn't considered such a drastic alternative seriously. At least, not too seriously.

That spring plodded well along into summer before I got things running anywhere close to the way I wanted, before I had any free time for my second and more personal project—to locate a site for my own retreat. My parents' empty house wasn't mine, and I hated to go there, although I still did, but the dust just grew deeper.

I must have looked at every cliff ledge in the Bardwalls before I settled on a location. I couldn't say how long it took. Seemed like years, but probably only took seasons, since the new shoots were coming out when I finally found it. Even I was tired of looking at rocks and more rocks.

I'd figured out what I needed before doing my surveying. The location had to be physically inaccessible except through an undertime slide right inside the structure.

I intended to build the exterior stone by stone in order to put it out-of-time-phase—like the Tower of Immortals itself. That way only some-one with innate directional senses and the ability to dive into an out-of-phase building could get there. Not totally foolproof—Sammis and maybe one or two others might be able to do it—but it sure would cut out Heimdall and his goons and most others.

I settled on a site under the peak called Seneschal, a small granite ledge jutting from a sheer cliff. Although Seneschal is a quarter of the way around the planet from Quest, I figured I could cope with the sun and the time differential.

There are no real seasonality problems because the axial tilt of Query is almost negligible. That's one of the reasons some of the older histori-ans in the Archives theorized that Query was not the planet we evolved on.

Who knows? We've never had the manpower to develop archae-ology—not since the Frost Giant Wars, and there's virtually nothing that predates that in the Archives or anywhere else. And, equally im-portant, who cares?

Any other race we could trace back for over a million years by time-diving and looking, recording what the Guards who went there saw. Maybe that doesn't follow, but I thought it did.

Building the retreat wouldn't be as difficult as it sounded. Queryan houses and quarters are generally small. It follows. We could dive for any luxury item we wanted from anywhere in time and space we could reach. But nothing big could be carried over the timepaths.

Post-Guard Query had a nonexistent industrial base, with the few public buildings and all housing built by hand. The better houses resist the elements well because the duplicators allow anyone to use the best materials for anything but planks and timbers and because any com-petent diver can partly warp the exterior edge of materials slightly out-of-time-phase. Only the most violent thunderstorms or electrical swirls cover more than the now.

All of this meant that I could build a small retreat, I thought, and one where my privacy would have to be respected. We all have been lovers of privacy, except for the inquisitive souls in the Guard, and most times they've been kept in line—most times. I wanted to make sure of the rest of the times.

Still, we're also a snoopy people—we clearly like looking in on other cultures and people.

Curiosity and privacy . . . an odd combination, perhaps. But perhaps not. A curious cat walks in shadows all the same.

Construction wasn't what I'd expected. My father had built his own home, and if he had, I knew I could. But I might not have been so eager, not if I'd known literally the years it would take.

First, I had to borrow a power projector to deepen the ledge. That meant holding a split slide in the middle of the sky with the wind whipping around me, trying to focus a projector weighing half what I did, wondering when the nearest night eagle was ready to start a dive at me.

I had to clear the area above the ledge of rocks that might decide to fall on me or on the structure. In addition, I fused the sheer walls around the site smooth enough to prevent any climbing into my retreat. I planned to mesh the walls exactly with the cliff edges on the sides, the edges of the ledge at the base, and decided to top it off with a smooth slanted roof that melded with the cliff.

After the ledge work alone I was drained. I lost count of the evenings

I carted that projector undertime and balanced in mid-canyon.

Just the beginning, that was.

Each foundation had to be cut precisely, and even with the mech section of Maintenance at my disposal, figuring out the proper pattern took I don't know how many days. I managed to work it down to three kinds of stones, and once I had them, I could duplicate as many as I wanted. But I still had to transport each one by hand on a time-slide out to the site of my aerie. Aerie, that was what I decided to call it, perched as it was over a sheer drop from the needle peaks to the canyons deep below, nestled over the lightning storms that blasted the lower levels of the deep valleys.

Then there was mortar. That meant carrying water and using a trowel. I discovered that there is a technique to laying stone, and I didn't have it. Not for a while. Sometimes I tore out whole rows.

During the days, I worked at trying to increase the ability of Maintenance to do more repairs. While it was too early to draft him, I had my eye on a second-year trainee named Brendan, who had a sense for mechanics. In the interim, I struggled with the overflowing repair bin, and with Narcissus, who had the unnerving habit of polishing metal to look at his reflection, rather than to clean it in order to repair it. He also tended to ignore work on the plastic or composite-covered items, honing in on the shiny stuff.

Both Maintenance and the Aerie struggled along.

After I finished laying the stonework and warping each stone out-of-time-phase, I began to lug the beams in. I carted the timber all the way from Terra, piece by piece.

I wasn't building a castle on the heights. The Aerie was scarcely close to that—just two levels, three rooms, plus a kitchen and a hygienarium. The power supplies were the easiest part, and I was finally glad for the pocket fusion generator I'd lugged back from Sinopol, because it was a hell of a lot easier to break down, duplicate, and assemble than the bigger Murian fusactors. The kitchen and hygienarium were simple, but I ended up adding some extras to take care of waste disposal, rather than letting it run down the cliffside, and that was another bunch of days hanging in midair digging out another cave underneath the ledge and struggling with installing the equipment. Then I had to lay more stones.

The structure was the hardest part, especially warping each stone, each beam, out of time.

It all was worth it. On the evening when I moved in the last of the furnishings, stood on the glowstone flooring, and watched the sunset below, I swallowed hard to push down the lump in my throat.

I had built something lasting, something of beauty, and with my own hands. My own hands . . . that was important.

XVII

MAINTENANCE COULD BE a challenge, as well as a pain in the neck. Once in a while, I fixed something that even Baldur wasn't sure could be put back together.

The Guard attitude toward machinery made it difficult. Frey and his people were the worst. They used and abused equipment until it broke, pounded on it to see if it were truly broken, threw it in a storeroom or an unused corner until it was needed again, and then and only then carted it down to Maintenance for repairs when they realized they couldn't just duplicate it. They even failed to understand that to duplicate a larger piece of equipment requires breaking it down and replacing the defective part—and that you have to find the defective piece.

The first few times I got long-broken equipment with demands for immediate repairs, I made the repairs without comment. The next dozen times, I grumbled, suggested that Frey send equipment when it broke, rather than waiting. The gear went back to Domestic Affairs with notes making the same point.

One fine winter morning, after a frost, when the air was clear and I had a breathing spell, I surveyed the Hall and watched Narcissus over-polish the sides of a small ethylene-powered auxiliary generator. He still polished too much, although he had actually finished training nearly a year earlier and been promoted to full Guard status.

Hopefully, I'd get less spit and polish and more repairs out of Brendan when he completed training. I already had my eyes on some other trainees to track into Maintenance.

In the meantime, I was struggling along under the repair burden and not diving nearly as much as I would have liked. I wondered how Glammis had held it all together—except I knew. She'd essentially given up diving, and I wasn't about to do that.

As I was speculating about the future, Ferrin arrived with a set of battered Locator portapacks. The hair on the back of my neck rose, but I ignored it for the moment.

Ferrin never carried gear down from Domestic Affairs. It was always some trainee.

I smiled.

"Oh, skilled god of forge and iron, of the fire and the energies that flow . . ." began Ferrin lightly.

"Skip the high-flown rhetoric. What's the dirty work?"

"Frey wants these immediately. No more than one hundred units. He needs to track down a miscreant, and he's headed foretime out-line— beyond the finer capabilities of the base system."

I nodded. "Who's the miscreant?" I really didn't care, but I wondered at all the haste.

"Remember that Ayren character? Some woman bushwhacked Hightel and Doradosi as they were bringing him back from Hell for his chronolobotomy and rehab."

Ayren? Ayren? It took a moment before the name registered. The woman had to be the one who had collapsed at Bly's hearing.

"Ferrin . . . how long have these been lying around your storeroom and not functioning?" I picked up one sensor and blew a cloud of dust from it.

"Couple of years, probably."

I slid off the stool, leaving the Locator packs on the bench, and marched across the Maintenance Hall. Baldur was in. I'd seen him earlier.

He looked up with mild surprise as I put a clenched fist down on his table hard enough to disarrange the papers, even to rattle the styli in their upright case.

"I've had it! Had it! This is the tenth time in less than a year that Frey's done this. I've recommended, suggested, begged, pleaded . . . everything. Let him do his own repairs."

"He doesn't know how," Baldur said calmly, as if he were used to Guards banging his workbench every day. "Glammis had the same problem, you know. I'm assuming you're referring to the fact that Frey doesn't ask for anything to be repaired until after it's needed?"

"Of course!"

"Is it worth getting that upset over?"

I didn't understand. Baldur, of all Guards, should understand. He was the one who taught me the value of maintenance, of care.

"Yes. It is!"

Baldur raised his eyebrows.

"Are you unwilling to make the repairs?" cut in a new voice, and I knew it was Heimdall's from the cold tone of menace. What I didn't know was why he was down in Maintenance, unless Frey had told him.

"No, honored Counselor," I replied, turning to face him and bringing my voice under control, "but I do feel that a disciplinary action should be brought against Supervisor Frey for the continued misuse of Guard resources and his failure to use properly the tools with which he is entrusted."

I didn't know how I'd managed to pull that one out, but it might work, I figured, even though my mouth was running ahead of my brain.

Ferrin's mouth dropped open. Heimdall was silent. Baldur smiled a smile so faint it wasn't.

"We could take this up informally with one of the Tribunes," said Baldur. It wasn't a suggestion.

Heimdall, who had appeared ready to speak, closed his mouth.

The four of us marched up to the two ramps from Maintenance to the Tribunes' private Halls.

Eranas invited us into a sitting chamber and summoned Frey.

"I should be supervising the hunt for an escaped miscreant, but I am waiting for equipment which should be repaired and is not, and now I find myself summoned here."

"Perhaps Loki should summarize the charge," commented Baldur.

I went through the whole thing, how year after year Frey never took care of anything, how I'd recommended, sent notes, pleaded, and how the situation never changed.

"So you refused to repair the Locator equipment?" cut in Eranas.

"No, honored Tribune. I refused to repair it until note was taken by the Tribunes that this kind of procedure not only is detrimental to Maintenance but inhibits the timely performance by Domestic Affairs. If I had started immediately on the damaged equipment, it would not be ready now. And the Guard Ferrin informed me that the defective Locator packs have been damaged for years. Yet they were never turned in to Maintenance for repairs."

"I see your point," said Eranas dryly, "but we really don't have time to play around with this. Guard Loki, you will, of course, attend to repairs immediately."

He turned to Frey.

"Senior Guard Frey, you will consider yourself reprimanded, and after the conclusion of your search, you will inventory all equipment within the coming season to assure its function. You will eliminate the unnecessary equipment and turn all necessary but nonfunctional gear over to Maintenance for repairs. Loki will endeavor to make or arrange for those repairs or replacements as soon as possible. Baldur will oversee the Maintenance aspect, and I will personally oversee Domestic Affairs."

Frey was white, absolutely white, whether from rage or fear, I wasn't certain. I knew he'd hear about it from Freyda as well.

Heimdall hadn't said anything, just had his head cocked at a calculating angle.

Me—this time I could read between the lines as well as anyone. If I'd had repairs to do before, they were going to be as nothing compared to what would be landing in my incoming bin.

Repairing the Locator packs wasn't all that difficult, took maybe fifty units after I got back to my spaces. I sent Narcissus across the Square to Domestic Affairs with them, and, to be fair to him, I carried two waste bins out to the dump on Vulcan. I didn't even mind the bitter smell or the hot wind ripping around me. It was a lot more pleasant than personally delivering the packs would have been.

I wished that had been the end of it, but what made Frey's attitude toward me even colder was that Ayren escaped, didn't register on the Locator screens anywhere, as if he'd vanished from the galaxy. Orpheus had been the last time a miscreant had vanished, and that had been millennia ago.

Then everyone raised the question about doing chronolobotomies before Hell, conveniently forgetting that the operation just about makes it impossible not only for someone to leave the now or Query but also for almost anyone else to carry them, because the undertime drag is so great.

Frey was called on the Tribunes' glowstones for the whole business, and Eranas made the point publicly that it might not have happened if Frey had taken better care of his equipment.

Needless to say, outside of the coldly necessary, Frey wasn't speaking to me, and for some reason neither was Heimdall. That might have been because he and Frey were friends. Frey was a disciple of sorts of Heimdall's, and like Heimdall, felt that Guard discipline should be stronger, that a more authoritative leadership was required, and that the routine dirty work ought to be done by non-Guard Queryans.

The way I translated that, they wanted to run the Guard and conscript a bunch of young citizens to be their private slave corps. In the back of my mind, I wondered if that weren't exactly how the Guard started.

Unfortunately, there isn't any real history. Literally everything on Query was blasted or frozen in the Frost Giant Wars. What little history we have beyond that point is mostly records of dives and discoveries, because the Guard had to be functional.

I asked Baldur about it once, because we have computers and data lattices to store more information than we'd ever need, and he answered with a simple question. "Who had time to put it on the computers when people could still remember it?"

Given the inability of the average Queryan to do much more than request duplicate equipment from Domestic Affairs, it made a sad sort of sense, and even explained why Heimdall could even rationalize such a scheme.

Eranas and Kranos turned a white eye on Heimdall's pretensions, I understood, but I had my own suspicions about Freyda, although she never treated me other than kindly.

After the turn of the next year, Baldur spoke to the Tribunes, and Brendan was assigned to Maintenance. That was before Frey had gotten his equipment housecleaning under way, and for a time I thought I might be able to keep ahead of the flow of busted junk flowing down from Domestic Affairs.

But the word spread, and I started seeing long-broken equipment coming in from odd places like the Archives and Weather Observation. Nobody else wanted to end up like Frey.

The hours I spent got longer and longer, and the sleep became less and less.

I shouldn't have tried to undo centuries' worth of neglect in less than a year, but where would I have put all the junk? Besides, Eranas kept dropping in to check on me.

Usually, I staggered into the Tower bright and early, right after dawn, helped by living where the sun rose earlier, but the morning came when I slept late. Not that I had slept well, tossing and turning on the Dire fur pallet which was warmed by the yielding glowstone floor of the Aerie, but the shadows of the canyons below were already shrinking into black traceries when the midmorning sun hit me full in the face.

Even with the continuing lack of sleep, I had been an early riser, but that night or morning my dreams had been filled with visions of crimson skies and screaming night eagles tearing at my guts.

I ran through a quick flame shower, threw myself into a black jumpsuit, grabbed my equipment harness, and slid to the Tower. I broke out as close to the South Portal as a late Guard dared and tried to slink down the ramp to Maintenance without attracting much notice. I should have dropped tight into my spaces and broken decorum, but I didn't.

Most mornings I could have overslept my own time limit by fifty units and still arrived before I needed to, but I'd overslept by more than a hundred. I was halfway down the ramp when I met Heimdall coming up.

"Loki's here at last! Good day, night owl, or is it night eagle, hidden away in your secret perch?"

I bit my tongue and wished I'd never let slip the existence of the Aerie, but Heimdall had overheard my explanation of needing some equipment when I was asked by Baldur.

"Good morning, honored Counselor."

Heimdall wasn't through, and blocked my path on the ramp. "Being in charge of repairs in Maintenance, taking advanced instruction, living up to your responsibilities aren't too important—is that it?"

I kept my mouth shut. Heimdall was out to get me. I wondered how long he'd been waiting.

"Rather go out and fly with the angels of Heaven IV than stay in and do the dirty work? Rather blame others when your own lateness could be the cause? Is that it?"

The glint in his eye told me he knew it was unfair and was daring me to refute it. Damned if I would.

Someone was heading down the ramp behind me, but Heimdall didn't look up. "Lateness shows no respect for the Guard and its traditions, and you show little enough, Loki."

"Enough," cut in Freyda.

"Don't take the youngster's case, Freyda," boomed Odin Thor. "He may have all the talent in the universe, but he needs discipline."

By this time, Baldur had shown up as well.

Heimdall had succeeded admirably in drawing a scene to highlight my lateness, and Hell only knew what he would come up with the next time I committed a minor transgression.

Baldur stared at Odin Thor, who lowered his eyes and mumbled, "Not like the old days at all. Any youngster these times thinks he's got the talent to be a god. No . . . not like the old days at all."

"Loki . . ." spoke up Heimdall, and his tone was all business, no malice, which set me further on edge.

I nodded.

He handed me a wrist gauntlet.

"The tracking functions are off. We've replaced what we can, and it still doesn't function. Nicodemus can't figure it out either. Obviously, simple replacements aren't the answer. It needs to be fixed."

I took it.

"We need it today, before you leave."

Set up, I thought, and no way out. Heimdall had provided the scene, pointed out that he had made an extraordinary effort, and given a rationale why no one else could fix it. I thought about strangling him on the spot in front of witnesses, but let it pass.

"Now, I certainly hope you'll find the time to do it right," was his parting shot, "since you've made such an issue about the importance of directional and Locator equipment."

Dumb statement by Heimdall. He couldn't find his way out of his quarters without an electronic arsenal and five different directional fixes. But because I was late, I'd have to shove everything else aside to fix what was obviously a problem gauntlet, which meant more time. And

I'd end up working even later for days or falling further behind with Eranas always looking over my shoulder.

I could have protested again, but I didn't think either Baldur or Eranas would have stood for it—especially not when I'd been late. Thinking about the fiendish nature of Heimdall's little gambit really burned me. How many others did he have waiting? As soon as I got caught up, would there be something else? I could bet on it.

Baldur had already left. Freyda didn't even smile as she passed. Odin Thor had forgotten what he'd been saying and went back up the ramp with a blank expression on his face. Heimdall turned and left without a word.

I carted the gauntlet to Maintenance and dumped it on my work-bench, although the continually cleaned and sterilized surface no more resembled a conventional bench than I did Odin Thor.

Suppressing a groan as I took in the overflowing repair bin, I called up the gauntlet specs on my console. On the off chance the malfunction might be simple, I placed the wristband in the diagnostic center, punched the stud, and waited.

"No circuit malfunction," the console informed me in its precise flowing script.

That figured. The gauntlet didn't work and didn't seem to have anything wrong with it. Was there anything really wrong?

I scanned the area around me. No one else was near. Ducking behind one of the old behemoths that bordered my space, I slipped on the gauntlet and dived backtime. I couldn't break out, but I could do a partial test anyway. After what was perhaps a quarter million back, I reversed and forced myself foretime until I felt shrouded in the bright blue of high speed. The idea was to see if diving speed had any impact.

When I broke out from right where I'd left, the face of the indicator was black. No one was around, not that there should have been with a virtually instantaneous dive and return.

Back at my bench, I tossed the gauntlet into the diagnostic center, black indicator and all. I punched the stud and was greeted by a fizzling sound and totally dead diagnostic center, followed by heat and the smell of burned and fused electronics.

Right there I was ready to stomp upstairs and throttle Heimdall. I didn't need to rebuild a diagnostic center at the moment. I swallowed and tried to think.

Item: The gauntlet hadn't done anything to the center before
  my dive.

Item: The dive had created enough power to overload the center,
    but not burn me.

As it dawned on me, I looked down. Down at the insulation laid over
the out-of-time-phase flooring.

Of course, I wouldn't get burned—not in Maintenance. I shivered.
The innocent-looking gauntlet didn't seem so innocent any more.

First, I fixed the diagnostic center. That took a good fifty units, even
with massive black-boxing, and more waste to cart off to Vulcan.

Next came a data search on the console, about insulation, time energy,
and the like. I finally located an obscure section buried under the other
citations which mentioned the need to check the insulation built into
the gauntlets and other equipment designed to "catch" temporal energy.
Put into the data banks centuries before by a Guard named Baldur. I
didn't understand the theory, but the diagrams were helpful, and after
studying them and rereading the explanation, the functions of some of
the strange blocks of material in the gauntlets became clearer.

With all that in mind, I began to break down the remnants of the
gauntlet step by step. It was close to mid-afternoon before I found what
I knew had to be there.

Someone had removed the power source insulators in a narrow line
on one side and wired a microfilament antenna across the underside of
the gauntlet. If I'd broken out anywhere outside of the insulated confines
of the Maintenance Hall, I'd have been lucky to escape with as little as
severe burns around the arms and wrists.

Since Heimdall didn't know the extent of my diving ability, the
gauntlet had to have been a damned setup. Without a timedive, the
problem couldn't be detected, and since no one had been burned before
I got the equipment, it wasn't a real problem, but a phony one foisted
off on me.

The more I thought about it, the madder I got. Heimdall wasn't just
out to bury me under a pile of work. He was out for blood, and, if that
was what he wanted, that was what he was going to get.

First, I fixed the gauntlet, after carefully recording how it had been
altered. Then I refixed it, with his microfilament antenna keyed to a
false boss. Anyone besides me who wore the gauntlet and didn't set the
boss correctly, would get the treatment that had been scheduled for me.
After a moment, I took out the boss and worked in a sort of timer, so
that the antenna didn't cut in until the second dive. If Heimdall went
somewhere and didn't make it back . . . Besides, I wanted the bastard
to get burned in front of witnesses.

Late afternoon arrived before I completed my microengineering, and

I was proud of it. Heimdall would still be waiting in Assignments. The devious Counselor must have been confident to set it up, must have figured that he had me either way.

Either I couldn't fix it and got fried on a test dive, or if I did, and complained, he'd merely claim it was a test of my abilities—and come up with something even more devious that I might not catch. No . . . I had to send a message that put a stop to the whole thing.

Heimdall was at his desk, leaning back in his high padded stool.

"Heimdall," I said respectfully, knowing that the failure to use his title would infuriate him, "I think I've got it fixed."

"Just 'think'?" he snapped. "You should know!"

"I've rechecked and replaced the calibration, which was defective. I've replaced the power cell, which was sending an uneven flow to the instrumentation, and replaced the missing insulation."

"Are you sure it's fixed?"

"As sure as I can be without a test, but time was running short."

"Why didn't you test it?"

"It's not mine, and I'd be reluctant to test equipment that's not my own."

"Well," drawled the master of the sarcastic, "you don't think I'd try it without a test, on just your say-so, would I?"

"No. But would you trust it if I just said I'd tested it?"

Heimdall frowned. "I'll tell you what. Let's go over to the Travel Hall. You test it, and if it seems all right, I'll take it."

Heimdall could be so smooth.

I trooped after him, down the ramp, and out to the Tower wing, keeping up with him, even though he was a bit taller and certainly more than a bit wider, stocky as I am.

I slipped on the gauntlet, adjusting it and making sure the false boss was in the correct position.

The dive was uneventful. I broke out on backtime Almaraden to pick a bouquet for the all-seeing schemer, but Heimdall laid the flowers aside when I presented them to him.

"You didn't notice anything unusual about the gauntlet when you fixed it?" he asked as I handed it to him. I'd already twisted the boss to its loaded position.

Strangely enough, Frey arrived at the Travel Hall about that time.

Circumstance, my foot. Frey had hot-slid over to pick up my pieces.

Heimdall stood there with the gauntlet, and I decided he needed a push. Besides, with Frey standing there, Heimdall just might hand the gauntlet to him and let Frey take any fall I had cooked up.

"Heimdall," I began, trying to irk him further with the lack of formality, "it was simple to do. Tedious but simple. The dials were out of calibration. In addition, some fool had left some stray filaments running along the inside of the gauntlet. These caused some problems. I cleaned up the loose ends, checked the insulation, and made the recalibrations. You want to take it back to the shop and check my work, fine. I did what you asked for, the way you asked for, in the time you asked for it, and it works fine.

"I know you have better things to do than stand and check over the quality of my workmanship, and your talents are better suited for that. So, if you've made your point about the need for me to be careful and timely, just take the gauntlet. I understand fully that it has probably been a while since you did test dives . . ."

At that point, Sammis and Wryan showed up. Wryan grinned at the last of my remarks. "Would you like me to test it?" she asked.

Heimdall glared at her and yanked on the gauntlet. He disappeared, but reappeared within less than a unit at the far end of the Travel Hall. As he broke out, the gauntlet exploded off his wrist, and blood and fire spewed all over everything.

"Loki!" he screamed before he collapsed.

I slid to the end of the room, catching his still form before he even hit the floor, and made a second undertime slide straight to the Infirmary. Had to have been less than two units between Heimdall's return to the Travel Hall and the instant Hycretis started transfusions with Heimdall's shattered wrist and broiled arm under the tissue regenerator.

About that time, the floor rose up and struck me down.

When I woke I was in the cell block under the Tower. Lovely place it was, with a single bright and recessed light in the ceiling, solid-glowstone bunk without furs, a barred door, and a handy-dandy automatic restrainer field to scramble my thoughts and keep me in. The all-too-solid walls were slightly out-of-time-phase, and the whole cubicle had barely enough space for four steps in any direction. There was a stone necessity consisting of a square hole and two taps above it. Very efficient.

When I'd seen Ayren Bly years back, I hadn't anticipated being on his side of the bars, and it seemed as though his cell had been more comfortable than mine, but that might have been a matter of perspective.

What was done was done. I'd been about as subtle as a sledgehammer in trying to get back at Heimdall. That might have been a mistake, but I still wasn't sure that anything less subtle would have worked.

With no one around and nothing better to do, I began trying to concentrate hard enough to negate the scrambling effect of the restraining fields. Because they were automatic and machinery, it didn't seem to take too long before I could shunt the effect aside and slide into the corridor outside the cell. I heard footsteps and slipped back into my cell.

I got back where I was supposed to be just in time. Freyda, Odin Thor, Eranas, and two hefty Guards I didn't know arrived to march me up to the Hall of Justice.

For the time being, I decided to cooperate and let them lead me along.

Since it was a Guard affair, the proceedings weren't public. My father would have had some quiet comment about the dangers of power, except with his disappearance, I had no way to find him.

Freyda, Kranos, and Eranas, as Tribunes, sat up on the dais facing the Hall. I was placed at one side in the red-railed stone box reserved for the nasty malefactors. Frey was seated across from me behind the silver podium reserved for the prosecutor on behalf of the good people of Query, who would never hear a word of what happened.

Although the Hall could seat thousands, only a few Guards sat in the front rows, and the slow-glass was undamped enough just to light the front of the soaring area. Baldur sat in the second row, but he wasn't looking at me.

"This is an informal Guard procedure," announced Eranas in his raspy voice.

Frey bowed and scraped, and my two Guards yanked me to my feet so that I could bow and scrape. And I bowed and scraped.

"Counsel for the Guard requests disciplinary procedures for Guard Loki."

I was on my own. Under disciplinary procedures, I didn't rate counsel, not that it would have mattered. The procedures were greased to zap me.

"Senior Guard Loki," I began, automatically promoting myself for no good reason except I was angry, "declares his innocence by reason of extreme provocation and fear of grave physical and bodily harm planned by Counselor Heimdall."

Odin Thor, sitting in the front row, snorted loudly and looked at Eranas; Eranas nodded at Frey.

Frey climbed back to his feet, for once without the light saber, and made it very simple, and he was good at being simple.

Loki was a Guard. Loki was responsible for important repairs. Instead, one Loki had booby-trapped a gauntlet which had harmed a Counselor seriously. Guards did not attack Counselors directly or indirectly.

Frey used the big wall screen sparingly and basically to display shots of Heimdall collapsing in a shower of fire and living blood, followed by another series of the poor assaulted Counselor lying in the Infirmary surrounded with all types of medical-support equipment.

As Frey continued, I realized the dope had been used. He honestly didn't know, I could sense, that the gauntlet had been double-trapped for me. Only Heimdall knew, and he wouldn't be saying anything.

That meant I had a chance because I'd recorded my original findings about the way the gauntlet had been tampered with.

Finally, it was my turn.

"Tribunes, my defense is simple. First, Heimdall intended that what happened to him should happen to me. Second, he waited for perhaps seasons for an excuse to administer such an assault disguised as routine maintenance. Third, when my repairs were completed, he knew there was a chance I would still be hurt, and he forced me to test the gauntlet . . ."

"Can you prove any of this?" rasped Eranas.

"Yes, Tribune. First, I carefully recorded the internal structures I found in the gauntlet I received from Heimdall, and the records from my diagnostic center will show that the gauntlet was altered to focus time energy on the wearer. You might also note that much of the equipment is new. That was because the energies built into the gauntlet destroyed half the original equipment before I discovered Heimdall's efforts. I suggest you examine both before they become unavailable."

I took a breath and glanced at Frey and Freyda. I liked the lady, but blood is often hotter than fire.

Eranas might have been thinking about stepping down, but he was nobody's fool—and a better diver than I realized. He disappeared from the dais, presumably sliding straight to the mech shop.

Kranos sat there and frowned.

"We wait," noted Freyda. She looked at her son.

I thought she had been unaware of the trickery and was more than a little angry that Frey had been linked to such a blatant scheme.

Eranas was back in place at the center of the Tribunes in a handful of units. He didn't even ask for more explanation.

"Loki, you are a damned fool, a double-damned fool, to go off on your own. Being a Guard has responsibilities—serious ones. Yes, too often you young ones joke about being gods, but what we do can create or destroy more than many gods of many people. There is no room in the Guard for half-cocked impulses.

"Heimdall had no business pulling a stunt like this either, and he may have gotten what he deserved, but you cannot appoint yourself High Tribune and play god. You cannot slide around trying to blow up scheming supervisors. Without order, the Guard has nothing, and if your example were followed, there would be no order—"

"But—" I protested. I wanted to say that no one at all was watching Heimdall.

"But nothing," rasped Eranas. "Heimdall will be in the Infirmary for five more days, and then he will spend five days on Hell. You will spend all ten days on Hell."

He flipped the black wand out of its holder and jabbed it at me to emphasize his point. Neither Kranos nor Freyda had said a word.

I started to my feet to protest, but didn't get very far. It felt like the entire Hall of Justice hit me in the face.

I came to in Hell, or rather, on it.

The sky is a scarlet black so blood-deep it curdles your soul. The ground is all sand and rock, and little scavenger rats scurry out from under the rocks to bite with needle teeth anything that is there to bite— insects, grubs, legs, toes, fingers, what have you.

I couldn't see much of that, chained as I was with rock links to a large black chunk of mountainside. The links are the same stone as the mountain, although the clamps around the stone are steel—they thought of everything. Unlike them, I could barely think, because the Guard hadn't taken any chances. This time, unlike the period in the cell block, someone had set up an entire bank of restrainer fields and focused them all on me.

I wasn't thinking the same thoughts twice, but four or five times, and in fragments.

The restrainer fields were supposed to prevent enough coherent thought to keep me from time-diving off the planet of the damned, and the regenerator gadgetry was supposed to keep me in mostly one piece and suffering, but the water tube in the mask that covered most of my face didn't function. With all that, I still could have dived clear, but clamped as I was to the black stone with the matching links, the whole mountain was one piece, and I couldn't carry it all with me.

Every so often—I didn't keep track—a large night eagle would come screaming out of the scarlet night that was day and rip a hunk out of me. I didn't see much, not with the face mask protector, the partial helmet, throat guard, and extended breastplate.

Not mercy, but practicality. The regeneration gear can't keep a body together if the eagles get the eyes, head, throat, or some large mess of guts.

Strapped there to suffer as these lovely beasts and birds rip away, most victims have a tendency to scream. I did—until I was too hoarse to continue. Then I whimpered.

Who in Hell wants to be proud and silent while your extremities are being tortured?

The rats, scorpions, eagles, give their dinner guests periodic rests. Not because they're merciful, but because the restrainer fields scramble their pea brains as well as the victim's.

Gravel-throated, sandy-whisper-voiced, unable to move, unable to scream, unable to dive, I built a cold fire within me, focused on the absolute injustice of Guard justice, and between the lapses of consciousness, between the stabs of pain as a scavenger rat nipped off a toe, snipped through an Achilles tendon, I concentrated on my future, my destiny . . .

There was the course of diligence, errand boy to barbarians, the path of out-and-out resistance, and the path of desertion. But was there another course?

If I had to strike, strike I would not until I wrenched bloody suns from their orbits . . . by god, by Hell, by the eagles of the night that screamed and ripped, and ripped and screamed . . . and my screams from a dry throat, my whimpers from a savaged body, merged with theirs and the blackness within that drowned me . . .

XVIII

I WOKE UP in the Infirmary, alone, cellular regeneration equipment attached to both arms and legs and with heavy wrapping around my too-tender midsection. My fingers and toes burned, like they were being roasted.

Glowstones and slow-glass, white panels and sunlight, all came out gray in my sight.

I slipped back into hot sleep, dreamed.

A man in black, the black singlesuit of the Guards, and a man in red stood on mountaintops across a cloud-filled chasm from each other. Gray clouds framed the scene; no sunlight intruded.

The black man threw thunderbolt after thunderbolt at the red man, who never responded, never ducked, accepted each blast without moving, without effect.

With each cast, the man in black laughed. Each laugh infused the clouds beneath his feet with a darkness, a growing ugliness. The clouds of darkness began to climb from the depths below, to tug at the feet of the man in red, who stood, as if asleep, untouched, unmoving. But his eyes were open, unseeing.

With a laugh that echoed through the gray skies, that shook the clouds until they trembled, the black figure leaned forward and released a last thunderbolt, terrible in its power, a yellow sword that shone with blackness, mightier than all that had come before.

The sound of the laugh reached the man in red, and his eyes filled with knowledge, and, as they filled with understanding, that last thunderbolt struck his shoulder, and he staggered, dropping to his knee, swaying on the mountain tip. And as he swayed, the black clouds clutched at his arm . . .

Someone touched my shoulder, and I woke.

Loragerd was sitting in the stool next to the high bed.

I tried to croak something.

"Not yet," she said softly, laying her hand on my forehead.

There was plenty I wanted to know. I knew, just knew, I hadn't spent any ten days on Hell, that no Guard, especially me, should have lost it that quickly.

I couldn't say much. Loragerd filled me in, sensing the well of questions.

Simple enough. The Guards who had dragged me off to Hell had been Heimdall's tools and hadn't been especially careful about the breastplates or throat guards, or the water tube, or the regenerator fields.

Eranas, crafty old schemer, had figured as much. He, Kranos, and Freyda had waited until the damage to me became apparent, until I had suffered about as much as I could take, recorded the scenario on holo, and rescued me before I joined the ranks of the departed.

Evidence in hand, they'd held another Guard hearing, discharged the Guards involved, one of whom was my ferret-faced acquaintance of years past, gave them a dose of Hell, and subjected them to that surgical procedure that ensured they would never dive again.

Underneath my cocoon of bandages, I shivered.

The Tribunes had let me go to the point of death, destroyed the lives of the Guards who had blindly followed Heimdall, and never let it go beyond the Guard. But the word would filter around. People could just disappear.

I drifted back into sleep, exhausted, sweating, with Loragerd stroking my forehead.

Another four days drifted by before Hycretis let me out of the Infirmary. Baldur insisted I take another four before showing up in Maintenance. Loragerd and I spent the last day on the beaches beyond Southpoint.

Back in Maintenance, I found the backlog wasn't bad.

"That's because Baldur came over every night and whipped of a bunch of repairs," Brendan explained.

I wondered about that. I couldn't ever recall seeing Baldur at night, and yet he often looked tired in the morning. He didn't have a special someone, and he never talked about his life outside the Guard.

In my absence, despite Baldur's help, Brendan and Narcissus had been in a dive-or-die situation. Narcissus had done neither, just plodded along, polishing away.

Brendan had dived, right into the business end of Maintenance, and learned plenty more on his own, though he was still strangely lacking confidence in his abilities.

I settled back into my work space, back into the routine.

Somehow, the backlog didn't seem quite so impressive, quite so over-whelming, not that I took it at all for granted or didn't keep whittling it down—or looking for new trainees who even understood the word "mechanical." Unfortunately, most of them made Narcissus look like a brilliant engineer.

I shrugged, so to speak, and waited. A new perspective, I guessed.

Some scars heal quickly; some do not.

For days and days after I returned, I was sore, especially by the end of the day, but with daily sessions under the regenerator the exterior scars from Hell faded.

But the memory of Heimdall asking me to fix that trapped gauntlet, and of the scarlet skies and black rocks of Hell, was as vivid as when the events had exploded upon me.

Heimdall had set me up. If I'd done as I'd been told and goofed, I would have been dead—or one badly injured Guard. If I'd fixed it prop-erly, played it straight, then Heimdall would have delivered the message that he was the one in charge—even that he could dispatch me at any time.

Except that my stubbornness and Eranas' craftiness had changed the equation. By giving an even greater punishment to Heimdall's tools, Eranas and the Tribunes had tried to put the conflict on a personal basis between the two of us. The message had to be clear—get involved with Heimdall or Loki and you'll end up worse than dead.

I didn't like it. In fact, the more I reflected, the angrier I got. Heim-dall had gotten a slap on the wrist for plotting to commit murder, and the only one who'd stood up to him they'd almost let die on Hell.

That meant that I'd face another confrontation with Heimdall, and another, and I intended to be ready in more ways than one.

I set myself the goal of mastering every piece of equipment in the entire Maintenance Hall—even the old stuff dating back to the Twi-light/Frost Giant Wars. That would be one step.

The second step would be more difficult, but I put some stock in the dream Loragerd had interrupted. I identified with the man in red. I needed to wake up, but that meant becoming vulnerable, and if I did, I needed to learn my own full capabilities.

Besides spending more time badgering Baldur, I petitioned Sammis to tutor me in everything he knew about hand-to-hand, weaponry, and that vague field he called "individual resources." Not only had he done the attitude adjustment course, but he had also led more advanced training in our final year of study.

Sammis had been around a while, so long that no one remembered when he hadn't been there. He also didn't have a Locator tag code—or not one on record—and the only codes that weren't on record were those of Counselors and Tribunes. Had he been a Counselor centuries before? I wondered. It was certainly possible. With him, there was more than met the eye.

The basic hand-to-hand instruction was where I had discovered that I could half time-slide and speed my movements while staying in the now. Sammis could not only do that, but detect and anticipate that skill, I had discovered, much to my chagrin. I had tried to catch him with a partial slide, and he'd caught me, flipped me on my shoulders, and delivered a solid thwack to my rear as I'd gone down.

"First," he had lectured me, "you learn how to fight. Then you combine it with undertime abilities. Right now, a really good hand-to-hand fighter could beat you without too much difficulty, no matter how you jumped through time."

I hadn't believed him, and it showed on my face. As a trainee, particularly after that attitude adjustment test, I'd been pretty cocky.

Sammis challenged me. "Go ahead. I'll stay put. Go on."

I had been upset at being put down in front of Ferrin and Patrice, perhaps because they'd done so well with the classroom stuff. I hadn't thought, just charged Sammis, sliding at the last instant and figuring to come out behind him.

Instead of surprising him, my chin had arrived on his open palm. I could have ended up with a snapped neck. From that point on, I had listened to what he wanted.

Now, with Heimdall waiting in the shadows to do me in if I gave him half a chance, I needed more than basics or the smattering of better techniques. I wanted everything Sammis could give me.

I decided to do it formally. I went to Baldur and asked his permission to spend part of each day training with Sammis to improve my skills.

"That's no problem. I'll enter it on your training record in the proper doublescript," Baldur said, almost kindly.

I was confused.

"Loki, you're feeling that you've neglected something, and that you need more skills. Your work here is superb, and I think the Guard would benefit from your efforts to broaden your capabilities. Let's leave it at that."

Baldur must have gotten to Sammis before I did, because Sammis said "Of course" . . . with a catch. The catch was that he and Wryan worked as a team, and that as a team they would train me.

"Besides, it would take two or more to really force you to upgrade your skills," Sammis noted.

Always the veiled hints, the messages within messages . . . I had never thought how many times this sort of information was passed in the Guard.

Working with Sammis and Wryan, even for just a hundred units a day, was more pleasure than toil. Each of them sensed what the other was about to do and reacted. According to the rumors, they'd always been together. No one could remember them not teaming.

One night at Hera's, Verdis told me that they predated Odin Thor in the Guard. I hadn't thought that much about it, didn't have a chance to draw out Verdis because of the noise, and didn't get back to it because for a while our schedules just didn't coincide. At the time, Ferrin was delivering a formal oration in high Weindrian about the subject of uncovered ankles, which had most of the juniors in stitches. It was funny, but not that funny.

Verdis, Tyron, and Loragerd were all enjoying it when I left.

The next afternoon I broached the subject to my tutors. "Odin Thor has been hanging around the Tower for centuries. When did he last take a diving mission?"

Wryan screwed her elvish features into a wry gesture. Sammis stroked his chin and looked at the equipment room floor. Finally, he answered. "I couldn't say exactly, but I think the follow-up work to the Frost Giants. He had some problems then."

Wryan gave a tiny headshake, but my jaw dropped open. Two million years back. How could anyone retain sanity over two million years even with memory therapy and the regenerator?

"How . . . his mind . . . I mean . . ." I stammered.

"Not that bad," commented Wryan. "Even when he started he never had much of one."

Sammis glared over at his partner. I wasn't certain if the glare were real or fake.

I faced Sammis. "You're older than Odin Thor."

"No." He grinned. "But she is."

I looked at Wryan. Never would I have guessed it. With Freyda, and

I thought Freyda was only a couple of thousand years old, I could see the darkness of age behind the clear eyes in a way I couldn't precisely explain.

Wryan seemed just a bit older than I was, and Sammis looked like her brother, sort of.

"You two are still taking missions."

They glanced at each other, then back at me.

Wryan spoke next. "Who wants to sit around and let their minds rot in front of a useless fireplace or an unused console? You keep young by doing."

"But . . . you could be Counselors, Tribunes . . ."

Dead silence. Sammis pointedly stared at the floor once more. Seemed embarrassed. Why did he seem so flustered?

"Loki, you rush in . . . don't you?" Wryan asked gently, humorously, but her smile held a trace of sadness.

"You two confuse me. My span is measured in tens of years, not hundreds of thousands, like yours."

I was missing something, but the more I tried to pin it down, the more it skittered away.

"Perhaps . . . perhaps we are confusing," concluded Wryan briskly. "But now," and she changed the subject, "you've got more to learn about knife work."

She and Sammis started buckling on protective armor. I stood there holding mine.

Tribunes . . . Sammis and Wryan . . . when . . . and then it hit—the Triumvirate! Odin Thor and the two others, the first three Tribunes. I swallowed. I'd always thought that the Odin Thor who rattled around was just named after the first Odin Thor, not the original article. But that meant that Sammis and Wryan were among the first of the Guard.

I started to strap on the armor, but my motions were slow because my thoughts were stirred up.

The legend was all I had to go on, because the Archives records, at least those which were open, were sketchy at best. There was a sealed section, but that had been sealed by . . . Sammis and Wryan and Odin Thor.

According to the tales, the Triumvirate had created the structure of the Guard, with the Counselors and the Tribunes, to fight the menace of the Frost Giants. More than half the Guard had perished in the long battle, and in the end, entire systems had been reduced to molten slag. But the legends never really dealt with afterward. The war had been won.

I put down the armor. "I can't practice."

Wryan looked at Sammis. He nodded. She smiled.

"How about Loratini's?" she asked.

We stowed the armor and slid.

I'd never been to Loratini's Inn, the oldest inn on Query. You had to be invited to be welcome. Rumor was that no Counselors, Tribunes, or trainees were ever invited.

An odd place, it seemed to me, with separate balconies for each table, with each balcony, maybe twenty in all, set in stone and overlooking the Falls. Officially the Falls were called Loratini Falls and had been well visited once upon a time. Only the inn and a small outbuilding farther down on the edge of the canyon remained.

The three of us sat around the circular table. I had opted for firejuice. They had beers. Wryan's was dark, and Sammis's light.

"What do you know about the Frost Giant Wars?" asked Wryan.

"Only the legend—that they almost destroyed Query and the Guard fought them and destroyed them."

Sammis snorted.

A pair, a real pair, they were, like a set of gauntlets perfectly matched. Even looked like each other—both with the light brown hair, the faint tiny lines close to the corners of their eyes, with pointed chins and elvish faces, though Sammis's features were a shade heavier, and Wryan seemed a trace bigger physically.

Both had piercing green eyes, set off by even tans. All of us tan easily and fairly darkly with a bronze cast.

I studied Sammis and waited.

"Legends never tell the whole story," said Sammis.

The more I thought about it, the more confusing it became. There I was, with two people who were former Tribunes, who'd controlled the Guard and given it up to work for millions of years at standard Guard assignments. Why? And why didn't anyone say anything?

"Because," Wryan answered my unspoken question, "no one really wants to know the full history. Because they don't, and because you won't either, let's just call it a story, a child's bedtime story, like those your father told you."

I shifted my weight on the stool, wondering whether to protest that I was better than other people. Instead, I just listened.

"Odin Thor is the strongest diver—except for you—the Guard has ever had. Unfortunately, he came out of the worst possible back-ground—the Marines of the Imperial ConFederation—and his morality is nonexistent, and his directional senses are worse. But let's guess a little bit more about the Frost Giants—it was called the Twilight War for a time because it was the twilight of Westron, the only unified

government in Queryan history before the Guard. Remember, this is a
story, and only a story."

Wryan paused, and Sammis continued where she had left off even
though a word had not passed between them.

"It really wasn't a war. It all started when the Imperial government
sent a planoforming expedition to Mithrada—"

"But why? We don't need to change planets around . . ."

"Listen," suggested Wryan, and I took a sip of firejuice.

". . . and parts of Mithrada began to freeze. That was because the
Frost Giants lived on heat energy, and when they fed, they withdrew
all the ambient energy from their surroundings. What made it worse
was that the Giants traveled through space and time, and there were
only a handful of divers . . ."

"Only a handful? But . . ."

Sammis held up a hand, before continuing.

I was beginning to believe that it *was* just a child's story.

The Frost Giants stood only a head or so taller than the tallest Queryan and were not giants in any real sense, though they had four arms
and considerably more mass.

The Frost Giants demonstrated another adaptation of the time-diving
talent, noted Wryan as she took up the tale. While they had definite
range limits, a Giant could time-dive to any point in the Galaxy which
existed during his, hers, or its own objective life. Giants seemed to have
lived several millennia. Not only could they time-dive, but basically the
adults had to because they would have starved if they had been restricted
to one place or time. In effect, they were cosmic energy grazers, although
considerably brighter than most grazing animals.

I hadn't asked for a dissertation on the Frost Giants, and I certainly
found it hard to believe that they were mere dumb animals bouncing
through time. But remembering my training thrashings from Sammis,
I decided to let them make their point in whatever obscure fashion
pleased them.

Giants went through two phases. In childhood they were planet
bound after their parent left until they physically matured. Adults had
the ability to time-dive and place-slide. If a maturing "child" did not
learn time-diving or have the talent, he, she, it, died of old age in less
than a century.

The Frost Giants needed no gross physical food, but absorbed heat
energy. How they drank it in without burning it up none of the Queryan
scientists could figure out.

"Yes, we had scientists," explained Wryan.

The more the explanations went on, the more confused I got. "The

Frost Giants were big, and when they matured, if they matured, they
could time-dive, and when they dived they fed and absorbed energy,
which left some planet or locale with a frozen chunk. Is that the idea?"
I asked.

Sammis nodded and kept talking.

Then, time-diving was a talent new to Query, so new that only a few
seemed to possess it and were often called witches. The empire of Westron ruled the planet and about one billion people, with a civilization
based largely on solar and satellite power and complex nonmetallic technology.

"Why isn't this in the Archives?" I asked.

"Someone has to have the time, the ability, and the desire to write
history," Sammis said gently. "By the time the disaster was over, there
were few indeed who could meet those qualifications."

When the abnormal temperature drops on Mithrada threatened the
expedition, some bright scientist plotted the drops, located a handful of
Frost Giants, and lobbed a thermonuclear warhead into the area. Energy
grazers or not, the Frost Giants retaliated by freezing large chunks of
Query, including all of Quest, then the Imperial capital.

The longer the story got, the more questions I had. I bottled them
up. But I really wanted to know why a planetary government at peace
needed a military establishment with thermonuclear weapons.

Sammis took another sip of the light beer and continued.

Among the survivors were two military factions, one headed by a
ConFed Marine colonel named Augurt Odin Thor. Odin Thor used the
military structure to attempt to reestablish order in Westra, the central
part of Westron, the western continent that had been the basis of the
empire.

At the same time, the other military faction had been seeking out
and eliminating the old educated aristocracy that had administered the
empire for the Imperial family.

Just prior to the expedition to Mithrada, at a relatively isolated government installation, the Imperial government had also begun a project
to investigate the time-diving talent that existed in perhaps a dozen or
so documented cases. The program, under the direction of a Dr. Wryan
Relorn, had been employing the timedivers to scout out possible interstellar colonies . . . since it appeared that the majority of the Queryan
people could not travel in time or use mental abilities to place-slide.

Threatened by one faction, Dr. Relorn had opened the installation to
Colonel Odin Thor. Odin Thor then used the divers to scout out the
other military faction, eventually to destroy its underground headquarters, and to consolidate the marines' hold on central Westra.

"None of this is in the Archives," I tried to point out reasonably.

"Certainly not in the open section," Sammis agreed.

"Let's just keep calling it a story," said Wryan, "just a made-up story."

"All right. But we've got Frost Giants freezing chunks of Query because somebody bombed one of them, military adventurers taking over the planet, and a few scattered timedivers under a nutty doctor . . ."

"She's still not nutty," said Sammis quietly.

I'd almost had enough. Now Sammis was insinuating that his partner Wryan was this Dr. Wryan Relorn and that she had sailed to the rescue of the Query by creating the timedivers, right? Sammis and Wryan were good Guards, and maybe they'd been around since forever, but nothing quite matched. I must have muttered my objections half-aloud without realizing that I had.

"No. The Guard came later, much later," said Wryan. "Try to understand, Loki. Millions of people lived within kilos of where we sit. Most died with the first wave of freezings. Those who were left were the less educated, or the well-off and isolated farmers, or the people in small towns. There was nothing holding anything together. Add to that a tremendous suppressed hatred of the educated aristocracy, and when most of the larger cities were frozen, everything disintegrated, literally and figuratively. When the Giants froze something it went to almost absolute zero, and when it thawed it fell apart in rubble and dust. Going that close to absolute zero does that, you know."

I just had to shrug and take another swallow of firejuice.

So the Imperial Marines under Odin Thor just cobbled together a regional government and tried to work with Dr. Relorn to keep things going. They tried to step up time-diving abilities, although they had only thought initially about the ability as place-sliding until a young ConFed Marine appeared from nowhere in Dr. Relorn's laboratory.

The diver suggested trying to find technology on other planets to support the marines and the attempt to hold things together.

"And this was Sammis?" I asked, not quite sarcastically.

"Of course," Wryan said, continuing almost as if I had not asked.

Technology was hard to find, especially without directional guides, gauntlets, and all the other gadgets later bought, borrowed, or stolen by the Guard, and the small towns resented the troops, and the farmers resented the townies and the troops.

Towns refused to support the new government, and fighting broke out between townies and farmers, and the townspeople even attacked marine outposts. Finally, even scarce seed grains and livestock were torched and looted and burned.

"People just wouldn't do that!" I protested.

They both stared at me, and I began to feel how old they really were. For that instant, the masks of youth that covered the depths of their eyes slipped, and I saw another kind of Hell, one a lot more lasting than my brief torment.

"Just say they did," I temporized. "What happened next?"

The timedivers recorded the chaos, the lootings and the burnings, and showed other towns, and for a time, the rebuilding progressed. Sammis found the duplicator and the Murian fusion generator. A start was made on building the Tower, and a village for the divers begun. Odin Thor began to arm his marines with more and more deadly weapons and to assert greater authority.

Then the Frost Giants returned—just one, but it froze a diver's family, and the divers and the marines panicked, demanding that Sammis and Dr. Relorn do something. But the weapons which Sammis had found could not concentrate energy enough to immobilize or kill a Giant.

Odin Thor used the incident, and his power as head of the sole remaining military force on the continent, to whip up sentiment among the other divers to develop a crusade against the Frost Giants, with him in charge. He ignored the advice of Dr. Relorn and the young Sammis, and used one of the remaining thermonuclear warheads to trap and destroy another Giant.

"That doesn't make sense," I protested again.

"A great deal of what people do when they're scared doesn't make sense," said Wryan tersely. "Remember that everything most of these people grew up with had been destroyed, and that a Frost Giant could appear from nowhere and freeze you solid before you could flee. Was it the wisest thing you ever did to blow off Heimdall's wrist?"

I shut up and listened some more.

The shadows crossing the mists from the Falls were getting longer, but more than half my firejuice remained. I took a sip and concentrated.

The Giants returned and froze most of Query solid.

The total of the disasters mounted, and the population of Query dropped from nearly a billion people to more like fifty million within a few years. The divers could avoid the Frost Giants, but most Queryans could not.

In the meantime, Sammis Olon kept scouting and trying to find better weapons, even as the Giants milled around Query, freezing more and more of the planet into dust.

Finding the Giants was the easy part. In the undertime, they left a jagged vibrating trail. The difficulty remained in figuring out what to do with the Giants. Past experience indicated that no known energy weapon short of a thermonuclear warhead or a dreadnought-class laser was effective. And there were far more Giants than warheads. Besides, no diver could carry either a warhead or a powerful enough laser.

In the end, with all the grubby persistence that the Guard still personified, Sammis Olon himself found the device . . . nothing more than a glorified sun-tunnel with special circuitry.

I looked at the two. It was almost evening, and the shadows were so long they were beginning to merge into twilight.

"It doesn't end there, does it?"

"No," said Wryan.

She condensed the story into what took perhaps no more than ten units, a short history of a bitter time.

"By tossing a sun-tunnel linked to a sun into the proximity of a Frost Giant, an energy overload was created which destroyed the Frost Giant. Odin Thor and all the others were overjoyed. And they all went hunting.

"The western continent was still the most heavily populated, even after the collapse, the riots, and the Frost Giant counterattack. With the Frost Giants still milling around Query, to kill them required sun-tunnels. The tunnels baked parts of the planet into cinders and black glass, and you can still see some of that devastation today. The Giants tried to retaliate and froze even more. No one knows how many millions more died.

"That fueled more anger and hatred, and Odin Thor and the angry divers chased the Giants across the galaxy, using sun-tunnels to destroy every Giant they could find, young or old.

"In the meantime, those back on Query tried to begin the rebuilding process, raising a Guard center and the Tower on the ruins of Inequital, the old Imperial capital. And Odin Thor continued to arm his trained marines with weapons that could destroy any diver in view, and there were still far more marines than divers."

"So what happened?" I asked in spite of myself.

"Why," answered Sammis, "Odin Thor decided to set up the present structure of the Guard, and to integrate marines and divers into it, with three people at the head. As the rebuilding of Query along the line of smaller self-sufficient individual communities progressed—supported by copies of the Murian fusion generator and the duplicator—it was becoming apparent that many Queryans were not aging . . . and either they or their children had the time-diving ability.

"So, in time, once there were more young divers, the three resigned to pave the way for elected Tribunes to carry on the work of reconstruction and the rebuilding of Query."

"That's it?"

"That's it. Remember, it's only a story," Wryan said gently.

"But the legends make . . . them . . . you . . . seem like gods . . ."

" 'God' is a very relative term," Sammis snorted. "You could easily think you were a god. You can strike down people with thunderbolts from your wrists. You can change the course of cultures and civilizations. You can cross oceans with a single step. For many people, that's a god. Think about it, young god."

They both got up.

"Stay as long as you like, Loki. Don't be late tomorrow. You still need more work with the knife."

I scarcely felt them leave as the thoughts swirled through my mind. No glorious Twilight/Frost Giant Wars? The cataclysm that leveled Query brought on by our own stupidity? Why would they tell me such a fantastic tale? Why on Query would they? What purpose would it serve?

And why had Sammis used such an ironic tone in describing Odin Thor's supposed change from a clear military autocrat into a democrat of sorts? From what I already knew, especially from watching Heimdall, people just didn't change that readily. I certainly didn't.

I watched the stars above the mist for a while, listened to the roar of falling water, and tried to digest it all.

What kept coming back to me was the question of motive. If it weren't true, why had they told me? How could two people tell a story like that, alternating without words, if they hadn't lived it?

I toyed with the now-dry and empty beaker that had held my fire-juice, attempting to puzzle things out. I even shook my head sternly to clear it, but shaking didn't help.

At some point, I gave up and slid back to the Aerie. Even there, I couldn't sleep, tired as I was. Gazing down into the deep valleys, knowing what caused at least some of the fused and splintered canyon walls, I asked myself about the cost of revenge. Yes, we had destroyed the Frost Giants, but what had it cost us? Did revenge always turn on the re-venger?

Somehow the thoughts made me think of my father's questions, and I wondered how he would have answered them. But he and my mother had been gone for a long time, and I still didn't know why. Or where. All I had was a bronze bell. In the end, I asked what my father would have asked. Was I any different?

I was different. That was how I answered my question. I wasn't a thoughtless pursuer like Odin Thor, at least I wouldn't be after my taste of Hell. No, I was different, but I would have my revenge on Heimdall.

Would that be enough? Was revenge on Heimdall really what I wanted?

Eventually, I drifted into an uneasy sleep in the early morning hours.

XIX

I GUESS I got a lot quieter after my long afternoon with Wryan and Sammis. I still worked with them, but we never talked much about the past after that.

I still had to deal with the backlogs generated from Frey's outfit, and, belatedly, Justina and her Weather Observation crew decided they had lots of old equipment—years' worth, even allowing for the stuff Baldur said we could dump on Vulcan.

For the next couple of years there were few trainees—it happens that way—and none with any mechanical ability, let alone interest. So Narcissus, Brendan, and I plodded along.

Heimdall sent all his requests through Nicodemus, which was fine with me, and my scattered diving assignments were from other departments. Usually, Heimdall left Assignments when I showed up to get briefing tapes. Either that or he buried himself in his console.

He was still cooking up things, I suspected, but he was waiting, and I kept trying to learn more about everything, but it wasn't exactly easy all the time. Like checking out the story I got from Sammis and Wryan.

Even when I fiddled with the blocks on the Archives consoles, and twiddled through some of the sealed sections, there still wasn't much hard information.

Sammis had put something in, but it had a scramble code that I couldn't figure out. There was one history text, obviously copied, about the monarchy of Westron and the conflicts between the dukes of Eastron and Westron, but a lot of the cultural references I just didn't have, and some of the words clearly didn't mean what they used to. I mean, what was a limited chartered monarchy? Or a solicitor general? Or an investment capital shortage? I could figure out things like the metals shortage or the infeasibility of further deep-seam mining, and the mention of the lack of metallic asteroids prompted my borrowing of some deep-space armor and some sliding around our own solar system. Why no one had seriously considered factories on Query made more sense after some of my digging.

Overall, as Baldur had indicated, there was plenty of information, but it was almost all about places other than Query, even about cultures that no longer existed. The stuff about Query was boring and routine, like changes in Tribunes. So what if Saturnis had been High Tribune before Martel? Or that someone named Kerina was the first High Tribune in the records? While I kept poking around, I wasn't finding much useful.

Of course, I kept diving, but the assignments weren't exactly scintillating, like the one I got for Doffissn. That came from Justina, of all people.

"These weather formations that the balloon scanners show just can't be natural, Loki."

"Why not?" I'd foolishly asked.

She explained, in excruciating detail, about orthographic trends, topography, and prevailing winds, and how clouds could not and should not replicate identical or similar patterns under dissimilar circumstances.

I got the message—the clouds on Doffissn were weird.

So I went to Doffissn. It was a water planet, mostly, and I had to wear breathing gear, because there was crap in the air that wouldn't have been really very good for me, besides leaving me dead for lack of oxygen, because most of the oxygen was tied up in the water, and I don't mean as water.

First, I watched clouds form over what looked like a cobalt-blue ocean, and I sweated, because it wasn't quite as warm as being steamed in a sauna. The hot winds didn't help cool me, while I hung split entries across the sky.

A few other things became clear quickly. I was the only nonweather object in the sky. There were clouds and rains and winds and me.

Then I checked out the few islands and peaks. There wasn't anything bigger than shrubs, lichens, and the local equivalents of moles and scavenger rats, and the rats, from what I could tell, fed on nodules that grew on the shrubs.

But Justina was right. The clouds were definitely weird, spinning sometimes into the sky in whirling patterns, or flattening into low walls that often arrowed toward each other, even against the wind.

I went back to Maintenance and cobbled together an energy field/ flow detector. Baldur said it should work, and it certainly indicated energy flows in and around the Tower.

It didn't indicate anything from the skies of Doffissn.

My next bright idea was to look under the almost opaque cobalt-blue ocean. To begin with, I tried it from the undertime, but have you ever tried to look into the water from beneath another layer of cloudy water? I couldn't see much, but I got the feeling something was there.

So I dug out some space armor, then had to modify it so that it resisted inward pressure as well as outward, and that meant I could barely move in the stuff. Back to Doffissn—this time with a pressurized water-resistant energy detector.

I broke out, looked at the detector, but nothing happened, except it showed a faint background, more than in the air. I studied the needle and slid westward, away from the islands and toward, I suppose, the deeps, although I was staying in relatively shallow levels. The water was just as cobalt-blue opaque underneath, and I wondered if it were filled with some form of copper.

Halfway to the deeper water, I broke out again. The detector registered markedly higher, and I could sense some background vibration.

On my next breakout, I looked at the detector once more. It pegged off the end and then expired. I didn't really have a chance to see that because the water seemed to turn into vast roaring and churning cascades of steam around me, and I went head over heels, as if I were being yanked to the depths of the ocean.

The suit wasn't built for the depths of even a shallow ocean, and I certainly wasn't. I left the suit behind, and appeared in underclothes back in the Aerie. I wasn't going to show up that way in the Travel Hall.

With that, after some Sustain, and a shower to clean off the sweat and fear, I put on the more conventional jumpsuit, the breathing gear, and bounced back to Doffissn.

A rough cloud replica of my suit had formed in the sky. So I went back to Baldur, and we talked about cloud generators, but that would have taken a while. I tried a gadget that made smoke, but whoever or whatever was beneath that cobalt-blue water didn't respond to smoke, and I recommended against taking any more dips in the ocean.

I'm extraordinarily able, but I barely got out with my skin, and I think whatever sculpted clouds from beneath the ocean was basically curious or friendly. What can you say or trade with something you can't see, can't talk to, and can't even describe?

For a while, some of Justina's trainees worked with water vapor from a squirt container I worked out, but they had to use a balloon platform, and it wasn't very safe, because they couldn't handle split entries. After I had to dive from Maintenance the second time to yank someone out of the water, even Justina gave up.

In the end, I guess that showed why the Guard mainly meddles with humanoid cultures. We're opportunists, not real knowledge-seekers, and we just don't have the knowledge base to go beyond humanoid contacts.

So, between oddball observation assignments, I plugged along in Maintenance.

One day, Baldur asked me to give him a hand with a generator. At first, I didn't recognize it. Then I swallowed. It was an even smaller version of the generator we'd brought back from Sinopol.

"How . . . ?"

"It wasn't easy. It's taken a long time."

What he wanted was really just someone careful enough to recheck some work that he'd done on the intakes. By repositioning the water feed lines and a few other things, he'd been able to shrink the generator more.

"What about the insulation?" I asked.

He shook his head. "It doesn't have any. It never did. It's all field-contained. You can't have power without the field, and if there's no power, there's no emission."

I had to take his word for it. For something that small it generated a lot of energy.

After more tests, we took it apart and duplicated it section by section until we had five. Baldur put two in Special Stores and gave one to Justina, with instructions on how to break it down and duplicate it. She thought they'd be useful in some of her smaller out-of-the-way observation posts.

Baldur also insisted I keep one. He kept his original and one other, and stored them in the big lockers adjacent to his space.

"I feel better with this than the big Murian fusactors," he said.

How you could consider something the size of a closet big was beyond me, and I said so. "It's big for a nomad culture that has to carry everything." He laughed. "Call it my contribution to ensuring our future."

"Ensuring the future?"

"Loki, the duplicator is portable; the Murian generators aren't. This uses water and is. With a duplicator and a generator that a lot of divers can carry . . ." He just shook his head.

I thought about it, and he was right.

A small square object shimmered on the side of the work space. I looked at it, but it seemed curiously almost out-of-time-phase, yet it wasn't, and it had a small screen like a console screen, except the screen was less than half the size of my palm. There were studs on it with symbols. When I picked it up, it was light, weighing less than a stylus.

"What is it?"

"A calculator," Baldur admitted.

I looked at it, at its shimmer, and back at him. I didn't recognize the symbols, but it looked like a decimal system. At least there were ten studs with single symbols on them and two others with multiple symbols. Around the twelve central studs were larger studs, probably for mathematical operations, assuming it was an advanced calculator.

"It really hasn't been invented yet. It may not be."

I looked at him. The Guard frowned on lifting objects from foretime pararealities. They didn't duplicate, and we usually didn't have the ability to model and build them from scratch. After all, there is such a thing as materials science, and we've never had it. Or if we did, the records didn't survive the Frost Giant catastrophe.

He grinned. "It still works."

That bothered me, but I tapped a stud, and the symbol appeared on the screen. "Why do you need it?"

"It's handy. I can't carry a console."

The portability thing again. It appeared like Baldur was getting a portability fetish. But why?

"You're spending a lot of effort on portability."

He shrugged. "According to the legends and a few of the old records, time-diving was initially employed to scout out other solar systems and planets where Queryans could live."

"There's more than enough space here," I pointed out, more from contrariness than anything.

"But suns don't last forever," he responded. "What would happen if our sun decided to explode?"

He had a point, a long-time future point, but definitely a point, and we are a long-lived race.

He smiled. "I know. It may be a long time, maybe never, for all practical purposes, but . . ." He shrugged.

We talked a little more, and then I went back to deal with all the beat-up Weather gear, hoping it wouldn't take too many more years to drudge through it all.

XX

IN A PARATIME that waits for a favorable change wind, the Grand Commander stands in front of the star plot.

She is impatient, and her tail lashes behind her in subdued swings.

The priestess, her scales yellow with age, enters, bows a bow that is more token than real, and presents the eternasteel tablet to the Supreme Commander of the star fleet.

The Commander's violet eyes flicker, and her tail is still. The ratings plugged into the command center are aware of the tension. Their green scales stand on edge as they wait for a reaction.

The Commander's eyes dart from the tablet that may be ancient to the star plot and back again.

Thump! Her tail strikes the deck with a single crash. She is pleased.

The ratings relax as the Commander begins readying the order of battle. The target is the second planet of an obscure system with a yellow sun.

The arrays of black ships accelerate toward their jump point. For now . . . for now . . . they are not real, only smoke in a paratime reality, owing their existence, such as it is, to the set of one god's mind, that god who may or may not deliver the tablet that rests before the star plot . . .

XXI

A LONG DAY, one that stretched out under the high ceilings of the Tower as if it would never end—that was the kind of day the morning promised.

Most technical peoples think that time passes at a uniform rate. It doesn't. Any good timediver knew that. A chronometer will measure intervals precisely, but not the passage of time. Usually, the difference isn't that noticeable, unless compared to biological processes. According to the chronometer, biology varies, not time.

Scientists explain the variance, if they try at all, by citing biological eccentricities, anything but the real answer, which is that time doesn't pass at a uniform rate. In most places, it doesn't vary much, it's true, but time is not an interval.

What is it? It's time. Simple answer, but the most accurate.

On that morning when time had dragged itself out, I left my work space to find Baldur, figuring I'd have to wait before he roused himself out of his deep concentration and recognized me. Even after all the years, he still made me wait.

Baldur wasn't in his space. One look, and I knew he wouldn't be back.

Baldur never left loose ends, and his old-fashioned writing platform was bare. Only a few standard manuals remained in the shelves by his stool. Baldur liked printed references. Most Guards preferred console scans. The tape access cabinet and record file cases had been polished.

I tiptoed over to the writing platform and opened the single drawer. Empty. The whole space was empty.

To make sure, I checked everything. Not a single sign of the blond giant who ran Maintenance. I debated trying to track him down before letting the Tribunes know, but decided against it. Better to keep playing it safe and not give Heimdall and company any free shots.

I rushed up the ramps to the Tribunes' chambers and asked for Freyda or Eranas. I didn't really want to deal with Kranos, not that I had anything against him, but he was so silent I hadn't the faintest idea where he stood.

I was tapping my feet by the time Eranas appeared.

"Baldur's left. Permanently."

"How do you know?"

I told him about the tidy way in which all the loose ends had been tied up, about how that would square with Baldur.

"I can't say I'm surprised," Eranas mused. "Thank you." He turned to go.

"Aren't you going to do anything? Locate him?"

"Yes. We'll have to do something about Maintenance, I suppose. As for Baldur . . . as a Counselor, he can leave the Guard or Query anytime he wants . . . and how could I compel Baldur to do anything? Nor should I." He smiled at me. "Even if you found Baldur, what would you say?"

Eranas walked back into his private chamber, leaving me there open-mouthed. Something had to be wrong. Even if it weren't I wanted to hear it from Baldur.

After thinking a unit, I crossed the Tower and walked into Personnel to tell Gilmesh.

"Figures," he growled. "On your way back to Maintenance, take this. I'd appreciate it if you could do something." He thrust a dented wrist gauntlet at me. "It's Lorren's. Damned fool left it on during hand-to-hand with Sammis."

I didn't have to take it, but there wasn't much point in upsetting Gilmesh. So I did. Lorren was Gilmesh's latest addition, a young blond senior trainee with an insipid smile. I couldn't help but grin at the thought of what Sammis could do to a trainee's arrogance. I had felt lucky to get through his course with a few bruises, and they were nothing compared to what I still got in my less and less frequent sessions, with him and Wryan.

The corridors of the Tower were quiet in the morning. The youngsters who visited and the citizens with business usually arrived in the afternoon. I never did figure that out, since people lived all over the planet and could slide in from anywhere, but there seemed to be a custom about it.

I waved at Loragerd as I passed the Linguistics Center, but she didn't
see me, and I didn't want to interrupt her.

Back at my own space in Maintenance, I dumped the wrist gauntlet
on the bench, sat down on the high stool I liked.

Baldur was gone. That was it, and whether Eranas or Freyda or Gilmesh cared, I had to find out why. To locate Baldur, or see if I could, I
needed his assignments file and a Locator check. The question was how
to get either.

Gilmesh ran Personnel and didn't seem interested. He'd agree with
Eranas. On the other hand, Eranas wasn't going to run around immediately announcing Baldur's disappearance. So maybe I could play it
dumb, if I moved quickly. Once again, I might be risking a bit, but
safer to play dumb aboveboard than sneaky and get caught.

I needed an entree, so to speak. I got to work on Lorren's gauntlet.
Took only a few units to fix it, primarily because I replaced the microcircuitry, lock, stock, and barrel. Wasteful but quick. Later I'd have to
break down the damaged modules which I'd set aside and fix them. I
didn't care much for total black-boxing as a standard repair technique,
but it did come in handy when I was in a hurry.

Gilmesh was a creature of habit, and one of his habits was sipping
cuerl at midmorning with Frey and Heimdall. That was one of the
reasons I hurried.

With the gauntlet in hand, I trotted up the ramps to Personnel and
loitered around the bend in the corridor until I heard the quick clump
of boots heading toward the small lounge where the Senior Guards often
took a break.

Time to present Lorren with his gauntlet.

He was sitting at the small console in the back corner, with his blond
hair hanging over his heavy brows and that insipid smile planted firmly
and unwaveringly on his face.

Verdis was hunched over a worktable in the adjoining room, oblivious
to my appearance.

"Here's your gauntlet," I announced.

Lorren nodded, didn't even open his mouth.

"I need to run down Baldur's whereabouts. Can you run out an update
on his past assignments?"

"I need Gilmesh's approval."

"Look, Baldur is my supervisor. If he's upset at my running him
down, he'll take care of me. You don't have to worry about it."

Lorren shook his head.

I picked the gauntlet up from his console. The smile disappeared, to
be replaced with a half-pout.

"What are you doing?"

"If you don't want to cooperate, fine. As a full Guard, I can require any trainee to fix his own gear. All I have to do is supply the guidance and the equipment."

"But it's fixed," protested Lorren sulkily.

"I black-boxed it, as a favor. All the components I replaced need to be checked out and repaired, if necessary."

I stood there. Lorren thought about it. Gilmesh certainly wouldn't let him off from his duties to fix the result of his own carelessness. He'd have to come down to Maintenance on his own time. And what I was asking for wasn't Baldur's current location, but where he'd once been.

"All right, if you're going to be that way about it . . ."

With that tone, the Senior Guards would have had his head, but he was young, and I wasn't a Senior Guard. He punched a series of commands into the console. I held onto the gauntlet. When he handed me the printout and the tape, a few units later, I let go of the gauntlet.

I left, and I didn't even run into Gilmesh on the way out. In a corner down the ramp and around the corner, I took a quick look at the printout. The earliest dive entry date was over two hundred centuries back—real-time.

I hadn't thought Baldur had been with the Guard twenty thousand years, but I supposed it wasn't all that surprising, particularly considering how little he spoke.

Frey wasn't around when I marched through the archway into Locator. I hadn't planned it that way. It just happened. Ferrin was doing most of the real work anyway. Without a doubt, Ferrin was the worst diver in memory to have passed the Test. He had more than redeemed himself in the running of the Locator system, which was a definite blessing to the Guard, and at least Frey was smart enough to let him do it and take all the credit.

One of the things Ferrin had done was rearrange the rotation system for all trainees and Guards by figuring their actual diving abilities into the schedule. That way, there was always a strong timediver on Locator duty.

Sitting in front of a pile of tapes, Ferrin was hunched over in his high-backed stool.

"Ferrin, can you run a Locator cross-check for me? Baldur went off without explaining some Maintenance scheduling, and, frankly, I need some of his technical expertise. Won't take long, but no one seems to know where he went." It was a lame explanation, but the best I could come up with.

Ferrin's eyebrows lifted. "He's a Counselor."

"I know. I don't have his code. But Locator must have some way of finding Counselors."

"Loki, since I am a literal-minded and very junior administrator, and since you undoubtedly have a worthwhile purpose in mind, I will indeed facilitate your search. Former fellow trainee, you have been so imploring that your search must indeed be pressing and necessary."

I tried to restrain a smile. A diver Ferrin might not be, but he knew I was skirting the edge. Ferrin, perhaps more than anyone I knew, could smell where dead fish would turn up long before they were hatched. But he knew, and I mean *knew*, what would hurt the Guard and what wouldn't.

He slipped off the stool, took the tape data bloc, and eased it into his tracer console. "I suspect that this is totally unnecessary, and that's one of the reasons I'm happy to do it."

I couldn't believe that. Baldur disappearing and a tracer unnecessary?

Ferrin sensed my questions. "I'm a snoop, Loki. Surely you remember that. That's why I can keep this place going—because I know more than I'm supposed to. News does have a way of spreading, you know." He turned back to the tracer screen. "You take a look."

I looked.

The console had printed in its stylized script, "No present trace. Individual does not register outside previous locales."

Baldur couldn't disappear. Not like that. But the console said his back- and foretime traces existed only in the places his assignment tape said he'd already been. Ergo . . . he'd disappeared. Right?

Something tickled the back of my mind, a nursery rhyme from the past, something about the little man who wasn't there. Yesterday he wasn't there, and today he wasn't there again.

My eyes burned, because two other people I had relied on, even as I had fought them, had also disappeared. They didn't register on Locator, and their house was slowly losing its time protection and falling apart, but no one but me had ever visited, not that I could tell.

Ferrin waited while I struggled.

"Loki," said Ferrin gently, very gently, "whatever Baldur's done, he deserves to be left alone. If he went to all the trouble of disguising his trace enough that we can't locate him, you can certainly see he doesn't want to be disturbed. And if he were dead, wouldn't the change in the signal show?"

"Maybe." I was still suspicious.

"You suspect everyone and everything. You should. But nobody disliked Baldur. Nobody, not even Heimdall."

What Ferrin said made sense. I just didn't want to believe that Baldur, who was so concerned about the future of Quest and Query, would off and take a dusting. But my father had.

I left the data bloc with Ferrin, pocketed the printout, and headed back to the Maintenance Hall. I sat down on my high stool, trying to puzzle it out.

Finally, I walked over to Baldur's spaces and looked at his console. Then I turned it on. The standard directory appeared, with a few others listed—one being Maintenance. I accessed the Maintenance files. Everything seemed pretty organized except for one file, entitled "High Sinopol," just at the bottom of the main directory. That wasn't Baldur. So I punched it in, and instead of seeing whatever was filed, I got an almost blank screen with the notation, "_____ Bazaar of Chance."

The file or whatever had to be for me. I tried to rack my brain for the name of the casino, or what have you, and was debating whether I should just dive back there again—it wasn't beyond my range—when the name popped into my head—Rafel's. I punched it in, and I got the message.

LOKI—

    BY NOW YOU ARE TRYING TO TURN THE GUARD UPSIDE DOWN TRYING TO LOCATE ME. IF I HAVE BEEN SUCCESSFUL, YOU WON'T. EVEN IF YOU CAN, I WOULD ASK THAT YOU DON'T. I HAVE SPENT A LONG TIME IN THE GUARD, PERHAPS TOO LONG, AND IT IS TIME TO DO SOMETHING NEW, AND PERHAPS MORE CREATIVE.

    YOU CAN LEARN STILL MORE FROM MAINTENANCE, AND YOU DO HAVE A GIFT FOR GETTING THINGS DONE. YOU ALSO HAVE THE CURSE OF NOT WORRYING ABOUT THE IMPACTS OF A SUCCESSFUL JOB. REMEMBER, SUCCESS CAN OFTEN BE MORE DANGEROUS THAN FAILURE, ESPECIALLY WITH BARBARIANS. THIS IS TRUE EVEN OF GODS. ODIN THOR WAS ONCE A GOD, DESPITE THE CURRENT JOKES ABOUT HIM, AND WHAT HE CREATED HAS DESTROYED HIM. KEEP THAT IN MIND WHEN YOUR TIME COMES.

There wasn't a signature, but I didn't need one. But why hadn't he told me, only left a hidden message? I looked at the console, and another line blinked into place.

"Have you read and understood this?"

I read it again, then tapped in a Yes.

This time another question scripted out, an obscure calculation involving the Sinopol generator. I didn't remember one of the parameters, and I went to the storage locker where Baldur had kept the two of them. Neither was there, and that meant I had to go back to my spaces.

Even after I got the numbers, it took me a unit or so to work out the calculation, and when I inputted it, the screen blanked back to the standard directory—without the High Sinopol entry. I tried again, but the whole file had disappeared.

I went back to my space and slowly plowed through repairs, trying to digest what Baldur's note had meant. He'd been planning for a long time—and the portable generators were certainly part of it.

I was still pondering two days later when the Tribunes arrived—all three of them—Freyda, Eranas, and Kranos. After scrambling off the stool, I bowed slightly in welcome.

"We have a problem," began Eranas.

I knew what their problem was, but decided to let them tell me.

"With Baldur's departure, the Guard is left without a Maintenance supervisor with appropriate knowledge and seniority. While no one doubts your unquestioned technical ability, to say nothing of your skill as a diver, your impetuousness and lack of seniority are equally demonstrable. At the same time, no Senior Guard having mechanical talents is available, and it will be a number of years before you will be eligible for Senior Guard status."

Eranas obviously wanted some acknowledgment from me.

"I can understand the problem."

"We explored a number of alternatives—including making you the nominal head of Maintenance with supervision by the Tribunes personally. But the unwise precedent that could be set by making a junior Guard a department head and the fact that such supervision could be somewhat time-consuming . . ."

In short, Loki, young fellow, I translated, you've already given us too many headaches.

". . . leads us to another temporary expedient, which we will review on a periodic basis. Assignments and Maintenance will be consolidated under Heimdall, but you will in fact take charge of and be fully responsible for the daily operations of Maintenance, and Heimdall will continue to direct Assignments."

All three waited for me to react.

I couldn't say I was surprised. Heimdall was a Counselor, and no other Senior Guard would have touched the job for anything if what Loragerd had told me about the gossip was half-true. Hell, I didn't understand why everyone thought I was so difficult to deal with. I just wanted to do it right. Except, as Baldur's note had said, success was dangerous.

"Not much I can say, honored Tribunes. While Heimdall and I certainly have not seen eye-to-eye in the past, I am confident we will develop a working relationship of mutual understanding."

Translate that any way you want, I thought.

"So long as that remains a working relationship," commented Kranos in his deep bass voice, "all of us will be pleased, I am sure."

Freyda moved her head minutely. Eranas stared at me.

I bowed slightly once more. "I appreciate the trust you have put in me."

With as little ceremony as when they arrived, the three left.

One or two things would happen, I decided. Either Heimdall would ignore me while figuring out how to undo me, or he would be politely civil and wait for me to fall on my face. Neither would change anything.

As Baldur had said so often, most of the Guards were barbarians, even the Tribunes and Counselors. None of them appreciated the power in purely mechanical devices, not even Heimdall, and since Baldur hadn't made that point, I certainly wasn't about to. But I still wanted to at least find where he'd gone. Was that to prove that I could or to ensure he was all right? Or some of each? I wasn't sure, but, after the entourage of higher-ups departed for their sanctified quarters elsewhere in the Tower, I studied the printout of Baldur's past assignments.

On the average, he had taken a diving assignment once a year, and that worked out to over twenty thousand. At first, it seemed preposterous, until I thought about it. The Guard monitored well over a million systems on some sort of continuing basis, and that, of course, was why we were often backtiming to solve problems. There weren't that many Guards.

The physical printout was notational, with each assignment and its duration, objective time, on a line or less. Twenty thousand assignments meant twenty thousand lines, or a few hundred thin pages.

How was I going to find him when the Locator tag system couldn't? The Locator got a fix on every fore- and backtime point where a diver is or has been. The now position was determined mainly by eliminating past assignments with a cross-index, which is why the records of all dives were rigorously maintained by Locator.

The rules of Time are inflexible. No diver could occupy the same time slot in more than one place in one solar system. I never understood why a diver could occupy the same time point in different solar systems, unless time is a partly subjective property of each sun, but that was the way it worked. Since the diver's "self" in an objective locale has "priority," no breakout is possible in a time area where the diver has already been.

That meant Baldur couldn't be where he'd already been, not at the same time. But what if he'd recorded a dive he'd never made? Baldur was certainly capable of planning that far ahead—and how could I ever find out which one it had been?

But because Baldur was hung up on doing something constructive, I might be able to figure out something. Constructive work, given his background, meant a mid-tech culture and someplace he wanted to stay for a while. Might even be coincident with the objective now, but I doubted that.

My first step in trying to track down Baldur, after polishing off the continuing maintenance waiting in my bin and farming it out to Brendan and Narcissus, would be to program my idea of Baldur's ideal home into the Archives data banks and request a list, hard copy. If it weren't too lengthy, I could compare it at leisure with his past assignments.

Might have been simpler to use the Locator system again, but Locator, unlike Maintenance, was staffed around the clock. If Baldur had gone to such pains to circumvent Locator, I would have felt lower than a grounded gopher if I'd tipped off Frey to my ideas.

Great insights or not, I still also had a day-to-day job to get done, and Heimdall would probably be looking over my shoulder.

The Maintenance load suddenly became greater. A lot of it was junk, dusty, unused for decades. Coincidences like that weren't. Some of it I did dump on Vulcan, and I was ready to explain that it was either obsolete or so old that we couldn't even justify the time to create spare parts. But no one asked. I wasn't sure whether the Tribunes wanted to keep me busy or whether Heimdall was up to his old tricks.

I rated midday breaks, regardless of work load. So when I got things halfway stabilized, I took the time to trot up to the Guard section of the Archives, instead of sliding out to an inn or the Aerie to eat.

I'd already decided to ask for the narrowest search possible, figuring I could widen it step by step if the parameters didn't touch on one of Baldur's earlier assignments. Sitting there in the golden glow of the black-walled cube, waiting for the screen display and ready to punch the print stud, another thought struck me. I asked the Archives data system if anyone else were indexing the same data.

"Affirmative," scripted the screen.

"What command?" I pursued.

"Duplicate all requests, LKI-30, Red."

I struck the side of the cubicle, hammered my fist against the un-yielding plastic, but the sharp lance of pain up my arm dissuaded me from further banging. That plastic was hard.

If they wanted to know what I was up to, I'd give them more than enough information. Scramble their schemes that way.

In the meantime, the information began displaying on the screen. Theoretically, each time/culture met the parameters I'd outlined. All in all, there were about two hundred.

I ordered a printout, then went ahead with my decision to muddle the waters by widening the search. I lowered the tech level by one magnitude which boosted the numbers considerably—up to two thousand time locales. Then I canceled the hold on the first group, ordered a printout on the second, and left the second list on recall hold under my personal code. I hoped that would give the impression that I'd found what I wanted in the second grouping, rather than in the first.

I ambled back down the ramp to Maintenance. The repairs piled in the bin seemed to have grown even in the time I'd been gone.

Another thought occurred to me as I pitched in on a portable atmosphere regenerator which had definitely seen better days—it reminded me of uptime Terran manufacture, lots of plastic, excess backup circuits to cover the sloppy construction, but it was from Weindre.

Baldur had been a Counselor, even though he'd missed his share of meetings. Certainly, Gilmesh, as his replacement, wouldn't. But maybe he'd gotten tired of the plotting, the maneuvering. He'd always preferred what he called real work.

I plowed through the work on the regenerator, finished it off, improving the workmanship in the process, and started in on a set of camp barriers, followed by what seemed to be a child's deep-space suit that hadn't been used in centuries. More and more of what had recently landed in the bin was no longer used or necessary for the Guard, but I wasn't in the mood to argue. What I could toss safely I did. The rest got fixed. Argument had turned out as a very poor survival technique.

I gritted my teeth and did the best I could, making a pretty good dent in the pile. Some of the easier garbage I continued to farm out. The nature of the stuff in the bin told me that sooner or later I was going to get ahead of them because even Frey couldn't break things as fast as we three could fix them. And it would look pretty stupid if they all went around breaking things to keep me busy.

The equipment the Guard used was durable and resisted most bumping and thumping—and the average Guard just didn't have that much equipment. He or she couldn't carry it.

The night when I got the printouts, when I left the Tower at twilight, I smiled at everyone I passed, even Heimdall. I place-slid to the Aerie, the two sets of printouts tucked into my jumpsuit.

At the Aerie it was dark, but I'd grown used to the sun position differences over the years. I set the printouts on the table next to the permaglass window and grabbed some fruits and nuts from the keeper, along with a beaker of firejuice.

After pulling up the stool, I started in on a quick comparison of the Archives' short list with Baldur's assignments. I'd expected only a few matches, but I was disappointed. A quick scan showed ten matches— requiring dives and explorations and searches of ten planets—if not more.

By the time I made ten timedives, someone in Locator—and by then I felt everyone was monitoring my every move—would figure out what I was doing. One or two I could get away with, but not ten planets or more.

Dive smart, not often, Sammis had said. I might have to do more thinking, I figured as I munched my way through the printouts. I laid out a couple of assumptions. Number one: If Baldur really liked one culture, he would have made more than one dive there. Number two: The culture had to be something where his knowledge and his type of knowledge were useful and likely to be accepted, and that meant not a totally closed system.

I went through the ten assignments that seemed to match the short list and came up with two systems that might match. Baldur had visited both more than twice.

The Atlantean Empire on Terra, twelve centuries back, real objective time, was the first. The second was the third early mech period of Midgard, five centuries back.

Both were within Baldur's time-diving range.

My guess was Midgard. Baldur just seemed that he'd opt out with the hope of bequeathing a future on the culture, a pass-on of some sort.

The Atlantean Empire of close backtime Terra, as I recalled, ended up playing too loose and fast with plate tectonics, and hadn't left much of anything to anybody.

So Midgard was tops on the list, if I went searching at all. But I was missing something. I just wanted to pull on equipment and go. I didn't have to go to the Travel Hall. That was just a formality for me anyway.

I had duplicates of most of the equipment I used stashed in the spare room in the Aerie. As soon as I'd finished building it, I'd begun to stock the back room with supplies pilfered from the back storerooms of the Tower, and once I'd installed my own duplicator, I'd begun to copy a lot of normal gear. Not everything—I hadn't seen the point in mindless copying.

Midgard was a relatively small and dense planet, and the backtime era where I suspected Baldur had grounded himself was relatively underpopulated. But even small planets are huge when you're looking for one person, and it would take forever just to look for some sort of hints.

So I curbed my impatience and looked into the darkness, resisting the urge to chew through my fingernails. I didn't have much practice at analytical thinking about people, but it was clearly time to start.

Item: Baldur liked to think and work with his hands.
Item: Baldur disliked the continual backtime tampering of the Guard.
Item: Baldur could make an impact in any early or midmech culture.
Item: Baldur had taken both portable generators.
Item: No winds of time-change had accompanied his departure.
Possible conclusion: Baldur was playing a longer-range game, and the closer to the objective now his retreat was, the less likely the impacts of his efforts were to be discovered.

Thinking done, I stood up and unloaded an insulated warm suit from its insulated pack. I had it half on before I stopped. I still kept forgetting. I had all the time in the world. No one else was searching for Baldur, and I didn't have to find him that night. I could stretch it over years . . .

. . . and I still didn't have any way to locate him. I took off the warm suit and paced around some more.

The generators kept popping into my mind—the damned generators that had bothered me from the first. They were the key. Sometimes I'm slow, but in the late evening that answer hit me. I already had the locator gadget I needed.

Baldur took two generators, and probably a duplicator. That would allow him to make more generators, or parts to keep them running at least. That meant he was generating power, and when I'd gone to Doffissn, he'd helped me build a broad-scale energy detector. I'd given the original to Sammis for something, but the specs were still in my console.

With everyone watching me, I wasn't about to dive into Maintenance that night. So I pulled off my clothes and went to bed, but I didn't sleep for a long time.

The dawn snaked its way over Seneschal all too soon after my eyes actually closed . . . and later than I would have liked to rise, but I managed to grumble myself together and onto my feet. From that point, it wasn't that long before I slid to the Tower and walked into Maintenance.

During the day, the backlog shrank a bit more, perhaps because

Heimdall and the Tribunes were running out of things to repair. Never, I suspected, had so many odd pieces of equipment been in such good condition.

In between the repairs I pulled out the detector specs and began to replicate the device, with a few simplifications, since this one didn't have to function underwater and under pressure.

Right after a quick evening meal, I pulled on the insulated suit and dived from the Aerie, straight back to Midgard and the time of Baldur's last objective assignment, in the city of Fenris. The wolf-city was more like a town, with narrow streets and open sewers.

The detector detected nothing, not even in sweeps around the area, as I froze in the ice-splintered skies, despite the warm suit. So when the chill finally got to me, I timedived back to the Aerie and fell into the waiting furs and a few hours' sleep.

I made it to the Tower and into Maintenance at my normal time, a feat in itself after a long night of freezing in the skies of Midgard. As I studied the new additions to the repair bin and congratulated myself on making all the ends meet, Loragerd cornered me.

"I've been thinking . . ."

I didn't want her thinking. "Dangerous occupation, thinking."

She avoided the hint. "I know Baldur's disappearance has upset you, but are you going to chase his ghost all over the galaxy?"

"Why does everyone keep thinking he's a ghost?" I turned on her, grabbing her shoulders before I'd realized I'd even moved. "Is everyone so glad he's gone? Was his honesty too much?"

"Loki! Loki! Stop yelling at me. You're hurting my shoulders. I'm not your enemy, and I liked Baldur."

I let go of her shoulders and found she was inside my arms, holding me. Holding me.

"Loki, for such a strong man, you're such an idiot."

I finally put my arms around her, but as I did she pulled back and brushed something out of her eyes.

She cleared her throat, and the sound was swallowed in the morning emptiness of the Maintenance Hall. By that point, all the Halls seemed empty, but I suspected it was me. The Guard was functioning the same way it had for centuries.

"Why is it so important for you to find Baldur?"

"Because it's not like him to leave."

"From what you've told me, it *is* like him. No fuss, no outcry, with all the loose ends tied up. You're the one who likes the theatrics."

That hurt, even from Loragerd, and she must have realized it. She looked at the glowstone floor.

We avoided looking each other in the eyes. I gestured toward the two stools by my bench. She took the lower one.

"There's something more on your mind," I observed.

"You'll never love anyone, and you know it. You may be fond of me, or want Verdis, even Freyda. Yes, I know about that. Everyone knows about that. But you won't let yourself love."

"What does that have to do with Baldur?"

"Everything. Baldur loved. He loved everyone. And he just couldn't stand it any more. He left. He didn't tell Freyda, or Eranas, or Heimdall, or Odin Thor."

"How do you know?"

"Because they've been following you, tracking you, wondering if you can find Baldur, half hoping you can, half hoping you can't."

I wasn't exactly surprised.

"They don't have any ideas?"

Loragerd brushed whatever it was out of her eyes again, cleared her throat, and went on. She seemed hoarse. "Freyda said . . . she said you ought to leave the poor bastard alone."

"What?" Manipulating Freyda wanted anyone left alone? I didn't believe that for an instant.

"I'd better go, Loki."

"You just got here."

"You have work to do, and so do I."

She slipped off the stool into the quiet side lights and was out of Maintenance within instants.

I watched, not quite believing she had either come or gone. Finally, I swallowed, then dropped off the stool, walked over to the bin, and studied the backlog piled there. With the exception of the shield unit, Brendan and Narcissus could handle it all.

I dumped the shield assembly on my own bench and pulled up the stool. I should have left it for Brendan and gone over it with him. It would have taught him something new, but I needed something to do besides think.

Despite my intentions to farm all the repairs out, I kept a lot and ended up working straight through. Not much left to do by late afternoon.

After picking up a quick meal at Hera's Inn, I tried to puzzle it out as I watched the sunset from the Aerie.

Baldur gone, and no one able to track him, no one wanting to. Loragerd's appearance in the Maintenance Hall and the business about my not being able to love anyone. That had hurt, along with the crack about my theatrics.

Sammis had said to dive smart and not often, but as the twilight deepened, and the sun-reddened snow fields of Seneschal turned purple, I found myself suited and ready to timedive back to Midgard. Another night, another city—this time, Isolde.

My luck, skill, whatever, wasn't any better in Isolde. No energy flows, and no backtime trails or other signs of Baldur.

Somehow the days and nights passed. Every night I tried a different locale on Midgard. I knew I was being monitored by the Locator section, but no one said a word.

Fifteen cities, towns, and villages, and no sign of Baldur. Isolated high forests, and rocky crags surrounded by ice, and no sign of Baldur. Day and night, and night and day, repairs and searching and sleeping, the pattern repeating day after day. Fall came and went, but I didn't notice much of the mild change in season.

The morning after my last dive to Midgard, and I knew it was my last because there wasn't anywhere else to look, I was staring blankly at a warm-suit power pack connection block.

"Loki."

I knew the voice and swiveled on the stool. Dropping to my feet, I gave her an overelaborate bow.

She seldom beat around the bush. She didn't then.

"Haven't you tried enough?"

"Enough of what?"

"Baldur—what else?"

"What did you do to him to make him leave?" I tried a glare, but was too tired for it to make much of a dent against Freyda's composure.

She shook her head slowly. "In such a hurry, trying to solve the universe as if you had no tomorrow. I had hoped . . ."

"Hoped what?"

She smiled faintly. "That is neither here nor now. I thought I might be able to help you. Why do you want to find Baldur so badly?"

"Because he shouldn't have disappeared."

"Did you know that Ferrin has tried every possible Locator cross-check? That even includes comparing the time length of past assignments, trying variations on Baldur's Locator tag signal, and sending Sammis back-and foretime with portable Locator packs. There is no trace of Baldur."

I swallowed that without commenting. No wonder the Tribunes had been content to let me poke around Midgard. They knew he wasn't there—and were happy to let me waste my time on nonproductive searching.

"And you let me waste time . . ."

"Would you have believed me without trying it out yourself?"

I wasn't sure I believed Freyda even then. "So what do you want now?"

"For you to stop wasting your energy chasing him."

"What did you do to him?"

"Nothing. We had nothing to do with it."

"He was a threat, and you got rid of him."

She looked at me for a long time, eye-to-eye, and her gaze never wavered. "I was the second choice to replace Martel—a very distant second. Baldur was selected almost unanimously on the first ballot. He refused, without explaining. If you want, I'll even open that section of the Tribune's private records to you."

Put in that light, I had no reason to disbelieve. I didn't understand, but Freyda was telling me the truth—at least, the truth as she knew it.

"Why?" I caught myself just about ready to pound on my workbench. "Why would he just walk out on everything?"

"I have an answer, but I think you'll have to find your own, Loki. Guards are human—even Counselors. We are all human, too human, for all our experience, all our ages, and all our abilities. You can exercise the powers of a god or be a human, but not both, not and stay sane. Somewhere you make a choice. Baldur chose one way, and I may have to choose another. You will too, if you haven't already."

The words whirled around in my head. I heard the words, about choices. And I knew my parents had made that sort of choice, and maybe Baldur had also. But why did it have to be so? Why couldn't we be what we were born?

Looking into the darkness of the shadowed and shielded machinery, asking why, and not having any answer, I let the time ebb and flow past me before I understood that Freyda had left.

I wondered if she had ever even been there. Was her appearance a creation of my own mind?

I had to dismiss that, but I wondered how much of what I saw and heard was "real."

Baldur had dropped from the sight of the Guard, had turned his back on me, and I had to accept that. But I still had trouble with accepting Freyda's logic.

If I understood more behind Baldur's reasons, I might have been able to find him. Somehow, and in some way, it had to do with the old issue of barbarians. Baldur didn't like cultures where the "elite" were barbarians, where only a few understood the technology that underlay the civilization. But even I understood that the cultural factors came far before the technology, and I couldn't see Baldur running off and playing god in some pre-tech place in order to foreshadow his own kind of technological society. Besides, those changes would bring the cold change winds blowing—unless the time and place he had chosen were foretime from Query.

The only places he'd shown great interest in were Midgard and Terra, and personally I thought the Terrans were just like us, maybe worse, and too damned ruthless for someone like Baldur.

I took a deep breath as I considered the possibilities. The change winds didn't blow backward, and there was no real way to track Baldur, or my parents, or anyone through all the foretime possibilities.

Baldur was gone. I had to accept that. So were my parents. The old names were fading from Query. Martel had stepped down. Odin Thor was a shadow growing fainter by the century. Orpheus was a shadow in the mist. My grandfather Ragnorak had been missing for centuries— had he done what Baldur had? Was he living out a meaningless life somewhere on a dustball in the void?

Were the ranks of the immortals thinning, to be replaced with techs like Ferrin, Verdis, Loragerd? Or did the system just create new names, like Gilmesh, Loki, Freyda?

XXII

I WAS PERCHED above my workbench, pondering over more changes in the layout in Maintenance. After I had moved into Baldur's former spaces, for a time, I had left things as they were, but the fact that Baldur had been a good head taller than me had made more and more changes necessary.

Nicodemus tiptoed in. I never did understand why people tiptoed into Maintenance as if they were treading around eggshells. I was always civil, and I was still a pretty junior Guard.

"What is it?"

"Counselor Heimdall would like to see you, sir."

"I'm not 'sir,' Nicodemus. I'm Loki, first, last, and always."

"Yes, sir."

I sighed. I wasn't really even a supervisor, and I couldn't understand why I rated a 'sir' from other junior Guards or Guards who'd been serving for centuries. Still . . . while Heimdall was the nominal supervisor of Assignments, which now included Maintenance, it had become apparent that I was running most things. Heimdall had larger birds to watch, although one of the older Guards might ask him to ensure I did something quickly. Such requests were generally meaningless, since we did everything as quickly as practicable.

As Nicodemus stood there waiting, stiff, as if I were going to snap his head off, I climbed down from my high stool and straightened my black jumpsuit. I followed him up the ramp to Assignments.

Heimdall was waiting, calm, assured, with his long black hair in perfect place. He frowned and kept pulling at his chin, as he flicked his long fingers over the console in front of him while I stepped up on the platform and settled myself in the lower stool across from him.

"Do you know Patrice?" he asked without looking away from the screen.

"Went through training together."

"She is a good diver, I gather?"

"My impression was that she was very good."

"Sammis agrees. It makes this very disturbing."

I waited, wondering why Heimdall wasn't being his usual direct and blustery self.

"Locator has a fix on her twelve centuries back. A place called Toltek. She was supposed to have returned—two days ago. We sent Derron after her, fully equipped. He hasn't returned. Both signals appear to be in the same place."

"Toltek? Derron?" I hadn't heard of either.

"Derron was the best diver from the Domestic Affairs Strike Force. Sammis thought someone with that sort of experience might be helpful."

Heimdall's assignment struck me as simple, and nasty. If Frey's most accomplished goon couldn't rescue one of the better divers, I wasn't sure I wanted much to do with it.

He hadn't answered my question about Toltek; so I asked again, politely. "I've never heard of Toltek. Should it be familiar?"

"Toltek?" Heimdall seemed amused. "No. It's out beyond Faffnir, in a small cluster. Patrice did the preliminaries from deep space, then orbit, and brought back some holo shots. She went in for a closer scan."

"And never came back, and he never came back. Now you want a double rescue?"

Heimdall's fingers flashed over the console again before he answered. He didn't look straight at me.

"It may not be that simple. Archives evaluated the holos Patrice brought in. There are signs of a mid-tech culture, maybe even high-tech."

High-tech civilizations are rare, with only a handful in the time and locales surveyed by the Guard.

"High-tech?"

He nodded.

That meant that if I didn't drag them out, at some backtime point a large sun-tunnel would be funneled through the undertime to Toltek. What was left of the planet would resemble a large cinder. So might any Guard on it—or be left breathing sudden vacuum or dust.

The idea was to destroy anyone bright enough to stumble onto the Guard, and theoretically an alert Guard might have a chance, but how much of a chance depended on a lot of variables. Sounds cruel, but it was necessary. With really good divers scarce, the Guard couldn't afford to have them whittled down through rescue attempt after rescue attempt. We weren't organized for massive assaults, and we really didn't like the idea of even gadgets like wrist gauntlets and their thunderbolts falling into high-tech hands—or paws, or claws.

Moving a big sun-tunnel usually took two divers, and it took a while to plan and coordinate. Plus, if it were used, we lost access to a possible high-tech culture and goodies we might be able to exploit. All in all, it would be better for the Guard if I could pull the two out. That might not be better for me.

"Briefing?" I asked, mentally trying to catalogue what I might have to take along.

Heimdall tapped several studs and pointed to the adjacent console. I changed stools, on edge because he moved to stand behind me, and watched the script and holo shots unfold in front of me.

Patrice had blown it. Obvious to a dunderhead like me. You take it easy with planetary cultures that build lots of structures you can see from space. While some tech societies have visible long-distance-travel systems—rails, canals, roads—some do not. The difference is power. Invisible systems take far more power, much more—whether they're tunnel ways or air transport.

Toltek was too regular. The forests, rivers, coastlines, fit into a definite pattern, almost a sculpted one. Any culture which shaped a planet for aesthetic purposes had one hell of a lot of power to spare.

"Stinks," I said to Heimdall, more to get his reaction than to state the obvious.

"Do you recommend forgoing a rescue and implementing a sun-tunnel?" he asked in a level tone.

Common sense said yes, but I wasn't ready to do that when I hadn't even seen a single member of the species. If you're going to destroy something you really ought to know what you're destroying.

"No. I'll see what I can do."

I would have liked to travel back to Toltek equipped like a deep-space dreadnought, but that wasn't possible or practical.

According to data Patrice had recorded, the air was breathable, if higher in water vapor and oxygen. The temperature was a touch higher than on Query, and so was the gravity.

How was I going to decide on equipment? No information on planetary dangers, no description of the "people" who shaped an entire planet and imprisoned two timedivers who should be able to escape from most places—that made it difficult.

I needed a small Locator pack to narrow down Derron's and Patrice's shoulder tags, plus demolition cubes to cover any tracks I might leave— assuming I could pull it off.

"When are you leaving?" Heimdall interrupted my mental planning with his question.

"As soon as I gather what I need," I replied, slipping off the stool and heading out the archway toward the ramps.

I stopped by Maintenance to pick up a small laser-cutter and some spare power cells in case Derron and Patrice needed them. I sent Brendan over to Locator for the portable directional packs and told him to meet me at the Travel Hall.

Hard as I concentrated, I couldn't think of anything else of a special nature I ought to have taken—and if it were really special, I could always come back.

I reached the Travel Hall before Brendan and began to assemble what I needed. Improvisation was the order of the day. I started with the black bodymesh armor I'd worn to Sinopol and put it on under a standard jumpsuit. I added the laser to the equipment belt, plus a stunner, some additional ration packs, and a sheath knife.

By the time I finished, Brendan arrived with the Locator packs.

"Ferrin says good luck."

I had to grin. "If you see him—don't make a special trip—tell him that luck is a luxury too chancy for me."

Brendan nodded. Seldom could anything I said surprise him.

I ambled out into the Travel Hall from the equipment room, taking my time, wondering if it were another Heimdall setup. Finally, I dived, smashing through the time-chill and arrowing out and backtime toward Toltek.

I took a flash-look at the planet from altitude.

Patrice's holo hadn't conveyed the greenness of the place, from the green-tinged atmosphere, to the long green grassy stuff that covered the regular fields, to the persistent green cliff walls that outlined the symmetrical green sand beaches.

After three, four, five flash-throughs around the edges of the daylight sites, I had not gotten a glimpse of a native, although the evidence of continuing planetary maintenance was always clear.

Nocturnal—that was my next thought.

I flashed through the undertime, and was rewarded when I passed over a beach on the night side. I came back for another look.

Several figures were standing on the glowing green sand under the stars. I broke out, silently, on the sand almost under one of the squared-off cliffs. I stood there for several units trying to make out the shapes—definitely not humanoid.

Abruptly, I was seized and shaken. That's what it felt like, but there was nothing around. Just as suddenly, I was tossed head over heels into the sand. My whole body was being vibrated. I could sense that the shadow figures were moving across the sand toward my prostrate form.

The shaking and the high-pitched whine that accompanied it made concentrating as hard as hell, but I knew if I didn't slide quickly, I wasn't going to be sliding anywhere. I managed to blot the distractions out and stagger undertime.

Too close . . . way too close . . . and stupid. Just because I had trouble seeing at night didn't mean they did. As usual, dumb old Loki had slid right in and announced, "Here I am."

I broke out momentarily with a split entry high overhead, just long enough to lose the aftereffects of the whine, and dropped back into the undertime to try to get an impression of the Toltekians from a safer perspective.

Not even roughly humanoid, that seemed certain. Through the time-tension barrier, I could make out a solid "trunk" with pseudopods, I thought, propelling it, and with a fringe of tentacles at the top. The "trunk" glistened like the cliff walls around the beach, which made me think it was solid.

After gleaning what I could from the undertime and watching the Toltekians swirl around where I had disappeared, I decided on a temporary retreat. I plunked myself over to an isolated spot on Faffnir, settling on a knoll above the lifeless black sea. I sat down on a raised and smoothed chunk of ironglass, which probably dated back to the fall of High Sinopol. Hoped the rest would cure my shaking legs. They hadn't appreciated the reception they'd gotten from the inhabitants of Toltek, or their watchdogs, or whatever.

In the atmosphere of quiet antiquity, in the afternoon light of Faffnir, I began to put together what little I'd picked up.

Item: Toltekians were nocturnal and nonhumanoid.
Item: I was assuming the beings I'd run into were Toltekians.

Item: They had picked up my appearance in the dark within
     unit-fractions and had shaken the hell out of me.
Item: I had barely managed to think my way undertime with
     the scrambling my thoughts had taken.
Item: Most divers wouldn't have gotten clear.

My first guess was energy projection, but I hadn't felt the power, and
with my sensitivity to energy concentrations, I should have.

Second guess was directed sonics. That matched the high-pitched
whine I'd heard.

If the Toltekians were a sonic-based culture, that would explain a
number of things. They could have picked up my arrival, even my
breathing, and reacted. The sonic assault could have been a natural
defense mechanism, and an effective one, at that.

I postponed further thought while I pulled a ration stick out of my
belt and munched it to quiet my shaking legs. If my assumptions were
correct, and I saw no reason why they wouldn't be, the Toltekians would
be limited in how long they could and would maintain such a sound
attack. Patrice and Derron should have escaped and reported. They
hadn't.

I only knew of two basic ways to imprison a good diver—either
scramble thoughts or tie him or her to a chunk of something too big to
carry into a dive. The second method was likely, particularly if Patrice
and Derron had been rendered unconscious by the initial sonic blast.

I reached down and checked my own equipment belt for the laser-
cutter. It was there. I wanted to make sure I hadn't lost it when I'd
fallen all over the beach.

Knowing the kind of Guard employed on the Strike Force, I'd have
bet that Derron had homed in on Patrice's signal and tried a frontal
assault of some sort. The Toltekians had apparently been ready for Derron and potted him as well.

Sitting there in the early afternoon light of Faffnir, once I was recovered, I decided that waiting any longer wouldn't solve my problems. I
didn't know of any equipment back on Query that would provide a
defense against sonics, and the subjective clocks of both Patrice and
Derron were still ticking. So it seemed like speed was the best answer.
Speed and the willingness to zap a few Toltekians along the way.

I checked the Locator packs and activated them, diving undertime
back to Toltek and emerging quickly and periodically to home in on
the signals. They led me under one of the larger structures on the northern continent. Both signals were from the same point, from what seemed
to be a chamber carved from solid rock well beneath the city above.

The objective "now" for Patrice and Derron was close to local midnight. I could have waited until day, but I didn't know what shape they were in, and that far underground I doubted it would make any difference to the locals.

With both the darkness and the undertime barrier, I couldn't see more than shadows, but I got rough images of two figures chained to opposite sides of a long wall with Toltekian sentries stationed or planted or whatever at each end.

Hit and run was my idea, to slide up from undertime behind one sentry and stun him, her, or it, then to do the same to the other, disable the weapon gadget in front of the one guard, cut the divers free, leave a mess of demolition cubes, and depart. The charges would make a thorough mess of the chamber and cover our tracks to some degree.

I slid from the undertime behind the Toltekian sentry closest to the gadget gun and thumbed the stunner. It hummed. Nothing happened. The sentry stood.

At that instant, both sentries "screamed," and the whole dungeon began shaking. I dropped the stunner and threw a thunderbolt at the far sentry.

That energy bounced off and around him, skittered around the tentacles, and they were purple tentacles. The sentry shrank back, winced. In the intervening instants, the sentry I'd failed to stun had turned toward me, "screaming," and grabbed at me with his tentacles.

For a fraction of an instant, the vibrations distracted me, but I mentally pushed them away and slid around the grabby Toltekian. I threw another thunderbolt, this time at the weapon. The pointed nozzle wilted, and the sentries froze at the flash.

A deep gong chimed in the background, kept chiming.

So far, I'd alerted the entire city and accomplished nothing. I was beginning to see red. Damned if a bunch of tree-snails were going to stand in front of Loki!

Light! That was the answer. They didn't like light.

I began firing off thunderbolts in every which direction, pulling the laser cutter off my belt as I dashed/slid toward Patrice. She was out cold, slumped against the chains which linked her to the wall. Her arms were tight against the stone, and the links were shaped rock which seemed to be the same material as the walls. That explained plenty.

I cut through two sets of links and let her slump to the floor.

Mindlessly, I fired off another round of thunderbolts in the general directions of the sentries and slid to the other side of the chamber.

Like Patrice, Derron was unconscious. It was harder to cut the chains from his arms because he was bigger than me, bigger than Baldur, and had his whole weight resting against them.

I used the cutter to blaze through one while I threw a bunch of lightnings behind me. I had the feeling that the Toltekians were closing, ready to enter the chamber, but I finished the second set of links and let Derron collapse on the rock floor. I could hold him, but not carry him.

I glanced up to see a procession of Toltekians coming through the oval door in a high-speed glide. My body felt like it wanted to shatter, but damned if I were going to let it.

I froze the tree-snails in place with all the power I could throw, and as the chamber flared with that light, I saw they were unlimbering some ugly hardware.

I flash-slid to the other side of the chamber and tossed Patrice over my shoulder, glad she was small, and slid/dashed back to Derron, feeling like I was moving in slow motion.

Using my free arm, I blasted the Toltekians again, concentrating on light. The thunderbolts may not have hurt them personally, but all the power I was tossing blinded them and made a mess out of their equipment.

Before I picked up Derron, I had enough presence of mind to yank out a handful of demolition cubes, one at a time, ripping the set tab on each one as I scattered them across the chamber. One was supposed to bring down an average-sized dwelling into dust, and the bunch I scattered had enough power to punch a good-sized hole in the citadel around us and the city above, if that's what it happened to be.

With the last cube gone, I grabbed Derron around the waist and forced my way undertime. Forced, because it's difficult to carry a co-operating and consenting adult undertime, let alone two unconscious ones. The unconscious mind resists *any* change, has a tendency to lock itself into the here and now, wherever that is.

But I managed, clearing the undertime of Toltek as fast as I could, which was the subjective equivalent of a slow crawl under large and heavy rocks. I wasn't about to try a straight dive foretime to Query, not lugging all that baggage. I struggled forever to get just as far as Faffnir, and Faffnir was only a fraction of the time and distance home to Query.

I broke out on the knoll I'd found earlier, not that I'd been looking for it, but somehow we ended up there. Local time was late afternoon, with a breeze sweeping up from the sea, carrying a tang of ancient metal.

Legs quivering, I eased both Derron and Patrice down and laid them out so they'd be as comfortable as possible on the hard ground. Both were breathing and, outside of a few reddish welts, had no obvious physical injuries.

I sat down on a low hump next to them. Didn't have any choice. My legs refused to support me any more. I dug out my ration sticks and gobbled two bone-dry before I even thought about being thirsty. After a few units, my body stopped trembling, and I began to take stock.

Patrice and Derron, unmoving, slept like small children.

I surveyed my own gear. Both my wrist gauntlets were fused and inert plates. Everything from the directional readouts to the power cells and thunderbolts was gone. Probably overused them, I figured, in the continual throwing of power at the Toltekians.

One arm, my left, had a red line. I peeled back my sleeve slightly to trace it, but the scratch only ran up to a point below the elbow, much like a fine scrape that a briar thorn might have caused me when I was growing up and running through the woods.

I dismissed the scratch. Everything else was accounted for except for the stunner and the laser-cutter. I'd dropped both. That couldn't be helped, but I hoped that they were safely buried under a pile of rock.

"Uunnnnhhh," someone groaned.

I glanced at the two. Derron was not moving, but Patrice was shaking her head and trying to get up. She was still wearing a canteen—more thoughtful than I had been. I was surprised that they still had their equipment, but hadn't thought about that before then.

I unstoppered the canteen and helped her take a swallow. For several units she sipped and pulled herself together.

I waited.

"Hell! It had to be you, blood and thunder. Break out and assault the sentries and carry everyone off. I suppose you fried the planet after you left."

"Patrice!"

"Did you?"

"No. Just blew up part of the city, or whatever it was. That's a guess. Took everything I had to drag you two here. Didn't have the energy to stay around and see what happened."

"Where's here?"

"Faffnir."

She cocked her head. "How come they didn't get you with their shaker-upper?"

"They almost did . . ." I told her about my experience on the green sand beach at night.

"No reinforcements? And after *that*, you decided you could handle it?"

In retrospect and put that way, it did sound stupid.

"Why not?" I replied, not wanting to admit it.

Patrice was about to tell me, but Derron started groaning, and I was spared another lecture.

The three of us sat there while Derron recovered. After a few units, he started in with his questions. From the tenor of his comments, I gathered he'd been in some tight spots.

"Never seen anything like it . . . those trees, snails, didn't react to stunners, warblers, darts, nothing," Derron lamented. "Just how did you manage it?"

"Lucky, I guess." I didn't have real answers, except for one. "I used thunderbolts to blind them."

Patrice looked at me, then climbed to her feet, studied the area around us for a long unit or so, then jumped, pointed at a nearby rock, and screamed, "Loki! Quick! Blast it!"

I fired and blasted the rock into powder.

She turned absolutely white, sat down in a heap like a pile of stone fragmenting into gravel.

Derron looked around as if he'd missed something. "I don't get it." I was afraid I did.

"I must be seeing things . . . Better get back, before Heimdall thinks we're trapped here," said Patrice. Her color was returning.

After we finished the last of the water from Patrice's canteen, we all dived.

Hycretis insisted on putting all three of us through a barrage of diagnostics and retaining us for a night's sleep in the Infirmary before he'd let Heimdall debrief us. The head medical tech with the twinkle in his eyes also insisted on feeding us breakfast before he'd let us go. All that was relative, of course. Any one of us could have left, and no one could have stopped us, but he was so insistent we stayed.

After eating and cleaning up, we made our way to Assignments.

Nicodemus intercepted us at the archway into the Assignments Hall.

"Counselor Heimdall would like to see you individually, starting with Guard Patrice. He suggests that Guards Loki and Derron avail themselves of the lounge."

I shrugged. Derron frowned.

Patrice smiled faintly. "Don't worry."

I hoped I didn't have to, but Heimdall was sharp, and I still didn't have everything figured out. Derron and I wandered down the corridor to the vacant Guards' lounge and sat down. For a time, neither one of us said anything, just sat there, me looking at him, him looking at me. But he wasn't, not exactly.

As the silence lengthened, Derron cleared his throat.

"Loki?"

"Yes."

"Remember one thing, no matter what happens. I'll never cross you."

I swallowed. I hadn't expected that. Finally, I stammered, "All right, but there's nothing to worry about."

There was a seasoned Guard who'd probably been tracking down malefactors for centuries and who outweighed me and overtopped me, asking me to remember that he'd never cross me.

"I mean that," he insisted.

"I'll remember," I promised, when it became obvious that he was sincere. But why was he that worried? Just because I'd somehow thrown a thunderbolt without gauntlets? A thunderbolt was a thunderbolt, and both kinds killed.

We sat for a few units longer before Patrice tripped her way out of the archway and down the corridor.

"Derron, Heimdall wants to see you next."

"See you around, Loki," he said as he got up.

I stood and bowed slightly. "Good diving, Derron."

He deserved that much.

Patrice waited for Derron to enter the Assignments Hall. "I didn't tell Heimdall, because it would hurt the Guard, I think. But have you got it figured out, Loki? Do you finally understand?"

I understood all right. At least I understood the how, if not the why. If timedivers could use their minds to move their bodies across distances, why couldn't we use our minds to move energy? After all, a body is merely stabilized energy. From the beginning I could dive while in motion, and that was handling a form of kinetic energy.

Personal thunderbolts? Theoretically practical, since there is some energy virtually anywhere, and a thunderbolt is only the manifestation of passage from one point to another. It does leave a lot of damage in the wake of its passage, but that was another question.

What Patrice and the others didn't seem to see was that it made no difference. If I did a series of quick split entries in the atmosphere, it looked like I was flying. If I thought hard, I could throw thunderbolts. If I concentrated hard, I could avoid getting disrupted by restrainer fields and sonic shocks. So what?

My talents were only the logical extensions of already existing talents, and in some cases, the difference between what I could do and what equipment could do wasn't detectable. What was the difference between a thunderbolt from my fingers and one from a gauntlet?

As the Laws of Time have decreed—dead is dead.

"I understand that you're worried, and that there's no reason for it."

"Loki . . . you think too much like Baldur. If there's a mechanical explanation, why, you figure everyone should see it—"

"There's no difference between a thunderbolt and a thunderbolt," I protested.

"Probably not," she admitted. "But I'd rather that you didn't forget. So . . . would you do me two favors?"

I nodded. The favor business was getting old quickly.

"First, when Heimdall's through with you, check your gauntlets again, and remember that it's you, not the equipment. Second, remember that technology is an acceptable way to be god for most Queryans. The real thing upsets people . . . a lot. Think about it."

She hadn't quite come out and said it, but it was close enough, and she made sense, too much sense.

The gauntlets would have to wait. Brendan had already carried all my equipment down to my bench for repairs while we had stayed with Hycretis for observation. There wasn't much I could do while I waited for Heimdall to debrief Derron.

That didn't take too long, and Nicodemus came after me.

Heimdall was leaning back in his stool right where I'd left him— had it been one or two days before? I wasn't sure.

"Derron and Patrice have filled me in on what happened to them, except for how you got them out of the dungeon. The Toltekians 'screamed' when you appeared, and that knocked them out, I gather. What happened?"

I told Heimdall what I'd done, from the point where I'd broken out on the green sand beach at night until the time when I staggered onto the knoll on Faffnir with Patrice and Derron in tow. I did not mention the state of my gauntlets.

He nodded as I recited, muttering at one point something about "sheer brute force." A matter of opinion, I thought. At least, I hadn't used any more force than necessary, nor destroyed the planet.

I stopped.

"You all agree on the sonic control," Heimdall noted. "What sort of follow-up would you recommend?"

"Do we need any? I'd have to revise my earlier judgment. I don't think the tech level is as high as I figured, and the Toltekians are so sensitive to light that they could certainly be controlled if necessary. From a safe distance," I added.

Heimdall smiled at that.

I added a last judgment. "I think the planetary engineering is more a result of extensive social control and sonics than ultra-high-tech."

Heimdall punched a code on his keyboard and leaned back so that I could see the picture that formed. The holo shots zeroed in on one of the Toltekians cities. As I watched, a whole section collapsed in on itself, thundering down into a crater filled with rubble.

"Sammis and Wryan went out last night to get a series of follow-up shots. I thought you might have left a trail." He laughed, a short bark that wasn't expressing humor. "Your demolition cubes covered your tracks adequately, although they may have been an overreaction."

Overreaction? Heimdall hadn't been out there getting himself shaken apart.

"Sammis does agree with all three of you that further retaliation is totally unnecessary, but that further monitoring should be undertaken— from your safe distance, Loki."

I repressed a sigh of relief. Even if they weren't human, I really wouldn't have wanted to have fried them out of existence.

"There's one question that still hasn't been answered."

I stiffened.

"When the Toltekians 'screamed,' the others were stunned. You were hardly affected. Why not?"

"I don't know. The first time, on the beach, it was hard, really hard, to get undertime. The second time I was mad, wasn't thinking much about it, and it didn't seem to affect me as much. I don't know why. Hycretis gave me some hearing tests, but my ears are fine. Maybe the effect isn't as strong after a while or if you can concentrate." I shrugged. My guess was that I was just stubborn enough to be able to concentrate a bit more. "I don't know, Counselor. I just don't know."

The title seemed to help, and Heimdall relaxed a trace.

"Is that all?"

"That's all."

I got up from the lower stool and went out through the main archway. Started down the ramps to Maintenance, but I wasn't really watching where I was going and barely avoided crashing into Sammis. Wryan was next to him and smiled.

Then they were gone.

I was still mulling over the gauntlet bit. I had checked them on Faffnir before Patrice had awakened, and I was certain they were so much fused metal. I could certainly tell busted equipment from functional. I'd thrown a thunderbolt without a gauntlet—just one for certain. But could I do it again? I wasn't about to try in the Tower, or with anyone around.

I nodded at Narcissus, but headed straight for my bench, where the gauntlets lay, fused. One chance remained. One of them still might be operational, for all the melted exterior. I studied them, then removed the power cells, and had to cut away metal to get one free. The cells had no charge. I placed the left gauntlet in the diagnostic center. "Nonfunctioning" the console scripted out, following the caption with an extensive list of malfunctions.

The right one was diagnosed the same way.

So I had another problem—and Patrice's point about gods and technology. I still didn't know if I could do it again, if I had any control, or if it had all been a fluke. My guts told me it wasn't, but I didn't know yet, and Baldur's philosophy of checking and testing told me to take it step by step. Somehow I thought I'd better. Even if she didn't think so, I had listened to Patrice.

Heimdall, also, had been too polite and deferential, and that nagged at me. In the meantime, I had to get back to the day-to-day business of Maintenance, because Brendan was working with Justina's people on console malfunctions, and Narcissus had gone back to more polishing than repairs.

That evening came quickly, but tiredness even sooner.

Diving, especially rescue diving, takes a toll, and after Toltek one night's sleep just hadn't been enough. It couldn't have been more than fifty units after I'd walked out of the South Portal of the Tower before I was on my pallet in the Aerie, feeling my eyelids close.

Most nights I slept without dreaming, or if I did dream, I didn't remember. Once in a while, I had a dream so vivid it was real, no dream at all. I could tell that kind only because the subjects were usually so unreal. The dream I had after the Toltek rescue was different, if indeed the events were part of a dream.

Some sense of energy, of power, a tingling in the air around me, pulled me from sleep, but I felt so light, so filled with energy, I knew it had to be a dream.

It couldn't be happening, not when I'd fallen asleep so exhausted.

With the exception of the muted light from the glowstone floors, the Aerie was dark. I looked around, half sitting, trying to puzzle out what had brought me from such a deep sleep.

Nothing . . . no one . . . but an uneasy feeling grew, centered on a point in the middle of the room.

I eased to my feet with a fluid motion so swift it had to be unreal. The walls, each glowstone, the permaglass overlooking the cliffs, all stood out in the darkness in relief, outlined with a reflected energy from somewhere.

I walked across the room, hovering above the glowstones, trying to pinpoint that sense of danger. I couldn't explain it, but the energy that outlined the room, the same energy that filled and refreshed me—that unseen force that coursed through my veins like fire—was the danger. As I waited, at the absolute center of the Aerie, a point of starlight burned, pulsing, pushing its way out from the undertime. The room filled with blinding light, heat, and power.

Without thinking, I gestured, pushed the light back where it came from, banished it into the undertime. I couldn't have explained how, but I did. I wanted it gone, and it was. Realtime wavered for a few instants, rippled by the vanishing energy, before stabilizing, and the remaining energy lingered in the Aerie, the outlines which had put everything in relief fading slowly. The heat dissipated even more slowly. I felt sleepy, filled with warmth, and curled up on top of my sleeping furs.

When the sun struck me full in the face at dawn, I was still curled on top of the furs. The Aerie was warm and the dream still clear in my mind. As I uncurled I felt better than I had in seasons, relaxed and refreshed. After wondering exactly what the dream had to do with the feeling, I washed up, dressed, and downed some biscuits and firejuice, ready for a quick slide to the Tower and the work that was waiting.

The Tower was quiet, the ramps vacant, when I arrived earlier than normal, and bounded down the incline to Maintenance.

I had zipped through several routine jobs, a gauntlet that might have been wedged in a corner for millennia the circuitry was so old, a pair of stunners that a synthesizer had been dropped on, by the time Brendan rushed in.

"Loki, have you heard the latest?" He stopped and whistled. "Where did you get that tan?"

"Tan?" The time on Faffnir hadn't been enough to darken my face that much. Was I more tanned?

"What's the latest?" I didn't really know what to say about the tan.

"Sun-tunnel blew on some of Frey's people. Hycretis has them closeted in the old wards of the Infirmary. Hush-hush, that sort of thing, but Lynia had duty last night, and I wouldn't let her in until she told me."

Lynia must have been his contract, but Brendan hadn't mentioned her before. Even as a full junior Guard, he was too young, by custom at least, to enter a full contract.

"Told you what?" I was thinking about Lynia—barely out of training—and about how it had been with Loragerd.

"Loki, were you listening?" He laughed.

I grinned back. "Sort of. Lynia had to work late . . ."

"No . . . she had duty. Hycretis and Gerrond had to work most of the night patching people up. Some of the divers were badly burned. Must have been something . . ."

"What were Frey's people doing with a sun-tunnel? How could one do that? It either works or it doesn't. And if they dropped it into real-time where they were, there wouldn't be even cinders left."

"I know," mused Brendan. "But Lynia said five had to stay in the Infirmary, and all the regenerators were in use. One of them was scream-ing 'impossible' over and over."

"Strange." I tried to keep my voice level. "Very strange. But we still have some backlogged stuff."

"Strange" wasn't the word. I felt a cold fear rising in the back of my mind, like a wave. While it couldn't have had anything to do with my dream, I knew the sun-tunnel did, and it was part of the gauntlet ques-tion. While it might have been coincidence, with my subconscious tun-ing in to the disaster, I didn't think so. And I didn't like the idea of Frey playing with sun-tunnels.

"About that tan?" Brendan asked again.

"Got stuck on Faffnir after the mess on Toltek."

He nodded.

No one else I ran into ever mentioned the Guards in the Infirmary, and I never knew their names. Frey would have been the only one I could have asked, besides Hycretis.

But when I cornered Hycretis, he just nodded and said, "I get so many odd injuries, Loki, I just can't remember." He looked sad, and that bothered me, but Frey, or Heimdall, had gotten to him.

I got on with reorganizing Maintenance and trying to figure out exactly what I could and couldn't do with and without equipment.

XXIII

THE HAIR OF the man dressed in black flashes like flame against the dawn sky. "Man" is a general term, not entirely appropriate.

Thunderclouds mass to the west, growling at the puny figure who hangs motionless in the empty air above the mountains. The sun peeks over the lower hills to the east, as if uncertain about entering the conflict. For it is a conflict, a confrontation between forces.

The storm roars and rears its hammer over the man, who, suspended like a black candle between the clouds above and the rocks below, would block the descending arm of nature.

The eastern heavens pink, and to the west, under the fringe of the thunder-

storm, the distant horizon skies have the black shades pulled down.

A blast of energy lances from the mountain tip below the man toward the clouds.

He lifts his left arm. The jagged fire smooth-bends, and he gathers it unto him. He glows momentarily in the dawn like a sun-point.

His left arm straightens as he hurls the lightning against a more distant peak.

His sudden laugh would shatter the towers of the cities of men, were they near, for all its moderate pitch. The mountains shrink beneath that laughter, though they move not, and his insignificant figure standing on nothing but air between the mighty peaks somehow dwarves them all.

With a third thunderclap, the man in black is gone, and the dawn proceeds on schedule, with only the echo of his laugh reminding the sundered stones and the wilted storm that a god has stood above them.

XXIV

SEASONS, YEARS, CAN often pass before a Guard knows it, even an impatient one with a purpose. Much always had to be done, and there were few enough Guards to accomplish the mere monitoring of our corner of the galaxy, small as it was in comparison to all the stars in the night sky.

Through it all, I kept puzzling out the old equipment and machines in the Maintenance Hall, determined to uncover the principles behind each design. That was a straightforward task, and more unfortunately, generally disappointing. Despite their size, they were uniformly simpler than they appeared, with one or two exceptions.

Harder was the effort to master the material left in Baldur's console.

Not so direct as mastering either hardware or technology was the self-imposed goal of increasing my own personal abilities. At first, the hardest of tasks had been working with Sammis and Wryan. As the seasons passed, the sessions had become more and more sophisticated and less and less frequent. Finally, Sammis called a halt.

"You know more than either of us, and probably more than any Guard does, and that's far too much for your own good. You've attained too much ability, too much raw knowledge, and not enough wisdom. Try to take a break. Watch things happen, and let a little time flow around you."

By then, I'd already decided that I needed more than mere improvement in physical or diving abilities.

Some of the stunts I attempted after Sammis and Wryan called off physical training were stupid, like catching thunderbolts, trying to tap solar flares through the undertime, or trying to string together continuous split entries to fly in real-time. I could fly, sort of, but it was more work than it was worth. Overall, I didn't spend that much time on experimental stuff, but it was fun to try, and playing with the storms above the Bardwalls was exhilarating.

When I wasn't in the Aerie, still adding to it or fixing it up, I spent a lot of time around the Tower, mostly in Maintenance. I picked up a new trainee, finally, a woman named Elene, who rated somewhere between Narcissus and Brendan in ability—another redhead, but a lot calmer than I had been, than I still was, probably.

I took some considerable pride in the fact that we had everything in the Tower working. Heimdall couldn't find anything to complain about, but he still did. Getting on top of the repairs gave us time to redesign the entire Maintenance Hall and to dig up some better repair consoles, suitably modified, from Weindre. I got rid of a few of the totally obsolete behemoths that no one had ever used, and I don't think Heimdall ever noticed. To him, a machine was a machine was a machine.

A messenger interrupted me on a morning no different from any other spring morning in Quest. He was one of the newer trainees—Giron. He arrived as I was puzzling over the design of an incomprehensible, for the moment, Gurlenian "artifact" brought in by Zealor.

"Tribune Kranos requests the honor of your presence, sir."

"I'll bet."

"Sir?"

"Tell the honored Tribune I will be there as soon as I get the grime off my hands."

What did Kranos want? He normally avoided me like the plague. If the Tribunes wanted something, Freyda was the one to drop it on me, usually. Once or twice Eranas had.

I sighed, flipped the artifact partly out-of-time-phase to make sure no one else casually fiddled with it. Narcissus was getting too damned curious for his own good, fueled by the fact that he'd learned a bunch of repairs by rote. He still didn't understand, and he didn't have the talents, either mechanical or diving, to get himself out of the jams his nosiness created.

A few days earlier, he'd tried to discover the purpose of the back-row machine that assembled atmospheric shield units, and if I had been any slower he would have had one planted in his shoulder. It worked on a mass-focus assembly system. While uptime Weindrian equipment took one-third the space and power, I was still trying to figure out the theory behind mass-focus systems. I'd forgotten to refocus the time protection, and Narcissus was trying to energize the equipment with his shoulder halfway into the focusing point. Narcissus had almost paid for both our curiosities, but he hadn't, and that was what counted, I supposed.

I wiped off my hands, straightened my jumpsuit, and marched up the ramps to Kranos's chambers.

Blunt as always, he had a proposition stated before I sat down on the stool across from him.

"Loki, I'd like you to take a short leave of absence from Maintenance and see if you can give the admin people a hand in designing a better personnel system. You've done wonders in Maintenance."

"Why?" That was a question I'd asked too often. "I know as much about administration as this stool does."

Kranos's stern face was always smooth, and with his thick and unruly hair, made you think he was an animated statue on loan from the Archives gallery. We didn't have much sculpture, and none of it was animated. People with such long lifespans don't need as much to remind them of the past they've experienced. Besides, if it were really old, no one outside the Guard really cared—except people like my parents, and even they'd left all the traditions behind when they vanished.

Kranos didn't blink an eye at my question. "You have a different outlook. We need new perspectives to make sure the system keeps working."

"You've got plenty of new blood. What about Verdis or Lorren? I would certainly think Gilmesh would run a tight shop."

Kranos smiled a smile that wasn't real. His eyes stayed level while the corners of his mouth turned up. "Too tight. No one wants to think about change. But he's going over to Locator for the same time to give them a shake-up."

In the whole time I'd been in the Guard, I'd never heard of such a switch. Suggestions were freely offered between supervisors anyway, except to Maintenance, but that was different, I thought. So why did Kranos want me out of Maintenance?

"Why do you want me out of Maintenance?"

"I don't. I want you *in* Personnel. If you want, I'll even seal the Maintenance Hall while you're gone."

Although that was unrealistic, I believed the spirit of his offer. The question was why he wanted me in Personnel, and it looked like the only way to find out was to agree. "When?"

"As soon as you want to."

"Fine. How about tomorrow?" The sooner I went through whatever the Tribunes had in mind, the better.

Kranos's expression didn't change, but I had the distinct impression that he was relieved, as if he'd been asked to play a role for someone else and was pleased to have carried it off.

The next morning I was sitting on Gilmesh's padded stool, looking at Personnel tracers. None of it made any sense. I had to start asking questions. At first, even the answers didn't make sense. Finally, I commandeered Verdis, set her stool across the worktable from me, and got the system explained from scratch.

She had entered training a year or two before I had, and like many of the key support people, wasn't much of a diver, but as I had begun to discover, without her or Ferrin or Loragerd or a bunch of semi-divers, the Guard organization would have been hard-pressed to function.

Verdis was a redhead, with shoulder-length hair verging on a shade of mahogany, black eyes, and a shortish nose. She often expressed her feelings with her whole body.

She was expressing impatience.

". . . we take the exact time periods of each assignment. That gives us a backup to the Locator system. The accuracy is important, and that's why divers are taught to check and verify the wrist gauntlet readouts immediately upon return . . ."

I understood that need. What I didn't understand was another backup to the computerized Locator system.

"But why the backup in Personnel?" I finally asked.

"Because Locator only handles diving records of active divers. If they want to sort for a rescue, it would delay things too much, and priority goes to active Guards . . ."

I frowned. In a way that made sense, but there were only around four thousand active Guards, including Guards like Verdis. All of the records were stored in the Personnel system computer and in the main Archives data banks.

It still seemed like a lot of duplication, especially since five people essentially ran Personnel—Gilmesh, Verdis, Lorren, and two trainees. The trainees basically ran duplicate data blocs into the system daily.

The rest of Personnel dealt with assignments and history. My record showed the times in various duties, from the time I was a trainee onward, but that didn't take that much space in the records. After they became Guards, people didn't shift that much, or at least not often.

And even updating the diving didn't take that much effort, it seemed to me. All in all, about four hundred timedivers were out on continued assignment at any one time. Another two hundred were involved in short or routine dives.

Why were there more divers on extended dives? I hadn't thought about it, but the answers became clear as I thought. First, a diver handling short dives could handle a lot more than one on a continued, say, linguistics assignment. Second, the Law of Real Elapsed Time comes into play. If I dived to Atlantea for ten units of holo-taking, I could not return to Query and break out at any time except ten objective units after my departure. I couldn't gain or lose time on Query by backtiming or foretiming and then returning to my point of departure.

Like most of the time laws, no one had a good explanation why it worked that way. But it did. My own theory was that, because Time requires a biological synchronization between objective time on Query and objective time experienced by the body, the Law of Elapsed Time is merely a reflection of that synchronization.

Because of the impact, and because deep time-diving is exhausting, Guards on remote assignments are often better off staying on location.

Time flows differently in different parts of the universe. Our body clocks are set by where we are born and run in tune with our home system, by and large, give or take a few time rushes.

If a Guard were caught in a time-flow rush, or more important, missed one, the personal consequences might be severe, I suspected. I thought that a few divers never made it back to Query because their biological clocks got desynced and they couldn't break out.

Once or twice, I'd noticed that a breakout on return was more difficult than usual. I attributed that to the getting out of phase with the in-system time flows.

No one had done any work on it, not that I knew, despite the Archives' creation of a time research section—that was one person. Practically speaking, neither Query nor the Guard was big enough to maintain a meaningful research base. We had to borrow our ideas from others, and since the Guard sidetracked any research by other cultures into the nature of time, we didn't know very much about the "why" of the Laws of Time and only a relatively small amount, I felt, about the "how."

I hadn't realized how small Personnel was—and how little real work they did. Compared to Personnel, Maintenance was a bigger operation. I had Narcissus, Brendan, and Elene, plus me, working full-time, and a lot of the simple dings and dents were fixed by second- and third-year trainees.

Maintenance had four full-time personnel; Personnel had three; Assignments twenty, and that included all the divers who did background research; and Medical had close to two hundred spread across Query.

But all that meant that Guard headquarters had perhaps four hundred people. Where were the other thirty-six hundred Guards? I asked.

Verdis gave me an exasperated look. "What does that have to do with tracer forms?"

"It doesn't, but the question popped into my head."

"It should have popped into your head in training. Look . . ." As she talked, Gilmesh's old trainee sermons began to come back, and the picture made more sense. And she was right; my own experience in Domestic Affairs should have answered the question.

What it boiled down to was that the support functions of the Guard far outweighed the Temporal "police" functions. Query had roughly ten million people, roughly two thousand towns, five thousand villages, and one city—plus a lot of people living where they wanted. All told, Quest wasn't really a city, not with less than 25,000 scattered around. The largest of the towns, Elysia, contained 8,500; the average village less than 500 people. So Quest had to be called a city, but only relatively.

That was part of the point. Queryans enjoyed the fruits of stolen technology. Even stolen technology has to be distributed, and as I had discovered in Domestic Affairs, even law-abiding people need some police system. The combination of duplicator offices and Domestic Affairs offices took almost three quarters of all Guard personnel.

If someone needed a cooker, for example, or a synthesizer, he didn't need one more than once every five or ten years, if that. He went to his local Domestic Affairs office, which had mint copies of standard household items, plus a duplicator. Some of the larger offices had several duplicators.

The range of appliances was narrow. Large and small cookers and synthesizers; washers; dryers; hygiene appliances; a variety of hand tools, saws, hammers, wrenches; communits; wordwriters; small hand tractors; a few hunting weapons; and that was about it.

The catch was . . . it was free. Any adult Queryan could request those items as needed. He might need several friends to slide one home, and if someone wanted a bunch of items all the time, Domestic Affairs was likely to investigate.

Guards also often dived into other cultures in search of their own personal luxury items or tools. Technically, it was frowned upon, but the hierarchy didn't seem to mind if the Guard was fully briefed and he or she could get it without notice or creating cultural change. Had to be that way with a headstrong bunch of divers, I supposed.

". . . you can see that leaves the Guard spread thin . . ."

"Thin" wasn't the word for it. Roughly four thousand active Guards supporting the technology and culture of ten million. It almost didn't seem possible, and I said so.

"Maybe it's not," retorted Verdis, "but we do it. Sometimes I wonder whether the power grubbers and the egotists around understand it."

"You don't think Personnel is given enough credit for ensuring we have the right people in the right places, then?"

"Loki . . . don't patronize me. I'll never be the hotshot diver you are, and I'll never understand why a gauntlet works. But I have to ask if you understand at all how fragile the system really is, how much depends on the Guard?"

"I understand." I was irritated, irritated for some reason I couldn't quite explain. "What I see is a stream of broken equipment that none of the divers understand, that few of them pay any attention to, and it all gets dumped on Maintenance. Every time we come up with something a little better, everyone wants it and abuses it, and the repairs get heavier. If I should get caught up, Heimdall or Freyda or Kranos invents a mission that is designed to fry or freeze someone and assigns it to me.

"And by the time I get done with that, there's even more busted equipment stacked up—all waited for eagerly by a bunch of would-be heroes who don't understand the difference between a screw and a bolt or an integrated circuit or . . ." I paused to catch my breath, but hurried on before she could interrupt.

"Now, maybe I don't remember how important the Guard is, but no one on this planet, in or out of the Guard, can make much of anything. If you want to look at it honestly, we're a bunch of parasites supported by a group of glorified thieves. We're the thieves, and it's a bit much to puff out our jumpsuits and tell the galaxy how important we are."

Lorren was peering around the corner, mouth open as if he couldn't believe what he was hearing.

Verdis had her mouth half-open, and her color had changed from what I'd call flushed to cold livid.

"I didn't say the Guard wasn't vital to Query. Sitting here and seeing how it's all held together brings it home. But it doesn't make us heroes. We pull down or change whole planetary systems and destroy peoples who might threaten our monopoly of time. We pride ourselves on slaving to pamper ten million Queryans who are handed the necessities of life on a silver platter. We discipline them with an iron hand, to ensure that the end justifies the means."

Verdis rocked on her stool, ready to flare. I quit talking. I'd said way too much.

"How can you wear the black? You don't really believe in the Guard. I think all you believe in is Loki, first, last, and always."

"I don't even believe in that. I don't have the answers, and I'd like to know what comes next."

She let out her breath with a hissing sound. "Next?"

"The present structure isn't going to last forever. Have you noticed that we rattle around in this Tower?" I shrugged, waiting for a response.

Verdis shook her head slightly, and her mahogany hair slipped forward over her left shoulder. She didn't seem quite as angry. "So what do you think comes next, Loki?"

"I don't know. Assignments to fewer planets, more off-planet assignments per Guard; fewer local offices and more people thrown onto Hell? Have we already reduced the number of high-tech cultures within our range in order to keep control? I'd bet we have, but I don't know how you'd prove it."

"You're paranoid."

I smiled, hard as it was. "Probably, but it doesn't have much to do with Personnel. So let's skip it for now." I wanted to, and wished I hadn't blithered all over the place.

Verdis nodded slowly. She wouldn't forget, and who knew who she'd tell? I wanted to kick myself in the ass. Instead, I changed the subject. "Now . . . have you considered a direct link of the Personnel computer to the Archives data banks?"

They hadn't. It wasn't surprising. I'd already gathered that little new programming had been done. I guessed that the original designers, whoever they had been, had kept the system simple to ensure its continuity.

"Why do you think so?" Verdis asked, with the emphasis on *you*.

"Because simple structures last longer. A centralized administrative and records system could be handled with a fraction of the people now used. But if it failed, I doubt anyone could rebuild it from scratch. Right now, the present system could almost work with stylus and permabond."

I wouldn't have been moderately amazed if the Tribunes had been quietly blocking too much computerization. But if that were the case, why had Kranos sent me to Personnel? Did he really want simplification from simpleminded Loki?

Wheels were turning. Wheels within wheels, and my formerly clear picture of Guard operations was definitely being muddied. Who had put Kranos up to the switches? Was it all to put the focus on troublemaking Loki while Gilmesh investigated Frey's private empire?

"Verdis, I need to take a walk. Be back in a while."

She just watched me go.

When I looked into Locator, Gilmesh was standing up, listening to Ferrin explain some facet of a Locator trace he probably already knew. They both broke off and looked at me politely as I plodded though the archway.

"Mastered Personnel already?" flicked out Gilmesh.

"Hardly," I lied, since there wasn't much else to master except the evaluation process, and I knew about evaluations from writing them. "I just needed a break from the wealth of administrative detail."

I was sounding dumber by the instant, and both Ferrin and Gilmesh were having trouble not shaking their heads. So I smiled, turned around, and left. Let them think what they would.

Verdis was staring at the wall when I returned. "Loki . . . I'm sorry."

"So am I." I smiled. "Ready for something to eat?"

"I don't go out to lunch," she answered.

"You don't have a rough-edged Maintenance type fouling up your records all the time either. Let's go." I hoped she wouldn't argue. I disliked arguing, even if I did too much.

"Where?" she asked softly.

"Demetros's or Hera's . . . take your pick."

"Demetros's."

"I'd like to take a quick check in Maintenance. I'll meet you there in twenty to twenty-five units. All right?"

I presumed the delay was fine from her slight nod. By the time I was headed out the arch and down the ramp, I was feeling paranoid, but becoming paranoid didn't mean that someone wasn't out to get me. I'd left a few microsnoops around the Maintenance Hall, and I wanted to see what had happened in my first day away.

They all fed into a storeroom, but what showed up wasn't all that interesting. Narcissus, Brendan, and Elene had been plugging away industriously. The only surprise was that they were handling space armor. Most Guards use it very little.

The snoops were tiny, the best designs I'd been able to locate. The problem was that I'd had to build them from the design, rather than copy them, because they were uptime Terran. The post-atomic Terrans left the rest of the low high-tech cultures so far behind in sneakiness that it was unbelievable. What was most amusing to me was they believed that they were totally straightforward.

Their microcircuitry was almost as good as that of the old Ydrisians, but since it was uptime, we couldn't copy it, and I certainly didn't have the time or the skill to create much from scratch. The single snoop I'd built to copy had been bad enough.

Whether the Terrans got even better was, like the Ydrisians, in doubt, since they seemed to tread on the verge of blowing themselves away. In those few times when I walked the streets of Washington, or Denvra or Landan, I could feel the change winds whistling around me. There was always an uncertainty about Terra that seemed more extreme than in other foretime locales, a conflict between what was apparently about to be and what might have been—a conflict that almost invaded the undertime.

Maybe it was the attitude of the Terrans, the fact that they held little or nothing sacred. Baldur had said that none of their gods were perfect, and yet that they required gods all the same.

Once, right after I got my gold-pointed star, Baldur had suggested I track one of the northern hemisphere's Terran cultures, a bunch of apparent barbarians who built sophisticated wooden ships with hand tools.

"Why?" I'd asked.

"So you understand how much some cultures can do with so little."

I'd understood that before I'd ever left on the tracking dive, but, just like on High Sinopol, I'd gotten too curious, and when I broke out I damned near got my skull split by a steel ax.

Those fellows on the longships swung first, worried later, even when someone appeared from nowhere. I'd blasted the ax, of course, but didn't zap the ax-wielder. Typical Terran, he wanted to know who I was.

I told him, not that it would matter.

That incident was representative of the Terrans—attack, bow to superior force, apologize, and then try to find out enough to get you the next time. But it still didn't explain the uncertainty or the continual change winds that swirled across the place. Baldur hadn't said much when I told him. He'd rubbed an eyebrow.

Change winds usually meant the Guard, but according to Locator no one was working Terra, not after we'd taken a look at the level of normal violence in the society. It wasn't a very safe place to be, and they had a lot of long-range personal weapons on even the safest streets.

Baldur hadn't had much of an explanation for the uncertainty on Terra, but that uncertainty might be why the Terrans could end up better weaponeers than the Ydrisians. But the uncertainty was also why we couldn't duplicate their equipment. Some places, like good stable Sertis, you could. Not Terra.

I shook my head. The nifty little Terran-derived snoops indicated that no outside Guards had been in the Hall but Heimdall. He and Nicodemus and a trainee had delivered the space armor and left.

My snooping completed, I planet-slid out to Demetros's. "Early caveman" best described the decor. The inn was comprised of a series of interlocking caverns, but each chamber was holed through the cliffside and provided a gull's-eye view of the north coast breakers.

I arrived before Verdis, despite my stop in Maintenance. I wondered if she were reporting to someone—but who?

I could see the actions—Heimdall finding space armor to repair; Kranos fronting for someone; Gilmesh investigating Frey's domain while all eyes were on me; Frey and his efforts with the sun-tunnel years back—but I couldn't see the pattern.

Had such subterranean maneuverings always been part of the Guard, and had I just been blind to them? Were Gilmesh and Kranos out to thwart the Heimdall-Frey collaboration? I'd just have to watch more closely.

I still had gotten to Demetros's early enough that most tables were vacant. I picked one on the shadowed side of the third cavern, far enough back from the edge, but not in the deepest corner where everyone looked to see who was hiding there.

Verdis came in with an emotional swing to her step that indicated she was pleased about something. The way her body indicated her feelings, I had to ask myself if she could possibly be involved in any of the plottings. While I didn't know her all that well, I doubted her ability to counterfeit her entire body posture.

"Very discreet, Loki," she observed after she'd toured or studied most of the inn trying to locate me.

"Didn't some wise type say that discretion was the better part of valor?"

"Probably." She sat down in the earthy way that said she was all there, giving her hair a sort of settling-down shake as she eased into the low stool.

Wishing I knew what more to say to her, with all my new-found concerns about wheels within wheels, I kept my mouth shut and hoped she'd dive right in. I needn't have worried.

"You've never had a contract, Loki, or shared quarters with anyone— just about the only Guard who hasn't. How come?"

"Snooping in my records, Verdis?"

She had the decency to blush, and it was becoming, perhaps in that it showed a shyness I wasn't aware she had. The sudden change of color, the redness, climbed her body like a wave and receded as quickly. If I hadn't been watching, I might have missed it.

"Well . . ." and she actually left the sentence unfinished, the first time I'd seen her at a loss for words.

Was she really interested, or was another role in the offing?

"Are you really interested?" I asked.

"I don't know. I would like an answer."

"Never hit it off, I guess, not well enough to contract."

"I find that hard to believe. Not even short-term?"

"With my background . . ." I found myself telling her about my parents, with their single life contract, totally in love and totally faithful, so far as I knew, for I didn't know how many centuries. I didn't tell her how they'd disappeared together as well. ". . . and with that sort of example, anything short-term seems, I don't know, so . . . so . . . why bother with a contract if it's not for a while?"

"You do make it difficult, don't you? Do your parents believe in a series of absolutes?"

"Probably. They don't believe much in the Guard, that's for sure." I went on to spill the story of my disappointments when I'd been accepted after my Test.

"So you have to believe in the Guard and its traditions, don't you?"

That was too stiff even for the best side of my better nature. "Do you always carve up people when they unbend and reveal a bit of themselves?"

"Sorry." She didn't sound sorry, just amused, as if she'd uncovered a rare and unusual species of some sort.

All the inns are self-service. And it was a fine time for a break from the inquisition. I got up and strolled over to the synthesizer to pick out a grilled Atlantean fishray, whatever that was, and a beaker of firejuice.

The synthesizer hummed, burped, and presented me with the beaker and a steaming platter of something that wasn't defined but smelled pretty fair.

Verdis selected something from Gorratte and a dark ale from Terra. We ate without conversation.

Finally, Verdis broke the silence. "Why do you accept all those impossible missions, especially when you and Heimdall don't get along?"

"Someone has to do them." That wasn't totally true. I didn't know what to say. Besides, there hadn't been that many, maybe only a dozen.

"Why don't Sammis and Wryan do some? Or Gilmesh? He's supposed to be a good diver." She took another bite from her plate, not quite looking at me.

"I don't know about Gilmesh, but Sammis and Wryan do." I shrugged. "Sometimes the hard ones . . . I don't know . . . I feel good when I can do them."

"You like proving you're the best?"

Answering that could put me on very dangerous ground. "It's more that I like accomplishing something that can be measured. Maybe that's why I like Maintenance. If I build something or fix it, I can look at it and say I did it."

"That implies you aren't too impressed with Personnel."

I wasn't, but I wasn't stupid enough to say so. "I think each Guard has to do what fits him—or her," I added quickly. "Maintenance fits me. It wouldn't suit most people."

"I suppose that follows," she said after a bite from her plate. "You seem to like hard facts and answers and results." She paused. "Is life really like that, Loki? Is everything so certain?"

I swallowed a too-big mouthful of fishray before answering. It scraped all the way down my throat, and I had to gulp down some firejuice. "No. But I have trouble when I get on shifting sands. Why is it all right to meddle with one culture and not another? Do we only play with those that would be a threat? Who defines what that threat is?"

"So you just do the job as well as you can and try not to deal with those thoughts?"

I winced. She was probably right—except I hadn't done that on Toltek. "Not always. I think more now, and I did persuade them to leave Toltek alone."

"Hmmmm . . ."

I didn't like the sound of the "hmmm," but I couldn't think of anything to add.

"Don't people live and die whether we meddle or not?"

I nodded reluctantly.

"So . . . if you don't kill any of these beings personally, what's the difference? They'll live and die just the same."

"There *is* a difference," I said even more reluctantly. "What that says . . ." I had to grope for the words, and the instants dragged out, but Verdis waited. ". . . is that it's wrong to kill one being face-to-face, but it's all right to destroy cultures. I don't believe that."

"You do have a problem, don't you?"

We talked some more, but that was it. It seemed to me that she really didn't understand that the idea of dead being dead applied to whole groups of people, whether they were born on Query or not.

I didn't go out to eat with Verdis for the rest of the time I was in Personnel. I stayed there for five days, and that was too long. I didn't get any new insights, just more aspects of the same questions, and there wasn't much else I could suggest to improve the place, because form follows function. No one was about to change the function.

Somehow, someway, something I had said had turned Verdis completely off. She was friendly, friendlier than when I'd first showed up in Personnel, but behind the pleasantness was a definite reserve.

Gilmesh returned to his empire after the six-day period, and I went back down to Maintenance with a head full of unanswered questions, still not knowing where to find real answers, feeling like all my communications were being monitored by "them," whoever "they" happened to be. I was far from certain even how many "theys" there might be.

I settled back into my space in the Maintenance Hall with a sigh of relief, however temporary it might be.

XXV

THERE WERE NEVER any alarms, no shrieking sirens, clanging bells. The Temporal Guard proceeded at a measured pace—with few exceptions. With eternity to work in, the Tribunes could afford the luxury of actions planned quietly in their secluded conference room—the one that no one had ever seen but the Tribunes—except I'd looked once from the undertime.

It had seemed normal except for the table, which somehow shimmered black even in the undertime and almost threw sparks beneath the surface of the now. What it was, I didn't know, except that it was definitely connected with time and diving, and with such connections, I was reluctant to break out where I wasn't supposed to be. I was also sure I wasn't the only one with snoops around.

Still, "eternity," even as practiced by the Tribunes, was a relative term. Practically speaking, most Guard actions had to be restricted to the past. I could manage time-diving not quite two million years back and about six thousand forward. But trying to work anywhere foretime was confusing. At the forward end of my range, I felt like everything had multiple images and shimmered as if it weren't quite real, or hadn't been quite nailed down into reality. It hadn't, of course, and foretime changes didn't always take. It's hard to change what might not even be.

Sometimes, over dinner at an inn, we'd discuss the questions of whether what we did had to be done, because in the overall scheme of things, because we did them, they then had to have been done—a sort of pre-ordained predestination. I didn't believe it—mainly because of the change winds. If it were all to be the way we made it by Guard meddling, there would never be change winds, because the universe couldn't be any different.

The present is the result of what happened, but some of what happened can be changed by outsiders. I can't go back and kill my grandfather, or the grandfather of anyone else on Query, but I could go kill the former Grand High Vizier on Sertis. Sometimes it changes things. Sometimes not. Time doesn't like to be changed, which is why Guard actions can get pretty violent.

The most violent ones I seemed to get, and more and more often they were heralded by the arrival of Nicodemus. As the years passed, even after he became a full Guard, Heimdall's assistant entered Maintenance more and more gingerly.

"Sir . . ."

"Another screwball mission from Heimdall . . . right? I'll be there shortly."

Heimdall wasn't in Assignments, and Frey was seated beside the supervisor's console. Sammis was seated next to him in a low stool, and Nicodemus eased into another one.

"Heimdall will be right back," offered Frey. "But this one is tailor-made for you." For once Frey had the light saber stowed someplace, and he wore a standard jumpsuit instead of black nightmail.

The phrase "made for you" triggered all sorts of mental alarms.

"Hmmm . . ." I responded cautiously, glancing around the Assignments Hall.

Sammis sat in his stool almost stiffly, looking at the glowstones, and there were deep circles under his eyes.

"Let's get on with it," groused Heimdall from the archway.

Frey damped the slow-glass panels, darkening the room. A full-length holo flashed onto the wall screen. Simple real-time star plate— I studied it, but I didn't see anything remarkable, not that I probably could have told a remarkable one from an unremarkable one.

"Sammis was scouting the fringes and came across this," Heimdall said as he climbed back into his high stool.

In the dimness, Sammis looked blankly at the screen.

I waited.

"Typical star plate," observed Heimdall, "except what's important is what's not there." He flicked a stud on the controls, and another holo appeared beside the first one. It seemed similar, virtually the same shot, but there were differences.

My first conclusion was that the same point had been taken at different times, but that was so obvious there had to be more.

"Midway down . . . on the right," cut in Frey, trying to be helpful, but sounding officious.

As it penetrated, I gasped.

In the first holo, what Frey had called our attention to was a brilliant star cluster. In the second, the cluster was overshadowed by a trio of even more brilliant points of light.

"Times?" I asked.

Heimdall grinned, pleased that he'd gotten some interest from me.

"The first holo is now, roughly. The second holo is uptime about ten centuries."

"Three stars going nova simultaneously is pretty rare. You're implying that it's not natural."

Heimdall shut down the grin before he turned toward Sammis, who remained stone-faced. Heimdall's voice lowered, almost with a syrupy sound. "This next series shows a season's span in a few units."

I watched as one star flared, then another, then the third.

"What happened?" I asked.

"Several things," Heimdall said. "First, you should know that there's something there extraordinarily dangerous." He nodded toward Sammis. "Do you want to add anything?"

Sammis shook his head. He looked like hell.

"The cost of these shots was high. Wryan got in the way of these creatures . . ."

Heimdall may have said more, but I missed it, as my eyes went back to Sammis. No wonder he looked like hell. He seldom went anywhere without her, or vice versa.

I swallowed. These things happened, but I found it hard to believe. They'd been around so long, and seemed so much a part of each other. I shook my head and looked back at Sammis. Poor bastard.

Wryan and Sammis—the long-contract pair. Maybe the only ones I knew besides my parents . . . and they were severed—not even together.

"Loki?" Heimdall's raspy voice brought me back to the wall screen— sort of.

I was still thinking about Wryan and her comments about my deficient knife work.

". . . anything that's quick enough to get Wryan . . ."

Heimdall was droning on, but I still had trouble concentrating on the mission, whatever it was. Wryan . . . gone?

"Loki?"

"Sorry . . ." I shook my head and looked at Sammis again. He wouldn't look at me or Heimdall. He just looked as if he wanted out of there. So I swallowed and listened.

". . . Sammis and Wryan made the foretime holo first, then went real-time into the cluster. It's out beyond Terra, by the way, beyond the Guard's current fringe, you know," Heimdall explained. "They tried to be cautious . . ."

At that point Sammis stood up and left. Heimdall kept talking, but I tried to wave, gesture something of sympathy, but he wasn't looking my way. I really wanted to throttle Heimdall. Instead I kept listening.

". . . out in deep space near a G-type star . . . within two units of breakout, a warship fried Wryan . . . almost as if they knew she was there. Sammis managed to get away and took a few more shots on the way back."

Heimdall undamped the slow-glass and pointed to the table across from him. "There's what he got on the ships."

The hard-copy holos were laid out for me.

For all my fiddling around back- and foretime, I'd never seen anything resembling them. Shark ships, shining black in the darkness of space, were caught in the act of destruction, destroying smaller ships of another type, annihilating crippled ships of their own fleet, blasting a moon station. There were others—one frame of a purple planet under a normal yellow sun; a frame of a series of orbit fortresses, deserted, pitted, and holed; a frame of a planet with a molten surface, circled by an ancient and cratered moon.

Destruction . . . fire . . . that was the theme.

For a long time I sat at the table. No one said anything, not even Heimdall.

If anything, most scouts brought back too many shots, but it was apparent that Sammis had struggled to bring back a handful from the cluster, the shark cluster.

I finally looked at Heimdall, the question on my mind.

"Because the sharks are getting out of the cluster, and they seem to have some way of detecting in the undertime."

That set me back in the stool. I didn't like playing god, but, if the shots brought back by Sammis were accurate, and I trusted Sammis a lot more than Heimdall, the sharks made the Guard look like philanthropists.

Heimdall raised his eyebrows.

I knew it was going to be messy . . . and long—if I could even do it.

"I'll look at it." Then I got up and walked out of Assignments. I wanted to find Sammis, but he wasn't anywhere around, and no one had seen him.

As I walked down the ramp to Maintenance, for the first time I was face-to-face with an assignment that looked like genocide, pure and simple. Sure, I'd heard the stories about Odin Thor, even as gory as depicted by Wryan and Sammis . . . I stopped again, wondering what Sammis would do. They'd been such a pair.

I swallowed and kept walking. In all the stories, though, the changes had been almost by-products, allowing peoples to destroy themselves, opportunities which they had willingly taken.

In recent times, though, and maybe never, no Guard had gone out to remove a race. Now Heimdall and company, sitting around their consoles like the sweet young ladies of bygone High Sinopol, were going to urge on their current candidate for hero.

Great, I thought to myself. So I was going to be a hero—if I made it. Wryan hadn't, and she had so much more experience and knowledge than I did that there was no comparison. The only advantage I had was that I knew the shark people were there and vicious, while she hadn't.

The shark people were something else—destroying anything that wasn't theirs, frying their own cripples, melting down planetary surfaces, undertaking target practice on research stations. A charming bunch, and I really hadn't even made their acquaintance yet.

I was a coward, and ready to admit it. If there were any easy ways to get the job done, I'd try them. Dead heroes were just that—dead.

I cornered Brendan as soon as I got back into Maintenance. "I've been drafted as a hero. Going to take twenty, thirty days, if not longer. You've got it."

I left him standing there flat-footed. He'd keep things running. I didn't have any doubts about that.

The next step was to go back to Assignments and get the rest of the briefing. That didn't take long because there wasn't much more available, basically the temporal and spacial coordinates.

After that I had to round up the equipment I needed. I'd already decided that I would be deep-diving, not that I was about to tell Heimdall that, and I intended to be prepared. Since I was limited in what I could carry and still function, I was selective: warm suit with sealed breather option, a belt nav-recorder, miniature holopak, and most important a remote life/energy detector that I could drop into real-time while staying undertime myself. The detector just might help me avoid the same fate as Wryan.

After lining it all up in the Guard's equipment room, I walked out of the Tower and slid home to the Aerie. The next morning was early enough for a reluctant hero. As I sat behind the permaglass, watching the twilight spread across the Bardwalls, everything seemed sort of empty, meaningless. Was I going to be assigned more and more difficult diving missions, year after year, until I was either dead or resigned from active diving?

What was the purpose of it all? And why had Frey been there at the first briefing?

I sipped firejuice until long after night fell. In the end, I decided that the questions were just a way of telling myself that I was scared—more of the unknown than the sharks.

For all the fuss and furor of the day before, only Sammis was at the

Travel Hall the next morning when I arrived to suit up.

"I'm sorry," I told him, now knowing what else to say.

"Thank you . . . Loki. I appreciate the thought." He looked at the floor, and he didn't say much more, just pleasantries, to which I responded with other pleasantries.

Still, it was funny how he was always around, and on good terms with everyone. Wryan had been too, and I had to admit that I missed her. But I swallowed and pulled on the rest of my gear.

From the instant of mind-chill with the departure from the Hall, I was tense. Wryan was the first immortal I'd known closely who had gotten zapped, and the holo shots Sammis had brought back had conveyed all too starkly the sheer destructiveness of the culture I was tracking.

I had planned to backtime to the limit of my range, a good two million years back, and work forward, trying to reduce the risk factor. I used an angle approach dropping backtime as I neared the cluster, because I didn't want to be near the present, even undertime, when I reached it.

When a diver reached range limit, it felt like the paths and time branches were all curling back with a searing red-fire edging. I stopped as soon as I sensed the curl, dropped into the now on a cold airless moon for the instant necessary to check the register, and my blood chilled—more than the temperature around me—and I dropped undertime. The readout had registered at a touch over a million years back, half of what my spinning mind insisted that it should.

The rest of the equipment had registered normal. Some sort of time-blocked cluster, and that wasn't exactly wonderful. Still, it could happen, I supposed, and I began sliding around the undertime looking for a likely shark-people planet.

Dull—that was one word for it. *Tiresome* was another. *Careful* was the third. There were close to a hundred thousand systems in that small cluster and I was trying to find the one that would erupt into mayhem a million-plus years foretime of my search.

With the life/energy detector and my own senses of probability, I felt I should have gotten a quick feeling for which systems had any possibilities at all, but real day after real day, I'd go from the Aerie to the Travel Hall, deep-dive and slide out to the shark cluster, pushing my detector out into the now at each system I located. At first, Heimdall waited patiently. Then he began to suggest less deep dives.

That got to be a pain, and I set up a staging point backtime in the cluster itself, only checking in with Heimdall occasionally. I kept track of my progress and got past sixty days without finding anything.

It took work to be a coward. The rest of them seemed to believe that they were invulnerable to the forces outside Query, but being immortal has nothing to do with that. I was the one being called upon to stick my neck out, and I didn't like what I was finding—or wasn't finding.

First, there wasn't *any* intelligent life on any of the planets I checked, even those with oxygen atmospheres. Second, I was blocked from going deeper in my backtime range at a million years, half my normal, and that half took full effort.

I was skip-scanning a couple of hundred systems a trip, and when the first fifty systems turned up blank on the detector, I took the gadget back into "our" territory and retested it. The detector worked fine, even a million years back.

Then I studied several of the cluster systems more closely. Sure, there was low-brain animal life, plenty of plants, but nothing big, nothing smart. I had hunches, but I kept them inside.

The few nights I spent on Query I spent alone. Loragerd was off somewhere, and Verdis avoided me. Maybe I was driving everyone off.

I wasn't sure. Maybe my whole approach was stupid, but I was scared. The more I looked, the more the pieces didn't add up.

Item: Three suns going nova simultaneously.
Item: A star cluster filled with ships that tracked undertime.
Item: An intelligent race that appeared to destroy all other life on sight, and the injured of its own species.
Item: A cluster in which time-diving is difficult.
Item: A cluster that has large numbers of inhabitable planets and no intelligent life—nearly a million years before the sharks start to spew from the cluster and across our galaxy.

The last item really bothered me. All inhabitable planets, with exceptions too rare to consider, develop at least semi-intelligent life. Even some gas giants, I knew from my experience on Anemone, had intelligent life.

For that reason alone, the surveillance boundaries of the Guard were limited to one sector of one galaxy. A substantial section of a single galaxy is too much even for immortals with the equivalent of instant travel. Too often we forgot how big the universe is.

I kept at it, though, and skip-scanned through more than a thousand systems in sixty days, feeling proud until I realized that it amounted to about one percent of the cluster.

On my few check-ins, outside of a few glances and a gently pointed remark from Heimdall, everyone left me alone. When you got right down to it, the Guard had to work that way. There just wasn't that much surplus for second-guessing timedivers.

Along the way, I adopted a quartering technique, relying on feel and knowing that, somehow, when I got close I'd know it. That was what we all based a lot on in the long run—feelings, plain and simple. If necessary, I'd decided I'd spend four years plus on it—that would amount to twenty percent of all the systems—and that was a lot easier on my life expectancy than the way Wryan had done it.

It didn't take that long—only another thirty-seven days of skip-scanning before something clicked. It was a plain, seven-planet system with a normal G-type sun, hard-core inner planets, with two small gas giants farther out. The detector showed a slightly higher reading, as well as energy flows on a different level.

Planet number three had an aura, and I slid in, following the feel, the shading of time toward the ancient. The Tower of Immortals had that feeling, like the Sacred Forge of the Goblins on Heaven IV, or the Priest-King's palace on Sertis.

I was careful, even a million years backtime, recalling the holos Sammis had collected.

After tracing my strange feel to its strongest point, I set my own holopak for instant exposure and made a flash-through. I repaired then to my staging planet, the vacant planet of the blue seas, to study what the holo showed.

The one frame I had taken was stark enough, and ugly enough. The years of erosion, wind, rain, hail, fire, and time itself had scarcely blunted the edges of the black fortress. The structure was a good kilo on a side, if not more, and nearly as high, as if a giant god had plunked it down in the middle of a flat, grassy plain.

Black it was, so deep a black that there was light in the space between stars, by comparison, black enough to swallow light. And old—that black monstrosity dripped years. The Tower of Immortals had been built yesterday compared to the black fort.

I sat down on a grassy knoll of Azure. I might as well give it a name, and I did, after its blue seas. I looked at the holo frame again.

On a second study, other details stood out—like the laser which was sweeping toward the holo center, or the absolute smoothness of the plain.

I shivered. Big, strong Temporal Guards who could leap centuries with a single dive and catch the thunderbolts from storms weren't supposed to shiver, but I did.

What sort of weapon was a mere thunderbolt against a mechanism that could last millennia and track and attack an object that appeared in real-time for only milli-units? Could this old fortress track under the now?

The first contact, strictly with an artifact, and it was hostile.

I forced myself to keep concentrating on the holo frame. The regularity of the distant hills behind the fortress, virtually all the same level, was another disturbing note.

I closed both eyes, took several deep breaths, and tried to concentrate, letting the feelings come as well. Sharks, shark people, staging base, sterile planets, weapons . . . all ran through my mind. Yet I had still not seen an actual shark person—I just thought of them as such from the shape of the ships Sammis had caught. Was that really accurate?

The sharks, or whatever, had been there longer than Sammis or Heimdall had figured. I was tempted to go back and tell everyone, but mad enough to decide against it. Damned if I was going back with my tail between my legs after one slightly scary brush with an ancient fort.

I checked my equipment, stuffed the holo frame into the equipment chest I'd brought to Azure, and closed the flaps on the bubble tent.

After a deep breath, I slipped through the mind-chill of the time tension and headed back to the planet of the black fortress. I stayed in the undertime beneath the structure, grasping for a link, a direction. In a funny sort of way, all created objects in the universe have time links, shadow paths, branches linking them with their creators. Call it an outgrowth of the fact that none of us can tamper with our own pasts.

The black fort, staging base, whatever it was, had a thready link farther backtime. I couldn't follow it far because I was near the end of my own backtime range, but I grabbed a damned good feel for the direction, and I slid along the directional I'd picked up, keyed and ready for anything.

I could pick up the deadliness of the second contact from well beyond the system's geographical confines—a dark feel stronger than the glow from the Tower of Immortals.

I noted the location and let myself drift foretime toward Query. After that I rated a solid sleep in my own Aerie, and there was no way I was tackling that second contact without feeling completely refreshed. I hadn't kept track of objective Queryan time, and when I broke out in the Travel Hall, it was close to local midnight.

A trainee I didn't know was waiting.

"Sir . . . you're Loki?"

"Yes," I growled at the girl, wondering why Heimdall, and it had to be Heimdall, had left someone to contact me.

She paled, but didn't flinch. That alone recommended her for hazard duty, considering the mood I was in.

I took the folded sheet she handed me, stuffed it into my jumpsuit thigh pocket, and walked straight for the exit portals of the Tower. Outside, I planet-slid straight to the Aerie.

I collapsed into the furs as soon as I had my boots off.

Sleep didn't last all that long, and I was awake not long after dawn. Not that I thought at first, just looked at the rising sun throwing light on the peaks and the canyons below, watched the weak light splinter off the ice fields of Seneschal, and let the silence penetrate—and with it the realization that I was afraid. Scared. Fearful. Names didn't matter; the feeling was the same.

When I returned to the cluster, I was headed for a breakout where beings or machines reacted with incredible speed. For the first time, the ability to dive, even to throw thunderbolts, didn't seem like that much of an advantage. I wouldn't be captured, never again, but I could be killed. Zap.

I remembered the folded sheet I'd wadded into my jumpsuit and retrieved it. Simple it was, and to the point. Finish or report your progress within a ten-day. Heimdall must be getting nervous. I crumpled the sheet and tossed it into the recycler end of the synthesizer.

Took my time cleaning up, rechecking my equipment, putting in new power cells—in general, stalling. I had to face the fact that I was putting off a return, and I had to return and finish the assignment, either that or beg off and let someone else get killed.

I had no doubts that any other Guard who undertook a mission to the cluster and found the sharks would be dead within a unit of contact—except maybe Sammis, and it sure as hell wasn't fair to dump it on him. He'd lost enough already.

I might be dead also, but I pulled myself together and dived—straight from the Aerie. There was no real sense in going to the Travel Hall. Heimdall could grouse all he wanted to. So could Verdis. No matter what happened, there wouldn't be any rescues. I was going to succeed or get zapped.

The first dive was to Azure, my staging point, where I curled up in the bubble tent for a catnap that turned out longer than that. A million-year dive was tiring, even if it took no objective time.

When I woke up, I felt better, and I knew I couldn't put it off any longer. I decided to call the second shark planet Lyste, for reasons unclear to me, except that the Sertians have a god of destruction with the same name.

I set the holopak and made a flash-through of quick points on the system's fourth planet, the one that reeked of age and shark. Then I slid back to my bubble tent to survey the holos.

The single frame of the first breakout displayed a perfectly cultivated row crop of some sort, not a single straggle of grass or weed showing.

The second flash-through was from what I'd figured from the under-time to be a small city. The holopak had come up with two frames.

In the first was a cart, apparently fueled by a stack of logs that seemed to be individual plants. I could discern no other machines, but several "people" in the background. They looked healthy, strong, and purpose-ful. Semi-humanoid was as good a description as any—smooth black skin, hairless, scaleless, short and stocky pair of legs, upright carriage, two arms ending in a hand of some sort, and a head.

The second holo frame had a detailed head-on picture of a "shark." I'd lingered a fraction of a unit to get that second frame. That could have been a mistake. The pedestrian marching down the street had seen me, recognized a threat, and turned in the space of less than half a unit. The reason the shot was head-on was that he/she/it had been caught in the act of firing a hand-held dart gun. The holo caught the dart emerging from the end of the gun—and I had no difficulty in grasping its barbed and hostile intent.

As I sat on the grassy knoll, I shuddered. What was I getting into? Why did even urban pedestrians react with instant violence to strangers?

I studied the second frame again. As I looked over the face, with the nostrils, if that's what they were, between two heavy-lidded eyes and with a virtually neckless head set on the squarish body, I could see that a number of other bystanders had reacted to the flash-through.

It was no fluke—they all had micro-unit reflexes.

Fine—I'd found the home planet—maybe. Now what?

I ate and took another nap after I found myself shaking. Was sleep a way to escape? I didn't care, and when I woke I munched through some more dried ration sticks before considering my options.

I couldn't very well eliminate their progenitors. I was at the backtime limit of my range. That meant frying the planet, but I still didn't know how many others there might be. I didn't believe that the people who had built the black forts had built only two—or what shape the one on Lyste was in, since I hadn't looked at it yet. And that meant I really didn't know enough.

I headed back to Lyste and made three more flash-throughs at ran-dom, plus a series of high-altitude recon shots, before retreating to the quiet grass of Azure.

Some conclusions leaped out at me from the holo frames.

The population density was high. On all of the run-throughs, there were crowded streets, and several sharks spotted me. At least one shark on each run had managed to unlimber the ubiquitous dart gun.

On the other hand, I received no interference from aircraft, which seemed strange, since the ground technology was sophisticated enough, fossil-fueled or not, to have suggested their presence.

I checked over the recon shots again and again, looking for some more clues. I just didn't want to go back to the Tower for technical assistance, not from Heimdall, since I wanted to jam the whole thing down Heimdall's throat one way or another.

Reluctantly, I decided I needed more holo shots of Lyste. I dived back to get them. On the last pass, I found myself within body lengths of an atmospheric fighter that definitely had been looking for me. He tried to lift a wing to whack me, but even his reflexes weren't fast enough, and I was gone.

With that, I took another rest stop on Azure, the staging planet that was beginning to feel like a second home. I slumped down next to my ration pack. Sooner or later I was going to be an instant too slow if I kept up exposing myself.

I glanced over the last set of high-altitude panoramas, letting my thoughts wander over the regularity, the gentle contours of the mountains, the direct lines of the rivers, the low and small cities, the rail-like transport, and the comparative lack of aircraft.

Finally, it jumped out of the pictures and pasted me between the eyes. Lyste was an old, old planet, probably gutted of easily mined minerals, fossilized hydrocarbons, and even natural radioactives. Yet it wasn't in some post-civilization crash, and it was populated by an almost insanely aggressive species more likely than we were to shoot on sight.

I studied the holos more closely, and, in the next to last one, found what I was searching for—the regular blackness of another fortress. I reloaded the holopak and dropped under the now.

Between the holo and the pull of the fort, locating it in the undertime wasn't at all hard. Still, at the edge of breakout, I hesitated. It seemed stupid, but it felt like someone was waiting, but how could that be when no elapsed time was occurring? Besides, I wasn't that close, and nothing was obvious through the time-tension barrier. So I went ahead.

I got the first holo frame, and a second—just as an enormous surge of energy flashed toward me. I tried to push it away and dive undertime simultaneously. I threw up my arm just before I penetrated the undertime—but not quickly enough. When my forearm shattered, I thought I screamed.

The dive foretime to Quest was a red-blurred agony, and when I popped out in the Travel Hall, the glowstones came up to meet me.

Next thing I knew, I was propped up in the Infirmary with a regenerator over my arm and a mass of tubes hooked into me.

"Loki?" asked a voice.

Focusing was difficult, even though it was the second time I'd ended up like that.

"Loragerd?" I croaked. My throat felt like I'd been swallowing sand.

I couldn't hear the response, if there were one, couldn't see the formless faces, and fell, twisting through the nightmare country into a dark pit filled with shiny black shark people who swirled and gobbled and chomped, mostly on me, but on each other when they got tired of tasting me.

Later, and I had no idea how much later, I woke up to find a young Guard sitting across the room.

"Good morning, or is it good afternoon?" I asked.

He seemed surprised.

"Morning . . . sir . . ." he stammered.

"Loki," I corrected him.

"Yes, sir."

"So what happened?" I asked, as if nothing in the world had gone wrong. Even though immortals recovered quickly, I was feeling a lot better than the time after Hell. I glanced at the arm that I'd felt explode, but it only rested in a dressing. I could wriggle my fingers, even. I frowned. Regenerators didn't work that fast.

"Tribune Freyda should answer that, sir."

He left, presumably to run down the honored Tribune.

I wriggled my fingers again. They burned, and the whole arm felt bruised, but it was all there. There was a beaker of Sustain on the table, and I swallowed the whole thing, ignoring the kick to my guts when it hit. I just wished there had been another beaker.

Freyda arrived shortly.

"All right, superhero, you've left us on blasts and bolts . . ."

"Did you leave me much choice?" I interrupted.

I was still sore about the whole situation, but whether I was sore at me or sore at the Guard—that I wasn't quite sure.

"From your instruments, we figured you went back a million years, but the energy drain on the equipment shows two million. Locator pinned the spot, but no one can get anywhere close, and Eranas gave strict orders that no breakouts were to be tried until you were in shape to report." She glared at me.

"You realize that no one could have pulled you out if you hadn't staggered back under your own power?" Her eyes narrowed as they flicked to the loosely dressed arm.

"I suspected it, but there wasn't much choice."

"You also couldn't have survived the energy blast that your equipment took, but there was only the damage to your arm." She looked at the arm again. "Hycretis still . . ." She broke off.

"I heal quickly," I said.

"No one heals that quickly."

I shrugged, then changed the subject. "Did the last holo frames come through?"

"There were three. That's another thing. Where's the rest of your equipment?"

I held up my good arm, my right one, to stop the questions. "I had to use a staging base. I imagine the stuff's all there. Do you have the holos?"

Freyda handed them over. I took them with my right hand; the left still felt shaky, although the Sustain had helped. The top shot was the last one. It showed raw energy and my forearm exploding in blood under the pressure. But the wave of energy, laser beam or particle beam, stopped cold at the forearm. Too bad I hadn't reacted sooner. When I thought about it, energy was energy, and if I could handle thunderbolts, why not lasers? Except—learning under fire you sometimes make mistakes.

I laid that frame aside.

Frames one and two showed what I had been looking for—and afraid of finding. The installation, though more eroded, apparently also deserted, was a match to the ancient fortress on the deserted planet, down to the regular hills and the flat plain in front of towering black walls.

The evidence was enough for me. The same culture built both.

The sharks on Lyste were also avoiding the black fortress, which indicated to me that the automatic defenses were not terribly discriminating about who or what they zapped. The more I learned about the sharks and the cluster they inhabited, the less I liked them.

Freyda sat through my studies in silence, finally clearing her throat. "Unless you have objections, I would recommend an immediate sterilization of that planet."

"Whose murder or suicide?" I asked brightly.

She looked at me with the cold expression that demanded an answer because she was Tribune.

"Besides me, who can get there? Does anyone want to try it farther foretime? And there's also another point—a rather important one. So far, I've found traces on other planets. My gut feeling is that these people already almost destroyed themselves once across the entire cluster—or someone else tried to, for the same reasons we're considering. Without looking where else they might be, frying one planet won't help much."

Freyda digested my objections. "We'll discuss it, and you can think about it while you recover. Hycretis says ten days or less."

"It'll be more like twenty or twenty-five," I countered. I wasn't going anywhere until I was not only fully healed but thinking. Those people were *mean*.

Freyda frowned. Her eyes looked at my nearly healed arm. I ignored her look. She wasn't the one who would be trying to counter people with micro-unit reflexes.

Meanwhile, everyone discussed the sharks. Heimdall thought genetic poisoning might be a good idea. Freyda still wanted to sun-tunnel the planet or nova the sun. Odin Thor wanted to send the whole Temporal Guard back with thunderbolts.

"Do the Guard some good! Shake up these softies! Give 'em some real field experience, that's what I say!" insisted the old warrior.

He conveniently forgot that he and I were the only ones with the time-diving range to get there or that he'd have to be led.

I just listened, and thought. And I wondered how many planets were inhabited by sharks, even that far back. Despite the problems I'd had getting information, we still didn't have enough.

Before I came to any conclusions, I wanted to see if I could track undertime from the second fort—the one on Lyste. I hoped there weren't more, but I really doubted that there were only two in the cluster.

Neither Loragerd nor Verdis came to see me, even when I was puttering around Maintenance, doing routine repairs while thinking about shark people. I had to keep telling myself that I needed some quiet duty and more sleep before I should dive into that cluster.

Brendan had done well in my absence, and outside of one or two ticklish jobs he'd left for me, Maintenance was current. Baldur hadn't been indispensable, and, it appeared, neither was I. That must have pleased Heimdall no end.

Practically, however, the time came when I couldn't put off the resumption of my shark assignment.

"Fit as a thunderstorm, fire and flash, ready to go . . ." was Hycretis's assessment. I wished he hadn't used those terms, but I grinned and gathered my equipment and headed for the Travel Hall.

Nothing had changed at my staging camp on Azure, since I broke out only a few units after my last exit. I didn't have to leave the interval between, but leaving blocks of time can be very useful, especially in emergencies. If you use up all your time, sometimes it can kill you.

My next stop was Lyste. I didn't break out, didn't have to, just centered on the undertime feel of the black fort that had potted me. From the undertime I could feel the continuity of the fortress and the flat plain in front of it, which meant that both had been there for one *long* period.

Hanging there, letting my thoughts drift out, I caught it—except it wasn't "it." I could pick up at least a dozen threads out- and backtime. Good and bad. Good because Lyste once had been a regional center for the shark predecessors who built the forts—assuming the builders were sharks or their predecessors. And bad because there could be a dozen other planets or systems inhabited by nasty sharks.

Rather belatedly, another thought crossed my mind. No one said immortals have to be smart, but I wondered why it took me so long to get to the point. Although the sharks were nasty in the now, they still couldn't do anything in the undertime, and I could certainly look at the inside of the fort from the undertime, perhaps flash through even.

After the initial inspiration, some of my enthusiasm faded. There were such things as internal defenses . . . but they couldn't put high-powered lasers inside—not if they wanted a fort left.

So I wandered through the dim outlines of the chambers in the undertime, trying to find the right spot for a flash-through, if I needed one. In the center, nearly a half-kilo underground, I sensed what I sought, what seemed to be a control center.

Scared enough that my flash-through was fast, I returned to Azure hoping the holo had gotten a shot or two. There was one frame—underexposed. On the grassy knoll, I studied the image from all angles.

Most of the chamber wall I had faced was bare and black, but the center section was blurred, like a holo of the Tower of Immortals. Even with the blur, the console, the chair, and the panels were clear enough, and I added another piece to the puzzle.

Item: The control board of the ancient fort was abandoned, and out-of-time-focus.

I made three more, equally quick flash-throughs, fast enough to avoid any internal defenses. That also told me that, if I hurried, I was faster than the machinery—but I worried about running into a live shark.

From the shots I compiled a sketchy outline. None of the gadgets looked familiar, except in the general sense that almost all extensive equipment built by humanoids seems to have a general similarity.

With that, I began tracing, as I could, the other backtime links. The first three turned out negative. Number one was a sterile planet with a flat dusty surface and the faint outline of what probably had been another fort. The hills were fused but regular. Number two wasn't around any longer—just fine dust in a ring around a G-type sun.

Number three was worse. I couldn't even get close, but from the undertime pressure I suspected the equivalent of a black hole where the sun had been—and G-type suns aren't supposed to do that.

My first impressions were being reinforced. Someone or something had played rough—very rough.

Numbers four, five, and six were repeats of my very first contact with the black forts, complete with a grassy plain, a welcoming laser, and no higher life. In all cases, I avoided the fireworks.

Number seven was another dust ring.

Number eight was slightly different, breaking the pattern. No intelligent life, but I did find a perfectly circular inland sea, deeper than anything on the planet, with what seemed to be fused shorelines.

By the time I got around to following the ninth trail, I was expecting some sort of local disaster, but through force of habit, dropped the detector out. I couldn't get it back, because, even from the undertime, I could feel the energy cascade. I left—quickly—without even breaking out anywhere.

On Azure, I thought about it, munched on some ration cubes, but stopped when my stomach threatened not to hold them. I sat down on the grass.

Whoever or whatever inhabited the planet—my ninth lead from the Lyste fort—had located and blasted out of existence a small block of metal in literally fractions of a unit. They'd used enough force to shake the undertime. From my point of view, "hostile" wasn't descriptive enough.

I thought about going back to the Aerie, but I was too damned tired. So I climbed into the bubble tent, and I slept. I also dreamed, dreamed of shadow sharks spitting flames, swallowing me whole with gaping black jaws. When I finally woke in the dim glow of a gray morning I was drenched in sweat. The nearby stream took care of that, and ration sticks helped clear my mind.

First, I needed to trace down the remaining leads to see what other shark planets existed—or that I could find. I decided to begin with the last three leads from the black fort on Lyste, rather than from Lead Nine, hoping they were relatively harmless.

All three were negative, for which I was grateful. The tenth lead, the first one I tried on this round, was another black hole, neutron star, what have you. The next one was another asteroid belt, and the twelfth lead from Lyste was a dead moon pocked with a series of deep, regular, and very artificial craters.

I still didn't want to trace the leads from the three other deserted black forts or dig into the mysteries of Lead Nine . . . and I felt grubby. So I dived back to Quest to resupply, clean up, and get a good night's sleep in the Aerie.

Heimdall hit me even before I cleared the Travel Hall. "Progress?" he asked in that slimy, extra-polite manner of his.

"Another inhabited shark planet, more high-tech than I thought, and a bunch more forts to check out. Now I need sleep and more supplies, and a lot more time."

"Any chance of a tissue sample?" he asked, obviously still hung up on his nutty scheme of genetic sterilization.

I turned on him, almost blasted him right on the spot with a thunderbolt. "Don't you understand? These people have faster reflexes than you or I do by a factor of between ten and a hundred. I might be able to shoot them in the back—maybe—but unless I could find an isolated individual, and I've never seen one yet, no, you aren't getting a tissue sample."

He fell back, pale, whether from rage or what, I didn't know or care.

As he departed, Freyda glided up, a cold flame, standing there in her black on black of a Tribune. "Another ten-day?"

"Maybe." I wasn't committing to anything.

I didn't sleep that much, perhaps because of the shifts between the cluster and Query. Most of the next day, I just rested, watching the view from the Aerie, enjoyed the eagles soaring in the shadows, the rose light of sunset reflected on the ice fields of Seneschal, and the silver rivers in the canyons below.

The following morning I left straight from the Aerie with a deep dive to Azure. It had rained, lightly, and the bubble tent was streaked with dust and pockmarks, but the grass around the tent was dry.

Gritting my teeth, I tightened my equipment belt and plunged through the chill of the time barrier. While not exactly eager to get on with the investigation of possible time leads from the other three forts on the currently uninhabited planets, I wanted to get it done.

In about three days objective, I managed to finish that part of the task. All the time-ties from the forts on leads four, five, and six, led to three times/locales. The first was Lyste. The second was Lead Nine—I never did call it anything else. And the third common contact point was the planet with the pretty circular sea.

When in doubt, try the easiest way first. That was my operating principle. So I scoured the empty planet with the pretty circular sea first, and tried to track things every which way. Nothing.

I felt I knew enough about Lyste, and that left Lead Nine, where I'd never even broken out. On the fourth day after promising Freyda I'd try for answers within ten, I geared up and dropped back to Lead Nine, knowing I couldn't put it off any longer.

With my experience out in the open against the sharks, if that was what they were, I decided that investigating the black fort of Lead Nine from the undertime was definitely the best way to start.

I located what seemed to be the control center where, unlike Lyste, there were people present. Gambling that they wouldn't destroy an entire control room to get a momentary intruder, I flashed through with my holopak set as quick as possible.

After a quick retreat to Azure, I congratulated myself on making a breakout against the sharks and remaining in one piece. Sitting on my grassy knoll in relative safety, I studied the single frame.

First, the center was operated and functional. Second, the sharks present looked a bit less humanoid than the bunch on Lyste. Third, I was lucky to be back in one piece, since all three sharks in the control room were looking at me, with sidearms up and ready. I rocked back and forth on my knees, wondering how they had managed it.

The holo frame was out of focus around the control board, the same way the frame I'd taken of the fort on Lyste had turned out.

I looked back at the frame, concentrating on the chairs and the consoles, evaluating the differences between the two forts.

Item: I could have used the chair on Lyste, but not the one on Lead Nine.

Item: The sharks of Lead Nine had access to and control of their fort.

Item: Lyste and Lead Nine were on opposite sides of the cluster.

I didn't have exactly what I needed. After resting a bit, and eating some ration sticks, of which I was getting more than tired, I pushed my range a trace more—just a year or so backtime—and went back to Lyste, a place a little safer than Lead Nine, my thoughts groping for antiquity, for a glimpse of the past.

Exactly how long it took, I didn't really know. In a trimmed and ancient grove, in a ring that exuded age, on the side of a hill carpeted with grass and shaded by trees so old that they held time in their needles, I found what I needed, drawn as I was to the spot by ages of thought trapped in the smooth stone walls of the temple, if that indeed was what it was.

I checked the area from the undertime, but not a single shark was near, and I stepped into the local dawn for a look. On the frieze above the heavy stone lintel was a procession of figures. The frieze was the temple's only ornamentation.

The procession was simple enough. At the left end, the first figure was a human woman, or close enough to fool me, and at the right end was a female shark. The figures in between showed, to my way of thinking, an evolution from strung-out and slow-witted humanoid to solid and fast-reacting shark people.

I took several shots of the frieze with the holopak, knowing the Tribunes would appreciate any more evidence, although I had no doubts that they already wanted the cluster rid of the sharks.

From Lyste I dived slightly foretime toward Azure—and almost broke out, until I felt a slight buckle to the undertime. Instead, I paused. Breaking out would not have been instantly fatal perhaps, but definitely uncomfortable, since where Azure had been was mostly molten and shattered rocks.

I fiddled around undertime until I could sense what happened. The whole undertime buckled, and a squadron—eleven ships—appeared from nowhere and delivered something—antimatter bombs, whatever. You don't swallow in the undertime, but I felt like it. Instead I went straight back to Query, and the Aerie. I needed to think, and I didn't want to deal with Heimdall yet.

As I cleaned up, I tried to think it through.

So . . . the sharks from Lead Nine were nasty, but would the nastiness last a million years? And how dangerous would they be? I had some evidence of a highly developed defense reaction, but as far as aggression went . . . all I really had were a few scattered holos from the present time and Sammis's and Heimdall's concerns that they would overrun the galaxy.

Would they?

I thought for a while. I didn't want to do it, but did I really have much choice?

I ate some more pearapples and finished off the firejuice. Then I pulled on the space armor—I hated space armor—and attached the holopak to my belt.

Then I slid out toward and beyond Terra, heading foretime perhaps two thousand years, looking for the bending in the undertime that might signify the undertime ships of the sharks. In itself, I didn't like the combination of space warships and time ships.

Once again, the business was time-consuming, but not so bad as the original search. It took five days—objective—before I found the first battle, except it wasn't a battle but a slaughter.

The sun was G-type, yellow, and the fourth planet was a water planet, except the oceans were boiling when I found it, and a squadron of black ships orbited.

One found my under-the-now track and began following me in real-time, presumably to blast me when I emerged. I didn't—instead dropped back several days, then popped farther foretime. The sterilization of the planet completed, black ships were doing things to the biosphere. What it was didn't matter at that point; so I dropped a few hundred years back.

Under me twirled a peaceful-looking planet. I didn't care much for the purplish ocean or the thick green-tinged air, but there were lights on the night side that had to be cities.

I dropped lower, and under the now.

From the darkest shadows I could find, I watched the equivalent of a street, a long straight grassy strip. In the middle was some sort of moving ramp or way, except that it didn't move, exactly. Rather, the people on it did, and what they stood on flowed and carried them. And they weren't exactly people, but sort of triangular floral tripods.

I tried another location, a smaller group of angular buildings, along a lake, but I saw nothing moving except a small six-legged creature that reminded me of a segmented cat.

I flashed through several other locales. The overall impression was of people, some violent, some bored, some working, some playing—even if they were floral tripods.

Then I slid foretime to the first buckling of the undertime, and I watched, not that I could have done that much against the attack.

Hundreds of the black ships appeared in orbit, frying several local satellites, and anything that flew toward them, and began assembling massive lasers, or maybe they were particle beams, turning each on the planet below.

They turned the oceans to steam, superheated steam.

I kept having to duck and dodge, not being able to maintain position more than a few instants in any one time or locale. At that point, with at least four smaller pursuit ships screaming toward me anytime I came close to breaking out, I left, simultaneously shivering and sweating.

I dropped back toward the now quickly, hoping to lose the trackers, and I did after perhaps a century, certainly not far back in terms of my range.

Why didn't the sharks travel far back- or foretime in their ships? It had to be for two reasons. First, they were bound as we were—they could use their mechanical control of time for instant travel and for scanning of other times and other systems, but once they linked into another system, I suspected that they couldn't affect their own destiny

in that system. All they could do was watch the undertime and patrol
the now.

Second, carrying material gear undertime takes tremendous power,
and power had to be a limitation of some sort. The buckling of the
undertime around them signified that.

I tried the next system over—but it didn't have shark- or people-
inhabitable planets. Three systems later, I found another planet—low-
tech, just into the steam age, I thought. These people were more catlike,
if you can imagine a four-legged, two-armed cat, with a brain in the
top of the torso.

It didn't matter there either. This planet was perhaps a shade too dry
for the sharks. They bombarded it with water asteroids and superheated
the resulting water and the small seas. One more sterile planet ready to
be reseeded shark style.

Maybe a doubting type would have insisted on more, but my guts
wouldn't take more, and I now understood the regularity of all the
planets in the shark cluster.

After another night's sleep, I marched into the Tower, but Heimdall
apparently had his orders, and we ended up in the Tribunes' chambers.
Freyda, Kranos, and Eranas were waiting.

"We would be interested in your report . . ." began Eranas.

Heimdall scurried in, followed by Sammis and two hefty Guards who
blocked the entrance.

I presented everything I had, not taking sides in the presentation. I
didn't have to. Sammis added a few remarks about what he and Wryan
had witnessed.

Heimdall immediately suggested their destruction.

Freyda ignored the suggestion and asked, "Have you any further observations, Loki? You have been inventive enough to survive and prosper
in the face of what these people have attempted."

"Prosper" was not a word I would have used.

"They once were like us," I offered, "perhaps even related or descended from the mythical forerunners. Now they rely on machines . . ."

I went on for a bit, pointing out that their limited control of mechanical time-diving/sliding had led to a totally self-centered and ruthless race, one that destroyed others on sight, and one with little respect
for their own wounded and disabled. Even as I spoke, I wondered if the
difference between the sharks or the Hunters of Faffnir, or the Guards
of Query, were only in degree, and not in kind. The sharks destroyed
anything that could oppose them; the Hunters enslaved it; and we
merely manipulated it.

"That may be," noted Kranos, "but the question is of action. What should we do?"

In the end, it came down to destruction. I would try to use the sun-tunnel to fry Lyste and Lead Nine before the remnants of the sharks spread.

After Frey's unfortunate failure with the sun-tunnel some seasons back, I had decided to investigate the technology employed by my apparent opponents and spent time digging into the sun-tunnel.

Unlike many cultures, where beneficial technologies come out of warlike beginnings, the sun-tunnel first came out of a peaceful use—a simple high-powered matter transmitter used by the same Murians from whom we had stolen fusion power. The early Guard made some adaptations, and, for theoretical reasons I didn't quite understand, having to do with the need to synchronize the varying energy levels of the universe, whatever was pushed into the input end was tossed out the receiver end as chaotic energy—searing, blasting, and pure destructive power.

The sun-tunnel assembly I put together for the sharks weighed half as much as I did, and it took me several jumps to carry it back.

Not even I could break out in a sun, nor was I crazy enough to try. I slid close enough to shove the input terminal through the undertime and let the sun suck it in. Not all the terminal was in real-time, since the equipment was twisted partly out-of-time-phase.

With that done, I zeroed in on Lead Nine, carting the output side. I decided on a frontal attack near the fortress, and there I half flashed, half tossed the output end into real-time.

Even from the undertime, I could feel the disruption. But it dropped off too quickly, even as I could feel the undertime buckle.

I drifted foretime quickly, perhaps a hundred units after the tunnel collapsed, and did a quick flash-through. Most of the nearby planetary surface was a mess—with the exception of the black fort, which remained intact, if slightly wilted around the edges.

Several black ships, shimmering out-of-time-phase, sat beside the fort, and I had the feeling all sorts of energy were headed in my direction as I vanished under the now.

The sharks were tough, and fast, and very able technically.

I made another dive, foretime about a local year. I almost hung there too long, because the installations surrounding the black fort had been totally rebuilt and the vegetation restored.

Suddenly, I could feel the damnable laser sweeping in toward me, and I was angry, flaming with rage, that the sharks were trying to kill me again.

I had brushed aside Frey's miserable sun-tunnel, hadn't I, and a laser was nothing compared to a sun, and this time I was ready. Hardly thinking, I stood there in the air and wrenched the energy away from me, hurling it back at its source in the black fort, drilling it right through the control center.

Then I dropped undertime and back until I found another time buckle—this one strong enough to bend the undertime around the entire planet—just after the sun-tunnel collapsed.

I followed the black path like a highway—right back to one of the black holes—not exactly, but to a moon, asteroid, something, in an orbit. The whole base was shivering on the edge of the undertime—but how?

I didn't get terribly close, but I got the idea. Somehow, like the spirals of Anemone, the sharks were using the gravity of the black hole as a basis for accelerating or fueling their mechanical time-diving.

It also meant that a sun-tunnel or two in the cluster wouldn't solve the problem. How could I char an out-of-time base into nonexistence?

I went back to Query, not at all pleased.

Neither was anyone else, especially Heimdall.

"You're just going to let them take over the galaxy, steam every planet they can reach?"

"I didn't say that, honored Counselor. What I said was that a sun-tunnel or two won't do the job. Just let me work on it."

They did, because no one else had any better ideas. Finally, I cornered Freyda and told her that, if they wanted anything left of their kind of galaxy in another million years, they'd better leave me alone. They did, except for Sammis, who occasionally looked at me with a sad expression. I didn't mind him, for some reason.

I went back into Baldur's references. Then I even went foretime to Terra. If anyone had ideas about destruction, it was the Terrans.

Terra was worse than ever, almost strobing through foretime realities, and the only way I could do any research was actually to break out and read it before it changed.

If I'd had more time, I would have liked to dig into the uncertainty that surrounded Terra, but the sharks kept preying on my mind, and I kept dreaming about oceans being steamed.

It took nearly three ten-days before I gathered enough information. According to Terran theory, it ought to work. All galaxies, or clusters, have more highly concentrated suns near the center. Clusters are usually more highly concentrated, and the shark cluster was—with a stellar concentration averaging far higher than even galactic centers. With that it became a matter of applying power in the right spots.

I simply intended to plant linked sun-tunnels across the cluster center, particularly in suns that seemed unstable, and by funneling energy flows, nova the cluster-center stars. From there the process would feed on itself.

Even with their time-sliding ships, I doubted that the sharks would escape, not if it had taken them a million years to get out of the cluster without such a disruption.

It wasn't that simple. The data banks and my calculations indicated I needed a sun-tunnel with a cross section four times the output we had been using. That created other problems. Baldur had once mentioned the problems involved with stepped-up power requirements, that they increased geometrically as the power increased arithmetically. I shuddered at a tunnel sixteen times bigger. I couldn't carry one, let alone the numbers I would need. But it didn't work out quite that way.

What I did need were intake and output ports with four times the cross section. While awkward for me to carry, even in a collapsed form, and even more awkward to use, the increase in mass was minimal—provided I dropped the design safety factors a magnitude.

Even after I got back from Terra, the modification and building process took Narcissus, Brendan, Elene, and me almost two whole seasons, and a lot of minor repairs piled up. No one said anything about that but Frey, and I just looked at him.

It took a while longer to calculate the tunnel linkages, and I insisted on including the stars for Lyste and Lead Nine. I also worried about the linkages—everything was theoretical except the tunnels themselves—but this sort of gadgetry wasn't exactly something I intended to test on suns in our own galaxy.

When the time came, I didn't tell anyone except Brendan and Elene, and I started it at night, Quest time. All told, I had to set up more than twenty linkages within a hundred-and-fifty-unit period—objective. That didn't include the tunnels for Lyste and Lead Nine, which could be done outside the time parameters. I used a corner of one of the deserted planets as a staging base to ferry the tunnels to, because I figured there was enough time energy around a fort planet to conceal what I was doing.

Then I did it. It was that simple. Twenty dives in time dropping forty time-protected packages into forty suns. And I finished with a good fifteen units to spare.

After a quick nap, I repeated the process with Lyste and Lead Nine and then strapped myself into deep-space armor, picked up my trusty holopak, and foretimed ten thousand years to see the results—really to show the results, since the moaning of the change winds and the buck-

ling of both time and the undertime provided a good indication that
something had worked.

As I foretimed, I could sense almost endless swathes of the black
ships, but they died out halfway to the foretime end of my dive. Being
time-protected is fine, but it generally takes planets to reproduce and
prosper, and the ships, at least at the beginning, had limited ranges.

I broke out in quiet desolation, floating in the equivalent of cosmic
cinders.

A few white dwarves peered out from the swirling nebula composed
of the remnants of the once-glittering cluster. I dropped back and picked
up frames showing the pulse of destruction, the stellar winds pushing
out ahead of the front of fire. What the holo frames didn't show was the
howling winds of time-change that echoed through the undertime and
the anguishes as planetary sentiences were snuffed out.

While some of the sharks theoretically could have escaped in their
time and space cruisers, I *knew* none had, just as I knew I could bend
energy away from me and use energy to help rebuild injuries.

When I hit the Travel Hall, one person stood in front of those waiting.

Heimdall.

"Congratulations, Loki!"

I knew the moaning, heaving change winds had preceded me. And
I knew, for whatever reason, Heimdall was planting the whole thing
on me.

I nodded curtly. There wasn't much else to do. It was my doing. I'd
just done what I'd destroyed the sharks for doing. And I had destroyed
a hundred thousand systems and a million years of lives because I had
no other way of dealing with the sharks. Maybe we were meant for each
other, the sharks and me.

Even Brendan and Elene shrank away from me. Why wouldn't they?
Who wanted to welcome back the god of destruction, the lord of fire?
They knew me, knew me all too well, as I was coming to know myself.

I walked heavily through the corridors of the Tower, still fully
equipped, wrist gauntlets and all. Where I walked, Guards shrank, eased
away as if I wore the very flames I had kindled, and perhaps I did.

Massive as it was, the Tower seemed small and tawdry in those moments, insignificant against the night skies I had left units before, and
infinitesimal against the searing point of light I had created in distant
heavens.

Since there was little enough to be accomplished by returning to
Maintenance immediately—Brendan and the others could start to catch

up without me, and I needed to unwind—I spent the next few days at the Aerie and on the empty places of the high Bardwalls, watching the eagles, the clean lines of the knife peaks, and the winding shadows of the clefts below.

XXVI

THE TWO MEN *and the woman study the picture presented by the black crystal table.*

She frowns, and the face of the taller man is blank. The shorter man glares at the image in the center of the table.

All three are dressed in black, in one-piece uniforms with high collars. On the left collar of each is a four-pointed black star edged with silver.

The image in the crystal wavers, but the lack of absolute clarity cannot obscure the basic picture of a statuette suspended in flames and being worshipped by a winged humanoid. The statue is of a god without wings, cast in a shining metal.

Even through the distortion of the crystal table, the power represented in the flame-bathed statue fills the watchers' chamber.

"How probable is this paratime?" asks the tall man.

"It will be real, before long," answers the woman.

"Can we destroy him?" asks the shorter man in black.

"Not without destroying the Guard. He is viewed as incorruptible."

"Ridiculous . . ."

"But true," corrects the woman abstractly, "and our days have been counted and limited."

"Why didn't we act sooner?"

"You might recall the people of the cluster . . . who else would have destroyed them? We do have some idealism for the race, not just for ourselves, you know?" She touches a flat plate on the edge of the black crystal table, and the image fades.

"Nonsense, all of it," snaps the squat man with the curly hair.

No one answers him.

XXVII

THE SEASONS PASSED. Like Baldur before me, I kept myself in Maintenance when I wasn't stalking thunderstorms in the passes of the Bardwalls or bending lasers into light sculptures around the Aerie. I even got so I could heal cuts and scrapes—maybe more, but who's crazy enough to put a slash in your arm to see if you can heal it?

Why not? Energy is matter, and vice versa, and if you can control energy through your mind, theoretically the rest follows. How far, I hadn't figured, not beyond what I could do.

Once in a great while, Loragerd and I got together, but the spontaneity we had enjoyed as younger Guards remained in the past, and we drifted apart on the gentle waves of the present.

Heimdall no longer assigned me missions—he suggested them, perhaps because the Tribunes very quietly gave me the silver star of a Senior Guard, and because they disassociated Maintenance from Assignments.

I let Brendan, Narcissus, and Elene do most of the day-to-day work, and Brendan had another trainee or two he was working into Maintenance. I tried to dig more into theory, both through the Archives and through some field research on the side—sometimes on Weindre and sometimes on uptime Terra, except that Terra was still so unreal that staying there very long gave me headaches. Along with the engineering and physics theories, I looked more into history. Most of the history in the Archives was crisp and gory. Reading between the lines, I gained the impression that the Guard had made more than its share of blunders, at least in the earlier days.

I hadn't realized that world deaths or total depopulations happened so often, although I certainly wasn't one to make judgments along those lines.

If some idiot decided core-tapping was a good way to get heavy metals and energy, and miscalculated, and pieces of real estate went flying all over creation, messing up orbits and incidentally ripping up any time-diver who was caught unaware—that was one thing. It may have been a tragedy, a disaster, but the planetary cultures did it to themselves.

If the Guard saw something like that developing, and thought the culture valuable, the Tribunes sometimes tried to head it off. But the Guard could fail. That happened when Eranas, then a Senior Guard, was tracking the Nepturian Civil War.

He didn't get to the right people and place quite in time, and someone dropped a hell-blaster down a core-tap. Now, when a planet comes apart, it bends time in a way that's difficult, if not impossible, to put back together. With planets, like Guards, dead is generally dead. There may be a way around it, but we haven't found it.

I really didn't have too many second thoughts about the sharks—only about other innocent races that got zapped years before the sharks would have gotten them. But Gurlenis was another question.

Giron had fetched me up to Assignments for Heimdall. Heimdall never came down to see me, probably just as well for both of us.

"Sammis thought you might like an easy assignment, for once," Heimdall announced.

"There must be a catch."

"No catch . . . none whatsoever, except it might take some tricky diving," Heimdall said. "The data is on the end console."

"What's the general idea?" I asked before heading over to the console.

"Holo update before a cultural change."

That translated into getting holo frames of a time/locale just before the Guard meddled. I asked myself what the Gurlenians had done to merit the Guard's decision to alter their culture, but didn't verbalize it, since it was doubtless on the briefing console. I walked over to the stool and keyed in.

Gurlenis was an Arm planet, orange sun, long low hills bronzed with grass, cities built with a green glass that held the light for hours past sunset.

Heavy transport was based on a subsurface induction rail network or by solar-powered craft that skimmed the shallow seas. The people who built it all were bipeds, covered with a fine bronze-green fur that streamed behind them in the continuing and gentle winds.

The reason for the mission, and the cultural alteration, was one publication by a scholar. The professor, although the Gurlenian term more accurately translated as "knowledge-intuiter," had presented a rather scholarly paper on a unified time theory.

Corbell, the head of Archives, evaluated the contents and predicted, based on the data bank's analyses, that the probability of the Gurlenians developing time-diving abilities approached unity, given further development. In short, like the sharks, the Gurlenians would challenge the Guard's monopoly of Time. But since the Gurlenians were peaceful, so to speak, and the occurrence a one-of-a-kind thing, a minor alteration was recommended, if possible.

Zealor had been assigned the job. All I had to do was record the last moments of the existing culture, the moment of passage, and the results.

I'd never stood in the middle of a time-change before, but based on past practice, it wouldn't affect me—so long as the planet stayed put, and I did a little checking on that to make sure exactly what sort of alteration Zealor had in mind and when.

All he intended to do was move one native where he wouldn't meet another, thus ensuring that the professor never got born. As changes go, it sounded mild, and I got the coordinates down and headed to Special Stores to pick up the recording equipment.

Halcyon was an assistant supervisor at Special Stores, and I thought Athene relied on her more than on any of the earlier assistants. Like

Loragerd, she'd been a trainee with me, but she'd never developed much beyond rote time-diving. She could dive anywhere she'd been taken, but couldn't strike out on her own, even with detailed instructions.

I guessed that Baldur had gotten to all of us in that group of trainees, though I would have been hard-pressed to explain it. Halcyon had taken special care to update the equipment they supplied, and that was important, not so much to me, but to the others.

If something failed a crack diver, he or she could usually get back and get it replaced or repaired. But then I could dive while falling through the air. Most divers have to have a momentarily stable platform. Anyway, Athene was lucky to have Halcyon.

She was waiting. "Nicodemus said you'd be the one, and that you'd been in a hurry." She handed me a set of what appeared to be goggles. "Try these."

The gadgets had a thin cable that led to a belt pack. I struggled to make the goggles fit, but with them in place, I couldn't see.

"Silly," she murmured. "You wear them above your eyes."

Halcyon had long, fine, blond hair, green eyes so dark they verged on black, and clear tanned skin. Her voice tended to break slightly when she was amused, and she giggled—even after all the years.

"Why?"

"To get the best spacing for an eyewitness view."

It made sense. You need depth with holos, and the sight perspective is the easiest to watch for long periods of time.

"Remember—try not to jerk your head around. Make long slow movements."

I nodded, strapped on the belt pack, and headed for the Travel Hall and Gurlenis to make the last record there might be of a culture before Zealor reoriented it.

The Hall had a few Guards popping in and out, but the far end was clear, and I strapped on gauntlets and equipment, not that I thought I'd need them. I dived toward Gurlenis, only a shallow trip because I was almost heading for the now.

I didn't follow the timepaths, but skipped branches and intuited my way to the destination. Only a few Guards tried straight shots. The rest used the equipment, popping into the now to reorient themselves along the way—at least for longer dives.

Breakout on Gurlenis found me hovering over bronzed hills bathed in light from the orange sun. Late afternoon, I guessed, and the readouts confirmed that the local season was late summer.

Picking a low hill above the nearest city, I made sure the holo "goggles" were in place, and made a series of short split entries down to the empty hilltop. There I panned the valley and ended with a view of the green glass city at the other end of the grassy lands that filled the valley.

It probably almost looked like flying, and I grinned as I thought of Heimdall watching it. After I finished on the hilltop, I cut out the holo and slid undertime toward the city, ducked into the shadows, and reset the holopak.

From outside the tall evergreens that edged the city, I could see that the place was a town, rather than a full city, and laid out in a definite plan.

The first close-up I caught with the equipment showed three youngsters playing on a triangular grass court of some sort. On each corner of the playing surface stood a tall pole with a balanced crossbar and three metallic rings of various sizes.

Apparently, the idea was to throw an oblong object through the rings in some predetermined order. The crossbar was vaned and changed position with the breeze, moving with minimal changes in wind direction or velocity.

I watched.

The smallest youngster, and I guessed he or she or it was young because of the size differential and an air, a feeling, that I associated with growing up, moved toward one of the corner standards in a hop, step, step, step, hop pattern.

The other two tried to block the advance by anticipating where the patterned zigzag would lead and setting themselves in a blocking stature. No physical contact took place, and it was more like a dance. A couple of body lengths out from the corner standard, the one carrying the oblong made a double hop and tossed it toward the standard. I thought the crossbar swung before the toss was completed. The vanes fluttered, but the light steady breeze hadn't changed.

The oblong tumbled through the middle ring and was recovered by the tallest, who began moving toward the corner away from me in another stylized pattern—more of a hop, hop, step, hop, step.

The game, if that's what it was, seemed strangely noncompetitive, but I wondered about the way the crossbar had moved against the wind. I kept the holo going until I had a representative section of the game.

Then I slipped under the now and toward the more heavily structured center of the town, where a number of incomprehensible activities were taking place. I could tell that some of them were commercial transactions, and some seemed social. All the Gurlenians I saw and caught on the holo radiated an impression of purposefulness, but the town was quiet, much quieter than I expected, even considering the attitude of gentleness I had begun to associate with the bronze-furred people.

I recorded everything I could, gazing from unobserved corners, sometimes doing split entries on ceilings to get the best possible view.

The town stood on a low plateau, and from the gradual slope down and into the cropped and cultivated spaces below, it was obvious that the Gurlenians planned their environment carefully. The town center was linked and intertwined with grassy paths. The more heavily traveled routes were paved with a soft green pebbled pavement that gave underfoot.

Not a single garish display showed anywhere, although some of the buildings were labeled with distinctive script, which I couldn't read.

Even as I watched and recorded, kept cranking away, I noticed that the number of Gurlenians out and about was shrinking. Strange, I thought, because with their wide eyes and cupped ears and lithe bearing I would have suspected them to be at ease at night, even a nocturnal race.

I flicked in and out of the undertime, flashing though the corners of the city, trying to pinpoint activity. As I slid from place to place, something began to nag at me.

As I stopped to holo a scene of the Gurlenians filing into a central structure, I recognized the feeling, or rather the absence of a feeling. Fear—the Gurlenians, or the ones I was watching, didn't demonstrate any signs of it. In most cultures, somewhere, someplace, there is an aura of fear. Even on Query it exists, and certainly within the Guard, but not where I looked on Gurlenis, it didn't.

Not a single Gurlenian had looked around as I popped in and out of time to record scenes for posterity. Most races are at least subliminally aware of surveillance—or, like the sharks, violently aware. Either the Gurlenians weren't aware, or it didn't bother them.

I shelved that analysis as I began to take stock of the number of graceful souls gliding into the building I was observing. My first thought was a government or town meeting. My second was a religious observance, but I wasn't sure either fit.

Item: The city was six-sided.
Item: The only six-sided building in the town was the one
       where the Gurlenians were gathering.
Item: The six sides of the building were parallel to the town
       boundaries.
Item: Both the grounds of the building and the boundaries of
       the town were delineated with trimmed coniferlike trees.
Item: The temple was in the exact center of the town, and I
       could have drawn a perfectly straight line from each

corner of the building to each corner of the town
boundary.

Curiosity cornered the mountain cat. I ducked undertime and slid
into the temple. Fuzzy as it was in the undertime, I didn't want to break
out inside a wall or a heat source. Those hurt.

I located an open space away from the assembling group and broke
out, ready to dive, if necessary.

Face-to-face with me was a Gurlenian—an older one with white-
streaked and flowing body hair and a mantle of age wrapped around his
very being.

The old Gurlenian looked at me, not at all surprised, bowed slightly,
made some cryptic motion in the air with a single sweeping gesture,
and waited.

I stayed where I was, tense, taking it all in.

And after that gesture, I received a feeling of peacefulness, and that
was the only way I could describe it.

I nodded back, and slid undertime to a darker corner of the meeting
hall between where two beams met in the ceiling. I kept the holo running.

A slight shiver shook the undertime, and the hall wavered, and it
seemed to me that there were slightly fewer Gurlenians, and that those
who were left no longer sat in chairs.

Instead, row after row of Gurlenians sat on wide and flat cushions,
equally spaced from each other. The entire hall was dead silent, yet filled
with that same feeling of peace that I had received from the old Gurlenian.

What had happened? I could feel the whisper of a change wind, but
little had changed. I swallowed, and ducked undertime, sliding higher
into the sky before breaking out.

There were definite differences. The town was still six-sided but
smaller. The hills looked wilder, with fewer trees, but the place felt the
same.

I shivered. The Gurlenian mind was attuned to time, and someone
else besides the professor in the briefing had addressed the time issue,
in his absence—or nonexistence. Zealor would know it hadn't worked,
just as I had. If Zealor's simple alteration didn't work, what would he
try next? Should I leave?

For whatever reason, I decided against it. Instead, I panned the town
and the surroundings before dropping back to the beams in the temple,
at least for another few moments.

As I recorded what I felt would be the last moments of that unique culture, my thoughts kept drifting. Why was I the one with the holo-pak? No specialist was I, not speaking the language, not even having been sent for a Linguistics briefing. It didn't make sense.

Sammis thought I'd like an easy assignment, and Heimdall had given it to me. Why?

I didn't have time for more reflection, because the cold wind of time-change blew, creeping up my spine like the paralysis that followed the sting of a rocksucker.

Like a picture seen through falling water in the twilight, the temple melted around me. The town evaporated in mist, and the Gurlenians dressed only in their golden, fine-flowing hair who had been seated within body lengths of me instants before became smoke, and then less than the memory of smoke—and were gone.

The chill of the time-change winds howled past me and barked its way down the trail to the future. I slid to a rocky outcrop and gazed out over sparsely vegetated hills and wild grasses. A few scraggly bushes had replaced the cultured and trimmed conifers.

With the abrupt drop in temperature, I shivered.

Some animal howled in the distance.

No more Gurlenians. They were gone, for good, and I could feel it. That wasn't quite it. Rather, they and their sense of peace had never been, and Gurlenis was now a wild planet.

I hit the stud on the belt pack to stop the holos, lifted the goggles, and dropped them into a belt pouch.

I slid back to the Travel Hall. It was deserted.

I stowed my equipment in my own chest, including the holo gear. The equipment would go back to Special Stores in the morning, but the holo frames would go to Assignments, directly to Heimdall's console, before I left the Tower.

The Tower itself was generally empty, except for the trainee watch staff, and I could hear my own steps echoing in the silence as I climbed the ramps.

The Assignments Hall was dark, except for Giron, who held the watch console, and the figure at the main console.

"Sammis?"

"I told Heimdall I'd wait for your return. How did it go?"

"Fine, if you care for that sort of thing." I didn't much care what I said. Sammis wasn't likely to repeat it. I might have been more careful if Heimdall had asked, but at that point I might not have been.

He smiled, I'd have to have said sadly, and answered, "Sometimes that's the way it goes."

I didn't want to hear more.

I handed him the holo tapes, said good night, and left, wondering about Sammis—why he was there. Was it just that he had nothing better to do with Wryan gone?

After I left the Tower, I slid straight to the Aerie. There I sat on the edge of my cliff in the darkness, warmed by my glowstone floor, sipped firejuice, and saw the eagles circle, far from the Tower, far from Quest— and yet not nearly far enough.

The eradication of the Gurlenians wasn't going to vanish, no matter how long I stared out the permaglass of the Aerie, no matter how many busted pieces of equipment I fixed, no matter how much I learned about solid-state theory or Terran physics.

And how many others had we wiped clean from the slate of Time? I knew about those that had impinged on me—Gurlenis, the shark cluster—and a few others like Ydris. But how many others had there been?

That answer was in the Assignment files. I didn't want to go through Nicodemus or Heimdall to find out. The data banks of the Archives probably had most of the same information, maybe more, but the results of my last efforts to access such data, when the entire Guard knew I was trying to find Baldur, indicated that the Tribunes, or Heimdall, or someone was following my every move.

Would they still be looking after all these years? Probably. Patience had to be a virtue learned by the powers-that-be in an immortal society.

Real analytical thinking had been difficult for me, unlike Ferrin or Sammis. If I were Ferrin and wanted to find out information without broadcasting my intentions, how would I do it? That was the question. How did the Tribunes know who accessed data? The last time, they'd simply asked for copies of the requests off my personal code.

As I'd discovered in my brief time in Personnel, and in my own supervisory work in Maintenance, not many cross-checks were used. We didn't have enough time or people.

Clearly, the simplistic answer was not to use my own code, but another Guard's. The next question was whose and how to get it.

I tilted my stool back, letting my thoughts ferment, and looked out into the darkness, trying to pick out the shadows of the night eagles, soaring in the blackness. They flew with such little effort, a flap here or there, riding the thermals.

Ask someone? Hardly—that would be the same as announcing it. Whatever I did had to look as though nothing had changed.

How about microsnoops?

I was always working on small stuff at my bench, and, if I could plant them in the course of normal business, who would know? But where?

Suppose I planted one focused on each console screen used by Guards whose codes I wanted?

That sounded simple enough, provided I could get the focus angle wide enough to cover the entire screen and keyboard. And it wouldn't do to use a Tribune's code, even if I could get it, since they probably talked to each other.

If I obtained ten codes, or at the fewest, the codes of four or five individuals whose requests for trend data might not seem strange, I might obscure exactly what I was after. My main targets were Heimdall, if for no other reason than to get someone chasing him, Nicodemus, Gilmesh, and Frey for starters. Corbell's code would be ideal, but too dangerous because he'd likely be one of those checking data requests, and all I needed was for him to find out that he was making requests he hadn't made.

With that, I ended my plotting for the moment.

The next afternoon, I rounded up the smallest of the microsnoops I'd built to cover my back when I'd gone to Personnel and began redesigning it to shrink it further and use wider-angle lenses. Between repairs, that took almost a ten-day. Then I duplicated fifteen.

I still had to decide on the best way to plant them. Since I couldn't back- or foretime on Query itself, I had two choices—either to mosey into each of the areas in the coming days and place them in broad daylight, so to speak, or to use the undertime to flash through during periods when the spaces were empty.

The first alternative, while superficially attractive—no sliding around in the dark of night—had a few drawbacks. How was I going to plant a snoop near someone's personal screen while he or she was using it?

Number two didn't appear much better. If anyone was naturally suspicious, and a lot of people seemed to be, wouldn't someone have remote sensing devices—or something to monitor work areas?

When I'd joined the Guard, never would I have considered that the honorable Senior Guards, Counselors, and Tribunes might have snoops in their Halls. While some of them, such as Frey, might not have the ability to find, plant, and use such devices, I had no such doubts about the abilities of others, such as Gilmesh, Freyda, and Heimdall—or Eranas.

Although there were night watches in the Tower, only certain Halls were manned—Locator, Domestic Affairs, and Assignments. The Tribunes had to know that some divers, like Sammis or me, could dive within the Tower, and I couldn't believe that there weren't at least holo records being taken of some areas all the time.

So how could I plant snoops without getting caught?

If anything went at all wrong while I attempted to place snoops during working hours, I'd be caught red-handed, and then some. If on the other hand, if I tried a flash through night-slide, I might end up as an image on a holo screen. I wouldn't be caught immediately—just whenever someone reviewed the records. That wasn't much help.

What if I didn't look like me? That was one idea worth pursuing. In most snoops the focus wasn't too clear, and a general suggestion of someone else might do the trick.

That conclusion led to another series of questions, but in the end only one pseudo-identity made much sense, because he was roughly my size and his mannerisms and especially his outfit were easily counter-feited.

Nightmail is easily procured, even black nightmail, from the deep storerooms. At one time many of the Guards used it. Went to show how much softer things had gotten over the centuries.

While I couldn't obtain a real light saber, I could duplicate its sil-houette and exterior appearance with materials right at my own work-bench, and it would even glow. A dark cloak, a big black chain, black high boots, a swagger, and who would know I wasn't Frey?

That left one screen to get—Frey's own in Locator/Domestic Affairs. I would have to use the direct approach there. Frey wouldn't go skulking into his own office.

It was hard not to dash off that afternoon and put it all together, but I refrained, refrained for almost a ten-day, getting each piece of my costume as a part of daily routine, or concealed within it, with no sudden trips to Stores, no odd requests.

The night I picked, the planting went as smoothly as a dive to Vulcan or Haskill. Flick undertime, then out in a shadow, walk to the console and place the snoop, ruffle through papers and drawers, clink the night-mail, and walk away before disappearing in the shadows.

I got snoops into Heimdall's console, and those of Nicodemus, Ferrin, Tyron, Verdis, Gilmesh, and Athene. I even used the same routine to plant one on my own console.

I slid away from the Tower wearing the outfit and left it in the Aerie. If anyone could track me that far, it didn't matter—they'd already know. During the whole bit, I avoided going fore- or backtime, because the Locator consoles were programmed to throw out real-time locations on Query.

Later I'd need to retrieve them. I'd opted for self-contained units, since I didn't want broadcast energy flows running around the Tower—besides, over time, I wasn't sure how they'd work and how they might be traced. The self-contained types were less likely to be detected, easier to operate, and had no overt ties to me. The ones I placed looked like rivets, raised plates, screws—that sort of stuff.

The morning after I planted my snoops, my ears were wide open, alert to any change in the pulse or gossip around the Tower, but nothing seemed to have changed.

At least, no one was wandering around asking, "Did you hear that someone was snooping around the Tower last night?"

In some ways, it was an anticlimax.

I buried myself in the little world of Maintenance, worried about divers' gear, fixed warm suits, power packs, stunners, gauntlets, and even recommended greater use of Baldur's small fusion generator for a couple of isolated weather remote stations.

Two or three days passed before I could plant a snoop on Frey's console, and I practically had to pick an argument with him to do it. I didn't dislike him, not exactly, but if anyone had been granted status beyond ability, that was Frey.

On that morning, I loitered my way past his archway, and if anyone had asked me why I was on that side of the Square and not in Maintenance, I'd have been hard-pressed for an answer that made sense. I always have had trouble in coming up with out-and-out lies.

Frey was in, toying with his black light saber, obviously bored. His boredom could be laid at Tyron's and Ferrin's arches. Neither could dive worth a damn, but Tyron handled Domestic Affairs and Ferrin effectively ran Locator. Together they did their work and Frey's, which was good because Frey probably would have made a botch of it. Still, Frey was technically the effective chief constable of Query by virtue of being the supervisor of Domestic Affairs/Locator.

Since Frey was alone, I ambled in.

"Got an instant?"

"Infinity and some," he flipped back as he sheathed the light saber and sat up straight in the work stool.

"Why don't we put some trainees into Domestic Affairs earlier in training?" I asked. "They'd understand how the system works better, and the real role of the Guard in holding Query together would be clearer."

I edged toward his console.

He leaned forward and put both elbows on the table, crowding me back and away from the console screen.

"Loki, the system's worked fine for umpteen hundred centuries. Let's not meddle with a good thing."

"We lose a lot of trainees who opt out for the admin obligation."

"No guts," snorted Frey.

I circled around to the other side of the table and leaned against a heavy wooden case with no apparent function to account for its presence.

"At ten trainees a year or less, we're not exactly burning up this corner of the galaxy—or replacing the giants of the past, like Ragnorak or Odin Thor."

"With Guards like you," laughed Frey, "who needs the past? But then, with more Guards like you, the future wouldn't have a past."

He chuckled so thoroughly I almost felt like stuffing his light saber straight down his throat. I didn't, instead slipping between him and his console as he reared back howling over his joke. It wasn't that funny, but I smiled and slapped the snoop in place.

". . . future wouldn't have a past . . ." He chuckled again.

"Maybe not," I admitted. "But that makes an argument for more other kinds of Guards, doesn't it? Anyway . . . think about it, would you?"

"I'll talk it over with Heimdall."

He'd talk anything over with Heimdall if it involved thought or words of more than two syllables.

I bowed ever so slightly as I left and wandered back to Maintenance.

The days drifted by quietly, like the eye of a storm on Faffnir, and I knew a storm was swirling around unseen, but the more certain I was that something had to happen, the less that did.

After a couple of ten-days, I redonned my costume imitation of Frey and picked up all my snoops.

To get the one from Frey's console was harder, but not impossible. I waited until he left one afternoon, then barged in and dropped a report on the status of repairs on his table, picking up the snoop along the way.

When I inspected the snoops, I discovered that not one had been damaged, tampered with, or even touched. Such miraculous disregard alerted my cautionary feelings. Either I was way off base, or I was missing something, maybe a lot. But what?

With no answer apparent, I began to run out the scans from the snoops, tedious enough to keep me occupied for a while between repairs, since I had to study each frame under the magnifiers of the miniwaldo setup.

In the end, though, I identified the personal codes for Frey, Heimdall, Nicodemus, Verdis, Gilmesh, Athene, Loragerd, Halcyon, Ferrin, and a few trainees. The biggest problem wasn't getting the codes, but identifying which code belonged to whom.

I'd placed all the snoops with decent focus on the console keyboards, but they were so small that the peripheral scan was tight. Some of the codes were simple enough. HML-10 had to be Heimdall, and FRY-27 had to be Frey. But who was XXF-13? And which Tribune—if it were a Tribune—was TRB-002?

I supposed identifying them all didn't really matter, since my goal was to get enough to use them for specific data requests. I also had to assume that the Archives could track the console from which data was requested, and that meant I had to use other consoles—or one of the research consoles in the Archives. They were secluded enough, for the most part.

After making that decision, I stood and started to leave for some refreshment.

Brendan caught me.

"What do you need?"

"I'm having trouble with a generator, and the schematics all check. But it won't run. Could you take a look?"

"Be right there." I tucked the code list into my pocket and followed him back to his space.

He brightly expected me to put it all to rights, even though he could do it himself, I was convinced.

"You can see. I've replaced all the fused circuits, rerouted the control lines . . . matched all of it . . ."

At first glance nothing seemed wrong, and I could understand his frustration. Nothing more upsetting than to work your tail off and not be able to get something to work that should. If all the circuits were correct, and I assumed for a moment that they were, what could be wrong?

I began to chuckle, not nastily, but almost sympathetically.

"Brendan . . . think about it . . . What's the first thing you do when you repair a generator?"

"Remove the . . ." He blushed.

"I'm not laughing at you, but you went to all this work, and you thought you'd made this terrible and intricate mistake. You didn't. Nothing works without fuel."

The generator worked. Brendan was torn between embarrassment and pride. Embarrassment because he'd forgotten to reopen the water intake, and pride because he'd basically rebuilt the generator from scratch.

"Good job," I told him. "Don't make a big deal about the intake. It's just the sort of thing we've all done at one time or another."

I thought about it as I munched a small pastry. You could go through the most complicated procedures and forget the simplest and most vital things. Why did I want to find critical turning points in other cultures? Did the answer lie in high-tech cultures that might impinge on Query?

Would finding out how many cultures we'd exterminated really tell me anything I didn't know?

That night, in my high and secure Aerie, as I watched the dark canyons, everything seemed so small. There I was, perched behind permaglass over the depths of needle-thin canyons, with the bottoms so far below that two cloud layers often obscured the river that twisted its way under my roost. And I felt cramped.

I could walk the air between the peaks, catch thunderbolts from the skies and throw them without gauntlets, heal small scratches by looking at them—but I felt cramped. Had Baldur felt that way after all the years?

Heimdall was continuing to build a private group of thugs, and even after they'd tried to kill me on Hell, I'd done nothing. Gilmesh was plotting through Kranos, it seemed, against Heimdall, yet no one said anything. The Tribunes had a hidden time-linked table of some sort and told no one. A fake Frey wandered the Tower, and nothing happened.

And some things didn't fit at all. I mean, with a long-lived culture, I could see the need for or at least the rationale behind long, slow plots, but why had I been sent out to make the holo record of Gurlenis? That was a job for a junior Guard—or was it?

And Baldur, his insistence on getting the Sinopol generator, not all that long before he disappeared—with both generators. What was he doing with them?

Even the sharks. Why had the Tribunes pushed for my destroying the sharks—it would have been millions of years before they reached Query. The only place they were really close to was Terra.

Was the Guard winding down, like the mechanical toy I thought it was? Or was I seeing what I wanted to see? Or was someone else showing me what they wanted me to see?

I went to sleep without any real answers. Morning's arrival didn't provide them either.

Deciding more information was necessary, and hating myself for thinking so, I ate and slid to the Tower. Baseline data came first, and I spent a portion of the morning—after I'd tackled a small atmospheric generator for a weather satellite, and gone over the remaining repairs with Brendan, Narcissus, and Elene—in one of the Archives' shielded booths.

I plugged in Nicodemus's code.

"Has the number of trainees per century increased or decreased in the past million years?"

"Increased." The figures followed. Summed up, the Archives' data indicated that prior to 1,000,000. A.T. the average number of trainees per century completing the first two years of training was 300. The current moving average was 530.

I tried another tack. "Has the time-diving ability of the average trainee decreased over the period?"

"Negative . . . Subjective analysis of performance reports indicates significant improvement."

I sat back in the padded stool. I'd spent thirty-plus years figuring the Guard was on the way out, and the damned data banks were saying the opposite. I assumed that the business of tearing down high-tech cultures was to eliminate challenges to an ever-weakening Query.

If the Guard and Query were stronger, why the increased destruction? Just because we could do it? Would we end up just like the sharks? Or was data being falsified?

I asked another question.

"What is the current number of active Temporal Guards? Of all currently living Guards and former Guards?"

The Guard, including trainees, numbered 4,156, with approximately a half million current and former living Guards and trainees.

A half a million? I couldn't believe that. Where were they? I asked about former Guards.

There were 480,000 residing on Query and 5,000 on Sertis. Statistical probabilities indicated that 15,000 resided elsewhere.

I was convinced the numbers didn't match. An average of four hundred new Guards a century over a million years totaled four million. Guards were supposedly immortal. So what happened to three and a half million Guards? I was dumb enough to ask that one.

"Inquiry included trainees. Sixty percent of all trainees select administrative option. Guard mortality/disappearance averages twenty-eight percent."

One in four Guards died or disappeared? Even if it were true, the numbers still didn't make sense. That meant twenty percent of Query's population had basic Guard training and experience. And they just went along? Or did they?

I canceled out, asked for a total erasure, and walked back down to Maintenance.

The Guard was bigger than it used to be? Why did we all rattle around in the Tower? Who could answer the questions? My father would have been happy to—except I had no idea where in the galaxy he might be.

What about my own experiences? When I had started in Maintenance, there had been Glammis and Baldur. Now I was there, with

Brendan, Elene, and Narcissus, and we were slated to get one of the current trainees, Dercia.

I slammed my fist on the worktable so hard the slap echoed off the walls.

Both Brendan and Narcissus were there before I knew it.

"Are you all right?"

"What's wrong?"

Elene just stood behind them and waited.

I grinned, hard as it was. "Nothing. Just amazed at my own stupidity."

They exchanged looks. Brendan shrugged at Narcissus, who smiled back at Brendan. Elene nodded.

"If there's anything we can do," said Brendan, "let us know."

They were gone. Too bad the entire Guard wasn't like them.

I'd tried to pass on Baldur's understanding and appreciation of the mechanical basis of cultures, but wasn't sure I'd gotten it across to them or any of the trainees I'd lectured. Compared to old silken-tongued Heimdall or smooth Gilmesh, my halting lectures were probably as dry as centuries-old dust.

The only other person who could and might answer my questions was Sammis, and it was time to look him up, if I could find him.

Not so strangely, he was in the first place I looked, in the corner of the Assignments Hall. When he wasn't diving, that was usually where he was, often using a console. Why he spent so much time there, I couldn't understand. He and Heimdall had little enough in common, but Heimdall did seem to listen when Sammis made a suggestion.

"Loratini's, Loki?" he asked before I could more than open my mouth.

Back we went to Loratini's, the inn overlooking the Falls. Didn't seem right without Wryan, but Sammis didn't say anything. I decided not to raise that one.

Sammis picked out his food even before we sat down at one of the individual balcony tables. I followed his example.

"It still has the best food," he said, "or the best templates in the synthesizers."

I nodded as I put down my beaker of firejuice.

"What's on your mind?"

I swallowed and asked, "How big was the Guard when it started?"

He grinned momentarily. "You're assuming that I know a lot. No one kept detailed records that far back. If I had to guess, I'd say there were perhaps a thousand in the original Guard—but only about fifty were timedivers."

"Fifty?" I blurted.

"Even a million years ago, not everyone in the Tower was a diver."

"Do you think divers today have different abilities from the older divers?"

"That's hard to say. Take the two of us. You can dive a bit farther fore- and backtime than I can. Not much, though. The biggest overt difference is that you can dive to and from a wider range of environments and lug a lot more mass with you. Of course, as we both know, you can do more than that, not that I'm terribly surprised. Diving is a matter of mental control over both energy and matter, and it was probably only a matter of time before someone showed up who could. Good genes help, though."

I had trouble not choking on my Terran steak. Here Sammis was politely telling me he knew about my ability to handle thunderbolts without gauntlets, just as if it were common knowledge.

"Have you talked about this," I stumbled through the words, "with . . . ah . . . anyone . . . ?"

Sammis snorted. "Give me a little credit, Loki. Even if anyone believed me and didn't think that old Sammis had finally lost it, why would I want to give Heimdall or the Tribunes another reason to worry about you?"

I chewed on the steak, digesting the implications of his words. Then I tried another tack. "Am I just late discovering it, or have people always been plotting and checking up on each other—in the Guard, I mean?"

Sammis actually sighed and put down the light beer he had been sipping. "People of any species have been plotting in any organization ever put together, so far as I've been able to discover. What happens in the Guard is generally more subtle and long-range, because nobody really wants to go to Hell, and because most troublemakers and revolutionaries either bite off too much as divers or give up and disappear."

For some reason, I thought of Wryan. "Did Wryan bite off too much?"

He sighed again. "Loki . . . yes, she . . . yes."

"Sorry." I took a sip of firejuice. "The other big question I had, one of them, was about the Guard. Why do I get the impression that the Guard is getting weaker and tearing down other civilizations because it fears them, when all the statistics show that it's actually stronger?"

"If I were being cruel, I'd tell you to wait a few centuries. Or that impatience was the problem with Orpheus, or that it takes gods longer to understand mere human thought." Sammis stroked his chin for a moment. "But that would only tell you I was playing games, or trying to manipulate you." He paused. "How about this? The bigger and stronger an organization becomes, the more it has, and the more it has to lose. The more it has to lose, the more it fears anything that could challenge it. The early Guard was too busy just trying to keep people alive right then to worry about potential future challenges."

I didn't like the answer, even if it squared with some of my thoughts. Would the same thing happen to Query as the sharks? Did it have to? Could I do anything? What?

"Do you think that other peoples besides us should travel the stars?"

He laughed. "Does it matter what I think? Others have, and some still do—just not in our corner of the galaxy."

That bothered me, but I wasn't quite sure why. I didn't want more sharks running around, but was the Guard the best entity to make that judgment?

I had a last question. "What happened to Baldur?"

"He disappeared, voluntarily, from everything I know."

"But where would he go? And why?"

Sammis smiled sadly. "Did anyone besides you really listen to him? Does anyone listen to you because of the value of your words? Or do they listen because you're so powerful that they're frightened to death of displeasing you?"

"Frightened of me?"

Sammis snorted for the second time. "Cut the false modesty, Loki. You're the closest thing to a real god ever invented, and you're the Guard's creation. They destroy you, and they make the Guard a farce. Besides, now it would be rather difficult."

"I damn near died on Hell—and getting back from the shark cluster."

Sammis smiled. "They needed you to stop Heimdall, and the sharks, and now you're a worse threat to them than either. That's the problem when you create heroes and gods."

I shook my head. I had been set up to stop Heimdall?

"You didn't think it was an accident that Heimdall was allowed to foist that gauntlet off on you? Or that Freyda was right there?"

I swallowed, hard.

"But Heimdall and Freyda seem more friendly now . . ."

Sammis had finished both his beer and his meal. "Of course. Times change, and he's no longer the greatest threat to the Tribunes."

We talked a bit longer, but Sammis had said all he was going to say, and just talked pleasantries.

After the meal, I went back to Maintenance, and I presumed he went back to Assignments.

A lot of people clearly thought I was dense for not seeing what was obvious, but I saw plenty. Seeing wasn't my problem . . . Heimdall's schemes to become a Tribune, Freyda's power climbing, Gilmesh's ef-

forts to weaken Frey, and Corbell's use of analyses from the Archives to
ensure his indispensability. What I had problems with was believing
. . . how could so many people talk about the good of Query, and the
good of the Guard, and then act in ways basically immoral or destructive
just to be a little higher, just to get a star with silver edges instead of
gold edges?

Hell, I had destroyed peoples—the sharks anyway—but I did it because I thought they were deadly to the rest of the galaxy. Maybe I'd
been wrong . . . maybe not . . . but I hadn't been doing it to become a
Counselor or Tribune.

That still didn't answer my questions, and I wanted to double-check
what Sammis had intimated. So I went back to the Archives. This time
I used Heimdall's codes.

I'd decided on exactly what I wanted, and that was a printout of
twenty cultures within the last million years that could be shifted up
to high-tech or cultures which had been high-tech and reduced by the
Guard's meddling. To that, I added the criterion of possible development of interstellar travel in some form or another.

The data banks balked at the additional condition, ending up with
some garbage that scripted, "No basis for evaluating particular isolated
technological phenomena."

That might make it harder for me to go ahead with my half-formed
plans to end the monopoly on the stars—or at least to see if it was a
good idea—but I got a list of times/cultures, plus a smaller list of low-
tech planets that offered long-shot possibilities and empty planets suitable for some types of colonization.

The three lists might cover all the possibilities. For all the ideas I
had, I had a growing feeling that I wasn't going to have the time to
develop them.

Still . . . twenty-plus cultures that should be out among the stars . . .
and weren't. Ten that had been pulled out of time or star travel by the
Guard—and the precedent I had set in destroying a whole cluster. As
I saw it, the trends were becoming critical.

XXVIII

THINKING ABOUT THE best way to throw a monkey wrench in the machine led me to study the aftereffects. I didn't want to get caught in
the act—or afterward.

That was the basic reason why the Guard had such a hold on Query.

Domestic Affairs/Locator could track any Queryan through the Locator tags planted in our shoulders at birth. They weren't mandatory, but most parents opted for them, simply because they could see the necessity—how could they find a place-lost child without them? As it was, despite the Locator equipment, we still lost a few every year.

The exact composition of the tags was a closely held secret, supposedly only known by the Tribunes. I doubted that, but it was closely held enough that there were no records in the Archives or anywhere else that I could find.

Not that I intended to let that stop me. I had the equipment necessary, and the lack of interest in things mechanical among most Guards had to work in my favor. Who would consider a mechanical solution, or understand one as I worked it out?

Except for a few in Domestic Affairs and Assignments, or maybe Special Stores, most of the Guard were fumble-fingers when it came to technology. Use it, break it, and ask Maintenance to fix it, or duplicate it and don't tell anyone—that was the operating philosophy. Most of those who really understood the technology were mine, like Brendan, Elene, and Narcissus. All Brendan lacked was a bit of self-confidence, and that was coming.

Narcissus was so proud of his profile or face-on image that I sometimes thought he'd polish stuff to a fine gloss just to see his reflection. Never mind if it worked—just get it to shine. If I let him admire himself long enough, he worked with a will. Barely passed his diving test, though.

Through it all and despite the abysmal level of technical understanding in the Guard, Maintenance was holding up its end, with all of Heimdall's efforts to pour repairs at us.

Heimdall, in his spotless black, delighted in seeing me with greasy hands or in a messed jumpsuit. I was always the sort of technician who couldn't paint or repair anything without picking up every stray bit of paint, grease, and general grime. The work product was spotless, but I never was.

To deal with the Locator system, I needed an analysis of a functioning tag. That was the priority, and I got down to it.

Setting up the heavy equipment scanner to pick up my own Locator tag was the hard part, but I managed it by shorting out a safety access circuit and removing one wall from the inspection chamber. Then I had to design a special shield to screen everything but the square of my shoulder blade where the tag was embedded.

I rechecked the circuitry to make sure it would only take a flash scan, then chewed my fingernails a bit farther.

Why didn't I get the parameters from the Locator section?

The Locator signals are sealed, automatic, and the parameters are limited to the Tribunes. While Locator can track the signals of any Queryan with a Locator tag, the composition of the signals is secret.

Why didn't I take a blank tag from the maternity ward and analyze it? I did—and found out that the signal is a twisted helix, so to speak, and combined the basic temporal Locator signal with the individual aura and sent it back in a scrambled pattern. The combination was set at random by the master Locator computer by remote after the implantation at birth, and once set, remained set—forever. That immutability might work in my favor, provided no one found out what I was doing.

Not that anyone who would understand my actions was likely to be wandering down into Maintenance. Both Freyda and Heimdall were happier to see me repairing, analyzing, or traipsing around the galaxy than thinking.

Repair facilities, even ones like the Guard's, with the sophisticated air and light scrubbers, with superclean technology, microcircuit duplicators, and the rest, still have that atmosphere or edge of grubbiness that no amount of cleaning can totally remove. In the Maintenance Hall, it wasn't so apparent at first, but after years I became aware of it, more of a feeling associated with technology than anything else.

A light meter would tell me that the Hall was as clean as Assignments, but the floor-to-ceiling slow-glass panels seemed dimmer. The air had a faint tinge of something—ozone, graphite, oil, heated metal—that no other section of the Tower had. The rows and rows of equipment that I had reorganized, some of it under time protection and unused for centuries, added to the impression of raw mechanical power.

I tried to picture a time when the Guard had employed all the equipment, but failed. Some of the bulkier pieces dated to cultures no longer accessible, a few back to the time of the Frost Giant/Twilight Wars, sleeping under their time-protectors, shining as brightly as they had two million years before when they had turned out fire swords and rain shields. I laughed softly, as I caught myself lapsing into belief and repetition of the legend which Wryan and Sammis had said was untrue. According to them, the equipment had been gathered, but most of it had never been used.

According to the myth, that had been the first, last, and only pitched battle fought by the Guard. I found it hard to understand how they could all coast through twenty thousand centuries on the memory of one war—particularly when it hadn't been all that glorious.

I cut off the dreams and historical analysis, knowing I was only postponing sticking myself under the modified analyzer because it was going to hurt.

With a deep breath, I pushed my not quite totally shielded shoulder under the beam head and punched the stud. After I had wiped the blood from my chin and slapped some heal paste on the lip I had bitten through, I checked the analyzer data. There was enough, for which I was glad. I wasn't certain I could have gotten through it another time.

I managed to smear some more of the paste on the burned shoulder and to cover the burn with a sterile field dressing in order to slip my jumpsuit back on. I knew the wound was sterile, but the pain marched across my shoulder like a shark army might have. Then I tried to concentrate on having the muscles and skin heal. I thought the pain lessened, but that could have been wishful thinking.

Sitting down on the operator's stool, I put the circuitry back in its normal patterns, although I doubted that anyone would have tried to use the equipment or figure out why it had been changed. Still—Narcissus was just curious enough to poke his nose or fingers in the wrong place, and the last thing I needed was for him to get burned. With my luck, Heimdall would have started asking questions.

I kept thinking of the Guard as an enormous clock, designed for eternity, but ever so slowly wearing down, missing an instant here, counting two units instead of one there, while the clockmaker's children and grandchildren kept oiling it and polishing it, afraid to tinker or replace any of the fine pieces within.

I knew the Archives data said the Guard was growing, but I found it hard to believe the numbers. Even so, greater numbers of more talented Guards didn't necessarily mean a better Guard.

I debated leaving for the Aerie to let the shoulder recover, but decided not to wait. I walked back to my spaces and fed the data into the master analyzer. One tape had my own aura recordings; one had the data from the blank Locator tag, and the last had information from my own tag.

The console screen seemed blank forever, though it was only several units before a complicated formula appeared. I made several recordings of the formula and tucked it away under several dummy files in my system, plus two copies on data blocs that I tucked into my belt. I pulled my heavy red cloak over my jumpsuit.

The next day would be the most risky, I figured.

Then I walked up the ramps to the South Portal, still concentrating on trying to heal my lip and shoulder.

For some reason—Heimdall's displeasure with me, my own introspectiveness, my reputation for not suffering technological idiots, or the rumor that I didn't need gauntlets to throw thunderbolts—few of the Guards struck up conversations with me within the Tower itself.

I was the only Guard in centuries to openly oppose and injure a Counselor, go to Hell, and return. For similar reasons, I suspected, Heimdall also had few conversations. After all, he had attempted murder and gotten away with it with the equivalent of a slap on the wrist. Heimdall led a lonely life, both public and private. The born-again Glammis found him too cold and had turned away, finally leaving the Guard.

In that late afternoon, as I walked through the echoing and near-empty corridors, glancing at holos of past glories standing out from the main walls, feeling the warmth and light of the slow-glass panels from a thousand suns, I wanted the silence, trying not to strain or bite my lip at the combined pain and itching from my shoulder.

"Loki?" called a light voice. Verdis had left Personnel for the day apparently, and waited by the South Portal.

She tossed her mahogany hair back over her shoulder. Usually, she expressed her feelings with her entire body, but now her eyes were filled with concern. The rest of her body might as well not have been there, and that bothered me.

"Hera's Inn?" she asked.

I wanted to go anywhere like I wanted to dive through a black hole, but Verdis was up to something, and my gut instincts told me that refusal was not a good idea.

Verdis was well regarded, and now that Gilmesh, Heimdall, and Freyda were closer than ever, she could easily start inquiries with the newest Tribune. She might also have some news about what Freyda was up to.

Freyda and I had long since cooled on each other, but I liked to think that a fondness remained. Not that Freyda would hesitate a moment to consign me to Hell or worse if she thought I were a danger to the Guard.

"I'll be just an instant. Meet you there." I nodded to Verdis and slid, not to the Inn, but the Aerie. A quarter way around Query, the sun was low, almost dropping behind the peaks, and the light glittered off Seneschal.

I staggered over to the mirror and stripped off my jumpsuit and dressing. The dressing burned as it came off, but already the deep burn looked more like a combination of old bruise and scab. Still, I put on more heal paste and a clean dressing. It still hurt, stabbing into the shoulder.

Maybe it had been a stupid thing to use an equipment analyzer, but a standard tissue analyzer wouldn't have been equipped with the necessary energy scanning levels. More important, the medical equipment was more closely monitored by the Tribunes.

I washed my face, spent another few units taking care of bodily necessities, and arrived at Hera's Inn to face Verdis's scowl.

"You took long enough."

"Sorry," I apologized, and she nodded, relaxing slightly.

Inns were peculiar to Guard and Queryan life—at least our kind of inns. In the first place, the doors and inner walls were time-twisted, which limited entry to better than average planet-sliders—although a diver who could barely pass the Test could struggle through. The decor was usually some variety of technological sword and sorcery, with holos and displays from the more spectacular planets visited by the Guard.

Hera had been a fair diver, but had retired into a quieter way of life, if the hustle and bustle of running an inn could be termed quieter. She was plump, the closest thing to a fat diver or ex-diver I'd ever seen, with brassy blond hair she swore—and could she swear—was natural.

Her inn was done in wood—real wood—mostly polished cedar from a place called Lebanon on Terra. Must have taken a good-sized forest, just from the expanse of the inn, and a lot of divers to bring it all back— either that or a few planks and the biggest duplicator I'd ever heard of. With her connections, either was possible.

The floors were blue glowstones, also unusual, and the illumination was provided by light-torches from Olympus.

Inns wouldn't have been possible without a sharing based on a sense of honor. Hera or any innkeeper left a list of items she needed on a tablet by the door. Guards brought them back as they saw fit. Haphazard as it was, it worked. The inns not favored perished or were taken over by more congenial proprietors.

Power came from the ubiquitous Murian fusactor, and Hera's synthesizers, adaptations of the duplicator really, would copy the master dishes in the files—really just energy patterns stored in lattices similar to those that supported the data banks of the Archives.

Verdis claimed a corner booth as I followed her, although all booths were essentially corner booths. I sat down gingerly to ensure I didn't hit my tender shoulder.

Verdis offered a smile that didn't quite make it. Mine was about as genuine as hers.

She cleared her throat, and I waited.

"Loki, you've spent years now, since you were in Hell, aloof from almost anyone . . ."

"Me? Charming Loki? Aloof?"

"That's what I mean." She shook her head. "I'm hungry, and I don't

think well on an empty stomach." She rose and headed for the synthesizers.

It sounded like a good idea, but I winced when I bumped my shoulder. No one saw. I got a Weindrian flameray, and Verdis got something
smothered in cheese.

Mine took longer for the synthesizer to deliver, and Verdis was sipping a glass of Atlantean Firesong when I eased back into my side of
the booth.

She ate for a while before she tried again.

"For all your power and fame, you distrust the very people you work
for. They distrust you. You bury yourself and the fire that springs from
you in that cavern with your machines. When you do emerge, Odin
Thor and the Tribunes shake. All the younger Guards worship the glowstones you walk on, and if you deign to favor them with a word, they
feel honored. Everyone always wants to talk to your people, trying to
figure out what you might do next. But you never do anything—except
improve the machinery of the Guard, occasionally go fight a thunderstorm, and take impossible diving missions."

"And that all means?" I asked, after swallowing the hot-bitter meat.

"You could run the Guard, Loki, and yet you do whatever Heimdall
or Frey or Freyda suggests. I wonder if they didn't go beyond the call
of duty to plant the shark cluster on you. After all, I've looked at the
charts, and it's a good distance beyond what we usually patrol." She
smiled crookedly. "Much good it did them."

I still had no answers about the shark mission. Who had put Sammis
and Wryan up to that? Sammis certainly wouldn't have intentionally
done something to cost him Wryan, and Heimdall never ordered Sammis to do anything.

"Do you want to be Tribune?" she asked.

I had thought about being Tribune, I suppose. What Guard hadn't?
But for all of Verdis's talk about running the Guard, I was fiftyish,
looking twenty, and the Tribunes had tens of centuries of experience.
The Counselors did too. Heimdall was waiting and plotting to be Tribune, as was Gilmesh, and Freyda of the cool voice and fires within was
certainly not about to step down. Nor was Eranas for all the decades of
rumors that he might. Unlike Heimdall, I certainly wasn't up to murder
for ambition.

At that, I laughed aloud.

"Loki?"

Loki, the man who destroyed a hundred thousand suns and a million
years of life; the man who watched Zealor wipe out a gentle people at
the behest of the Tribunes; the man who booby-trapped the gauntlet of

Heimdall—good old thunderbolt-throwing, storm-stalking, fire-breathing Loki was the Guard who couldn't even consider killing the greatest tyrants in time.

Two hated my guts, and Freyda would be very sorry and shed a tear and stamp me out like an insect if she could and if I threatened the Guard or her ambition.

I looked at the planks above my head.

"Loki, can't you hear?" Her eyes were hard.

"Hear? What do you mean?"

As she pointed to the back room, the singing became clear.

"Who's the Guard that fired the stars and sank the sharks?
Who's the Guard that wired the gloves and gave them sparks?
Who's the Guard that went to Hell and almost died?
Who's the Guard that told no truths and never lied?
Loki! Loki! That's who, the Immortal God for me and you!

"Who's the Guard that tamed the techs and stole the sun?
Who's the Guard that faced the Tribs and made them run?
Who's the Guard that stood on air without a wing?
Who's the Guard that lives for life, the Guard we sing?
Loki! Loki! That's who, the Immortal Guard for me and you!"

There was more, but I lost it in studying Verdis. I wonder if she'd composed the damned song—awful lyrics and all—just to put more pressure on me.

I hadn't realized how many young Guards there were who could sing, and they turned that doggerel into a solid drinking song. They belted it out, and when I peered around the corner of the booth, I thought I saw a glimpse of Dercia and Kyra in with the other young Guards.

Verdis was attacking me with a cold stare. I wanted to shrug, but while the pain was decreasing, my shoulder still hurt.

What was the purpose of it all? Had Verdis arranged the whole scene, song and all, to suck me into some sort of conspiracy? If so, how had she managed to convince all those younger Guards to participate? But what could she want with me? Why even raise the idea of my running the Guard? Assuming I was crazy enough to want to be Tribune, I certainly wouldn't have listened to her if I did get to be Tribune. As if I wanted to. Who the hell wanted to run a funeral procession? That's the way things were headed, and I clearly wasn't the only one who thought so. My parents had dropped out decades earlier, and so had Baldur—and those unnamed and "lost" Guards. I wasn't good at intrigue or reading between the lines, and I was tired and irritable. So I asked.

"Just what are you asking?"

There was a long silence between us, though the inn was filled with noise as the trainees and the young Guards in the adjoining room launched into another round of song. Thankfully, it was a ditty about the seamier side of Odin Thor's past.

"Loki, few of the really good divers know anything about how important the Guard is to Query. I'm not talking about temporal meddling or about the trappings of power. I'm talking about supplies. The duplicators, the generators, the equipment bank, the simplified mechanical basis of Query, make it possible for a few thousand people to support millions. What happens if anything goes wrong?"

Verdis should have been a political agitator somewhere, sometime. Maybe she was, and I didn't know it. Her eyes flashed as she threw the questions at me, demanding that I believe what she had to say.

Oh, she was right in a way, but was the situation all that pressing?

"You have to know I'm not terribly sympathetic to the Tribunes," I responded, "nor Heimdall, but what could go wrong? Query is still a fruitful planet, and we have a low population and a low birthrate.

"If the Guard disappeared tomorrow and never carried another item back to Query, it would be centuries before the system fell apart, if ever—unless the diving ability totally disappeared, or unless someone destroyed all the power generators and duplicators. So," I concluded, "what are you diving for?"

Verdis opened her mouth, then shut it, paused as if to catalogue the arguments filed behind her smooth forehead and dark red hair. "You've been underestimated, Loki."

"I doubt that," I demurred. I didn't expect or need any more gratuitous flattery.

She sipped the Firesong for a while, and I finished the last bites of my dinner.

"All right," she said quietly. "Let's assume you are right—that Query will survive without the Guard. Will it survive *with* the Guard in its present outlook?"

"What do you mean by the present outlook?" I wasn't about to commit to anything, not until I knew what she had in mind and why, and maybe not then. The itching in my shoulder was worse, but when I leaned against the booth cushions, it hurt. I shifted my weight and waited.

"That increasing the Guard's power is a desirable end in itself."

Her words almost echoed those of Sammis, and that bothered me.

"Are you saying that the Tribunes' goal seems to be to make the Guard more and more powerful?" I wasn't about to admit that was my view, not publicly anyway, but I was already convinced that the present course of the Guard would pull down a round lot of cultures, whether or not that destruction was really necessary.

"Loki—after what you've been asked to do, is there really any doubt?"

"I've learned that the more obvious anything seems, the more there is to doubt." I tried to keep my voice wry.

She set her empty glass on the table and stared at me. "Don't tell me you're still supporting every little thing the Tribunes propose?"

"As you may know, I am supporting Loki, past, present, and future." Someone had told me that, and I played the quote back, hoping that it hadn't been Verdis. If she had been the one, she didn't comment.

"With that," she said slowly, "I need another drink."

That, at least, was a good idea, and I followed her, hoping the walk would relieve the agony of itching in my shoulder. I pushed the synthesizer stud for another firejuice. This time I reached the table before she did.

As soon as she sat down and took a deep swallow, she started in as if she hadn't left off. "Someone, or a number of someones, has been asking the Archives questions about history and parahistory, questions about critical turning points in any number of cultures which rivaled or could rival Query."

"So?" I asked with a sinking feeling in my stomach.

"We don't know who it is, but the fact that *someone* is asking that sort of question is ominous."

I leaned back into the padding behind me, trying to focus on Verdis, but the intensity of the itching in my shoulder distracted me, and I missed some of what she said.

". . . may mean that since Query has so much inertia and so many Queryans outside the Guard are like sheep that this group wants to set up a man-on-a-white-horse situation—"

"A what?"

"Man on a white horse—great Black Father to take over in a period of crisis. Whoever it is doesn't want to wait centuries for a real crisis and may be searching for a crisis to create."

"Seems pretty farfetched to me," I commented.

"It doesn't to the Tribunes."

That hit me like a flash of deep-space cold.

"Why do you say that?"

"Personnel has been asked to devise and issue priority codes to the Guard for the historical data banks, with a system so that no one, not

even a Tribune, can use someone else's code. The other little feature
we're working on is a way for the Tribunes to track data requests without
knowing the new code."

I shook my head, not for the reason Verdis thought, of course. Someone was monitoring the data banks and my innocently programmed
requests. I was glad I already had what I needed.

"We're afraid that one way or another this power game between
Guard X and the Tribunes will bring down the whole Guard structure."
Verdis had that intent look in her eyes again.

"Isn't that overreacting? I mean, the Guard has survived centuries of
power plots."

"We don't think so—not this time."

"Who's we, and why are you so convinced this time? Or are you
afraid that the Tribunes may find your little group?"

"Dive again?" she asked.

"You keep talking about 'we.' And you keep avoiding my questions.
You still haven't answered what you want from me. You haven't said
why you think this rumored plotter, who could merely be a student of
history, could do what no one else could do. And you haven't identified
your mysterious group that's so involved with tracking down this rumored schemer."

As she cocked her head to think up an answer she hoped I'd accept,
I had another thought. Was the whole meal a gimmick to see if I'd
reveal anything? Verdis didn't want to tell me much, for all her supposed
openness.

"I'd rather not say more, not right now. A number of us are concerned.
As for what we want from you—that's simple enough. You keep your
word, and we want your word that you won't meddle in the domestic
affairs of the Guard and Query."

I had to laugh, and that surprised Verdis more than anything I could
have said. "You don't even understand what you're asking. If I repair
one gauntlet, I'm meddling in Guard affairs. Or do you mean I should
promise your vague conspiracy that I won't try to set myself up as High
Tribune? You make me sick. As if I wanted to become emperor of this
time-flying gopher hole!" I wanted out of the inn, then and there. "Or
does it mean that I should stand idly by as you and your company take
over the Guard?"

"Loki, that's not what I meant at all!" Her protest was pretty loud
at that. "You plod on in your own world, buried in Maintenance, oblivious to almost everything. Eranas is making noises about stepping down,
and Heimdall is using every tactic and favor in the book to ensure he's
selected to replace Eranas. Everyone wonders who is staking out past

history and why. Gilmesh is trying to untrack Heimdall by showing Frey's incompetence, while Ferrin and Tyron are trying to save their hides by covering for Frey. People still ask what happened to Baldur and Wryan, and the Tribunes ignore Sammis because he advises Heimdall, and Heimdall gathers more and more loyal goons. And you don't pay any attention at all."

I wished I'd left earlier. I could tell Verdis I cared, and blow myself out of the water, because what I intended certainly wasn't what she wanted. Or I could say I didn't care and be lumped in with the status quo she loathed and distrusted.

Like so many times before, I struggled with conflicting thoughts. What could I say?

The songfest in the other room had degenerated into assorted conversations. Phrases drifted through the archway as I looked down at the empty plate and glass and as Verdis looked at me.

". . . Guard'll last forever . . . Loki for Tribune . . . never happen, not with the bitch goddess . . . fly Kyra . . . sheep, and they'll never care . . . who'll do the dirty work . . . Domestic Affairs in Hilgar . . . shit work . . ."

"Put that way," I said finally, because I had to get out of the inn, "I guess I don't. Not the way you mean. But maybe I ought to. Maybe I should."

I pulled myself together and walked out into the antechamber, wanting to claw at the endless itching in my shoulder. I jumped back to the Aerie and collapsed.

XXIX

By MORNING THE violent itching had subsided to mere irritation, and the scab had dried to the point where it looked like it was almost ready to come off. I concentrated hard, and it seemed to help enough that the scab fell away. The skin was still pinkish and tender to the touch, and the purple green of a bruise underlay the new skin. Still, the ability to heal myself was improving. I supposed it took practice.

I was still stiff, though, as I discovered in hurrying to get cleaned up and dressed. As I dressed, my eyes flicked to the bronze bell. I hadn't looked at it in a while, but the inscription was still unreadable, even with the handful of new languages I'd picked up. With so many in the galaxy, where would I begin?

I wanted to get to the Tower early, and I did, early enough that no one was there except the duty trainees.

The production equipment I had set in the corner of Maintenance didn't take more than a few units to ready. Shortly after I fed in the parameter formula, little black boxes, each with a Locator tag and an uncharged power cell within, began popping out of the other end of the system. From there they went into a converter that charged them, and right into a time-shielded bin.

The shielding might have been an unnecessary precaution, but I had warped the plastic edges out of time enough. With all the rumors being circulated, it would save me some grief. Who wanted Locator to register one thousand "Lokis" in Maintenance—assuming the real-time parameters were even lifted?

After the first units dropped into the bin, I took one and ducked behind one of the older machines for a quick timedive backtime to Abelard. I dropped off the little black box there, stuffed it under the roots of some plant, and dived back to Query.

As I broke out in the Maintenance Hall, I checked around, but saw no one. If my black gadget worked as designed, it should already have been registering my continuing "presence" on Abelard. Later, I'd have to verify that.

I walked back to the compact production machine, a modified duplicator and mass focus assembly unit and watched the output build up. Then I began my regular work by assigning the repairs which had been brought in by the duty trainees. Brendan arrived within units and carted off his share.

I carried Narcissus's to his space, and Brendan came back and delivered Elene's. Before he got out of sight, I gestured. "Would you start to work on setting up what Dercia will need? No hurry, but I'll leave that up to you—unless you run into something strange."

"I'd be happy to."

Brendan could be a real pleasure to work with, and probably would be a better Maintenance supervisor than I had ever been. As I ran through the routine and not-so-routine jobs I'd assigned myself, the equipment behind me continued to produce black boxes.

I needed to work on access to a Locator terminal, preferably when no one knew what I was doing.

Terminals existed in three places—the Personnel Hall, under the scrutiny of Verdis and Gilmesh; the Tribunes' spaces; and the Locator section, which had a full-time duty staff.

With all the concerns Verdis had mentioned, especially that bit about the Tribunes' interest, I wasn't too interested in a repeat of my imitation of Frey and the nighttime follies. Sliding and entering is officially classified as thievery and merits a sentence on Hell. While no Guard or Tribune would ever get me back on Hell, skulking around after hours was definitely being watched more closely.

Paradoxically, my success in Maintenance had denied me the one legitimate access to a Locator terminal I used to have. When the Tribunes had made me a Senior Guard and given Maintenance back to me, my name had been lifted from the emergency divers' watch list. That particular watch list had been Ferrin's innovation to ensure a first-class diver was always on call, but supervisors were exempted.

Somehow, I had to get myself back into rescue work, at least occasionally. I turned off the phony tag producer and covered the bin, setting out to corner Ferrin.

He was still in charge of the watch list, despite effectively running all of Locator. He was also struggling along by himself at the moment I walked in.

After pleasantries, I hit him. "Look, you script-pusher. First, I've gotten tied into support and administration. I never get anything routine or moderately interesting in diving missions—just killers when Heimdall cooks up something designed to fry or freeze me."

Ferrin didn't even flinch. "So what do you want?"

"The only diversion I ever got was occasionally rescuing someone. Now I can't do that."

"Loki . . ." Ferrin sighed. "Far be it for this lowly personage to question the ways of the high and the mighty, nor would I ever wish to cast aspersions upon the god of forge and metal, whose mighty hammer fuels the weapons of the Guard . . ."

"Ferrin, can't we discuss this straightforwardly?"

". . . nor would I wish to be faulted by the powers that were, are, and ever shall be for dissuading the mighty Guard of fire from his appointed responsibilities . . ."

"My responsibilities are minimal, and, besides, we're all caught up. Even Frey can't find anything more that needs repair."

". . . and his duties as a supervisor . . ."

"Ferrin!" I must have sounded desperate enough. At least, he stopped the high-sounding obfuscation and looked at me. "I'll have to check."

"Then ask Eranas, or Freyda, or Kranos. Just let me be an occasional fill-in—a backup."

Ferrin finally grinned, and that meant he'd look into it. So I went back to Maintenance and resumed the production of black boxes. By the end of a ten-day, I had nearly a thousand stashed behind a time-protected wall in the Aerie and had disassembled the equipment back into less obvious uses.

Days passed, and I was about to take another whack at Ferrin when a trainee showed up late one afternoon with a polite request from Ferrin, asking if I would stand in for Sammis that evening in Locator.

That bothered me. Sammis rarely, if ever, missed a duty, even after Wryan's death at the hands of the sharks. But I was in Locator for the night watch.

The standby diver, unfortunately, doesn't have a console, and I couldn't get near one.

Duty was uneventful, as it usually was, and by the time I left I was tied in knots. A run across the training fields before I slid back to the Aerie helped calm me down.

The false Locator tags were still stacked up behind the phony wall, showing, if they worked, and if anyone cared to disable the Locator "now" cutouts, that I was always in the Aerie. I didn't want to proceed until I knew they did in fact work.

As the time dragged out, what Verdis would do was another question, and I hoped she wouldn't try to drag me into whatever she had in mind.

I didn't escape that easily.

Several days after my standby in Locator, she showed up in Maintenance after the others had already left—even Brendan. I was closing up.

"You've been avoiding me. Why?"

"I've been thinking."

"There's a time for thinking and a time for action."

I tried not to swallow, since I didn't like the implications of what she was saying. "I'm not exactly up for snap decisions that might overturn two million years of relatively successful traditions. Also, you haven't said what you want and what you have in mind."

And she, or they, hadn't. The only general concern that they'd expressed was the wish that I not try to take over things. I didn't believe that for a moment. There was more involved—much more—but I was a lousy snoop. Not one sign of what was going on had surfaced anywhere. Or if it had, I didn't know what to look for. Probably the latter.

"Caution doesn't fit your image," Verdis suggested ironically.

That was another way of saying my courage had deserted me.

"Have I ever shown I was a coward? Where was your courageous group when I was shark-hunting at the end of time? Or rescuing divers under sonic assault? Or getting squashed by heavy-planet spirals?"

I'd been fearful and cautious plenty of times, not that Verdis would know, but I decided to defend my image.

"It's easy when you're not dealing with real people," she said, before turning away.

Real people? That bothered me. Both Verdis and the Tribunes seemed to think that no one outside of Query was real. Just because they couldn't control time they weren't real?

The other thing that nagged at me was the lack of certainty. I still had no real idea of what was going on—just bits and pieces and parts of people's reactions. I had flash-slid through most of the Tower, avoiding the Tribunes' spaces, time and time again, and never found a trace of anything. Neither had my microsnoops. The only strange item was the time-shrouded table in the Tribunes' private council room that I'd viewed from the undertime. Still, finding almost nothing meant nothing. Anyone in the Guard could slide somewhere and meet. They didn't need the Tower.

Days passed, but Verdis didn't come back, didn't press me, and that bothered me as much as being pressed.

I waited for another standby in Locator, and finally got it. The night was an uneventful one, starting out just like the first duty I'd taken from Sammis, until close to local midnight.

A figure appeared on the public slide stage, a woman who started screaming. Helton, one of the two console operators, got up and headed across the stage to her. I slipped into his seat and accessed my own Locator code.

The console began scripting all the past locales. I wasn't interested in verifying the whole mess, but just looked to see if the phony tag I dropped backtime on Abelard registered. It did.

I blanked the console and hurried over to Helton and the distressed woman. She was pouring out her tale of woe—one of those screwy and, thankfully, very rare cases.

The woman's first contract-mate, and father of her ten-year-old daughter, had slid into her quarters, grabbed the daughter, and threatened to kill himself and the daughter unless she renewed the lapsed contract.

She refused, and the father disappeared with the daughter.

"He's crazy. I couldn't ever renew . . . not with him. He'll kill her . . . I didn't think he would . . . but he will . . ." she gasped out between sobs.

"What's her name, your daughter's name, her personal code?" Helton pursued.

I stood there looking sympathetic and helpful. Wasn't much I could do until they'd come up with some sort of location.

"Regine," the mother stammered. "RGE-66-MC." The MC was stan-

dard for "minor child" and would be replaced with a color code once
she matured, generally after she was the age to take the Test.

Giron was on the other console and plugged the codes into the Locator system.

"Undertime, Lestral, near the top of the Sequin Falls!" Giron announced.

"Looks like he means it," commented Helton, sotto voce.

I leaned over Giron's shoulder to scan the coordinates and dived right
from the spot. I knew where I was headed. I'd been there before. Most
Queryans have also. The Falls are quite a scenic attraction, drop straight
down for kilos into the Lestral Trench. The Trench makes the Bardwalls
look like the mounds around a flying gopher hole.

The water of the Sequin Falls is black, coal black and cold, if not
freezing. The chunks of ice that dot the waters bob like stars on that
black expanse and fall like meteors to the Trench below. They glow with
a light of their own because of the ice worms and glittering microor-
ganisms that are so common on Lestral.

Any delay on my part was out of the question, regardless of whether
I needed a warm suit or not. The father wasn't a diver—at least he'd
gone for real-time Lestral, and he had already broken out.

With the coordinates in mind, I was undertime, and instead of following the time-lines, I was crossing, vaulting, trying to minimize even
the minute crossover delay from the undertime to the now.

For all that, "lucky" was the word.

The father had thrown Regine into the water near the brink, and the
conditions helped me locate her even from the under-time, because bodies glow like the ice against the black water.

She was heading over the edge by the time I located her, frozen in
fall as I studied her position. From there it was straightforward. Not
easy. Sounds matter-of-fact, but to break out in water cascading verti-
cally, thrashing me around, while trying to grasp a child in the space
of less than a unit and dive safely undertime as we both dropped toward
the biggest pile of sharp rocks on the planet was not an average dive,
or a typical rescue.

I lost Regine in the cold water, and it took three quick undertime
slides before I got a grip on her, and just as I touched her arm, a chunk
of something stabbed me in the shoulder. I kept hold of her night robe,
but I had to have a firm grip on flesh to be able to carry her undertime.

I grabbed with my other hand. My feet somersaulted over my head,
but my left hand closed over her wrist, and I dived, wrenching her out
of time.

We got back to the Tower Infirmary before Helton or the mother had left the Domestic Affairs section, I figured.

Regine was bright blue, but breathing. The duty Guard medical tech had run diagnostics on her, stripped her out of the night robe, and wrapped her into a thermal quilt. She had a small gash above one eye, and a line of blood was dribbling down her cheek. Her damp hair was plastered back above her ears in a blond wave. Her eyes studied us both without much expression as the tech focused the end of the regenerator on the cut. Regine might have come to my waist if she stretched.

The tech turned to me, insisted on a quick check.

"Hell of a bruise across your shoulders," she commented.

"Ice, I think."

She pushed me into the nearest diagnostic booth. Nothing showed but the bruise, and the tech left me to my own devices as she went back to Regine.

I wrapped myself in a quilt. I still felt like I was a paler shade of blue, but I wanted to see Regine. She had seemed so somber. As I caught sight of her from the archway, I decided against joking.

She was sitting on the edge of a bed, her color close to normal. The Guard tech was wheeling away the portable regenerator. My entry rated a glare from the tech, but she didn't try to throw me out.

"I'm Loki. How do you feel?"

"Wet . . . cold. Where's my mother?"

"She'll be here in a moment."

Regine's lips had a faint bluish tinge, but the thermal quilt had restored most of her body heat. She didn't want to talk.

Standing there made me feel awkward, but I shifted from foot to foot for several units . . . waiting. Regine ignored me. Finally, I drew the quilt around me and went back through the archway to recover my jumpsuit.

I finished wringing it out and slipped it on. The fabric dried quickly, so it was only damp. Some of the stuff on the equipment belt was shot, but I'd replace that later.

I was getting ready to leave the Infirmary to check back in with Locator when the mother arrived with Freyda and Helton.

"Loki?" asked Freyda, the Tribune.

"None other," I said with a forced smile. "If you'll excuse me, I need to report back to Locator."

She nodded. The mother said nothing, her eyes darting around, looking for her daughter.

"Through the archway," I offered.

As I walked toward the exit portal to cross the square, I could hear Freyda's voice. ". . . the only one on Quest who could have saved your daughter . . ."

In that, at least, she was right.

Probably I didn't have to, but I finished the remaining few units of the standby duty before sliding back to the Aerie for a solid night's sleep.

Sleep didn't come immediately, because I'd had one of those after-the-fact realizations, something I should have thought about earlier, much earlier.

I had gone to elaborate lengths to manufacture nearly one thousand phony Locators, to get legitimate access to a Locator console, gone over Sequin Falls to save a child who wouldn't talk to me. And I'd approached the whole question backward—as usual.

How had people like Ayren disappeared? People who didn't have backtime records to hide in or machines to duplicate tags?

Somehow, they'd had the tags removed. How could I have it done?

Have a surgeon somewhere cut it out, of course.

With that thought, I fell asleep, sound enough not to be troubled with dreams or fears.

Once I got into Maintenance the next morning, I turned my concentration to finding a surgeon who could do the job under local anesthetic. I want to be able to watch, and, frankly, I didn't want it to hurt too much.

The Archives had some data along those levels, but I did want to show some care. I traipsed up to the study cubes for a bit around mid-morning and used Giron's code to ask about medical progress levels.

The Tribunes hadn't implemented their new code plan; in fact, for all of Verdis's explanations, nothing of the sort had even been rumored elsewhere, let alone announced, which made me wonder how she knew what she knew. Who was telling her? And why?

In the meantime, Terra, late early atomic, northern western hemisphere, about halfway up my foretime range, seemed the best place. Sinopol had the medical technology, but I wasn't willing to undergo what they might have in mind for strangers or imposters.

Before I dived foretime to Terra, I absconded with some medical equipment from the back rooms of the Infirmary. I also rigged a gadget with a miniature surgical laser which would cut the small chunk of metal clear of my shoulder. Rather involved technically, but as foolproof as I could make it. I added to that a miniature Locator that would point directly to the tag.

With the gadgets in hand, and after wheedling yet another Terran language implant—the Terrans had more languages than some small clusters—out of the duty trainee late in the afternoon, when Loragerd and the regular Linguistics staff had left, I departed for Terra.

I could feel the moan of the change winds around me, not the violent shudders and twists that ripped through the undertime when the Guard meddled, but the little tugs, the fleeting flashes that weren't quite there—except they were.

Terra equaled change. I wondered about the source of that flowing change, and while I couldn't have said I knew the reason, I would have bet that some of the "missing" Guards could have been found scattered around Terra, stirring up the gentler time-changes by their presence. At that point, I wished I'd brought an energy detector, just for curiosity, but I hadn't.

Most Guards probably wouldn't have picked up the little indicators, the blurring around the edges of each entry or exit from the undertime, but the signs of changes were there. Certainly, neither Heimdall nor Frey would have sensed a thing, and because the change winds don't blow backward, unless the Guard set up a foretime station on Terra and continually recorded, it would be difficult to determine exactly what changes, if any, were taking place.

Just because a change impacts a town or a village doesn't mean that it changes much overall, and even if it does, the impact of such a change may not blossom until later. That way you have a whisper of the change winds for a time, before they become a torrent, and it can be difficult even to track. While it's easy to find a change in a stable culture, Terra is far from stable.

For a moment, I thought that if my own plan didn't work, I might be able to do something with Terra. I pushed that thought away— changing the future wouldn't change the past wrongs of the Guard.

Besides, there was no time for maybes or alternatives. One thing at a time. I didn't want to compound my errors, and I'd dithered around too much already. So Terra was merely a stop on the timepath I'd charted.

I knew what I wanted, preferably a small health-care facility isolated from any other with no one else around.

Despite the penchant of the Terrans to label every building and structure, and to number those they didn't label, I had difficulty Locating a medical facility, taking roughly a hundred slides before I found what seemed to fill the bill.

The sign read, roughly translated, "Dr. Odd-Affection, clan (family?) practice."

The front room of the structure was filled with hydrocarbon replicas of plants—and empty. I had hoped so, and had chosen the late time of local day for that reason.

Dr. Odd-Affection looked older than I was and was surprised to see me in his office. That may have been because the front door was locked.

"Did you have an appointment, Mr. . . . ?"

"Loki," I supplied, not answering his question. "You will not have any patients for the next few units, and I do need your skill. I am willing to pay handsomely for it. No, there is nothing illegal about it, and I would do it myself, but the location involved means that I cannot."

I wasn't certain I could have cut into myself even if I could have seen what I was doing, but I wasn't about to let him know that.

The good doctor looked more puzzled than intrigued.

"I can pay you with any of these." I flashed a diamond, a flat gold bar, and a small eternasteel scalpel.

His eyes widened most at the scalpel, perhaps because of the glow, and he struggled with his tongue.

"What . . . how?"

"Simple. There is a small metal plate on the flat of my shoulder blade. I need it removed. This device would remove it virtually painlessly, but I cannot expose the bone."

"In my office? I'm really not set up for surgery."

I handed him the spray container and the scalpel-laser. "This will sterilize and numb the area instantly." I thrust the miniature Locator at him. "This will point directly to the metal square."

The doctor seemed a bit glassy-eyed as I tapped the end of the surgical laser.

"That will cut the plate clear. Then sew me up and bandage it loosely. You will never see me again."

I put two of the diamonds on his desk, plus the gold bar. "You can also have the scalpel and the local anesthesia."

I could see the conflict by the workings of his face, but I guessed he finally decided that anyone who appeared out of thin air and wanted to be cut open was crazy enough to listen to.

"Why?" he demanded.

"Because I was tagged with this tracer plate while I was unable to resist, and I'd like a bit of privacy." Which was true as far as it went.

"But I can't do it here," he protested.

"Where?"

He told me, and it didn't make much sense—something about a hospital and his license and the government. I supposed I could have gone elsewhere, but he seemed so conscientious that I decided to solve the problem for him.

A squarish machine with a keyboard rested on a table next to the wall. I gestured at it and fused it into junk.

"Doctor, I really would like some help."

"But you want me to cut you open while you're awake." He paused. "You're acting like you're some sort of criminal."

"I am a fugitive of sorts, but I can assure you that I am not a criminal, nor am I wanted for any crime." Not yet, at least.

It took me a while, but, in the end, the combination of rhetoric and thunderbolts convinced him. He was a bit unnerved when I insisted on an arrangement of mirrors to watch him, but I figured he couldn't be too bad because he didn't seem to be motivated primarily by greed.

Even with the anesthesia, it hurt. Dr. Odd-Affection wanted to immobilize it, but I requested stitches, the temporary kind, and a sling. I was diving back to the Aerie, where I could concentrate on healing it, with the removed Locator tag in my pocket.

I placed the rest of the diamonds and the medical equipment on his table, hoping the good doctor could put it to use. Then I ducked undertime right in front of him. That way, no one would ever believe him if he tried to explain it all.

I staggered along the timepaths and broke out in the Aerie. My legs were shaking, and recovery was a top priority. I fell asleep.

There wasn't too much I could do for the next day, except recover. The itching was so bad, it was even hard to think, but the healing was faster. Maybe cuts healed faster than burns.

The next day, as I lay there and itched, and willed the shoulder to heal, staring at the clouds that obscured the canyons below, I tried to take stock.

Item: I had one thousand phony Locator tags stored behind the wall not two body lengths away.
Item: I wasn't going to need them.
Item: Verdis and company were unhappy with the present Guard structure.
Item: Contrary to what I had thought, the numbers of Guards were increasing, and so was the amount of high-tech destruction.
Item: Eranas was the last of the old-line Tribunes, and was talking about stepping down.
Item: Despite all my maneuverings and everyone else's, nothing was obvious.
Item: Verdis was impatient and pushing.

Item: Heimdall wanted to be the next Tribune, and Freyda was
    talking to him frequently.
Conclusion: The present quiet was a lull before a terrible time
    storm, and I was going to have to act before long.

Verdis and her allies were pressing. Heimdall was continuing to build
a private army, and Freyda had some plan of her own. Kranos hadn't
said a word, but I couldn't bring myself to trust him either.

One conclusion was simple. If the Guard survived in its present form,
Freyda would be calling the shots. Heimdall might think he was, but I
had a good idea who would be, and just one part of Heimdall's price
would be a lot stricter Guard. Eventually, of course, Heimdall wanted
to make the Guard's corner of the galaxy his own playpen.

I didn't want that, whatever happened, and I already didn't like the
excessive meddling. I could see the need for dealing with the sharks,
but there had never been a need to destroy the Gurlenians. And I
couldn't undo things like that by backtime tampering with Query—
that wasn't possible. Likewise, tampering with other cultures piecemeal
to create rivals to Query wouldn't work. All Freyda and Heimdall had
to do was send back unquestioning young divers to undo what I had
done—and we'd end up with a time war that would make the Frost
Giant Wars seem insignificant.

On the other hand, if I grabbed the rocksucker by the tentacles and
eliminated Heimdall, the structure would sooner or later create another—was Gilmesh any different? And Freyda might do the same sort
of thing, more gently and not with the same intention, but to make the
galaxy safe for Query.

Plus, I didn't have the resources for an extended war—let alone any
way to survive if the entire Guard came after me. Hell, I still didn't
know exactly what I wanted to do, or if I really wanted to. So far, all
I'd been able to do was to set it up so I could disappear and not be
tracked—like Baldur.

I told myself I needed more information, but I wasn't sure I really
did, or that I had time to get it. First, I needed to recover, but two days
after the ministrations of Dr. Odd-Affection, I planet-slid to the Tower
and popped out of the undertime right in front of the South Portal.

I walked into the Tower wearing the mesh armor I'd gotten so long
before from Sinopol under my jumpsuit, gauntlets, and a stunner
strapped under my forearm, ready to drop undertime at the slightest
provocation.

Edgy?

And how! Who knew what had gone on while I had been absent?

I trotted down the ramps to the Maintenance Hall, nodding to the few trainees I passed, but prepared for anything. The only surprise was the empty bin by my space and the note Brendan had left.

Not sure we did it as quickly, but decided you didn't need to come back to it all.

B—

I had to smile. Brendan would fill the bill fine. Narcissus would even do an adequate job if anything happened to Brendan, and Elene was coming along fine.

If . . . if I were going to go through with my mad scheme, I needed a few props. Both could be fabricated elsewhere, but I needed information from the Archives.

So . . . back to the Archives and a theoretically shielded booth I went, where I keyed in my request, using Heimdall's code, asking for hard copy.

"Galactic Sectoral star chart, normal space, centered on Query."

The second query was shorter.

"Field theory . . . enabling equations for FTL drive . . . with universal math addendum."

I stopped back in Maintenance to leave a note on Brendan's console, telling him I was still somewhat under the weather, but hoping to be back as soon as possible. I also asked him to convey that to Heimdall.

Following that, I marched up the ramps and across the Tower to the Travel Hall, where I picked up my personal equipment chest and slid it and myself back to the Aerie. So heavy was the chest I staggered out of the undertime wobbling.

My next step was to confuse the issue.

I began pulling phony Locator tags from their hiding place, time-diving straight from the Aerie and placing them on planets scattered both fore- and backtime, but making sure I avoided the systems listed on my printout of possible high-tech cultures. By objective nightfall at the Aerie, I'd dumped—and I had literally dropped them—several hundred "Lokis" throughout the Guard's corner of creation.

Those left I unloaded into the Lestral Trench. The ones I'd planted would have to do.

I tumbled into my furs for some sleep, but sleep didn't come, and my shoulder still itched.

In a culture where life was short, decisions had to be made in a hurry. You would never have enough time, might never live to see the consequences of a wrong action—or a correct one. On Query, it was different. At the back of my mind, the thought kept recurring—you can always wait and see what happens. So far, nothing you've done can't be undone.

The thoughts eventually merged with dreams, and neither were clear.

I was up with the dawn and time-diving slightly foretime and clear to Sertis before the sun broke from the horizon. I'd been there dozens of times before on routine procurements, but this was different. For one thing, I carried no Locator tag.

Three of four establishments turned me down cold.

"Copy that on metal . . . no. That's out of my line. Try . . ."

I tried whoever they mentioned.

Despite the fact that I was no longer tied into the Locator system, I had the feeling that Heimdall's blood-seekers wouldn't have too much trouble tracing me through Sertis, burnoose draped properly or not, not with the signs I was leaving. I felt that every metalworking shop and jeweler on the planet would have heard of the red-haired fellow with the accent who wanted a screwball map copied on one side of a metal plate with funny squiggles on the other. Still, without a Locator signal, they'd have some trouble trying to find out when on Sertis, and by going forward, there wouldn't be obvious change winds.

All I needed was one basic plate. I could duplicate from that.

After more than a dozen false starts, I found a woman who dealt in exotic metals and engraving who promised the plate within a ten-day local. I left a substantial deposit and the promise of a more exorbitant payment.

Needless to say, I merely time-dived ahead and picked it up. I studied the result carefully, and as far as I could see, she'd copied both the map and the equations exactly. She also wanted more money, claiming that she'd had to use a diamond stylus to do it properly. She probably had, and I didn't quibble.

A second study confirmed to me that a trained astrogator or astronomer could pick out the starred system without difficulty. The starred—I guessed it was really highlighted—system was Query's.

I was back in the Tower by nearly normal working time, even so, and had managed to duplicate more than thirty of the plates on thin eternasteel by midday.

Packing them into a light carrying case was no problem, and I studied the Hall to decide what else might be useful to cart along when I skipped out.

The thought of leaving caught me. Ferrin or Heimdall would have planned something like that down to the last unit and realized it sooner.

But why should I skip before I had to? In my case, that amounted to leaving a signpost.

I regeared mentally, tucked the case and star plates into the big bottom drawer under my workbench, and dragged a repair job into position. A simple one, which gave me a chance to think.

What a circular path I had been treading. First, I had decided to confuse the Locator system by duplicating my personal tag and strewing it all over the galaxy. Then I had reversed tracks and had Dr. Odd-Affection remove the tag. In the meantime, while on Query I was wearing the removed tag on a chain with the appropriate gadgetry to ensure that the Tribunes did not know I had removed it.

I had gotten the information necessary to use outside cultural pressure on Query, but hadn't done anything because I figured it would start a time war if Heimdall weren't removed. Then I'd temporized by saying to myself that Heimdall would only be replaced by someone else just like him.

Sooner or later, and probably sooner, I was going to have to make up my mind. What was I going to do?

As I struggled over the questions, and automatically knocked off the gauntlet repair in front of me, Verdis glided in with the warmth of a blizzard and smiled.

"I'm glad you're still here." Her smile wasn't genuine because her black eyes weren't smiling with her mouth.

She twisted her body to flip her heavy red hair back over her shoulders.

"So am I, I guess," I answered, smiling a phony smile to match hers.

"Have you heard the rumors?"

"Which rumors?"

"Facts, actually," admitted Verdis. "Frey's been charged with high treason by Gilmesh."

"What?" I was afraid of what was coming next.

"The Tribunes placed snoops around the Tower. They have frames of Frey rifling desks and recovering snoops of his own. He swears it's a plot, that he's been framed."

"When did this get out?"

"Last night. The hearing is set for late this afternoon. Frey's in the holding cells below. Heimdall is demanding that Freyda not sit on the Tribunal. In the meantime, he's also charged that Gilmesh has been using his personal code to obtain culture information. It's a mess." With that, her smile became real. Verdis was pleased.

"You're pleased," I noted.

"Not displeased, but I never thought Frey had the brains to think up something like this."

I decided to muddy the waters by being honest.

"He doesn't. Nor the mechanical talent to handle snoops."

"You sound awfully certain, Loki."

I shrugged. "I've no great love for Frey, but either he's telling the truth, or someone else is in it with him."

Verdis pursed her lips.

"Could be . . . could be. And who might that be?"

"Verdis, I'm scarcely up on intrigue. As you so pointedly reminded me at our last meeting, I bury myself away from what really goes on. You already know the answer. You just want me to answer for you. Count me out of the games, thank you."

She shook her head. "You amaze me, Loki. The biggest scandal in centuries—one of the Guard caught plotting—and you want out." She glared and mimicked my voice. " 'Count me out. It's getting a bit complicated . . . Yes, count me out, Verdis.' "

I chuckled. Her imitation was good.

"Young lady, just what do you want me to do? Go up before the Tribunes and declare, 'I have no basis for my statement, honored Tribunes, except that I do know that Frey is a mechanical idiot and incapable of higher thought. So either he didn't do what you've charged him with, or he's someone's dupe.' Is that what you want, Verdis?"

She actually stamped her foot on the glowstone flooring.

"Loki, you're impossible! I don't know if you practice density or if it comes naturally. If you can think all that up, everyone already had. Who handles all the microcircuitry? You do! And who could dig up Heimdall's codes? And how soon do you think it will be before Heimdall persuades the Tribunes to send someone down here for you? He's already arranged to take over Domestic Affairs because Frey's been relieved of duty, and because Kranos said it would be a conflict if Gilmesh did." She stepped back from the workbench. "Good luck. You're either the culprit, which I can't believe, because it's a bigger mess than even you could create, or you're going to be Heimdall's way of getting out of it all. But I suppose you'll sit here and wait and go to Hell again, like always."

She turned and marched out, heading for the ramps.

How long would it take Heimdall to act? Not long, and he'd be arriving before long too, if Verdis were right. But was she? Or was she trying, again, to panic me into something so that her little tech group could fill in the breach somehow?

I left the repairs stacked around and reached down and pulled out the case and set it by my table. Then I looked at the copy of my cultural meddling printout. My request had been coded to request the easiest changes first, followed by those which would take more and more dives and effort. The whole project would be even more difficult than a normal cultural alteration because I intended to point the finger of time right at the Guard and at Query. That would probably require additional dives and doubtless some ad hoc improvisations.

Altara IV was the first planet on the list, as I began to study what would be required. I didn't have much time to study it then.

Brendan came flying into my spaces. "Loki! Get out of here! Heimdall and the Strike Force are gathering, and they've got a big laser. There must be a dozen of them, and they're coming after you."

"Thanks!" I meant it. "Now get the Hell out of here, and take everyone else with you."

Brendan got.

Fight now or later? My guts said now. But someone had wised Heimdall up about needing more than gauntlets or stunners. Gilmesh? Freyda? Not Sammis. He knew a laser wouldn't be enough, not anything portable.

I didn't know enough, but what was clear was that I was still getting pushed around. Did I want to stand around and get tied to a rock on Hell? Not exactly, and staying there meant either blasting away Guards or getting locked to a rock.

I jammed the printout into my jumpsuit, grabbed the plates from beside the table, and slid straight undertime from the Maintenance Hall—sidetracking for an instant to drop my Locator tag into the Sand Hills—to the Aerie.

If . . . if I had to straighten things out, I could always claim I wasn't there—while if I fought it out, a lot of people would get killed, and there was always the possibility that I might be one of them. Not a high possibility, but real, nonetheless.

Standing in the Aerie, I surveyed my small nest, from the permaglass to the stores of destruction, the power cells, the equipment I had gathered over the seasons.

I had been considering action for years, putting it off, planning and replanning in my dreams, but I was down to a decision point, with Heimdall, and probably the Tribunes, close behind.

I had wondered why he couldn't have arranged my death when I was unconscious after losing my hand in the shark mission, but Hycretis belonged to the Tribunes, and I suspect I just wasn't unconscious long enough. Besides, I hadn't finished off the sharks yet, and the Tribunes probably wanted to keep me around until that was resolved—there had certainly been the chance that the sharks could have done it for them.

Verdis's plotting had probably forced the issue. She wanted me to support some tech-based internal reform or revolution, and that was the last thing the Tribunes, or Heimdall, or Gilmesh wanted. By trying to arrest me, Heimdall or the Tribunes removed me one way or another. They probably had my own words on Frey's incompetence recorded somewhere, as well as Verdis's assessment of my complicity. I either got sentenced to Hell or left the Guard to wander in the outer reaches of some part of our galaxy. Either way, their empire would remain intact.

I shook my head. That was what they thought. The time for dreaming and speculation was past, and so were the times for scheming and plotting. As I thought, I changed from the black Guard jumpsuit into something else, glancing down at the river and the deep canyons. I needed to hurry, before they mounted enough equipment to break into the Aerie—if they could or would.

With a start, I realized I had changed into a totally red outfit. That fit. I would challenge the fires of time, perhaps whatever gods of time might be, and red was my color . . . red for the fires that burned within.

XXX

THE NAME AT the top of my list was Altara IV, supposedly the planet where time-changes would be the easiest to make. The natives called it Rephala, later in their parahistory.

Wrist gauntlets fully powered, eternasteel tablets in the carrying case slung under my shoulder, I squared myself for the first of the timedives with which I would wrench Query's history into a different mold.

I slipped into the undertime with scarcely a ripple, hardly aware of the mind-chill.

The backtime for which I was diving contained a turning point. All histories have them, a place where an "almost" culture might have emerged. Given a push at the right times, or a mailed fist on the opposition, the prognosis for events leading to a high-tech development was favorable.

On Altara IV a bronze age evolution on the small island continent had been wiped out by the invasions of a barbaric bunch of ax-wielders who outnumbered the lizard people of the island ten to one. The barbarians hadn't even bothered to stay on the island, but had eaten everything, looted, and departed rather than work at agriculture and silvaculture.

My first breakout was to locate the barbarian encampment. After three scans through likely twilights, I found campfires scattered around the sandbars and the twisting land bridge that led over the horizon to the land I had chosen to protect.

With a skip, flick, flick, flick through the undertime, I centered on the narrowest segment of the unstable rock and sand that composed the causeway.

The destruction was simple enough. I pushed the small antimatter cube out into the now at the proper juncture of fault lines and shifting rock and retreated into the sky and the now to watch. The sand shifted; a line of fire spewed heavenward; the sand and grass sank; and the waters rushed into the new channel that would block the island continent from the mainland.

And I flamed into view over the camps of the ax-wielders.

AND IN THE twilight appeared the god of fire to his people, and thence to their enemies. The lightnings were his cloak, and the sparks dropped like the rains of winter, and the enemies of his people knew him not, for the god of fire had long been absent from his place.

The multitudes of the enemy did not bow down, nor did they cover their eyes, nor show any sign of respect.

And the god of fire was angered, and his lightnings, they rained upon the unbelievers, and few were spared. Few of the males, or the females, or the neuters, or the children.

Their screams spread upon the night and were not heard, for they had not believed. They had seen and not seen; they had been shown God and did not worship.

The night was as day, and the lightnings struck the land as the hammers of the smith pound upon the forge, and there was heat, and many of the waters bubbled and seethed.

And the people of the island, the chosen ones, kneeled upon hard rocks and marveled, and their tails were stilled, and they were amazed. By the hammers of God were they astounded, and they worshipped, and then, then did the god of fire depart.

WITH A SHIVER, I slid undertime along the chill wind of the time-change I had created, riding the creaking surges forward.

A city shimmered with lights, beckoning through the time-tension barrier.

I answered the call and broke out.

The city section I saw first was squalid even in the night, gas lights

throwing shadows across low stone huts. But where gas lights existed,
so did emerging technology.

I skip-slid into the following day and toward the harbor, looking for
a warship, certain of finding one.

Not one, but a squadron, small fleet, powered by some sort of fire-
steam system, attested to by the smokestacks. Crude metal plating and
gun ports proclaimed they were intended for combat.

*THE GOD OF time and fire arose from his slumbers, and in the twilight of that
evening gathered his thunderbolts that the ships of that king, and the pride of
that people, be brought down to the fishes of the sea, and along with the vessels,
also the soldiers and sailors who defied the god of time by their blasphemies.*

*For no harbor was yet safe from God, and no city escaped his judgment of
fire; and his judgment was, and it was that the warships of the sea should be
no longer. And raised he his mighty arm and collected the flames of the sun and
the lightnings of the storms and once more, as he had in the past, made the night
as day, and brighter than noontime it was as the fires fell from the heavens unto
the ships and the waters. And the ships were no more.*

*The people were sore afraid and remembered the tales of old and the prophecies
they had mocked, and they prostrated themselves before their god and prayed for
his forgiveness.*

*Unto them who prayed was their god merciful and upon the black rock by
the waters which still seethed gave unto his people his holy tablet, and departed
then the god of fire upon the lightnings and the flames.*

WHERE ONE FLEET sailed must have sailed another, if not several, and I
began a quick slide-search of Altara IV. In my haste I was not strictly
impartial, searching only for warships of apparently different origin.

*AND UNTO THE enemies of his people visited also the god of fire and rained
upon their vessels also the fires of the sun and the lightnings of the storm. And
those vessels also perished.*

THE CHANGE WINDS around Altara IV moaned more loudly as history
changed into parahistory and parahistory became history, even as I rode
those winds forward into time, looking as I was from the undertime for
the signposts of development.

I whisked through local centuries to break from the undertime into
objective time. Differences were evident, with canals, intensive culti-
vation, and the lines of what might have been quick-transit systems all
visible from my commanding view. Those were not what I needed.

I slid undertime and scanned the planet, hunting for the energy concentrations that must have existed. They did.

Three power plants were ideally spaced, and I girded myself for the next step.

FOR IN THEIR *pride, his people had builded themselves towers to store the fires of the sun and to trap the lightnings of the storms, and to have each do their bidding.*

And they said, we are like the god of our fathers, mastering the fires of the sun and the lightnings of the storms, and flying like the eagles, and there was no god, but only foolish writings of ignorant peoples.

And for this arrogance, the god of fire was displeased, and in the space of an instant hurled down the towers of power, and they were stone and dust.

Yet the people were still proud, and in their pride, dared their god and the heavens. And, behold, they crossed the skies faster than eagles, and their craft of the air made the sun stand motionless in its course.

And a craft of the air approached the god of fire even as he had toppled the towers and flew nigh unto the god and turned not.

The almighty one drew unto himself, and from the thunderbolts of the storm made first a signal; so might all the peoples of the earth know his displeasure, and the red of his fires surpassed the green of the sky.

And those who had forgotten recalled again the tales of their god, and trembled, and were fearful.

Another sign displayed the god, and yet another, for to warn that flier who had dared the heavens after the fashion of his fellows and challenged the god of fire. But the defiant one struck at God with an arrow of flame.

And God was angered and turned upon the flier, and the defiant one then fled, faster than the sun itself. But the lord of fire suffered not that his erring servant should escape, and he gathered unto him his flames greater than the sun of the noon, and cast down the defiant one.

Many feared, yet saw not. Because the people did fear and did see with their eyes, but understood not what they saw, the god went to the high place of his peoples where gathered the most mighty, and so cast it down, making the hills like plains, flat and smooth as the finest ice, and in the center of that holy place, left the last of his holy tablets that his people might read, and reading, might learn what was to lie before them.

DEPARTING IN A column of flame, I rode the screaming, wrenching change winds for parainstants before racing ahead, back to Query, back to my Aerie.

I shuddered, but I dared not feel for those who had suffered . . . not and redress the balance of Time.

Standing over the cliffs, my Aerie seemed poised over the canyon of destruction, but I knew it was all illusion.

My power packs were dead, and I replaced them, not that I was sure I even needed them longer, tapping as I was the energy underlying the now.

My supply of miniature antimatter bombs was depleted, and I restocked.

One gauntlet was fused, and the skin beneath red and tender, and I willed it to heal, and it did.

I looked around my Aerie, my weapons storeroom, cluttered and jumbled with implements of destruction, before setting out for the second wrench I would make in the machinery of time.

I replaced the eternasteel tablets with their message, star chart, and formula in my carrying case, pulled on another gauntlet over my healed right wrist.

Three swigs of firejuice, a battle ration cube, and I was prepared to dive. Rationally, I knew that much of the sustenance, except for the liquids, was unnecessary, but it made me feel better. Already I could sense the change winds in the back distance over the curve of time, blowing ahead of the now toward Query, and I knew I had much to do before they arrived with their messages.

After a stint as the Lord of Destruction I would become the Lord of Creation, before I donned the mantle of Destruction again.

I time-dived and slid out the black branches into the backtime, three hundred centuries or so, and out to Heaven IV.

Heaven IV was not on any printout I had gotten from the data banks. That alone might have kept Freyda, Eranas, Kranos, and Heimdall buffeting in the change winds, even if they had copies of the list.

I forced my way down the backtime paths toward the planet of the angels, with a specific aim in mind—an angel nursery. With a sense of feel and three quick slides across the blue heavens, I located it.

Although the term "nursery" sounded formal, it wasn't, because the place was more of a sheltered cliff on one of the tallest peaks I'd ever seen, but overlooking, as always, the goblin's hell smoldering far below under the dark clouds and seething heat.

For the god of fire and time had come unto the place called Heaven, to take his due from the angels and from that mount where the children were gathered.

Yet a single angel protested and raised his lance against the god of fire, and that angel was no more, for against the thunderbolts of the god he could not prevail.

And from that place called Heaven the god of fire departed, time and time again, carrying the children, two by two, to a far place that is strange no more, but was strange unto them, until he had gathered there two score and more.

And to guard them, against the cold and against danger, further provided were they with angels to succor them, for they grieved and their hearts were heavy, and they were alone.

THE PLANET ON which I had placed the uprooted angels had a slightly heavier gravity than Heaven IV, and the atmosphere was thinner. Intelligent life had not yet evolved, but my data indicated the biosystems were compatible.

Statistically, it was a long shot, but I *knew* it would work out. That is the business of gods.

Flying would not work well, except for short distances, and more metal meant a tech culture.

That I did not intend to leave to chance. I slid foretime on the first murmur of the second change wind I had blown into our stuffy corner of the galaxy.

Twenty centuries up were towns, small cities, boats, and beasts of burden, fires—enough for a first appearance.

I lit up the sky at twilight over the square of a town, cast a few thunderbolts into the town center, and deposited a tablet.

After repeating the performance over a more distant village, I then departed up the line. I did not expect much more from the change wind, but the murmurs were swelling as I rode forward, peering from the undertime at the changing surface of the planet.

At fifty centuries foretime from the objective time of the transplant, I found iron ships upon the shallow oceans and laden power wagons upon the roads.

AND THE FALLEN angels had prospered, but in their prosperity had disregarded the words of their god and had taken up new ways, and sailed the seas in ships of metal and turned the soil with metal beasts, and had in truth forgotten their god.

Yet he laughed, and his laughter shook the forests, and drew thunder from the skies.

And the fallen angels stopped, and they listened, for they feared, for the sound was strange unto them.

But the strangeness of that laughter did not turn them; they listened and did not hear.

And their god was angered, and in his anger cast his thunderbolts upon the highways and upon the wagons that traveled them and upon the seas and the ships that crossed them, and put his mark upon the very stones of the hills ere he departed.

He waited in the shadows of time unbeknownst, and bided his time until the millennium had come.

For again, the people who had been angels had forsaken their god and were proud in their handiworks and their contrivances, and raised their wings against their god.

The god of fire strode across the heavens and flattened the cities, and struck the ships from the seas, even those which were mighty, and picked the ships of the air from the skies, and twisted the iron ways into forms that confounded their makers.

All that and more did the god of fire, who laughed at what he had wrought.

For lo, the fallen angels did not cower, nor were they ashamed, nor were they filled with fear, but instead shook their wings against the sky and against the fires.

And they seized the eternal tablets of the god and were filled with wrath, and in their hearts they plotted and directed their ways against the very stars.

The winds of change wailed, and reached into space beyond the firmament and behind the time and twisted both and brought chill and the cold that was beyond chill onto the gales that reached even unto the home of the god of fire.

XXXI

"SO NOW YOU'RE a god?"

I realized that it was Sammis I had tied up in the slope chair and linked with a unit chain to the Aerie itself. The chain was loose enough that he could have escaped the moment I let go of him. But he waited.

I shook my head. The stillness was deafening, and it seemed like I was two different people—maybe a poor way to explain, and it didn't excuse anything. Just easier, I guessed, to destroy and remold world cultures while letting the god side of me take the blame.

"Hardly. Just doing what's necessary."

"Eagle crap!" he snorted. "I saw the look on your face when you surprised me. You came in here like the god of fire. Wryan would call it psychotic disassociation or some such."

I swigged some firejuice and finished off two battle ration cubes. One was a full day's nourishment, but diving like I'd been doing was *work*.

The change winds were blowing. The sounds from downtime distance were nasty.

"It's really much easier to manipulate poor unsuspecting sapients than face the real problem, isn't it, Loki? Or should I still say, God Loki?"

Sammis or not, I could have punched him. He was right, at least about it being easier to deal with out-time cultures, and I might as well face it. I'd have to sooner or later.

"I didn't notice you doing much about it, great original Tribune."

"You're right," he sighed. "One stint as the god of death was almost more than I could handle." His eyes turned black, as if they had seen an even deeper Hell, and never forgotten. "That's a problem we all have, those of us who decide to stay sane, Wryan says. Life is often too easy and too long to face the hard decisions. We plan and watch and wait and hope, and go along to some degree with the schemers. I'd hoped you'd be different, especially after your head-to-head confrontations with Heimdall."

I was ready to go and was replacing my power cells, another burned-out gauntlet, packing up more eternasteel tablets, and finishing off the firejuice in the beaker.

"What do you mean?"

"You're strong enough to take on the entire Guard in a single battle, I sometimes think, and win, and yet you never raised your voice after you came back from Hell, never said a word."

"Neither did anyone else," I reminded him. Hell, the ones who thought the Guard had done wrong just hung back and hoped I'd do their fighting for them, and the others hoped they wouldn't have to fight. Well, now it was my turn.

I swung on the carrying case.

"How will you stop Heimdall? Unless you do, he'll stop everything you're doing."

I halted, caught in midstride, but both riddles were crystal-clear, oh so clear, and with them, the response to Sammis's questions.

Sammis insisted I was a god. So did most of the Guard, both those who supported me and those who opposed me. And with that lineup I had assumed the choice was simple—either you're a god or you're not. *I* knew I wasn't, not in terms of my own definition of a god. But the definitions weren't the real questions, and I'd been hung up on definitions, just like everyone else.

Without even understanding my questions, Sammis had flamed that right to the point. "Who" wasn't the question. Nor "what," but rather "how." Like "How are you going to deal with what you are?" Like "How will you stop Heimdall?"

That second "how" I could answer. Now. The other would come, had to come, and soon. But first—Heimdall and the Guard, for Heimdall was only a symptom of what the Guard was becoming.

"Actions speak louder than words. Or definitions, Sammis."

"Wait."

His voice was lost as I slid across the skies of Query to the Tower, glittering as it rose from the Square to challenge the sun.

Without their tools, their sources of information, Freyda and Heimdall could not undo what I had done. They could not locate, except by trial and error, the turning points to which they would have to send other Guards.

I ducked under the edge of time and broke out in Assignments, flaming, lightnings gathered to my chest, but only Giron stood at the main Assignments console, his mouth opening wide at my appearance.

"Out!" I ordered him, for I did not wish him harm.

Without fanfare, I unleashed my energies across the consoles to leave fused metal, twisted plastic, and acrid smoke as witnesses to my visit.

Assignments was only the beginning, only the start, for the information remained in the data banks—two million years of data on history and parahistory. In the deepest depths of the Tower, levels below the Maintenance Hall, locked in behind walls that would halt a battle cruiser, were the memory banks, the lattice crystals that held the information amassed through millennia.

I bypassed the walls, breaking out inside the sterile confines, skip-sliding down the dim rows of lattices, flinging lightnings before me, and dropping animater cubes behind me.

With a final toss at the core, I ducked fully undertime and slid into the sunlit sky above the Tower.

Though the muffled sounds of explosions rumbled through the ground and the Tower trembled, the massive, buried, and time-protected walls surrounding the physical storage area held firm. The data banks themselves had not been so lucky, I knew.

More as a gesture than anything, I gathered more power from the air around me and flung a last thunderbolt at the steps in front of the South Portal and scored the glowstones with a line of black fire that would live within the stones for eons.

I turned my attention to the past I must create anew. I needed to choose from the possibilities left on my list, for the moments of hard decision would be coming soon. Heimdall and Freyda and their cohorts would be grouping already, and would be scheming on how they could stop my efforts.

Mightier men than I—Tribunes and rulers of sharks and peoples—had deceived themselves into thinking that their works were permanent, and I was only a man, whatever immortality, whatever weapons of the gods I might bear, whatever delusions it might take for me to remake a small corner of a single galaxy. To myself I would have to answer, not for what I might be called, or for the name I refused, but for what I had done, and would yet do.

Along the way I had a score to settle, somewhat indirectly, which might cloud the change winds more.

I time-dived from the sunlight and the sky above the Tower toward Gurlenis back until, flicking in and out, back and forth, I could sense another link to Query, a figure breaking out into the sky above nomads' tents, where gentle wanderers camped—or at least ancestors of the green-bronzed philosopher I had met in a paratime instant . . . an instant that was not and would not ever be, yet would.

To break into another's previous past-time was a feat thought impossible, but determined as I was to do it, I bent and broke the fabric of those instants to my will.

AND THE PURPLE of the night was sundered into fragments, and each fragment was a song, and the peoples of that time bowed and prostrated themselves then before the song. For not only was there music in the heavens, but fire.

The god of fire, he who was called Loki, raised his arm against the other, who was called Zealor, and a god of time in his own right.

And Zealor called upon Loki and begged of him mercy, and asked that his days not be numbered. But Loki the god of fire was not dissuaded and turned the lightnings of fire and the powers of time against Zealor, and Zealor was no more.

The wanderers who beheld the fires that exceeded the stars saw, and covered their eyes, and were filled with awe.

He who was called Loki laughed, and the sound of his laughter brought waves to still lakes, and caused the leaves of the trees to tremble. When he had laughed and lowered his hand, behold, where once there had been a mount was a holy place, and thereupon the god of fire placed his holy writ for his chosen people, lest they forget.

AS I DROPPED undertime, shivered, the die was cast. After having killed my own, knowingly and deliberately, even though he had refused to turn from his mission, and no matter how noble my reasons, the time of denying my own responsibilities, my own failures to take stock, had passed, and passed forever.

Sertis, good old stable, always mid-tech Sertis, was next, and the revolution of fire would strike the unexpected to fan the no-longer-gentle winds of time-change into the true hurricane of time.

The king-emperors of Sertis had ruled because they controlled the water, and thus, the minds and power of Sertis.

Water enough existed, but it was locked into the polar caps and the plateau glaciers.

I headed for the fiftieth century before my own birth.

THE GOD OF fire appeared and struck his lances upon the ice that had been, that had crowned the far poles, and the ice and the snow were no more, but became as boiling water, and broke their boundaries and sundered the mountains that confined them.

Pillars of fire and soot were there also, of red and of black, and when the ruler of the place called Sertis felt his throne quake, asked that ruler of his generals the cause.

And they knew not, save that the fires of Hell had appeared at the far poles, and that the ice had departed, and the water had come.

Then the soldiers of the armies were afraid, and heeded not their commanders, nor the voice of their ruler.

And when the priests appeared before the assembled peoples, neither were they heard, but were offered by the peoples as sacrifices to the god of fire; and the god listened and left unto them his holy book that his will might be done.

THE WINDS OF time-change screamed as I crossed them on my time-vault back to Query.

Would I exist when I was done? Had I become as a man who had never been born or died, a god with no beginning and no end, and neither worshippers nor deniers?

From the undertime the planet Query would be shaken, twisted, bent like a leaf in a tempest assaulted by the change winds out of time. For each wind from the pasts I altered would create its own winds, and the second winds would blow unto the third winds, and no man or god would know his place while blew the wild winds of time.

In and out of time, solid as I approached, stood my Aerie, as stood the Tower of Immortals.

"And now?" asked Sammis, as I broke out and began to replenish my stores of destruction.

"The rest will come, Sammis. The rest will come."

I noticed he was free of the chain. He had been waiting for me, and he was waiting for me to speak again.

"By the way," I asked, "how and why did you and Wryan fake her death? Little lapse of tense, old god. And why did you provide all the behind-the-scenes assistance?"

In retrospect, all of it seemed so clear. Only Sammis could have maneuvered so cleverly. Sammis gently provided suggestions, and the Guard listened. Stupid of me not to have seen it. Wryan planned, and Sammis executed, even that first test to determine my capabilities. I saw not just what Sammis was, for he was Sammis Olon, but the others—my parents and Baldur.

Why had it taken me so long to see the obvious? How my parents had stayed on Query long enough to give me what I needed. And Baldur—from the generator to the time-changes flickering on Terra—how he had left for Terra to create legends and shape all the differing Terran cultures with facets of our own, and with his insistence on the importance of understanding technology. Or how—the list was long, too long.

"It wasn't that hard," answered Sammis, who stood there nearly forgotten, "not with all the distractions you and Heimdall and Gilmesh provided. Wryan and I were ready to leave earlier, probably would have, except that when you came along, your father asked . . . and we kept hoping—"

Sammis wasn't that pure, and I cut him off. "How many did you test? Over how many years? How many were too scared to dive again? Old god, don't dwell too much on idealism! What kind of will does it take to follow the same course for centuries upon centuries? What kind of power is that?"

All the time I was talking, I was replenishing and watching the man I had accepted as Sammis Olon.

Time, subjectively and objectively, was short, and I girded myself for another dive, another series.

"Goodbye, old god. Where's Wryan?"

"Where she's always been, great-great-grandson and young god. She and I wish you the best."

That stopped me. Why was he finally admitting openly that he was my great-great-grandfather? "Why are you finally admitting it?" I snapped.

"Because you always want someone else to admit things first. If they won't, you hide it. Part of that is the brute strength of youth, but when you grow up it tends to become just stupidity. Things are, whether you want to admit it or not."

I swallowed.

As he talked, the memories were there—"great-granddaughter of Sammis Olon," the stories of the Guard—and other remembrances . . . looking up at someone crying, seeing a look that might have been concern—or fear.

While I struggled with his words and the memories, and his logic about my wanting to force others to admit things, I could hear the change winds howling toward the now like night eagles swooping in for the kill.

"Your saving grace," continued Sammis implacably, "has been your willingness to undergo punishment for your mistakes, even to punish yourself. And to try to avoid deluding yourself—even as you have."

Sammis delivered the words quietly, as if he were stating well-known facts or established truths.

"Where's Wryan?" I wasn't quite grasping at straws.

"You'll be able to find us. You always could. Just look at the bell." He pointed at the bronze bell. "It's a wide universe. Treat it kindly." He vanished as I watched. He was diving to Wryan.

I looked at the bell, and I recognized the script—Terran—courtesy of my last language implant, the one I had needed to find Dr. Odd-Affection and remove the Locator tag.

I shook my head to clear it. Duty, if I could call it that, would be to finish what I had started before the change winds unleashed their all-too-long-thwarted fury on Query.

I could not meddle with other cultures as devastatingly as I had on Sertis, Altara IV, or the offshoot of Heaven IV. Time was short, its noose tightening, but at times knowledge can be enough of a lever.

I had eleven tablets left. I intended to deposit each one on a different planet, each in one of the times/locales identified by the now-sundered data banks as promising for high-tech development, knowing that my very appearance in a cloud of flame would spur something.

Midgard was first, close-time, and I dropped the tablet on the ceremonial steps of the Asgard, thunderbolting the statue of the Serpent as I did.

The next nine were a blur, and when I struggled across the bucking timepaths to the last, Weindre, and forced my way into the Technarchial Center to deposit the last eternasteel tablet, I could hear the creaks in the warp of reality while still undertime.

As another last gesture, I etched the black thunderbolt across the front of the Technarchate's Fountain of Power and placed the tablet under it.

For better or worse, the Guard's corner of the galaxy would not be the same—and no one would undo what I had done.

Hell and Timefire! No Guard, no god, but Loki, could tread the paths of time in those instants against the wild change winds. And next would I assure that none would so tread after the winds passed and the worlds and stars settled into new histories.

Some things I could not have avoided, no matter how I pretended, and some matters were not to be handled by stealth. Nor would I have had the appellation "coward" stand in the memory of those who cared, and those who survived.

I broke out in Assignments.

Heimdall was absent.

"Loki!"

Nicodemus reached for a stunner. I knocked it clear of his hand with a trickle of fire from the gauntlets. Not exactly, for I looked at my wrists, and the gauntlets were fused metal encircling my lower forearms—merely metal decorations. I knew I no longer needed them, but I left them in place.

"Where's Heimdall?"

"Tribunes' spaces," answered Nicodemus, with a look that demanded I destroy him.

I refused to oblige his whim.

Before, always before, I had avoided the Tribunes' spaces, at least in real-time, but power blocks or no, I had no intention of avoiding them, and I did not, smashing through the physical and paratime barriers as if they did not exist, hurling myself into the center of the once-sacred Tower.

Heimdall, Eranas, Freyda, and Kranos stood around a black crystal table, waiting—waiting for me.

Heimdall wore gauntlets. The others were dressed in their black jumpsuits and were without overt weapons.

"Greetings, fallen gods, and Heimdall, whom I shall call false god for the sake of convenience."

"Proud of yourself, Loki? Happy to destroy a million years' worth of dreams in an afternoon?" That was Kranos. He'd never understand.

"The sins of the father's sons." That was Freyda.

"Why?" demanded Eranas, in anguish, face twisted. He thought he had been fair, and he had, in his own way.

Heimdall didn't bother with words. He just pointed and fired, and Freyda smiled. His aim was good, but it didn't matter.

I let the energy sheet around me. I walked toward him, around the black crystal table filled with images from time, and he leveled another thunderbolt at me. I gathered the energy to me, and kept walking.

Freyda smiled sadly and vanished undertime. No matter, she would accept what came, trying to twist it to her advantage somehow.

Heimdall backed away.

Kranos also stepped back, almost drawing time around himself, until he froze into a time-locked cocoon, withering as I watched. I shook my head, not realizing such a death existed.

Eranas stood motionless, the blackness growing in his eyes, as I moved toward Heimdall, who retreated step by step until his back was against the time-protected wall.

Heimdall, the honorable, the Counselor, the Guard who would have been Tribune, turned the full power of his gauntlets upon me. And though I could feel the power sheeting around me, it was as nothing, and I took another step.

As both gauntlets separately had failed to destroy me, he linked them together and blasted the thunderbolts of Hell toward my face. They flared around and past me as if they were no more than smoke, and in the slowness of that "now," I took another step toward the false god who would have been king of a battered corner of a beaten galaxy.

He lifted his hands to strike me, and with two fingers I crushed his wrist into powder.

Heimdall, the once-mighty, the schemer, the demigod who would have flattened Query and countless worlds to lift himself, gasped once, gasped twice, squared his shoulders, and dropped his arms.

"Do your worst, with your hands dripping blood and fire! Do your worst and feel righteous in your slaughter!"

I broke his neck with a single blow.

I took in the black room, the crystal table of time, for that was what it was, a tool of the Tribunes sheltered and used in secret. Then I stared at the black crystal, willed it to shatter, and it did, with the falling shards themselves exploding into dust that was no more.

Where Kranos had stood was but a pile of dust.

Eranas, who looked and would not see, who saw and would not complete his actions, stood rooted in his own private and forever "now," his vision locked into a universe that soon would never have been, darkness creeping over his soul.

He, too, would vanish when the change winds whistled around the Tower and stirred the silent dust of time, for his mind could not bear the weight of its own past.

Some things I had to finish, and I slid straight for Freyda's mountain hideaway, the one overlooking Quest that had been in her family for millennia.

As I broke out of the undertime, the invincibility broke also, and I was scared, or sore afraid, as my would-be-god persona might have said. I was sore afraid, for the changes I had wrought could have been far beyond my own conception. How small that conception was had just begun to dawn.

Freyda was sitting in the hidden balcony, watching a hawk circle over the valley in the afternoon sun, sitting a bit too upright to show as much ease as she meant to convey. She acknowledged my entry without turning, staring at the city below, still wearing her Tribune's black, star and all.

"I assume that's you, Loki—god of fire, god of destruction and madness."

"You expected me."

"Sooner or later. I was one of the few who didn't underestimate you. Gods take longer to grow up and learn the extent of their powers."

I didn't correct her assessment of me as a god. For Freyda, in some ways, things were simple. Either I was a god, or I wasn't, and I'd unconsciously accepted her frame of reference, until Sammis's questions, while somehow knowing it wasn't correct and fighting the simplistic definition.

Now definitions didn't matter. The actions, my actions, mattered.

"Why didn't you stop me, then, if you were so wise?"

"Ten years ago, it was too late to stop you. Your mother said it was too late to stop you when you were born. You don't think people didn't try? Heimdall tried the sneaky way, and you were sneakier. Gilmesh tried to ignore you, and got ignored. Eranas tried to awe you with the power of the Guard, and you not only refused to be awed but proceeded to awe the Guard with your own power. The technicians tried to use technical expertise to reform the Guard, and you used greater expertise to confound everyone." Freyda sipped from her glass.

I waited. It was her turn to talk, and I owed her that.

"I'm not sure the entire Guard could have destroyed you after you recovered from your sentence on Hell. Sammis was convinced that you went only as a penance. One way or another, with your birth, the Guard we knew was doomed."

"I think that's overstating things."

"Loki, don't you see? It didn't matter. If the Tribunes had strangled you at birth, the guilt would have rotted us from within, at least those of us who counted—assuming Sammis would have ever let us, and he was the god of death once." She shivered. "If you had died on Hell, or we had let you, no Guard would ever have trusted the Tribunes or Counselors again. And what about you, the real you? Have you ever really been forced to do what you didn't agree to?"

"I'm sure I have," I answered, but Freyda stopped and sipped her drink.

The sun flashed through her hair, and the effect as she turned was the instant impression of silver, of age before her time, which disappeared even as I noted it.

"Sit down, young god. Sit down and watch the end of our era and the beginning of yours."

I sat.

"What's the insistence on the god business?" I protested. "I'm no god." I knew how she thought, but I had to try.

"Oh, not in the theological sense, but with your powers of mind over matter, in practical terms it doesn't make much difference. You throw thunderbolts without bothering to use microcircuits, use the undertime to walk on air and water, heal yourself, destroy with a glance, go when and where you please regardless of barriers raised against you, and you cast down and raise up whole planets and cultures."

Her dark eyes pinned me where I sat.

"Now . . . define a god for me," she finished.

What could I say that she would accept? Yes, I could certainly do most of what she described. But I was certainly not all-knowing, nor all-understanding, and certainly not all-powerful.

"Then I guess you'll have to call me a god."

Her attitude made one decision, or sealed it for me. Living legends, particularly those reputed to be gods, never live up to their image. And I had no desire to remain on Query—it would be fair neither to Queryans nor to me.

Freyda turned full face to me. "How does it feel to destroy the oldest institution in galactic history? Does it make you feel grand?"

That was the first real bitterness I had heard from Freyda.

I shook my head, not caring if Freyda believed me or not, thinking more of Verdis, Loragerd, Brendan—all the technicians who had hoped that solid work make the Guard better, even while the old schemers plotted, and Loki destroyed.

Whatever happened, if it continued, the Guard would not be the same meddling force that the Tribunes had sculpted from the original model of temporal restraint formed by the ancient Triumvirate. I had seen to that. Yes, I had seen to that.

Freyda, the last of the Tribunes, sat on the balcony of her retreat in the hills overlooking Quest and pointed to the City of Immortals.

"Can't you feel it?"

I glanced at Freyda, seated in her sculpted chair and gazing out at Quest from her protected terrace. So crisp she was, every white-blond hair in place, golden skin smoother than glowstone, black eyes glittering.

"Can't you feel it?"

The change winds were boiling just under the horizon of now, their black chill building.

I nodded, and in that instant when the winds of time-change struck, everything went out of focus, from Freyda, the firs framing the view of Quest, to the Tower of Immortals rising from the central Square. And the wind of time howled; the icicles marched up my spine as I stood in the sun, the golden sun that hid behind the clouds that were not there; the very ground trembled; and black cracks in the fabric of the instant splintered across the sky.

The histories, the might-have-beens, the was and the were, the is and the are, warred upon each other. Through the black windows of time hung in front of us, battles never fought were fought, all at once, all together, and the new turning points of history and parahistory, of space and paraspace, were hammered out in the fires of paratime.

Freyda sat, her face frozen, for she did not see the windows of the brand-new past opening into the new now.

In one window, and I called it that, for what else could I call a vision of a past that was inscribing itself on the present as I watched, a ship swathed in light burst over the eastern horizon and streaked on a downward course toward Quest.

From the central Square rose the Tower that glittered with the muted light of a thousand suns, soaring out of the perfect lawns and walks, out of the rows of scarlet fireflowers.

Before that first ship reached the city, the cool green air of that instant-past Query was wrenched apart with the sounds of a second ship. That one, tubular and black, somehow shrouded in darkness in full sunlight, dived at the city from out of the west, barely clearing the distant Bardwalls as it plunged toward Quest.

I looked again at Freyda. She was motionless, staring at the City of Immortals, waiting to see the results of the mighty cataclysm she felt, but had no sight to watch, for the windows of time were closed to her.

She did not see, for all her looking, for all her feeling. She did not see as the ship of light unleashed lightnings at suddenly deserted streets.

That vision did not happen in the now, was only a picture of what had transpired in a past we never knew, but it was *the* past from henceforth.

Under the light of the golden sun as it emerged from the clouds that never were, I was cold, not just from the chill of the change winds that swept over Query, for they had passed into the future, twisting and shaping it into new patterns.

No . . . I was cold . . . and not just from the winds of change.

I gazed, and beneath us on the plain that was suddenly filled with the rubble of old buildings still rose the Tower of Immortals. The remainder of Quest, a city raised around it, was jumbled humps and lumps.

Yet around that wreckage the ways and walks of a wide park wound, and fireflowers bloomed. There was order, and there was power without the arrogance of the old Guard. Query still challenged time, but not to subdue others for the mere sake of preservation and conquest.

The Tower stood, as a memorial, as did the rubble, both as a reminder of a past that had needed change—and that had been changed.

And while the dead, such as Heimdall, Eranas, and Kranos, were still dead, the others, perhaps among them Loragerd, Verdis, Narcissus, or Brendan, or others like them, would chart the new destiny of Query. They deserved that honor, and that challenge, without my heavy hand.

All that I knew, and, though I could not say how, I accepted that knowledge, for I was of Query, and would always be so, in whatever corner of the universe I found myself.

A question remained.

Freyda and I stood on her balcony, a balcony changed slightly, but the same, and with the world changed around us, we were yet the same—except that there was no star upon Freyda's collar.

"Us?" I asked.

Freyda understood.

"Because you made this present, this 'now,' you cannot be changed. If you were, it would not be. I suppose I am unchanged because you have willed it so, young god, or because of some other quirk of time, about which we know so little. That is both a gift and a curse."

She smiled faintly, and her smile said "Goodbye."

"What will you do in your new universe?"

I did not know, only understanding what I would not do. Understanding that I would not play god without accepting the responsibilities and burdens that went with it. Understanding, too, with bittersweet certainty, that I would fail at times to meet that commitment, and that even those with the power of gods can fail.

I made a jump, a final slide across the skies of Query, to the Aerie, which remained untouched. A thin layer of dust blanketed the glowstones, the empty rooms as though I had left them long ago.

Under Seneschal I let the afternoon wane, the twilight rise around me for my last goodbye before I ventured forth into the galaxy I had remade, out from Quest, out from Query. Out following all those who had left without the trumpets of fire I had summoned, out after Baldur and his Terrans, out after Ayren Bly, out after my parents, out . . . the list was longer than I knew, with no real need to go on.

The first star of night, the night before the dawn, appeared.

Greetings, Baldur.

Greetings, Wryan . . . wherever you are.